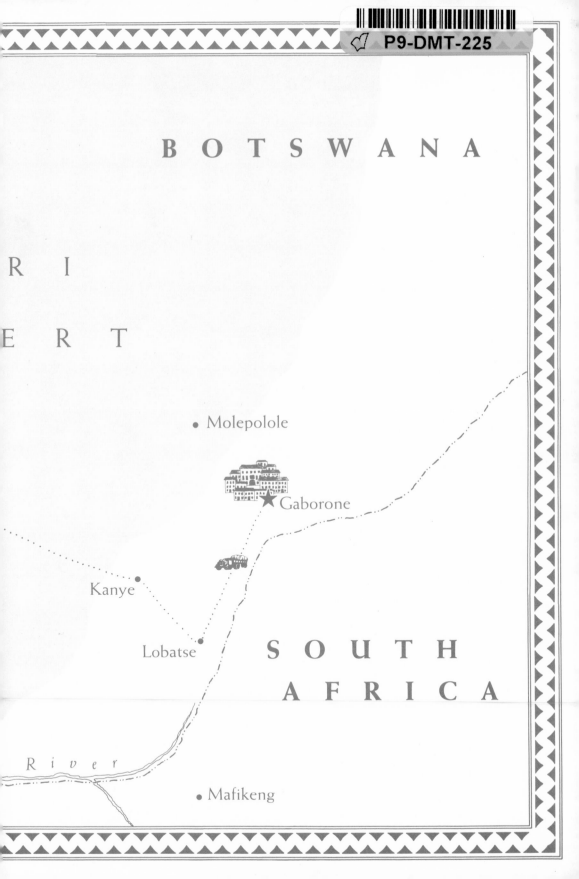

Also by Norman Rush

WHITES

MATING

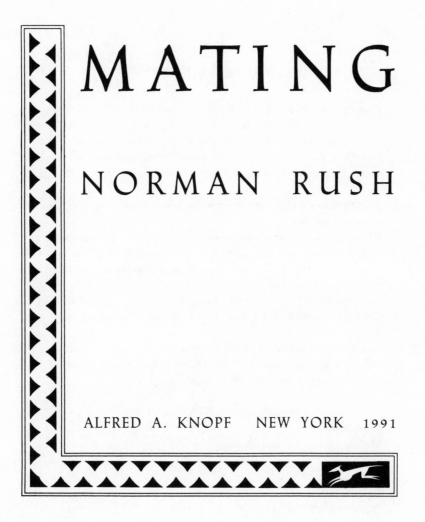

MATING

NORMAN RUSH

ALFRED A. KNOPF　NEW YORK　1991

THIS IS A BORZOI BOOK PUBLISHED BY ALFRED A. KNOPF, INC.

Copyright © 1991 by Norman Rush
All rights reserved under International and Pan-American Copyright
Conventions. Published in the United States by Alfred A. Knopf, Inc.,
New York, and simultaneously in Canada by Random House of Canada
Limited, Toronto. Distributed by Random House, Inc., New York.

Grateful acknowledgment is made to the following for permission to reprint
previously published material:
Farrar, Straus and Giroux, Inc.: Excerpt from "Songs for a Colored Singer"
from *The Complete Poems, 1927–1979* by Elizabeth Bishop. Copyright ©
1979, 1984 by Alice Helen Methfessel. Reprinted by permission of Farrar,
Straus and Giroux, Inc.
Random House, Inc.: "Dishonor" from *The Complete Poems* by Edwin Denby.
Copyright © 1986 by Full Court Press. Reprinted by permission of
Random House, Inc.
Special Rider Music: Excerpt from "Blowin' in the Wind" by Bob Dylan. This
arrangement copyright 1992, Special Rider Music. All rights reserved.
International copyright secured. Reprinted by permission.

Library of Congress Cataloging-in-Publication Data
Rush, Norman.
Mating: a novel / Norman Rush.
  p. cm.
ISBN 0-394-54472-2
I. Title
PS3568.U727M38 1991
813'.54—dc20 90-2572 CIP

Manufactured in the United States of America

FIRST EDITION

Everything I write is for Elsa, but especially this book, since in it her heart, sensibility, and intellect are so signally—if perforce esoterically—celebrated and exploited. My debt to her, in art and in life, grows however much I put against it. I also dedicate *Mating* to my beloved son and daughter-in-law, Jason and Monica, to my mother, and to the memory of my father, and to my lost child, Liza.

Contents

MATING

GUILTY REPOSE

Another Disappointee

In Africa, you want more, I think.

People get avid. This takes different forms in different people, but it shows up in some form in everybody who stays there any length of time. It can be sudden. I include myself.

Obviously I mean whites in Africa and not black Africans. The average black African has the opposite problem: he or she doesn't want enough. A whole profession called Rural Animation exists devoted to making villagers want more and work harder to get it. Africans are pretty ungreedy—elites excepted, naturally. Elites are elites.

But in Africa you see middleclass white people you know for a fact are highly normal turn overnight into chainsmokers or heavy drinkers or gourmets. Suddenly you find otherwise serious people wedged in among the maids of the truly rich in the throng at the Chinese butchery, their faces clenched, determined to come away with one of the nine or ten half pints of crème fraîche that arrive from Mafikeng on Wednesdays at three. You see people fixate on eating wonderfully despite the derisory palette Botswana offers. Or they may get into quantity sex. Or you can see it strike them there's no reason they shouldn't take a stab at getting rich before they have to leave Africa. Most expatriates only stay for a few years. And like clockwork when they get toward the end they start buying up karosses or carvings to resell, or they decide to buy real estate through Batswana proxies or in one case to found the first peewee golf course south of the Sahara. I knew someone who was an echt mama's boy in real life who took insane risks smuggling wristwatches into Zimbabwe on weekends. He was at the very end of his contract. He was teaching law at the University of Botswana.

In my case, disappointment was behind it. I got disgusting. I was typical—avid, and frantic. It was fall 1980, meaning spring in Africa. Africa had disappointed me. I had just spent eighteen months in the bush, all by myself basically. My thesis was in nutritional anthropology, and what I had been supposed to show was that fertility in what are called remote-dwelling populations fluctuates according to the season, because a large part of what remote dwellers eat depends on what they can find when they go out gathering, which should affect fertility. Or so I had been led to believe. It was unso. I had to hunt for gatherers. Gathering was a dead issue in my part of the bush. Normal-type food seems to have percolated everywhere, even into the heart of the Tswapong Hills. One way or another, people were getting regular canned food and cornflakes, or getting relief food, sorghum and maize, from the World Food Program. So nobody bothered with gathering much, and I had an exploded thesis on my hands.

On top of which I had been a bystander during something interpersonally very nasty in Keteng, the main village in my research zone. A Dutch cooperant had been hounded to death by the local power structure—old Boer settler families who'd become Botswana citizens when independence came. It still bothers me. Then on top of that I was having irregular periods, which turned out to be due to physical stress and my monochrome diet, which was as I suspected but which I needed to do something about, not be worried about. It intersected my turning thirty-two. I gave up and retreated to the capital, Gaborone, ostensibly to regroup but in fact to regress.

When I find myself in a homogeneous phase of my life, I like to have a caption for it. Guilty Repose is what I came up with for my caesura in Gaborone, which softens it: I went slightly decadent. It only lasted a couple of months.

I had no real excuse for not going back to the U.S. I told myself it was the prospect of another birthday at the hands of my mother. The more birthdays with her I missed, the more grandiose and excruciating the catch-up birthday always was, and I was years overdue. I had de facto promised to spend my thirty-second with her if I was back in the States. I knew it was her guilt—over being poor when she raised me, over being gigantic—that drove her to be so Wagnerian about my birthdays, but that wasn't enough. I was enervated.

Wanting company entered into it. I was tired of my own company and there was no one I had left behind or even on the horizon in the States. I was feeling sexually alert. There's no place like Gaborone for a detached white woman with a few social graces, even someone feeling very one-down. In fact for a disappointee Gaborone was perfect, because you circulate in a medium of other whites who are disappointed too. Nobody uses the word.

Accumulated Whites

There are more whites in Africa than you might expect, and more in Botswana than most places in Africa. Whites accumulate in Botswana. Parliament works and the courts are decent, so the West is hot to help with development projects: so white experts pile in. Botswana has almost the last hunter-gatherers anywhere, so you have anthropologists and anthropologists manqué like me underfoot. From South Africa you get fugitive white and black politicals, the whites mostly passing through, except for the bravest and hardiest. The Boers can reach out and touch anyone they want in Gaborone. Spies of all kinds are profuse, since everybody wants to know when the Republic of South Africa is going to combust and Gaborone is only five hours by road from Pretoria and Johannesburg. The Russian embassy is huge. And then Botswana is a geographical receptacle for civil service Brits excessed as decolonization moved ever southward. These are people who are forever structurally maladapted to living in England. This is their last perch in Africa. Tories from the Black Lagoon, or Paleo-Tories, Nelson Denoon called them, their politics are so primitive-right. They're interesting from the anthropological standpoint, but there are too many of them. Then you have white cooperants and volunteers, a hundred in the Peace Corps alone. You have droves of white game hunters and viewers heading north. Botswana has the last places in Africa wild animals have never seen a white face. There are only a million Batswana. And there are the missionaries.

I think I tend to exploit missionaries, which I really have to not do if I'm going to be negative toward them behind their backs. The Carmelite sisters in Keteng were unfailingly nice to me when I dropped in on them for a place to stay where I could get a hot bath and some fresh vegetables when I couldn't take it anymore in the bush. That happened periodically. A Seventh-Day Adventist couple put me up for two weeks when I decided to malinger in Gaborone instead of going back to the U.S. I don't know if I should omit missionaries from my globalizing about disappointment or not. I don't think so, although their absolutely seamless cheerfulness is designed to keep you from even conceiving the possibility. On the face of it they seem to get what they want. They do entrench their sects and denominations and keep Africans flowing into them. But they've got to be at least queasy over the tremendous and steady defections to the Spiritualist churches, which are syncretist Christian enterprises created and run by Africans and distinguished by certain doctrinal novelties, like drinking seawater for your ulcers. All the missionaries I stayed with showed a certain interest in my, shall we say, spiritual orientation. I don't think I teased them. I didn't misrepresent myself, but I didn't give them the full frontal, either. I used to think of myself as anticlerical but not antireligious, but that was before I met Nelson Denoon, who was both, and violently. He worked on my attitudes, directly and otherwise. It was an interest of his. I think I'm being fair. It was automatic with him to try to get people he, shall we say, loved, to agree with him on such matters. I still need to concentrate on how much of where I am now is Denoon's influence and how much is normal personal evolution. Denoon is pushing into this before he's historically due, naturally.

So I stayed with my Adventists, in a reclusive way initially. First of all I had to confront a resurgence of the conviction that I was academically accursed. Was I really so marginal? Why had I had to wait a week before hearing whether I'd passed my orals when the norm was to be told the next day? I felt intelligent: what was wrong? Why was everything so protracted and grudging with me? Why was I unable ever to figure out how you get to be someone's protégé? It happened all around me at Stanford, but never to me. After a few days in Gaborone I was able to reconvince myself, again, that everything was in essence bad luck or the aftereffects of the genteel poverty I grew up in. I got under control.

In those days the people at Immigration were more than easygoing. It took me less than an hour to get my visa extended for a year. Then I was ready to circulate.

Wherewithal

I remember when greed struck. It was at the first party I went to that spring, a garden party.

I was eavesdropping on a vehement argument between two Brits over whether Zambia or Botswana has the world's greatest climate. This during a killer drought. I respond to sun, but then I come from Minnesota and had years of being disappointed by northern California with its indeterminate weather and freezing surf. I'm overdetermined for life in Africa. I love the sun bursting up every day of your life like some broken mechanism. Even during the socalled rainy season you have sun until two or three in the afternoon and then again after your trivial little five-minute dusting of rain. Even in high summer in Botswana you barely sweat. It's hot but so dry you can feel your sweat actually cooling the surface of your skin as it flashes into nothing. You're in a desert three thousand feet above sea level, after all, although it doesn't look like the usual desert. Denoon's theory was that people get biologically adapted to the stupendously regular southern African climate, which he called "metronomic."

Out came our hostess, in chartreuse, pleased with the day. The drought had something for the festive classes. Outdoor functions are easier because of the multitudes to be fed and managed. The median party in Gaborone is very large. If you can count on fair weather, it's a relief. And partygivers could afford to keep their landscapes green by hiring day labor on the cheap to do handwatering so as to get around the ban on watering by hosepipe. On the cheap and hosepipe are relics of how Briticized my speech became. I have either a talent or a weakness for mimicry, depending on how you look at it. I knew I was sounding half British. It didn't bother me. It related to my being able to pick up languages easily, which I can, and which was one reason I'd thought anthropology was such a natural for me. I blend in, if I want to. A core fantasy of mine from before high school was that members of the most puzzling cultures were going to divulge secrets to me out of hardly noticing my intrusion, or thinking I was almost one of them.

There was an opulent sunset. I was standing under an acacia in bloom and the words "shower of gold" came into my mind, followed by a surge of feeling. I call it greed, but it was more a feeling of wanting a surplus in my life, wanting to have too much of something, for a change. I didn't want to be a candidate anymore, not for a doctorate or anything else: I wanted to be at the next level, where things would come to me, accrue to me. It was acute. I looked at the people around me. The woman giving the party was extremely ordinary physically. She may have been with the British Council. She was plain. Not that I'm so beautiful, unless hair volume determines beauty. I'm robust, shall we say, but my waist is good. I apparently look Irish. I was glad I'd kept my hair long all through my fieldwork, an ordeal in itself and against the advice of the entire world. It is a feature. And I do look good when I'm as thin as I was then. This woman could afford to feed fifty people. The starters were miniature sandwiches made with genuine Parma ham. I had been living on cabbage and mealie porridge for eighteen months. She was serving cashews as big as shrimps. I remember pearl onions and white asparagus. Little perfect fillet steaks were coming. She lived in a two-bedroom house and had a cook and a groundsman. The grounds were the usual impeccable. She never had to iron. She was at most five years older than I. I know how this sounds and don't defend it. It was depletion speaking.

I was attracting male attention already. It was premature. Braais and cream teas are given by women. Invitations were going to be my bread and butter. I had to avoid being typed as someone out to browse the local male flora. There could be attachments, but not yet. Somehow I was going to expropriate the expropriators so softly they would never notice, but how? I needed a métier, but the right métier. Then I knew.

I would be a docent, presenting Botswana as an institution with obscure holdings. It was clear I was perfect for addressing a true need. Whites in Botswana needed to feel they had come to an exotic place. After all, they were in Africa. But Botswana is frustrating. Gaborone was built from the ground up in the nineteen sixties, and except for the squatter section along the Lobatse road, it looks more like a college town in the American Southwest than anything else. There's no national costume. In the villages cement block structures with metal roofs are driving out the mud and thatch rondavels. English is an official language, along with Setswana. For entertainment in the towns you have churchgoing, disco, karate exhibitions, ballroom dancing competitions, beauty contests, and soccer. The interesting fauna are in the far north, unless an occasional ostrich or baboon excites you. Except for the fantasy castles of the rich and the diplomatic corps in Section Sixteen, housing in Gaborone looks either modular or pitiful. The culture looks familiar but feels alien. The Batswana are not what you would call forthcoming. They murmur when they talk to whites. They have a right to be sick of whites and to show it a little. They want to be opaque at the same time that they're working on their English and ordering platform shoes from South African mail order houses. The Batswana won't invite you to dinner, so another avenue to enlightenment is closed to whites. Batswana will without fail accept your invitations to dinner, although they frequently won't show up. Meal reciprocation is not in the culture. This puts whites off, and they regard the general assertion that Batswana would be delighted to see you if you just dropped by at mealtime as a canard. Weddings and funerals are big deals but very crowded, and even when whites are invited nobody talks to them or bothers to explain that, for example, the reason the bride is staring at the ground in misery the whole time is as an expression of sadness at leaving her parents. There are barriers. Americans suffer the most. They come to Botswana wanting to be lovely to Africans. A wall confounds them. Behind it is something they sense is interesting. I could help them.

I had the specific wherewithal for this. I spoke good Setswana. I had anecdotes. I could demonstrate that beneath the surface the culture was as other as anyone could ask. I would be being useful. Why did Batswana babies have woolen caps on during the summer? On the other hand, why did some Batswana shave their heads in winter? I knew. Why did Kalanga men let the nail on the little finger of the right hand grow to an extreme length and then sharpen it? Why did the Batswana hate lawns and prefer beaten earth around their houses? Why did schoolgirls so often try to sleep with their heads under the covers? I could also help at the mundane level. What American cut of beef did silverside correspond to? What were the Diamond Police? Did anyone care that not far from Molepolole there were Batswana who had serfs? People would have material for letters. I could bring them a sense of the otherness that was eluding them. It would all be informal. A brunet was stalking me, I noticed.

Bring your wife over, I called to him, which unsettled him. I was standing at the fence, musing or trying to, and realizing that a troop of Zed CC marchers was approaching. He didn't like going to get her.

The spot where he'd noticed me was rather secluded and bosky. I remember he had a sleek brown beard and what the Batswana call a pushing face. He brought a little group with him when he came to the fence.

Fifty marchers went slowly by. Men in taut tan porters' uniforms and garrison caps led. Women followed, all in white. The women wore ordinary sandals. I pointed out the footgear of the men. They wore sneakers that had been cut apart and reassembled around a section of canvas tubing to extend the toe box by eight or ten inches. The purpose of the shoes was to make a thunderous slap when the men landed from the leaps they made during these marches. They would go up and descend en bloc. I also explained that once they started singing they sang without pause for as long as a couple of hours. My group said things like Where do they get the energy? The marchers were through leaping for the day. But I told my group where they could catch them some other Sunday. I knew what routes they took. I explained how the Zionist Christian Church originated, why it was interesting, some of what its adherents believed, how the main body of the sect in South Africa had sold its soul to the Botha regime.

I must have been fascinating. Before I left I'd been offered a very decent leave house to sit, a type two house on the edge of Extension Sixteen. My duties amounted to feeding some budgerigars. I was delivered from my missionaries. Two women wanted me to go with them to the tapestry workshop at Lentswe la Oodi. I had the next day's lunch and dinner in my pocket.

A Period of Surplus

It became a peculiar time for me. The original conceit was that I was going to be hedonic, think passim about my life and next steps, repose on the white utopia Gaborone was, inevitably use up my savings, fly home. I had my return ticket. So my period of guilty repose would be self-limiting. Barter would supposedly carry me only so far. But something went wrong.

I began nicely. To avoid any substantive contact with my thesis abortion I wrapped up my notes and records in layer upon layer of kraft paper, tied the parcel with cord, and dropped hot wax on the knots—a thing still done in southern Africa. I left the object in plain view as a memento mori that my academic life was not going to go away but was only lying in wait. My days were fine. There was no typical day. Some days I was up at dawn and watching the sunrise while I sipped rooibos tea. Other days I got up at two or three or worse. Sometimes I played tennis to extinction.

I had never allowed myself this kind of hiatus. I was deliberately planless. I was even able to suppress the vague internalized lifetime reading plan that always nags me when I read trash. I decided to let myself read only whatever turned up in my vicinity. Fortunately the shelves in the house were loaded with Simenon. I think it was Denoon who said that the closest you can come in life to experiencing free will is when you do things at random. There is no free will. Everything is still determined when you make random choices, but you stop noticing. Counterfeit freedom is still something you can enjoy in the right frame of mind. It was perfect being in someone else's house.

What went wrong was the surplus I began to run. So many things came my way. I had virtually no expenses. I edged toward being extravagant in small ways. When I could get crème fraîche I bought as much as I could conceivably hope to eat before it spoiled. I bought some ostrich-eggshell-chip chokers. I tried to be less driven re eating leftovers. I was still in surplus.

For example: my medical care was gratis. The Peace Corps doctor took a Platonic interest in me. I got a superb parasitology workup from him. It was boring treating volunteers for nonspecific urethritis and sun poisoning and not much else. He felt underutilized and would treat anybody who would let him talk about the medical abysses he had stared into elsewhere in the third world or the shortcomings of the Botswana Ministry of Health. He considered me very clean, based on my having chewed my nails short when I was in the bush. I let him think I agreed with his central conviction that everyone, white and black, was cavalier about sanitation to the point of madness, except the two of us. He lived exclusively on canned food or food that could be boiled. When he went to parties he took his own boiled-water ice cubes. Paper money was infectious because so many Batswana women carried it in their bras, next to the flesh. He lavished free medical samples on me, some of which I still have. I liked him. His name was Elman—after the violinist— Cornetta. He was short, forty, unmarried, normal about sex except for his conclusion—I intuited this—that even the most carefully regulated intercourse was unsanitary. He was at ease in Africa in a generic way: he felt he was performing in what was essentially a hopeless situation. You see variants of this in whites in other hopeless situations. Elman was a genuinely calm person. I interpreted his coming to Africa to be in the midst of infection, the thing he feared most, as purely counterphobic behavior. That made for a bond between us because I could be considered counterphobic in a way myself. I have topological agnosia, a condition somewhat akin to dyslexia and meaning that I have great trouble finding my way around the topography. And I had come to a part of the world where there are almost no landmarks, "Driving through Botswana one is struck by the unvarying landscape stretching into the distance" is a line from the *Guide to Botswana* expatriates seem to remember and quote.

Elman thought the sanitation problem in the capital was doomed to worsen as the population grew. It would get like Lomé, where the main outdoor sign you see is Défense d'uriner le long des murs. Something needed to be done. I thought I should try to steer his phobia in a constructive direction, and the way that worked out illustrates both how Africa disappoints people and how my attempt at self-impoverishment kept failing. I suggested we produce a comic book presentation on basic sanitation. I would translate his English text into Setswana and find him an artist. He was enthusiastic. We did it. We produced an eight-page black-and-white comic printed offset on newsprint. It was crude but he was delighted. He paid for it himself and he insisted on paying, overpaying, me, which was ridiculous. But he was overjoyed with the thing and it turned out to be a hit. Batswana were dropping by the office and asking for copies. He couldn't believe it. We had to reprint. For a while he was a new man. Then an enemy of his enlightened him. There are public toilets in central Gaborone but no toilet paper in them. The poor make do with whatever kinds of wastepaper they can lay hands on. Actual commercial toilet paper is a luxury commodity. I tried to comfort him with the news that the same thing was happening to the Watchtower publications the Jehovah's Witnesses were being mobbed for in the mall. I tried to console him. The money he gave me always smelled sweet. I suspect he swabbed the bills with an astringent before putting them in little plastic bags.

So it went. No one could do enough for me. I would do a favor for a wandering scholar, such as typing or indexing, and invariably I was overpaid. When it got around that I had very good shorthand there was

a surge of offers to send me to conferences and gatherings as a rapporteur. Taping is not appropriate in every setting. When I said no I was
just offered more money. I also became a favorite recipient when people
came to the ends of their tours and gave away whatever was left in their
pantries and liquor cabinets. At some level whites felt sorry for one
another at being assigned to a place and a society so unforthcoming,
which showed also in the tonus of the grandiose parties thrown to welcome new arrivals or say goodbye to the reassigned. I don't say that
valedictory giftgiving didn't include Batswana, particularly domestic
help: it did, but the degree to which it didn't is significant. Unstated
emotion had a lot to do with it. Anti-makhoa feeling among the Batswana
was fairly vocal around then. There were letters in the papers alleging
that white experts were misrepresenting their qualifications in order to
hold on to jobs Batswana should have. Some of it was absurd. An MP
from Francistown was upset that young Batswana were wearing sunglasses in the presence of their elders, which was disrespectful since their
eyes couldn't be seen clearly, and whites were responsible for the vogue
of sunglasses. In any case, it wasn't my reciprocations that made me
popular. All told I gave maybe six functions, all of them smallscale, two
of them Monopoly evenings that only involved snacks.

Why Do We Yield?

It's an effort to recapture the detail of guilty repose, because what I
want is to plunge into Denoon and what followed. But the prelude is
important, probably. I feel like someone after the deluge being asked to
describe the way it was before the flood while I'm still plucking seaweed
out of my hair, Denoon being the deluge. Despite my metaphors, the
last thing I want to do is fabulize Denoon and make him more than he
was. I hate drama. I hate dramatizers. But it was distinctly like a building
falling on me when I met him. Why? Why do we yield, when we don't
have to? I'd like to know, as a woman and a human being, both. What
did the sex side of my life in Gabs up to then have to do with it? This is
British: Gaborone equals Gabs, Lobatse Lobs, Molepolole Moleps, und-

soweiter. If I seem to convey that everyone I was involved with sexually pre-Denoon that summer was a clod or worse, I take it back in advance. That wasn't it.

I won't be exhaustive about my carnal involvements. There were more than the three main ones, but not many more. To start off with, probably I should indicate who I didn't sleep with—or wouldn't, rather. It was principled and there were categories. One was Rhodesians and South Africans, nonexiles. Another was anybody I considered wittingly rightwing. Reagan was going to be president and I regarded anybody who was even close to neutral on that as a limb of evil. My final category needs some explication because I feel defensive about it, because the category was African men as in black African. Partly I was being self-protective. Male chauvinism is the air African men breathe. They can't escape it. They are imbued. They are taught patriarchy by every voice in their culture, including their mothers'. That was a predisposing thing. I was not going to devote my energies to educating a perfectly happy Motswana as to my exquisite basic needs. But beyond that there was the danger of something happening, possibly, that would turn out to be permanent—meaning, for me, staying on in Africa forever. It may seem coldblooded, but if I was clear about anything in my life I was clear about not staying in Africa forever. By the same token I was not going to find myself in the position of seeming to offer somebody a way of getting to lefatshe la madi, the country money comes from. Most younger Africans want to get to America so badly you can taste it, as someone said. I couldn't help being seen as a potential conduit. I was not going to be involved in raising or blasting hopes, either one.

Giles

First was Giles, whom I met at a party given by some Canadian volunteers. He was physically stellar. He wasn't Canadian, he was British but had lived for long stretches in Canada and America and was very homogenized. His chestnut hair was long and in actual ringlets. It was a hot night. CUSO is very hairshirt, so naturally the air-conditioning was unplugged and we were all outside under the thorn trees fanning our-

selves with scraps of cardboard. Canadians thought it was funny that
Reagan was likely to be elected president. We stopped playing Jimmy
Cliff records and started a desultory game of proposing the people Rea-
gan was no doubt going to name to his cabinet, all Hollywood stars,
naturally. It was puerile. I didn't distinguish myself. John Wayne was
going to be Secretary of Defense and Boris Karloff was going to be White
House Science Adviser. I had to explain when I said Lloyd Bridges for
Secretary of the Navy. Apparently I was the only one present low-level
enough to have spent time watching the stupid television series in which
Lloyd Bridges went around underwater. Giles was so thick he proposed
Jean Gabin for Director of the FBI. The consensus being that nominees
had to be American citizens, Gabin was rejected. Another cinéphile then
counterproposed Basil Rathbone, in honor of his long experience as
Sherlock Holmes. Giles insisted that Basil Rathbone was British. We
were unanimous against him. Basil Rathbone had been naturalized. It
was typical that nothing would move Giles on this point. His obstinacy
brought the game to an end, but in an unconscious tribute to his physical
beauty, we all immediately forgave him. He was a beauty. He was self-
consciously leonine. He was wearing a sheer batiste shirt that let his
golden chest hair show interestingly through. The kneesocks he wore
with his safari shorts were doubled down just where his blocky calves
were thickest, for emphasis. He let me admire the camera he had with
him at all times. Later in our relationship when I asked him how old he
was his reply was *Under forty*. He was what he was. His beauty made him
unusually goodnatured. You could revile him and be sure he wouldn't
mind for long because when all was said and done he was still going to
be the beautiful six foot plus guy you or somebody else wanted. This was
not vanity. It was reality.

He was a professional photographer. The last I heard, he was unknown, although I still think he was very very good. He was someone
totally permeated by his vocation. He related to the world composition-
ally. I was already inclined against the visual arts as a hunting ground for
mates, but Giles clinched it. Two women I knew married to painters
were supremely unhappy in an identical way. Men whose raison d'être is
to wring images out of everything around them range from mute to gaga
when they stop doing art, such as at breakfast, lunch, dinner, and bedtime. Giles's stance was to be always alert to the parade of images that
constituted the world, because one of them might be classic, like the
Frenchman weeping when the German army marched into Paris. The
trick was to never stop taking pictures, which is what he did. He was

working on several contracts simultaneously. One was for documentation for the UN, one was for the firm in South Africa that supplied
Botswana's picture postcards, and one was for un unbelievably crude
men's magazine put out in Malta. And then he was always adding to
his personal portfolio, which I promised to someday review for possible
classics.

I intrigued him enough that he followed up to get my suggestions
about picturesque spots near Gabs, mostly in the hills along the back
road from Kanye to Moshupa. It was a little greener there. Goats kept it
parklike in the small villages. He was grateful and started offering me
tiny fees, which I refused, which seemed to overwhelm him somehow: I
became sexual to him. Suddenly he wanted to turn our picnics into
something a little different. I had been bringing chicken sandwiches and
milk stout along on our photo excursions. The idea of making love al
fresco was suddenly to be discussed. He was likable, possibly because he
liked his subject, which was everything, oneself included. To some extent I was responsible for the direction things took, but it was my duty to
point out that outdoor love was not a good idea. I explained about dispersed settlement patterns in Botswana, that what looked like blank veld
could erupt with boys herding cows or goats right past you, how there
could be homesteads or cattle posts functioning in the midst of spectacular desolation, miles from anything. I also knew of two anthropologists
working out of Kanye who were cataloging stone age settlement sites,
which could be anywhere. He got it. He was not an aggressive man and
the question went away, leaving an undertone in our outings that was to
my advantage. Pastoral sex is exclusively a male penchant. I guarantee
no woman ever proposes it if there are quarters available. Even Denoon
had a vestige of a tendency in that direction until I mused pointedly a
couple of times that the tendency must have something to do with exhi-
bitionism.

I had an objective where Giles was concerned. He had an assignment
pending in Victoria Falls, which I was in danger of never seeing before I
left Africa. I not only wanted to get to Victoria Falls but to stay there in
splendor at the Vic Falls Hotel, the way the colonial exploiters had. This
was less greed per se than it was wanting to visit or inhabit a particularly
gorgeous and egregious consummation of it. I was convinced that under
Mugabe accommodations would be democratized and establishments
like the Vic Falls Hotel would cease to exist, which of course was only
one of a number of things that didn't happen under Mugabe. I had a
fixation on seeing the greatest natural feature in Africa and seeing it at

the maximal time of year, which was just then, when the Zambezi was still in spate. I might be going back home to exile in the academic tundra, but I wanted to have seen the world's greatest waterfall from the windows of an establishment amounting to a wet dream of doomed white settler amour propre.

I teased Giles to this end. I'm against what I did. I didn't enjoy doing it. A utopia I would join in a minute is a society which could be communist or capitalist, anything, except that no woman member of it ever underwent sex unless she was hot. Pretending to be hot bears a distinct resemblance to self-rape, but it's a rape accompanied by boredom instead of fear. Everyone raved about Victoria Falls and in fact I was right to want to go there.

For his postcard project Giles wanted bucolica—happy faces in rural places, as he put it—but he did point his camera my way now and then when the mood struck him. He decided I was a good subject. Would I let him do some indoor studies in his suite at the President Hotel? His promo was that shooting me indoors would be clever because I was so plainly an outdoor type. He had some ideas about how to exploit that, involving some props he had, antique veils and fans. There must be a term for the faint whining sound the fingers produce as they slide down the strings of a guitar to make a chord lower on the neck. I heard the equivalent in his voice. I agreed on condition he not buy me dinner first, just as a genuflection toward professionalism.

I arrived about eight one evening. All was in readiness: the photofloods, the reflectors. He thought it would be helpful if we each had a touch of brandy. He had been married twice, each time to a flawless woman, if their photographs were to be trusted. One of them was Thai. The pictures of his exes were propaganda: who were you to resist a man who had won such human gems? Denoon once said that if Martians conquered the earth and ran an ethnic beauty contest to decide who should be given control of the planet on the basis of sheer beauty, it would go to Thai women and Cretan men. I remember I said Speaking for my fellow colleens I am outraged. He began absurdly backtracking and trying to say something nice about women of Irish descent, but this was Denoon before I managed to tone up his sense of humor. Could there be a little deshabille? Giles wanted to know. I couldn't see why not.

I let things stretch to the point where he wanted to neck. At that point he wasn't being untoward, so when I said no way Raymond and told him what the deal was—which was that I was his if he took me along to Vic Falls—he was in shock. I was absolutely naked about it.

Obviously my no was a first. He bridled all over the place. I was prepared, though, and had a few things to point out.

To wit, he was forgetful. Very goodlooking people are as a rule more forgetful than the median. Their mothers start it and the world at large continues it, handing them things, picking things up for them, smoothing their vicinity out for them in every way. I on the other hand remember everything. I'm practically a mnemonist of the kind people study. My mother forgot everything during the raptures of misery she was always involved in, so I had to remember everything for both of us, perforce, before we sank. She also used to lose things as a strategy against people like creditors and landlords. Academically my memory starts out a blessing and ends up a curse because it carries me into milieux where people have been led to make strong assumptions about my core intellect based on it. Recall is not enough. Not that I'm stupid. I don't know if I am, yet. But my photographic memory was useful to Giles. The panoply of things I had been keeping track of for him constituted everything except his camera. I gave him some recent examples.

Then there was Africa. His experience was the Republic of South Africa plus a little Rhodesia during UDI. He seemed to feel this qualified him for all of Africa. He walked around as though he knew what he was doing, but I knew better—as I had proved. Black-run Africa is different. He didn't take Botswana seriously. More than once I'd stopped him from shooting scenes with public buildings in the background, which is not appreciated by the Botswana police. Also I had convinced him it was not smart to be continually using the adjective "lekker" for great, terrific. He had picked that up in South Africa and it was doubtless okay at the bar in the Grenadier Room at the President Hotel but not out among where the people could hear. He slightly disbelieved me when I told him the Batswana disliked Boers, because he had been overwhelmed by Boer hospitality, which is a real entity, if you happen to be white.

He said he needed to think about taking me along.

After a little swallowing he came around, but would I mind paying for my own breakfasts and lunches at Vic Falls if he picked up my dinners and everything else, all the travel? That made it perfect and crystal clear all around. We shook on it. I can take breakfast or leave it anyway. I could tell he needed some kind of reassurance that I found him physically attractive, our negotiations notwithstanding. Finally I just told him so, and that worked. It was all set.

Bulawayo

The train trip from Gaborone to Victoria Falls is in two stages—a night and half a day to Bulawayo, then a layover until ten and then overnight to the falls. There is no Rhodesia, I had to tell Giles over and over, to grind into his brain that we were going to a country called Zimbabwe and only Zimbabwe. I made up a rhyme to help him.

We toyed with the idea of doing it in our compartment but decided to hold off until Vic Falls and luxury. There's no hot water on the train, only cold water that comes out of a little tap and down into a zinc basin that folds out of the wall between the windows and which you know has been used as a urinal by people not eager for the tumult you standardly get in the corridors on your way to the toilets. This is the case with basins in any accommodation not accompanied by a private bath, so this is not a third world failing. I liked the wood paneling and all the glittering brass fitments, but if you looked at the carpeting you were not seeing something pristine. Also the berths were a little short for a beefeater like Giles. We agreed about amenity being important. We held hands.

The ambience got worse in a more global way at our first stop inside Zimbabwe, at Plumtree, where Zimbabwe customs and immigration people get on and check you out. They weren't dreamy like the Batswana officers. Giles found them aggressive. His appearance was against him because he looked so classically proconsular, with his tailored safari kit and opulent wristwatch. I saw it coming. He was the epitome of what they had overthrown, and here he was again. He had never ever until then had his passport taken out of his presence, he told me, when that happened, vibrating. Eventually it was all right, but it developed he had chewed the lining of his mouth till it bled while he was in anxiety, which he showed me evidence of on a serviette.

They had only recently resumed the run from Bulawayo to Victoria Falls: there were still bullet holes in the sides of some of the coaches. Political euphoria was the air we breathed once we were under way. I had luckily forewarned Giles to expect this. People who were already pretty boisterous surged out of third and fourth class and got more so

fooling around in first class trying to find empty compartments if they
could. There was full-blast camaraderie going on. We were the only
whites in our car. You could lock your compartment, but anyone could
get into it by taking the piece of slate with the compartment number on
it out of its holder on the door and inserting it into the gap between the
door and the frame and tripping the catch, which the conductors routinely did when they wanted for any reason to check out a compartment
and didn't feel like fiddling with different keys. They weren't secretive
when they were doing the trick. The corridor was a mêlée of people
carousing and singing freedom songs, which I liked—the singing, not
the carousing. Giles wouldn't undress, in case he had to repel somebody.
In fact he dozed sitting on the floor with his back against the door and it
woke me up when he did finally fall backward out into the corridor.
Somebody had gotten the door open who then vanished—apologizing,
as I pointed out. Giles roared briefly, mainly because by two a.m. the
corridor was aqueous, shall we say, and he'd gotten his shirt befouled.
He tore his shirt off and I got up and soaped his back for him.

Of Surfeit One Can Never Have Too Much

We got to the hotel before seven. It was perfection. It sits alone high
up in ordinary thin woods and bush. The grounds are perfection. The
hotel is huge, cavernous, and quiet. Staff was everywhere, but there
were no other guests in evidence, which Giles incorrectly assumed was
because people were still asleep. I had to tear him away from a fixated
perusal of a placard that told you what the drill was in the event of a
terrorist attack, which was taken down the next day along with the sign
commanding you to turn in your firearms when you registered. This no
longer applies, I had to tell him firmly several times.

We were in an apotheosis of whiteness. The hotel was white inside
and out. The white paintwork in our room was like porcelain. When you
turned up the white ceiling fan to maximum you were under a white disk
that seemed symbolic. Our bedspread was white. At meals there were
white sauces to go with the cold meats, the vegetables, the trifle. Later I
would see a woman, white, eating spoonfuls of béarnaise sauce directly

out of a gravy boat. The cleaners and porters, not kids but mature black men, had to wear juvenilizing white outfits like sailorsuits—shorts, and jumpers with tallywhackers. There were other white statements I forget. Our bed was contained in a trembling white cone of mosquito netting, and delicate white lace curtains were lifting and sinking at the open windows as we dropped our bags. This is practically sacral, I said. But Giles wasn't hearing me. That should really be asses' milk, I said as he was drawing his bath. He was so tired he got into the tub with his socks on. I thought I'd await him in bed, having acted tartish enough unpacking to suggest that the gates of paradise were ajar. I felt sorry for Giles so far. I was patient, but where was he? Eventually I found him asleep in the tub.

I got re-dressed and headed for the falls, hurrying because I realized how pleased I was to be going by myself and also because if you stopped to muse for a second anyplace on the oceanic front lawn of the hotel you were pursued by drinks waiters with their little trays, even at nine in the morning. If you pause on the lawn and concentrate you can feel the vibration from the falls through the soles of your feet. The path went to the left through the woods. I was excited.

I was excited to the point that I was able to ignore a handful of baboons who seemed to be shadowing me for a while. I normally hate and fear them, based on personal experience. They sometimes shy off if you make a throwing motion. Not these, though. But I proceeded. I was on the verge of a confused but major experience.

Weep for Me

Well before you see water you find yourself walking through pure vapor. The roar penetrates you and you stop thinking without trying.

I took a branch of the path that led out onto the shoulder of the gorge the falls pour into. I could sit in long grass with my feet to the void, the falls immense straight in front of me. It was excessive in every dimension. The mist and spray rise up in a column that breaks off at the top into normal clouds while you watch. This is the last waterfall I need to see, I thought. Depending on the angle of the sun, there were rainbows and fractions of rainbows above and below the falls. You resonate. The first main sensation is about physicality. The falls said something to me like You are flesh, in no uncertain terms. This phase lasted over an hour. I have never been so intent. Several times I started to get up but couldn't. It was injunctive. Something in me was being sated and I was paralyzed until that was done.

The next phase was emotional. Something was building up in me as I went back toward the hotel and got on the path that led to overlooks directly beside and above the east cataract. My solitude was eroding, which was oddly painful. I could vaguely make out darkly dressed people here and there on the Zambia side, and there seemed to be some local African boys upstream just recreationally manhandling a huge dead tree into the rapids, which they would later run along the bank following to its plunge, incidentally intruding on me in my crise or whatever it should be called. The dark clothing I was seeing was of course raingear, which anyone sensible would be wearing. I was drenched.

You know you're in Africa at Victoria Falls because there is nothing anyplace to keep you from stepping off into the cataract, not a handrail, not an inch of barbed wire. There are certain small trees growing out over the drop where obvious handholds on the limbs have been worn smooth by people clutching them to lean out bodily over white death. I did this myself. I leaned outward and stared down and said out loud something like Weep for me. At which point I was overcome with enormous sadness, from nowhere. I drew back into where it was safe, terrified.

I think the falls represented death for the taking, but a particular death, one that would be quick but also make you part of something magnificent and eternal, an eternal mechanism. This was not in the same league as throwing yourself under some filthy bus. I had no idea I was that sad. I began to ask myself why, out loud. I had permission to. It was safe to talk to yourself because of the roar you were subsumed in, besides being alone. I fragmented. One sense I had was that I was going to die sometime anyway. Another was that the falls were something you could never apply the term fake or stupid to. This has to be animism, was another feeling. I was also bemused because suicide had never meant anything to me personally, except as an option it sometimes amazed me my mother had never taken, if her misery was as kosher as she made it seem. There was also an element of urgency underneath everything, an implication that the chance for this kind of death was not going to happen again and that if I passed it up I should stop complaining

—which was also baseless and from nowhere because I'm not a complainer, historically. I am the Platonic idea of a good sport.

Why was I this sad? I needed to know. I was alarmed. I had no secret guilt that I was aware of, no betrayals or cruelty toward anyone. On the contrary, I have led a fairly generative life in the time I've had to spare from defending myself against the slings and arrows. Remorse wasn't it. To get away from the boys and their log I had moved to a secluded rock below the brink of the falls. At this point I was weeping, which was disguised by the condensation already bathing my face. No bypasser would notice. This is not saying you could get away with outright sobbing, but in general it would not be embarrassing to be come upon in the degree of emotional dishevelment I seemed to be in.

What was it about? It was nothing sexual: I was not dealing on any level with uncleanness, say. My sex history was the essence of ordinary. So any notion that I was undergoing some naughtiness-based lustral seizure was worthless, especially since I have never been religious in the slightest. One of the better papers I had done was on lustral rites. Was something saying I should kill myself posthaste if the truth was that I was going to be mediocre? This was a thought with real pain behind it. To my wreck of a mother mediocre was a superlative—an imputation I resisted with all my might once I realized it involved me. I grew up clinging to the idea that either I was original in an unappreciated way or that I could be original—this later—by incessant striving and reading and taking simple precautions like never watching television again in my life.

There must be such a thing as situational madness, because I verged on it. I know that schizophrenics hear people murmuring when the bedsheets rustle or when the vacuum cleaner is on. The falls were coming across to me as an utterance, but in more ways than just the roar. There seemed to be certain recurrent elongated forms in the falling masses of water, an architecture that I would be able to apprehend if only I got closer. The sound and the shapes I was seeing went together and meant something, something ethical or existential and having to do with me henceforward in some way. I started to edge even closer, when the thought came to me If you had a companion you would stay where you are.

I stopped in my tracks. There was elation and desperation. Where was my companion? I had no companion, et cetera. I had no life companion, but why was that? What had I done that had made that the case, leaving me in danger? Each time I thought the word "companion" I felt pain collecting in my chest. I suddenly realized how precipitous the place I had chosen to sit and commune from was. The pain was like hot liquid, and I remember feeling hopeless because I knew it was something not amenable to vomiting. I wanted to expel it. Vomiting is my least favorite inevitable recurrent experience, but I would have been willing to drop to all fours and vomit for hours if that would access this burning material. It was no use saying mate or compadre instead of companion: the pain was the same. Also, that I genuinely deserved a companion was something included. I wish I knew how long this went on. It was under ten minutes, I think.

Who can I tell this to, was the thought that seemed to end it. I may have been into the diminuendo already, because I had gotten back from the ledge, back even from the path and into the undergrowth. It all lifted. I sat in the brush, clutching myself. I had an optical feeling that the falls were receding. Then it was really over.

I hauled myself back to the hotel feeling like a hysteric, except for the sense that I had gotten something germane, whatever it was, out of my brush with chaos.

A Datum

What kind of person gets into bed still dripping wet from his bath? I had to conclude that this was what Giles had done, from the condition of the bed I now needed to share. I was ready for sleep. I put towels down over the damp on my side. I thought I'd try nudity again.

The most I could distill from my crise was that it was somehow rubiconic for me, that I had passed up an exit and so now more than ever I should fight, fight like a man, fight the world—which I was under the impression I had been doing all along—but fight harder, possibly. This seemed banal to me and probably a self-mystification. There was something far more deeply interfused, so to speak, but I couldn't get it. Did it have something to do with an association of maleness I had for the falls as an entity? This also led me nowhere, and even now when I raise it it has the feel of a confession. I only mention it because the point is to exclude nothing.

Giles was the first man I ever knew who actively preferred the left side of the bed (as you face the bed). Was it meaningful? I think I consider the right side of the bed, which I always prefer, dominant. In my future of course was Denoon, the only man born of woman with absolutely no preference for which side of the bed he slept on. I watched Giles asleep. In fairness I have to admit he slept quite beautifully, mouth closed, no musicale. It should have been soporific, but an edge of chagrin was tinting my feelings for him. I have always wondered why the fact that men have to sleep has never been really utilized by women, who are basically insomniac, when men transgress. Why have men never intuited that sleeping next to a woman you abuse all day might be hazardous? Drifting off I got into a fantasy of haranguing some feminist friends of mine with: Men sleep! We don't! Power is lying in the street and nobody bothers to pick it up! But I'm fabulating, because the power part of the harangue is a quote from Trotsky via Denoon.

We woke up in unison at seven thirty and scrambled to get some dinner. Afterward he wanted to read. We both ended up reading something. This time I was the culprit in that I dozed off. I could have been nudged out of it. I slept lightly and brokenly and have a distinct memory of Giles getting up a couple of times, going to the door, and stepping out into the corridor and looking up and down it, presumably for other white people. I fell asleep for good with him outlined that way in the dim corridor.

The next day was all work and no play. He was dead to the falls except visually and was preoccupied with how moist it was around them and what that might do to his apparati and film. He was not his usual perfectionist self. In fact he was slipshod, I thought. We had box lunches and worked straight through to dinner, where again the impression was of a sprinkling of whites and a vast chorus or gallery of black help. Let me pay for all my meals, why don't you? I said, to see how he would respond and if saying it would key something. But he said No no no. Apparently a deal was a deal.

At bedtime I pressed my availability fairly far. He noticed, and we got into the foyer of something, but there was a sense of his going through with it that was impossible to mistake. He was not getting hard and I wasn't prepared for heroic measures, nor, to be fair, was he asking for them. We stopped without discussing why we were stopping. The only comment I retain from that night was his saying that there were entire abandoned luxury hotels somewhere in the bush in Mozambique being kept going by former staff and where there had been no guests for years.

He saw them as shrines being kept pristine for a vanished white clientele against the day it might return. Like cargo cults, I said. He looked blank. He was fascinated to hear all I could tell him about those.

In the morning it was more work, quick quick, the last of it. He wanted to shoot other things in the vicinity than the falls. I had absorbed the falls, so I didn't mind. They were in my list of great sights seen, along with Mont-aux-Sources and Table Mountain.

Then at lunch, which we ate at the hotel, there was a change in the matrix which I thought might prove interesting vis-à-vis Giles. A substantial party of white Rhodesians was eating and drinking. These were diehards. Giles lit up slightly. He wandered over and mingled with them at the buffet and came back saying they were real Rhodesians and still pissing steam about the war. I was astonished at how public they were about the way they felt. Their main man was a guy with a Wild West mustache and a tee shirt with a very congested legend on it saying Rhodesian War Games 1960–1979, Rhodesians 100, Terrs 0, The Winners: Terrs. Giles kept looking their way during lunch. The group adjourned to play cards and drink more on the veranda. They waved to Giles as we left to continue shooting.

See this as perfect was what I was trying to make myself do. But Giles's physical uninterest in me was inevitably a kind of insult and was also making me feel like an exploitress. There was no question Giles had been normal toward me in Botswana, so I was forced to the hypothesis that it must be the starkness and recency of the overthrow of white power here that had done something to him at the level of the lower self. What a datum! I couldn't help thinking over and over. Was this an instant new thesis topic presenting itself? I had actually noticed a kind of aggressive sullenness among the white wives of Zimbabwe in several settings. Could this be it and could it be gotten at? You could never get it through male testimony—that I knew. But was this a thesis just going begging, even if it was social psychology and not nutritional anthropology? Couldn't it be cultural anthropology? Giles had been energized by having the ex–Selous Scouts or whatever they were turn up. If there was anything in this it ought to surface in greater warmth should I return to the attack.

By dinnertime the Rhodesians were gone. It had been a stopoff en route to Chobe. Giles was back to his lows immediately. I didn't even try to get anything to transpire. I suppose my embryonic thesis was quasi confirmed, but that whole speculation was a little lurid and a sign of intellectual desperation more than anything else. I tried to think of who at Stanford I could even conceivably give an aesopian hint of a sketch of my idea to, and had to laugh.

We flew back to Gaborone by charter the next day. You go diagonally across the central Kalahari, where there is nothing to see beneath you once you get past the Sua Pan area. Nevertheless Giles had stopped stroking his camera case and was suddenly staring down intently. When I asked him what he was looking for he said there was supposed to be a strange place down there run by an American where women went around naked. I felt like saying What's it to you? but refrained, sportswomanlike to the end. What was he talking about? Was it some kind of nudist colony? I asked, thinking of his connection with the cheap soft porn magazine in Valletta. But no, it was some kind of project. It was secret. I let him know how bizarre I thought he was being. Now of course I know that this was the deformed version of Denoon's work at Tsau produced by male gossip, because except for the women of Tsau, and the very few male dependents with them, it was only a handful of prurient men in various bureaucracies in Botswana who knew what was going on.

When we got back to Gabs we lost touch directly. He went to Mauritius, I heard, and was loving it.

Martin Wade Leaves a Party

Except among the elderly you rarely see healthy white people as thin as Martin Wade. He was only in his late twenties. He looked like a Tenniel illustration, with his biggish head. All the diplomatic wives wanted to feed him.

He was a celebrity among the South African exiles in Gaborone. His nickname was Mars, which was what the Batswana neighbor children in Bontleng called him. Martin Wade itself was a nom de guerre. He had been significant in the National Union of South African Students at Wits and had done something spectacular enough to get himself conscripted out of turn and sent to the "operational area." Then he had done something spectacular in the army, after which he had deserted and made his

way to Gaborone. In Bontleng he lived in a genuine hovel on some kind
of subsidy from the Swedes. People still in South Africa got information
to him on strikes and jailings, which he published in a little mimeo
newsletter that went out to different newspapers in the West, to be ignored. He was said to be ANC but sub rosa. He was myopic and wore
glasses, which like his weight had an effect on me. I have a certain
inordinate feeling toward revolutionaries who wear glasses, because
there is the sense of how easily they could be unhorsed in the slightest
physical confrontation with the enemy just by someone flicking their
glasses to the ground and stepping on them. So you assume such people
have unusual amounts of courage.

He had crossed my peripheral vision at one or two parties, inspiring
in me the universal response: how much was he getting to eat at that
particular occasion? Why didn't he eat more? Was it political, à la Simone
Weil? I knew that he was famous for giving away food to the Bontleng
urchinry, because one or two hostesses had complained that that was
what was happening to food packets they'd put up for him. I thought of
approaching him in a light way with something like You give new meaning to the term ectomorph. But then I would have been imbricated with
all the other maternal presences in what he doubtless experienced as a
nightmare.

The entrée was going to be roast pork the night we finally met. In the
universe there is nothing more inciting than pork, garlic, and onions
roasting. You could tell he was salivating because his Adam's apple was
on the prominent side and was moving like an animal.

I was having to control my body language with the hors d'oeuvres
when he came near. Of course diet is always with me and the psycho-
drama of why is not mysterious. The script reads along the lines of
needing urgently to know what it was about food that turned my mother
into an exhibit and might, unless I prevented it, do the same to me.
Everything is an artifact. I was in graduate school before I realized that
all her innocence about how little she actually ate was a sustained lie,
propaganda. So voilà, nutritional anthropology for me, which combined
the two things most compelling to me, food and man. Martin was the
guest of honor that night.

The couple giving the dinner were Americans, decent people teaching on local contract—which is not munificent—at the university. He
was biology and Margaret was setting up a pharmacy curriculum, if I
remember. They had been there a few years. They had two junior high
age boys in a boarding school in Johannesburg. They felt suitably guilty

about it, but they had looked at the alternatives in Botswana and decided it was the only fair choice they could make for the boys, who would be going on in science back home someday, the usual.

Dinner was virtually served. Several of us were commiserating Margaret, who was upset. A couple of days earlier she had picked up the Rand Daily Mail and lo there was a story about St. Stithian's, the boarding school, to wit, the police had organized a ratissage to drive some squatters out of a wooded area on the school property, with dogs and clubs and all the standard paraphernalia, and they had included boys from the upper forms, including the sons of our hosts. So it had been a tear-stained couple of days and there had been violent phone calls to the school, and so on. It would never happen again. But the boys were going to stay at St. Stithian's.

Hereupon Martin joined us, a samoosa half-raised to his mouth. He hadn't heard about the incident. He put the samoosa down.

I admired the way he approached the thing. First he made sure he had all the details right, and in particular that the boys were not going to be withdrawn. Then he said You will have to excuse me. The maid came in to say dinner was served just as he walked out. Margaret's husband tried to fix things by saying they might do something next term, if they could think of something, and reminded us how impossible it had been when they tried correspondence school for the boys. But Martin had picked up his daypack and was gone.

The only scene like it I had been through involved a dinner destroyed when a guy left abruptly as some veterans of therapy were all agreeing how much they hated their parents. He was European and had apparently never mentioned to anyone present that his parents had died in a concentration camp. It was no help, but anyway I followed Martin out into the street. May I stride with you? I asked him when I caught up with him.

So then we began bantering. He was very cockney, to my ear. I told him that as a South African male he was better off avoiding a meal that was too fatty anyway. They're at hugely high risk for heart attack, genetically. He said he knew that South African males up to age forty-five had the world's highest coronary rate but that his explanation was different to mine, as he put it, he would bet. He said Did you know the rate in South African men is the same to the second decimal as the rate for prison guards as a class around the world, and what does that say to you? I said I wouldn't deign to reply, it was so obvious. Then I asked him if he knew that the best gene pool against coronaries was living right next door to the Boers in the form of the Bantus and especially the southern Sotho. I mentioned studies showing that a tendency to early coronaries had been concentrated in the Boers by inbreeding but that all around, you had the Bantu tribes, with the lowest coronary rates in the world. Only apartheid stood between them. We agreed on the irony of it all: Boer and Bantu, made for each other. I can eat anything, he said, not being a Boer. He was from Natal. His position was that he was responsible for my leaving the dinner, so he would take me to his place and feed me. He knew I entirely understood why he'd felt he had had to leave.

His place, his one-room cement hut, was in a poor neighborhood but not the worst. He had his own standpipe in the yard and his own outhouse. He had a paraffin stove, used mainly to burn letters and documents. He had almost no chattels. Everything had to be kept to the minimum, so that he could decamp instantly and so that there would be nothing in the place he would ever have to come back for. This was another world to me. He was a musicologist. He had taken up the recorder, but only because it was portable. He could play beautifully. His real instrument was the viola da gamba. This whole time we were getting acquainted he was looking for food to serve us, including stepping out to check with his impoverished neighbors to see if they could lend him something when he discovered he had nothing except an ancient orange and two cans of pilchards. This was a man who loved to talk. We fascinated each other. Finally he permitted me to take him to a restaurant—only the most nominal, poorest, most working-class restaurant would do—where we talked endlessly some more. It emerged that he had conflicted feelings toward Americans, which I discovered my working-class origins had a slightly mollifying effect on. I highlighted them and it was all right. He came back with me to my place.

My Mortal Life

I could never get a coherent relationship going with Martin. I wanted to. I tried different modes with him. I tried just making his life more normal and less protean. He would stay over with me sometimes for as long as three days. But even then the clandestine side of his life would superpose itself and he would have to slip off to meet someone in the dead of night or go somewhere. I was helpful to him in small ways. For instance, right away I discovered he was afraid he was losing his hearing, a tragedy for somebody who expects to be second viola in the All Races National Symphony someday in a reborn South Africa. It occurred to me that he was having an earwax buildup, which is mostly a thing of the past for people who regularly take hot baths and showers. But in Bont-leng he was essentially reduced to sponge baths, even though he was methodical about them. I purged his ears with Debrox and he was over-come with the result.

We could have been serious. It was seductive that he enjoyed sex with me so much. He could be lyrical about my breasts. He was not widely experienced. If he ever got to a normal weight he was going to be striking rather than alarming. We were both starved for talk. I admired him for what he was doing. He was enrolled in a war against something that was totally evil, and he was fighting in a disinterested way—because he was doing it all for his black countrymen, a third party. He thought of himself as a realist and was the first to say he expected that even the whites with the best credentials would go into a period of eclipse once there was majority rule. The question of what I was doing with my life kept coming up by implication more and more overtly.

This reminds me that later Denoon would say there were only two completely self-justifying occupations in the contemporary world that he had personally run into: one was fighting the Christian fascists of South Africa and the other was being a fireman, because you can never have the slightest doubt that you're doing something totally socially valuable by pulling people out of burning buildings. Medicine he excluded be-cause people got rich doing it, and anybody who lived a life of service to the church—say in a ghetto or medical mission—also got excluded be-cause ultimately their work was acquisitive and inwardly intended to increase the temporal power of their particular denomination. He said firemen were the only people he knew with no self-doubt and that they went into their vocation knowing they had a thirty percent likelihood of ending up with a damaged spinal column.

But what was I doing with my mortal life? The question kept rearing up in my mind not because Martin tried to make me feel disadvantaged or trivial but because when you came down to it what I was trying to do with my anthropology was first to get a job in a halfway decent university and then get tenure. This was a marxist analysis of my situation but it was correct. Along the way, of course, I was going to be adding to the world's knowledge of man, no doubt. But there was already a lot of that, to put it mildly. Possibly there was enough. The government of Botswana, at least, thought there was enough for a while, it looked like. This was late January, because Reagan had been elected. The government announced a bombshell, a moratorium on all foreign-sponsored anthropological research in the country. Studies were piling up faster than anybody in the ministries could figure out what they were supposed to conclude from them. Most of the projects the government approves have something to do, however remotely, with getting the agricultural economy to work better. My colleagues were in a frenzy. They had had visions of coming back and doing follow-ups into infinity. I found it liberating but kept that to myself. My colleagues were fuming over a threatened investment. Who would ever have heard of Isaac Schapera if he had been permitted to do only one monograph of the Bakgatla? was something said endlessly. I was even in the unfamiliar position of feeling one-up, because my stupid exploded project at Tswapong was considered ongoing and I could stay in Botswana relatively indefinitely. I was grandfathered.

I was attracted by the intimations of danger around Martin, thinking initially that I was dealing mostly with atmosphere. It was inconceivable that the Bureau of Special Services had nothing better to do than infiltrate agents to harass this aesthete so thin he looked like a weather vane. I was also attracted by the sense he gave me of being able to see into the world of power hidden behind the public world. This was a little addictive to me, and I felt it. The conviction that the world is secretly corrupt is dangerous to certain temperaments because it rationalizes cutting corners and being selfish, an impulsion I was not in need of. But we would sit on the balcony at the President Hotel and a permsec would come by who was a lion of opposition to South Africa in the press and Martin would tell me that this man had children in school in Pretoria in a fancy place like St. Stithian's and that he owned chicken farms near Mafikeng, which made him in effect a hostage of the people he was constantly attacking. Martin knew exactly who was related to whom in government and convinced me that nepotism is not a useful construct for anthropologists to bring to the study of African government. He knew who all the undercover Special Branch operatives were and who were the intelligence people from the different embassies. In fact, although I had no way of knowing it at the time, he pointed out in some connection the Brit who would turn out to be my next lover. Martin compared Gabs to Lisbon during World War II. He had a pearl of great price: he knew whom to trust. When black exiles came over for a drink, it was wonderful. He was trusted, even by the Black Consciousness people, who are so edgy usually. He knew who was with the Diamond Police, which is almost a state within a state in Botswana. He especially loved pointing out the undercover South Africans, who all looked like burghers or successful farmers, which fed my taste for irony. I have a weakness for irony, and it was supreme irony that if anyone was, in the long run, going to salvage something for the white South African bourgeoisie, it was going to be people like Martin, whom they were, according to him, surveilling and thinking of killing. The future of a few million guilty whites was going to depend on whatever goodwill a handful of decent white colgrads like Martin could generate in the breast of the victorious black masses.

A *Fatal Proposition*

Let me not omit certain impurities in the man. Whole genera could get on his hate list if certain members of it did something antithetical to the cause. He was homophobic, or tended to be, because, he claimed, they had been overrepresented in Rhodesian information services during the liberation war. So that was it for homosexuals. I tried to point out that there was a logical error consisting of making the part stand for the whole, which he was committing. I drew back from trying to make headway against his anathematizing tendencies because that indirectly raised a question of why he was associating with me, an American whose CIA had told the South Africans where they could find Nelson Mandela when he was underground.

My being American was a serious issue and came up also at one point when I asked him why he wasn't proselytizing me more than he was. My feelings were a little hurt, frankly. I hated South Africa, which he didn't dispute. But there was the fact that I had not done anything politically strong enough to suit him in my life to date. I had never been a member of anything that was specifically against apartheid. I asked him how many women there were available to him in Botswana who had done everything he demanded politically. It was no use. We and the West Germans and Israel were the worst. We had given the Boers the bomb, and so on.

There would always be a coda waiving my responsibility for the actions of the American power elite when we had these malentendus, so we could get on with dinner or bed, but the strain was there.

We could never close a certain gap. Everything I was doing in that direction, like fixing up his diet, raising the creature comfort level, I did innocently and because I didn't think it would hurt anything for him to live a little less exigently. He, for instance, had no stereo. The house I was sitting did, a good one, and a good collection of tapes of Renaissance music. He started listening to them but then made himself stop, abruptly. One evening we were playing Albinoni and making sex—I won't say making love—nice and protractedly. He couldn't help turning on me afterward. Clearly the whole thing was too voluptuous for his image. He demanded I stop making custard for him, because it made him feel like a child. Blancmange was another thing I had just learned to make and had to stop making. I had been trying to find out what his favorite foods were and cooking them for him, not such an insidious thing to do. It took ingenuity because of the limits of what can be bought in Botswana: I made clever substitutions. I think I deserved appreciation, not what I got, which was an outburst against Americans for breeding a taste for luxury wherever they went. I tried to be more Spartan. I wanted to avoid fighting. It was too hot for it.

Even if somehow I had been able to overcome being an American, being hypermaternal, being a few years older—which he was sensitive about—there would still have been the question of what discipline meant. I was fascinated by the concept of being under discipline. It took force to get him to discuss it at all, and even then everything was couched so cryptically it was agony.

Martin was under discipline. He would never say whose, even though he knew I knew it had to be ANC. What he seemed perpetually unable to comprehend was that our relationship gave me the right to know something about this situation. I was also interested, in fact initially interested, from a social science angle. If he had been the least bit forthcoming when I first raised the matter we might have slipped past it. Over and over I told him I had no interest whatever in who it was he was under discipline to or what being under discipline was requiring him to do. I was curious about what it meant to be part of a social organism in the way I assumed he was. I wanted help conceptualizing it, was all. I knew his movements were to some extent controlled by orders he got. One reason he put in so much time at my place, I concluded, was because he could get and send phone messages there. There are no phones in Bontleng. But my questioning was never exquisite enough for him. If I asked something like Could you be a member of the movement against apartheid in a *contributory* way as opposed to the way you are now? he would fly into a rage and treat me like a spy.

Could someone who was under discipline ever be an appropriate mate? This was of course the underlying question I wanted answered. I had serious feelings for Martin. Most of the obstacles between us were probably erodable. I wasn't prepared to spend a life with him in permanent atonement for being American, but I was confident that if he loved me, it would denationalize my image. But I could never be hypothetical enough to have our discussion come off. I had long since given up asking naive—and, he thought, leading—questions like Do you have to have been born in South Africa to join the ANC? But a question like Suppose someone gave someone an order to kill someone he had nothing against except as a symbol? was also inadmissible. Being under discipline was something I may have reacted to too strongly, as a woman, and I told him that. But nothing helped.

I think he needed our relationship to come apart nastily, to make it easier for both of us.

We almost couldn't break it off, because just when I'd made the decision someone killed his cat. He had adopted a stray. One night he went home and found it strangled on his kitchen table. The house had been locked. He was very shaken. Then letters to him started turning up with razor slits across the address, just that, the contents not touched. I was terrified, but I kept making mistakes. Here was my heinous suggestion: I thought he should get away for a while and I proposed he come with me to a game area. I had some contacts in the safari business in Maun and I knew how we could do this for next to nothing. I told him it was ridiculous of him to be in Botswana for whatever reason and never see the last and greatest unfenced game area in the world. He looked at me as though I were a criminal. I tried to argue him into it by saying he was missing a unique experience, because camping out in a game area was the only way you could get the frisson of what it must have been like to be a lone human being who was the subject of predation by stronger, bigger, and more numerous animals. This was deeply stupid, and he let me see it. He was already a prey. My heart was in the right place, but that was the end for us.

Nothing happened to him, finally. People I met glancingly through

him were ultimately killed by the South Africans, not in Botswana but in
Angola or Zimbabwe, where they had gone for safety. He got to England.
The ANC has a choir, which he has something to do with.

The British Spy

My last relationship before Nelson Denoon rose in the skies of my
life was with a spy, Z. Z is for zed, meaning the last in a series of things
of a certain kind. It took me awhile to get him to admit it, but the reason
he initially sought me out was because his information was that I was
going with Martin Wade, in whom the British High Commission had an
interest. I was no longer seeing Martin but I was still trying to keep track
of him, see how he was doing, regretting things. It even occurred to me
that I could use Z's attentions to me as a way to get back with Martin by
offering to disinform Z, if that was appropriate.

Z didn't know that thanks to Martin, I knew Z was a spy. I felt I had
enormous leverage, for once. Everything I do is so overdetermined. I
was moved by the feeling that this was just what I deserved—a spy. He
pulled up beside me in a black Peugeot as I was walking home with a
netbag of groceries over my shoulder and offered me a lift. Whites do
that for one another. I hated to accept free lifts from fellow whites: the
Batswana notice it and I empathize with them standing waiting forever
for jammed taxis or vans while the whites slide off into the sunset. But I
got in. I got in because I had some dairy products I needed to rush to my
refrigerator, but I got in even more because Z was a spy.

He must have been mid-fifties. I found him attractive. I don't despise
people for fighting old age tooth and nail, which he was. I like the
impulse more in men than I do in women, though, which I should
probably explore sometime. He was still well built but showing a little
gynecomastia, which didn't really go with his rectilinear, almost colum-
nar midsection. Later, his first evasion on that subject would be that he
was wearing a truss. Then it came out that it was a girdle. He was wearing
the usual safari shirt and shorts, and I noticed he had touched up a
couple of varicosities with something pink. He was a leading-man type
who was just over the line into paterfamilias roles and hating it. He had

gray hair worn long on one side and carefully articulated and spray-fixed over his bald crown. His eyebrows were like ledges. I wondered if wanting to be sexually plausible, which he clearly did, had anything to do with needing to be able to do his job, id est extracting confidences. He seemed very tan, but there was something off about the hue, which was another secret of his I ultimately extracted.

What would a spy be like personally? Would a spy compensate, say, for the duplicity of his working day by being the opposite in his free time with his loved ones or one? What kind of spy was Z, in the sense of how far he was expected to go in corruption or surveilling or whatever his job description required? Just as a feat, how much that I wasn't supposed to know might I be able to get him to tell me? I was getting ahead of myself, but I could tell Z was in a state of appreciation toward me. I gave him a couple of minutes to arrange himself before he stepped out of the car at my place. I had invited him to come in for iced tea.

A little breeze had sprung up, and it did a cruel thing to him, lifting the lattice of hair up from his head like a lid. I know he noticed it, but he was stoical and ignored it, which went to my heart.

He had an intelligent line. All the vital statistics were delivered in passing, while he was ostensibly talking about other things. He was divorced. He was lonely. He found the anthropology of the country fascinating but unfortunately in his circles there was no one of like mind, perhaps it was just a British failing. Here he was showing me that he was atypical and not imperialistic. Nota bene: he liked to eat out but he hated eating alone. Nothing interested him more than anthropology. He was virtually an amateur anthropologist. All this was like marbling as he talked cynically about the economics of the country. I saw him pick up that I liked a slightly cynical approach to social reality, and he went more with that. There were some clichés. He missed West Africa, which is what everybody says who was ever posted there—the Gambia, the color, the markets, the people so happy they're practically giddy. I couldn't tell him enough about my time in Keteng and the Tswapong Hills.

The only thing he did that I didn't like was to try to strum a little on my possible fear of being alone in the house. He went on about break-ins increasing, until he saw he was in the wrong pew. I told him I positively enjoyed living alone and the single thing I didn't like about it was stepping on millipedes coiled up like coasters on the kitchen floor. There were a lot of them getting indoors somehow. Re the break-ins, I assumed he was trying to cast himself as a protector type I could count on.

He took me to dinner a few times. It was all liberal arts. And anthropology. He represented himself as a voracious reader and he went out of his way to read a couple of things I recommended. He took me to a place I didn't even know existed, a deluxe restaurant connected to the golf club. It was run by Portuguese who had owned a sumptuous place in Beira before the liberation. Z was not boring, or rather his footwork was not boring. He stopped flashing his avuncular side bit by bit. He started me out reading Arnold Bennett, which I'm grateful to him for. The whole thing was very much like synchronized swimming. We wanted something from each other but we kept going elegantly side by side, not saying what we wanted. He still thought I was seeing Martin, which I had somewhat led him to assume. Finally it was all too leisurely for me, and I struck.

Gratitude Is a Drug

I was after his secrets. I had some already, but so far they were all in the category of personal vanity. The girdle was one. His tan was another. He took a carotene product you can get in South Africa. It gives you a terra cotta appearance and makes your excreta gaudy. He used alum on the backs of his hands for age spots. I was finding myself in a game. It was like deciding to have an obsession. The game was roughly that I would get more out of him than he wanted to tell me—but not in exchange for what he wanted from me, which was yet to reveal itself but which probably meant tidbits about Martin and his friends. From me he would get nothing, not even fabrications on that score, although it might be necessary to start the game with fabrications. I would trade sex, if I had to, but I would get more points, the game would be more consummate, if I got his secrets by trading something else, something that hadn't defined itself yet. I was greedy for his secrets, and I construed secrets as embracing everything he would rather not tell me—personal, political, what have you. I'm willing to call this decadent. The fact that spying is an execrable and stupid thing had nothing to do with why I wanted to play this game with Z.

I feel putrid when I go over my nexus with Z, but so be it. What I

did, I did. Greed misrepresents my motives, which were complex, but is
what you would come up with as an outside observer, because of the
wining and dining that continued, the entrée into upper echelon white
teas and potlatches. Overhanging me from the breakup with Martin were
heroine fantasies, my somehow starring unexpectedly in the struggle
against apartheid. Breaking with Martin meant losing someone who had
something important, which was significance. I felt deprived and retrograde. I had begun letting my eating inch up. When I was with Martin I
was almost never hungry, partly out of involuntary corporeal sympathy
with what he was and partly because there was a limit to how disparate
from my skeletal boyfriend I could stand to be. When it ended with
Martin it was like a spring being released, evidently. I was in the Star
Bakery and suddenly the bread available in Gaborone was intolerable. In
the Star you could almost imagine you were in a bread museum, the
display of types of bread was so broad—baguettes, braided loaves, rolls.
But interiorly everything was made from the same spongeous cement-
colored stuff. I had to bake. And what you bake you eat. I was eating too
much and felt like a zero because of it, or a doughnut, rather. Here came
Z, a worse bread maven than even I was, someone even more famished
for good bread. We fit. Moreover, when the time came for me to regroup
on my weight, the odd physical relationship that had evolved between
us was perfect for that too—because of the quantum of sheer exercise
in it.

We'd had some minor postprandial necking in the car, in the course
of which I'd wondered if he was uncomfortable kissing in a sitting position. Or there might or might not be a goodnight kiss at the door as he
left following a nightcap ceremony during which he had not been insistent on accelerating the physical pace, far from it. In retrospect I think
the kissing was more a recurring declaration that in spite of the continued decorousness of our relationship, he was not unsexual toward me.
He would occasionally get mild erections, nothing full-blown, though.

But once I'd faced what I wanted, I knew it was time to stop skirmish-
ing so much. His back was his Achilles' heel. One night as he was coming
in I insisted he bring his back pillow. He was chagrined that I'd even
noticed it. It was an orthopedic pillow he always tried to twitch out of
sight into the backseat before I could spot it if I was getting into the car.
I put it that since he had to know I knew about it he should bring it in
and use it, because then he might be disposed to stay longer. I think he
said You notice everything, and I said Oh you've noticed, so we laughed
and he brought the thing in. This is how reduced I was: I took his You

notice everything as a compliment conceivably containing the suggestion
that he thought I might somehow make a good spy. This is how much,
at our lowest, we suck after the male imprimatur for some completely
congenital quality we might have. This is how I know I was on the plain
of the abyss.

I said Your back is a mess, am I right? He couldn't agree more and
was prone on a sheepskin in front of the fireplace almost before I asked
if he would let me see what I could do. I acted knowing in the area and
that was all it took. I sat on my hams next to him and said I can't do this
through cloth, and he, in a sort of frenzy, said Yes, yes, and violently
worked his shirt up to his neck like an escape artist, not even getting up
to do it. Then with just the heel of my hand running lightly once up his
spine I said I think this isn't from parachuting, to which he burst back
with No, it's scoliosis, oh god—just as I was saying It's scoliosis, isn't it?
He torqued around to look at me as though I was extraordinary.

The truth was that the man was in concealed distress most of the
time. Nobody at the High Commission could know the extent of it lest
the idea of his retirement arise. I had the key. What developed from this
was a profound physical relationship without sex, although there was
sexual feeling here and there in it. If you need professional massage in
Botswana you're in the same position as someone who needs periodontia.
It isn't there. I'm not a masseuse, but I have strong hands and arms and
the conviction that massage is all logic and feedback, which, so far,
checks out. With Z I was brilliant. I changed his life, briefly.

I mastered his back. I developed a rapport with it, is the best way I
can describe what I did. I dealt with his back as though it were an
autonomous entity like a face or a frightened animal. For two weeks we
had nightly sessions and at the end of it he was close to reborn. He had
decent cervical mobility again, which meant he could look over his
shoulder for the first time in years, which had to have professional value
to him—as I was kind enough not to point out. He was overcome with
what I was doing for him. He would do anything for me, I only had to
say what, why was I refusing his gifts? I was the only American he had
ever met who made him want to see America, no woman had ever done
for him what I was doing and I was doing it during the hottest part of the
year like an angel of mercy and on and on, and did I know that he himself had been very anti-American and did I know how very much anti-
American feeling there was among British Overseas Territories staff,
which they hid, and he had to confess he hadn't been totally uninterested

in America until me because he had always been curious to see the Grand Canyon, and on and on.

By about the third session I had figured out what the protocol needed to be. The frame around the process was that we should both understand his back as our antagonist. He had to grasp that the process was cumulative. I was assembling my mode from what seemed to work, unknown to him, and it was clear that an authoritative tone was a winner. There would be two things we were going to ignore during this intensive, as I decided to call it. First of all, I said, we are going to ignore any erections you get and call them manifestations and laugh at them. Second of all, there are going to be incidents of flatus and we are going to ignore them and refer to them as queries. There was a genuine therapeutic notion behind both maneuvers. I wanted to abort the tension that would come from his thinking he, in the circumstances, ought to be getting aroused. And also the first time I had sensed I'd gotten him deeply relaxed a fart had escaped him. He was horrified and got tense. I presented the protocol on erections as a coin with two sides in that I would also be ignoring any feelings of desire that transpired in me. The regulations were that he would be in his undershorts and I would be in my mom-type lentil-green one-piece South African bathing suit. Finally, because I was the one who was in communication with his back, I would control the rhythm of the sessions. He was a bystander. He might have to be silent sometimes, and if he spoke to me I might not reply, because my mission was to preserve my concentration.

I could do anything with him. I could sit on him. I could walk on him if I was careful. I could put my heels in the nape of his neck and grip his arms at the elbows and pull until he gave a groan of pleasure that was absolutely specific. There isn't just one all-purpose groan of pleasure, as we assume. His back acclimated to me. There was something about being able to manhandle a male body without having to treat the experience as foreplay. I wasn't rough with him. In fact it became very domestic. He was suddenly sleeping wonderfully, he told me. I didn't mind this man. I gave myself to his back. Gratitude is a drug.

But what I do resent, still, is Denoon for trivializing the experience when I told him about it and he, in one of his litanies about the normalization of the bizarre in the U.S., asked if I knew that in sex tabloids there were ads from women making themselves available to men for wrestling purposes, no penetration involved. It seems men with a taste for being bested by big, strapping women had been allowed, through the magic of late capitalism, to constitute themselves as one market among others. I hadn't heard about it. But it was worse when he tried to get away with the canard that what I had been doing was nothing more than soft core SM whether I knew it or not. And was I aware of some famous datum showing that the largest vocational category resorting to SM-specialized prostitutes was law enforcement personalities, not excluding the judiciary? I pointed out that Z had had nothing to do with law enforcement that I knew of, but Denoon insisted—out of jealousy, no question—that spies were in the same ballpark. I mocked him into re-tracting that, finally, as beneath him. I said something like I revere the level of argument you impose on others and now you come up with something like this? His real problem was that he thought my ministra-tions to him along the same lines were a pale reflection of what I had depicted myself as doing for Z. He was right, which I never denied. You are a different moment, I told him. Your back is fine, for one thing.

Denoon couldn't understand that there was a feel almost of paradise about being absorbed so completely in a project of personal alleviation. This may be a strictly female view. And it is not the same as saying it wouldn't be boring as a lifetime repetitive vocation. One difference be-tween women and men is that women really want paradise. Men say they do, but what they mean by it is absolute security, which they can obtain only through utter domination of the near and dear and the environment as far as the eye can see, how else? Most men. In any case, aside from the exertion involved, which ultimately I was able to think of simply as good exercise, I liked the ordeal, down to the details—perspiration, flesh smells, towels all over, his rather charred breath, insects banging inces-santly into the window screens.

It began to bother him that there was apparently nothing he could do for me in return. We had even stopped eating out, so that we could have longer sessions. He was grateful across the board. He was cutting back on his smoking, he noticed. It was a byproduct of feeling better and was something he had wanted to do for a long time. My merest hints were helping him. I'd advised him to stop his housekeeper from picking up vegetables at the prison garden, beautiful as they were, because night soil was used in cultivating them and he was running definite gastroin-testinal dangers in eating them. Whatever his original interest in me had been, I had blasted it into nothingness with my attentions. Martin Wade never came up once.

I did accept one gift, a beautiful ethereal blue and white yakuta. I couldn't believe it was cotton. But this was a bagatelle to him, and as I pounded and wrenched he would lie there free associating on my virtues and uniqueness and how hurtful it was that I was refusing his generosity.

As to secrets, I had more than I wanted on the personal side but nothing that counted from his professional side, yet.

Tell Me Something I'm Not Supposed to Know

I was liking Z. His improvement made him cheerful. We had certain things in common, such as both being natural mimics. After one particularly acute but cutting impersonation of his, I said Remind me to warn my daughter about going with someone's who's a good mimic, because they aren't necessarily the kindest, as in my case. Ah, do you have a daughter, then? And I said No, I mean when I do, someday. And then he said So it wouldn't be a good idea for two mimics to marry, would it? Even through his carotene I could tell he was blushing. I was touched. We both were.

I remember I was sitting on the back of his legs, resting, when I decided it was time to shorten the game. My Martin Wade fantasies were fading. I decided to be a little reckless.

You're unique, he was saying, apropos his having come to the conviction that I could tell people's nationality at a distance at a glance. Recently there had been a couple of lucky shots in the dark doing that. And then, at a tea the day before, he had asked what the nationality was of a rather Syrian-looking woman who was new in town and new to me. I'd said Oh, British, flooring him. But it had been easy because I'd overheard her say arvacado for avocado earlier, unbeknownst to him.

You're unique, he said. No woman in my life has done for me half what you have, and yet you've asked nothing. Please, what can I do for you?

Really nothing. I enjoyed this. Nothing, unless you wanted to satisfy my curiosity about something.

Anything. What?

I don't know. Tell me something I'm not supposed to know.

He got tense instantly. I said Now don't do that and ruin our work. Let's drop it.

But what did I mean?

I began kneading him while I vamped. I said I know this will seem perverse to you. But in a way—and I understand it has to be this way, don't think I don't—in a way there's something in you I can't reach and never will and probably it can't be helped, but it's a hindrance, really. I know how involuted this sounds. But you are obviously some kind of spy or operative, which is all right, but you are. I happen to know about it. But of course life puts us in the position where you have to deny this to my face, so feel free. But you know what I am and I can't know what you are, which I accept, because your mission is to playact the commercial attaché for me and what is resulting is false consciousness, inevitably.

He got very upset. We had to talk. I had to get off him and we both had to dress and talk properly. He wanted a drink.

We sat at the kitchen table after he had washed his face twice and made me look around to see if perchance there were any cigarettes about.

He didn't immediately deny being a spy but took a line which I didn't honor with a reply. He wanted to know where on earth I had gotten such an idea, and from whom.

Then he did deny it, to which I said Fine, but I know otherwise for a fact, and you might consider admitting something just for the sake of our relationship.

How did I mean? Did I mean he couldn't see me, all this couldn't continue, if he didn't confirm what I was saying?

Then we circled around my assertion that of course I was not saying anything like that and of course we could go on, however imperfectly. And then of course I invited him to reassure himself any way he liked that there was nothing clandestine going on with me, no tape recorders or surveillance cameras, which he dismissed curtly, saying I know who you are.

Then it was theme and variations, theme being tell me what I am, then: I'm an anthropologist, I have a hobby which is related and which is putting together an understanding of the real world and trying to live in it. He should consider it a quirk.

Somehow I knew it was no longer touch and go. He continued looking stricken for a while, then said Well, suppose I were to go along with you and we carry on together and I endorse this fairytale that I am whatever you like: what would you be expecting then?

We could do that, I said. It would be up to you. This is symbolic anyway. You could tell me something I'm not supposed to know, and it could be anything. It's a token of something. Let's forget it. There is no way I would do anything with what you told me, or repeat it, which you know. You could tell me something obsolete but that I'm still not supposed to know. Let's stop. This is making me feel neurotic.

I kept on in that vein, urging us to drop the whole thing and continue on bravely but by implication lamely in whatever relationship would survive my cri de coeur–type outburst, continue on in a relationship that —since I was using the past tense and the conditional a lot—looked as if it might be coming to an end sooner rather than later.

Then he cut me off with You mean to say you have no particular field of inquiry, no particular set of questions, no particular question at all? This I find strange.

So I laughed and said This is how you tell a thing is a quirk. This is what you call humoring a person. Tell me something quote unquote forbidden. Make it something pointless, useless, out of date, anything, just so it's something somebody thinks I shouldn't know. You have the choice of seeing this as a caprice or believing that I'm not what I seem and what you know I am.

You have been an absolute angel to me, he said. Now, how would you know if I made something up in order to pacify you? How would you know?

That would be up to you. I probably wouldn't know. Who am I? That's what a clever man would do, probably. You could.

It was late, so I said he should go home, that I regretted the whole thing and he should come back the next night for dinner and he should forgive me if he could for yielding to a feeling of wanting to get something from some deep protected nonpublic part of him. It was an impulse I said I was sure many other women had had with him and been smart enough to suppress.

I'm not good at being rueful, so I curtailed things. I made myself say the whole thing was about being open, and I nearly gagged. The world is what it is, I said, and you are what you are, and if I'm a neurotic about the fact that men have all the secrets and I have an impulse and want to get one, then that's what I am. I said I'm not saying to tell me the worst thing you ever did, although who wouldn't love to hear that, or tell me something filthy about the queen or something defense related or something that puts perfidious Albion in a bad light—did I say that? I wanted to get a smile out of him before he left.

You thoroughly confuse one, he said. He left, thinking.

What Was I Doing?

Once he was gone I felt like a lunatic. I was engaging in something deluded and worthless. What was I doing? How stupid a goal could you set for yourself?

I suppose I had a dark night of the soul. I had no relation to anything that had meaning. It was like an experience Nelson would tell me about that was similar. He was in New York, where he had a couple of hours free between appointments or appearances. He was in the vicinity of the New York Public Library so decided to stop in. It was going to be an enormous pleasure to be there. I don't know where he'd been living just before that, but it had been remote, someplace without libraries, and he was famished for print. He was filled with anticipation, he would be flooded with choices of things he wanted to look up or catch up on. He stepped into the main reference room, a vast place where every wall was lined with banks of card catalogs, where he would have access to every written thing in the Western world that was worthwhile, virtually. He steps into the room and begins to sweat from every pore, as he put it. *Nothing interested him.* Not only had he forgotten what it was he'd intended to follow up on, *there was nothing of interest.* He called it the abomination of desolation. *There was nothing he wanted to read.* He felt cold but not faint. He felt he was real but that the material of the world had changed into something like paper ash that would disintegrate if he touched it. Paper ash was all he could compare it to. He was in terror. He felt he had to walk carefully in leaving, not touch anything. Then he left and it stopped. I walked him through it again when he told me about it because I thought the paper ash was a clue. It may have been. One of his chores as a boy was to endlessly burn newspapers and periodicals in a backyard incinerator. His father subscribed to everything, but by the time Nelson was fifteen or so his father's reading had become haphazard and was in the process of stopping altogether, so Nelson would be burning a lot of periodicals unopened, in their mailers. And it had been painful for him, and he had a strong image of stirring the ashes and of whole intact pages reduced to black or gray ash with the print still read-able. He denied there was a connection.

Finally I got myself in hand. Not proceeding would be even more demoralizing than seeing where this would come out, even if it was ridiculous. And so to bed.

Two Feints

He came in glum. I was rehearsed.

I saturated the first half hour with protestations that I repented the whole thing, that I had been incredibly jejune, that the little nips of Mainstay I had taken while I was massaging him had been part of the problem, that I was distraught. I looked the part thanks to my dark night of the soul. My plea was that we forget it. It was just that when he had said Please let me do something for you it had been the equivalent of someone inviting you to make a wish, no more. Also I didn't want things to end uglily because I had to start thinking about getting home and I wanted to not leave a stain behind.

Also, I said, I know you can't help but worry this is something that however circuitously could endanger your job. I want you to know I'm not cavalier about jobs. You can fall into a fissure between jobs and never be seen again, because of your age, for instance. My antecedents are one hundred percent working class, I said, by which I mean just barely arrived there and glad of it. Here I was exploiting my having got-ten him to let slip that he was Labour, which people at his level in the ministry he was in are supposed to reveal only on pain of death, I gathered.

I forget what I made for dinner, but I remember he toyed with the entrée. Not the bread, though. He could never keep his hands off my baking.

We sat in the heat. I was supposed to pick up that he'd made some brave decision that rendered all the preambling I was doing irrelevant.

Might we talk as friends, or family? he finally asked. He was going into a role.

I know what you're doing, I said: You have an instinct for the avuncular. But go ahead anyway. He smiled.

Well, there are so many things of interest, aren't there? The Bushmen. Let us say you were concerned with the Bushmen—everyone here is, it seems. The fate of the Bushmen. Sad, isn't it, that the South Africans are turning them into trackers to hunt down guerrillas in Ovamboland?

This annoyed me no end, because it was such common knowledge. But I just said that I knew about this because it had been in the Rand Daily Mail, and it was more than sad. Patronize me at your peril, my attitude said, and he got it.

So sorry, he murmured. I could feel him punching the reset button.

Then, Um, did I think there was anything to the stories that the South Africans were bribing certain Kwena chiefs to get them interested in joining up with the five million Kwenas the Boers already controlled through their thug Mangope across the border in Bophuthatswana, thusly threatening to partition and wreck Botswana for being so uncooperative? Mangope's agents were working everywhere. I am summarizing. Halfway through this I started finishing his sentences for him. I read the Economist too, I said. But I didn't need to read the Economist to know about Mangope. I reprised how serious I was about forgetting the whole thing, how embarrassed I was that I had ever said anything, especially if this was the outcome.

Next I got a disorganized series of asides, essentially, to the effect that I was really a rather terrifying person and did I know that? I seemed to be a sort of monster who remembered everything—an allusion to something that happened rather often where I would quote him to himself if the situation called for it. Did I also remember lines of text, as I seemed to? But then I was also an angel. I was saying all was forgiven, but I was not projecting that. It was pro forma. He was no fool.

I briefly considered showing him I could tell him a thing or two myself. I knew from my time in Keteng that the South Africans had spies and stooges absolutely everywhere and were behind the big abrupt movement among the Herero to go back to Namibia and take their cattle with them. They had come over with nothing after the German massacres in 1905, and they had built up their herds from scratch, being genius cattle raisers. The government was saying begone but leave your herds. But this kind of thing is what the Boers do for fun. There's nothing surprising about it. They are breeders of strife. But I held myself in because I could tell by his expression that something new was impending.

Sekopololo

Well, he could pass on something he would wager I hadn't heard of.
Possibly this would come under the heading of scandal. Someone rather
famous was in Botswana incognito, so to speak, and had been—off and
on, but now on—for some years, eight to be precise. He paused to see if
this was going to be old news again and was relieved when it was clear I
had no idea what he was talking about, unless he meant Elizabeth Taylor
and her putative hospital project, which would have been completely
risible.

I wasn't to think that this was by any manner of means an official
secret. It was more a gentlemen's agreement among people who had
to know about this person's presence. This person had exacted highly
unusual conditions from the government of Botswana, outrageous conditions, in setting up his project, which was what he was doing in Botswana, something very avant-garde, supposedly very major and massive,
a whole new village built from the ground up, in point of fact, somewhere in the north central Kalahari. Clearly he hated whoever this was.
Did I still not know? He was surprised.

Go on, I said.

Well, what else could he add? He considered. This was an American,
a difficult individual, and there was division in government vis-à-vis all
the latitude granted him, particularly in the matter of oversight. His idea
was that evaluators and visitors were parasites whose only function was
to deform and corrupt the development process. Some unspecified day
this New Jerusalem would be complete and only then would the world,
including the donors who had financed it, be allowed to see what they
had wrought and carry back the secret word that would put paid to
poverty in Africa. There was even a Tswana code name for the project,
which was Sekopololo, which no one could pronounce. I knew that
Sekopololo translated as "The Key."

When he said Nelson Denoon I could hardly believe it. Denoon was
a bête noire of mine, in an abstract way, from the first of my endless
years at Stanford. Initially I associated him with earlier tribulations at

Bemidji State, but that was wrong. I had been tantamount to a fan of this man's work. There were several of us. He had come to Stanford to run a colloquy on the etiology of poverty. Too bad, it was restricted to faculty and a select few students. You had to have passed your quals and or you had to know somebody. You could get in if somebody liked you. When we were noninvited we even went so far as to appeal to him directly via a fanlike note. No reply. Naturally afterward all the attendees reported a truly scrotum-tightening experience. Their worldviews had changed. One woman couldn't get over his voice. It was a voice you could eat, she said.

It all came back, the bathos of trying to be nonchalant about trying and failing to get at least a glimpse of the great man. He had written a classic that undergraduates loved and most of the professoriat hated: *Development as the Death of Villages*, with its jacket portrait of someone reminiscent of the white actors they use to play the Indian chief's head-strong eldest son in westerns. You couldn't tell in the photograph because it was full face, but he had his sleek black hair in an actual ponytail. He was wearing it that way when he came to Stanford, as I learned from one of my female colleagues who attended the audience and whose name I forget but whom I think of for some reason as Whoreen, which is close. Whoreen is at the University of South Dakota, but on tenure track. Colleague is of course a misnomer: you only have colleagues once you get hired. As of early 1981, Denoon would be mid–late forties, I calculated.

So it was none other than Nelson Denoon! He was so famously sardonic! So heretical! He was so interdisciplinary! Economics, anthropology, economic anthropology, you name it in the policy sciences, not to mention development proper and being in actual charge of a sequence of famous rural development projects in Africa! In fact, he was supposed to be in Tanzania at that very moment or until just recently and arguing with Julius Nyerere, or was I out of date or was he just everywhere?

Here was someone at the level of Paulo Freire or Ivan Illich, but nonreligious, totally, therefore not dismissable as a mystic. Here was the ultimate beneficiary of the academic star system and a star himself, who was somehow against it and reviled it at all times, which only made him more of a star, more in demand, more invited to conferences, always a panelist, never a rapporteur. Here was the acme of what you could get out of academia: teach where you like, get visiting fellowships and lectureships, grants, get quoted, jet around, rusticate a few years in the bush if you felt like it. This is how I saw him. I remembered that in fact

I knew he had left Tanzania after—what else?—a famous harangue against the revered head of a sovereign country that was the left's darling, a polemic that—what else?—had been published in hard covers, something that was essentially a pamphlet. Which had been met with the most pleasant eruptions of praise and rage, per usual.

He was at the pinnacle of whatever vineyard I was laboring in as a groundling. I'm not proud of the vibration the image I had of him created in me. It was a textbook example of ressentiment. I was thirty-two and a woman and no doctorate yet, no thesis even, and closing in on my thesis deadline. I had been working my tits down to nubs in the study of man, with the result that my goals were receding farther the faster I ran. So it seemed.

Z sensed he had something I wanted more on. He was acute. I was so labile it was ridiculous. It would be about as hard to read me as being in the kitchen and noticing when the compressor went on in the refrigerator.

Did I know the party, then?

Only by reputation, I said. What else could he tell me?

Now he was cagey. He was adamant that he had no idea where the project was, exactly. That was very closely held. But he held out the faint possibility that in a pinch he could find out. Ho hum, I thought: for a consideration, he means, and what might that be?

I was having the berserk and faintly triumphant feeling of having cornered Denoon, just because we both happened to be in Botswana. This was not absolutely stupid, because for the white presence Botswana is like one big very dispersed small town. There are only a million people all told, black and white together, in a country the size of Texas or France, as the intro paragraph of every project proposal on Botswana reads. But Denoon's being there felt like providence. I was certain I could get his attention this time. A king can look at a cat for a change, I thought. This shooting star had apparently been sedentarized in my bailiwick—so, good. I wanted to see him in the flesh, see how he was holding up. Was he the same black Irish kindly Satan persona with hair like a Sioux, black as night, dispensing piercing glances left and right, or not?

People felt so strongly about him. When he was the topic of conversation you got sick of hearing the cliché that either you hated his positions or you loved them, there was no middle ground with him. Friendships had broken up over his book. The development business is full of suppressed hatred between schools of thought, and the passion arises because money is involved. Developmentalists are competing tooth and nail for project money to enact their theories someplace. This is the only way to know you're on top. It isn't like English History, say, where the prize is getting into every bibliography until the end of time because what you figured out about Tudor statecraft subsumes and overturns everything anybody else wrote, up until you. Development is more like research medicine, where you rise and fall according to the grants you rack up. In regular scholarship what you get is the joy of subsuming your predecessors and peers: they thought they were rivers but you turn them into creeks, tributaries to your majestic seaward flow. And Denoon not only pierced competitive theories on paper, he did live projects, lots of them one after another.

Anthropologists were particularly conflicted about Denoon because of his celebrated scorn for the field as a whole. But anthropology needs development and gets dragged perforce into taking sides on schools of thought or on projects. There is hiring involved. You need feasibility studies, you need sensitivity monitoring, you need impact evaluation, you need retrospectives of various kinds and degrees of thoroughness. For some reason he had basically a left academic constituency, which was odd because he was notorious for taking the position that marxists had no development theory worth the name: from Lenin onward development was just whatever took place after the spokesmen for the proletariat took power. But still they loved him. How did they like his famous Capitalism is strangling black Africa: Socialism will bury her! I wondered. He was the theorist you hate to love. I had to know how he was doing. Was he still the equivalent in development terms of Orson Welles in the movie world when he was at his zenith between *Citizen Kane* and *The Magnificent Ambersons*? Had he slipped at all, since we all slip? I wanted to see him in the flesh.

Tell me at least if he's married, I said to Z. He had been, the last I'd heard. I couldn't help it. Eminence is not the best medium for marriages, is what I was thinking.

I can tell you something about that another time, Z said. It's an interesting question. I would say yes and no. It's an interesting story. But there was the question of our um prognosis.

I was slightly unforthcoming.

Well, there was more he could tell me, possibly. Denoon kept his movements in Botswana, when he was offsite, very private. But he thought Denoon was about to be in town for a short while. Z might be able to find out more about that too.

He had me and knew it.

Could we not just go on seeing each other for a time, at a pace of say once a week, since I had gotten him well over the hump with his back? It's your hands I'm going to miss eternally when you leave, he said, your marvelous hands, your great gift.

Another choppy night ensued after he left me alone with my new fixation. I slept minimally, then got up and cleaned the premises and wrote another lying letter to my mother.

2 THE SOLAR DEMOCRAT

A *Fête Worse Than Death*

I was wound up when I met Denoon. The night was muggy, with freak intermittent blasts and lurches of hot wind, which was fine somehow when I was walking over to the reception with Z but nerve-wracking during the aeon we had to wait in a mob outside the locked gates of the house we were invited to. The hosts who were keeping us in the street were the USAID mission director Arthur Bemis and his wife, Ariel. Apparently we were waiting for the receiving line to complete itself.

Just getting into the AID director's house was considered a coup, because of the decor. People said it was like being in Asia. From the street the place looked Moorish: there were high pink perimeter walls, polychrome tiles outlining the arch around the locked gates, palm fronds visible lashing back and forth above the walls. There was a huge attendance, half of it Batswana out of the state bourgeoisie. We were very dressy. Z was wearing an actual cummerbund, my first. I was wearing a black skirt with kick pleats and a tank top, also black. I needed a full skirt at that point in time. Cursing was going on in several languages as women hunched and swiveled in the wind while their coiffures came to pieces. We couldn't see Denoon in the line, which prompted Z to tell me again that it was only a rumor that he would be there at all.

We were let into the grounds but not yet into the house. The walls were no help when it came to the wind. The grounds had a very lunar feeling. Floodlights cast a bleaching glare over everything, and the estate lights dotted about the grounds were so fierce they left afterimages. You had to watch where you looked. Wife Ariel was the leading malcontent in the American community. The watering restrictions that came with the drought had been the last straw for her, and she had had all her lawns scraped up and replaced with beds of white pebbles imported from South Africa. I have removed the brownsward, she is supposed to have announced. There was a paucity of chairs, and the ones there were were metal and forbidding, unpadded. Ariel was identified with Asia, where they had been posted repeatedly. In the receiving line she was easily your

most unforgettable character. She was perfect for the electric-blue
Chinese silk sheath she was wearing, being anorectic. She was sharp-
featured and made you feel she had been shanghaied to Africa but was
making the best of it. When he got up to Ariel, Z looked as though he
feared he had gotten it wrong and this was perhaps a costume party.

Bemis was a big soft bankerly man reputed to be very shrewd, which
was possibly true because his eyes were everywhere. He and Ariel were
in their early sixties. There was some jagged non-Western music coming
over the public address system, maybe from a field recording of a game-
lan orchestra. Anyway it was vintage and scratchy. Z said there was
feeling against Ariel across the board for underentertaining. She would
put off entertaining for long intervals and then try to catch up, with
mammoth and unsatisfactory events like the one we were at. Word came
that we would be outside awhile longer because they were running late
with the buffet, which was going to be authentic oriental treats that all
had to be done at the same time. We were starving. Wife Ariel was also,
Z said, renowned for small portions. He predicted what we were likely to
get: jellyfish entrails—a joculism for cellophane noodles—in tiny bowls
of acrid broth with leaf shreds floating, and pebbles of meat called saté,
in a searing sauce. The saté would get between your teeth. He had
toothpicks with him and handed me some proleptically. Z had a fixed
bridge of not the greatest quality. There was plenty to drink. The occasion was in honor of the corps of district commissioners, who were in
town for a pep talk on the Tribal Grazing Lands Policy. Z said Denoon
had been ordered not to say anything on TGLP under any circumstances
in public. It figured that he would be against it since it was only the single
most important ingredient in the whole land tenure reform exercise the
government was committed to.

It became the kind of scene that makes you want to be a writer so
you can capture a transient unique form of social agony being undergone
by people who have it made in every way, the observer excepted. The
bouts of wind continued. Z turned out to be right about the saté, but it
appeared during the appetizer phase. Emissaries came out with salvers
of skewers of it but never made it to our neck of the woods. Where are
these *treats*? a Motswana said plaintively. Overhead there were strings of
paper lanterns with real candles in them, a poor idea because the lanterns were jerking around and spilling hot wax on selected prominent
people. We joined a move to get into a pergola that had been erected on
a platform over a drained swimming pool. AID directors are forbidden to
live in houses with functioning swimming pools. Had this thing been

constructed for this number of people? I wondered, thinking I could feel the floorboards yielding. I got out. I pulled Z back out into the teeth of the gale with me.

Everything was adding to the mad hatter tenor of events. In every collation of at least two hundred Brits there will be several people with hysterical surnames. I think this is the result of coming from a culture which has yet to wake up to the fact that it's a thinkable thing to do to go down to the name-changing bureau and rid you and your offspring of these embarrassments. Or possibly they don't do it just because Americans do, when they notice that people start falling about laughing when they introduce themselves. Anyway, they were all there: Mr. Hailstones, Mr. Swinerod, I. Denzil Quorme, Mr. Leatherhead, and a plump couple, the Tittings. Anyway, there we were with all the Brits with ludic names all in one enclosure. The feeling of being under guard was enhanced by the presence of lots of actual guards, Waygards in specially cleaned maroon uniforms, spaced like caryatids around the edges of the incipient riot we were becoming. I had to get myself under control. I kept thinking This is the world created for us by grown men, n'est-ce pas? This was the human comedy. I warned myself that a perfect way to go wrong in the real world is to assume that because someone looks like a fool he or she is unintelligent. Someone at this point turned up the PA so that the authenticity of the thing we were hearing would be more unmistakable. Expectations were raised when Ariel seemed to be running for the house. The receiving line had dissolved. But then she was among us frantically on another matter, finding her pet, her dog.

Why would Denoon attend a carnival like this, with not an underdog in sight?

Finally somebody relented and opened the house up. It was all true about the splendor within. Welcome to Macao, somebody to my right murmured. I was staggered by the furnishings and what it must be costing the government to ship them from one end of the earth to the other, because these were massive articles like teak chests, lacquer screens, bronzes, a vast gong, celadon vases. The food was along the lines Z had posited. I ate as I scanned every room in the place, trying to look desultory. Ariel was ubiquitous, cringing on behalf of her possessions when anyone got too close to one of them. I utilized Z to monitor the late arrivals outside, which he was sweet about despite the wind comedy problem. I said to him Explain something to me: this is the second most important representative of the United States in this country, after the ambassador. What does this place say? Suppose you went to the Chinese embassy and it turned out to be a replica of an American log cabin circa 1830? You'd be flummoxed. Is everything ultimately a camp experience, is that the message? I asked him. There was no sign of Denoon.

I pretended a fixation on seeing every piece of chinoiserie there was, which naturally took me off the beaten track and into the private rooms at the back of the house. Obviously I was drivenly trying to satisfy myself that Denoon wasn't secreted somewhere. This came to an end when I opened the door to a tiny room and was met with a blast of freezing air-conditioning and the sight of an aged chow on a quilt, an animal never intended for life in Africa. When it barked it was more like a cough than a bark, but it still attracted the attention of a maid who got stern with me and said Mma, it can die. This by the way was the only airconditioning in use anywhere. Everywhere else, massive floor fans swept the different scenes, continuing the meteorological theme of ceaseless wind underway outdoors. All the rippling and undulating produced made for an under-sea feeling. It was time for me to circulate normally.

It was also obvious that my usual associates came from a lesser stra-tum than was being represented that night. I didn't know many of the attendees, except for a handful, and those glancingly—like the brother-sister act from Montreal who had been brought to my attention a few days previous by the screams of a tot pursuing them through the mall. He wanted his pushtoy back, which his older brother had sold to the Canadians without his permission. They ran a gallery devoted to naive art and were on a buying trip, focusing on the scrapwire toys the children in the squatter sections and the periurban villages make. The one the tot wanted back was a beautiful specimen, complex, a bicycle with wheels that revolved and pedals that rose and fell and a rider devised from a stuffed and twisted yellow hypermarket sakkie with blue text where the eyes should be, saying that refunds were impossible. The legs pumped when the thing was rolled along. The toy was a masterpiece. They were holding it up like a chalice while the tot leapt at them. I meandered after the brother and sister into their bolt-hole, the British Council reading room, and watched while they tried the toy out and exclaimed about it until some Batswana began politely hissing. We chatted at the fête. They were in Botswana on a mission. They had reason to believe that some-where among the squatters in the Old Naledi section was a blind child who was an artistic genius who made things out of scrapwire not to be believed, such as radios, locomotives, dirigibles, large scale things. Had I heard of him? So far they hadn't found him, but they were certain he was there. I left open that I might be able to help them: they were an example of the clientele I was reposing on in those times.

It was not a comfortable scene and I was saying the wrong things, out of distraction. Things were going on that I felt I had to understand, like the maid who was darting around and doing something to each lamp. It was nothing, but it was odd—and I was in discomfort until I knew what it was. She was drizzling liquid incense onto lightbulbs with an eyedropper. I edged my way into a group of women talking about their recent vacations. One woman was just back from Greece and was mildly wondering why every Greek woman over forty seemed to be dressed in black. Someone told them it was slimming, it came to me to say. They had no idea I was being amusing.

At about this time I observed that a particular woman seemed to be shadowing me from group to group. She was a wreck.

I let her catch up with me at the shrimp tree.

Do you know me? I asked her. Because you seem to be following me. It wasn't hostile. She admitted immediately she was following me.

She was following me because I was American and seemed so at home and she was looking for someone she could impose on for something. Underneath the extremis she was in she was the way you would die to look at forty, forty-two. Sorority person, I said to myself. She was in a couture version of safari attire, which she had to know was a mistake. The invitations had specified formal and she was barely touching smart casual. She definitely looked rich, which made me not sisterly toward her. I have a vulgar marxist reaction to the rich, which is part of me. Not that I'm a marxist of any kind. I would have made a wonderful marxist if I'd been born into it, probably, which is the only way it could have stuck. Too bad for marxism. I feel toward marxists the way you feel toward Greek Orthodox people when New Year's Eve comes and they get to go to this fantasy mass with basso priests droning, candles flaring, gold leaf all over. If only you could believe it. Also my temperament is marxist in that analytically looking for the cui bono or materialist explanation is nearly always correct in retrospect. Also I love marxist academics because it turns them into such absolute bloodhounds when it comes to critiquing actually existing capitalism. But as for the dungheap states these bouquets of humane thought have turned into as they decomposed, no thank you and again no thank you. Denoon knew everything about marxism and loved to talk about it. It was Marx and Engels's fault that when Lenin took power he had no idea what a socialist state should be like, because they had never bothered to describe it. Engels supposedly thought full communism was going to be like the Shakers, without the celibacy. Denoon told me the name of the actual person who thought up the Russian state socialist system. He is now totally forgotten. It may be Pashukanis. It was definitely not Lenin. I have the name written down somewhere. But to this day I resent it that Denoon never credited me with having had my own view of marxism. I maintain that my attitude had always been pretty nuanced. He also knew by heart some letter of Marx's where he bewails that it is too late for him to open a small business. The skin of the rich is different and the woman before me had it. She was also ash blond.

She was about to be a spectacle, unless I helped. Her eyes were red and her left hand looked like one of those claw feet on nineteenth-century furniture clutching an orb, except that the orb in her case was composed of damp Kleenex. I realized that her safari coatlet was in fact perfect for her situation because of its accordion pockets. Even as I watched she reached into one for yet another Kleenex, which she passed across her nostrils before adding it to the orb she was creating. My first act was to gently relieve her of her collection and force it into a stone-ware urn.

I want to go to my husband, she said. But I—

What? I said.

But I, they—

What? I said.

These men. There are men.

Be more consecutive, I said. I don't know why I was so butch with her, but she elicited it, and she also seemed to respond to it. She seemed unsteady. Thank god the shrimp tree is empty, I thought, because it looked as though she might collapse into it.

Would you go with me? she said.

For a second I could see something a little ulterior in her distress, but I lost my grasp of it when she said she was Grace Denoon. Instantly I was her sister.

There was a party or gathering within the party, it seemed. Denoon was there. She knew where it was. She wanted to go there. She had a right to go there. Throughout she was making the correct assumption that the name Denoon would be a major thing not needing explication. Was I a person who would go with her? I was.

I was elated, but now I felt shabbily dressed, next to her. Nothing could be done about it. I perceived that her skirt was in fact expensive

culottes. So definitely that night I was among the avec-culottes, a joculism I would later use on Denoon and that he would praise. She was
wearing a very sheer lime green thing for an ascot, brilliantly obscuring
her throat lines, if any. Her nostrils astounded me, they were so small,
like watermelon seeds. How could she breathe?

Then will you go with me? she said.

Of course.

I'm not actually invited, she said.

All you have to do is show me where it is. You're his wife. You have
the right.

Thank god I found you, she said.

Z came up just as I was going off with her. He was holding out a just-
popped Castle Lager with a knob of foam in the mouth, and saying that
Denoon wasn't coming after all, so far as he could tell.

Serious Men

Exactly what is it I enjoy about situations like finding myself the only
or almost the only woman in a roomful of men trying to ignore me? They
energize me no end. I used to fantasize about slipping into a burlesque
show someday just to see how the rest of the audience took it. Anyway,
at the door was a slight gauntlet of reserved personalities for us to run. I
felt like a tugboat because Grace had physical hold of my waistband. It
took a little effort to make her let go before we forged through. This is
his wife, I said, to get us through the anteroom and into the symposium
proper.

The venue was rather improvised, I thought. It was the guesthouse,
deep at the rear of the property, with the regular furnishings removed
and the living room set up with folding chairs for the audience and a big
armchair for the man of the hour. It was a very bare white space in a
concrete block building with windows standing open on three sides
apropos the heat and the definite attar of mankind arising. The room
wasn't big enough for the thirty or so of us.

Spare me is what I said to myself when I got my first look at Nelson.
I meant Spare me the heroic in all its guises.

Because here was a genuinely goodlooking man, alas. He was of course older than in the photographs of him I'd seen. The lower part of his face was softer. There were plenty of crowsfeet. He still wore his hair pulled back aboriginally in a short ponytail, which was brave because the style forfeits any camouflage for a receding hairline. His was still good. His hair was still black, although it had the slightly dusty look of hair that is going to be definitely gray someday soon. There was some distinct gray along his part. His cheekbones were still carrying him. Fullface he looked more Slavic than Cherokee now, but this was a matter of weight. This man is not vain, I thought, when I noted that on one side his hair went over his ear and on the other behind it: so here was a serious man, in all probability. Serious men are my type. That was why Martin Wade had been painful for me. But there was a difference between them, and of course a lot of this is retroanalytic, in that Martin's seriousness was narrower and more guilt-driven. He had moments of definite irritation at his fate: there was no escape from his obligation, but he was so good at music it was unfair.

Possibly I should have been a sculptor specializing in busts. I appreciate the head as an aesthetic unit—the weight, the poise, the shape. Most women don't. Or rather they respond subliminally, but at the conscious level they apply a hilarious planar aesthetic, as in Those eyes, Those lips, That smile. Denoon had a beautiful head. I date my more advanced sense of the head to my brief flirtation with physical anthropology, with all its front and sideview photographs and cephalic indices. I thought I was smart not choosing physical anthropology as my specialty. There had been openings. I think I can honestly say I was once even faintly solicited by what amounts to a star in the field. But I thought This is a doomed subfield if there ever was one. Everyone in it is suspected of having chosen it in order to prove something about the godly white race. I did know at least one unquestionable racist in the field. Also, every single male I met in the specialty was married. But I could have gone into it to wreak intellectual havoc, I suppose. This could have been one of my numerous career gaffes. I can get into throes of self-doubt and accuse myself of opting for nutritional anthropology for stupidly female generic reasons, because nurturance is natural to me as a woman, la la la, going the way I did for the same reason so many women in medicine wind up in obstetrics or clinical dietetics. Denoon was thicker through the neck and middle than he needed to be. He could be helped.

I immediately misjudged the way Nelson was dressed. He was wearing a garish dashiki with a red and black naive floral motif, some kind of unisex gray muslinoid drawstring pants, and elaborate leather sandals of a kind I'd never seen. I of course leapt to the conclusion that he was dressed to show how little dressing up meant to someone of his degree of seriousness and inner direction. I thought it was pointlessly combative or provocative. I even got a pang when I realized that only an objectively goodlooking presence could transcend the implications of such a costume. Later on when I discovered that he was dressed that way for a perfectly good reason I felt callow. He was acting as a manikin. Everything he was wearing or carrying represented something the people in his project were producing. He was even taking orders for things. All his accessories were from the workshops at Tsau, including a peculiar spade-shaped cowhide sidebag and some hideous leather bracelets. Not only was his costume defensible, it was self-sacrificial. But for the time being I took comfort from my snap judgment that, at least in this, he was a bit of a fool.

A Great Reckoning in a Little Room

What was my attitude? So far Denoon was impressing me with his performance of absolute repose in the midst of turbulence. We had arrived during a break. The audience was pure agitation—guys machinating, exchanging greetings, checking the time, organizing couriers for more drinks. It was the usual male smokefest, but no cigarettes for him. He was at rest even though he was standing up. He was leaning on one palm against a window frame, gazing out into the night. He was roughly my height or a little under, which was fine because I regard caring about height as a kind of fetishism, which is easy for me to say, I recognize, being tall myself. He looked very strong and I know why: I associate big wrist and elbow knobs with unusual physical strength. Actually it was Nelson who elucidated that to me about myself, in the life to come. The light was fluorescent, very harsh. No matter what he thought he could stand on the basis of his dark complexion, he was getting too much sun, in my humble opinion. But had he noticed that his wife had entered the room? In fact, where was she? Had he taken the lost-in-thought pose he had in order not to have to interact, or was everything accidental?

Grace had found the only place to hide that there was. She was sitting on a camp stool behind a big potted arboricola near the door. Since I owed my entrée to this scene entirely to her, I went over. She waved me off, violently, but keeping her movements tight. I tried again and produced what I can only call a paroxysm, so I stopped. She put her head back against the wall, which lifted her tiny nostrils once again into my field of vision. The effect conveyed was of unspeakable refinement. I left her alone. All I wanted next was to hear Denoon speak. I am apparently voice activated. I judge inordinately by the voice. And there was the promo his voice had been given by Whoreen.

This might be good, I thought as I studied the crowd. There were several definitely intelligent guys present, not strobe-light intellects but people who could make you uncomfortable in a debate if you got too much beyond what you absolutely had the facts on. My preference is always for hanging out with the finalists, and there were some there. What did I want? I wanted Denoon either to turn out to be the definitive elusive great man or I wanted him to turn out to be an open-and-shut fraud—that is, mediocre—so I could go on with my lifelong headlong flight from the unintelligentsia and all its works. I don't know which I wanted more, although I've thought about it. I was well aware this was chapter nine thousand in the supremely boring unfinished comic opera *The Mediocre and Me,* and also aware there was nothing so superlative about me as to justify my stupid elitism. But there it was, crazing me as usual. The psychogenesis of this is not a mystery to me.

I loved the averting of eyes my presence seemed to stimulate.

I finally found a couple of people willing to overlook my interloping and talk to me. One was an Ethiopian underling at UNDP. I love Ethiopians for their almond eyes. And they remind me of Siamese cats, they're so sinuous. I gathered from him that the left was fairly joyous over Act One, which was devoted to excoriating the capitalist development mode for Africa. The country representative of the Gustav Noske Foundation looked happy, and the Swedes did too, insofar as you can detect emotion in them. I said Act Two, where he attacks the socialist mode, is going to be good, especially if somebody remembers Denoon once said socialism is like knitting with oars. But just then an overling from UNDP saw me talking with my contact, who thereupon slid off.

I got next to a Motswana from Commerce and Industry, who I expected would be unhappy but wasn't. This was surprising in a way. Botswana is capitalist. There is plenty of socialism—subsidized housing, car loans, and so on—for the civil service, but the political class in toto is whole hog for capitalism red in tooth and claw, which is why the West loves the country so much. When the man who had just become president of the country was vice president he had gotten up in parliament and said, apropos a proposal to regulate the number of bottle stores in the towns, If a man can get rich selling liquor let him make the nation drunk. So how did they feel at Commerce and Industry about someone they were sponsoring, Denoon, pissing all over capitalist Botswana, a jewel in the crown of capitalist success right up there with Malawi and the Ivory Coast? I took it they were just very pleased. Everything was just all right, which is idiomatic for superb in southern Africa. I had a flash of the feeling I used to get from time to time of the Batswana as spectators at a great game played by whites called Running Your Country.

Meantime I was trying to keep something of an eye on Grace and figure out what was going on with her as she made herself small behind the arboricola. She still looked crazed. Remember this is Africa, I said to myself, where hospital patients run around the streets of the city in pajamas. Grace's glittering eyes were nothing. In West Africa the foux were part of the cityscape. Also I was certain that there was something subsidiary going on with her, something involving cunning, which I chose to take as reassuring. I should have been more sisterly toward her, but I couldn't be. She was extremely goodlooking, which I had to push aside a little if I was not going to be affected by envy of her derisory little hips and just right bosom. My breasts are the wrong size for an active person. They would be fine for someone restricted to lounging. I am built for childbearing, which was the last thing I wanted to happen to me, but—but looking at her I comforted myself with the idea that should I fall pregnant, as the idiom goes over there, I'd be in better shape than she would. Her bust was perfect in that it was perfect for galvanizing oafdom if she chose to stand up straight and inhale, and perfect in that she could let a succession of males pass by her in a narrow train corridor without having to keep her back to each one that passed. Of course apparently something unspeakable was going on between her and her husband. She had something planned relating to it. A talent I have is being able to step into a roomful of people and fairly instantly classify the majority who are just walking around in intake mode and the handful who are bent on something.

I should have been a better person toward her. I was blocked. She

had one of your true heart-shaped faces. I loved her teeth. She was a
perfect representative of whatever size she was, all in proportion, what
have you. Was she possibly originally southern? Because there was an
effluvium of flirtation about her, even though she wasn't doing it: all she
was doing was being miserable and hatching some deluded plan. She
would have been one of the girls in my high school with nine hundred
cashmere sweaters, cashmeres coming out of her closet like Kleenex. I
never asked Denoon if she was southern. Status in my high school came
from how infrequently you wore the same clothes, and especially how
infrequently you wore the same sweaters. In my humble opinion life
shouldn't be more painful than it has to be. I remember all the desperate
improvisations and camouflages it took to disguise the dreadful brevity
of the little cycle of clothes I had to wear. This still has the capacity to
freeze my heart.

What was Denoon, by the way? I wondered: what class, what background? Denoon was just an Irish surname to me, and there were no
particular indicia glaring at me. Of course a nice thing for him was that
as a celestial intellectual he was now hors class. I had to remind myself
that the information I wanted was not obtainable by staring.

It was time to resume.

A FARCE WRITTEN IN HUMAN BLOOD: THE DESTRUCTION OF AFRICA ACCELERATED BY HER BENEFACTORS, PRESENT COMPANY NOT EXCEPTED

ACT TWO

DENOON:

Now I know very well if I say the word socialism I'm talking about
a commodity that's fairly popular in some quarters hereabouts.
Understandably.

A CLAQUE OF YOUTH FROM THE BOTSWANA SOCIAL FRONT:

Hyah hyah!
*Semiparodic rendering of the cry Hear hear as heard in the Parlia-
ment of Botswana.*

DENOON:

Ehé. But just because I was so uncomplimentary about what capitalism is doing to Africa I hasten to not leave the impression I

embrace socialism as a remedy, just in the event anyone here might think that.

A MARXIST, ISAAC MBAAKE, YOUTH SECRETARY
OF THE BOTSWANA SOCIAL FRONT:

Never mind, because we all know what you are for. You are for suigenerism, so you must never suppose you can be surprising to us. *He finished with his famous hacking laugh, a trademark.*

A SWEDE:

I think no one was interrupting until now, isn't it? I think we can all put questions in good time. . . .

DENOON:

No, it's fine, it's just all right. I know Isaac. We're comrades. He wouldn't say it, but I say it. Interruption is just all right, but in moderation, comrades.

Ehé. First I always say I am not the enemy of any system per se. I collect systems. I am an agnostic about systems, but I love them. What I say is we should ask the same questions of every system we consider. What are its fruits, number one, and two or even possibly number one, How much compulsion of individuals is required in order to keep it working.

Voilà, here was the famous voice, a bass baritone with a beautiful grain to it, as advertised. What an asset! But even better was that he seemed to have no idea what he had. When I alluded to it for the first time, down the line, it barely detained him. He was pleased enough and he did remember that there were people who had said something like what I was saying, but even as I was complimenting him his mind was moving on to something else. There are actors who have magnificent voices, but it means nothing because you know that they know how beautiful their voices are: Stuart Whitman is one. When they talk it's as though they have their voice on a leash, like a borzoi they're taking to the dog show.

There was more about having the right attitude to systems. There was for example a great book called Guild Socialism Restated, *not that he was a guild socialist. . . . People should be pluralists and take what was good from one system if it passed certain tests. . . . All systems are ensembles or mosaics.*

What he was doing was well-intentioned but pro forma. He stayed too long with this.

DENOON:

So then, just to balance my books, I want to give the five most serious objections to the socialist remedy for Africa, but by socialism I mean what the comrades mean—the orthodox model you find in Cuba or East Germany or Burma or that you had until lately in Guinea. *I think this was the area where he lost everyone with a pun about Cuban socialism being social cubism.*

But he would not get to it. He was too proleptic and too ingratiating. The comrades were supposed to be glad that there were only five objections, whereas he had given nine objections to capitalism. He thought it was nine. Then everybody was to remember that if socialism came to Africa, it would be to an Africa already three quarters integrated into the world capitalist system, the point being that making socialism was not like going to a desert island with your best friends and starting de novo. He was driving us mad with caveats. And by the way did the comrades know that Karl Marx had never set foot in a factory?

DENOON:

Every student who writes for UBScope ends his or her article with FORWARD WITH SCIENTIFIC SOCIALISM in big letters.

But then the article writers go forward into the civil service, never to be heard from on this subject again, except to keep a certain flame burning in their hearts and maybe to vote for Botswana Social Front sometimes, for Boso.

I am saying that people who say socialism and nothing but socialism are using that as a pretext for doing nothing—and, worse, in the meantime they are reaping the fruits that fall to them as a class to whom capitalism directs its benefits even as it drives the mass of the people into worse misery than before.

And I am saying that if by magic one day the streets turn into rivers of fists and the people themselves come to the guys who today are shouting Forward with Scientific Socialism and rouse them from their desks and say The day has come, then, I am saying, you will have reached the first stage of a calamity.

Because your socialism is a rhetorical solution to real problems.

Now I'll tell you why.

Thank god, I thought. I felt for him because up to now he had been having trouble getting the right level of discourse going. One problem was that he had too much to say. Also I could tell he liked the idea of proceeding by having enemies, manipulating people into goodnatured enmity toward him. I was on to him. Also showing through, I thought, was that he liked the people he was trying to jockey into antagonistic self-definitions. Also he was dealing with a very mixed group and was essentially uninterested in communicating with the most sophisticated members of it, for the obvious reason that their minds were already made up—yet he needed to retain their respect and was resorting to little tricks of allusion to show that he was only using some portion of what he knew or could say. It was the youth he was going for, but there were pitfalls in that. One danger was his seeming to talk down to them. Either because they were young or because they were Africans they had a less extended set of political referents to hang things on, or a different set, I should say. His speech pattern was adapting toward African English. Anybody who denies you talk more slowly and deliberately when you speak English to Africans is lying. The fact is that the English they learn in school is a very deliberately enunciated English, with the consonants stressed. You know this and yet you still feel like you're condescending when you do it, and you sweat. A final thing he was struggling with that was apparent to me was the conviction that he had all the answers. He had thought these questions into the ground. This wasn't manifesting as arrogance but as an unsuppressible certainty, which can be just as irritating. There is some degree of hindsight in all this analysis, I admit, but most of it came to me in bits at the time, even if it was reinforced when I discussed it with Nelson later.

MBAAKE:

Ehé, so now we must just perish whilst makhoa dispute about which way we must live.

DENOON:

Just what I'm saying—you are perishing *now*, not you personally but many of your countrymen, and waiting for socialism is not the way to stop perishing.

Again he was detouring. It was a reprise about capitalism, having to do with the fact that the white West or the market system, whichever, was taking down the forests of West Africa at the rate of five percent a year, and this was nursing the drought that was throttling everyone in the south. I could imagine Denoon starting an appearance by saying Hello, first may I digress? which I told him.

DENOON:

There is no socialism without water. *He let this sink in, the intent being to show that somehow capitalism in its application to west and southern Africa was like a pincers, leading to desiccation. It was not carefully crafted. I could have done better. It was a confused amalgam of market-driven deforestation on the one hand and borehole pump peddling in the south on the other.* So the white West says Ah, drought, then here—buy some borehole pumps and we will even loan or give you the rigs to drill with, and take your cattle deeper and deeper into the Kalahari and go destroy the grasses there, and in the meantime put in a wellfield in Lobatse and pump out the last fossil water in that part of the country so that construction can resume and more people can be accommodated on land that is turning into a husk. Ah, and in the meantime keep buying more and more diesel from us to run your pumps, thank you very much.

Nobody is saying to wait and watch. The reverse is what I'm saying. You, we, must look immediately around and see how we can stop being destroyed <u>as of now</u>.

By the way, Karl Marx was a lakhoa, if I recall. And unfortunately in his scheme, which many of you prefer to cling to, the natural world is only a <u>factor of production</u> and is inexhaustible. Now—

A VOICE:

So you must hurry and catechize us as to <u>vernacular development</u>, isn't it? So that we may be saved in time.

DENOON:

Oh god *grimly*. I haven't used the phrase vernacular development since 1968. And I am not here to catechize anybody on that or on any scheme to save the third world or the world overall. Not tonight. Tonight there will be no exercise in hubristics.

But I just want to say I could feel another involution coming. I felt like joining Boso on the spot. This man needed editing. I wanted to scream at him to give us the five sins of socialism or sit down.

But I just want to say that if you are bystanding waiting for the dispute between capitalist makhoa and socialist makhoa to come to a victory for one side *he was now talking practically pure para-African-English and not realizing it,* then please stop waiting for that. Because capitalism has already won. The world capitalist republic is here. Mother Russia is in debt to the great banks, more so every day, not to mention Mother Poland. The market is coming! the market is coming! one might say. Socialism is decomposing.

Ah, but the argument goes on, of course: in the universities.

All I am saying is that the conversion of Russia is happening behind the backs of the generals and commissars. It has happened.

Moans and hums of disapproval from the left.

DENOON:

But just let me try again to go in order as to socialism.

Let us say you want to clear away private ownership of productive property and put everything under the state. Well and good, but then you must be prepared to pay five surcharges, very heavy surcharges. These are permanent recurrent costs that never go away. They are intrinsic to your system.

Also, these are costs not given very much prominence in the literature, or should I say reiterature.

But to proceed.

Cost number one is that since you have lost the use of the market, which allocates everything gratis, you must set up a mechanism to allocate things by command. And you must pay people to do that, a lot of people. Historically it has taken somewhere between twenty-five and thirty percent of the total workforce just to do this. You have to remove this large bloc of workers, take them away from productive work, the making of things, just to do this one function, allocating by command, as well as it can be done, which is not very well for the most part. You have to find the people to do this—which is not so easy in Africa, which capitalism is very much but not wholly to blame for—train them, and pay them. And many of them will be among the most talented people in any generation. And they will have to devote their intelligence to this function. So, number one.

MBAAKE:

To my comrades *pronounced comraids in African English* I am reminding that our comrade speaker has said Oh yes, socialism, it is the same as knitting with oars, at one time. You can do it but not for very long at all and the garment leaves something to be desired, he has said. As well, our comrade speaker *reading from a card now* has said, and not long time ago, not 1968, Oh yes, capitalism is strangling black Africa and socialism must bury her. He has said this.

DENOON:

So I did. I said it to provoke. But just let me advance to number two.

Number two is that under socialism you are going to have to lay aside money to buy technology, ever newer and better technology, from the market states. And forever. Because under socialism unfortunately there is no invention, that is to say innovation. If you ask why this is so, I have to say I can't tell you. I have guesses about it. But this inventing of new things is very low in all non-market societies, not only in socialism.

So if you want the latest thing you have to steal it or buy it or do without.

But at the level of the government, we discover, our rulers would rather not do without, especially if what is on offer is a better kind of weapon. And you can be sure the West is going to keep on creating newer and more gorgeous guns and baubles. I hope we all can see that.

MBAAKE:

If you can please say about all these <u>intrinsical</u> troubles about socialism more timeously, so that we can have our voice as well. If you don't mind to. Because we can say that you are just telling us some claptraps. Because we know that socialism is coming, never mind about what some makhoa tell us. Because Africans have always been socialists, in our villages we were socialists when

Karl Marx was not yet born, not even less his grandfather. We are socialists by our blood. *Mbaake, rather than continuing to have to stand up to intervene, now went to lean fulltime against the wall.*

BOSO VOICES: ,
Hyah, hyah!

DENOON:
Well, this is a moment of temptation for me. *I could tell.*

I would love to talk about African socialism and was the village a truly socialist institution, ever. *I willed him not to.*

Very many untruths have been written on this subject. *In my mind I* begged *him to stick to his checklist. It was partly because I was interested.*

Three is a cost you will never see in a Boso pamphlet and is the cost of suppressing possessive individualism. One could say socialism is an annual, but possessive individualism is an iron perennial. This is a cost superadded to the costs of dealing with general crime, which has not gone away yet in any socialist country. I am referring to the cost of suppressing a novel class of activities designated as economic crimes, such as giving people the death penalty for speculation or hoarding. All crime, but especially this new kind of crime, was supposed to fall away when capitalism was overthrown and the new socialist man was allowed to flourish. But there is no new socialist man, no homo beneficus, and never was. Of course when anyone complained to Lenin about the harsh blows being dealt to his own people his answer was that you could not make an omelet without breaking some eggs. So but now the omelet is cooked and his successors are still breaking eggs. Number three.

I hope you believe me on this, if on nothing else. Note that I am not saying that making cooperative economic institutions work is impossible because we have to rely on our friend homo economicus to sustain them. Well. I am just saying you can do it, but you have to be wise as serpents. . . . But now number four.

Four. Whatever idea you might have—one might have—about giving Botswana a socialist industrial economy, remember that it, and all of Africa, is an agricultural economy. Show me a socialist country and I will show you a net food importer. Even now you, we, are living on gift food from the West. I notice that Boso is talking about collective farms and ranches. But believe me that the application of socialism—that is, making farmwork into wage labor—has been everywhere a disaster. Industrial socialism is one thing. Socialism in agriculture—the special case of the kibbutz excepted—is nonworkable. The last of the many group ranches set up in Kenya at independence closed down last year. If you choose only one single proposition that I have made tonight to study up and refute, choose that one.

One reason you'll have to import food and pay cash for it is that as a socialist country you'll only get gift food if your people sink to the point of starvation as they have in Mozambique.

Five was a mess. He couldn't get it schematic enough, and during it some people got bored to the hilt. My notes, which I made when I went home that night, say that there are two ways to extract the social surplus— confiscatory via the state, or individual and voluntary, whereby people sweat and compel themselves to save. I think the point was that the rate of capital accumulation was much lower in systems where you have to rely on only the first method and that this will express itself in the need to rent capital in perpetuity from the more fecund market economies.

There was something related about the adaptive slowness of socialist systems in general, with efficient units subsidizing inefficient ones to an unconscionable degree. Exit and entry of firms was not controlled by efficiency, and since people would have political entitlements to jobs, the inefficient units would accumulate and encumber the economy. In this phase I was listening to the voice more than the man.

I caught Grace looking at me. I must have been being somewhat rapt. I think I caught a gleam of triumph in her eye before she looked away.

His wrap-up was good and was to the effect that in a nutshell orthodox socialism, which one was welcome to choose, was a system that was slower, more rigid, and more fragile because decisionmaking was centralized and there couldn't be any risk-spreading, and had extraordinary recurrent costs not characteristic of the economies of its socalled rivals. And it was a system that would in all probability be permanently <u>dependent</u> on its socalled rivals. And even though the distribution of benefits within *socialism was more equal—its sovereign virtue—there was a long-run tendency to inequality that could be argued about. And there was what he had said about the incompatibility of socialism and agriculture to remember.*

There was a mixture of for and against outcries. Somebody from the Russian embassy was suddenly present and I gather was expected to say something—but he was shrugging. He had been out of the room, unfortunately. Mbaake was all set. In fact he was making the up and down waving motion Batswana use when they hitchhike instead of putting their thumb out, which conveyed sarcasm.

DENOON:

I just want to say—

More cries, including "Ow!" and the word "Menshevik."

DENOON:

Comrades, I just want to say—

If I search my mind for permanent marks I left on Denoon rather than vice versa, this is one I can be sure of: I made him stop overusing the intro "I just this" or "I just that." I convinced him that it was always taken as preapologetic. I warned him especially about beginning phone conversations that way. He got the point and after a couple of false starts completely stopped.

MBAAKE:

Now please hold on, my comrade *said sardonically,* for you are just catering for confusion. For you first cry down capitalism as making slaves and next time you say we must turn from scientific socialism lest we pay five great surcharges. So then we must just set to idling and look at our hands whilst all about us white guys are undertaking everything. It is just that Karl Marx was only very late to find out about all what we have been stopped from doing since many years by whitemen. And once we begin again with socialism you forgot to say how whitemen always kill us, as with Asegyefo Nkrumah.

So now you must tell us what is this underline: suigenerism where we must turn and what is *said very bitingly* underline: vernacular development.

DENOON:

But again I repeat I have not used the phrase you just used, for twelve years.

And I just want to say I am straying from my brief, which is just to talk about villages, can we somehow right away devise a few things we can do to save the village.

And what I have been doing up to this point is to say, One, capitalism is killing the village everywhere, bleeding it, killing it, throttling it, stealing its young men. So I hope I established that, because I think I saw my comrades very much agreeing at that point.

So then, Two, is socialism the way you save the village? Which I was prepared to hear said and to which I wanted to say no in advance to save time.

So tonight I am not talking about general systems except as answering objections in advance. So, One, the first question is, What is destroying the village? Answer: capitalism. Two, What can save the village? Answer: wait for socialism. The first answer is true and the second is false. Now about villages—

A VOICE:
So then we are just deceived if we see revolution upraising before our eyes.

DENOON:
Ah, revolution.

Nothing is more interesting than revolution, or should I say insurrection, because all the imagery of revolution comes from insurrection, which is a different thing.

I'm getting so far outside my brief it makes me nervous.

I should just say that even if you think socialism is the way, a way, to save the village, then revolution is the worst way to bring in socialism—positively, hands down, the worst.

This is what I meant when I said, also long ago, Socialism is the continuation of the romantic movement by any means necessary. This was a parody both on Clausewitz and on some people, socialists, who no longer exist, called the Black Panther Party. Revolution equals insurrection and insurrection is the icon at the heart of socialism.

You can see why! Socialists, especially young socialists, love the idea of revolution. Every circle of sociology majors and bookstore clerks wants to call itself the Revolutionary Party of the Left or the Party of the Revolutionary Left or the Left Revolutionary Party of the People—anything so long as revolution is in the title. We can understand this. Everything we want in a society is what we find brought out in people in the moment of insurrection. Spontaneity! Spontaneous hierarchy! Self-sacrifice! Staying awake all night! Working until we drop! Audacity! Camaraderie! The carnival behind the barricades—what it feels like when the police have just been kicked out of your quartier! Free eggs, free goods . . . until the stores that have been sacked lie empty. One man one gun! And don't forget what it feels like to throw open the gates of the prisons! What a great moment! This is the moment the true socialist worships and thinks will be incarnated in the society on the morning after.

This is intellectual loneliness showing, I thought. It was evident he had a kind of hysteria to talk that was getting worse the more he was interrupted. He was veering all over. Who was Clausewitz to Mbaake? Denoon was supposed to be aiming himself at youth and he was talking about Clausewitz! The man was too lonely. I had no idea who he had with him out in the bush, but this scene suggested that they left something to be desired as discussants. The same sort of hysteria was familiar to me. I had experienced the same thing coming in from the Tswapong Hills to Keteng. I could be useful to this man. I love to talk, needless to say. Also I was pleased at how much of his rap I was getting, even if it was slightly outside my academic bailiwick. I love to talk. For a woman, I'm even considered a raconteuse. I remember jokes, for example. But then I also remember everything.

Also he was doing something else I considered compulsive, saying things that might constitute laugh lines in other settings, but not here. Who cared if he was willing to say of himself that he was wellknown to be gung ho for half measures and that if he had been in the October Revolution he would have been saying _some_ power to the soviets?

And it was also compulsive and part of the same thing to recommend books in passing like Soil and Civilization *and* Evolutionary Socialism *that no one in Botswana could get if they had a million dollars. They were hard to find in London and New York. He fought me on this. He had only*

mentioned Soil and Civilization *because it contained the key phrase* Man
is a parasite on soils, *which had been a strobelike experience for him the
first time he read it. I agree that man is a parasite, but I made the point
that mentioning books when he was proselytizing that people could never
hope to get their hands on just drives mankind crazy. This is the third
world, I told him. Mention books you have copies of or offprints of the
main passages of.*

DENOON:

*Making the point that the feelings that abound at the onset of
insurrection fade away.* The moment is artificial and based on
adrenaline and so forth. The prisons refill. Look, if you look nowhere else, at Algeria. Of course there is much more to say on
this, and I see my colleague from Local Government and Lands
not smiling.

So as much as I appreciate the opportunity you have all given me
to spontificate *he was doing it again,* I should return, I mean
rather I must return, to my topic—which is how we can, all of us,
of all persuasions—join to redeem and preserve Botswana's villages. We must get back to the village.

BOSO VOICES:

Yes, back to the village! Back to the village! Yes, go back to the
village! *Go back to the village! won out as the predominant cry.
Denoon was patient until that stopped.*

DENOON:

Back to the village—

MBAAKE:

So but you will not tell us what is vernacular development and
nor will you tell us what is your great scheme, even in some some
some short terms. *Mbaake was excited, which showed up not as a
stutter but as a word repetition syndrome. I sensed he had something up his sleeve en route.*

Nor about our ancestors as to if they they were socialists or whatnot.

DENOON:

My brief, as I said, is to talk about some few things that can be
done right now, today, in the villages, in particular some low

tillage schemes I can describe, some specialty crops that makhoa in Europe want and will pay for very handsomely, some—

MBAAKE:

Ehé. Oh, all about how we can grow some some flowers in the sandveld and such things, yah.

Well, these are things we like to know, as well.

But but you see it is just the same as always with whitemen because once again a lakhoa is saying what we must hear and whatnot. So it is just the same.

You say comrade, yet you take us as small boys.

DENOON:

Comrade, I am under the instructions of your government in this, as you well know.

I would love nothing better than to stay long into the night to talk about all these matters.

But, Rra, I am a guest in this country. I—

MBAAKE:

Ah, my comrade, but what can you say at all as to your your holy of holies, your your New Jerusalem, not can we raise up some flowers in the sandveld?

What is . . . what is, what is, if you can say . . . what is this *very slyly* solar democracy?

Or must whitemen just time and again produce more secrets that we in our own country must beg to know in our own country?

DENOON:

If you suppose there is anything sinister in—

MBAAKE:

No, my comrade, because when have whitemen done ill to us or made schemes behind our backs? Can you think when?

Some kind of transgression had occurred involving mentioning solar democracy. Denoon was steely for a change.

MBAAKE:

So what can you say is this this *city of the sun*, yah?

DENOON:

>After a long pause. There is no such thing. *Another pause.* Solar democracy is . . . is still . . . *He trailed off. He drank some water.*

The peculiar passivity of the white presence was patently determined by their interest in seeing if Boso's heckling was going to jab Denoon into revealing something about his project that they were interested in knowing. But under the passivity was a palpable intensity. We were all excited.

The permsec of Local Government and Lands, I noticed, had left. This meant something.

It was even more exciting when the permsec came back leading his boss, the minister himself, Kgosetlemang. This raised the stakes immensely. Kgosetlemang was new as minister. He was very tough. He had worked his way up through the ranks of the Botswana National Party on the strength of his performance as an enforcer for the reigning BNP faction, the Serowe faction. The Botswana National Party hated the Botswana Social Front, who were upstart marxists who had astoundingly won two seats in the parliament at the last election. Moreover, Kgosetlemang hated Mbaake on a personal level. Mbaake was reputed to have seduced, if that's the word, one of Kgosetlemang's mistresses, which I had heard from Z.

The tension accompanying the positioning of the various antagonists was almost sexual. Would Kgosetlemang bring everything to a stop, or, more likely, make a speech of some kind? At the moment he was trying to get his permsec to do or say something. Everyone there had his or her own mosaic of what Denoon was up to in the Kalahari, made up of true and false tessarae. Solar democracy was new and sounded overweening and interesting, so would Denoon say more or not? Memcons would be written tonight. Would there be enough substance for a cable, maybe?

Something fleeting passed across Denoon's face that I loved. It was subtle, like a cloud shadow passing over something in a landscape you're contemplating. Overall and considering, I thought Denoon so far had done fairly well, my cavils notwithstanding. But a change of state was coming. Heraldically speaking, he went from sedent to rampant, but all inwardly. He was, you could see if you were me, going from play to work. I loved it. It was so male.

Of course now I know Nelson was responding to yet one more proof that he had enemies in high places, because the solar democracy barb pointed to a document supposed to be genuinely secret and speculative and some-

thing only two people in the cabinet were supposed to have seen. Mostly he had been speaking ex cathedra, but now he got up and went around behind his armchair and faced the audience, gripping the finials or whatever they are that stood up from the back. Grace was missing this. Kgosetlemang was starting for the front. Denoon loves the line For the night is gone and the sword is drawn and the scabbard is thrown away, which is something his father, who was a sot, liked to quote—and this is what I associate with the next moment.

DENOON:

What could that mean, solar democracy?

To my colleagues and good friends at LG and L, I apologize for what I see I am about to do. I ask forgiveness.

But suppose that we imagine a country the size of France, its borders not in danger because it is beloved of the white West for its prudence and uprightness and its parliament, with only a million inhabitants, and millions of hectares in public lands, mostly empty and unused. Imagine also that this country enjoys averagely two hundred and twenty days a year of pure sun pouring down, streaming down, a downpour of gold that no one stops to hold a bucket to.

There are some whites in this country, in fact too many. Whites who are in the wrong skin for Africa. The sun is poison to us and we should probably say so and depart. Many of these whites are experts and advisers, who leave the iron skies of the north to come here with a lump of coal in their hands for you to worship, or petrol to sell. They think the sun is pretty, no more.

Now suppose the Batswana, or rather the inhabitants of this country, for any reason, wanted to base every mechanical process without exception on the free energy of the sun. Heating, cooling, cooking, transport, water pumping, any process you might name, could be run directly or indirectly from this great tireless source. Industry as well, should they choose to, since there is space to run collectors of energy many times exceeding the demand of any industry one million people might need.

The sun is wasted on these people unless they one day see it and use it. They could, you could, be rich, but only if you choose something better than being rich.

Now as philosopher king of the country described, with only one million citizens—what would I tell these people?

I would say to them that it could be done in a generation. Your children, if you train them, could be masters of the power of the sun. They could be a better thing than rich: they could be free.

Expats here and there were rolling their eyes notably. He seemed not to care.

You could be the first nation to give its people lives of freedom to devote to art, science, scholarship, sport if you like that. Work could be as you liked, by agreement: half a day, a week at a time, one year on and one off, different times and kinds of work in different towns, different regions, however you wanted. You could be the first nation to make self-directed individual development the first goal of your political economy.

Your villages could be like the great universities of Europe during the dark ages, and there is now a dark age of its own kind: your villages could be like suns or stars shining, because you could teach the use of the sun to the rest of Africa and beyond. Botswana—this country, rather—could be a garden of beautiful villages, each one different. You could be the first nation to tell your children to ask themselves what work in the world would most become their souls and to prepare to do it.

Of course I am a lakhoa telling you this, of the race that brought you the hut tax to drive you into money slavery and is even today telling you that the point of life is to get rich, how the best use of your mortal life is to perfect a system in which a fraction of you can get rich, only a fraction, but never mind.

But I am saying that you could make villages that are <u>engines of rest.</u> The ratios are there, if you control your numbers, if you seize your schools by the neck and change them. You can be the first whose women can say I work at what I please, the same as men, and as I determine. You can be the first whose children say We shall do this or that because it pleases us and not because the makhoa or the church say you must, or your father or the state or the iron hand of hunger or the itch to be richer than your neighbor and live behind walls protected by dogs and Waygards.

Of course, these people could only build such a democracy, should they choose to, if they saved and redeemed their villages instead of emptying them into the swamps of Old Naledi, where all you hear all day is I have no money, I'm begging for money, Ga ke na madi, Ga ke na madi, Kopa madi. Day laborers, beggars, small boys besieging you in your money fortresses crying madi, madi, madi. Old Naledi, where you grow thieves. While over your heads every day a great machine goes back and forth and pours out treasure that nobody takes in his hands. Or her hands.

Here he made a slightly sacerdotal gesture with cupped hands and I thought the excursion was over. It had been choppy and maybe a little counterfeit in places, but I forgave it because it had been impromptu. The pastoral tonus bothered me, but given what he was aiming for, I had to admit it was probably not inappropriate. This seemed to be the end. I wondered where things would go, because now left and right both, if they came back at him, would have to either admit or deny that they were blind to the sun, this deus ex machina that certainly deserved more attention than it was getting in either of their literatures. He had changed the terrain.

But that wasn't all.

Amazingly he swung into perfect Setswana and did the whole cri de coeur again. And he was excellent. I said to myself You are in the presence of the extraordinary. He was as good as I was at the time. His tenses were impeccable.

In Setswana his spiel came over as an aria. In English the intoned quality bothered me, but not in Setswana. I was moved.

I had heard that the Batswana called him Rra Puleng, meaning Rain-like Man or Man as Good as Rain, the highest praise the Batswana can give. Rain also means wealth, as in the unit of currency, the pula. Mbaake was upset. In Africa the people who are involved in telling you what to do rarely speak your language. Denoon had shown him personal respect. My one complaint with the Setswana version was that Denoon stood with his eyes closed a beat longer than was absolutely necessary when he came to the end.

Later in talking to him about this moment I found out it had been a relief for Denoon that the solar democracy leak had occurred and led to his aria.

What he was afraid was lying in wait for him was the litany No Dams, No Roads, No Tourists, which represented a vulgarization of his early work on vernacular development. There was a defense for each element in the litany, but it was always strenuous. Meanwhile his thought had moved on. He did have a more general theory, even one more difficult to capsulize. There was a suigenerism.

I found this erotic. Is it erotic or not to be in the ambience of someone who offhandedly confutes the two systems that are dividing the world, is fairly convincing about it, and has in reserve something entirely his own and superior? Is it erotic or not that he is even diffident about going into it, not all hot-eyed to catch people by the lapels to make them listen, which is the usual accompaniment of such convictions?

Of course when I reflect back I realize I never got a full frontal of mature Denoonism, partly because we were so busy the whole time we were together, I think. Sometimes he would say he had a complete system and other times he would deny it, or half deny it. Or he would take the position that his strategy was to develop and propagate individual pieces of his system and induce the world to figure out how they could cohere beautifully in some transcendent new whole. I always had a rough idea of his provenance: it was visible even in his little aria about solar democracy. He was a radical decentralist the elements of whose system were composed of the odd amalgam of collective and microcapitalist institutions he had come up with at Tsau. I was after him a few times to get things down in a more extended way on paper, for example re what seemed to me his hubris about solar technology, but this ran up against the extreme position he had arrived at vis-à-vis literary-academic propagation of the faith, which was that it was a waste of time, or rather that everything was so exigent there was no time for that.

One thing was his inordinate fear of vulgarization. He was willing to be cursory or epigrammatic about other people's systems, but when it came to laying Denoonism out, you would need a seminar atmosphere, lots of time, la la la. He called certain people genre marxists, some of whom didn't actually deserve it. Partly his fear of being vulgarized came from the caricature people turned vernacular development into after the book came out. And he was cornucopious with examples of good ideas coming into ludicrous incarnations, like Positivism turning into a spiritualist religion in Brazil, one of whose saints was August Comte's mistress. There were other examples. His favorite thing to call himself in front of the student left in Botswana was scientific utopian: I am a scientific utopian. This was a calculated oxymoron built on Marx's famous loathing of the utopian socialists he thought he was so superior to and the absolutely unbreakable conviction among the students that socialism is one of the sciences. I should have pressed him more, I suppose. It would be nice if there were some great classic text. Of course now there never will be. Unless I'm wrong. I may be wrong.

The moment after he finished was wonderful in another way. It was not only erotic, it was nationalistically gratifying. Rra Puleng was an American. There have been a couple of other Rra Pulengs, and they also have been Americans. Nobody ever called me a Mma Puleng, but they would have if it had been the Batswana custom to notice the existence of women. No Brit that I know of ever got called Rra Puleng, and people say that even Sir Seretse Khama's wife hardly speaks the language. Also it was normally so embarrassing to be American. Reagan had just been elected, which was so embarrassing to Denoon—I would discover—that he couldn't speak his name and, for the first few months I knew him, would only refer to him as The Brazen Head, after the hollow metal idols the Babylonian priestcraft got their flocks to worship and which were equipped with speaking tubes leading down into the bowels of the temple whence the priests would make the idol speak.

We were having a distinct afterglow. Kgosetlemang had stopped moving purposively on Denoon. Mbaake was making his hitchhiking gesture, but halfheartedly compared to before. From the look on his face I think he was about to say something complimentary. And then everyone stood up, whites included.

It was not a tribute. A prodigy was happening. For a beat everything felt dead. The lights blinked and then resumed at a vaguer, almost orange level.

There was a sound like nothing in my experience. It was both a roar and a washing or seething sound. It was immense. And there was thunder all over, and ozone. It was a sound like the sea roaring back to reclaim the ex-seabed Botswana actually is.

It was a sand rain, my first. But it was a deluge. These have become more common now, with the drought. But all I could think was Africa! What next!

Grace Acts

The performance was over. Guys who had been hanging around outside wanted immediately to come inside, and guys who were inside wanted to go out. They were worried about their wives and their cars. Sand could get into the hood vents, and a fair number of the crowd had undoubtedly left their car windows open because of the heat. The Way-gards who had come in out of the storm were pulling their shirttails out and spilling sand all over and laughing greatly. I would have gone out to see, except that I was concentrated on Denoon. Normally I'm as inter-ested in a freak of nature as the next man, but I didn't move an inch. I was determined I was going to chat Denoon up, but I had to act fast because Z would undoubtedly come to see if I was drowning in sand and I did not want to appear for the first time before Denoon in association with Z.

Before I could think, someone was pushing me from behind. They were a woman's hands, and it was Grace. She had me by the hips and was steering me through the disintegrating crowd straight at Denoon.

The question is why I didn't punch her, since my middle name is noli me tangere if it's anything. Ever since I could do anything about it I have made it abundantly clear that nobody should touch me without being invited or until I make the first move. All the male-initiated touching and kissing currently going on is nonviolent aggression. It's training for do-cility and should be fought until the valence of things is equal between the sexes, since as it stands if women touch first it means come and get it. I could become a militant on this easily. God save me from ever ending up working in some Aquarian-type office setting where friendly patting is the religion. I have seen these places. For a while at Stanford I was not staunch about this. I was there when faculty-student relations got oh so casual. The odd thing was that all the touching never led, for example, to even a slightly more expansive comment than usual next to the inevitable eighty-seven on my papers. I think the kissing and patting was worse at Stanford because of the odious human potential movement and the vapors wafting over us from the twit factory at Esalen, which was not so far away and was going full blast. There could be a campaign saying women who work in offices and who want to be touched should wear a button saying so.

Nelson always complained about how hard it was to get kisses from me. So be it, I had to tell him finally. Because to me a kiss is a carnal thing. In fact he said Getting a kiss from you is about equal in difficulty with getting the average woman to sit on my face. Clearly I see my mouth as a stand-in for what he cutely loved to refer to as my je ne sais quoi. I would be lying if I denied the linkage. We had other antic names for my pudendum, of which his favorite was sí-señor. We got into a small fight over why only women have pudenda, why only one sex has something between its legs to be ashamed of. I had to remind him that pudere, the root word, means to cause shame. He insisted the term was unisex until I got hold of a decent dictionary and converted him. I noticed we were generating more funny names for my private parts than for his: so I put my mind to it and overwhelmed him. I'm all for fun. I think he had been a little cheated in the past in this branch of playfulness. He was good at it. For example, if I prickteased him he would say I was in danger of getting my comeuppance. He wasn't trying to be demeaning.

I think the main reason I was passive to her shoving was because I felt sorry for Denoon that this was his wife. He hardly needed the embarrassment of a scene such as my turning and punching her lights out. And also something else tranquilized me. The other thing that saved her from the disaster she was ignorant she was flirting with was a feeling of fatedness I was undergoing. The feeling was that this was supposed to happen, according to the stars in their courses.

When I think of being pushed toward Denoon it feels dreamlike and slow, and like the reverse of a short story whose title has to be The Kiss. I always remember titles and authors, unlike women in general. I make a point of it. I slipped up in this case because I thought The Kiss would be something I would always be stumbling across in anthologies. But it vanished, and now when I tell people about it they think it's some kind of feminist canard of mine. The Kiss is short, a two-page account of what a man sees when he keeps his eyes open as his face gets closer and closer to the woman he is kissing. Her eyes are of course closed per the custom. When he begins the descent to the kiss her face is a seamless mask of beauty. Then as he gets closer and keeps scrutinizing, it turns into the surface of the moon, cratered, with points of oil glittering and her lanugo showing up. Of course this is quintessential hatred of the female. Her metamorphosis into ugliness is a result of sheer proximity and nothing else: she is a normal beauty. I've tried to recapture where I read this and who wrote it. The author was British, I'm sure. When I ask women if they've read it and I mention that I think the author is British, they say Oh, then this has to be a gay thing.

Nelson had great difficulty adapting to my thesis anxiety. He was so far beyond that kind of question. And he was so antiacademic. And it had all been so easy for him. Once he stopped trying to shut me up with facetious suggestions for alternative fields of study and thesis topics, he could make an interesting suggestion now and then. He thought somebody could surely get a thesis out of the fact that if you ran a computer through the corpus of murder mysteries written since the genre began you would find a rising curve for female as opposed to male victims, which meant something. I objected that this was a paper and not a thesis. Then I could expand into other vital statistics, was his idea. He was convinced that the average number of killings per title had also gone up. And he was insensitive at first to something he refused to consider an issue in doing a thesis these days: that is, you do your thesis and discover that due to the enormous volume of theses being produced, you've duplicated a half or a third of somebody else's thesis. I said But you say that because you're an original thinker. This annoyed him.

In any case my slow progress toward Denoon was The Kiss in reverse. He looked better the closer I got. His jaws looked bluer, although this may have been the result of seeing him more directly under the peculiar fluorescent doughnut that lit that part of the room. His superfices were good. The whites of his eyes were models of whiteness. He was smiling at Kgosetlemang—the event was to be considered over with, clearly—and I could tell that his gingivae were as good as mine, which is saying a lot. I attend to my gums. People in the bush don't always attend to their oral hygiene, not to mention other niceties. There was no sign of that here. I of course am fanatical about my gums because my idea of what the movie *I Wake Up Screaming* is about is a woman who has to keep dating to find her soulmate and she's had to get dentures. I have very long-range anxieties.

He was appropriate for me and the reverse. I felt it and hated it because it was true despite his being around fifteen years older than me. What did that mean about me? I also hated it because I hate assortative mating, the idea of it. One of my most imperishable objections to the world is the existence of assortative mating, how everyone at some level ends up physically with just who they deserve, at least to the eye of some ideal observer, unless money or power deforms the process. This is equivalent to being irritated at photosynthesis or at inhabiting a body that has to defecate periodically, I am well aware. Mostly it comes down to the matching of faces. When I first encountered the literature, I even referred to it privately as faceism. I will never adapt to it, probably. Why can't every mating in the world be on the basis of souls instead of inevitably and fundamentally on the match between physical envelopes? Of course we all know the answer, which is that otherwise we would be throwing evolution into disarray. Still it distresses me. We know what we are.

He was in a state of health. His reflexes showed it. There was aplomb in the way he juggled getting closure with Kgosetlemang and turning to deal with a juggernaut consisting of me being driven into his very face by his crazed wife.

Being able to tell if someone is in a state of health is a knack or delusion I acquired when I was working as a receptionist for a charlatan nutrition therapist in Belmont. I predicted Denoon would have sweet breath, and that was right. By this time I was wanting Denoon to be what he appeared to be, or better. The only remaining question was his midsection. I wanted the power of impresarios or whoever they are who tell women trying out for places in the chorus line to lift up their skirts so their thighs can be checked out. A dashiki can cover a multitude of sins. A tense scene like the one that was developing makes you hold your belly in. I wanted to know how thick he was there, if I could. Knowing the extent of his problem would be calming. I am unbelievably cathected when it comes to fat, which works out well in that it impels me to be a good influence on friends who need to lose weight. But beneath it all is the undersea mountain of my mother and what her size is going to mean, ultimately, to me. A dashiki is like a smock. My mother always wore smocks, even long after she was persona non grata in the kindergartens of southern Minnesota for repeatedly eating food meant for the toddlers.

Grace had stopped shoving. I was kind. I provided cover by giving her a complicit or prankish look, which took fortitude on my part.

He said Hello, Grace. His voice was perfect for the occasion. It was wary, but also kind and faintly threatening. He was looking past me. So far he was barely cognizing my presence.

Here's someone you should meet, she said, in a ravished voice. Like him she was the lucky owner of an above average voice. Did this mean they had been meant for each other at one point? If only their voices could live together, I thought, and let their envelopes go their separate ways. I hadn't noticed her voice earlier.

One thing at least was clear: I was in the presence of a smashed mechanism: their relationship was over, whether she was ready to admit it or not. I was sorry for both of them, but also alas exhilarated, to tell the absolute truth.

We were now an appropriately spaced triangle.

She liked you tonight, Grace said.

Did you? Nelson said directly to me.

I love a tirade, I said. It came to me on the spur of the moment and once it was said I knew I was being shameless and attempting almost self-evidently to pander to his demonstrated weakness for wordplay. I blushed, it was so obvious. But I was also thinking To hell with it. The fact is you have about ten seconds to impress yourself on someone you meet de novo. People decide up or down almost instantaneously, without even knowing it. And the great and near great decide even quicker, because part of their eminence is based on a facility at classifying the people who are bothering them almost instantly into those who can do something for them and those who can't. So I struck. I also was aware I was not going to overwhelm anybody with sheer loveliness at the weight I was just then at. The iron was hot. I was the first to arrive at the scene of the accident, namely the wreck of their marriage. I know I flushed. My coloring is a strong point, so that was all right too.

Having been on the periphery of a certain number of the near great, I was in fear of a certain phenomenon transpiring, which is a dimming in their regard like a fine membrane coming down over their eyeballs. They keep looking at you but not seeing you if you aren't on their level or are a kind of prey not of interest to them. There is such a thing in nature. It's called a nictitating membrane and certain reptiles have it, as did the great Chinese criminal genius Fu Manchu, a hero of Nelson's boyhood reading as I later found out in the course of a discussion of the moment we met. Denoon denied he ever did it. My position was that the great can't help doing it, but I did finally concede that I'd never seen him do it, not even once. He considered himself a congenital democrat. This was urgent to him.

What tirade? he asked.

So I answered him in Setswana, very brisk, slightly parodically, saying The tirade about the sun being the cow that nobody troubles to milk. This was another shot meant to hit before the portcullis came down. It had several features. It gave a sketch of one of my powers. I was someone out of the ordinary. It also had the carom quality of indirectly apprising him that in his description of the sun he had missed a bet by not comparing it to a cow. In Botswana the most magnificent entity you can be compared to is a cow. It's true for all Bantu people, not only the Tswana. The god with the moist nose, is one way it's put. Also here or later I used the phrase "dry rain" for sunlight, which he loved and which can be found in the Setswana pamphlet on solar democracy that eventually came out. I must have said it later.

If I overdwell on this it can't be helped: love is important and the reasons you get it or fail to are important. The number of women in my generation who in retrospect anyone will apply the term "great love" to, in any connection, is going to be minute. I needed to know if I had a chance here. Love is strenuous. Pursuing someone is strenuous. What I say is if you find yourself condemned to wanting love, you have to play while you can play. Of course it would be so much easier to play from the male side. They never go after love qua love, ever. They go after women. And for men love is the distillate or description of whatever happened with each woman that was not actually painful in feeling-tone. There is some contradiction here which I can't expel. What was moving me was the feeling of being worth someone's absolute love, great love, even. And to me this means male love whether I like it or not. C'est ça. Here I am, there I was. I don't know if getting love out of a man is more of a feat of strength now than it used to be or not, except that I do: it is. It's hideous. It's an ordeal beyond speech. When I'm depressed I feel like what was meant by one of his favorite quotations: A bitter feast was steaming hot and a mouth must be found to eat it. Men are like armored things, mountainous assemblages of armor and leather, masonry even, which you are told will self-dismantle if you touch the right spot, and out will flow passionate attention. And we know that this sometimes does happen for one of our sisters, or has happened. This comes full circle back to my attitude to kissing, which he never adjusted to. You want kisses, obviously. But you want kisses from a source, a person, who is in a state. This is why the plague of little moth kisses from men just planting their seniority on you is so intolerable. Of course even as I was machinating I was well aware I was in the outskirts of the suburbs of the thing you want or suspect is there. But at this moment in my life I was at the point where even the briefest experience of unmistakable love would be something I could clutch to myself as proof that my theory of myself was not incorrect. Theories can be reactionary and still be applicable.

Of course, Grace was drunk. It was crystalline. I had led a drunk to this occasion but not seen it until now. How I had missed it was a case study in the effect of motivation on perception. He would have to be feeling that without me she would never have been there. Grace swayed.

How do you like her? Grace said.

I thought you were leaving on Tuesday, Grace. It was all set, I thought.

You thought I was gone, she said. But I found her. How do you like her?

He ignored that. He said Grace, it was definite when you were going to leave. I have to go back to . . . I have to go back.

Ah, but Nel I have a few things to do. He lets you call him Nel. But pretty soon I'll be gone.

Well. So when you do think?

Don't be so anxious, she said. He's divorcing me, she said to me.

He blew his cheeks out.

Everybody wants a divorce, she said. Why is that?

This isn't edifying, Grace, he said, sterner.

I never am, she said. Oh I know. So you two just talk instead of me. That might be edifying. *I* think.

She pulled herself up very straight, in a parody of girlish interest that didn't work. She tried to go up on her toes for some reason. She swayed badly and we all, reaching for her, somewhat grabbed each other. My elbow went against his midsection but it told me nothing.

I got a chair for her and she sat down. He poised his right hand over his head and then brought the nails down on his part, a self-calming strategy related to acupressure and something I only saw him do in absolute extremis.

It was now awkward or impossible for us to say anything to each other, unless I could come up with something.

Bits of the audience had come back. A nice, very meek, serious young Motswana guy who worked at the Botswana Book Centre was edging deferentially toward our viper's knot, all unknowing. I knew this guy because whenever I went to the bookshop he was reading Penguin Classics, like *The Mill on the Floss*, for some reason. His main job was to carry bales of the Rand Daily Mail and the Star up to the front of the shop and then to carry the unsold ones back, which he did. But in the intervals he moved quickly back to his studies.

He wanted to talk to Denoon, but Grace summoned him over.

Africa is huge, isn't it? she said. I find it huge.

He was dumbfounded, but said it was. Nelson rescued him.

He wanted to ask Nelson what could be done to stop the Boers. But I suddenly was interested in the question of whether Grace was stupid or just drunk. Was she caricaturing herself out of desperation or je m'en foutisme of some kind? How smart was she? Had her hold on Denoon failed because she was below a certain intellectual level?

I went over to her.

It was no use. She wasn't talking, apparently. It was all nodding or headshaking. She wouldn't have lunch with me. She didn't want me to go with her back to the hotel, no no no.

Denoon was concluding a very succinct proposal on sanctions. The way to produce a white revolt against the government in South Africa was to get the four companies in the world that manufactured automobile tires to make a boycott. South Africa would run out of tires in less than a year.

The LGL permsec was standing nervously next to Denoon and waiting for enough of the audience to reassemble for him to thank them for coming. Finally he drifted off.

Denoon went over to organize Grace. He said something, and she said something back like You think I don't think Africa is pleasant, but I do. I could be very happy around here. Very much so.

Old Naledi

I spent the better part of the next day trying to ascertain where in Gaborone Denoon was staying. Naturally I had to hear once again all the antinomies about him I had already heard. He had renounced his U.S. citizenship versus he was on the verge of going back to redeem the South Bronx. He was personally rich versus he had given all his goods to the poor at some point. He was a genius versus he was finished, a crank. His secret project was in the Kalahari versus being in the Tuli Block. His project was self-financing versus he had inexhaustible funds from Histadrut and/or Olivetti. It made me suspicious that there was consensus on only one point: it was all over with his wife, who had made this last desperate expedition to corner him and get him to reconcile.

In my case I was going to find him and offer myself as a volunteer, for a while, in his project. I had more to offer than he knew yet. When I was in the bush I had learned a few words of Saherero out of boredom. In fact it had occurred to me to greet him with a hearty Wapenduka! the night before, which I had rejected as a totally artificial thing to do, rightly. In any case the only way you can speak perfect Saherero is to have your two front teeth taken out the way they do, which is asking too much. But I knew there were Herero in his project, some anyway.

By seven in the evening I was brazening it out in Old Naledi. He was staying with a family called Tutwane. There are two parts to the squatter settlement in Gaborone, Old Naledi and new Old Naledi. New Old Naledi is where the World Bank has been razing shacks and putting up site and service shells for their inhabitants. Each shell has a standpipe and electricity. House shells are just that—walls awaiting ceilings, windows, doors.

But naturally Denoon would be staying in Old Naledi, where the mud shacks are falling apart, where holes in the house walls are plugged with wadded rags and the tin roofs are held down with cobbles. I was jumping over ditches and getting hoarse shouting Footsek! at the terrifying roaming ridgeback hounds. Footsek is Afrikaans and is the only thing that gives them pause, somehow. A peaches and blood sunset was over. It was getting dark. Nobody I asked about the Tutwanes would tell me anything. I couldn't blame them: I could have been anybody.

I was fairly desperate because I had a plan that required getting to the Tutwane house circa dinnertime to exploit the provision in Tswana culture that if you happen around dinnertime you'll be invited in. To whites, there is a slight element of scam in this provision as regards them, since it cannot have failed to be noted by their Batswana dinner guests that no white family has ever felt free to utilize it. Besides, the Batswana eat their main meal at noon and dinner is fairly catch as catch can. Nevertheless.

I was near defeat. There is a pool of woodsmoke from yard fires that hangs over Old Naledi and makes you weep. Any nostalgia you might have about woodsmoke you can say goodbye to after an hour of this.

Maybe the way I was dressed struck people the wrong way, as semi-official. I had decided it would be a smart idea to look bush ready, so I was wearing a new khaki blouse and skirt outfit. I would have worn jeans except that the further down you get in the Botswana pecking order, the worse people think it is for women to be seen in trousers. And Old Naledi is traditionopolis, because the squatters are the freshest and rawest refugees from the bush. I think also that the deeper I went into Old Naledi, the more official I acted, out of fear. I realized I was using my skin color more and more, but I couldn't help it. It was like a horror ride in an amusement park, where you proceed along okay in the dark and then a thing springs up in front of you to terrify you—a snarling ridgeback or an ancient guy trying to get you to buy something he has in a sack but talking in a dialect you don't understand. People go into their hovels and sit there in the dark and take care of business in the dark, which makes them seem like a different order of being, despite all your training.

I was in danger of clutching. I was deep in the maze of the bleakest section of Old Naledi, the part closest to Kgale Hill, where quarrying is going on and fine grit floats out over everything until it looks like a painting of bedlam in the sfumato style, where there are no real edges or outlines to things. I had fine grit in the corners of my mouth and in my lashes. I wanted to look decent above all and now this was happening.

No way can you overstate Old Naledi, which you enter by leaping across a ditch flowing with something black and viscous, probably dumped crankcase oil from the Central Transport Organisation work-yard nearby. No one had heard of the Tutwanes, let alone Rra Puleng. I tried virtually everybody—not excluding a gaunt character hurrying along with a netbag full of bloody cowbones over his shoulder, with blood incidentally soaking into his shirt and with a ball-peen hammer stuck in his belt. Three women were sitting in a dooryard behind a plot fence entirely made out of rusted auto brake-spring leaves sticking up like fangs. I approached them. They did in fact answer me but not without continuing what they were doing, which was simultaneously conversing a blue streak and masticating mouthfuls of sweet reed, id est chewing the strips into pulp and spewing the white waste out onto the ground, as if they were pieces of agricultural machinery. The directions they gave me were internally contradictory: I should be going both bophiri-matsatsi and botlhabats-atsi, west and east. The fact that I spoke Setswana was seemingly not wowing anyone. It only seemed to be making them more suspicious of me. Some even seemed to hate me for it.

I saw something ahead that looked from a distance like a play yard with blue and white blocks scattered over a wide area. I made for it, until I realized it was a shebeen and the blocks were empty chibuku cartons by the hundred. A couple of the nonrecumbent partakers were showing an interest in me. I would have to detour. A top homily about Botswana is that white women never get raped by Batswana men. This is pure embassy folklore.

Slips of the tongue are rare with me. When I make them I can be

sure I'm under strain. So I was horrified when I was describing to Denoon my odyssey through Old Naledi and heard myself say that when I
saw the shebeen I decided to give the guys at it a wide breast. It was
performance anxiety. Needless to say, what I did was mix up "give a wide
berth to" with "making a clean breast of." It was a true sign of delicacy
in him that he pretended not to notice my gaffe. Neither of us mentioned
it, although I was suffering inwardly. At Tsau at one point I thanked
him, in effect, for having let it pass and never teasing me about it. In
fact that turned out to be like releasing a spring allowing him to tease me
forever after with various permutations of the gaffe, à la Would you mind
giving me a clean berth, or Let's have a wide breast, and so on. But it
was a proof of gentility that he overlooked my first parapraxis in his
presence and is probably even one of the reasons I was moved to persist
despite an otherwise not-auspicious encounter at Tutwane's.

I was at the farthest edge of Old Naledi, where the shanties stop and
the bush begins. A footpath led straight into the bush and along it a kids'
game was in progress. There were six or eight bana arrayed on either
side of the path so that each one was facing a clear space. A kid from the
foot of the left hand row would go to the head of the path, where it
disappeared into the bush where his mission was to roll a paint can lid
down between the opposing ranks for them to hurl rocks at. Somebody
was keeping score. Everybody would move down a notch after each hit,
as in volleyball. These were little kids, between six and ten or so, all male
naturally, in ragged school shorts, with three little girls spectating. I had
arrived at a key moment. It would soon be too dark to play and they were
trying to speed things up so that the championship could be settled
before they had to quit.

Well, I said to myself. And with no ado whatsoever I stepped into
their game and like a genius snatched up the paint can lid as it was
rolling, before a single rock could be fired, and held it behind my back,
thusly amazing them.

They had an adult reaction. They stood up like soldiers and began to
consult. I thought they might scatter at the intervention of this giant
white woman. I told them all I wanted was to be told how I could find
the Tutwane place. Then I would return their toy.

I wish I had a videotape of the way they organized themselves. They
were very courteous, but then so had I been very courteous, starting out
with Dumelang, bo bana and so on. We had a deal in about three minutes. I tried to imagine American kids in a parallel situation. They would
go for the police or their mothers. One thing wrong with America, ac-

cording to Denoon, is that the society is converging to suppress unsupervised mass play, largely through the mechanisms of TV and adult-run sports like Little League. His theory was that if you leave young males alone they will go in play situations from fascism to feudalism to democracy. So now there is a diffuse and thwarted attraction to fascism that is getting played out at the adult level. He was fecund with theories. He also thought the increase in heart attacks in the white West could be traced to the decline in stair climbing, id est to the victory of the ranch-style house and the elevator. The switch from tub bathing to showers was a related public health disaster because tub bathing does something physiologically unique having to do with the vagus nerve. Part of his feeling about gang play for boys came from his own sense of personal deprivation in that area. When he was growing up in East Oakland there were vacant lots all over, and gangs of boys having mudball wars, building clubhouses, forming confederations. But his weekends had been eaten up with compulsory churchgoing and compulsory shopping attendance, which prevented him from engaging fully in these, as he called them, political experiments. His mother was the motive force behind his weekend captivity, and he tried in retrospect to be forgiving. She wanted him with her out of spiritual loneliness, was his guess. But he never forgave his father for not intervening to free him, at least from the shopping.

The Tutwanes were in fact wellknown in Old Naledi. Our deal was that two of the bana would take me there quickly, but first I had to hand over the paint can lid. I acceded, and we went off.

Intellectual Love

I hadn't wanted to offer money for information earlier, just out of prudence. I didn't want to be seen as a white moneybags careering around out of her depth. But now it was all right and I gave a few thebe to my little escorts as they prepared to flee.

The Tutwane place was a surprise. It was very shipshape and well-kempt. A low storm fence surrounded the plot. The house was a good-sized ovaldavel, recently limewashed, with a good thatch roof. There was an elephant grass enclosure to one side of the house, from which lustral sounds were issuing. At points along the fence were wooden tubs containing various bushy plants. The yard was beaten earth, neatly swept. And in one corner of the plot was an outhouse, also freshly limewashed. I needed to urinate desperately.

If I could go back in time and rechoreograph the first three minutes chez Tutwane I would. Of course I would still have to get into the outhouse tout de suite whatever choreography obtained, thanks to the accursed female bladder. If there is an evolutionary justification for the pygmy bladder assigned to the female race I would like to know what it is.

As I was knocking at the gate saying koko, the solar democrat backed through the elephant grass carrying a basin of graywater, which he began to empty delicately in a line along the edge of the planting. The pouring did it. My situation was extremely urgent.

He had been washing his torso, obviously, and was still barechested, wearing cutoffs and those egregious sandals that looked like cothurni. He heard me yank the gate clip up, turned, saw me standing there in the gloaming, then, oddly enough, stepped back through the elephant grass. I didn't know it then, but it was modesty. He was retreating to get a shirt on. It was unnecessary. His midsection was nice, better than I'd expected. There was some rondure, but nothing undue at his age or out of reach of the lash of diet and situps.

I ran to the outhouse. The interior was tidy and decent and there were squares of newspaper on a spike in the wall. It was dark. I proceeded mostly by feel. There was a candle on the floor I could have lit. There was, I could tell, something slightly nonstandard about the toilet seat itself.

I thought I heard Nelson say Wait, from a distance. Next I sensed him just outside the outhouse, agitated. I hurried to finish. As I exited I clarified for myself that the toilet opening was definitely not usual, being like a keyhole turned sideways.

He was annoyed and redfaced. He matched his lurid dashiki.

What have I done? I asked him. You remember we met?

Hello, yes. Look, did you just urinate? I'm sorry I'm asking you this. That thing should be locked.

I did, I said, astounded.

He was irritated, no question, but mostly at himself. The subject matter was on the intimate side for such short acquaintance as ours. I was mortified.

He explained while I apologized a few times, each time more fervently. The people who lived in this place, who were away, had been good enough to help him with an experimental trial of a composting latrine. The principle of the privy was to separate urine from feces, to conduct urine separately off. It seems I was the only educated human being who had never heard of the universally known fact that urea keeps feces from composting properly. Correspondingly, I had to be the only development-connected person unaware that the single most needed scientific invention in the world was not the wireless transmission of electrical energy but the compound that would neutralize urea when it got mixed with nightsoil. All this was true enough, to my shame. In the absence of such a discovery, there was this experimental Burmese toilet that so far only the Confucians of the Far East had had the discipline to use correctly over long periods of time, except for the Tutwanes. Denoon himself had somewhat redesigned the toilet hole. All you had to do was slide to your left for the urine phase and back to your right for the other. Third world agriculture was waiting for this cornucopia of natural fertilizer to be proved out, and I had been unhelpful.

Finally I said I am *horribly sorry* about this but I can't keep repeating it this way without starting to feel like a machine.

That made him see himself, apparently.

The celerity with which people recognize something is spilt milk is a main measure of their rationality. We were both quick in this way. He got over being mad at me very expeditiously. It was the same with me. I had shot myself in the foot at the beginning of the race, but the thing to do was to proceed anyway with as much vivacity as I could dredge up.

I thought that next he was probably going to make me state my business. Instead he was decent. He assumed I was there about his project. We could talk, he said, but up front I should know that there were no openings, volunteer or other, at the site. Tsau was always "the site."

Given the way things had begun, I was clearly not going to talk myself into Tsau that night. The lesser task I had to rise to was to convince him I was colleague material. I was not to be mistaken for a world traveler, for example, someone out of the self-made pauper stratum of first world young people bumming through the third world in search of cheap dope and the unspoiled in general and taking up space in the jampacked jitneys and ferries the involuntary poor are stuck with. He had to see I was a trained person. This was herculean enough.

He got tea for us.

We sat down. He faced me.

So do you like the Batswana? he asked. I sensed this was a precipice.

I don't know yet, I said. Apparently that was right.

We had a silence.

I took a chance with Tell me how you disappear into a project? I'm skeptical. You're a lakhoa. I don't see how knowing the language can be enough.

Oh, it can be enough, he said. You have to know what you're doing. For example, how to make a deal with Motswana.

I said Say more about that.

Makhoa make deals standing up and shaking hands. But the Batswana make deals with everybody squatting or sitting. It may have something to do with everybody being on the same level: when men are standing, somebody is always going to be taller. I think the feeling is that squatting people are at least temporarily all the same height. Be that as it may. A deal made standing up doesn't feel real to a Motswana, especially a deal over something major. He won't tell you that, but it doesn't bind him in the same way and he might follow through or he might not. By the way, I'm aware that I said men. I'm talking about traditionalists.

No question he was showing off for me with this—but why, if any further association with him was as out of the question as he seemed to want me to understand?

Not that there aren't problems to be avoided, he said. Do you want to know what the worst problem is in most projects once they start running decently?

I did. Of course I thought I already knew that the worst thing in the world was what urea does to nightsoil. Silly me, he was now talking at a more elevated level—the psychosocial. The correct answer was ressentiment, did I know the word? I thanked God I'd kept quiet. It happened I did know the word, which led to a small coup. There is a classic that touches heavily on the concept. *Envy*, by somebody Schoeck. I had read it and Denoon hadn't. He hated having to admit not having read anything describable as a genuine classic. He would routinely stoop to saying he *knew* a certain work. This was an unfailing sign that he was guiltily concealing that he hadn't read it or had only read part of it. He stopped doing it during my reign.

Of course I know about ressentiment, I said. It's from French sociology and means roughly rancor expressed covertly, especially against our benefactors. Then I mentioned the Schoeck and was surprised to see how much not knowing this particular book discomfited him. He took some comfort in my inability to remember Schoeck's first name.

Anyway, he said, so say we have some average collection of poor Africans, farmers, and here come some white experts to induce development, say by setting up an integrated rural development project in the most sensitive way anybody has figured out to date. Time passes. Things begin to work. But a funny thing: the best of the poor, the most competent, the ones doing best and the ones who're even the most like you spiritually, are the ones who are going to present you with leis and bouquets of ressentiment. Why? What can be done? I am talking about your mainstream development project here, by the way.

This had to me faintly the tinge of a crypto job interview. I told myself I was wrong.

No adult wants to be helped, I said. It's definitional. Probably I should qualify adult as male adult: it's different with women. But take the French and the British and us. You'd think they'd at least pretend to like us for part of a generation or so after we save them from being turned into provinces of the Third Reich. You can help women but beware helping men. Nations are male. I thought that here there was a slight change for the better in the quality of his attention. There was. Later he acknowledged it.

After a rather strained passage wherein he made it overabundantly clear that I should never for a moment think he had raised the question of ressentiment because it was rearing its head at the site, we got on to anti-Americanism. The exact nexus eludes me now. But he was making numerous fine distinctions vis-à-vis anti-Americanism. For example, British anti-Americanism was hardly worth noticing because it was just one more facet of the larger phenomenon of British self-worship. The only race the British had ever liked while they were subjecting it to empire had been those dashing pederasts of the Sahara, the Bedouins in their lovely robes. The French and British could go fuck themselves, especially the British. There were only two countries in Europe Denoon could stomach, Italy and Denmark, and that was because they were the only ones to attempt to protect their Jews during World War II. Everybody else had jumped in with both feet or, the same thing, studiously done nothing. Churchill, trying to come up with an especially thoughtful token of his esteem for FDR, had settled on a sumptuous little private edition of Kipling's anti-Semitic poetry. Now ironically the Israelis were making themselves unforgivable.

At intervals throughout this occasion I was undergoing an event like a blackout or seizure, but with text, where I would incredulously ask myself if it could possibly be true that I had begun this encounter by urinating into the main crucible of an experiment to save the poorest of the poor. It was like seeing titles in a silent movie.

Next he irritated me almost to the breaking point, which I deserve some kind of an award for concealing. Terrible as America was becoming, he wasn't responsible. Oh la, I thought. And why wasn't he responsible? One, he always voted, by absentee ballot if necessary, and always for the minority party candidate most perpendicular to what was becoming standard national operating procedure. There was a tiny relic of the original Debsian socialist party he had been partial to, but which unfortunately was no longer running presidential candidates. Not, he unnecessarily reminded me, that he, Denoon, was a genre socialist. And two, he hadn't paid federal taxes, thanks to the overseas exclusion, for nineteen years. I saw red. I swore inwardly this would come up again between us if anything would, in spades, when it was safe. All I could think of was the semi-immortal Edmund Wilson, distracted by being famous, failing to get around to paying his taxes for years out of pure sloth, then wrapping himself in the antiwar flag when the IRS knocked on his door. Anybody decent has urges against paying taxes when the realpolitik gets too egregious, but in America not paying your taxes is not an option for the average person. There is such a life and death thing as a credit rating. At that moment I could thank God I was never going to be famous. This man thought he was cleaner than thou despite the fact that it was only the luck of his genius that had brought him into this realm where he neither had to face paying taxes for the things he excoriated nor to consider renouncing his citizenship. Of course I agreed with him about Chile and Guatemala, but was I supposed to feel morally coarser than he was because under the Brazen Head I was going to be paying for crueler things than anything I had dreamed of yet? Not that I had ever had to pay that much. It was oblivious privilege speaking through Denoon, and elitism. I thought of that poor hapless blue-collar deserter being ordered shot by Eisenhower while Ezra Pound got to poetize and eat petits fours for the rest of his life. It was too breathtaking for me. But apparently my fate is to resonate against my will to representatives of certain elitisms I intellectually reject. Ultimately I developed a more tout pardonner perspective toward Denoon on this: after all, here was the son of a man so very pure he had demolished the family vacuum cleaner in a rage after reading in a newsletter that Electrolux was owned by a Nazi collaborator.

I needed to get from this tract of discourse over to something more restful and with fewer pitfalls, so I asked if there had ever been any anthropologists associated with his project. This was more than a mistake, because everything was wrong with anthropology, according to him. No: no anthropologist had ever been allowed near the site. Most of the official great names in anthropology were mediocrities. Some were creeps. Malinowski had screwed Trobriand women. Boas had made things up about the Tlingits: if you went back and looked at his field notes they bore only a glancing resemblance to what he'd put in his books. No advance in general theory in forty years. Anthropology: a bolus, anecdotal. The few interesting contributions to anthropology that there were had been made by rich dilettantes like Theodore Besterman. What is the conceptual distinction between anthropology and sociology? On it went. It was hard to keep up with his anathemas. I kept semiagreeing with him, although I felt like screaming due to the implications for present company. I told myself this must be an exercise to see how well I stood up under being told my specialty was somebody's bête noire and I was the torchbearer for a discipline that was turning into a social control system like industrial psychology, a figleaf for multinational corporations and the World Bank. Anthropology departments had given cover to CIA operations. He could name names. On it went. Does everything have to be an ordeal? I thought. The basic premise of doctoral programs is bad enough, to wit, driving the academic weak sisters out of the program through trial by ordeal until only the strong remain. He was right and he was wrong. I think I was judicious. He was wearing me out. I had to hold back. I think I showed I was reserving comment re some of his thrusts. I think I did. Anthropology is not negligible, even if it's still only information so far. The point was to be supportive of his general iconoclasm but not to concede I was a charlatan and knew it. Fortunately it stopped. I was saved by a woman screaming in a shanty somewhere close by. Denoon sprang over to the fence and listened into the darkness, but there was no repetition.

Intellectual love is not the same animal as landing a mentor, although women I've raised the construct with want to reduce it to that. I distrust and shun the whole mentor concept, which is just as well since I seem not to attract them. Nelson was not my mentor, ever. I gave as well as I got, with him. But there was intellectual love on my part, commencing circa that night.

Intellectual love is a particular hazard for educated women, I think. Certain conditions have to obtain. You meet someone—I would specify of the opposite sex, but this is obviously me being hyperparochial—who strikes you as having persuasive and wellfounded answers to questions on the order of Where is the world going? These are distinctly not meaning-of-life questions. One thing Denoon did convince me of is that all answers so far to the question What is the meaning of life? dissolve into ascertaining what some hypostatized superior entity wants you to be doing, id est ascertaining how, and to whom or what, you should be in an obedience relationship. The proof of this is that no one would ever say, if he or she had been convinced that life was totally random and accidental in origin and evolution, that he or she had found the meaning of life. So, fundamentally, intellectual love is for a secular mind, because if you discover that someone, however smart, is—he has neglected to mention—a Thomist or in Baha'i, you think of him as a slave to something uninteresting.

What beguiles you toward intellectual love is the feeling of observing a mental searchlight lazily turning here and there and lighting up certain parts of the landscape you thought might be dubious or fraudulent but lacked the time or energy to investigate or the inner authority to dismiss tout court. The searchlight confirms you. I'm thinking of Nelson's comments on the formerly famous Norman O. Brown, or on deconstructionism, although all this came much later. Denoon was an answer to something I was only subliminally aware was really bothering me, namely the glut of things you feel you ought to have a perspective on, à la core-periphery analysis or the galloping hypothèse Girardien. You are barely able to take note of the earthshaking novelties people are producing before they are swathed in bibliographies to be gotten through. But paradoxically you also want some tinge of provisionality about the most sweeping or summary judgments offered up for you. There was this feeling in for example Denoon's fairly straightfaced contention that Christianity was originally a type of police socialism, id est Paul was a Roman imperial provocateur out to undo armed messianic Judaism and replace it with toothless lovingkindness. There needs to be humor, also. And there needs to be unselfconsciousness, some degree of it anyway, about the quality of the propositions our hero is able to produce. Denoon was often quite aphoristic. By my standards he often said publishable things. But there was no great vanity attaching. He said things matter of factly, and he was scrupulous to the point of mania about crediting whoever the author was of something he was using that the hearer might think was his, such as Society—an inferno of saviors, one of his favorite quotations and one I told him he didn't have to keep telling me was by E. M. Cioran, a name I'll never forget.

Nelson was interesting on the Boers, which was our last main topic at Tutwane's. I was flagging, but this woke me up. In Gaborone, especially within the embassy penumbra, everybody talks about the Boers but nobody does anything about them, as I once said and which went over gratifyingly. The Boers keep coming into Botswana and killing people when they feel like it. They are still doing it. So we were always speculating about when the next raid would be, how far they would turn the screw, when they would close the railway at Ramatlabama, and so on. Anyone who had anything new or acute to say on the Boers was regarded with interest. I in fact jotted down key words from Denoon's take on the Boer menace as soon as I got back under a streetlight. I might not get invited to the site, but I would take this away with me against a rainy day. Waste not want not is my motto.

The craziness of the Boers comes out of nationalism, he said. The Boers have only had the feeling of being in charge in South Africa since 1948 or 1950, which is recent, when they finally overcame the British. They had just gotten their feet under the table, so to speak, when of all people the *kaffirs* start telling them it's all over, dinner will not be served. All they get is starters. The Boers reminded him of America, which only got to run a Pax Americana from the end of the Second World War until the sixties. Tantalized nationalisms are the worst. To which he added that, more than in any comparable case, the Boers *are* their state, since over half the adult Boer workforce is state employed.

Secondly, apartheid had to be looked at as an instance of a generically male form of madness having to do with sport. He said You're looking at a particular game of performative excellence, like the shepherds in Crete who base their hierarchies on successful sheep rustling. Oppressing blacks is a national blood sport. We should consider the handicap the Boers accept. A tiny minority is holding down a gigantic black majority getting larger and more furious by the day. If the Boers can do it it's better than winning every medal in the Olympics, which the Boers can't play in anyway. The game is called Triumph of the Will. I know a fair number of Boers, he said, and Boers *want* to go into the SADF and go to the border or ride like lords through the townships. The English speakers don't and are the ones who are conscientious objecting or slipping away abroad when the draft touches them. The white exiles you meet in Gaborone are English speakers, most of them. You strike up a conversation with a Boer and the first thing he wants to know is if you've done your military service, wherever you come from. Been to the army, then? is the first line out of their mouths. If you haven't, they'll still talk to you but from an emotional distance. I know them, he said.

There was no bravura about any of this analysis. In fact I could see he was depressing himself as he went on.

How is it going to end, do you think? I asked.

I don't know, but it is, he said, and there's something amusing the Boers have done to themselves that they won't appreciate until it's all over. Possibly the dumbest thing the Boers ever did was allow kung fu movies into the townships. They thought they were letting in cultural trash to distract the masses. Mark my words, someday somebody will trace the influence of kung fu movies on the liberation struggle and it will be substantial. Because kung fu movies, which are in fact trash, nevertheless teach over and over again an important lesson: you've got to get revenge. Christianity says you don't, the reverse, and for years the educated black leadership went with that. But here comes something else, a set of brilliant how-to illustrations that says to young men Join into groups, use your bare hands against the enemy—the corrupt kung fu clubs that support the gangsters or the evil dynasty—accept discipline and adversity, team up, never give up, avenge your brothers. And by the way, here and there include women as fighters.

I had done as much as I could for myself. It would be smart to leave before I was dismissed.

I got up and said Do you know the Batswana call the stars the same thing the Sumerians did, the shining herd, letlhape phatsimo?

I went to the gate. I had been a touch abrupt in leaving, slightly disconcerting him, which I liked.

Would he at least think about considering using me as a volunteer?

You tempt me, but I have to say no, he said. Of course what would make you irresistible would be if you know something about cooperage. Or taxidermy, say.

Sorry, I said.

That was all. He asked me if I had a torch, and I said no as if he were asking a silly question, the point being to show how acclimated I was to getting around in the dark the way you do in the village at night. It was bravado and in fact I was afraid. But I forged out into the black labyrinth of Old Naledi as though nothing could make me happier and as though I were a person with an actual sense of direction.

I enjoyed this, he said as I left.

All the way home I flattered myself that I had at least gotten into the foyer of his consciousness. Sometimes I believed it. In any case, he would see my face again.

Grace, Again

I was feeling tender and valedictory toward Gaborone, and even toward the mall, now that I was going to be leaving. It was set. I was preparing to get to Denoon's site. I was determined to do it. The surprise would be his.

I liked and hated the mall, a halfway-paved enclosure three blocks long which is the crux of retail and street life in the capital. The shops lining the mall are pseudomoderne, with go-go displays featuring Mylar and pinlights, with Muzak loops droning, and with typical third world inventories: gluts of what you don't want, voids where the most commonplace necessities—such as tweezers, my then most pressing need—should be. For the most part the proprietors are Chinese or Indians, with a few Batswana fronting for South Africans. The array of businesses is the usual: hardware and clothing stockists, chemists, takeaways, butcheries, a walk-in surgery or two. The only really big buildings are at the ends of the mall—the banks, the embassies. For amenity you have, on either side of the central and widest part of the mall, between the Capitol Cinema and the President Hotel, cement benches with umbrelloid metal canopies. There are thorn trees intermittently. I liked the mall for its comédie humaine but hated it because it so completely incarnates the Western good idea of what Africa should become and because the South African merchandise the shelves are overflowing with is such shit yet so overpriced. South African shoe manufacture is my personal bête noire. It is risible. A smattering of poor devils, mainly women, selling seasonal items like fried mopane worms or maize on the cob spread their karosses under the trees—but only a smattering. When the mall was put up, the traditional farmers' market was deconstructed and the shards moved into permanent stalls far away along the railway, where the market languishes but is definitely not an eyesore for makhoa, who prefer to shop in tidiness, on vinyl tile flooring, to the strains of the Melachrino Strings or some other dead orchestra.

I was crossing the mall, just passing the President Hotel, en route to a second attempt to secure a tweezers, which I was willing to be in stock at Botschem. My mode when I want something badly, and which has been known to work, is to proceed up to the absolutely last moment as though there could be no doubt I would get it. In three days of hard work I had succeeded in assembling everything I felt I needed to begin my expedition to Denoon's site, with two minor exceptions: tweezers and the actual location of Denoon's project.

I picked up a commotion on the grandiose staircase connecting the balcony of the President Hotel to the mall.

Oh no, I thought, more abnormal psychology. It was Grace, pushing her way roughly down through the ascending lunchtime throng and calling my name.

I stood stockstill to lessen her anxiety, and waved.

If we were going to talk it would have to be someplace else. It was bright and hot and we were already the object of the attention of the mall crowd. The Batswana love it when whites make spectacles of themselves as in fighting or showing affection in public. Grace looked as crazed as before. She was persisting in running, and it was clear she had decided to cast her bra to the winds as part of living life to the hilt for a while in the heart of darkness where nobody knew her, as can happen.

She came up, preceded by the distinct bouquet of Mainstay. She was wearing a different outfit in the same genre as the one she'd worn to the Bemises'. Her undereyes were puffy, but she was neat and clean and all fixed up.

She had to get her breath. Two things told me I was right about some affectional extravaganza going on. She had a leopardskin print ribbon in her hair. And I spotted the notorious extra-large Boer, Meerkotter, proprietarily following her movements from the balcony and holding a drink in each fist, one of them obviously intended for her. He was the local representative for some South African consortium of construction firms, I think. He was a tireless lecher and bon vivant who ate all his meals in the Brigadier Room at the President, usually buying rump steak for one of his various and numerous Batswana teen queen girlfriends. Going jet, as it's called, was his basic thing, but he embraced all race groups. He was very proud of what Edgar Rice Burroughs would have called his thews. He had forearms like bleach bottles. I immediately wanted to warn Grace about a couple of dangers attaching to him. I thought he must be infectious. But worse, lately the story was that he was steady with an actual beauty contest winner, Idol Mketa. She was famous for her hairdos, which really were art—the current one was amazing and looked like a suitcase handle display—and her violent jealousy. Meerkotter was considered a prize. One recourse of wronged Batswana women is to scald their rivals. I thought Grace should know these things, if I was right that she was with Meerkotter. There was also the story that Meerkotter's glass eye was the product of female reprisal, which possibly deserved mention if only as a clue to the sort of milieu Meerkotter swam in.

We greeted each other. She had something she so much wanted to say, she said.

She was wearing a little red scarf knotted around her throat. It made her look like a Brownie. I praised it.

I got it here, she said, as a present. It was a gift from a person.

I wanted to warn her that you get drunker on less alcohol in Gaborone, because of the elevation. She wasn't leaving spaces for me, though.

I know Nelson likes you, she said.

The sun is eating us up, I said. We should go somewhere, but not the President.

Where we could have a drink, she said. She got a death grip on my elbow and began leading me purposely across the mall as though she had a perfect idea of where to go. This was drink spreading its wings in her mind, which resulted in her walking directly across the mat of a woman selling cowpeas, almost treading on the woman's hand. Grace had no idea where she was going. I took over. She was odd. She looked labile to me. It occurred to me he had been giving her Mandrax, which the grapevine said he had access to.

I reversed our direction and got us out of the mall and across King's Road onto the long dusty path that takes you to White City, the shabby and unpaved shopping area where everything is on a far far humbler scale and some of the shopowners are actual Batswana. I was told it was called White City because most of the buildings had been white at one time.

I took her to the Carat Restaurant, a hole-in-the-wall place run by a Motswana woman I liked and which was doomed to fail because they gave you too much food for your money. It no longer exists.

Grace wanted a beer. I conspired in Setswana to get them to forget to bring it until she had started on her salad, id est shredded beetroot

and some baked beans, and also to bring us some strong tea simultaneously with her beer. I talked her out of getting chips, which at the
Carat came so underdone they looked like they were made of Lucite.

She was utterly drunk. She said Do you like the four seasons? Because
no one here does that I've talked to.

I said I did like the seasons, assuming she meant wasn't I nostalgic for
the snowfall and crisp fall mornings and so on, at which point she went
Dawn go away I'm no good for you, in a little deluded whining voice.
She meant the Four Seasons. I couldn't believe it. I let her sing quite a
bit of it.

When would she get to Denoon? And in retrospect her great love for
the Four Seasons is odd and may have played a part in why it didn't work
out with Nelson, because in his lexicon, one of the all-time stupidest
popular songs in history was Walk Like a Man, Talk Like a Man, sung in
piercing falsetto by the lead singer of the Four Seasons. I think it was in
first place for entire-song stupidity, with first place for single-line stupidity—to say nothing of hardheartedness—going to Now laughing friends
deride tears I cannot hide.

I was worried about Grace. She was underprotected. I talked circuitously about Meerkotter. She was seeing him, as she put it. I tried to fill
her in gently. This was unwelcome, I could tell. Either very little of it
was registering, or I was only making Meerkotter seem more exotic and
attractive. I let myself mention the glass eye business. There was an
explosive effect that astonished me. She began weeping.

She wouldn't stop. I wanted to know what I'd said to cause this.
Ultimately she told me.

People tell you things that make you wonder if the world is fiction or
nonfiction. She had started weeping, she said, because of the glass eye.
She hadn't been aware Meerkotter had one, but her father had had one
and it was one reason she was a feminist. She had a slightly younger
brother and her brother had been the one allowed to assist her father
with certain ministrations, including rinsing, concerning her father's
eye. She, never. And she was the one who had truly loved her father.
Her brother had disappointed him right and left. The news that she saw
herself as a feminist touched me in some way and helped me be a little
more patient with her.

It finally came to my saying What is it you want to say to me about
your husband—which is what you want to talk about, Grace, isn't it?

She sobbed summarily and then said yes. She wanted me to know
she and Nelson were finished. Nelson was free and she wanted him to be

happy, if he could. She had a sixth sense, she said, about who Nelson liked and would be good for him and she hoped I could forgive her for the way she'd introduced us, but time was short. Had I seen him again yet?

I said that I had and that I liked him and I was interested in his work.

Does he like you? she asked me.

I said I didn't know, but that it was moot because he was returning to his secret project, which seemed to be a genuine secret as far as location was concerned.

She held up a finger and made herself eat. I think she wanted to be soberer for this part of our talk. I waited. So far nobody would tell me where the site was, not even Z. I gathered there was some new uneasiness and clamming up ever since the solar democracy peroration. For some reason I wasn't desperate about it. I had faith there was some way to find out that had simply not occurred to me yet.

I know where it is, she said. My lawyers forced it out of him ages ago. I can even draw where it is.

I got out my pad. There was a God.

She did know.

It's somewhere called Tsau, she said, on a straight line east into the Central Kalahari Game Reserve from a place that sounds like it should be in China, called Kang. I corrected her pronunciations. I was breathless. I even knew roughly where Tsau was. It would be about a hundred miles from Kang. Everything was findable. She could see I was emotional.

You can't of course tell anybody, she said, because a part of what he's signed so far says I can't tell anyone. It has to go no farther. You have to swear. I was never allowed there.

I swore. We relaxed. But why was she giving me all this? My thoughts on this were a bolus, to use a word I owe to Denoon and that seems to have become indispensable to me. Was revenge in it somewhere or was she trying to involve me with him in order to get some legal advantage? This was my realpolitikal lobe speaking. My other lobe sensed this as something personal and unsordid. It was a bolus.

I know all about you, she said. I picked you out before I knew anything except the way you look, but I find out you're perfect. Everybody has an opinion about you.

I loved that.

You're like a strong person, I feel, she said. Someone like you must have a lot of siblings. I said no and she was surprised.

I made us go. She held my hand once or twice walking back to the President.

Her South African side of beef was waiting agitatedly for her at the foot of the stairway.

We had an effusive moment where she asked me a little wildly if I would write to her. Meerkotter was already pulling her to come with him.

I don't have your address, I said. She wrenched free of Meerkotter and fished up a minipurse out of her blouson and began rummaging through it. Again Meerkotter pulled on her. This enraged me, and I must have looked at him in some medusan way because he let go and permitted her to continue searching. Finally she came up with her checkbook and tore out a blank check, which she forced on me. This has my address, she said. She lived in Cos Cob. I didn't want her check, but in the tension of the moment I couldn't think of what to do.

Oh, she said, do you know what bruxism is? I forgot to mention this.

Grinding your teeth at night, I said.

Nelson has it. I knew you were smart.

It struck me that I could tear the address out of the check, and I did.

I had a sudden confused feeling toward her. I wanted to say I knew that what she was now was not what she had once been. I think I loved her for helping me. I wanted to say something like Neither am I always going to be like I am. There was no way to say it.

Meerkotter maneuvered her up the steps to the hotel.

I think I'm going to Milan, she said. I think it was meant to reassure me.

Kang

Once a week the government sends a flatbed truck, a monster Bedford, the two hundred and fifty miles north from Lobatse to Kang. The trip actually starts in Gabs, whence you go briefly south to Lobatse. The truck carries sacks of World Food Program cornmeal, building material, mail, and soap and other sundries. The load is a huge mound under canvas, which people have the privilege of clinging to the lashings of if they sign a waiver of liability at CTO. The trucks also provide a good deal of additional, nonapproved, bus service for people encountered along the way. At any given time you can have as many as eight or ten people and their chattels up back.

I was on the truck and waiting for the fun to begin, which would be when we got off the tarmac, at Jwaneng, and onto the alternating sand, washboard, and rubble track that stretches all the way to Maun. The time to think was now, in the predemonic phase, while traffic on the Gaborone-Lobatse road was keeping our speed down in normal range and even bringing us to a dead stop now and then. The sun came up while we were halted opposite one of the few raised landforms in that part of the country, the abrupt little massif with lime-streaked cliff faces behind Ootse, where the Cape vultures mate and roost. They only do it there or at a similar place in the Magaliesberg. Ergo, they're doomed as civilization creeps up the slopes from Ootse toward the vultury. I understand them, though, I thought. In love and mating, ambience is central.

All was well. I had tied up the loose ends of my life with a vengeance. I had given a jumble sale almost as a joke but ended up making money. I had mailed things off and reduced my possessions to what I could carry. I had said thanks wherever it was applicable. There had been some misdirection. It had seemed like a good idea to give the impression that I was going back to the U.S. I had everything I needed for my sortie including my Botschem tweezers. I was decently equipped for light camping. I had a map of the water points along the route I intended to take from Kang to Tsau, although it could have been more recent. It was six years old, but I told myself that since it had been made during a previous drought it was probably accurate enough.

We were going so fitfully there was even time, between lunges, to chat with my copassenger, a young pregnant woman from Mogoditsane who was under the impression her cousin could get her a job as a cleaner at the abattoir in Lobatse. Her questions showed she was sorry for me that at my advanced age I was unmarried and childless. She also was unmarried. In Botswana, in the villages, the practice is for women to produce a child first, to advertise their marriageability.

That's up to them, I thought, which reminds me that I have to stop using phrases meaningless except between me and Denoon. See what happen! is another phrase I have to stop using for the same reason. That's up to them arises from an older Jewish couple who had come to Botswana with the Peace Corps and had had a number of difficult cultural adjustments to make, the one they talked about most being that their Indian upstairs neighbors ate rice every day. The Roths believed strongly that it was more appropriate to eat potatoes every day as a starch staple. Mr. Roth agreed with his wife that the Indians were strange, but when she continued to wonder over and over at this matter in front of people, his attempt to get her to abbreviate her going on about this was to say—of the Indians preferring rice—That's up to them. I told this story to Nelson and he found it as obscurely funny as I did, and between us it became indispensable as a signum of the recurring problem of other people doing things you find peculiar or stressful but probably shouldn't. The provenance of See what happen! was a lake in a park in Oakland where there were flocks of geese and ducks. A rabble of Hispanic boys was there, with one ten- or eleven-year-old ringleader urging a five-year-old minion to try to urinate on a duck. The five-year-old was reluctant but began complying, running after some ducks with his tiny penis out, after the older boy had inspired him with cries of See what happen! The deed was being done in the scientific spirit, apparently. Where could you find a better emblem for dubious propositions being vigorously encouraged, and where is Denoon, who understands, and what is he doing now?

One attractive thing about me is that I'm never bored, because during any caesura my personal automatic pastime of questioning my own motives is there for me. I looked at my copassenger. Was it possible I was homing in on Tsau out of maternal urges I was incapable of recognizing in myself? Was that the kind of fool I was, underneath? I think and hope I'm averagely maternal, but I think I reject the idea that the repetition compulsion, which is my private phrase for the drive to reproduce, is shadowily behind every move we make while we're fertile.

I don't see myself as antimaternal, but I'm not under any compulsion to repeat myself, either. I think if I were laden with accomplishments to date or saw some on the horizon I might feel differently. Nor had there been up to then any particular male person I was so impressed with I thought I should contribute to his replication. Was I being attacked by this whole question now because the impetus of my drive to reach Denoon had slackened, physically, for the first time since I began it: I was on a track, being conveyed, passive, stopped, and had a pregnant woman as part of the landscape. Denoon was childless, so far as I knew: and that was interesting. But, next question, if the whole issue of repetition is so uninteresting, why was Denoon's childlessness interesting? Was he also waiting for the perfect missing jigsaw puzzle partner to complete his inner wholeness and so release him into wanting to reproduce? That I could be swept out of myself under the sign of absolute love and into embracing motherhood was something I suppose I was assuming, but this has to be bracketed with the population question, on which I'm a fanatic, still. In the cities of the third world your heart is constantly breaking for the children who are either homeless or next door to it, excess children that you feel in your heart of hearts you should be doing something concrete for, creating crèches or schools, something. Also who would want what I was as an adolescent? Pas moi. Denoon once said Do you realize that ninety percent of all the adolescents who have ever lived are alive today? I think I wanted the question of reproduction to be deliberative, as in Well, should we reproduce? or What are we that we should want to reproduce? and so on, à la Immanuel Kant. Of course, this would give you a minuscule world population.

Or was I in fact holding the repetition compulsion at bay at a deeper level with vague self-admonitions that there were more options available in my wonderful home culture than I could shake a stick at, more than there had ever been, e.g., single motherhood via a friend or a sperm bank. Or, just to mention everything, what about a relationship with another woman? This was happening. I have no inclination toward it, but then, presumably, neither had some of the women in my personal range of acquaintance who had astonishingly turned up in that category, mostly during their forties or fifties. In fact I remembered hearing about a woman who was seeing a psychotherapist with the object of overcoming her heterosexuality, presumably in response to the dearth of decent men. Wait, consider the source, I said to myself when it came to me that this story was a gem from the lips of a man with whom I'd had a short sharp relationship which ended when it dawned on me that he was a complete fool, an example of whose level of wit was his whistling or humming the first bars of Two Different Worlds whenever we happened to pass by an interracial couple. There was nothing interesting about Gary, or rather an index of his blankness was that the most interesting thing about him was that he was lactose intolerant. I think I like children. I know I like intelligent children. I might be impatient for a child of mine to talk. I never wanted pets. My mother wanted me to have a dog once, which I tried, and which I rejected because it couldn't talk to me. This may relate. Infants qua infants fail to produce faintness and emotional synesthesia in me. I might have bonded with my dog if my mother had gotten it for me when I was younger. I had too high expectations by the time I got it. I was precocious.

At Lobatse the drivers offered to let someone ride in the cab with them. All declined but me. The cab is roomy and seemed as though it might be restful for part of the trip and that at the very least riding in it would give me a chance to extract the hemp spines from my palms. It was all right until we got onto rough ground during a detour outside Kanye. There was a jack and crank sitting loose in an open box at my feet. On the washboarding we drove at a speed that was only a foretaste of what would be the norm later but that was still excessive, with the result that whenever we hit a bump thirty pounds of metal would float up into the air and rotate in the void between my knees before crashing back down. I'm attached to my feet, so I suggested to the reserve driver —who seemed like a sensible family man and not a daredevil like the fiendish shavenheaded adolescent at the wheel—that if we tried we could force the jack under the seat. But he pretended not to hear me. This was, after all, a suggestion from a woman. Also this continuous limb-threatening hazard probably helped keep everybody alert. So when we stopped in Kanye it was al fresco time for me again.

The tarmac ends at Sekgoma Pan, which looks like a lobe of hell, which is appropriate because driving through the bush on the back of a Bedford being operated according to the CTO theory of how to drive over unpaved road is identical with flying through hell. The pan had been ravaged by veldfires: what had been thorn trees looked like black candelabras and pylons. The ground was scorched black, with drifts of gray and white ash here and there. There were four of us on the load, all women. I couldn't help thinking of the pol-econ officer at the American embassy who liked to say that Botswana was missing its calling: his notion was that it was a perfect setting for day-after-the-end-of-the-world movies, with a few outnumbered good guys running around in post-wargasm desolations, protecting the last nubile woman from the dregs of the lumpenproletariat.

The Bedford isn't a four wheel drive vehicle, so the CTO full-tilt theory of driving may not be insane. The idea is to go, over the cross-rutted stretches, so fast that you're touching only the tops of the ruts, in effect making them a continuous surface. Also your intense speed is supposed to carry you through the intermittent tracts of pure sand. We began. This way lies madness, I thought, which became the caption for my experience between Sekgoma Pan and Kang.

The wind ripped out everything that was holding my hair in place, so I thought So be it. I was keeping my hair long for attractiveness' sake, against every rule about bush living there is. The blast made consecutive thought impossible. I stood up in the blast, the back of my shirt blown out taut like a turtleshell, and sang the Marseillaise. Faster! I frequently murmured. Denoon is the only non-French person I ever met who knows all the verses of the Marseillaise. He also knew other anthems, and specialized in ones from minor countries. He thought anthems were hilarious, as a genus. He thought occupations should have anthems. For chefs there could be one called La Mayonnaise. He did a hilarious English version of the Boer anthem, Die Stem, which I have on tape.

We stopped a few times before reaching Kang, once to pick up a hitchhiking young woman, a teacher, and to let all hands relieve themselves, and again when we hit deep sand outside Mabuasehube and the passenger-side door burst open and the teacher and the jack and the crank flew onto the road. The sand was soft, fortunately. She wasn't hurt. The same or a slightly preceding jolt had cracked a carton of Daylight soap, so that bars of soap were distributed down the road behind us in a long array. The drivers were scrupulous, I must say. They climbed up high on the load to oversee us, the passengers, as we retrieved every spilled bar, and were very encouraging with their shouts and cries. This was our main rest break.

There was a moment when it looked as though getting out of the sand might be a problem. The breakdown kit, when it was extricated, surprised us by containing only a spare carburetor—no shovel, no sand mat of the absolutely reliable and time-tested kind they use all over the Sahel, no first aid kit. In point of fact, it wasn't a spare carburetor but rather one that had given out sometime in the past.

Apparently our drivers would get us out through sheer experience. I was told how long they had successfully been driving this route, and it was years and years. The adolescent must have begun driving as a tot. I hoped they were right, because I wasn't happy at the prospect of camping right there if they were wrong. We would be okay: there was water, although drinking water was siphoned out for us with the same length of hose used to refill the gas tank from the spare petrol drum. I was asked why I was asking the most questions.

By a trick, which no doubt took years of life off the drive train, a violent shifting back and forth between forward and reverse, they got us out. So it was back to more of the same searing thing, Botswana passing in a sepia blur. Ultimately I was too parched even for mental singing. I had to give up on the private travel game of guessing when the glittering decor along the roadside, the cans and bottles and broken glass, would thin out and stop. It never stopped. My mind emptied.

I was exhausted but increasingly elated. This was travel at its purest.

This was velocitude, the feeling of wellbeing associated with being in prolonged transit. I had no idea this was a faintly contemptible thing. For someone who had traveled everywhere, Denoon was peculiarly scathing on people who liked to travel. Of all the enthusiasms, the one for sheer travel was the one he claimed to find the most boring. You could rarely if ever get a travel buff to tell you one thing of interest, he would say. They can tell you the names of the places they've been and the number of places they've been. If you're lucky they can tell if some-place was fabulously cheap or criminally expensive. The quintessence of it was something Robert Louis Stevenson wrote, to wit, I travel not to go anywhere but to go, which was imprinted, fittingly enough, on the paper the Banana Republic wrapped your purchases in. Nelson was against recreational travel. It was his puritanism. If your work compelled you to travel, that was fine. Then you could enjoy it, presumably. But he hated tourism and thought people should stay home and make their own back-yards interesting enough to hold their attention. There was something about Denoon not realizing he was having his cake and eating it too in this connection that drove me to distraction. He wasn't a good sport about confronting it, either, or not at first.

The roar stopped and we were in Kang. Day was done. It was abrupt. I felt like one of those disciples of Gurdjieff who demonstrated the depth of their servitude by freezing in midcourse of whatever action they were performing, at Gurdjieff's command, not excluding when they were run-ning from the back of a stage straight at the audience. Naturally many of them sailed into the orchestra pit in marvelously frozen postures, crashing down triumphantly among the chairs and music stands.

The moon was up. We were under the wings of a beautiful tree, or a tree whose stasis seemed beautiful. I was still vibrating and still a blur as I got my gear together and set off to find shelter with the nuns at a mission oddly called, as I understood it, Mary, Star of the Sea.

The Sisters

Kang has douceur. The village is very dispersed, but the heart of it is under the canopy of a healthy acacia grove in which lots of the trees are lordly mature specimens of the umbrella and cloud genuses. The red aloes were up. At one time Kang was a government camp, and there is still a handful of government officers posted there who are typically away hunting or attending conferences or on leave, which doesn't bother the Bakgalagadi farmers and herders who populate Kang. The dominant tribes tease and look down on the Bakgalagadi as hopeless rustics only one step above the absolute bottom dogs, the Basarwa. Sometimes in the most unimaginably remote spots in Africa you find a bemused lakhoa staying for years, unable to leave, gripped by the particular genius loci. I could conceive that happening in Kang. The atmosphere is drowsy and floral. Underfoot is fine dark-grayish sand, soft, almost a talc, overlaid with a lattice of some vine resembling trailing myrtle, with small tough white blooms you hate to step on. You have a silence decorated by occasional goatbell and cowbell sounds. All the housing is in the old style: the male and the common rondavels have trimmed thatch and the female houses have loose, weeping thatch. The people are ragged and the place is poor, but there is a sense that things are being seen to. Kang is not demoralized. The brush fencing around the lolwapas is kept tight.

Whites in Kang are few and far between. There is the Boer general dealer and moneylender. There are the Franciscan Missionaries of Mary, at Mary, Star of the Sea, where I was crashing, six of them. There were supposed to be whites out at the half-built new consolidated secondary school outside Kang. I stopped out to see the place. The school complex is very futurist, in pink cement. A considerable error was made in preparing the site: they tore up the ground vines and whatever grass they could find and consequently sand is everywhere and in everything, a real affliction. The Dane who gave me tea was obsessed with managing the sand. He was shaking out a rug when I came up. When we sat down he kept clearing the gleaming tabletop between us with the side of his hand. The other teachers had gone and he was about to go. He was bitter. He had been surcharged for a watering violation: he had been caught pouring pitchers of water on the sand around the front door of his bungalow, to keep it down. The Italian contractors who had been putting up the school had gone bankrupt. He was the one who had believed the longest that the government would restart construction any day. But that was his curse, he had decided: he was credulous. He was using the time to review his life.

In Kang you are definitely at the still center of nowhere. Facing north you have bush running hundreds of miles unto Angola. To your west is the Kalahari and then Namibia, which is emptiness folded into emptiness until you get to the Atlantic, except for the flyspeck of Gobabis. To your east is more Kalahari, but an even more restricted and empty zone of it, the Central Kalahari Game Reserve. The desert gets drier and stonier to the west, but in the north, south, and east the Kalahari is flat to rolling thornveld, with trees and brush occasionally clustered but predominantly hot, dry grasslands, no surface water anywhere, absurd succulents you would be wasting your time trying to find in any field guide. Tsau, the omphalos of my idioverse, lay dead east in the reserve, a hundred miles away. I was listening circumspectly to see if anyone had anything to say about Tsau or Denoon, but nothing emerged. Conversation was arduous in Kang, which was not what I expected. I think people on the whole preferred to be silent. I began to understand it.

I loved the silence in Kang. My time in the bush had made me think about silence in a concerted way for the first time in my life, but there my appreciation of the silence had been colored by apprehension: I was listening through it for anything that might mean danger, intruders. In Kang I was always safe. I had also just survived the aural battering of the ride from Gabs. In any case I discovered I had a craving for silence that Kang seemed to feed. Conversation among the sisters was minimal, not out of obedience to any doctrinal rule I was aware of but because people preferred it that way. I halfway wondered if part of the success of cloistered institutions comes from parasitic exploitation of a deep thirst for silence that certain people may have and be unaware of. Denoon thought there might be something to this idea, although he also thought the taste for silence was draining out of mankind under conditions of civilization, and at a cost, if he was correct that the price of lamb in the United States was getting prohibitive because fewer and fewer people could be found who were capable of enduring the solitude entailed by being a shepherd. He claimed there had been a scheme to train welfare recipients for the occupation—the pay is quite decent—which had foundered spectacularly on entrenched silence aversion among the poor. This may be why he seemed fairly interested in my positive attitude toward silence. Not only should I have been more distinctly marked in this area by my low-income origins, but there was my escape from the generalized hatred of silence Americans are trained in, as manifested in the freezing horror that seizes us when the conversation during a date or at a dinner party falters. This was when it became clear that Denoon hardly thought of himself as an American. What he did think of himself as was another matter. In fact, for all my rather earnest musings on the subject, he had deeper feelings re silence than I did. When I was getting to know Denoon during what I allow myself to think of as a courtship period, we drifted into the inevitable eddying exchanges about our happiest memories, our most unpleasant experiences. For my most unpleasant experience I had come up trivially with once having had nothing to put a grease fire out with except a tray of cat litter. I should have scanned for something higher level. His was seeing a young cousin reading *Lord Jim* for the first time while a Doors album blasted on the stereo, the same side repeated over and over. He related this passionately. Of course in his own way he was being trivial too.

All I know is that in Kang the silence was almost lyrical, or more precisely, the ratio of innocuous noise to silence was perfect. I think you have to be deep inland for that kind of silence. The susurrus of wind in the thorn trees was highly occasional, not predictable. Furthermore I was so sick of talking. My last days in Gaborone had been endless structures of talk—coy talk, promises, cajolement, white lies—from morning to night. I was very ready to have it stop.

The mission was a line of squaredavels along the crest of the high side of the Kang pan. The sisters ran a tiny, overwhelmed clinic and were attempting, without luck so far, to establish a hostel cum primary school for Basarwa children. I enjoyed the sisters, who ceased being at all curious about me when I said the word anthropology. Their eyes glazed. We are not exotic in that part of the world. One of the sisters took me down into the pan to impress me with the severity of the drought. The pan at Kang is pretty deep and I had a recurrence of skepticism about the standard explanation of the origin of the pans, viz. wind action over millennia scouring out these depressions, the proof being that the rim standing most counter to the prevailing wind is supposedly always the highest. They look so much like volcanic or impact craters, though. We went down into the blinding thing. There had been next to no rain for three years. A hand-dug pit at the center of the pan which had been briefly used for watering cattle was now full of bones. We went to it. The floor of the pan was baked and checkered, and walking across it felt like walking on potsherds. In certain cracks you could insert your arm down to the biceps and your fingers would touch a wet substance like paste which would have dried into a rigid plaster coating by the time you pulled your hand out. You had to knock your coated fingers against something hard to get it off.

From an anthropological standpoint I was very interested in there being female Franciscans, women motivated by yet another embalmed male dream to live out their lives in wilderness like this. I have nothing against St. Francis of Assisi, I don't think. I know him by image, exclusively. But it was an anthropologically interesting fact to me that the heavy work of this remote mission was being done exclusively by very nice women. And the same is true for Africa generally, for Lutherans and all the rest of them. Even when a woman gets her own order authorized, like Mother Teresa, it's women who end up doing the cooking and cleaning and nursing and little detachments of men who get to do the fun proselytizing. As I say, I was more interested in the sisters than they were in me. It may be because people who do good, to a self-sacrificial point and on a continuous basis, seem to exist in a kind of light trance a lot of the time. When we were down in the pan I realized I had been waiting for a thing to happen that I'd gotten used to seeing happen among missionary women, id est a brief peeping out of the sin of pride. They are consciously determined not to take pride in the afflictions they endure for the love of Christ, but they tend to slip. My guide asked if I had heard the news that a nun had been trampled to death by an elephant in Zambia. I saw the gleam. And I could hear chagrin when honesty compelled her to mention that it was a sister not of their order. I commiserated appropriately, feeling ashamed of the kind of person I am.

It took me a week to get myself outfitted and provisioned for my expedition, and I could have made it take longer. I was protracting the process. Kang was hard to leave. Apparently I wasn't alone in feeling that way, because one of the sisters was in rebellion against a command to return to Racine. The time I spent lending a hand in the clinic also slowed me down by inducing internal questioning along the lines of What would be so terrible about public health as a career for you and What is so compelling about the socalled study of man? What did I think was wrong with the idea of doing something for people whose cheeks looked like pegboard, as opposed to spending my life swimming upstream through the shrinking attention spans of the sons and daughters of the American middle class? I knew I was already too old for medical school. I knew a woman three years younger who had been told she was too old for veterinary school. The sisters were doing medicine, in effect. And they seemed happy and were living decently, male absence notwithstanding. They were all a little overweight, but were obviously content construing whatever weight they settled at as what God, in the form of interacting genes, diet, and exercise, wanted. It was not on their minds. In America the dominant female types seem to be gaunt women jogging themselves into amenorrhea or women so fat they're barely able to force one thigh past the other when it's time to locomote, like Mom. The problem was that there was no mystery, that I could see, connected with public health. Anthropology, even my rather mundane corner of it, seemed to me to connect with the mystery of everything, by which I think I meant why the world has to be so unpleasant.

What finally stirred me to get moving was the water in Kang. It was cloudy and had an acrid taste. The sisters were aware of it but, I thought, eerily sanguine about it. When I brought it up directly, finally, it was clear they were, it could be said, even rather proud of what they were drinking. It seems the water in Kang is dense with naturally occurring nitrates. The water has been tested by the authorities and found to be spectacularly above the danger level. Everything in the literature suggested that nitrates at this level should cause people to develop a kidney disorder called methemoglobinuria. But there was no sign of the disease among the local people, who had been drinking the water for generations, nor among the nuns. There was no feasible filtering, in any case, nor if there were would it have felt right for them to make use of it when the poor of Kang would not have access to it. It was a medical mystery and a sign that Kang was under divine protection. They said this. So then it was time to bestir myself.

My lie to the sisters as to my destination was that I was only going east about twenty-five miles to rendezvous with a team from the rural income survey, which should have made my undertaking seem unthreatening enough. Still they wanted to talk seriously with me about traveling alone in the bush. It was about sexual danger, although everything was put more than obliquely. First they wanted reassurance that I had notified the proper officials as to my itinerary, namely the district commissioners in Kanye and Maun, which I lied yes to. I had skipped doing that out of hypercaution: I thought Denoon might have some kind of early warning agreement with the Ministry of Local Government and Lands to deflect journalists and supremely cunning doctoral candidates. I let fall gems like Please remember that Batswana think white women have an unattractive odor due to the amount of meat in our diets. Lastly I felt I had to lie that I had a pistol, which, as soon as I had uttered it, seemed like not a bad idea. I hadn't felt the need of any sort of firearm when I was in the bush near Tswapong, but then that piece of wilderness was closer to town than anyplace I was going, and there were occasional farms and ranches scattered around there. The wildlife in the Tswapong Hills was sparser and smaller by a long chalk than what I might be facing in the central Kalahari. I inquired around offhandedly the next day, but there were no guns for sale in Kang, at least not to me. So I repeated to myself all the reasons I had originally concluded a gun would be super-fluous and that was the end of that.

MY EXPEDITION

The Hunchbacks

I have to begin to be more synoptic.

I thought it would take me four days, at twenty-five miles a day, to get to Tsau, which it has become emotionally convenient lately for me to refer to inwardly as Pellucidar, after a book in the Tarzan series. It took me six-plus or seven-plus days, one or the other, to get there. Toward the end I was in serious straits. Calling Tsau Pellucidar is partly distancing and partly apposite. Pellucidar sounds like the way Tsau felt to me in one respect: it was like being, for the first time in my existence, in a correctly lighted place. I've never read the book, but I assume Pellucidar was one of the numerous lost and weird but still functioning cities Tarzan visited, and it was in Africa, naturally, although possibly it was at the earth's core, with only the opening leading down to it being in Africa proper. So it all coheres. Nelson was a boyhood fan of the Tarzan series. The first meal he personally prepared for us was a curried dish he called Rice Edgar Burroughs because it had some of Tarzan's favorite ingredients in it, whatever those might be.

Somewhere I have a list of the authors of Nelson's favorite boys' books. Most of them were news to me, like Roy Rockwood and Talbot Mundy. I now think the reason I have so much detail about the boyhood phase of his life is because telling me about it was a form of misdirection it took me forever to identify as such. I wanted details of his marriage and serious attachments generally and instead I got the thousand and one nights of his life as a boy, Denoon again and again taking ingenious revenges on the neighbor pharisee boys, who seemed to love to torment him and keep him from reading without interruption in the treehouses he constructed as reading pavilia. On the other hand, and to be absolutely fair, reading was one of his religions. In fact he gave as an instance of a consummate experience of pleasure reading straight through a collected edition of Sax Rohmer one summer. This was also an example of not knowing you were having a peak experience at the time you were having it and mistakenly assuming that it was the forerunner of many equal experiences waiting for you onward in life. I gathered he wished he had read more savoringly, possibly stopping after each paragraph and going Ah. He seemed to think that the idea that you should know when you're having fun and concentrate on it passim was original. I tried to suggest that this looked to me a lot like our old Aquarian friend Mindfulness, but he wouldn't have it. I must be vulgarizing him a little here. In any case it was his reading of Sax Rohmer, in particular a book starring his favorite Sax Rohmer hero, Morris Klaw, the Dream Detective, a prodigy who solves mysteries by inhaling verbena and going to sleep, that redneck neighbor boys disrupted by vandalizing his treehouse. His family owned a summer place in a dank redwood grove near the Russian River. Denoon's revenge was ingenious, but it escapes me. I did drift off now and then, toward dawn, during the thousand and one nights.

There was a formula, I pointed out, to the way he had resolved his difficulties with his enemy peers. I asked him if he was aware what it was. He thought. He had no idea. I delineated it. I said Routinely after you got revenge you undid renewed persecution against you by becoming the leader of your tormentors, at least until you moved. I count several times that you turned your former enemies into a club with you as president and got the club involved in time-consuming activities you could partake in glancingly, as a supervisor, such as building grandiose earthworks in vacant lots in preparation for mud war attacks from boys in other neighborhoods that rarely eventuated. There are patterns in all our lives, I said. Saying this may have contributed to a decline in his preoccupation with telling me about his boyhood, or it may have been genuine evolution in our relationship. Something helped.

The day I left Kang I got up at five, dressed quietly, and was slipping out of the mission courtyard when the entire sisterbody waylaid me with godspeed and bags of hardboiled eggs and other treats. I was gracious even though I had trouble figuring out quickly where to put the additional provisions they were forcing on me. I had everything planned down to the last ounce. My two donkeys were already loaded to the point of being in danger of tipping over. This is pure cavil. But actually I did feel slight irritation at their interposing themselves between me and one of the great unalloyed solitary joys of life—being up at first light and setting out on empty roads to go someplace difficult and significant. I think this is best enjoyed alone but I don't know why I say that. It was a nice bon voyage despite its being imposed on me.

In the outskirts of Kang something happened that I took as a reminder not to interpret experiential oddities too quickly. I was approaching the path leading to the primary school, and I stopped to watch the children running to class, a stream of them, and I thought Oh god! No! because as they passed I was seeing a stream of little hunchbacks, every one of them hunchbacked. I thought So many hunchbacks in one little spot in the Kalahari! What a commentary! Why was this never reported? How can this be? But then I watched as one little girl's hump disappeared. A tin bowl appeared at her feet and one of her schoolmates kicked it in my direction. In Kang it was the custom to carry your mealie bowl to school on your back with your jersey pulled tight over it to hold it in place, that was all. So with that I set off into the unknown, telling myself to remember that there is less to the mysterious than meets the eye. Because of what was to come, this was salutary. I used it as a talisman in the desert more than once.

Lions

The first day went perfectly. The heat was moderate. There were clouds in the afternoon. My donkeys looked like galleons, with all the extra feed and reserve water I had felt compelled to bring in case we struck some burned-over tract that extended farther than it should or we missed a water point. They had names. The bigger and older one was Baph, short for Baphomey. The Herero guy who sold me the animals had been unable to explain the provenance or meaning of the name. Denoon later had a freakish reaction to it which I never fully understood. Baphomey may have been a corruption of baphoumedi, which means roughly a group of rash people, or it may have been a corruption of bapola, a verb meaning to stretch out and peg down a hide. Neither association was too comforting. The younger donkey was Mmo, for mmoduhadi or sluggard. That was clear enough. I thought of the donkeys as the boys, my boys.

The grass thinned and gave way to patches of hardpan and bare sand. The trees began to be fewer. I passed my last attended cattle at ten and by midafternoon I had seen my last stray cow. The boys seemed fairly catholic about the available kinds of grasses, which was a relief. Toward evening I found my first water point exactly where it was supposed to be, although I had to do more digging in the bed of the sand river than I'd expected. I finally got visible seepage in the trough I'd dug. We stopped there. I tethered my animals and uncorked my pop-up alpine tent and zipped myself into it. I made a meal out of the hardboiled eggs, which was a mistake. I have no idea what I thought about that day. I think I was subsisting mentally on the singing feeling you get from beginning a great action. I was even too tired to write anything. I sank like a stone into sleep.

At two a.m. I awoke, my mind on fire with the question of lions. I knew I was supposedly safe, myself, in my tent, because there were no cases on record of lions actually forcing their way into a closed one. Also the game migrations were over with, which were what drew lions, and the migration routes in any case went in a curve deep to the west and north of my itinerary. But of course now in the small hours I was asking myself how much of everything you're told in Africa is folklore. I might be safe, but what about my boys? In Gaborone there was a public attraction, a lion park socalled, and what the tourists came to watch was fresh donkey meat being flung over a chainlink fence to a couple of lions at feeding time. Was the lion-tent copula a piece of folklore? and were lions really so strictly nocturnal in their hunting? There was a man in Gaborone I had had drinks with, the lion man. He was one of my sources. He was one of the people who had been reassuring. But he himself had started out as a student of lions and had been turned into an obsessive on the subject. He was a bar character you bought drinks for. I remembered his descriptions of lions bringing down gigantic Cape buffalo: one would swallow the buffalo 's snout, suffocating it, while other lions tore at the buffalo's legs. The lion man never wanted to see another lion. It was pointless, but I spent a good part of the rest of the night listening.

A Brief Mania

The next day I got up tired and swearing that from then on every night I would do the prudent thing of building either a perimeter fire or at least a large campfire and staking the boys next to it. I was annoyed at myself for gorging on eggs and naturally getting constipated. So it was onward.

It was a long time before Denoon really took my vocational crisis for anything like the real thing. The world was my oyster if only I got organized, was his initial thrust. Why couldn't I write about travel, for example. I loved travel. Need Travel Constipate? could be a selling article in something. All this was in the context of his proposal that I should found a magazine called True Travel analogous to True Crime or True Detective. I should found a travel magazine that would tell the absolute truth, for a change, which would lead to more people staying home, a consummation devoutly to be wished, according to him. Tourism corrupts, was his tune. I would be perfect for True Travel because according to Denoon I had never been in a country I really liked. America the Beautiful included.

Of course I proposed my share of alternative careers for him. One of us would be depressed and the other would say Well, you could always do such and such, and it would be off to the races. This began as a benign device for getting out of moments of discouragement. It evolved. The concept was that the one who noticed the other was depressed was thereby authorized to select a new vocation the depressed person would be forced to follow thenceforward, and in the pursuit of which depression would perforce not be logical. This jeu maintained its facetious character, but there came a time when I began to resent it as a concealed way of short-circuiting my episode of depression, because he preferred me to be merry, naturally. Finally, when I'd had many more vocations imposed on me than I was ever likely to be able to impose on him, it was enough and I made us discuss it, with the interesting result that he realized our jeu was probably vaguely filial to a species of game he'd enticed his unfortunate younger brother into playing when they were on boring car trips as children. He would get his little brother to agree that each of them would have the right to pick out, from the array of housing they would pass as they drove, the house that the other would have to live in for the rest of his life. The idea was to saddle the other with the worst-looking, worst-circumstanced hovel they saw on that particular trip. But of course Denoon, being older, had more patience and knew his younger brother would choose precipitately, and that by biding his time he, Denoon, would find something infinitely more humiliating for his brother than his brother would for him. He always won. He found houses on eroding cliffs and frightening little houses in cemeteries, for example. Denoon always won, but he also won the more important metagame, which was to get his brother to play another time, and another. Nelson wasn't proud of this. Looking it in the face even interested

him. Through talking about it he remembered a parallel game he had
gotten his brother to play, out of his brother's desire to be in his zone.
Peter was four years younger. This was not a car game, because it involved recourse to lists and books. You're really good for me, Denoon
would say when we got into these purlieus. You amaze me. Nelson
would propose to Peter that they each have the power to name the
other's firstborns, always assumed to be male, interestingly. During these
accounts I felt fortunate having no siblings. I was seeing something
foreign. The name would have to be documentable, either by appearing
in the sorts of lists of names that are appended to big dictionaries—which
Peter was more or less restricted to by reason of youth and lack of imag-
ination—or by appearing in some other printed text. Again he could
count on his brother's being premature and going with something like
Percy, something that sounded unmanly, which in the early games Denoon might counter with something like Uriel, thusly bringing bodily
wastes associatively into the picture. So Denoon would win and his
brother in frustration would scream that all right then he was taking back
Percy and somehow was going to make Nelson call his son Shitler. Denoon was always on the lookout for humiliating names. In the last game
in the series, Denoon's greatest triumph, his brother was forced to accept
naming his firstborn Dong, as in Dong Kingman, the painter, dong of
course being slang in those days for penis. The protocol in these games
and the bait that kept getting Peter to play was that each new game would
allow the players to wipe out the results of the last preceding game in the
genre. I was seeing a true vortex of oppression. When they played cow-
boys, for instance, Denoon would inveigle his brother into calling himself something like Roy Mucus, Sheriff of Scrotum County, when these
words meant nothing to Peter. The games could go on for days. Where
were your parents during all this? I wanted to know. They were otherwise
beset, he said: beset is Afrikaans for occupied, and you see it on the
restroom doors on South African Airways planes.

   On the second day the terrain changed. There were long dips and
rises. I let the boys graze liberally anytime they seemed inclined. Around
noon I had my first phenomenological oddity, having to do with light. It
came suddenly. There was a surplus of light. I felt I was getting too much
light, despite the fact that I was wearing sunglasses that were practically
black. The sky was cloudless. An irrational sign or proof that there was
too much light was that I thought I could detect a barely visible flicker
in the sky just above the horizon. I tried to push this whole subject out
of my consciousness, but it persisted. I thought it might be low blood

sugar speaking, so I ate some raisins. Peculiar ideation about light continued.

My sunglasses began to feel heavy and irritating. They were preventing something significant from happening. I developed the conviction that they were keeping me from seeing the real colors of the Kalahari and that this was hazardous for me. I would be in danger unless I recharged my sense of the real colors of things by taking my glasses off at some regular interval. I yielded to this notion, mainly in order to exhaust it, but each time I pushed my glasses up onto my forehead I had a stronger sense of some suppressed vibration going on in the landscape which I would be able to see clearly if I looked more intently and for a longer period the next time. This is brain chemistry, I said, and squatted down and hung my head between my knees. I got up, pulled the visor of my kepi down tight, put my glasses back on, and thought about the hunchbacks of Kang.

I was then all right for twenty minutes, until the mania came back reformulated as the proposition that if I actually got rid of my sunglasses, and only if, I would be able to see the true and fundamental color of nature. I was to understand that what we perceive as beautiful individual colors are only corruptions and distortions of the true color of reality, which is ravishing and ultimate and apprehensible only in extremely rare circumstances. This was not a question of hallucination. It was analogous to dream knowledge, but different. I knew that for some reason at some deep level I was doing this to myself. But still I was tempted to act. I said aloud things like This is about self-injury, This is about self-worth, What are we to ourselves? and other pop-psych trash. The experience was strange in every way. Was I trying to get myself to turn around and go back to Kang before it was too late, because navigating in the Kalahari without sunglasses is one thing for Bushmen who have presumably been adapting their vision to a surplus of light for millennia and another thing for a lakhoa already in a state of anxiety? On any trip like mine there's a point of no return. So was this some ideational response to the fact, which I was already having to fight to repress, that I was over my head? Had my brilliant unconscious chosen the one thing that if discarded would virtually disable me for making the long trip to Tsau but be manageable for a quick retreat back to Kang and safety? I think what broke the grip of this mania on me was firstly just hearing my own voice, whatever it was saying, and, secondly, remembering reading about someone who had been lost in the Kalahari and survived it reporting that he had had to get past a point when he experienced the desert as an organism or totality trying to get him to become part of it, as in surrender to it. This would make my sunglasses mania an analog of the feeling people lost in the Arctic get that they would be more comfortable if they took off their caps and mittens. The mania left, also suddenly, and we went on uneventfully.

That night I did everything right. I wore myself out collecting enough wood for a ring fire, got us all set up inside it, went into my tent, and closed my eyes, and immediately there were lions in the neighborhood. There may have been only one. I heard a roar like no other sound on earth. I felt it in my atoms. This is my reward for taking precautions, was my first thought.

I made myself emerge. I peered around. My boys were standing pressed together and shaking pathetically. I looked for glints from lion eyes out in the dark but saw nothing. Everything I did I managed to do with one hand on the flap of my tent.

Again I went through my lion lore. Lions roar only after they've eaten, for example. The paradox is that ultimately I slept better that night than I had the night before. I fell asleep clutching my bush knife.

In the morning I found it hard to eat. There was terror in me. I could die in this place, it was clear.

I dawdled breaking camp because I wanted to give any lions there were a head start at getting torpid. Lions are torpid during the day, was a key part of my lore package.

Music

Anyone who thinks crossing the Kalahari by yourself is boring is deluded. It's like being self-employed in a marginal enterprise: there's always something you should be doing if your little business is going to survive. For example, you should always be lashing a stick around ahead of you through the thicker grass to warn snakes to get back. But this isn't enough, because there are adders, who pay no attention to noise and just flatten themselves when they hear you coming, the better for you to step on them: so you have to be persistent about watching where you walk. Then you have to be careful not to walk directly under tree limbs without looking keenly to see if there are mambas or boomslangs aloft. You also have to keep resetting your level of vigilance, because your forearm muscles, the extensors in particular, begin to burn, the lashing motion being one you're totally unaccustomed to. In addition to which there is the sun to be careful about. I was keeping myself smeared with something I bought for three pula at Botschem that was supposed to be a strong sunscreen, but I was turning red in strips and patches anyway. And you have to be watchful for ticks. In only one way was I in luck, and that was in regard to dehydration. This was mid-April, that is to say mid-autumn, and perfect walking weather. In summer you could expect to lose about three pounds of water in a day of walking in the full sun.

You do need mental self-management, though, as I'd already partially learned, to get through solitudes like the Kalahari successfully. Fear itself is not enough to fully sustain and occupy you. On the whole I think I did well, which would have amazed certain lightweight women at the American embassy whose name for me, I learned much later, was Party Lights, based on their interpretation of my way of life—lifestyle to them, no doubt—in Gabs.

I was nervous and so were my animals, postlion. I stumbled on singing as a means of calming them down. I was singing for myself, initially, and then noticed that it seemed to help the boys too, especially Mmo. This is ridiculous, but they seemed to prefer complete songs to fragments of songs strung together with humming. I discovered how few songs I knew in full and how few songs of the ones I did know I knew more than one verse of. I think I must have a more complete sense of my total song inventory than anyone else has of theirs, except for professional singers. I know roughly which songs I know only the choruses of. I know which songs I know but discovered I couldn't stand to sing in the desert, You Are My Sunshine being a prime example of a song I loathed suddenly to which I had never had any objection previously. And there are other songs you have sung only halfheartedly in the past which in the desert suddenly give you peace and seem indispensable, like Die Gedanken Sind Frei. You are astonished at the number of separate songs that have gotten fused together in your mind in some manner that makes it impossible to separate them, à la What do you want for breakfast my good old man? What do you want for breakfast my honey my lamb? Even God is uneasy say the bells of Swansea. And what will you give me say the bells of Rhymney? And there were songs I knew in full and perfectly but which I had no recollection of ever paying attention to when they were popular, like Heart of Glass, now a favorite of mine forever. Songs help when you're under duress, which is undoubtedly why the Boer geniuses of cruelty forbid people in solitary confinement to sing.

I was singing so continuously that I began to find I disliked it when I stopped—I disliked that ambience. I was briefly an aide in a nursery school for neglected children, and the best-adapted, happiest, and smartest children in the place were three sisters who had been taken from a mother who kept them chained to a radiator so they would be safe while she was out circulating, and who when I asked them what they did all the time when they were alone said We sang. The inspiriting effect my singing had on my animals was not an illusion, and it reminds me now of the period when I was feeling depressed at how commonplace and rudimentary my dreams were compared to Denoon's. He claimed to dream infrequently, but when he did, his dreams were like something by Fabergé or Kafka in their uniqueness. He would have noetic dreams, and when they were over he would be left in possession of some adage or percept that tells you something occult or fundamental about the world. One of these was the conviction he woke up with one morning that music was the remnant of a medium that had been employed in the depths of the past as a means of communication between men and animals—I assume man arrow animal and not ducks playing flutes to get their point across to man. Living with me made him more provisional about his dreams, especially after I compared one of his adages to a statement some famous surrealist was left with after dreaming, which he thought important enough to print up: Beat your mother while she's still young. I would always make Denoon at least try to reduce his insights to a sentence or two. The fact is I laugh at dreams. They seem to me to be some kind of gorgeous garbage. I have revenge dreams, mainly, in which I tell significant figures from my past things like You have the brains of a drum. On I sang.

Is it absurd to be proud of your dreams, or not? Denoon was.

Poetry let me down. I elided into poetry from time to time and discovered that I knew a lot of it. My attitude toward rhymed poetry changed utterly. Respect was born. Except for Dover Beach there was almost nothing unrhymed in my inventory. I know quite a lot of Kipling. I know some Vachel Lindsay. Finally one stanza out of Elizabeth Bishop got hold of me and kept inserting itself between pieces of other poems, truculently. It maddened me both by its tenacity and by what it said: Far down the highway wet and black, I'll ride and ride and not come back, I'm going to go and take the bus, and find someone monogamous. I used opera to drive this away.

Serious Trouble

Serious trouble began on the fourth or fifth day out. It happened because I was doing a thing I had been warned not to do in the desert: I was reviewing my life. Actually I was thinking about an aspect of my life, to wit, who would miss me the most if I was reported lost. Also I was thinking in general about how easy it would be to vanish physically in the Kalahari, how quickly you would turn into dust and be distributed, the usual. I had been advised by people like the lion man to keep my consciousness in my superfices, my skin and eyes and ears, my legs, to be a scanning mechanism and nothing else while I was in the desert. Also I had been told not to try to figure out everything that was odd that might happen to me, like an impulse to stand stockstill, which I had in fact had a couple of times but, naturally I need to point out, only after I had been apprised that this might happen to me. The reason I think I was letting my mind drift in these directions was that I was tired of the singing and chanting that had served me so well during the first leg of my madness. Also I had been told to forget all the Bushman notions I knew, the bizarre items. I hadn't known what these were, but I was curious to know, so I'd bought more drinks for the lion man, whose face was lined so authoritatively you could faint. Apparently Bushmen say they can hear the sun burning, to which I say So what? The lion man had been touted to me as the ultimate authority on the Kalahari. He did look like an authority, but he was an authority who was living to drink, insofar as I could tell. The Bushmen say they can hear a faint hiss from the sun, he said, as I wondered if this was something he had thought up because he had me in front of him squinting for the truth about the Kalahari. There was a woman who knew everything I wanted to know, someone I would have trusted, she had lived in the Kalahari, but she was no longer around. She had become unwelcome to the government. One thing I am sure of is that the lion man dyes his hair. I had been oblique with the lion man about whether I myself was actually going into the Kalahari, but he knew.

Just after breaking camp in the morning and going through agonies over whether I was giving enough water to the boys—we had missed at least one water point and were doing rations—I thought I heard a short sharp noise that must be a gunshot: like the lion roar, just the one event. Was this an everyday natural thing no one bothers to investigate? We were in a very barren area. When the sound came I felt faint. But then nothing. We proceeded again.

I was trying to buck myself up by reminding myself, apropos the lion man's stories, that the desire to tell stories is not always the same thing as the desire to convey the truth, when we came to a locale I hated from the outset. It was a grassy, thickly wooded basin. The grass was a coarse gray-green type I knew was unpopular with my boys unless they were at the very end of their tether. I felt I had no choice but to go through this place, which was extensive. The ground was spongeous in spots. The feeling was claustral. The trees, low thorn trees, struck me as very uniform, almost the way trees look in children's art. The trees were clotted with mud nests, weaverbird nests, sometimes six in a tree. But there was no birdlife. The nests were dead. Not only were there no birds but there was none of the mild almost subliminal background shuffling caused by animals like springhares and lizards you become used to sensing. I kept yawning, for no reason.

To be frank, I think that one thing that led me into the grove was a desperate feeling about my innards. There was a feeling of privacy. We would be out of view in this place. I was hoping and yearning for a sign that this might be the place where I would be restored to normal in this respect at least, that the enclosedness of the scene might summon something. In the normal parts of the Kalahari you are on display for miles in every direction.

There was a sinister gestalt that clearly I began cooperating with and adding to, as in finding the air not only thick but actually fetid, and so on. There may have been a barometric anomaly taking place, it now occurs to me. We went deeper into the grove. My boys were nervous and acting out, and this also affected me. If they'd been placid I could have used that to moderate my readings-in, but they were increasingly jangled and wired-seeming as we proceeded. What was the origin of all the folklore about dogs and horses being sensitive to the presence of ghosts? I wanted to know. It was multicultural, so did it have some basis in reality? The Batswana believed it.

But mainly I wanted to know why my life path had led me into such a frightening place, if I was as intelligent as I was supposed to be. It was because of a fixation on another human, a male. But why had the conviction that this kind of fixation befalls women much more often than it does men not been enough to deter me a little, stop me from acting so generically so precipitously? Somehow this place was worse than anything so far, worse than hearing the lion roar, which I was already pathetically recasting as possibly having been a dream in any case. Also it was abundantly clear I would never be able to relax enough in the grove to think of my bodily processes.

I was leading Baph by a rope attached to his headstall. Mmo was on a halter tied to Baph's pannier rack. Mmo was the one who was being the most difficult. I thought I could improve things, as I had a couple of times before, by getting between my boys and leading them as a team. So I untied Mmo and in the process lost him. It was instantaneous.

It happened because I had brought only one compass with me and I had developed a recurring anxious need to reassure myself that it was where it had to be, in my left breast pocket. It calmed me to touch my pocket. I let go of Mmo's rope for just the fraction of a second touching my pocket took. I must have done this before, without incident. Mmo shot away like a genius. I had never seen him move like that. It was fast and purposive. I was paralyzed. I thought I must have done something to him I was unaware of, hurt him. It froze me. What was he doing and what should I do? I had treated him well, I thought. I lost crucial time trying inanely to think what it was I must have done. There was also the feeling that it was unthinkable that he wouldn't reconsider in a moment and come back. I started after him, but Baph was only willing to walk and there was no way I could see myself letting go of Baph. The idea of tying Baph to a tree and then running as fast as I could after Mmo was not accessible to me.

I even took time to stupefy myself with a moment or two of class rage. I could never have been one of those adolescent girls who deified the horse family. You had to have money for that. If I had ever been exposed to horses for more than ten minutes in my life I might have had a better idea of what to do now or what I should have avoided doing that led my boy to bolt, which might be dooming me. Probably it would be a wonderfully empowering thing for a young woman to get to clasp her legs around a powerful naked male beast and make it do things, jump over obstacles on command, and so on. This could be one of the sources of the self-confidence you envy in rich women, not that the sources of self-confidence in the rich are not as numberless as the sands of the Gobi. I had known a few equestrienne darlings in their little caps who rode in shows. Or rather I had been aware of them. In the meantime Mmo was a hundred yards away, looking back over his shoulder at me.

Finally I did tie Baph up and try to run in earnest after Mmo. It was too late. I was now terrified to get too far from Baph out of fear that something might happen to him in my absence. Each sortie drove Mmo farther out of reach. Baph acted frantic each time I left. Worst of all, I realized that I had no idea what the equivalent of Here kitty kitty is for a donkey. There had to be something that Batswana drovers used. In my state of pride and momentum I had never bothered to ask. This more than anything demoralized me. Even if I got inside his startle zone, what then?

Mmo cantered out of sight. I tried to reconstruct what portion of everything he was carrying. It was some of the feed, some of the water, and my tent. Never do this again, was my main brilliant injunction to myself.

I suppose what I should have done was take Baph and trail along in the general direction Mmo had taken in hopes that he would relent and come back. But this was inconceivable. Mmo was going away from Tsau, not toward it. I had no idea how long such a game might go on, either. In any case I was convinced that I would be unable to plan anything until I got out of the grove and into some less accursed part of the landscape.

After the Gray Place

We got clear of the gray place, as I was calling it to myself, and stopped. I was petting Baph insanely. We had a very modest amount of water left.

I was full of guilt. Whatever risk he had imposed on me by decamping, Mmo was dooming himself. I must have been being too routine toward these animals, not loving enough, not enough in rapport with them. These were beasts of burden whose cargo was my survival. I had failed them, or failed one of them.

Now what would I do, other than what I had been doing, except faster? It was about now that I noticed with disgust a trace of elation in my reaction to what things had come to. Apparently I was furtively pleased that the level of difficulty had gone up. I reject this tendency in humanity. I had always seen it as a specifically male pathology, yet here it was, even if dilutely. A young ne'er-do-well attempts to kill himself by shooting himself through the head and when he only succeeds in blinding himself is galvanized with determination to get into law school, overcome his new disability, and become a millionaire lawyer, which he does. This was the company I was finding myself in in the Kalahari.

Remember the hunchbacks, interpret nothing, I said to myself. You are going to be abnormal until this is over, because no one crossing the Kalahari alone is going to be normal after the second day. I felt superficially better. It helped that we were back in a more standard part of the desolation.

The thing to do was to get to Tsau immediately. This was my new solution for everything. Nothing interested me but that. Ostriches crossed our path several times that afternoon and I barely paid attention, even though this is one of the few birds I have any kind of curiosity about. One reason we had to get to Tsau faster than planned was because my tent was gone, which meant having to stop early enough each night to collect enough wood to keep major fires going throughout the night without fail. Being lax or nominal about this would not be possible. We picked up the pace considerably, and Baph was good about it at first.

We went too fast. Going faster meant needing to rest more. During one rest stop I fell asleep sitting against a tree and was awakened by being jerked over by Baph, to whose halter I had tied my hand. We resumed. I pressed us. I even got Baph to canter for short stretches.

I never whine but was whining then. We aren't getting to Tsau, was what I was whining. It was as though I thought that by sheer urgency I could force Tsau to rise out of the ground. It irritated me that we would be unable to go in a beeline for Tsau because the remaining water points lay significantly south or north of our route. Why had I let myself make such cursory calculations of how much time would be consumed in deviations from our route?

Camping that night was macabre. What my map led us to was an abandoned cattle post, probably German, dating from the early protectorate and obviously derelict for years. There were tumbledown pens and stall fencing, a burst and heeling dip tank, piping, remnants of buildings, and at the center of the complex an ox pump, meaning a butterfly-shaped iron rig which two oxen could be harnessed to and then driven to turn, goaded to plod endlessly in a circle to raise the water. The nails I occasionally kicked up were antique. On the face of it this should have been a more sinister venue than the gray place, but it never registered that way with me. I was totally absorbed in hurrying.

I was manic. I threw myself into wrenching half-buried timbers out of the ground and dragging old planks and poles from the farthest reaches of the property to heap up in piles in a rough circle around the pump. Most of the wood went into a central dump which I would sleep next to and from which I would chuck replenishment into the barrier fires from time to time. What was left of the place, I virtually razed. This was arson, not camping. I hope the site had no historical value. Nothing could slow me, not even my cold fear about water. I had decided early on that very far down the well shaft something was glinting that must be water. How I would get it remained to be seen. The apparatus was rusted rigid, completely inoperable. But that problem was for the morning. Even when I sensed I had enough wood I went for more. I put off eating. I had failed to bring gloves of any kind, so in short order my hands had become rich with splinters I would have the pleasure of dealing with later. I know what I was doing. I was overpreparing the event because I dreaded my next task, which was to inventory my supplies and face what Mmo's defection had done to them.

I laid out what was left. I thought we would survive if Tsau was where I estimated it to be. Food for me was more than adequate, especially now that I was so anorectic. Water was the dilemma. I had two plastic five-gallon jerricans, one empty and one a third full of water that was reserved for Baph. I had two canteens, one full. There were enough oats for two skimpy feedings for Baph. If we got there, he would arrive hungry.

I had started a new journal, in a separate notebook, in Kang. That was gone. This meant I had no sure fix on the date. I hadn't paid attention to the date on the page I had written my farewell-to-Kang entry on. But all my Tswapong and Gaborone journals were safe.

A perfect index of the shape I was in was my reaction to losing my mirror. All my toilet articles had gone with Mmo. I couldn't stand it. It felt like I had lost my left hand. I would have traded my first aid kit for my mirror and my comb. It was irrational. How could I look at myself, check myself, before I got to Tsau? I would need to look at myself. It was urgent because I knew that through fear and exertion, weight was dropping off me. I was certain I was in ketosis, since I was living on protein and water—pilchards and water, tuna and water, ghastly Vienna sausages and water. When I lose weight rapidly it shows first in my face, then go breasts, hips, middle. This was why I needed a mirror. I felt stabbed in the back by life, by my foul luck. Now I was supposed to present myself to Denoon with only the vaguest notion of how I looked, and uncombed. I was wild. I thought of trying to devise a comb out of the nails in the sand.

So I lit the fire. It was a spectacle.

Baph was exhausted, clearly, because he got down on his knees as soon as we stopped. I slept half on top of him, or half slept, after pulling a tarp over us both.

April nights in the Kalahari are cold, but we were hot. I got up three times to renew my paean to heat, light, and destruction. I burned everything. Even as day fell I threw more into the display.

The Well

The day began with the ordeal of fishing up water for us.

This was by the spoonful, almost.

The casing the ox pump shaft went down into was about eight inches across. There was a clearance of at most three inches between the shaft housing and the casing wall once I had battered and levered the shaft over as far as I could through brute force. My canteen was too fat to slide through the gap. I was stymied. I needed a thing, ideally, like a bayonet case that I could reel down to get water by increments.

What I did was pound, crush, and crimp my canteen cup into a travesty of itself, beating the side in and folding the bottom up over it and praying to god I wouldn't pierce or break it. It was thinner than a pack of cigarettes when I was done with it, and it would hold about half a cup of water. I had dropped a ten thebe piece down the shaft and concluded that the water was forty or fifty feet down. I had a hundred feet of nylon cord. I made two holes in the rim to thread the cord through.

On my first try, the cup, crushed and compressed as it was, seemed to take a long time to immerse, even though I jiggled the line vigorously once it was in the water to tip it. So before the next descent I attached a sinker made of odd bits and pieces of iron fitments I scavenged from the area, and then we were all right.

It took hours to fish up enough water to fill all my vessels. I had to be in an excruciating position to do it. My knees and back were agonized. Whoever said he had measured out his life in coffee spoons was talking about me that day.

I made Baph slake himself before we left. That was difficult because I discovered a rent in the collapsible canvas bucket he very much preferred to drink from, which meant holding the rent pinched closed while he took his time, which could be done only by my assuming a position specially created to torture my already excruciated back. Finally we could go.

Walking erect was bliss for a while.

A Nadir

What transpired next survives in my mind as a medley, more or less. I was beyond writing things down. I may have had two identical days or I may have imagined one of them.

We went until late. When we stopped I had the strength for only one small fire, so we slept between it and a termite mound, which I thought I had heard lions disliked. I slept tied to Baph, as per usual. He was becoming very acclimated to fires, I observed. This time he stood all night. I remember this night scene, with the firelight flickering on the termite mound, happening twice, which is not possible.

In the morning I woke up with two songs I had forgotten I knew fresh in my consciousness—The Old Triangle, three verses, and Where Have All the Flowers Gone, all verses. They were both good trek songs.

The terrain was harder. We had to negotiate a sequence of lines of small dunes running straight north-south. The interdune valleys were gravelly, with occasional tracks of metallic-looking grasses growing in tufts. Now that we were regularly going uphill I had to pull Baph, whereas before he had been willing to go up or down anything with alacrity. My lips were puffing up because one thing I had kept in my toilet kit instead of my first aid kit was the zinc oxide. This brought on another, but weaker, episode of mirror anguish.

After the dunes the flatlands resumed, stretching away into the glare. Where was Tsau? Tsau should appear. It was built around and halfway up a substantial green koppie three hundred feet high and noted for its conicality. At the least I should be able to see the line of low red hills Tsau lay just eight miles beyond, or the sand river that cut through them and swung close to the base of the Tsau koppie.

East of us the ground was gray and yellow, mottled, with patches of thick shoulder-high brush we preferred to circumnavigate. To our north there had been fires recently. We began to encounter charred brush and prongs of black, burnt ground. The sky was a burning white, like the inside of an abalone shell.

Naturally when a windstorm came it would be from the north, plain grit and sand not being annoying enough for us: we would have to have ash and smuts too. Baph noticed that it was coming before I did, at least this is how I interpret his sitting down, like a person, on his rump. There was a dark blur to the north, moving. I could make out dust devils here and there. I put my back to the oncoming blur and hugged Baph's head in an attempt to shield his muzzle. The blast reached us.

Fortunately it was brief, if stinging. I tried, when I was brushing myself off, to be fastidious and flick away the dots and particles of ash on my clothes lest I mash them and make myself look camouflaged. But it was unavoidable. I brushed Baph off and dabbed his eyes clean. They seemed to be discharging. In fact he looked unwell. It was no surprise that he refused to move when I pulled on him to come. I didn't persist. This was serious. After one more bout of pulling as hard as I could made not the slightest difference I sat down with him.

This was my lowest ebb. Baph had to get up. I couldn't carry the water cans.

I had to remobilize. Venting was no use. I need a bath, I shouted, and Never do this again, but it was pro forma.

Then I impressed on myself that if I died there, no one in his right mind would regard it as a tragedy. I would be in the category of an aerialist falling to her death. Or I would be entitled to the species of commiseration people get who show up at parties on crutches but who got injured skiing at Gstaad or some other upper-middleclass earthly paradise. It would be sad but not that sad.

Enfin I made Baph get up by stabbing, or rather stabbing at, his hindquarters with a ballpoint pen—not drawing blood, but stabbing harder than I would ever have credited myself with being able to do. I still flinch at myself.

He got up and was angelic.

As we went I decided to wipe the peanut butter off my lips. The smell was making me nauseous. I had been using the peanut butter as a surrogate for my zinc oxide. I decided my lips were burned and swollen beyond repair anyhow, and for a split second I was able to feel glad that there was no mirror to see them in.

Night came and the idea of camping was unthinkable because, as I saw it, only impetus could save us. We had to reach Tsau. We would go with the water we had and forget about the last water point.

So long as Baph would walk, I would walk. That was another reason to keep going: he was proceeding at a dragging pace. And the final reason for continuing was that a vulture couple had picked us up during the day and was following us. This was not what we needed. And vultures leave you alone during the night. They go someplace and roost. There was a chance, I thought, that something more attractively protomoribund than we two might detain them on the morrow.

That night at last I became my body, my body and my breath, in about the way I assume the counsels of perfection I'd gotten from the lion man had meant I should. Walking was painless. I had no punitive ideation all night, none. It was very cold, and even that was pleasant. Undoubtedly this state was something devised out of the chemistry of threat, like Livingstone going into a religious rapture when a lion got him by the shoulder.

Tsau Appears

I assume I was in a fugue state until the moment the next afternoon when the reddish hills that were proof you were within eight miles of Tsau appeared. Appeared is the only word for the experience. They were not there and then they were.

Internally I experienced something like a profound but subaudible chord being played. And then I was alert. It was like falling back into my body from a height. Everything hurt at once: my insides hurt, my hands were pulsing with infection from unextracted splinters, my tongue for some reason felt like balsa, as did my lips. Baph stank, which I had not been noticing, and he was breathing in an alarming way.

Even now all I remember from the night before is walking through the dark through an intermittent, patternless wind. A couple of times, depending on the angle of the wind, it seemed to me that I heard, coming from a great distance, a sound like glass being struck. I assumed, wrongly as it turned out, that this was an anomaly like the phantom gunshot I'd heard earlier.

The hills appeared, and the sand river that was guaranteed to meander straight to the outskirts of Tsau.

Shortly I was at the hills themselves.

I wanted to see Tsau. I felt it as a physical emergency that I see my destination.

Up to my left on the flank of a hill was an odd, sharply higher hummock. There were trees on it that looked like parsley: albizzia, I guessed. A path marked with stones led to the hummock and up it, and there was what was clearly a hitching post at the mouth of the path. I tied Baph to it and went up.

The whole hummock was a devised thing. Chiming sounds came from the trees. The base of the hummock was encircled by a collar of dead broom plants. I could see some sort of furniture under the trees.

I was in a state of triumph.

It was clear that this eminence was something amplified by the hand of man and designed to be the place the traveler from the west got his or her first full prospect of Tsau. I gazed at Tsau.

Most koppies look like rubble pyramids with the apices sheared off and usually just a few bands or pockets of vegetation established on the slopes. The koppie Tsau was built against was different and classic. It was vast. It was a true island mountain rising splendidly alone in the plain. It was evenly and densely wooded almost to the crest, where enormous rouge-red bulbous boulders sat like ruins.

On the flats a tract of small houses lay like a fan open toward me. There was more housing, more structures in any case, on the lower slopes of the koppie. Not everything I could see was interpretable. I was puzzled by three flickering white bars or slots set in a row high up on the koppie, which would turn out to be the flanged cylinders that are the wind-trapping elements in the avant-garde windmills Denoon had installed in Tsau. I was also puzzled that Tsau looked almost sequined, owing to the profusion of glints and flashes of reflected light coming from all over the settlement. There was an explanation for this too.

One end of a sweep of fenced fields, all very geometrical, was visible far to the east. Where were the freeform Tswana mealie fields I was used to? I wanted to know. Overall I loved what I was seeing.

I was not emotionally normal.

Hanging from a chain in the crown of a large albizzia was the answer to the mystery of the crystalline notes I had picked up during the night. It was a glass bell the size of a half-gallon jug. It was beautifully shaped. I had never seen anything like it. The glass was thick and the same blue-green you see in utility line insulators, and the clapper was like an elongated iron teardrop. It seemed like the most beautiful object I had ever seen. I wanted it. I had to forcibly remind myself that the bell was there for a reason, although what that might be I was unable to imagine. Tsau was eight miles away and the idea that this bell might function in some way to give warning was ludicrous. Besides, it was hung so as to ring whenever a decent wind struck the tree. I shook the branches to make it drop its notes on me. They were like cool water. I must have needed some kind of release, because I went on autistically shaking the branches until I realized the blood was leaving my arms.

I seemed to see a pair of horns sticking out of the earth fifteen feet from the base of the bell tree, lower down on the Tsau-facing side of the hummock. Skulls of ungulates are common in the Kalahari, so I had barely paid attention. But these horns were too thick and in fact were carved out of wood and enameled white. I thought briefly then that this might be a cult item that would make some greater sense of the amount of work that had gone into creating this shrine area or whatever it might be.

I cleared the sand away from the base of the U formed by the horns. They were set into a hinged plug that opened on a narrow ceramic tank, glazed, with water in its depths. Resting in the tank was an iron dipper with a shank a yard long. The water seemed fine and sweet. I was out of halazone tablets, so I wouldn't drink it, but I could wash in it—or rinse off in it, rather, since I had no soap.

I was curious about this cistern, how it was fed, and went back to look more closely at the tree itself. It was a work of art. The tree had been converted into a device to harvest downpours. The cistern was fed by a system of polyvinylchloride tubes leading from ceramic basins sunk into sanded-out hollows in the main forks of the tree. All the small tubes were gathered together and stapled nicely out of sight on the Tsau side of the tree before joining at the base with the main collector, which ran underground to the capped cistern. I had no way of knowing it then, but this was my first brush with the jungle of contrivances Tsau so often felt like. This cistern was an elaboration of the Bushman praxis of using hollow trees as rain collectors. In part I was not impressed. The amount of labor involved in creating this thing was what bothered me. Other trees were also ducted into the system. How many people would ever use this? How could the labor of setting it up and maintaining it—presumably the collector basins would have to be cleaned and the tubing purged from time to time—ever be justified? I then proceeded to justify it in my case at least by lavishly using the water, of which there seemed to be plenty, for my purposes.

First I made several trips down to Baph to pour water over him and try to get him to come up into the shade with me. He balked. I cleaned his eyes and gave up.

I interspersed my ablutions with periods of gazing at Tsau. I rinsed my face and hands, which felt insufficient, then began sponging myself inside my shirt, which was no better. And so step by step, out in the blazing open, I disrobed and patted this lovely water all over myself. My feet were in unspeakable shape. I loved something about being naked in this place. It was done in contempt of the Kalahari and was a way of saying to it Go back to what you were doing before I interrupted the even tenor of your ways. It was adolescent. I think I also did a passage of invented eurhythmics whose real purpose was to wag my lower self in the face of the Kalahari, which I was letting myself feel fully as the organism that wants you to suffer that it truly is. There was also personal justice euphoria. I was rhetorically thinking How many women could have done this, women not supported by large male institutions or led by male guides? and so on. I had improvised and won through.

I put on new underpants and a new tee shirt, despite the Potemkin character of my toilette. I put on clean socks. My hair was irretrievable, just a wad on my head.

I was as restored as I could hope to be.

So it was time, wreck that I was, to impersonate myself as well as I could for Denoon and to get my husk of a donkey to Tsau and into the hands of others.

Wayposts, No Garlic

The path to Tsau was defined by wayposts. Every few hundred yards on alternate sides of the route, a wooden waypost about a yard high was set into the ground. On top of each post was a crossbar, from the ends of which hung clusters of dark-colored disks of glass threaded on fishline. You approached Tsau down a corridor of darling crepitation. I asked myself what the idea could possibly be. Again, all this represented human effort. The standards and crossbars were carved, not elaborately but carved just the same, spiral channels gouged into them, for example. Was the idea simply to go out and interior decorate the howling waste for fun? The wayposts were spaced irregularly, so that no purpose of measurement seemed served.

The wayposts I found depressing until I realized why, and then I was even more depressed. I realized they had ominous associations for me because, miniature though they were, the wayposts were homologs of the crosses and gibbets set up by characters like centurions to warn travelers arriving at a conquered city that the reigning power was cruel and rebellion not a thing tolerated, as in decline of the Roman Empire and rise of Christ movies. From this follows another perfect example of how marginal my state of mind had gotten in the desert. I suffered an attack of anguish over the amount of time I had wasted in movies as a girl. Getting into movies unaccompanied had been one of the few benefits of being tall for my age. But I thought Wouldn't I be calmer, and wouldn't I have less prefabricated imagery inundating me, and wouldn't I have somewhat less constant hubbub going on behind the arrases lining my mind if I hadn't gone running manically to the movies as a sop to my preadolescent miseries, as huge as they were? I could have taken out more records from the library instead, for example, and lost myself in music and at the same time developed a more systematic knowledge of the great composers, which would also have had the virtue of being free.

In the next breath it was an entirely new anxiety: I had the conviction, derived from nowhere, that there would be no garlic in Tsau. I felt I had to be able to look forward to garlic, by which I meant fresh garlic, not

garlic powder or salt. I do inordinately love that herb. My mother abjured
it for us because, she claimed, it didn't agree with her. But truly it was
because the poor she knew best, Italians, ate and smelled of garlic. We
might be poor but we would never be accused of smelling of garlic.
People would have to divine that we were poor via some other brilliant
deduction, like putting together the rents in our garments and my mother's missing incisor. Personal liberation for me was also incidentally culinary liberation, in which the great central discovery was the glory of
garlic.

Never say I am not mine own social worker. My liberal self now gently
tried to lead me to entertain the idea that my garlic urge was homeostasis
speaking, my body crying out for phosphorus, say. But then my true self
said that if I wanted phosphorus it wasn't garlic I wanted, it was water-
cress, and that marching fixedly toward Tsau as if the main point of
reaching it was to get a giant helping of boeuf en daube was silly. Denoon
was absurd on liberals and had a sulk I ultimately detonated him out of
after I told him his aphorism for liberalism—id est To alarm and soothe
in the same moment of policy—was a fake and groundless. I think probably we should all be liberals. When things were disintegrating between
us, and I regret this now, I even said I will give you a thousand dollars if
you show me why you shouldn't be defined as a liberal, given what we
have definitively established as your political baseline. In any case my
liberal incubus was now telling me that, la la la, maybe Tsau would be
the place, like a spa, where I could stop being operated upon by the
buried cultural mechanisms of my adolescence and/or absurd cravings
like this one for garlic. I and my rough beast staggered toward Tsau.
Meantime the chiming and jinking continued, the accompaniment.

I still, today, fault myself in the matter of Denoon's vitromania,
which I was just now beginning to endure the fruits of, all unknowing.
Nelson adored glass. Blowing it, casting it, it didn't matter: he loved it. If
I had pressed something home on this subject it might have had a clari-
fying effect. This was an example of something I could have done more
with. I don't know why I didn't, unless it was because I heard the keystone vitromania stories at a time when I was still grateful just to be
receiving this crumb or that from the table of his mind, or because it was
a time when he was feeling fragile in some other area and I refrained on
vitromania to be considerate. His vitromania was central, somehow.

What is clearly the core incident involving glass goes thusly. Denoon
is a boy, and his father has lately fallen, through alcohol abuse, from the
high estate of working in an advertising agency to the low estate of being

a salesman for a printing ink and industrial resins firm. The family is living south of San Francisco, on the peninsula. I think Nelson is fairly happy in school, and the house they're renting abuts some nice ex-farmland or an abandoned orchard in the shadow of the Coast Range. I think their place is near Belmont.

Two conditions conjoin. Nelson discovers a bottle dump out in the orchard nearby. Secondly he inherits a binful of corks, since his father has backslid from an attempt to control his drinking through oenophilia and home winemaking. Nelson's father was a devious drinker, a master drunk Nelson called him, who was at this point managing to spirit his empty fifths out into the woods and into this dump. I forget whether or not this might have been a preexisting dump with a trove of empty bottles already present when Nelson's father began using it. I think this may have been the case.

Nelson is eleven or twelve and is only in the most elliptical way aware of the extent of his father's drinking. He is on the verge of discovering how intense the war over his father's drinking is, but as yet there are only rumors of war, supposedly.

He saw no secret or unconscious impulse working beneath the surface of what he did. He was certain. His project was aesthetic, accidental. Looking back, he could plainly see the part his project played in proving that the agreement between his parents about his father's habit was a fiction. The agreement in force was that his father would drink set amounts at set times only. Obviously his father must have been drinking volumes of liquor in secret and using the permitted small amounts to mask his excesses. But Nelson's proof that the ultimate project was innocent was the ad hoc way he had come to undertake it in the first place.

Whatever else there was in it, there was an impulse against waste. The child is father to the man. His project revealed him ab ovo as the demon recycler and reuser he would become in adulthood. It occurs to me that one source of strain in our relationship was his aversion to the use of innocent clichés on my part, as in The child is father to the man. He subtly communicated that he wished people would avoid them and talk more individually and aesthetically, like the Irish or his father. When I said that Irish rural speech was in fact full of clichés, but clichés he was unfamiliar with, it annoyed him. I also argued that there is an aesthetic involved in the self-conscious use of clichés, which was the case in my case. He only nominally agreed with me, and I could tell he continued not to like clichés to figure in my presentation of self. I gather his father was a very elegant speaker, even inter pocula. A consequence of his attitude was that I stuffed my inner discourse with clichés from time to time, because he was making me feel deprived of something innocent, and that I got him a few times to engage in a game where we would talk solely in clichés, with the loser being the one who ran out of clichés not previously employed first. I always won, but he never played the game as committedly as I did. The project began with discarded bottles and un-employed corks. I felt like pointing out the interesting fact that a child will take the most monstrous of parents and pathetically ferret out and seize on the one or two things that might be considered conceivably admirable, like freefloating eloquence. But to the bottles and corks he added another waste commodity, crepe paper.

The family lives near a high school. In the football season when home games are being played, cars and buses arrive wreathed in crepe paper in the visiting school's colors. The home team is weak and usually loses. The custom is for the winners to drive through downtown Belmont af-terward blaring their horns and lavishly strewing their crepe paper decor into the streets to demonstrate victory and contempt. He resents this for Belmont and decides that a response to it would be to go out and strip the parked cars and buses of their crepe paper while the game is still going on. He organizes teams of junior high boys soon to be in Belmont High to do this, including Peter, his brother.

This is risky, but he continues. He becomes the repository for the expropriated crepe paper, collects it in one of the outbuildings at his place, and then incidentally notices that when rained on, crepe paper gives up its color. So he begins soaking crepe paper in jugs to get different colors. In his mind is the pharmacy his mother goes to, with two giant apothecary jars in the window filled with lovely colored water. I noticed that he seemed to have been forever being dragged along by his mother when she went to druggists and doctors, which was frequently. This caught my interest. Why was he always dragooned? The astounding, to me, answer was that his mother was irresistible to doctors. The family lore, which he as a young boy was included in, was that his mother was so attractive that doctors would lose their ethics and propose things to her. Apparently she was quite beautiful, in a meek and delicate way. She felt better if her son was there, even if only in the waiting room. And she would also take him with her into the examining room if the consultation was for something modest like her chronic rhinitis. I said to him Haven't you ever pursued the notion that with these doctor visits you were getting a specialized indoctrination in the notion that female beauty was powerful and dangerous? He hadn't. He was always sorry for his mother, was as far as he had pursued it.

Nelson's construct of his father was of a person using every ounce of his considerable intellect and force to maintain an outwardly middleclass productive exterior while secretly steadily raising the crossbar on the hurdles to accomplishing this by sinking deeper into the grip of alcohol. I granted that his father's trajectory was not a straight-line descent, but I was hardly able to credit that at twelve Nelson was still so steeped in innocence as he protested. At that age I knew everything that was happening to me in the pathetic matrix I was in. Why did the beginning of wisdom, which Nelson precipitated with his bottle project, come so late?

Nelson idly started a bottle collection, or more precisely a tinted water collection. He took empty bottles from his father's bottle dump, soaked the labels off, filled them with colored water of different hues created by soaking crepe paper in different permutations, and then corked them. All this industry was carried out in the depths of the property, not secretly, he said, but privately. At first it was desultory, but he began to work more concentratedly when he saw what the next phase of his project was going to be. These were not only liquor bottles, but any bottle with a mouth he could fit a cork into, such as fruit juice or soft drink bottles. It was a calumny that the bottle structure he made was composed entirely of liquor bottles, and one he would resent forever.

First there was simply an assemblage of bottles of colored water, an array he obscurely liked to look at. Then he began organizing them according to size and tint, variously. Then enter some stocks or samples of industrial resin made nugatory by his father's reascending yet again into advertising. Definitely here was something else that shouldn't be allowed to go to waste. What should be done with them, then? One thing several of the resins could do was bond glass solidly to glass. Out of this discovery came the objet d'art, a construction of bottles like a wedding cake, in tiers. It was open at the back in such a manner that you could install a sparkler or candles or a flashlight, or ultimately a Coleman lantern, into the heart of it, and sit back and enjoy the coruscations or whatever the ineffable effects were of lighting the thing up from inside. Nelson was even thinking ahead and considering introducing a phonograph turntable so that light sources could be made to revolve, producing even more formidable effects. This would be the ultimate. He was already saving his allowance to buy extension cords, of which many would be required. But the ultimate phase of his project was never to be.

I wish I knew why I keep worrying the question of Nelson's innocence in this. Partly it may be a kind of mental body language against his having to go through what finally transpired. I considered it a Götterdämmerung for him, even if he didn't. In a way I would have preferred his project to have been a conscious assault on his injurious parents. That would at least have made it slightly more bearable to relive. So I fixated on data like Nelson's mentioning that one thing he had disliked about his father from an early age was the man being a precisian about which libations go into which kinds of glasses, id est champagne only into champagne flutes, brandy into snifters, and so on, which had led to the necessity of maintaining what seemed like an infinite repertory of drinkware, in which one glass was only minutely different from the next but which when one type of glass ran out through breakage or mislaying would produce violent complaints and blaming scenes involving his mother. I established that this was something he had feelings on long before he created his, as he called them, bottlements. He admitted these were painful scenes. He admitted that, in retrospect, possibly there was some disparity in having a collection of wineglasses appropriate for a marquis and a family car whose running board trailed in the road and gave off sparks. But his father had no interest in cars, was all. The bottle project was a disjunct thing. It was the art impulse, the automatic elaboration of available objects into more and more complex and recognizably aesthetic structures tout court. I asked him what it had been like when he broke wineglasses from time to time, as he must have, doing the dishes. Terrible, he said, until he got expert at handling them and it ceased to happen.

So out in a clear space in a madrone thicket sat his concretion. I think his brother was at select times permitted to visit this holy of older brother holies. His father's bottle dump was much closer to the house, in an arroyo. Nelson's site is safe, he assumes, because both his parents are so demonstrably indoor-oriented. If his mother goes out, it's out the front door to shop or go to church or to the doctor. Nelson's father has a den and uses it.

It's early evening. Nelson has evolved the custom of going out and lighting up his bottle structure and looking at it for a while before dinner. He has latitude, because dinner is usually late because his father has important things to do in his den before dinner—id est drinking, in fact —which usually enormously protracts things. Nelson accepts but hates dinner being late, because he and his brother have to do the dishes, which he had no objection to except that there was never a fixed time he could look forward to when he would be free, done. Sometimes dinner is even brought to his father at his desk.

I wanted to know what his father had been doing, ostensibly, in his solitude. There were two things. One was keeping up with his important reading, meaning in those days the Socialist Call, which he subscribed to, and the Militant and the Weekly People, which he brought home with him and all of which he gave Nelson in a bundle once a week to burn for him. He also got somewhere the Despatcher, a publication of the longshoremen's union, which was then an organization terribly feared by the powers that were. In those days, Nelson said, this is how left San Francisco was: you could get the Militant and the Weekly People on newsstands the same as you got the Chronicle or the vicious Examiner. Nelson saw his father as a fan of the left, generically. His father belonged to nothing, did nothing left—either of which might have been dangerous. Nelson's explanation for his father's having become a passive admirer of the left had to do with his heart's having been broken when something called the End Poverty in California Campaign had been defeated through chicanery and vile propaganda tricks orchestrated by the movie industry, this in the thirties. Also he hated Stalin for what he had done to the good part of the left. When he could finally have adult discussions about socialism with his father, it emerged that the idea of joining anything openly had been impossible because he had a wife and children. Nelson believed him. The other thing he was doing was working on charts supposed to predict when the next depression would come. This entailed heavy use of an adding machine, whose noise, I pointed out, would also serve to remind the family that serious business was taking place.

In any case here is Nelson squatting down in the gloaming contemplating his creation. The dimensions of the object were considerable, with a bottom tier about five feet across and the pinnacle reaching four feet. The one not purely aesthetic impulse he conceded might have gotten admixed into his project was what he called cathedralism, the impression osmosing to him from his church-mad mother that the most significant human creation of all time is the cathedral.

Nelson hears someone coming furtively up.

It's his father, drunk, and, as he gets close enough to really discern the thing Nelson has built, incredulous, and then affronted, and then enraged by it.

Clearly he instantly categorizes this thing as a mockery of his drinking:

all his hidden fifths have been retrieved and refilled and lit up for all the world to see. Nelson cringes, but his father turns on his heel and strides back into the darkness toward the house. But this is not the end. Nelson knows it and stays there, frozen. No words have been spoken.

Nelson's father returns, this time carrying a Stillson wrench and a pickax. Nelson's heart clenches. He has never been physically afraid of his father. In fact his father has always been principled against corporal punishment, and Nelson has seen his mother reprimanded by him over her lapses in this regard.

Denoon's father was on the small side, faircomplected, with a blond toothbrush mustache, not threatening. Nelson had his mother's dark complexion, although she was rather slightly built, so where Nelson's bearlike form came from is unclear. She had a dead brother Nelson was supposed to be the image of.

Nelson hears the word cocksucker for the first time in his life.

His father slings the wrench at the bottlements.

Some damage is done, but the wrench has been badly aimed. The flashlight or candle is still burning, so there is still this illuminated statement.

Nelson was given no chance to explain his structure.

In any case the wrench has smashed through the bottles in the outer part of the lowest tier, but the heart of the insult is still glowing.

So now comes the time to wield the second weapon, the pickax.

Nelson is in agony, dancing around the perimeter but being careful to be ready to dodge when pater monster lets fly for the second time.

He said something to try to get his father to stop, but he has no memory of what it was. His father begins to swing the pickax around in the air.

All I could think the first time I heard this story was If you marry you will regret it, If you fail to marry you will regret it. This was one of the few things I was able to bring to Denoon's already topheavy intellectual armamentarium. He had somehow missed reading the great *Either/Or* of Kierkegaard, which is an ordeal except for the one small section whose name I forget that contains that gem. And what I was thinking, of course, was if you have a father you will regret it, If you have no father you will regret it: I was thinking of myself. This became one of Nelson's favorite quotes, somewhat to my chagrin as to what it meant vis-à-vis being with me. But if we had I would have gotten an agreement out of him not to use it in public when I was around. He always used the aphorism in the most general or comic sense as a way of saying nothing ever works out, but still it stung me slightly. There was a period when we were in effect married, by most criteria.

Did you scream or cry? I asked him. How did you feel seeing he was about to destroy this thing without showing even for an instant that he knew it was remarkable?

What adds to the pathos of this is that Nelson knew stories about his father's deprived early life—he was fostered to a farm family, for example, where he was told he had to drink the water for the animals as opposed to the water that was for the family—and that once he knew these stories a consuming fantasy of his was to go back in time and appear at his father's side, as a buddy, and to fight the injustices he was enduring, get him out of things.

Did you beg, did you plead? I asked him. He had protested, but he couldn't say how exactly.

Did he show any sign he appreciated even just the industriousness behind your creation, which is exactly the kind of creative thing you presumably want your children to do, if only to keep out of mischief? He was drunk, Nelson said.

His father whirls the pickax awkwardly around his head like someone tossing the caber but he is in fact so drunk that when he lets go, the pickax flies off, missing the bottlements altogether, through the madrones, down a slope into long grass where it is lost.

The detail is horrible.

Get me it, Nelson's father says or screams, meaning the lost pickax. Clearly this would be so he can have another try. And clearly he knows he is too wobbly with drink to go and find the thing himself.

Couldn't you have gone to get your mother? was my question. This is what we're for, I said. But he claimed it never occurred to him, which makes me suspect that his father's praxis toward Nelson's mother was cruel enough, whatever Nelson says, to make him want to leave her out of this, that it might be dangerous for her.

Nelson refuses to retrieve the pickax.

All right, his father says, then I'll do it with the wrench. At which his father begins reeling toward the partly shattered structure to pluck the wrench out of the shards it's lying in.

What drenches Nelson's consciousness is that his father could stumble and be hurt or killed, impaled on the spires of broken bottles—and he, Nelson, will have been responsible for it as the builder of the injuring structure.

He sees his only choice as being to go and find the pickax rapidly and give it to his father to use in the final destruction of his creation, which is in fact the outcome.

God leads him directly to the pickax in the blackness.

He furnishes the pickax to his father, who smashes the bottle sculpture into nothingness, drenching himself and wrecking a good suit in the process.

Never could I really convince him that his retrospective fatalism about this incident was false somehow and worth pursuing. Why is it, I asked him more than once, that when I hear this story I feel worse than you do? He once went so far as to say that it might have been worse: his father might have made him demolish the structure himself. So it goes among the males.

I don't know how many different ways I told him This is not just one incident among others in your life as a boy—this is formative. I might get a Maybe so out of him. Although once he did say, rather passionately before changing the subject, How many times can you imagine that it would happen that someone who is still basically a child could be in the position of saving his father from serious injury or death? I think this is when I gave up on the subject.

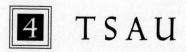 **TSAU**

The Prospect of Rescue Undoes You

 The prospect of rescue undoes you.

The closer I got to Tsau the more I decompensated. The eight miles felt interminable. I was feeling much worse. I lost all patience with my animal and abandoned him a mile from the gateway into Tsau. I wanted to run. I tried to, a little.

There was an actual gateway. The path I was on led straight to a crude square wooden arch about twenty feet high. It was a gateless structure like a torii, painted in alternating red and black bands like a coral snake and fringed across the top with bigger and better wind chimes. It was carnivalesque. Dark green waist-high rubber hedges straggled away from the arch to the left and right as far as I could see. In a yard to the right of the arch was a compound in which were two very tidy rondavels with peculiarly glossy thatch and other odd features I was too ragged to attempt to parse. This would have to be the gatehouse compound. I could see a kgotla chair set in the shade of a gigantic cloud tree in the yard, and I knew I had to get to it immediately.

I wanted to rest, but I also wanted to see everything. The path through the arch became a roadway leading to a complex of much larger buildings halfway up the koppie. In the flatland between the arch and the slope were neat identical rondavels in oblong fenced plots. There were thorn trees throughout. The scene was very busy in the sense you apply the term to a piece of printed fabric. There were novelties in the scene before me. There was the ubiquitous flashing and glinting, coming, it seemed, from all over and due, I was already assuming, to the various mirrors and solar instruments and other glass oddments that seemed to be specific to the place. There were repeated clicks of brilliant color observable at points along the upper paths: I had no idea what was causing them. I wanted to see everything at once, especially an ominous thing, something white and shrouded, hanging from a tree near where the roadway began to rise. Body, I thought. I was frightened and felt that at least I had to see what this was. In fact I was having a regressive recurrence of a feeling from kindergarten. I painted a sheet of newsprint with blue calcimine, solidly blue. I had never seen such a sublime blue and I had kept trying to fill my eyes with it by staring at it and by holding it close to my face. My teacher made me stop.

Goats all seemed to be either tethered or in pens, which I had never seen in an African village. There were no stray dogs. I could hear poultry but not see any—that too meant pens of some sort. The rondavels were not the usual monochrome red brown: they were painted in bright colors, sky blue being a dominant choice. There were people, but they were looking at me from around the edges of things.

The rondavel closest to the arch was magenta with a canary door. This door was flung open and a woman ran out toward me, stopped, turned and went back inside, and came out again with a police whistle in her mouth, on which she blew three skreels. Someone farther up the slope repeated the signal. This didn't strike me as unfriendly. The person approaching me with the whistle was a motherly older woman. I see that I'm using Denoon's or my neologism for the sound a police whistle makes, which was a byproduct of one of our personal games, called Filling in the White Spaces in the Dictionary. We satisfied ourselves that there was nothing in English for the sound except shrill blast, which was two words. Everything should have a name, according to Denoon. Decadence is when the names of things are being lost. He could be eloquent on this. He loved the Scots, who had had more names for everyday things in the eighteenth century than we do today. Greece was in terrible shape. He showed me an article in the Economist proving that groping for words among the general population was becoming a serious issue. On it would go.

Here things begin to fragment on me. The woman addressing me was in anxiety. Her costume, a gray tunic and long skirt and a white headscarf knotted to produce collapsed rabbit ears, struck me as beautiful. She was stocky. I believe I said something about vegetables or possibly even something about garlic. I know I sensed it wouldn't be against my interests to be a little incoherent for the time being, until I could see more clearly what kind of place I had come to: I was especially determined not to let anything slip suggesting a prior association with Nelson. I was going to present myself as a derelict traveler whose excursion had gone wrong. My story would have me doing ornithology. Tsau was a closed project, with an automatic exclusion rule for uninvited visitors. I would outwit this.

I knew she was afraid I had something to do with the Boers. The South African Defence Force does as it pleases in Caprivi and Namibia

and if they one day decided they wanted to drop down into the central
Kalahari like the wolf on the fold, there would be nothing to prevent it.
She had active eyebrows, but she calmed down once I convinced her I
was an American. I was sitting down and drinking broth by this time,
and fading badly.

I didn't want to fade out before I knew what this place was, or if not
what it was, what it was like, at least. In its symmetry and neatness and
Mediterranean color scheme it looked like a town in the Babar books,
but in its atmosphere there was something operatic or extravagant. I had
no referent for it.

Then two women were insisting I come inside and lie down. I communicated about my animal: someone had to be sent for him. They were
quick to arrange that. So I went inside and lay down on a platform bed
in a clean white room. There was some cool tea, my face was sponged,
and then I slept.

They woke me up to get more soup into me, a more substantial soup,
with macaroni in it. It was evening.

My hands felt huge. They had been taken care of medically, the
splinters extracted, and rather excessive bandaging wound on. I had been
cleaned up. They had done everything but shampoo me. I was wearing
a garment like a shift, very lightweight.

I was led into one of the wonders of the world, the Denoon outhouse,
and left there awhile. I used the facility correctly. When I came out I
was shown that normally I should dip my hands in a bowl of weak
antiseptic fluid on a stand next to the outhouse door. Because of my
bandages this was impossible, but they did somewhat brush and press my
bandages with a damp towel anyway.

Baph was safe, was the good news.

I was in a regulated place. They had put some kind of unguent on
my lips.

Being in this place and in the hands of women ran counter to my
main established refuge fantasy, wherein my father or uncle is a retired
judge or captain of industry with a giant Victorian house in an area like
Bucks County. He is there off and on. You can go to this house anytime
and collapse there for as long as you like, no questions asked. There
would be a staff. My father or uncle is powerful but also good, which is
one reason the place is so safe. He has goodwill extending to him from
far and near, either because his legal judgments were so wise and beloved

or because of unspecified other benefactions touching everyone in that
county. The food would be simple but good. There would be a farm
attached to the house. My protector is very diversified economically, so
that no depression would wipe him out. I could be a spinster if I wanted,
live in my beautiful room, use the extensive library and the piano, or if I
chose to I could moon around in my room and only come down for
meals. There was no mother in this. My uncle, though, would be devoted to the memory of my mother. I once said to Denoon, after he
denied he harbored any refuge fantasies whatsoever, I don't believe you,
but if this is true it's because the thing you as a white male will carry to
your grave is the feeling that you're safe anywhere in the world, in
essence, unless you have some particular physical handicap. I suppose my
position was that everyone has refuge fantasies. I said Saying you have
no refuge fantasies and even believing you don't is not the same thing as
really not having them in some way, shape, or form. He got mad. Was I
saying he was lying? he wanted to know. Only partially, I said. Then god
damn it, he said, I'll tell you again I don't and that I also doubt that any
fully mature human being does and also that if you do, you belong to
the one tenth of one percent of the female race who construct this refuge
fantasy because the automatic marriage fantasy, which is the real refuge-
fantasy people have until they try it, is repugnant to them somehow.

I scanned around. The furnishings were restful. There was a reed
mat on the floor. I could see a wooden table, a cupboard, a wardrobe, all
highly polished. I was covered with a cotton thermal blanket, light but
warm. My pillow was possibly a little on the hard side. My attendant was
sitting in a wooden armchair, reading by the light of candles burning in
a holder with winglike mirrors folded out from a spindle attached to the
base of the fixture. There was a heat source somewhere. All my goods
were laid out along the base of the wall where I could see them.

Just as I began to drift off again, it came to me that I had yet to ask
this woman in loco parentis over me what her name was. I was ashamed
of myself. I asked, and it was Mma Isang. Here I had an inappropriate
internal reaction. The fact that she was identifying herself in the completely traditional way as the mother of whoever her firstborn was, in this
case a son, should have produced no reaction in me whatever. It was
ordinary. But I wanted to shake her. Women were saving me, and why
wasn't this motherly woman more a separate being? I seemed to be wanting to say. Somehow it brought up the totally unrelated contempt I have
for all the apparatus of seconds and thirds and juniors specific to the
patriciate in America and applicable only to sons and never to daughters.

Denoon called this scionism. Also I wanted to know if Nelson Denoon had so much as looked in on me. He had to know I or someone very much like me had pitched up in his forbidden city. I had trekked across the plain of the abyss for a purpose. Where was Denoon? Who wants to feel like a tart, and an unsuccessful tart to boot? I felt like one of the loser sperms you see in Swedish documentaries shot inside the reproductive tract, one of the members of the shining herd, who only gets halfway up a fallopian tube when the Time Gentlemen bell is rung announcing that some other particle has made it to the ovum and the game is over. You aren't yourself, I told myself. Mma Isang saw I was agitated, and I believe I was then handfed some segments of orange, and then it was on to a marathon sleep.

Yliane

I awoke in total darkness in that state of intellectual fatigue that means you've been working things out violently and exhaustively in your dreamlife. I had had a dream—whose outlines I atypically still had hold of—with stature. I may have had six or so like this in my life, always at rubiconic junctures. My normal dreams are worse than run of the mill. But clearly you symbolically harangue yourself in your sleep when your inner self perceives looming danger. But was I in danger, or rather was I in any danger greater than making a fool of myself? Something in me seemed to think so. I felt as though I had just been excused from an excruciatingly long but absolutely essential lecture which I had had to listen to while standing up.

In fact the dream revolved around a lecture, and I knew who the lecturer was. She was a woman I'd known in California whose fate had made an impression on me. Initially she was interesting to me purely because she was a French émigré, of which there are not so many, nothing like for example the number of Israelis piling up on the two coasts. She was also interesting because she was in a ménage in which the union had to be based entirely on an uncanny parity of physical beauty. Her lover of many years was handsome and perfectly proportioned, the kind of type who models Norfolk jackets and handcarved pipes, but an absolute jerk. She was both beautiful and substantive but, hélas, nearly forty and therefore in terror of finding herself alone and having to start over in the search for companionship. She was an accomplished paste-up person and very much in demand among people who put out newsletters in the days before desktop publishing. He was intermittently a cad toward her. He was vaguely a creative person in magazine publishing. He had lost his touch. His career was disintegrating when I got to know Yliane, although he was disguising it by being on the phone interminably, talking to contacts and lining up minuscule freelance projects at greatly separated intervals. Maybe a bond between them was that he was Francophile. He was sickeningly Francophile, to the point that one of his projects was to write a uchronia based on the premise that the Louisiana Purchase had fallen through. This project meant that whenever she asked him where he had been when she needed him for something the answer was The library. How this most appeasing of women managed to irritate him so badly that he drove her out of their apartment in her bathrobe while lashing her with a straightened coathanger I have no idea. Drink played some role. Possibly one of her superb culinary efforts came in below par. It was the middle of the night and she was driven out without a sou, and ultimately she had to let herself be fucked by the cabdriver who took her some distance to a friend's house where she had expected to borrow the fare but where nobody was home. She spent the rest of the night cowering and crying in the rhododendra, waiting for her friend to return from the Mi Carême Ball or wherever she was.

So they stayed apart for a while. Then he showed up abject and swearing he wanted her back, would contain his drinking henceforward, would be decent. So he talked her back in. But there was just one thing he asked, as they were setting the ménage up once again, which was that she give up recycling for a month. She was a forerunner in ecological sensitivity and was serious about recycling. This would somehow make everything perfect between them. It had nothing to do with anything except power. He had no objection to recycling—not that he would ever bother with it himself. He sprung this codicil on her after she had already moved back in and he had begun being decent, so she negotiated. She wouldn't recycle for two weeks. That would do, he decided. Then things continued as horribly as before. I pondered this transaction inordinately at the time. She bore him a child, a boy, angelic-looking and destined to be a burnt offering if I was any judge. I lost touch with Yliane after this.

The message of the dream lecture was that there was something I had to avoid. It was a strain to formulate it. There was something I should beware, something that was not good enough.

What was not good enough was the usual form that mating takes.

I had to realize that the male idea of successful love is to get a woman into a state of secure dependency which the male can renew by a touch or pat or gesture now and then while he reserves his major attention for his work in the world or the contemplation of the various forms of surrogate combat men find so transfixing. I had to realize that female-style love is servile and petitionary and moves in the direction of greater and greater displays of servility whose object is to elicit from the male partner a surplus—the word was emphasized in some way—of face-to-face attention. So on the distaff side the object is to reduce the quantity of servile display needed to keep the pacified state between the mates in being. Equilibrium or perfect mating will come when the male is convinced he is giving less than he feels is really required to maintain dependency and the woman feels she is getting more from him than her servile displays should merit. In the dream this seemed to me like a burning insight and I concentrated fiercely to hold on to it when I woke up: I should remember this inescapable dyad at the heart of mating because it was not what I had come this far to get.

It was impossible not to sleep more.

You Should Be an Assassin

In all I must have slept for more than twenty-four hours.

Suddenly I was slept out. Unfortunately it was still in the middle of some night or other, either the one during which I'd had my homiletic dream or the one following. I lay there staring at nothing, being hungry.

I decided to use my time constructively by trying to figure my way out of the cleft stick of wanting to have Nelson think both that my expedition was a reckless ordeal undertaken under the influence of unmasterable feelings toward him and that an exploit like this was nothing extraordinary for someone of my experience and grit. But there was something amiss in my immediate vicinity.

I could hear someone breathing. This was not Mma Isang: it was excited breathing. I felt to see that I was modest. I felt around for the thermal blanket, but it must have been on the floor. My shift came just below the knee. I would have been happier with my underthings on underneath it, but this was all right.

I inched up to a sitting position and held my forearms in an X in front of my face. I held my breath so that I could hear where my intruder was.

Someone dove for me and got a hand across my mouth before I could yell. I knew it was Denoon and I was astounded. His hand was very hard and smelled of diesel and smoke, but his person smelled of soap. He had washed up before coming over to assault me, at least. He was pressing me hard against the wall and trying to tell me something in a whisper. My mind was blank with shock, but I remember managing to note that there was indeed garlic in Tsau. His fear was that I would thrash around in resisting and knock something over. He was tremendously strong and I sensed he was trying not to hurt me. He had me pinned to the wall, with his left arm stretched behind my shoulders and left hand gripping my arm at the elbow and his right hand clapped over my mouth. Once he had me bundled together the way he wanted, he held me that way and continued to whisper apologies into my ear, and then entreaties to say nothing, to promise to be silent while he explained something urgent to me.

The proof that I am a basically empathetic person is that I complied instantly. My essential nature is inclined to violence when someone touches me without being invited, and I am also physically strong. There were things I could have done. However, they would have prolonged the wrestling imbroglio we were in, which would have been okay with me except that the male constitution is a problem, or rather friction is a problem for it. The human penis is a thing like a marmoset or some other unruly small pet they carry around with them. An erection would hardly mean Denoon was in love with me or even desired me qua me, in all my wondrous dimensions. I wanted to spare us embarrassment. Also there would have been something faintly promissory in his getting an erection, which would have been unwelcome to me and unfair to him. If I was going to elicit an erection it should be nonaccidental. So in my enormous delicacy I went limp and began nodding violently yes to the question Will you be silent when I take my hand off your mouth?

He got off me like a shot then and slid over and sat up against the wall next to me, half on the bed.

You should be an assassin, I told him.

Even a low voice was too loud. He wanted us to whisper.

First there were more apologies. Secondly, was I all right? meaning all right after my expedition, which he couldn't believe I had attempted myself. He was not going to ask me to say why I had come to Tsau or how I had found out where it was, but he wanted me to know—and here he became halting—that he was impressed, he was flattered, if that was the right word, and he was glad I was there. We were both uncomfortable during this stanza, but I was also triumphant. As I read it, I was being admitted into a game neither of us could bear to be explicit about, and I had been right that the game had begun at Tutwane's. I was controlling joy.

There was a situation at Tsau I had to understand, was next. I no doubt knew that Tsau was a project for women. That is, he had started the project with women, destitute women from all over Botswana but mostly from the northwest, women cut off from their families for any one of a number of reasons and subsisting on one sack of mealie a month from the government. So they had been the ones gathered together to make Tsau. I am making this more compressed temporally than it was, because he was pausing throughout to get his breath and to listen to see if there was any sign that we might be being intruded on. But I am not misrepresenting what it was intellectually. What he conveyed in the dark in the time he had was a feat.

So these ablebodied destitute women had been gathered together to make Tsau. All the homesteads in Tsau were vested in women, meaning that the charter women owned the individual homesteads, and he had even worked it out with the government that in Tsau inheritance of the homestead would be restricted to female offspring and female collaterals or designees. Of course I would see men in Tsau, mostly relatives who had turned up miraculously after the fact, but they were a minority. But I should know all this. And there would be more men in the population down the road, of course. But the vesting of the homestead as an asset, and the entitlements that went with it, would always be in the female line. And of course the idea behind that was to demonstrate that at least here something could be done about the economic disenfranchisement of women that was taking place in the society at large as it modernized. Women were being impoverished wholesale because cattle herds, the main productive asset in Botswana, were being concentrated in fewer and fewer hands, all of them male, something he knew I had seen for myself in Tswapong and Keteng.

I love a concise mind.

So he wanted to be sure I grasped that there was a certain sensitivity about the presence of mates, since most women in Tsau either lacked them and were unlikely to get them or were beyond them and had strong feelings about those women still unhappy about the problem. As a matter of fairness he had been living alone in Tsau. He was not going to be seen as inviting special company for himself in the form of women or whites of his particular background. It was imperative that there be no suggestion of a prior connection to him and imperative that it be believed that I had gotten to Tsau sheerly by accident. It was an important source of strength to him that tourists and evaluators had been kept out of the project, and I must not seem to be either one of those things. He disliked dissembling, he said, but a great deal was at stake.

He paused. I was thinking that of course the spiritus rector of a female community would need to be a sexual solitary, at least during the foundational period. But such periods needn't last forever, it was my humble opinion. I wondered if this situation was the analog of western series on television where the female watchership shrank to nothing when the producers let the marshal get married.

He wouldn't describe the situation re the shortage of men as a split, exactly. On the whole the younger women were the more critical ones, unsurprisingly but not uniformly, and the older women were solidly on his side. If I could convincingly appear to be a lost traveler everything could evolve. He had no choice but to imply he'd never known me.

The sense of assumed collaboration was thrilling to me. The whole unstated side of our exchange was delicious. I felt brilliant.

I think men hate to whisper, because I noticed he found it necessary every so often to let his natural deep man's voice show itself for a moment or two before going back into hiding.

Be a lost traveler, he said. Do you have some story?

I told him. He thought ornithology was good and liked my lost donkey and lost scientific impedimenta flourishes. It worried him that I knew nothing—as I confessed—about birds. He would get a field guide to me, he said, posthaste.

Are we a conspiracy? I asked.

He circumvented with They don't know it, but the reason people are so pro bird is because ninety-five percent of bird species are monogamous.

I'm not, I said. I can do this but I have to overcome a sort of mocking feeling I have about birdwatchers. I figure Let the birds watch *me*. Of course this is me speaking as a higher life form.

Are your hands all right now? he asked. He felt my forehead and said Good. So he had been looking in.

Jesus, what am I doing? he said, I think with genuine feeling and apropos of nothing, to which I said Same here, and we laughed.

This place is going to generate wealth, he said. And men will be welcome, but by then the women will be where they should. You'll see. I think you deserve to be here.

This isn't exactly it, but he finished with something like I'm delighted you're here and now I have to crawl out of here on my belly like a reptile.

There was a brief, whispered exchange with someone, probably Mma Isang, who, I sensed correctly, was a confederate, outside the door.

I was already trying to recollect what little I knew about African birds and reflecting on how perverse it was for me to choose ornithology to misrepresent myself in. After all, I am the daughter of a mother whose humiliating favorite radio program was a thing called the Canary Chorus, wherein a Hammond organ droned for hours on end in a roomful of trilling canaries. She would recommend this program indiscriminately.

Mysteries Fall Away

In the morning I made a production of being concerned about my binoculars, digging fixedly through my goods until I came up with them —as any shipwrecked ornithologist would.

Mma Isang seemed to like me. It was mutual. She was in her fifties, built very blockily, with an unfortunate face. The root of her nose was sharply indented, her eyes were deep-sunk, and there were marked crowsfeet extending from her eyes around the sides of her face. Her face looked as though it had been crimped. I never learned if this was a congenital defect or just an unlucky but normal featural concatenation. There were residues of a Serowe accent in her Setswana, which I noted and which she acknowledged, impressed with me. All my clothes had been laundered.

I felt absurdly recovered but decided it would be prudent to conduct myself convalescently for the time being. I got dressed in my bush gear: longsleeved army shirt, jeans, boots. There was a mirror to use. I looked fairly banged up. I did a cursory toilette, which was all any toilette would be until I could get my hair clean. I borrowed a headscarf. At some point in the intervals in my sleepfest, I remembered vaguely I had been promised I could bathe.

We would be having breakfast with some women, Mma Isang said, surprising me by speaking in English. We would be speaking in English also when the delegation came. They would be bringing our food behind them, she said.

Waiting, I sauntered around outside a little, going up the main avenue, Gladys and Ruth Street, as far as the mysterious white object that had frightened me when I first noticed it. The main avenue was named for the wives of the first and second presidents of Botswana. An oddity was that at the gate end the street was Gladys and Ruth, but at the plaza end it was Ruth and Gladys Street. People were touchingly scrupulous about which name order they used, depending on which end of the street they were at. The white object was a gauze shroud covering a flayed carcass hanging from a tree, the meat tree, to age. It was to keep flies off. I had seen meat trees before, but never with this refinement. There was an attendant at the tree, and people were coming up and indicating which sections of the cow they wanted when it was cut up. The attendant, actually the cow's owner, was taking these orders down in a notebook, and chits or tokens of some kind were being handed to her. I observed all this from a distance, not wanting to overstep.

It was a cool morning, bright, no different than any other morning since Kang, but now I was able to experience the pleasure there was in it. Breathing was a pleasure. I'm sure I've never been so pleased with myself. All the innocent industry of the households getting mobilized for the day was a pleasure to see. And I loved Tsau from the compositional standpoint, from the pastel motley feeling of the rondavels to the red rock jumble crowning the koppie. I was already thinking of these rocks as the Citadel, portentously.

Another mystery fell away. Twice I saw children pushing light wooden two-wheeled carts whose sideboards were decorated with simple figures or symbols in enamels in spectrum colors. The wheels were bicycle wheels. In the case of the two carts I got a glimpse of the decor consisted of female imagos with pierced disks of glass screwed into the wood where eyes or a necklace would be. Clearly carts like these, in their shuttlings, were responsible for the vivid blurts of color I had seen recurring at odd points in the landscape. Why these rococo vehicles were always called dung carts when in fact collecting dung from the kraals and pens was the last and least thing they were used for is something I never figured out. The dung carts did well on the packed earth of the pathways and must have been strongly made, because I saw them routinely bumped very hard up and down the short intermittent runs of steps in the paved routes to the plaza without flying apart. Children personally owned these carts and could earn credits for conveying goods or messages in them. You might see a cart being furiously rushed someplace with a folded piece of paper in it and nothing more. This was not totally laughable, because there was always the possibility that something more substantial might be picked up for the return trip. As I was to discover, the explanation was that there was a greatly indulgent attitude toward the small, petted population of children. People sent the children on perpetual errands, many of them invented or marginal, out of love, essentially. The carts made a contribution to the visual agitation or liveliness you felt in Tsau, which was especially noticeable in late afternoon or during the innumerable holidays when the children were out of school.

Feeling unauthorized, I kept my saunterings close to home. The women I watched transacting at the meat tree watched back. I could tell I was being talked about, but it seemed friendly.

I had a moment of fear when all the women began, I thought, pointing at me. But they were only directing my attention to Mma Isang, who had come out into the yard and was summoning me by striking a thing like a glass sashweight with a ball-peen hammer. The notes produced were pleasant and musical, and did carry. What a genteel way to get somebody's attention, I thought, although it seemed to me you would have to be on the qui vive to pick out this particular line of sound amid the general aural glitter of Tsau—the jinkling of the wind chimes, the cowbells and goatbells and dogbells, the drivel of birds and poultry, and all the other as yet unidentified ingredients in the sinfonia domestica playing from sunrise to sunset in this intricate place.

The Mother Committee

Three women arrived. These are of the mother committee, Mma Isang said.

Breakfast would be al fresco, I had already observed, at a table under the cloud tree.

I wondered if everyone in Tsau was always beautifully dressed. I already knew that no one, children included, went barefoot. People wore sandals or moccasins. If they went out into the bush they were supposed to strap on leather leggings, like shin guards, as protection against snakes, but these were unpopular. There was a definite municipal costume. It was modular. People wore either a long sack dress, sleeveless, belted or unbelted, or a tunic and shorter-skirt combination. There was another type of skirt, much fuller and with complexly arranged buttoning panels that would supposedly permit the skirt to be fastened back into pantaloons, which only a few women wore any longer. It had been an experiment. Everything was made from the same material, a tan muslin. But here uniformity ended. Garments were individualistically decorated, either dyed in different solid or combined colors, or printed with motifs like eyes, crosses, stars, ankhs, letters of the alphabet—some quite majuscule. The printing, some dense and some sparse, was done with dies cut from different local tubers. There was some not overambitious embroidery around neckholes and armholes. Headscarves were universal but entirely individual as to color and tie-style. Headscarf art at Tsau would make a coffeetable book. Plain modes were the norm, but there were always triumphs of excess turning up: anything went, and stuffings were sometimes used to create truly startling ridged and tiara effects. When jewelry was worn it was usually glass, what else?, or the Basarwa ostrich-eggshell-chip bracelets and chokers that are staple trade goods all over the Kalahari. I felt quite drab and masculine as we went to the table.

Mma Isang muttered a Setswana phrase to me that translates as We are walking on our toenails. This equates to our Walking on eggs.

There were two women in Mma Isang's age range and one, Dineo, in her forties. Introductions were in Setswana. It was formal. I sat down with the delegation. There were only four chairs, regular European straight chairs, so Mma Isang went to get a chair for herself, placing it at a little distance from the setting around the table. We served ourselves tea. In English Mma Isang again said I should be patient because these sisters were bringing our breakfast behind them, which was meaningless to me until a young boy appeared propelling a vermilion cart into the yard. He was in the standard schoolboy kit of khaki shorts and short-sleeved shirt and appeared to be in a hurry to finish with us and get somewhere else. He was cutely officious, expertly prying the fitted lid off a sheet metal chest, inside which was straw, beneath which was another box, containing our breakfast of scones, socalled, and hardboiled eggs. It was done like lightning. The boy was given a token. He shot away. Everything was hot. We ate off cloth serviettes.

You must eat so many eggs as you please, Mma Isang said, again in English, for which she drew a reproving gesture from Dineo. I gathered that it would be Dineo who would determine when English would be spoken at this interview.

Dineo was clearly primus inter pares here. She was sinewy. Men would find her sexually interesting, I thought. She was tall for a Tswana, true black, Nilotic, with what the Batswana call long eyes. She had a hard, narrow face. Her dress, slit to the knee on one side, was printed with bands of tiny black crosses, black on tan, which gave a faintly sacerdotal air to her presence. She had presence. She was wearing an amber headscarf draped like the one the Sphinx wears. There was a trick, possibly starch, to the way the delta panels of the scarf stayed spread at the sides of her neck. This was her signature headdress. I only saw it varied a few times. She had force. I liked it that white though I am, she was looking me straight in the eye, unlike her companions, who were doing the more typical side-glancing and down-glancing as they absorbed themselves in studious tea drinking or egg peeling. Something in her expression reminded me how stern Batswana women can be about ma-lingering, and I readjusted my plan to look more done in than I actually felt. I felt myself involuntarily wanting to appease her.

The other two were subalterns. I came to think of them as the twins and then learned that other people used that term for them. These two women were fairly inseparable. One, called Dimakatso, had a ruined, white left eye. Joyce's hands were badly gnarled by arthritis. Dimakatso peeled Joyce's egg for her. Joyce was only a nominal participant. But I had the feeling that Dimakatso was listening keenly the whole time, and this was confirmed when at the end she took out a ballpoint pen and made some sort of notations on the flesh of the palm of her hand.

Mma Isang brought out oranges, honey, and paring knives. Dineo had some preliminary things to say to me in English about speaking English. I must not be misled to think that no one in Tsau could speak English save for very few women and Rra Puleng. But I must well understand, because there were some sisters still who could not speak English, that it was decided for all time to never have meetings conducted in English as they were at district council and parliament, where even should women attend it could never be told by them what was happening. That was an injustice I would never find in Tsau. At all events we must now speak in Setswana and later in English again.

The questioning was polite but acute, led by Dineo. There was interest in how I had learned to speak Setswana so well. I gave them a truthful Botswana curriculum vitae except that I substituted ornithology for anthropology. I especially disliked doing this to Mma Isang. I invented a Kalahari itinerary that would have taken me ultimately in a long curve to Lake Ngami—a place that is in fact a wellknown ornithological three-ring circus. They could well understand how I had come to grief on such a long expedition undertaken alone. Here I had to improvise about a companion who had been unable to join me at the last moment. Going alone into the desert was something for Bushmen, and my questioners weren't satisfied until I was more demonstrative about how foolhardy I had been to proceed with it. Then Dineo pressed me rather hard around my assertion that Tsau was a surprise to me, that I had never heard of it. She slipped into English. How was it that I hadn't heard any stories or whispers about what the people of Tsau were doing, making a city in which no one was poor, which no Europeans could yet say they had done in their own countries? Had I not heard whisperings of Rra Puleng, a man famous among Europeans, being at Tsau? I was steadfast in my claims of ignorance and finally she let up.

The coda was in English. Unfortunately Tsau was not yet ready to receive visitors of any kind except in cases of distressful accident such as mine, so that unfortunately the mother committee and Rra Puleng himself must tell me I must go away when that could be arranged and I was fully able for going. Unfortunately Rra Puleng was the strictest of them all as to this. Tsau was like a tree not yet ready to drop its fruits. No visitors could come except helpers like doctors at times. When Tsau was ready to drop its fruits, as many visitors would be free to come as would be pleased to. As for herself, she welcomed me as a sister, and she would be very pleased to have me stay too long with them and not rush away to be only with birds to discuss with.

I was asked what I wanted and if I was in eagerness to return elsewhere.

I said I had never been in a place I wanted to see more than I did Tsau and that I regarded everyone there as a sister or mother to me. I wanted to stay for as long as it could be allowed. I said that the birds would be waiting for me at Lake Ngami in any case at whatever time I got there. We were all nodding in accord.

Dineo said that in not above five days I would meet with all the sisters of the mother committee and they would say what must be. Until then I must go all about Tsau and look everywhere to see what kinds of works could be raised up by women if only they lock together as one.

My Journal

Today when I look at the journal I started in Tsau and see how microscopically I felt I had to inscribe my initial entries I know I was more than hyper. I must have been rather disturbed.

My normal handwriting is above average in size. The idea behind writing in miniature was to create something that would be unforthcoming in the case of someone giving a quick, furtive scan, which is also why I resorted so berserkly to abbreviations and code words as well as studding my text with bogus ornithological observations as further camouflage. The result is a bolus not completely intelligible to me without serious concentration and the effort to think myself back into the moments that led me to choose particular codes and evasions. I could have used Pitman's, which I know, but was afraid it would look suspicious to an unsophisticated person taking a quick snoop. Also I was speaking very little English for long stretches and found it a relief to use it in my journal: writing minutely served the need to enforce some selectivity on myself in dealing with the cascade of novelties and rarae aves Tsau confronted me with. There are also glyphs. Crossed swords mean sex. A truth about me is that when I visit a house where there are letters or other interesting-looking private papers lying around, I may have a quick look. I'm not convinced of my uniqueness in this tendency, although my excuse for it is anthropology. I would never do anything with information I got from my quick snoops, which are really quite disinterested. Anyone who could see into my heart would exculpate me and realize I was doing it pursuant to my consuming interest in the mystery of the world.

So the below represents an anthology, in effect, from my notes for early May 1981, up to and just through my full-dress meeting with the whole mother committee. I've tried to collect things under headings. Saying "the below" is yet another residue of Denoon, who thought that since people say "the above," as in None of the above, it was unreasonable not to use "the below" identically, and also amusing. The below is an impure text, in that I have, where necessary, drawn out and restored what I was concealing in my abbreviations and enigmatica.

▶ *200 homesteads, 12 new ones under construction, all laid out NE to NW quadrant on level ground and on slopes almost to the plaza terrace. Thus, at 2.5 persons per compound, circa 450 total population. 50 men, at most: uncles soi-disant, long-lost-type cousins or brothers, but some authentic prodigal husbands retiring from migrant minework in RSA. Children 40, up to preadolescence. All the rest women, 70 percent past childbearing age, 30 percent otherwise. Younger women known as queens or kgosigadi, older women aunts or aunties or mmamogolo: these terms used openly and not unfriendlily by both sides. Denoon's house a separate isolate cement octagon high NW on the koppie, above the plaza terrace. E below the koppie: sheds, workshops, kraals, mealie fields, nethouses, kiln, blockyard. S all the way around to W raw koppie, overlooking sand river as it turns due S. NE subterrace, on several levels, below plaza terrace: primary school, laundry, kitchen complex, infirmary, sewing house.* How are longlost male collaterals, who seem to be increasing, getting to Tsau? Not overland from Kang. Some were arriving one by one by plane, was part of the answer. Tsau had an airstrip to the southeast, where the Barclays Bank plane stopped every two weeks to bring in mail and exchange banking documents. This was a revelation to me. There had been a way into Tsau I had failed to discover, not that I would have been able to make use of it. The individual men who would occasionally be dropped off at Tsau were ones who had convinced the government that they were legitimate male relatives of residents of Tsau. I calmed myself over not knowing about the Barclays plane link by telling myself that it made my trek look even more heroic and authentic.

▶ *The longitudinal thoroughfares that converge on the plaza are called streets and are named for eminent African women, with one exception: there is a Blessed Mary Slessor Street. She was a Scots clergywoman who hunted through the bush in Ashantiland rescuing children, female infants, left out to die. There was a struggle over honoring her, which ended when it was decided that it was enough that she was a woman and that she had performed her good deeds in Africa. The names committee is apparently a hotbed of contention. Latitudinal thoroughfares are called ways. You live streetside or wayside. Ways are named after different social virtues, like Ipelegeng, or pulling together. There is a network of unnamed paths running everywhere, to the top of the koppie and throughout its wild slopes. Where trees are sparse along the streets and ways, efforts are being made to install lattices and to entice vines to grow out, creating stretches of loggia. The deep summer here is blinding and brutal, everybody says, and more shade is wanted. People use parasols in the summer and wear straw sun hats imported from Lesotho. There is a plan to set up toriis like the one next to the gatehouse at the mouth of each of the six main streets. But this is stalled because the gum tree plantation started eight years ago is just now producing trees of adequate height, and there are competing ideas of what to do with them. The gum tree plantation is deep SE, near the airstrip. Rra Puleng is the one who would most like the toriis set up, I sense. There is no map of this place. Everyone knows where everything is. The backlog of unnamed landmarks and venues is growing and causing grumbling.*

▶ *There is no modular outfit supplied to men. Men here look like men in any poor village: there is a range of quality in their clothing from new to fairly ragged, with self-evident castoffs predominating. Everything is laundered to a fare-thee-well, though, and clothes are changed frequently.* Men were never issued clothes gratis, as an entitlement, in the way women were, but a very serviceable coverall was made available below cost. All clothes went free to the washhouse. Urgings to men to sign up at least occasionally to take a turn in the washhouse came and went and were usually answered by the men asking when they could expect to see women taking turns in the tannery. The reek in the tannery was unbearable.

▶ *The political economy seems to go like this: Women are deeded their houses and plots. Ownership entitles you to a voting membership in Sekopololo, The Key: Sekopololo is a voluntary labor credit system. At your own discretion or inclination you exchange your labor or craftwork for scrip, which entitles you to anything in the stores house, where the range of imported and locally produced goods is surprising. The value of the scrip earnable at different tasks is continually under revision, to induce people to opt for the most needful jobs. Dineo seems to be in charge of this. With your house comes a share in the collective cattle herd and your own patch in the mealie fields. Sekopololo is also a mechanism for external trading: commodities exported run from knit goods to karosses to carvings and, I gather, glass oddments. There are some other items Tsau exports, the knowledge of which appears to be proprietary and which I am clearly not eligible to know about as an outsider. Men can only be non-voting members of Sekopololo. Unclear how this is justified. They seem to work like dogs.*

▶ *In most rondavels a soupçon of glass brick of the kind you used to see in moderne coctail lounge façades is incorporated. The bricks are embedded in the walls in random arrangements. If you look at Tsau at night from out in the plain or from the top of the koppie you can imagine the dots and dashes the lit bricks become constituting a message in code.* Apropos his vitromania I once asked Denoon to make the thought experiment of asking himself what he would have done with his life if he had been born into a world evolving on its own decently enough that his personal attention was not required: would he have been a glassblower or glass artisan of some kind? I meant this innocently, but it was taken as needling him. This was precisely the question to ask if I wanted to make him more seclusive about his glass projects, about which he was already defensive because it was so evident how lavishly his glass workshop was outfitted. He had a very expensive—in the thousands—solar crucible and a plethora of other devices and supplies, including sacks of rare sand. His glassworks was better equipped than the carpentry shop with its ludicrous pedal-driven saw. I had exclaimed the first time I saw his place. He didn't like my reaction. It was unfair to call glasscraft a hobby. He was forever going to find someone appropriate to train, although his maiden foray in that direction had gone wrong when the young woman who was his apprentice burned her arm badly. This had traumatized him and led him to keep the workshop as his own sealed bailiwick afterward. When I pointed out to him that it was odd that the glassworks was the only venue in Tsau, apart from the Sekopololo office and the post office, ever locked at night, he stopped locking it—but I think he never forgave me for making him feel he ought to. My last thrust at getting to the roots of his vitromania came when he told me the tale of going as a boy to the part of Oakland below Fourteenth Street where the Japanese flower growers and truck farmers had a settlement, just after the Japanese were taken away and put into camps at Tule Lake. There was absolute destruction. Mobs had come there. Acres of greenhouses had been smashed, houses trashed and vandalized. There were acres of broken glass. He was incredulous. It still depressed him to think of it. I suppose he partook in the cult of the working class his father followed. There was an important but tenuous connection here. Oakland and San Francisco were then, by our standards, citadels of union power, he claimed. How could the destruction have happened in a union town? was his question. I said The people who wrecked the greenhouses were hardly detachments from the Central Labor Council or the CIO, were they? No, I said, undoubtedly they were young boys. But no, he knew the mobs were men. I gather that the question was why the unions had permitted this, if they were what his father had said they were. I wanted to know where this episode lay in relation to his father's assault on Nelson's bottle sculpture, a reasonable enough thing to want to know. But with that the portcullis came down with a vengeance.

▶ *There is the credit system operating through Sekopololo, there is private barter outside that system, and there is a regular pula currency system operating, with regular banking through the post office. I keep looking for someone who is existing totally outside Sekopololo, something theoretically possible, but no one is, including the very hostile health post nurse assigned here by the government. She considers this exile, but people here are seducing her into liking the place by being unfailingly nice to her. Everyone says she was much worse formerly, which is hard to believe. They wish she would go if she is unhappy. The woman being trained to replace her is already more proficient at giving shots. The health post nurse is too young for this place. The government also wanted someone on government pay to run the post office, but Denoon succeeded in getting a Tsau woman deputized for that, if that's the word. But what the systems conjoin to produce is an amazing equality of condition. Equality is relaxing, Denoon liked to say. Certain powers only arise under conditions of equality, meaning absolute equality, and even then not at first, until people believe it is going to be permanent. Don't you feel it yourself? he would ask, and sometimes I did.*

▶ *Decoration rampant. No object too minor. Framing, lintels, all carved and stained. Crank handles on composters carved spirally. The dung carts. Sandal straps have designs burned in. Walkways in compounds edged with painted stones or mouth-down bottle butts. There is a tool here for sawing up scrap glass, bottles especially. Intaglio in the planking around the toilet holes identifies each one as to function, and at face level in the wall opposite as you sit is a wooden plaque bearing an eye-shaped piece of glass over gilt paint intended to glint at you and remind of correct procedure.* When I first saw these I thought what wonderful mementos of Tsau they would make, which I read as meaning that I already saw myself as leaving Tsau—as fascinating as I found it and despite the fact that I had just arrived. Do you belong anywhere? I asked myself. Denoon loved a book by James Joyce's brother in which their father is described as someone it was impossible to imagine as a happy, productive member of any society the mind of man had yet to come up with. I immediately thought of myself, of course. *Crockery heavily glazed in spectrum colors, but odd because the black-glaze floral motifs applied are clearly thumbprints. After the rondavels are painted a mastic is applied to the lower third of the exteriors to defeat termites: various herringbone and serpentine designs are created in the wet mastic, using the fingertips, including one design that looks very much like dollar signs.*

▶ *How serious is this place, au fond?* I once said to Nelson that he should call Tsau Occam's Torment instead, because he was always multiplying entities unnecessarily. This was during the long period when he could be teased pretty freely. *If it looks like rain you pull a string and a gutter made of overlapping flappets of wood flops down that extends beyond the edge of the roof thatch so that a drop of rain is never wasted. The gutter feeds a buried cistern equipped with an iron hand pump out of the nineteenth century. There is a box on a post next to the stoop: this is for messages, either in chalk on slate or in soft pencil on oblongs of frosted glass sealed to a wooden tablet: you rub out the message on the glass with a damp cloth or the heel of your hand. Reuse is king. Paper is precious here, so writing on both sides of a sheet is universal. You shower in the afternoon, having earlier raised a black polyvinyl sack of water up onto a shelf at the top of a stall, where the sun heats the water. The sack plug turns into a showerhead when you twist it. You raise the shower sack via pulley. The number of things that can be raised and lowered or operated at a distance via pulley systems is greater than I would ever have dreamed.*

*All tables are dropleaf, with very solidly made fly rails. All candle stands
and oil lamps have mirror reflector attachments.*

▶ I understand some things and not others. I can understand why the
proportion of older women with some visible defect or deformity is high. I
understand this in a general way because we know that illness in the
culture is interpreted as being the result of some transgression of what the
ancestors wanted you to do. So that permanent defects must mean serious
transgressions. But why is Dineo here? How did she get cast into destitution? She could be a model! Many of the younger women have been
shunned over prostitution coming to light, other patriarch-enraging actions or disobediences, or witchcraft accusations. Dineo is atypical in
some way. Her Setswana is pure, without dialect traces. When I ask what
tribe she is, people say Bamangwato, but on questioning it turns out that
this is an assumption, no doubt based on her self-confidence, and two
people have said Bamalete. She slightly obsesses me, which I have to
control because asking personal questions, especially about other people,
is très gauche in Tswana culture.

▶ *There is amenity here.* If you're white and you stay any length of time
in an African village, you can find yourself unconsciously counting the
moments until you get back to the properly upholstered white West.
Anybody can adapt for a while to perching on stools or sitting crosslegged
on mats when the time has come to stop standing up, but the feeling is
wholly interim. In Tsau you could be comfortable in the Western sense.
Mattresses were foam rubber slabs of the best density, although you were
welcome to sleep on one of Denoon's experimental palliasses made from
shredded maize husks if you were a total loyalist. He was also certain
there must be a way to make passable toilet tissue out of maize husks,
but he never was able to connect postally with the right expert. His drive
toward import substitution almost amounted to a tragic flaw. In Tsau
there was an adjustable chair, like an Adirondack chair, with a sling back
made of hide, in which you could attain what you never can in a normal
African village—the semireclining position. *Mopane wood furniture:
larger tables with marquetry: chairs have thong or strap mesh seats: chairs
and tables seem to be built slightly lower than the American norm, are
comfortable, suggesting that furniture in the West is built to a comfort
median set by the taller sex. Indoor temperatures fine. Rondavels have
thick walls, especially lower down, and are so thermally efficient you can*

*heat one up in fifteen minutes with a container of warm ashes, almost.
In the morning, in cold weather, you open your north-facing double-paned
windows and the sun heats the place decently all day and you retain the
heat for the night by closing the shutters and rolling down a thick feltlike
shade. There is a turtleshell-shaped smallish mud stove, vented to the
outside, which is mostly used for boiling water. There are larger mud
stoves outside, which people seem to use equally with the solar ovens they
complain continually about over having to keep adjusting the tracking
mirrors. Children can be gotten to do this if they aren't in school, but you
have to pay because it's boring. The children are darling fiends. There is
nothing wrong with this place so far.*

▶   *Tsau is permanently on edge over certain matters. Omnipresent mindfulness about water, not wasting it, conserving it. There is no such thing
as having a leisurely stroll off the beaten path anywhere on the koppie: the
entire upper surface is engineered for water harvesting: cement barriers,
damlets, sluices: these empty into two deep underground cisterns, one E
and one W. There is a supplementary system under construction on the
south slope below a broad face of bare rock—this system is not exactly an
afterthought, because the cistern was dug before the construction people
left, but the catchment structures are cruder, rock and cement rather than
the pure cement of the main system. A distinction is made between the
cistern water, called saved water, and the fresh water from the artesian
springs at the SE edge of the koppie, around which the fields and kraals
are laid out. Solar pumps and the three windmills move both kinds of
water into the huge storage tank sunk back in among the citadel rocks.
Public buildings and house plots are reticulated, house plots have standpipes, but water is released into the system only twice a day, morning and
evening currently, and then not for long. Each house plot has a cistern for
thatch runoff and a smaller tank for graywater. Finally, in the mongongo
grove deep south on the sand river is a primitive boom and bucket apparatus to get water from shafts dug next to the bank. These yield a little
rather turbid water which is trucked around on carts for various animal
needs. The supply of water is just above average for this time of year, but
people are hoping for a freak rainstorm or two, as has happened five times
in the last eight years on dates everyone can tell you. In addition to being
attuned to water, the community has to be alive to several other recurrent
threats, depending on the season. As I picture it, the entire settlement
convulses itself to get all its solar equipment and the netting on the
nethouses under burlap shrouding if it looks like hail or a serious sand-*

storm. The solar ovens in the yards have a wooden housing that is easily shoved over everything delicate, but shrouding all the solar panels that run pumps or do batch heating at the central kitchen is a major undertaking. There are teams for this. There is the equivalent of a fire drill, bells are rung, children rush out of school. Then there is the question of the very high level of maintenance going on: cleaning of the gutters in the water catchment, chlorinating cisterns, checking water levels, polishing mirrors on the various solar devices and oiling their joints and gears. People are also on the qui vive about public health. Flyswatting is done religiously, sometimes frenziedly. There are very few flies, in actual fact, especially in winter. But the feeling seems to be that there should be none. There is a kind of casual social monitoring, not only of children, over being sure that hands are dipped in the disinfectant solution outside the privies as you exit. It is perfectly to be expected that you will be shouted at from the next yard or the street if someone notices you being remiss. When you come to Tsau you take a virtual oath to do this faithfully. Is all this a tonic thing or not? Would you tend to wear down over time? Compare this to living at a less comfortable level but in a condition where you are free of the obligation to become part of a collective self-defense organism every time a bell rings. Or does that generate feelings of connection you can only get in some such way? Housefires not a source of anxiety because mud block is not flammable and thatch is impregnated with a fireproofing substance. Newly treated thatch smells like cinnamon, but this fades as the thatch ages.

▶ *Food en bref. Beef and rabbit irregularly, chicken and guinea hen more regularly, snake and game meats erratically, goat reliably, blood pudding all too often, lamb and pork forget. Fresh cow's milk usually only for children and pregnant or nursing women: powdered milk everywhere and stirred into everything, as is brewer's yeast and package gelatin. Yogurt, maas, and other clabbered milk products made from both fresh and powdered. Eggs off and on, powdered eggs available but not liked. Dried fish and biltong erratically. Cheese never, butter never unless canned. Scallions, cabbage, baby marrows, leeks, early and late carrots, various lettuces, parsley, spinach, kale, chard, sprouts of all kinds. Biltong scarce because only Basarwa can legally hunt game in the reserve: some fitful trade in this and fresh ostrich eggs from them is developing. Marmite and soy powder despised, but beloved by Denoon. Pinto beans, cowpeas, chickpeas. Stringbeans here should be treated as a source for string, period. Tomatoes very sweet, fluted sides. Much drying of vegetables. Fruit leath-*

ers. Sunflower oil and seeds, cashews, ground nuts, mongongo nuts. Melons, pawpaw, sour oranges, lemons, limes, granadilla. In every plot tub horticulture concentrated on dwarf varieties, always including peaches and tomatoes. Food is one of the things that put a subtle limit on how long you plan to stay in the rougher purlieus of the third world, unless you happen to be a saint of some kind. The variety of food in Tsau amazed me. Denoon had attended a lecture and heard a soil geneticist say offhand that he thought that Kalahari soils, mixed with sawdust and compost, would probably grow virtually anything. Denoon was out to prove this with a vengeance. The long growing season was in his favor. Sun was both friend and enemy, and the trick was to use plastic netting to shade the more delicate crops. Handwatering was the norm. Where any irrigating was done it was via the drip system. The fulcrum of our diet was maize or sorghum porridge done in monstrous vatlike pressure cookers at the main kitchen every day. You could take it away in insulated containers or have it delivered to you by dung cart if you chose not to hike up to the plaza. So that whatever else you added to the meal was recreational, in the nature of embellishment. People seemed delighted with this. Bread was baked every other day, socalled scones irregularly. Leftover bread was never thrown away but ended up as rusks to be eaten with hot milk for breakfast, or as breadcrumbs, another universal additive in Tsau. On the shelves of the Sekopololo stores house was everything you might want that the South Africans had ever bothered to can, from pilchards to lichee nuts. Of course, credit values on these items were kept astronomical both to reflect what it cost to get them to Tsau and to encourage consumption of local and cheaper foods. *Rice, groats, barley, pasta. Powdered coffee only, with chicory. Joko tea, rooibos tea.* I had been expecting a vastly more restricted food spectrum. There was also bush food, like wild medlars and various peculiar tubers, that kept inserting itself into our diet. In Tsau you could eat interestingly. The diet was light on fats, but there was nothing else wrong with it. Factors beyond my control were not, obviously, going to play their usual role in determining how long I stayed in a particular place, all of which raised my least favorite question, to wit, what exactly I was doing with my life. In Tsau I had been anticipating a palette that possibly a dedicated vegetarian could cope with for a while. This was otherwise. I'm not even against vegetarianism. At some level I think vegetarianism is right. It's certainly sound, so long as you watch your lysine and B_{12}. But I'm not a vegetarian. Something makes me resist. Why am I certain that males constitute a distinct minority of the total of vegetarians? I think I'm not prepared to concede animal protein to the striding-around master sex while I nibble leafage. I've certainly seen who gets the meat in African families.

▶ *Entertainments. A woman, a Morolong originally from Mafikeng, will come and stand outside your house and for scrip the equivalent of twenty-eight cents will play keening versions of Lady of Spain and Die Stem and a few other tunes on her violin. Her name is Prettyrose Chilume and she dresses up in tartesque town clothes to do this, eschewing the local sandals in favor of the towering platform shoes just going out of style in Gabs. She is very frail-looking, in her middle thirties, and was at one time a prostitute. Preceding that, she had been a kind of household slave to a Boer rancher, who taught her the violin as a joke. There are two choirs, one all queen and one all auntie, which are very rivalrous. Children get into traditional undress and do line dancing or have praise-poem-shouting contests. There are chess tournaments and speed contests with the abacus, which Denoon has introduced and popularized. There are reading circles, including several strictly for Bible study. In fact a surprising amount of reading goes on, in English and Setswana. People doing repetitive work can have someone come and read aloud to them. There are classes. Denoon lectures on almost anything. Afterdinner household intervisitation is somewhere between extremely popular and totally out of control. Since I moved to my own rondavel I've felt a certain pressure to light the welcome light each night, because if I don't I'm denying people access to a curiosity: myself. But I also feel compelled to preserve time for myself. This is a physical life and by nine I'm already falling asleep.* Also I felt it incumbent on me to try to memorize as much as I could from the *Field Guide to the Birds of Southern Africa,* for which I needed privacy. I think I have never hated a subject more. *I feel guilty when I hear people coming by, clearing their throats, milling around, and discussing why my light is off. People do have radios, but the reception from Radio Botswana is very weak here. There are tape players. Copies of the government newspaper arrive about a month late and are circulated, but we get only a sampling of issues. Illiterate people get read to.* I said something that led Denoon to feel I was being clinical or superior to what people did for entertainment in Tsau, which I denied. I said I fully appreciated that eight tenths of what our set did for entertainment back home we could do in Tsau. I meant reading, listening to music, going occasionally to a movie. I omitted eating out, which is in fact a major form of entertainment but which my circumstances had always kept me from doing very often, and shop-

ping. My concertgoing and playgoing had always been pretty much limited to amateur and college-level productions, so there was no great loss
there. Movies came in once a month from the British Council via the
Barclays plane. He grumbled about showing movies, and at first I
thought it was out of irritation at having to start up the big diesel generator with its inky smoke and general balkiness. But it was deeper. After
all, he had to start the generator to run his radio transmitter occasionally,
or for welding, and he did that without complaining. Gradually I extracted the bases of his objection to movies. His mind wandered during
them, he said. He only liked black and white. He only liked certain
recherché classics by Carl Dreyer and a few other early masters. He was
always aware of a blackish flicker: the frame speed was too slow for him.
Movies were ludicrous objects because background music told you how
to feel about everything. But even worse, movies were things that made
you passive, somehow. They happened to you. You couldn't make them
go faster, get on with it, even to the degree that you could with actors in
a play—by groaning, say. In any case, for the time spent, he would
always rather be reading. He never said so, but I think he hoped Tsau
would someday be above moviegoing. I treated all this as an eccentricity,
but I think now it was a form of puritanism coming from god knows
where. I told him I thought he liked reading because it was more like
work. He said something passé like touché. He wasn't annoyed. All this
was much later. He would say only slightly facetiously that the main
effort of arranging your life should be to progressively reduce the amount
of time required to decently maintain yourself so that you can have all
the time you want for reading. There was irony here, because until I
came and superintended some small upheavals in his use of time he was
always falling behind in his beloved reading and having to put it off,
falling months behind in the case of the Economist, which mounted up
in a stack that was always collapsing until I got an agreement out of him
that I could pull out and discard the bottom oldest few copies when the
stack got too high. That was fine, but I had to show him the copies I was
discarding. I would, and then and only then would he read them. Our
true entertainment was arguing, which we both loved. We liked to stay
up late and argue. If we started arguing while we were lying down, I
could always tell we had reached a serious point because he would want
us to proceed in a sitting position. He never knew I noticed this. We
argued about everything, but a lot of it devolved into arguments about
his basic philosophical anthropology. His assumptions were too romantic
for me. I wanted him to grasp something I thought I saw clearly, or to

confute me. We had various climactic arguments. I made some headway with him with my notion that, along with getting food and keeping warm, male competition for females and female reproductive power as a commodity is at the root of the hideous hypertrophied structures that keep renewing themselves and reappearing unstoppably in human affairs. Survival of the species is served by the best males getting to reproduce the most, tout court, was my point. So we are placed in the position of hating and trying to undo the results of something obviously imposed on us from the depths of our beings and, sub specie aeternitatis, a good thing. This is my definition of original sin. I am convinced that everything we really hate in society derives ultimately from this. Denoon would seem to grant me everything but then say something like You may be right, but it can still be defeated. He would say it passionately. I wanted to shake him on this and once said I doubt you'd be quite so sanguine about how much we can change things if you knew anything about fraternal interest group theory, which is a school of analysis in anthropology you only have glimmerings about due to your long absence from the groves of academe. Give me a syllabus, then, he said, mad at me. Besides, I read two or three years of Man at a time whenever I get near a decent library. They have it in Gaborone. No good, I said, because this school is American and Man is British. So then it was Then give me a syllabus, to which I had to say I'm not in a position to do that right away, obviously, but as soon as I can I will, I promise. Our arguments could get heated, which was all right, and once when he was becoming more recalcitrant than I had intended to make him I said, to close it off, Well, you can lead a horse to the river but you can't make him admire the view. I think this was one of the first times he looked at me with intellectual appreciation a cut above just letting me see he thought I was adequately smart. Another was during an early argument when I was defending Samuel Beckett. Death and approaching death are about as interesting a literary subject as peristalsis, was his position. But I said The fact is that people don't live as if death made any difference. There are innumerable institutions set up to encourage them in this, they spend years of their lives specifically defending against thinking that death is real and devoting themselves to the contemplation of various fictitious afterlives. But, I said, the world would be better if people incorporated the apprehension of death into the way they run their lives. Beckett makes you want to do that. Therefore he's a moral writer and important. He looked at me as if to say I had a point, and then said That's a very decent point. He would try Beckett again, he said.

▶ *Individual plots are roughly 150 by 100 feet, generous, but they feel crammed—what with two rondavels and a privy on each, plus chicken coops, animal pens, beehives, solar ovens, food dryers, composters, salad gardens, truck gardens, tub plantings, ornamental flowerbeds, maybe a parked dung cart or so. Plots are laid out in arcs along the ways, with dooryards facing, for neighborliness. There is something I am resisting about Tsau. Is there too much symmetry? I asked myself at first, but then asked Too much symmetry for whom? When you go into a real village everything is laid out otherwise, stragglingly, derelict compounds mixed in with thriving ones, stumps of rondavels next to flourishing setups. Materially Tsau is middleclass. I don't know what my question is, unless this is it: There are thousands of villages in places as remote as this, villages which are hideous, unsanitary, demeaning, but people are living in them about as cheerfully as the people here, which means what? Am I half identifying with the feeling that there should be more gratitude being manifested toward Denoon and the benefactions he organized to get all this going? This is totally reactionary. Also these women have come from gothic personal situations. I have heard the stories of the lives these women lived, and they have made me weep.* This shows my confusion as of then. I think what was bothering me had to do with political economy more than anything else. There was a question of amortization in the air that had to be settled before I could believe in Tsau. Enormous funds had gone into the setting up of the place. Tsau was no self-help settlement, not with slab concrete floors as level as ponds in every rondavel. This was not a perfect yet cheap idea working itself out. This was enlightened surplus capital coming in to lift a whole subclass of people up onto a pedestal and saying Go. What I was thinking over and over was This is all very well—but. Tsau was charity, or a species of it, which Denoon had to turn into something generically different or it was hardly worth doing. He needed more enthusiasm than I felt he was being given. I was very divided. You can only give what you can give. If you know in your heart something is in essence or origin charity you act differently toward it than if it's utterly your own creation. On the other hand, couldn't people see how extraordinary this could all turn out to be—in fact already was? I was in both camps at the same time. How happy should I myself be, was of course the unstated associated question. How happy should I be in Tsau? If I was holding that the average person should be more rapturous in this place, then all the eternal questions of what an average person is, what culture has to do with that, came flocking back, id est anthropology came flooding back.

What I really needed was to ventilate with Denoon on all this. But where was he? We were having brief, stiff public encounters and no more. Days were passing. The Tswana think you can routinely see ghosts for a second or two out of the corner of your eye. Denoon was ghostly to me. He was at the edges of my vision, always going somewhere else.

▶ *The sexual atmosphere of this place is normal, I think. But how can it be? You do see something covert and baffled in the faces of the men occasionally, which may relate. I would expect Tsau to be like what I imagine convents to be, in short, hells of incessant sexual stimulation and fixation, on the analysis that a convent is an institution devoted to an injunction reducible to Whatever you do, don't think about an elephant, the analog to the elephant being sex. The relative scarcity of men here should guarantee that, at least for the queens, you would think. I suppose there must be some sexual partnering going on between some of the women. I get the feeling that the only one here not sexually placid is me. I have fantasies in which I am hanging on Nelson's body like a langur, feeling inside his shirt. I think about his legs and the back of his head, the two main things of his I see as he skirts me and retreats from my vicinity with great celerity. Why is my meeting with the mother committee always being postponed? Why is nothing reaching me from him?* Everything was too slow. I hate trendlessness. I began dissecting the question of why Denoon was facilitating my being there. I could hardly attribute it to love, at that stage, or even protolove, or, given the snail's pace at which everything was occurring, to an opportunistic interest in me sexually. There were self-evident reasons, given his role in Tsau, for his not being sexually involved with members of the local nubility. And somehow he had managed himself sexually to his own satisfaction. I was not inclined to flatter myself that it was the unique charms concatenated in me that had wrecked whatever sexual equilibrium he had been enjoying previously. I asked myself what was the marxian, that is, selfish, interpretation of his apparently wanting me there? Light broke. It was obvious. Denoon wanted to know what he had wrought at Tsau. What was Tsau, really? I was an almost ideal vehicle through which he could find out. He would have had to be unaware of his own inner dynamic here, which meant that the little mating dance I was reading into our meetings in Gabs had been unconsciously allowed by him to ripen into whatever I had the force to bring it to. I was his ideal observer, and once I had been so persistent and brazen as to turn up in Tsau, there would be no way he

would want me sent off. As I suddenly saw it, his problem was how to
know truly what Tsau was. He was so immersed in the project and so
identified with it that his own reading of it would be suspect, to start
with. As for the actual beneficiaries of Tsau, there was a divide to cross.
Having the language would help only so much. There was the gulf of
gender, there was race, there was a culture tending toward evasion and
defensive courtesy, and there was the fact that the people of Tsau would
be insane to rock the boat: behind them was destitution, cruelty, hunger.
Ultimately when professional project evaluators managed to force their
way into Tsau, they would be looking for flaws and would be bringing
with them the understandable bias of orthodox developmentalists against
something like Tsau being a success. Nelson would not be being paranoid to feel this. He was celebrated in his field but not popular. So
although he could never have consciously orchestrated my getting
to Tsau without contaminating my ability to see things disinterestedly,
my arrival must have seemed perfect. Everyone has a demon of pride.
His was feeling deprived, and here was someone who could be helpful,
who had taken the trouble to cross the desert to get to him, no less.
There could, of course, be other motives supporting this one, I told myself to make myself feel a little better. But my insight seemed plausible and made me redouble my efforts to get everything down and
achieve an intelligent sense of what Tsau was as a synergy. This felt
like an assignment, and that felt comfortable. In any case it was what
I had to work with. *I find it difficult to probe people in re what they
may find unsatisfactory about Tsau. It makes me look ungrateful.
But there are certain perceptible areas of tenderness. There seems to be
no congregational religious activity of any kind. The Bible study that's
done is very ad hoc and people are slightly furtive about it. Botswana is
very Christianized, and very Zionist Christianized: so what is this about?
I gather that Denoon is regarded as the village atheist. He is known
for his jeremiads against religion, which seem to be regarded as just
another of the odd, lakhoa things he likes to do. There do seem to be
misgivings over the rule that housing be tribally mixed. Six of the thirteen Tswana tribes are represented here, plus the handful of Baherero. The
mixing of tribes in the wards and neighborhoods is for the most part defended as a good thing, and people tend to claim that feelings on it were
much stronger earlier on. I'm not so sure. Tomorrow I finally meet the
mother committee and get a chance to see how the deception I seem to
be embarked on is going over.* I hadn't actually written the word deception in my book, naturally. My surrogate for that was excursus in some

places and gavotte in others. Before my past cleverness makes these entries impenetrable to me, I need to make a glossary—either that or forget the whole thing. I am already guessing at what I meant, here and there.

The Plaza

With great regularity Nelson would regret and then not regret siting the public buildings of Tsau on a terrace one hundred and twenty-five feet above the plain. Everyone at one time or another would curse Tsau for not being laid out all on one level. I got used to seeing people dragging themselves around strickenly for a while after reaching the terrace, particularly if they'd had to get up to it in a hurry. This came across to me as largely pro forma, though. It was never long before the tonic elements in the setting would take over. The breezes were lovely there. You could promenade along the terrace rim and peer down into people's yards. And the actual ascent was very gradual, with benches along the routes.

The view was dramatic. You appreciated the greenness of Tsau, as against the burning grays and yellows of the Kalahari. When there were cloud shadows, the Kalahari looked like a leopard pelt. People would sit and commune with the view. What Denoon would say in defense of the location was that civically important events should take place in an elevating setting. I knew he had images of Delphi in mind. I also knew he thought stair climbing was cardiovascularly good for you and I found myself wondering if that had had something to do subliminally with the choice. My bet, still, is that, all things considered, no woman would have voted to have the washhouse, the stores house, the central kitchen, and the Sekopololo offices located at the top end of a long though gentle ramp. We inhabit male outcomes. Every human settlement is a male outcome. So was Tsau, which was seventy percent complete when the first women moved in.

Gladys and Ruth Street delivers you to the center point of the plaza, which is kidney shaped, half a city block in extent, flagged at the margins and raked sand otherwise. The concavity is toward you. There are several small mopane trees to the rear west side of the plaza, but most of the shade is provided by beach umbrellas, for which there are sockets in the ground irregularly distributed over the open area. Straight ahead of you as you arrive, and set far back, is the stores house, a huge rondavel connected via a covered passage to a cave in the koppie. There are two imposing sister structures, ovaldavels, one at each of the far ends of the plaza. I had looked only superficially into the stores house—the front section of the rondavel and not deeper into the cave—but I had been impressed by the density of the array of goods and tools stacked, racked, shelved, binned, hoisted up and hanging suspended over you, to be found there, everything labeled and tagged, seemingly. You would have to be lithe to get around rapidly amid the profusion of goods in the front room and through the back room and into the cave, where the crowding was supposedly worse. The stores house rondavel and its sister ovaldavels were magnificent buildings, voluminous, with high, open vaults under the steep-pitched thatched roofs. The construction was not mud block like the homestead rondavels, it was concrete block, but you could only tell this from inside: the exteriors were finished in heavy mastic and enameled sky blue. One reason that Tsau gave such a spangled appearance from a distance was that the thatching closure on the roof peaks is always protected by tin cladding, either a conical cap, in the case of the rondavels, or long, pieced shielding like an overturned racing shell, in the case of the ovaldavels.

The ovaldavel to the right I classified as general administrative, since it housed the post office–bank, the library, meeting rooms for the mother committee, the disputes committee, and the committee as to names. I analogized the mother committee to a town council, although the interlocks between it and something called the sister committee, which had to do exclusively with the economic side of Tsau, meaning Sekopololo, were for a long time obscure to me. Denoon had no office anywhere in the public buildings, I was surprised to learn. There was some mousy shrubbery around the administrative building, and some freesias, I think. A ship's bell hung from a hook next to the front door.

The ovaldavel to the left was Sekopololo itself—offices, record rooms, a veranda where the morning shapeups took place, and a combination shop and lounge devoted to stocks of the most commonly needed commodities, such as salt, toilet paper, cooking oil, and batteries. There were some smaller buildings behind Sekopololo, in one of which was the largest of the three generators in Tsau.

Wires could be strung across the plaza from high up on the different buildings so that, using support poles and sheets of burlap, large sections of the open area could be canopied for outdoor events in the hot season.

In fact it was possible to accommodate the whole populace under shade in the plaza. Risers would be packed in along the inner curve of the terrace, a canopied dais would be erected out toward the terrace rim, and the fun would begin. It was unique.

I was informed I should report to the plaza at seven in the morning for my meeting with the mother committee. I was prompt. Just off the Sekopololo veranda a circle of chairs had been set up around a low round table with a crockery urn and nine mugs on it. The mother committee was prompt. Just as I arrived the eight members of the committee filed out of the administration building. I was motioned to sit anywhere I liked. They were new faces, only Joyce and Dineo being familiar to me. We all said our names before beginning, but I was concentrating so on what I was going to say that only one of the new names stuck with me, the name of a woman who seemed fascinated with me, Dorcas Raboupi. Her eyes never left me. She had perfectly straight eyebrows, like dashes. She was short, not young but not yet in the aunt category. She was lighter complexioned, almost a coloured, her face lumpy on one side, as though she had a fat-deposition disorder. She sat in a huddled way that I thought showed hostility. The day was cool but not cold. Several of the women had brought shawls with them, and I had been told I could get one to borrow at the counter in Sekopololo. I didn't need one. Dorcas Raboupi was unnerving. She appeared to be someone's nemesis, probably mine for no reason I could think of. I was prescient.

I expected Dineo to lead off and handle the meeting, but instead a bag was passed around and people drew disks out of it, with the one who drew a notched disk beginning the proceedings. This was a heavyset young woman, Mma Molebi, evidently nursing: there was a milkstain in her bodice over one breast. Judging by the way she wrung her hands before she commenced, she was uneager for her assignment. My back was to the desert.

Mma Molebi began with the obviously obligatory history of Tsau. As she spoke, the other women got up one by one and served themselves tea. I was struck by this, because it would be usual for the youngest woman present to serve the older women. There is so much reflexively hierarchical behavior in Africa—the young serving the old, women routinely serving men—that this self-service feature of life in Tsau leapt out at me. It reminded me that I had seen something else that was atypical, namely young males willingly shoveling up animal manure to use in composting. Admittedly I had seen this in Tsau only a couple of times. But it was not the Botswana I knew. If manure had to be collected, it

would be usual for women to do it. I knew from my Peace Corps doctor
that there was perpetual sturm und drang with the boys the Peace Corps
hired as messengers over being required to take sealed packages containing stool samples from the medical office to the lab at Princess Marina
Hospital. One of the messengers had quit rather than demean himself
so. Finally the female receptionist had volunteered to take over the task
herself.

I got the feeling that our meeting was taking place in a circle out in
the open so that passersby would feel comfortable in hanging around to
see what was going on. People did drift up and listen for a while. I found
it both inhibiting and relaxing, more the second as time went on.

Mma Molebi was speaking too softly for the group, and people signaled this to her by holding up their index fingers until she spoke up.
She was either concluding or she was losing her way. Tsau was a jewel,
she said twice. And then she went into something that moved me, albeit
it was rather disjunct from what had gone before. She said Some women
in this place have even once been beggars, but never shall they be again,
because any woman who chooses to go away from Tsau can have money
to take and shall know catering as well as many other kinds of work, and
she shall never be seen working as maids or cleaners to others. The
degree to which I'm easily moved in the early morning must have something to do with my biochemistry. I remember bursting into tears the
first time I heard The Cherry Tree Carol sung on a record by Joan Baez,
also at that time of day. And I have had other attacks of piercing feeling
in the slot between seven and eight in the morning, including one over
Mother and Child Reunion, an incident that let me in for some substantial teasing. People noticed that Mma Molebi seemed to have moved me,
and were approving, I thought. The basket circulated again.

The winner this time seemed to have nothing to say other than that
I was to be praised for never forcing any sister to speak to me in English.

Dineo signaled that it was my turn to speak, which I did, saying who
I was and in essence repeating my pitch about being fascinated with
Tsau and wanting to stay as long as that could be permitted, but volunteering this time to work however much I was asked to in order to help
with any costs my presence caused. I laid in some filigree, but sincere
filigree, so to speak, about wanting to witness the extraordinary things
women seemed to be accomplishing in Tsau.

I could tell something was up with Dorcas. She said, out of turn and
under her breath, something to the effect that she hoped I would find
enough birds in Tsau to please me, and that if I was unable to find

enough birds to please me I should come to the mother committee, who would find birds for me.

Dineo cut her off and proceeded directly to what I took for the vote. She looked at each member of the committee until she got some response imperceptible to me. But apparently the vote was in my favor, because she went into a welcoming speech. A great exception was being made for me, she said, and I would be welcome among them only so long as I was seen as a friend of the struggle of poor women to gather strength and wealth. She put this with emphasis. I could stay where I was now, in the empty rondavel next to Mma Isang, who would continue to see after me and organize my meals, for which I would be asked to work at any tasks I would choose for a sum of fifteen hours each week. They hoped I would be willing to think of helping with teaching English to some of the older children. There was a great need. Finally, they thought it would be good for me to stay awhile because it was always a pleasure to meet persons from one's own country when one was in a far place, so they thought Rra Puleng would be glad to see me there in Tsau. If ever I wished to leave, it would be three weeks until it could be arranged with the Barclays plane. On no account would they assist me to go off into the desert again, even if I wished to. And as a last thing, was I pleased at how my donkey was being looked after?

I thanked them, then it was over. Mma Isang appeared from the wings and came to embrace me, which inspired a couple of rather more halfhearted embraces from two of the women, not including Dorcas.

I was elated.

Dorcas walked by me, saying musingly to herself the names of the local bird species she could think of, making a production out of not seeming to be able to think of more than six.

At Tea

A sort of municipal high tea was put out every afternoon around four on the Sekopololo veranda. There would be tea, powdered milk, fruit cut up into small pieces, sometimes bread pudding. Denoon would make cameo appearances at tea, often, but he hadn't been staying put long enough for me to get into casual conversation with him. I was tired of this and didn't understand it, really. My life is taking forever, I remember thinking.

I loved teatime. There was a moral point to it. Some days there would be a generous collation put out, some days it would be sparse. It all depended on what happened to be either left over or in good supply. If there was only a little fresh fruit, it would be cut up minutely and thorn tree spines would be stuck into each chunk, as in hors d'oeuvres. Tea was never intended to be a spread adequate for the whole population, should it choose to turn up. The point seemed to be for people to adjust to what was available each day, holding back from taking any large, personally satisfying amount in favor of everybody getting a little of whatever there was. One custom was for no adult to take any fruit until the children who were around in the first few minutes had taken what they wanted. An undeclared object of the exercise seemed to be for teatime to finish each day with something remaining uneaten on the table, no matter how much or how little had been provided. Everyone seemed to know what this exercise was about and to enjoy being part of it, even the children. You could see them assimilating the rules, deferring to each other occasionally, turning down morsels themselves. I never tired of it.

I managed to be in the right place when Denoon arrived that afternoon. I went up to him and we shook hands. His palms were like planks. We knew everyone was watching.

He had a talent, which was to be able to talk intelligibly while ostensibly merely smiling. It was remarkable.

They want you to stay, he said. Even a faction I felt sure would be against it wants you to stay. It's very funny. They think you're a spy sent here to get the goods on Tsau, and that suits them fine. Most people just seem to like you. But anyway keep doing what you're doing.

I said Yes, everyone was very nice at the mother committee. I'm definitely going to be here awhile.

Congratulations, he said. And then he said There was never any doubt.

Votaries of the Maggot

I forgave him that evening during corso, which was the correct term for the postprandial walking around and going into houses where the welcome light was on that he had inculcated in Tsau. He had gotten the idea for it out of Tolstoy's *Sebastopol Sketches*, he told me. It was apparently something done in Russian provincial towns during the nineteenth century, and it had seemed like a good idea, so why not?

In addition to the usual shooting the breeze, another thing that went on during corso was a scene that was a good deal like testifying, as it's called in fundamentalist Protestant churches. One woman might tell her tribulations up to the time of coming to Tsau and the listeners would chorically moan along, often making the speaker repeat the most painful episodes a few times. Many of the stories were genuinely harrowing, but there was something formulaic about the way they got told.

That evening I was in a house on Slessor where a woman lived whose name was Mariam Nene. She was under forty and seemed young for the chronology implicit in her story. She was the daughter of an accused witch. She had been fourteen when her mother died—poisoned, Mariam was sure—and it was widely assumed that Mariam had been initiated into witchcraft as a matter of course by her mother. So she was persona non grata, very, in her village near Pandamatenga close to the border with then Rhodesia.

She had an uncle on the Rhodesian side of the border in a village near Plumtree, and she set off on foot to find him. At this point Denoon slipped in and sat down. Members of the same tribe lived on both sides of the border, which meant nothing to them and which has still never been completely demarcated. I only remember the centerpiece of her story, which was her arrival in her uncle's village just in time to witness him being murdered. He was a herbalist but was also clearly believed to be a sorcerer. He had gone to a pond in the bush to dive for calcified lark dung, a powerful ingredient in magical concoctions, and enemies of his had been lying in wait. Mariam arrived at the pond and saw from the bushes, where she stayed hidden, her uncle being prodded with long

poles to the center of the pond and then forcibly kept under until he
drowned. This was a favored way of killing sorcerers because it left no
marks. White administrators would never bother about deaths that
looked natural. Denoon seemed to be strongly affected by her story.
Mariam started to tell this horrific part of it again, and Nelson got up and
stepped outside. I followed.

He was wiping his eyes. We walked around wordlessly. I felt close to
him.

I decided not to intrude on his state of being unless he made some
move to show that that would be welcome. He dropped me at Mma
Isang's and went off. I was being extremely careful. I think this was the
beginning of our courtship.

Of course, life being what it is, in fact the thing that moved him in
Mariam's story was not what I had thought. It was something more
abstract that her story had suggested. Much later I somehow brought
this scene up, and he, on his own, straightaway corrected my view of
what he had been feeling that night. I was saying, I think, how much it
had moved me that he had been so moved by Mariam.

The more abstract thing was manmade violence in general. Before
going to Mariam's he had been writing poetry, or rather trying for the
thousandth time to turn a very clear concept that he had into a real
poem. There had been an overflow of emotion at Mariam's because the
subject matter of her story was an example of what he had been trying
to get into his poem. He explained it to me. He wanted to write a poem
that would make the point that anyone who embraces violence should
be seen as an ally of all the inescapable natural enemies of humanity,
from earthquake through the panoply of diseases. It was so clear to him.
He obviously thought that if he could get this into a halfway decent
poem it might have some effect. He let me see some of what he had
done. It was Whitmanic. He was working with titles like Allies of Famine
and Victualers of the Maggot or Votaries of the Maggot. I remember
that Claymore and Gatling were characterized as allies of the maggot or
the blowfly. You're not a poet, I had to tell him. This is not a poem. A
genius could do it, he said. We laughed over it. Your problem is that you
want to be everything, I told him. That isn't the worst, he said.

I asked him what the worst was.

The worst was that in the course of things he had gotten to know
pretty well a couple of authentic poets, people whose names I would
know but which he was too ashamed to tell me. He had actually sent
them each a précis of his poem idea, in an attempt to get them to write

such a poem. One had never responded. One had responded politely. He seemed not to be friendly with either of them anymore.

You must be the greatest believer in the power of poetry there is, I told him.

More Courtship

Substantive courtship went on for a month, with me ultimately forcing the pace when I felt the balance between our public and private gettings-together was not improving. Public occasions far predominated, where we would find ourselves together at corso or some performance or other or at the movie. Our private occasions tended to be chaste long walks in the gloaming, which frequently turned out to end at some utilitarian destination such as a windmill in need of a touch of maintenance. Until the very end, there were no declarations toward me.

The studied pace of all this was something to be borne. I was working with the rabbits. On the few occasions Denoon and I were alone together I felt that he was more interested in how it was going in the rabbit pens than in getting to know all about me. He was always keenly interested in whatever I had to say analytically about Tsau, which served to confirm my notion that it was my reading of the place that he really wanted from me. We were going so ploddingly through the stages of courting—from handholding to a little mournful standing-up necking—that I for one found it embarrassing. It was quaint, not to say retrograde, for people our respective ages. But I went along with it, accepting the sickeningly familiar vigil for cues from the sovereign partner as to when it was time for the next plateau. There were great things at stake, I told myself, and his grasp of the ramifications of our getting together was greater than mine.

One thing I now know I was misinterpreting was Nelson's taste for bouts of self-communing, which I mistook as being longeurs for him just as surely as they were for me. He liked us to walk around together in total silence much more than I did. When we finally discussed it I made him laugh by saying I get bored when I'm not talking. I remembered that he had mentioned to me that a normal social occasion for his parents might be to invite friends over and sit around with them, nobody speaking for hours, while a recording of the Missa Solemnis was played. His mother and father, just the two of them, would often do the same thing. Mightn't seeing that kind of thing have had something to do with the development of your taste for silence? I asked. No, he said, because by the time he might have been influenced by it he had figured out that the scene was really only another device of his father's for having an apparently normal social evening while in fact being drunk: it was a sham, an excuse for sitting on a sofa with his eyes closed, only nominally present, making it to bedtime with the amount he had gotten away with secretly drinking going undetected. It was a con in every respect. For instance, his father's record selections ran heavily toward sacred music, a lot of Bach, which Nelson saw as a transparent inducement to his mother to partake.

Can't anything be innate? he wanted to know, objecting to my probing into his childhood yet again. Does everything have to be an exfoliation from the minutiae of our miserable childhoods? I happen to love silence, he said. Why do we have to be swamped in narrative? Our lives are consumed in narrative. We daydream and it's narrative. We fall asleep and dream and more narrative! Every human being we encounter has a story to tell us. So what did I think was so wrong with the pursuit of some occasional surcease of narrative?

In retrospect I suppose I could have pursued the reasons for his bouts of indwelling, but when you're being courted you develop such a gooseneck persona, even if only temporarily, that you're out of position to catch clues that would normally alert you to things you need to pursue. But of course nothing is more profitless than going back over what interventions might have changed the shape of things to come. I want to scream at myself when I do that.

I realize that I may have contributed to his wanting to be silent during our walks by my too concentrated and cathected soundings re the books in his life. I was groping gingerly for his intellectual keystone, but not gingerly enough. There are certain quagmires to be avoided with people. You can find yourself liking someone who appears intellectually normal and then have him let drop that his favorite book of all time is *The Prophet*. That wasn't the particular danger with Denoon, but there were others. A guy who tells you the best novel ever written is *Clarissa*, which also happens to be the first or second novel ever written, is also not unlikely to tell you that the only music he likes to listen to is motets and that art has never really advanced over the cave paintings at Lascaux. I

suppose I was on the qui vive for some variant of this reflex because
Denoon had said his favorite novel was *War and Peace*, so I was thinking,
Oh no, it's going to be Beethoven for music and Shakespeare for plays.
It isn't that these positions are not defensible, but taking them may mean
someone is not very individual. One thing you distinctly never want to
hear a man you're interested in say softly is that his favorite book in the
whole world is *The Golden Notebook*. Here you are dealing with a liar
from the black lagoon and it's time to start feeling in your purse for
carfare. Anyway, when I sensed the depth of Denoon's desire for a little
silence, I desisted. What I got out of this first attempt to look at his
literary underpinnings was a paperback called *L'Afrique Noire est Mal
Partie* to read and comment on.

The Octagon

Denoon was abruptly missing for four days, having said nothing
about going anywhere.

Unbeknownst to me, there was an innocent explanation for his absence. He had a custom of retreating once a month to a lean-to a mile
down the sand river for reading and reflection. The date had crept up on
him. He'd discovered it was time to go by turning a page in his daybook.
He'd looked for me, hadn't found me, hadn't wanted to leave anything
in written form for my information—the problem being, I was non-
plussed to hear, that written communications in Tsau weren't necessarily
that secure—and most of all he hadn't wanted to put off doing something
that everyone knew he had always done religiously, like clockwork, up
till then. These scruples related to his delicate stage-management of our
relationship in terms of the way it was important for it to appear to the
watchership of Tsau. Everything in our getting together had to appear
to be the result of accident and natural evolution. Everything had to be
convincingly gradual.

I couldn't ask where Denoon was because I felt I had to be wary
about the undoubtedly larger than suspected percentage of women in
Tsau who privately assumed I had come there with premeditation to
chase Denoon. So I couldn't ask, but what I could do was instanta-

neously convince myself that Denoon was involved in a covert liaison.
Somebody must have given him an ultimatum and forced him to go
away for a confrontation. There must be a grotto someplace, I thought,
or some other hideout where they were meeting. Who might my rival
be? I instantly had two candidates—Dineo, and Kakelo Modise, our surly
nurse. It seemed to me that both of them had been out of the public eye
sufficiently during Denoon's absence to make either of them plausible.
I, at least, hadn't seen much of either of them lately, insofar as I could
reconstruct.

It had to be Kakelo, probably. She was less than twenty-five and had
a very cute figure, which she tailored her nurse costume to exploit. She
went everywhere in full kit—always including her miniature toque of a
nurse's cap—lest we forget who she was. She had a beautiful au lait
complexion. In her presence you were never unaware that here was
someone in no doubt she was wasting her fragrance on the desert air.
She was in fact the sole user of perfume in the entire village, to my
knowledge. I had sympathy for her, but I was never able to exercise it.
She was tremendously rude. There was a protocol obtaining in small
groups in the event someone wanted to start speaking in English. It was
more pro forma than not, because I never saw anyone give the decline
signal. If you wanted to go into English you were supposed to lock your
little fingers together for a moment to give people the theoretical option
of signaling no with a thumbs-down. But whenever she had intersected
any group I was in she had tramplingly ignored the protocol and gone
straight into clipped, rapid English. Naturally if she was Denoon's secret
inamorata her rudeness toward me was more than explained. She was
clearly seething over something. And any lonely male would be interested in her, if she was interested, it seemed to me. I constructed a
complete psychology for her. I imagined myself in her place, nubile and
posted involuntarily to a city of women: what would make more sense
than trying to go sexually for the indirect author of my distress, to
wrench him down? Folklore vis-à-vis young nurses from my adolescence
helped me along. Thanks to the amusing reports on the male world I
extracted from a gay male friend, I knew what high school guys in my
day thought about nurses. My high school had been located two blocks
from a college of nursing. My friend described a locker room scene in
which a letter man, a lacrosse champion, becomes unhinged and begins
pounding the lockers: he has just gotten the news from the team physi-
cian that he has contracted a social disease. His worldview is crumbling
because he has contracted it from a nurse, or nursing student, rather.

Nurses were assumed to be sexually active both out of horniness—they lived under parietal rules—and because they knew all about hygiene and were contraceptively astute and could even give each other abortions if something went wrong. Nurses were supposed to be sexually sanitary in every way. And here a *nurse* has gotten him infected.

My suspicion of Kakelo was shortlived, though. I had a look around in her office and couldn't help noticing the thickness of the file of carbons of savingrams she had sent to the Ministry of Health appealing for transfer before her tour was up. Many of the appeals were recent. If she had ensnared Nelson, why would she be pressing so insistently for reassignment? Also a little inquiry revealed that her nonattendance at the health post recently had been due to bronchitis or hypochondria, both of which she had had spells of in the past according to everyone. And, finally, it was brought home to me that she bullied everyone about speaking English, whether I was in the group or not. Her first name translated into Obedience, funnily enough.

The last day Denoon was missing I went prowling around his place like a nut, very early in the morning. I had my pretexts ready in the event I came to anybody's attention, including his, should he be in situ. He wasn't. I got there circuitously, slipping down from the brushy hillside above the house instead of going publicly up the path from the plaza. Denoon had a terrace all to himself, an area about the size of two tennis courts end to end.

The house was a concrete block octagon, formerly the command center of the Belgian construction outfit that had built Tsau. There was something disparate and notional about the tall, double-peaked thatch roof. This was a feeling that turned out to be prescient: I was looking at something that would become a personal material headache. In fact the original perfectly good corrugated iron roof had been taken off at Denoon's instruction and replaced with this thatch fantasia not structurally appropriate to the shape of the building. He wanted to live under thatch like everybody else. At first my heart went out to Denoon over his having to live in such a peculiar albeit spacious building. It looked vaguely industrial, or even military industrial, like a blockhouse in World War I, or I may mean pillbox, except for the absence of guns sticking out of the narrow rectangular windows set horizontally at a higher than normal level in the walls. But then the more closely I looked at his house and grounds the more interesting and deceptive his choice of domicile seemed to me to be.

It amused me to refer to the whole yard area stretching away from the front of the house and ending in a precipice as the patio. Nelson never fully got the humor in the term. It came to me during that first reconnaissance. In truth what the yard resembled was a sculpture garden of broken or half-repaired or obsolescent machines and machine elements. In among the machines were other sorts of matériel—vats in which machine parts seemed to be marinating in solvents, piping bundled according to caliber, unopened crates. His yard was an antipatio, although there was a clear space near the outer edge of the terrace where any normal person would long ago have put a table and chairs or a hammock. This spot was shaded by the most perfect umbrella tree in Africa, incidentally. As a gardener, Denoon was nominal. There was a measly presentation of parsley and some other herbs in tubs near his doorstep. More could be done. To the back of the terrace, behind the house, was the privy and a sketchier thatched structure like the places you get drinks from on the beach in the Caribbean, except that it contained a huge authentic porcelain bathtub. The bathhouse walls were litani mats held together at the overlaps by clothespins. I marveled at this facility briefly, noting that here was the only place in all of Tsau where you could stretch out full length in hot water. Later I would discover that there was at least one other English bathtub in Tsau, at Dineo's. I tried the tap, and nothing. The bathtub wasn't reticulated to the water system. Water had to be brought in in canisters and emptied into the donkey boiler—essentially an oildrum set over a stone firebox—for heating. Here was exactly the peculiar amalgam of amenity and discomfort that I was picking up as a suppressed motif. You could have your own bathtub, but it would have to be somewhat of an ordeal to make use of it. It's an unfair simile, but what I thought of in scanning his accommodations was the signs you see protesters carrying in demonstrations in movies where the supposedly homemade lettering is so obviously the art director's version of what an enraged untrained hand would produce. This thought was unfair but I had it.

What Denoon had was space, privacy, the bathtub, magnificent views —especially the view west toward the red hills and the sand river. But clearly, as I read it, he was uncomfortable about any privilege at all and so the theme of perpetual work and study and basic austerity had to manifest everywhere. I was seeing it in the way the interior of the octagon was set up. Moreover, as he admitted later, he also was under a self-injunction against seeming to be a permanent fixture, against putting his roots down and elaborating his personal environment, because the deal was that he would be going away when Tsau was ready, id est perfect, which was a day bound to come sometime pretty soon. He had been there for eight years already.

I meant to limit myself to what I could pick up by looking in through the windows. First I had knocked violently enough at the door to be certain no one was home. The interior was divided up into a large cooking-sleeping-sitting front room and two smaller back rooms, one of which was mostly given over to a radio transmitter. For decor it was maps and planting charts. The walls were white, which was a relief, because it would have been totally congruent with the general spirit of austerity to have gone with the same lentil-green paint that was on the exterior, to show how above his intimate surroundings a person could be. I could see a few personal things of Denoon's in the front room: everything was very neatly kept. His clean clothes were wedged into compartments in a sagging wickerwork construct affixed to the wall. There was a sling chair. The mattress on the platform bed was going to be maize husk, I could sense. I had to go in, if only to get a better look at what passed for a kitchen.

I decided the kitchen was minimal but workable. There was the usual mudstove, and a camp stove with a goodly supply of bottled gas canisters. A surprise was that the tap over the tiny sink was not just an ornament. Denoon had the only functional interior sink I knew of in Tsau. All other houses had outdoor standpipes. I had to prowl carefully. There were neat stacks of books and papers on the floor in untoward places. Tables were in surplus, and they were loaded with more books, papers and periodicals, accordion files, and—in the rear rooms—utilitariana like surveying equipment, hand tools, and paper-cutters. Clearly the living quarters were just another part of the silva rerum the patio was.

Where would I be in all this? was the unavoidable question. I would need a table of my own, for example, at a minimum. How could I insert myself without becoming the longlost eternal feminine whose touch would now make everything cheery and comfy?

It was cold there. The floor needed more than the two or three mats in evidence. Leaving, I doubted myself, until from somewhere an image came to me of Nelson as being like a fig, something heavy in the hand and thickly seeded as opposed to light sweet things like seedless grapes. He was not watery. I had images of him going back and forth from room to room, or really of his burly legs going by me while I sat at my table.

Dineo

This was the same day. I had decided that my rival must be Dineo. She was someone it was impossible not to picture getting what she wanted and doing it without your noticing. She was purposive. She radiated purpose.

So it was electrifying when, as I was skinning some rabbits my nurturance had failed to save, I got a summons from Dineo to come to see her. The summons was on a slate in a bag in a cart rolled to me by my livewire favorite boy in the world, King James, the one who had brought breakfast to my first mother committee meeting. I was being asked to come to Sekopololo to meet with Dineo after lunch, id est during siesta, which was in itself interesting because, I had noticed, we were the two women who consistently worked through siesta, ignoring it. She had noticed the same thing. I sent back the message that I'd be there. King James seemed delighted to get the return errand. His mother was the young woman who had burned her arm apprenticing with Denoon in the glassworks.

Dineo was nowhere in Sekopololo, so I went searching for her through the stores house and then tentatively back into the cave. Finding her was odd, but only mildly in comparison to what came slightly later.

It was a hot day for that time of year, May, mid-fall in Africa. I was just inside the cave. To my left was what appeared to be a passage but was actually a narrow room out of Dickens, with pigeonhole racks on either side containing I forget what. There was light at the end of the room, which I perceived to be shining on some beautiful but unidentifiable piece of wooden furniture but which in fact was light from a paraffin lantern set on the floor shining off the bent-over naked back of Dineo as she rummaged through something. It was stifling and she had folded down the top of her dress. Only her back was lit: her head was bent down, out of sight, and so were her arms. What is that beautiful thing? I thought, until it moved when she heard my footsteps. A routine thing for women in the villages to do when the weather is scorching is to disencumber themselves down to the waist. There are famous stories of the consternation of male Peace Corps volunteers teaching in the upper forms of some of the remoter secondary schools turning around from the blackboard to confront ranks of young women allowing their nubile little breasts to show all innocently. This was before the headmasters had been appealed to by the various volunteer agencies to discourage this. Now it was rare. Dineo covered up like lightning, not turning around. She was surprised that I was there so quickly, she said, and asked if I knew the hour. I estimated. Time in Tsau was mostly by rough reckoning. Very few people wore wristwatches. Dineo was one of the ones who usually did. Denoon was sporadic with his.

We went back over to Sekopololo, to a dim meeting room where she motioned me to sit down next to her at a vast round marquetry table. I was very edgy, which I think she noticed and tried to dispel by mock-seriously locking her little fingers in the permission-to-speak-English sign. We smiled.

We talked about the weather, the heat. This sometimes can help us, Dineo said, referring to an overhead fan attached to the beamwork above us and connected by rods to a long box on the wall with a crank projecting from it. The fan ran by some variant of clockwork, some spring mechanism, I gathered. Dineo got up and cranked the thing tight, and the wooden blades of the fan began to feebly rotate. She had my file and started going through it, in the course of which a sheet of paper stuck to her arm. She peeled it off, grimacing, and wagged her hand in front of her face. We had both been doing strenuous physical work.

My interview seemed to be about the rabbits, who were not flourishing. Because of the climate, they had to be reared in small thick cement domes instead of the usual wire mesh hutches. This particular system had been a roaring success in some other arid place, like the Negev, and Dineo knew that Denoon was hipped on generalizing rabbit raising to the individual household level. She seemed relieved when I agreed with her that the idea was premature. The fan had stopped. She looked resigned, got up to recrank, and pointed out what I could already see— that the fan ran pretty briefly considering the effort it took to wind it up. Here was yet one more limb of Denoon's inventiousness.

Something suppressed and burning was going on with Dineo. I had the feeling she never stopped reading me. I felt it all through the cautionary tale she told about Denoon's enthusiasms for various husbandries, the latest being for ostrich husbandry. One message was that I should rely on the advice of women, certain women, and she named some who were active with the other animals. At one time Denoon had apparently been determined to raise pigs at Tsau. Ultimately the attempt had been given up. The heart of the scheme had been what Dineo called a moving house of pigs—a large, covered movable pen open at the bottom, with pigs in it. The idea had been that the enclosure would be moved around and anchored in different venues long enough for the rooting-around and defecating pigs to turn each locus into potting soil. The trouble was that pigs are very powerful animals, apparently, and also prone to cooperate among themselves. The cage was impossible to anchor satisfactorily, ever, so the pigs would shoulder the thing along over great distances to anywhere they pleased, such as the grounds of the primary school, where the children would see it coming and get hilarious. Not only was it beyond the power of man to anchor the cage, it was also impossible to construct it solidly enough to keep the pigs from, over time, bursting it apart and running off in all directions. Now, Dineo said, Rra Puleng wished to catch and raise ostriches, which were far stronger than pigs. In any case, I should proceed with the rabbits in the way I felt I should.

The other item to discuss was that I was accumulating a surplus of unused credits, due to my working more hours than were required to cover my necessities. I said I wondered if it might not be possible to donate some of my surplus credits to one of the older senior women, someone not able to work much who might enjoy some luxuries. This was a hit. I could tell because when Dineo was very happy about something she would wince, à la manière de Humphrey Bogart.

Then what unnerved me began. We were talking generally about how I liked Tsau, and she was, I thought, guardedly probing me by expressing surprise that I had heard nothing about Tsau in, say, Kang, where she knew that people told many stories about Tsau and in fact referred to it as the village where women eat before men do. But right in the midst of this she abruptly got up and said I should follow her to the bathhouse.

I had only seen the bathhouse from the outside up till then. It was one of the oversized rondavels sited in the broad stony shelving area lower down and around to the east, where the kitchen, the laundry, and the clinic were, as well. Why was she taking me there? Was I supposed to be taking a hint about my person? A facetious thought, but it shows how mystified I was.

The bathhouse was empty. The floor was stone, with movable wooden pallets scattered over it. You could see fairly decently by the wash of greenish light that came from two wide units of tinted glass brick set into the wall on either side of the door. Dineo pointed out that there were two kinds of tubs to use—standard squat plastic washtubs or tall wooden cylindrical tubs that you had to get into via stepladder and secure against tipping over by means of ponderous hook and eye catches around the bases. The purpose of the tall tubs was to make it possible to have warm water up to your neck. I gathered you sank down until your knees hit the tub side and that then you sat in this cocked position to your heart's content. All the tubs and pallets could be shifted around so as to bring your particular tub under one of the three spout pipes that supplied water warmed hot to tepid by a solar apparatus on the roof. You pulled your spout down toward you via a rope. You had to pull fairly hard. Three pulls were the limit per individual and would be enough for a good bath.

Remarkably she began matter-of-factly undressing as she explicated the bathhouse. In fact she handed me her clothes to hold. She kept talking. I should feel free to make use of the bathhouse anytime I was tired of having only the shower at Mma Isang's. For the present there would always be only women using the place, but soon the men would be given particular times of their own and a cloth would be hung by the door to say so. I should always cover, meaning lather, myself with soap before I pulled the water. And so on. There was no allusion to what she was doing.

There was no reason that I could detect for this scene to be taking place. She took off everything except her scarf. She pulled on one of the spout pipes enough to get a slight flow, but she didn't do much more with the water than pat her face and underarms. Her body was very good. Clearly she had never nursed. I think that for a few seconds I literally had no idea where I was. I was intensely uncomfortable. I was seeing something intentional and not casual, but uninterpretable. It wasn't sexual in any sense I was aware of. There is no serious modesty about the body among Batswana, except as regards the female pudendum, and even then it's pretty much the introitus soi-même that seems to be what counts. Tswana men aren't moved by the naked bosom or by female nudity generally to anything like the same degree as makhoa. Was it that she wanted me to know that, for her age, she had a body virtually in the hood ornament class? Her pubic thatch was the narrow and mainly vertical strip, not bushy, that you see turning up more and more in masturbation magazines like Playboy. Hers was natural, but I'm sure the ones in the magazines are artifacts created because the perfect fantasy for the male salariat is apparently a chimera with wetnurse breasts and a waxed and thinned preadolescent escutcheon. Where this leaves us more bouffant types is a question, I suppose, and just one more thing to feel imperfect about.

I did notice that she had a jagged, rough-textured scar starting at her navel and leading straight down into her escutcheon. This was wrong for an appendectomy, so I figured it meant that she had had a hysterectomy. It occurred to me that she might have wanted me to notice the scar. I was at sea.

This was not an extended event, interminable as it felt. Dineo got dressed quickly after her mock ablution was done. She never stopped talking. There was nothing languorous about the tone of things.

As we left, Dineo pointed at a stand of pawpaws next to the bath-house. They were watered by the graywater from the tubs. People are joking as to the rinsings of women being so sweet and strong, and they say if you want to taste what is a woman, taste these fruits, she said.

My notion that she was Denoon's lover seemed vapid to me after-ward, although I didn't know why that was.

Gaffe Fest

I treated his four days away as nothing when he came back. The last thing I was going to start off with in our relationship was a thrust that would stir up any phobias about personal restrictions, notifications, free-dom of movement. I couldn't help feeling that in his retreat there had been an intent to test me, to see if I was truly up for such an abruptly and highly mobile character as himself. Also I suppose I was thinking that if we did ever move in together and were going to avoid the inevita-ble claustral feelings that being confined within socializing on one koppie would entail, then he would—and maybe even I would—need to have recourse to overnights away from the hotbed of interactions Tsau ob-viously was. He told me that he usually stayed away at most three days on these personal retreats, but this one had been prolonged by being combined with a little fieldwork on an ostrich-ranching project he had in mind.

We had advanced to the point of his coming to dinner at Mma Isang's. For the first couple of times Mma Isang was included, but thereafter although for appearance's sake we would convene in her place, she would take her food and go off into my rondavel to eat. She insisted. She was part of the sector of women whose sentiment was that he and I should get together. I had a straightforward interpretation of this sentiment at the time: I assumed these were people who wanted Denoon to stay as long as possible in Tsau and who saw that ultimately his intimate status—if this was the truth about his status, which I was resisting accepting—his celibacy, not to put too fine a point on it, would drive him to leave town. After all, it was now generally known that he was on the point of being genuinely divorced. So change was in the air. Intellectually I could see why celibacy for Denoon was a plausible choice. Any liaison with a woman of Tsau would have meant compromising his role as above the battle, would have meant choosing a person from one tribe over all the others, would have complicated both his status and the status of the woman he chose. Also, Tswana women want children and they want them now. To all of which had to be added the question of his professional image as someone who tries to set up and then depart from self-sufficient politico-economic entities not tied to the coffers of the West and certainly not tied to the charisma of one man and a white man at that. Nor in the case of Tsau, where the point was female equality and dignity if it was anything, would it be very palatable to take a wife of convenience, a town wife so to speak, and then either leave her behind insultingly or take her with him when he left, thereby demonstrating to all her sisters that the real bingo in life was to escape to the metropolitan West in the arms of an icon. I could see that from some standpoints I would be perfect for him, if it could be assumed that I genuinely liked Tsau, as I seemed to, and was in no hurry to decamp, and that I was who I seemed to be.

There was one embarrassing dinner. I inferred that Nelson was feeling carnal by the way he was trying to keep abreast of Mma Isang's movements and when she might be returning. Patently he was trying to find out, without asking directly, if Mma and I had worked out a specific time when she might be expected back. I was unhelpful. I was teasing, partly because during our moonlight walk he had been so unforward, partly because of his four-day absence. So there was a mild revenge comedy in progress.

No question, teasing is regressive. I rarely do it, but when I do I justify it with the conceit that there's some allowable quota per woman I've never come close to.

Denoon was dressed up, for him. He was wearing his ludicrous billowing drawstring pants, a clean blue tunic, and he had shaved just before coming over and so looked rather gleaming.

The entrée was a baked carrots and groats dish I'd thought up. This was an all-solar production, which he was bound to love if only for that.

In my travels around Tsau I had heard that Nelson had drifted into the primary school and noticed that in a child's drawing of a horse tacked up in a display there was a cloud where the animal's penis should have been. The original outline of the penis was still dimly discernible under the erasure cloud. So Nelson had then established that puritanically a teacher had told the artist that the picture wouldn't be put up unless the horse was altered. And Nelson had taken the matter up heatedly with the schooling committee.

Is this really the issue level you want to be identified with? I asked him.

He said Are you saying I was ultra vires? which was the moment—we later agreed—we discovered we both had studied Latin. Later this was a bond. We both loved Latin.

I said Hardly, since I have no idea what your limits are institutionally, or rather juridically, around here. You seem to be ex officio on most of the committees I know anything about, or at least you turn up whenever you want and nobody asks what you're doing there. Also since this place is your idea, you presumably derive some rather indefinable kinds of powers from that. I do have the impression you're becoming slightly more emeritus, but that's just my impression. It's cloudy to me, is all.

Pointedly, I thought, he declined the opportunity to enlighten me in this area. He went on eating appreciatively, even murmuring that he wanted my recipe. So I just repeated my opinion that it was beneath him to be agitated over whether a teacher tries to keep a child from drawing a horse with a large penis. I in fact was aware that the penis in question had been of caricature dimensions in the original drawing, and also that the artist was King James, no less.

He said Isn't censorship an issue we should be concerned with?

It is if you're the Botswana Civil Liberties Union. Are you? Or are you more like an inspector general? This led to more silence.

I got frightened. This was close to nagging and he was uncomfortable. I klang-associated for something light to say and came up with Do you know how the Batswana describe a henpecked man? He didn't. I said They say he's a man who eats his overcoat. People laugh when they say this and I even laugh myself, but they can't explain why this is funny and neither can I.

I had stumbled on to something that interested him a lot—Tswana humor. Did I know any other Tswana jokes?

I was relieved that I did. I knew one other joke, exactly one. I do, I said. And then I realized what the joke was, too late.

It isn't a joke, I said, it's a riddle. It's not a joke, actually, at all.

He wanted to hear it. I couldn't believe what I had done. I even tried to instantly make up a joke or riddle to replace the one I was going to have to produce otherwise. My faculties were frozen. He was waiting.

Well, the riddle is Do you know why the penis always lands up in trouble? You don't know, and the answer is that it's because the penis has only one eye.

He laughed, and nondutifully. But I was mortified. So far everything I was saying hinged on the penis in one way or another. I am such a fool. But I was also gratified at his lovely laugh.

Brilliantly then I conceived that what I should do to defuse my apparent fixation on this item was show how little the subject meant to me, despite what he might think, by going even more for the jocular. I was trying to show insouciance.

So I said Along these lines, this might amuse you: when I was in high school and in a timeframe when the first names of my three best girlfriends all ended in the letter i, we used to ask one another if a particular boy we had been, say, necking with, had been *sincere*. Sincere standing for having an erection, naturally.

He thought it was funny, genuinely. This is new, he said. This is news.

How alone are we? he asked. But just then Mma Isang showed up. I maneuvered to let her know she should stay. I felt like a fool and a coquette, but this is where I wanted the evening to come to rest.

Causing active ongoing pleasure in your mate is something people tend to restrict to the sexual realm or getting attractive food on the table on time, but keeping permanent intimate comedy going is more important than any other one thing. Naturally it was living with Denoon that gave me this notion in its developed form as opposed to the bare inkling I got during the evening in question. I'm not talking about having a sense of humor you apply to the ups and downs of living together. I'm talking about being comedically proactive. Ultimately I was better at this than Denoon was. I don't know why being funny for someone was such a new idea for me. It had never occurred to me in connection with any other male I had been serious about. Denoon had early on made it clear I was free to include him and his foibles as ingredients and props in my routine if I felt like it, by not objecting when I did. So he was different. Or was it just that I was dealing for the first time in my life with an actual mature male, a concept which up until then I had considered an essentially literary construct and a way of not asking the question of whether or not in fact the real world reduced to a layer cake of differing grades of hysteria, with the hysteria of the ruling sex being simply more suppressed and expressing itself in ritualized forms like preparedness or memorizing lifetime batting averages that no one associates with hysteria. I was surprised at how pleased I felt to get such deep, easy, thorough laughter out of him.

Nelson was extremely nice when we discussed my penis gaffe fest much later. The way he comforted me was interesting and involved a conceit we used in later connections. He wanted me to know that the penis sequence had been sub-rosaly titillating, particularly so because it had been clearly so accidental. You never tease, he said. He said There is a school of thought, a heresy from the madhouse of heresies in the ninth century, that says God is good and is in control of every individual thing that happens, every event, but that unfortunately the devil is in control of timing. Hence, gaffes. Hence the actually existing world. Between us we could facetiously make use of this conceit, and laugh. Of course a conceit is different from something solid like the Stoic Maxim, Of all things in existence some things are in our power and some not, which is with me forever, also something I got from Denoon and made him defend as different from the pop variant of it in use in Alcoholics Anonymous groups.

Courtship

The below date from the end of our courtship.

▶ *Beware mood in men. N. palpably depressed by a split in some Spanish labor union. He is stalking around cursing a group called the renovados under his breath. His information is from a hectographed newsletter a year old which has just gotten here. It took a certain amount of temerity to extract even this much. All I wanted was to be able to help him reframe this bad news if I could, be less sad over it, be a shoulder to lean on once I had the basics of what was wrong. But I was told I would have to know the whole history of anarchosyndicalism in Spain from the Cro Magnon era, which he would have to take the time to tell me, before I could begin to understand about this. He's not disposed to do this for me, however succinctly, and the answer to the question of whether there is something around he can give me to read on the subject is no. Apparently he prefers to be down in the dumps about this, without any interventions by dear friends. I think I was brave to ask if there were also other areas in his life where tentacles of depression could suddenly shoot out and envelop him, turning him into a morose dinner partner without warning, to which he says no.* My aversion to mood in significant others is overdetermined and reality based. One centerpiece in my history is the three-month-long mood I plunged my mother into by accident one summer. I was going to do something pleasant for her. I had just gotten my driver's license via a long sequence of beggings and cajolings, borrowing cars, getting guys to teach me. It was a triumph for someone who was practically underclass. The first thing I was going to do with my license and the car I had borrowed was take my mother to a cabin on a lake for the weekend. It was going to be wonderful, one of the best things my poor barge of a mother had ever gotten to do. In any case what happened was that as we backed out of our driveway for our excursion there was a big thump. So I got out to see what was going on, and what it was was that I had backed up over my mother's suitcase, crushing and ruining it, the very suitcase, I was just about to learn, that meant more to her than any other possession she possessed, as she put it, because it had been a gift to her from her therapist and represented the only decent thing anyone had ever given her, allegedly, never mind my own pathetic outpouring of love objects from drawings to ashtrays to napkin rings to decoupage still lifes. The point seemed to be that the suitcase was brand-new. I assumed she'd put the suitcase in the trunk, and she assumed I would know she'd put it down where I could put it in the trunk, since bending to the degree necessary to stow the suitcase away would have been difficult for her. So then everything was off except misery. She was crushed. She was in mourning for the suitcase for three months at least. She was impenetrable to my apologies or the even more offensive offer that I somehow buy her an even better suitcase as a replacement. How could I conclude other than that emancipation meant liberation from people with moods. About the same time, my best friend Toni's mother went into a two-week funk because after the kitchen was renovated someone set a hot pot down on the new Formica counter and caused a faint brown semicircle, ruining everything, notwithstanding that Toni's father had the section of Formica replaced instantly. When later Denoon and I had a vehement contretemps over his assertion, during an up to then placid discussion of differences between men and women, that in contradistinction to men, women experience injury and injustice more strongly than they do good luck or surcease of sorrow, I had all this uneasily in mind but I still won.

▶ *He keeps asking me about morale here, which I tell him truthfully seems good overall as far as the women go, but that how happy the men are is ? We were out postprandially repairing antigoat fencing around the poplar plot next to the gum tree plantation. Young poplars are to goats as catnip is to cats. When I said morale among the men was a question, he was dismissive. All he would say was Men are only happy in prison or in the army. I am at a point where I suspect him of producing a few too many of these morsels and tidbits re the perfidies of the male race because he's under the impression I'll get off on them. So I'm being rather cum grano salis on these throwaway lines, for a change. How would you know men are happy in prison? I asked, and got I know men are happy in prison and the army because of what they fail to do when they get out. Most of them fail to avoid going back to prison. Second, they fail to say anything negative enough about what they've experienced to keep their affines and the young from risking going there. And you know men are happy in the army because when they get out they do nothing to keep younger men from joining up, and in fact they themselves join the American Legion to keep their memories of war and killing as fresh as possible and have circle jerks where they call anybody who's for peace commies, and a deep calm drenches the male soul when it feels the persona it inhabits being firmly screwed into a socket in some iron hierarchy or other, best of all a hierarchy legitimately about killing.* His misandry turned out to be a genuine if sporadic thing and continued, although accompanied by hagiographical asides re certain obviously countertypical men. In our exchange at the goat fence he picked up my skepticism about the sincerity of his attitude and abruptly and sternly went into an anecdote about a street performer who had been a fixture in his arrondissement when he was staying in Paris. This was an African guy, a magnificently muscled Senegalese who Nelson assumed at first was doing an escape act since he was bound up in chains and straining mightily against them. He was kneeling. But this wasn't an escape act, it was art. The guy straining interminably against his bonds was the show itself. What was interesting was the audience, which was made up overwhelmingly of fascinated men. Women would come by, take a look, shudder, be puzzled when there was no escape, and move on. But men were transfixed, and stayed, and kept putting money in the performer's skullcap. Explain this to me, Denoon said. Another time Nelson was claiming that there are almost no successful complete poems, that perfection should be looked for in fragments of failed larger structures, and I was suggesting he was conflating a human limitation—the tendency to retain only the more vivid fragments of poems—into a perverse cosmic judgment about poetry itself. In passing he quoted some lines he liked from an allegedly otherwise nongreat piece of poetry. An odd thing is that just hearing them that first time was enough to fix them in my memory. I think this is verbatim: The bald accountant back at his desk from vacation / Takes comfort in the president's angry order / The exile returning from honors in another nation / Feels a thrill seeing the first brutal face at the border. When I suspected disingenuousness on his part the most was when he told tall tales out of school about his gender and himself in particular. As: he was a freshman in college and he read a story by James Agee told from the standpoint of a cow en route to the slaughterhouse, a tour de force that affected him so deeply that his girlfriend gave up meat over the summer vacation— he kept on eating meat himself. So how to read this? As a confession of fundamental tendencies I should be forewarned about? As a demo of how clearly he grasped and disliked the traditional emotional division of labor between women and men? Or as something tendentious and mixed, ostensibly offered as a warning about even him while secretly intended to get me to appreciate him above all for his sterling evolution to the way he was now? I have fear and loathing of liars. I almost wish this were the nineteenth century so I could say something like You lie to me at your peril, to anyone who tried it. I had a glyph to indicate lying that I used in my journals, a circle with a line across it at different levels for probable different degrees of deception, id est an eye winking to different degrees. I see I even put a nota bene in my journal to watch for any reference by Nelson to himself as being a poor liar, which would be evidence that I was dealing with a real liar, in fact. This all makes me seem phobic on the subject. I was simultaneously trying to keep in touch with the fact that the approach of love can make you paranoid. I may lie when my back is against the wall. Obviously. Lies led to my existence in the world. I wasn't conceived through the association of ideas: somebody said to my mother that he liked her, was attracted, could be trusted. I think my personal utopia would be nobody lying.

We Engage

One evening after dinner chez moi he invited me to accompany him up to his place. There was a reason for it I forget, but it was really to show me the place: so far as he knew I hadn't seen it previously. It was changed utterly. He was being a bowerbird homolog. There was more furniture. The windows had been washed. Machinery and parts had been consolidated. Candle drippings had been scraped off surfaces where they had been prominent. There was now a significant water storage tank attached to the bathtub setup. I tapped it: it was full. Inside the house it was a wonderland of karosses, not only on the floor but tacked to the walls.

The song I hate most from the sixties begins I will follow him, follow him wherever he may go, and so on, whiningly sung. It epitomizes something humiliating. The prospect of moving in with someone always raises up fears of being the ignominious one, the supplicant, the camp follower, so it was very reassuring to see how delicately Nelson went about showing me his bower.

We held hands during the house tour and when we came out into nightfall both got the idea simultaneously of swinging our clasped hands in a parody of grade school handholding. Then came the embrace. There are ways to embrace a woman that are standard and there are ways that are perfect. This was the latter. If you're as tall as I am you begin to notice that men about your height always try to arrange for the first embrace-kiss sequence to take place while both of you are seated, so that they can subtly slide you down and deliver the coup de grace of the embrace, the declaratory kiss, from above, with your head bent back, and your throat exposed so you're like an animal signaling submission to a larger member of the species. The nice thing with Nelson was that no kiss followed. The embrace was not just the scaffolding for the great declaratory kiss. The best standing-up embrace is like that one, slightly off center so that you have his leg and not his actual téméraire up against you, one hand on the base of your spine, and you are brought in against him but not mashingly. His cheek is at your ear but not occluding your actual ear canal. His breath is in your hair. Then you want to feel him sinking against you, slightly, suggesting relief and repose: the embrace from something, not simply stage one in a campaign of possession.

So we hung against each other. I liked his smell. It was positive and faintly like a veal soup my mother made five or so times in my life when for some unknown reason she was elated about something. It was a trace smell subtending the soap, diesel, and smoke amalgam.

Who terminates the embrace is important also. It was up to me.

Not thinking why, I slid my hands down his spine and through the waistbands of his absurd pasha pants and his underpants. I spread his buttocks apart. I broke the embrace. I think he was amused. He asked me something like where I got to be so playful.

Anyway, there we were with Africa sliding into night, bats starting to circulate, the village turning into a brilliant code message as lights came on. It was up to me if we wanted to go further, but I held back. I would have liked to touch his beautiful sternocleidomastoids as thick as back-pack straps. I was happy. I was so happy. The feeling I had was that whatever else we could do for each other, we were going to be physical friends, friendly bodies. I determined when it was time for me to be escorted back home. I made some joke about having to get to bed early because I was probably going to be awake all night. I left him to figure out why this might be the case.

Snake Women

Some of the intervening steps to my moving in have to be left out, fascinating as every inch of the process is to me still. When we were looking back and talking about his Achilles-and-the-tortoise approach, I made him laugh when I asked if he didn't think my narcissism was the most interesting thing there was. I got control of my obsession with not exactly having been rushed off my feet as such as soon as I got to Tsau when Nelson said I was becoming a werewife. That is, for long stretches I was a normal companion, and then voilà when the moon is full I am an echt wife nostalgically fixated on the details of our sluggish courtship.

He claimed that it had been a distraction for us both when I became a snake woman. Being a snake woman was very honorific. This group earned huge extra credits at Sekopololo if it came back from a snake alarm bearing the culprit physically intact or, better yet, still alive. Joining the snake women was purely counterphobic on my part. I hate snakes.

The events the plaza bell was rung for were births, deaths, storm and hail, plenary meetings, snake sightings. Everything was supposed to stop and everyone gather.

I got to be a snake woman with very little ado. I was standing around during the shapeup that took place every morning outside Sekopololo. There was a blackboard propped up advertising the most deserving tasks —and the jacked-up credits you could earn by doing them—and there was a woman acting as a barker, touting particularly urgent tasks in a comic bravura style. I became friendly with her later out of sheer admiration. In action she reminded me of the traffic constables in Bermuda. Her name was Leto Mayekiso and she was the ex–household serf of a Bakwena headman. People acted knowing as to the exact manner of her manumission, which had something to do with the frequency of the unexplained minor fires that had seemed to plague her vicinity, although she was always able to show she was totally innocent. She had been freed but had suffered from some kind of informal blacklisting. There could be raillery from the crowd when she was touting work in the kiln or laundry, which she would never fail to describe as hotter than any woman should be expected to endure. In fact one of her main pieces of shtick was to dwell on how physically unbearable certain tasks were, obviously as a dare. The crowd would ululate appreciatively. I loved it all. She was about my age. She was very canny. If she saw Herero or Kalanga women coming to shape up she would dip into their languages. So far as I could tell she was a genuinely happy and satisfied human being. Anybody who can make the dour Baherero laugh has to be a genius. She was single. Happy people fascinate me.

So on a cold morning the bell rang and the scene around me dissolved madly: there was a snake sighting. Leto dropped the flywhisk she used in her performance and shot into Sekopololo. In the normal villages of Botswana snakes are taken care of by men, who go about it, in my opinion, fairly hysterically, their efforts usually culminating in burning down the perfectly good tree the snake has retired to and then hacking the carcass to bits with mattocks. The snake corps was made up of six trained women and two novices, one of them quite young. There was a fixed routine for dealing with snakes. Whoever spotted the animal was to stand there and blow a police whistle. The snake women would rush to Sekopololo and get into special, rather medieval-looking leather gear: there were greaves that you strapped to your shins under your skirt, a pipelike tube you slid onto your right forearm, heavy gloves, and a skimpy helmet or cloche that not everyone bothered with. Your armaments were like hypertrophied fireplace equipment—staves, tongs, long rods with pitch on the ends that you lit to smoke your quarry out of crevices, plus machetes, weighted nets, sacks, a stick with a wire slip noose attached. Dozens of snakes had been caught since the founding of Tsau. Several snake women had been bitten, none fatally. Beside the great aim of bringing the snake back alive or at least intact, there was an additional bonus for snake eggs. The skins were cured and sold, the skeletons were sunk in polymer and sold to biology departments somewhere, cobras and boomslangs were kept and milked for venom, for which there was also a market. The snake meat ended up grilled and cut into fragments and served as canapés at a celebration in the plaza.

On the spur of the moment, apparently, Leto came out and began pulling at me to come with her. She was inviting me to come fight snakes. There was some supportive ululation around me, so I said yes, hardly knowing what I was agreeing to. Then there was an adventure, at which I was essentially a nerve-wracked observer, ending in our trooping back with an only slightly damaged eight-foot-long rock python bound to a pole carried by our youngest novice and the little girl who had discovered the snake. I had been in terror throughout, but my companions claimed I had done a few helpful things, and they said they wanted me to join the group. I said Yes, you honor me.

Afterward I was extremely elated. There was an impromptu lunch set out for us when we got back. Denoon claimed all this happened on the very day he was going to ask me to think about moving in with him but that seeing me so elevated and involved with the group, he had decided to hold off. I think I do recall him contemplating me avuncularly while we were eating and being told how valiant we were. He even insisted he'd felt an extra attraction occasioned by my amazonesque accessories and general look. Only a fetishist would say that, I said. In any case, it would be a few days more until I was asked, and asked poorly, if you ask me.

I Am Asked

I was enjoying working. For one thing, I was very approved of for working more than I had to and for being goodnatured about volunteering my brawn for some of the heavier jobs. I liked being able to skip work altogether if I felt meditative. I especially liked shifting from one phylum of work to another and also that from time to time spontaneous singing would break out during certain kinds of gang work. These songs were real inventions. They were topical. There used to be something like them in rural Mexico. They were far removed from people robotically lip-synching along with the top forty, which was my closest workplace experience analog. Also work was transparent, unabstract. I was halfway into a state at right angles to my usual American median state of being in which you are in perpetual anxiety about the next thing that's supposed to transpire in your lifeplan, to the point that you can barely enjoy the thing you've just done or the plateau you've reached. Can you get pregnant? You do, but then will your child be healthy? Will it be popular, productive, and if it's a girl will she be assertive but not abrasive? And so on unto whether she is going to abandon you or not when you get old and burdensome. It resembles being a writer and having each book you write being judged essentially on how promising it is, what it augurs about how well you might do next time out. In America there are people who spend all year in agony because they don't know what quality of New Year's Eve party they're going to get invited to. Even in summer camp, which is supposed to be a respite, it was impossible to relax, because the Lutherans who were so charitably giving me a scholarship fixed it so that I was striving the whole time to rise into the next and less humiliating grade of the swimming competence hierarchy or be the object of subtle scorn—not that they realized it. All this was falling away. Partly it was just being with Africans, who are so much the reverse of the American anxiety. And who knows how much of my luxe and calme may have been my romantic reaction to the idea of the experience I was having rather than the result of the experience itself, by which I mean reaction to received ideas about the beauty of communal labor, women being in charge, and so forth. Another perfect fragment from a different imperfect favorite poem of Nelson's describes pretty well the way I was feeling: Zeno's arrow in my heart / I float in the plunging year. Basically the reason I don't know why I felt the way I did is because unfortunately we don't know what we are, anthropology notwithstanding, even though the reason I clutched anthropology to my bosom was because I believed that academic disciplines did what they said they were doing rather than being hotbeds of dominance behavior where disagreeing on the simplest point gets you into a Götterdämmerung with somebody or his disciples. Another layer of it all was the problem of my knowing that Nelson would no doubt love me more if I loved his system, which Tsau was, tout court. He would be happy if I was happy, he would be seduced if I was seduced, and so on into the night. So it was another bolus.

It was public when Nelson asked me to come and live with him. He chose a cream tea which happened to be particularly well attended. I'm still annoyed. He strode over and drew me to my feet as in some period movie. It was done to be observed. I suppose I betrayed myself to some extent, because I could have said We should talk this over later, but in fact my relief that the moment had arrived was too much. I did want it. I'd sought it. It could be seen as just one more instance of Satan controlling the timing. I accepted with a nod. Some women at my table said Ow! which signified surprise, pleasant surprise, and was just short of ululating on the applause meter.

We embraced. On my part it was dutiful but numb, and brief. A kiss, which I was in no mood for anyway, would have shocked the Batswana, who still mainly regard the act as outré.

I brought up his peculiar choice of venue much later. Horrifyingly his shortlived initial position was that he had chosen the moment on impulse and not out of any public relations consideration. I controlled the rage I felt, but I said You are a liar. It was over almost instantly, with Nelson admitting everything and apologizing and concluding by saying what a bad liar he had always been.

You are? I said in a tone that must have been more underlined than I intended. It made him look warily at me for a long time. He sensed something.

A Deluge

Nelson came to dinner that evening, bringing gifts for Mma Isang that served as a sort of joke surrogate for lobola. It was a nice touch. There was a small crowd hanging around. Individuals wandered in and out, giving good wishes.

The joke brideprice Nelson brought consisted of various delicacies of which I remember particularly a can of mandarin orange segments and a jar of marmite. He was trying to promote marmite as a spread. I had intimated to him that it would be advisable for there to be a general increase in B-complex intake. Marmite is yeast, so Nelson was reviving an earlier failed effort to get people to like it. He would say things like This is very popular in Australia. At our little leavetaking ceremony he was eating marmite demonstratively himself on water biscuits and buttering biscuits with it and passing them around the way hostesses do at parties where they've put hard work into a gourmet dip that isn't going over at all well. Mma Isang told me emotionally she would always be my mother.

We had a friendly entourage all the way to the octagon. King James made a thing out of saying the dung cart service was free. All my things were in his dung cart.

I thought I heard some distant ululating vaguely below us and assumed, wrongly, that it was just more good wishes for the hymeneal party. You get very used to ululating being the normal expression of high spirits and best wishes in Africa. In fact after you adjust to ululating as the norm, it makes applause seem strange and less delicate. Denoon agreed. Once during rest and recreation he had been privileged to hear Vladimir Horowitz playing sonatas in London, and it had been sublime. And then the applause had begun and he had experienced the bashing together of hands as a way of expressing appreciation as being animalistic, crude. In all my time in Africa I never learned to ululate, but not because I didn't try. Self-consciousness blocked me. I took the ululations I was picking up as equivalent to scattered applause for our getting together, leftover enthusiasm like the firecrackers you hear being set off at wide intervals on the fifth of July. Nelson stopped our progress a few times to look and listen. He had a different idea of what was transpiring, clearly, and so apparently did our entourage, which departed rapidly once they got us to our doorstep. What's going on? I asked him as we started my moving in. Maybe nothing, he said.

We kissed a bit, and I complimented the way things looked. The interior was changed utterly. I was extremely happy. He had applied himself to making the house something that would be more amenable to my needs, as he conceived them, down to placing little bouquets variously about. He was happy too, but I sensed I was holding him indoors and was proved right when he said Just a minute, and went out. I followed and found him standing at the edge of our terrace, gazing north.

All at once I was aware of the thick feel of the night. Denoon pointed: the stars were disappearing on a broad front north of us. A feeling like the one you get descending in an express elevator came over me. My shins prickled.

He said Do you have any idea what everyone is going to think if we get rain tonight? It would be the best omen you could imagine. He was elated. It was June and not a time when rain should be expected. Good, he said, they see it. The plaza bell had rung to warn people to get things covered up in case of hail.

He wanted to watch the storm descend, if it was indeed going to. The distraction was fine with me. We were shy. We had both been very shy discussing the bed. He had been apologetic. The mattress was new, double size, but it was still maize husk and not foam. There were a few foam mattresses in the stores house, but new households had a claim on them. I had insisted the mattress felt fine to me and that he should stop going on about it. What we both knew was that we had the moral equivalent of a wedding night looming. We were volatile. Our feelings, my theory is, were exceeding what we'd expected them to be. Mine were.

We got footstools and sat touching, facing the storm. The first lightning, like filaments, shone far away.

I took his hand. Are you willing the storm to come this way? I asked him. He smiled and said Of course. I am too, then, I said.

It crawled toward us, magnificent and immense. It looked organic, I thought, more like an electrified placenta than anything else. The breadth of the lightning display was amazing. It was transfixing. Earlier it had been cool, but now for long moments it was tropical and there were hot surges of air in the trees. The magnitude of the storm had not been lost on anybody in the village. Doors were being slammed, there were outcries, commands were being shouted.

Never have I seen any natural event like it. I shuddered and had pop philosophical insights, viz. human beings are microcosms of this vast oncoming system in that the thing that allows us to salivate and think and embrace is also electrical, in essence. We were related, this behemoth air beast and myself. I was its pale affiliate. Also I felt I was being acted on at some constitutive and possibly electrical level. I was terrified and wanted to get out of there, but something was preventing me from doing that, I mean besides Denoon's presence.

Tremendous thunder was involved, guttural at first but like metal ripping as it got closer. We stood up. Denoon put his arms around me. I happen not to be one of the many women who find thunderstorms sexually arousing. My associations with thunder, or more specifically long sequences of thunder, are, for some reason, with experiences in which you are helpless, the involuntary in general, and throwing up in particular. I've always been more or less phobic about vomiting: having to vomit, feeling it coming on, being in the grip of something wherein you're a bystander at some animal internal event, some overriding need of the systems that constitute you and that aren't your mind. As a child I resisted throwing up when I was ill, and regarded anyone who told me just to let it come as strange. If they went further and urged me to elicit the gag reflex, I knew they were insane. I would keep my head between my legs until my face turned black rather than surrender. During my first adventures in overconsumption of alcohol, when I realized that vomiting was frequently among the sequelae—which others might accept—I became pretty much a lifelong abstainer. Thunder is obviously a metaphor for something happening that no one can stop, which a good number of women I've talked to admit they find erotic, the idea of being overwhelmed, as by passion, notwithstanding how counterrevolutionary they know that whole thing is. But so are we made, some of us.

For me another link to vomiting is the destruction of my mother's last best chance to secure a better life for us. Through a friend my mother had gotten recommended for a job as a receptionist, with the prospect of moving up to bookkeeping. She was prepared to demonstrate that she knew bookkeeping. Her friend had coached her for a month. Concurrently my mother had been crash dieting in a pathetic attempt to get within armslength of normal overweight. My mother is not stupid. She is accursed but not stupid. She learned bookkeeping. But on the eve of her interview she had lost a trifling amount of weight and was still, by any standard, terribly fat. So in a moment of hysteria she decided that the thing to do to get the last ounce of fat off her that she could would be to induce vomiting. So she had gone into the bathroom and stuck her finger down her throat and, because she'd eaten virtually nothing, got almost nothing up. So she had performed the act repeatedly, enough times to burst every capillary in the whites of her eyes, thusly guaranteeing that she would show up at the interview as a certifiable movie monster with eyes like embers. In the morning, there she was with this condition. So it was her one big chance, she just knew, down the drain. After that it was aide positions in playschools. Don't miss your one big chance, was the message to me my whole childhood. Of course the one-big-chance-lost proposition is often a lie. Nelson's father had a one-big-chance story too, which was supposed to explain his ending up in advertising. He had been given a partial scholarship to a place called Brookwood Labor College, which had he gone to it might have changed his life. Other people who came out of Brookwood had gone on to do significant things in the labor movement. But his mother had either refused to give him the little extra he needed to support himself at school or in some even more insidious way had put a spoke in his wheel—she was a follower of Father Coughlin—so that naturally he had been forced to drink his way through life thereafter and apply his genius to being a brilliant sellout in advertising, the obvious antiprofession to leading labor for a living.

The storm was a cage sliding over us. I wanted to retreat to the octagon, but Nelson wanted to stay put until he felt rain. Staying there was ridiculous. The thunder was so shattering you wanted to get down low. The ozone smell was cutting, a stench and not just the usual tinge. I relinquished our embrace and decided it would be better to annoy him by pulling him back with me than see him electrocuted before my very eyes after I'd come this far. Lightning was streaming over us and striking the summit of the koppie. I swore to him I could hear rain coming.

There was a roaring overhead I could hardly credit, and then the rain smote us—there's no other word for it. Nelson gave a cry of utter joy as the blast hit. He was overcome. He swung his arm in a circle like a demented softball pitcher winding up. Then he froze, spun around, and dashed past me into the house, shouting something over his shoulder.

He had remembered about the roof. When I got inside he was manically unfurling plastic sheeting everywhere. Water like a jagged blade was already coming down from the roof join. I helped.

When that was done we went back to huddle in the doorway, jammed together like people in the hideout cave behind the waterfall in B movies. He was ecstatic, and it was a lovely sight and, to me, proof that Tsau was not just something he was doing with his left hand or in an exhausted or pro forma way or as his final practical joke on someone or other. Come on, he kept saying to the deluge. We all want a passionate man. This may be the man, I thought. I realized you never see a man in a state of public joy except in connection with professional sports, stupidly enough. His arms disappeared to the elbow when he held them out into the solid glassy sheet the rain made, pouring beyond reason, and when water from inside began purling out between our feet he was the happiest yet. I went back in and started peeling up the karosses on the floor before they got too saturated. I heard him singing. He did come in to reascertain that the roof over the radio area was sound and holding.

The rain roared on. Now there was the secondary roar of the flow in the catchment systems above and all around us. For twenty minutes, we watched while the rain went from a sheet, to vertical lines, to diagonals. With his hair matted down, I could see that Denoon had the beginnings of male pattern baldness. For his age it was slight.

There was a certain divergence in our attitudes now that the rain was slackening. It was hard for him to contain his elation at the drenching Tsau had gotten and what it would mean. But I was thinking about the mess our place was in. Water was still coming in from the back someplace. Was this supposed to be my particular province, when I could hardly be said to have even moved in properly? Incredibly he was making as if to go out, leaving me with flood relief responsibilities vis-à-vis all our goods while he went to see about damage elsewhere, how particular sluices or channels had held up. I asked myself what a genius would do in my situation. Ordering him to stay and help on our first night as a ménage seemed dubious. But then so was the idea of my meekly becoming a charwoman while he attended to the putatively greater needs of the populace, then my fixing myself up nicely and then waiting for him to come home so our intimate life could commence. I know myself, and I knew that that experience was almost designed to leave me in a carnally unenthusiastic state.

So I said something on the order of Do me a favor and don't go off to check things out until we get the basics under control here, and if you do I'll tell you something interesting about thunder I bet you don't know. I guaranteed he'd find it interesting.

He went for it. One of the virtues of studying anthropology is that you collect hoards of information on intriguing subjects not strictly germane to your specialty. He knew this about me already. How many students of computer science or, say, communications know that all over Europe the corpses of hanged men became the property of the executioner until late in the nineteenth century and that executioners conducted a lively trade in bits of flesh, selling them to apothecaries who used the morsels in various nostrums. How can I ever regret going into anthropology? The blood of freshly hanged persons was popular as a medication for epileptics, also. I had leverage over Denoon with informational sweepings like this because his anthropology was out of date and because his, I would say, premature rejection of the discipline meant there was lots he didn't know, thanks to the information explosion. And not to know something that might be somehow germane to his hubristic project in the world made him alert and uneasy instantly. He knew I understood this position he was in, but it was okay.

So as we worked I told him what I could remember about findings showing that infrasound waves just below twenty hertz associated with approaching thunder seem to have strange effects on the temporal lobe in some part of the population, to wit producing feelings of baseless awe and ecstasy. The theory is that certain types of chanting in the special vault acoustics of churches, the sounds certain ritual horns and bull roarers emit, certain organ notes, reproduce the same effect. And then by a miracle I remembered the names of the seven or eight out of ten founders of major religions who were suspected of being epileptics, epilepsy being a temporal lobe disorder par excellence. I have to say he loved it, which was because he loved the idea of a biometeorological cause for the existence of one of his bêtes noires, religion. This was right up his alley, as of course I'd guessed it would have to be. He questioned me pretty closely. My thunder theory immediately ousted the theory he'd previously liked, also biological, which has religion resulting from consumption of the Amanita muscaria or some related mushroom. This was a theory he was glad to relinquish because the case was weak but also because it was the brainchild of a wealthy person whose occupation in life he highly disapproved of. I think he was a banker, or bankster, as Denoon found it amusing to call them.

Then he did go out, but he surprised me by being back in forty minutes, having obviously resisted the urge to wander more exhaustively through his beloved infrastructure. It was because I was there.

All was well, then and almost immediately thereafter.

After the Rain

The next morning when we went down into the village quite a few of
the women we saw shoveling and bailing and wringing things out were
wearing the peculiar skirts that could be buttoned back into pantaloons,
I observed, which prompted me to admit to Denoon that my previous
attitude that the design was silly was wrong. This was clearly a practical
costume for vigorous manual labor. He was pleased. You take things
back, he said. There may have been an implication that not all women
did, but I didn't pursue it.

People seemed to be elated about the rainstorm almost to the point
of hilarity. Everyone was out. Everywhere we went I got credit, naturally, allusively, for bringing this fortune of rain, as it was put, by moving
in with Rra Puleng. It was genuine. Some of it was fairly bawdy. I forgave
Denoon for wanting to get going so early, seven o'clock, so as not to miss
seeing the body politic up and mobilized and talking about the great
storm. School was canceled. My only problem was that after a while I
didn't know exactly what it was Denoon and I were doing. We just
seemed to be making a royal progress, looking into things. Supposedly
that was all right because Sekopololo was closed down too. There was a
good deal of singing. Two groups were singing hymns. Ke Bona I heard
sung a few times.

I can hardly say our first breakfast at home together was intimate,
since Nelson ate standing up while I slowly gave up on being fetching in
a reclining mode in the face of his determination to get downtown. He
thought my calling the plaza downtown was amusing.

The smell of the Kalahari after sudden rain is something you never
forget. What blooms up, especially when the sun gets to work, and even
in cool-tending June weather, is an odor so powerful and so elusive that
you want to keep inhaling it in order to make up your mind which it is,
foul or sweet. It seems poised midway between the two poles. It's resin-
ous or like tar, and like the first smell of liver when it touches a hot pan.
It fades as the dryness returns, and as it does you will it to persist until
you can penetrate it. It's also mineral. Nelson thought I was hyperventi-

lating, until I explained. I think he said he agreed it was remarkable—I had gotten to the point of claiming the smell was red, or maroon, somehow—but that if he didn't react as strongly as I did, there was a reason. I've been here longer than you, he said.

Exuberating

Our mobile dolce far niente continued all morning. I was very conscious of his body as we went around mutedly reveling in the effects of the storm. We had made love twice so far, majorly once and then minorly, so to speak. I wanted him to be as attuned physically to me as I was to him, be in my aura. He was a good lover, a very comfortable lover, and also courteous as hell. In fact he had rather formally thanked me both times, as though there was only one beneficiary in our exertions and not two. I wanted him to be comfortable, now that it was settled that he was fine, and not feel he had to mark our getting together by being nonstop about sex. He was not in the first flush of youth, which I had to be sensitive to to some unknown degree. He was a young forty-six or seven or eight, was my guess, but which was it, exactly? I had a quasi right to know. I suppose I felt this as one of the threshold questions. Some others were What about Grace and what was all the grimness and unpleasantness in their breakup due to? Had he loved her? Also, what had he been doing about sex lo these several years? Had he masturbated, for example, as one answer, and how would I feel about it? I have complex attitudes, not all rational, on the subject. These were questions I could pose only after getting as close to Denoon as I now was. I had to be inside the moat. There was nothing violently preconditional about this. I was not going to rush. But I am at the opposite end of the spectrum from someone I know who, the morning after the first night with whoever her new friend is, says Tell me what I have to do to keep you.

Siesta that day was nice, and showed Nelson wasn't under a compulsion to complete lovemaking each time certain customary points of no return were reached: he understood about promissory occasions and seemed to like them all right. He had a proposition about cooking. If I didn't mind, he wanted to cook our dinners unless something came up

or I specifically asked to. Was that all right? I said Does Julio Iglesias own
a sunlamp? but I had to explain that this was in the genre of Is the Pope
Catholic? Nelson had never heard of Julio Iglesias.

He wanted to go out again in the afternoon and continue exuberat-
ing, and he wanted me to come with him. We had already done the few
really necessary things like checking on the nethouses and the windmills.
People were saying that the rain had been so heavy that standing water
could be seen at some low places in the sand river. They were organizing
parties to go and exclaim, so we went too. It was true. We had also
already toured the few trees, mostly on the summit, that had been struck.
There were loaves of sand and silt at the mouths of the main north-south
streets, but by midnoon they had been shoveled away. The supports to
some of the overhead lattices had slumped, and in places pavings had
been undermined. No hail had fallen, luckily. Mainly people were ex-
travagantly occupied with putting drenched mats and karosses out to
dry. The day off was an excuse for celebrating this huge influx of water
to the community's supply, essentially. Nelson reminded people about
stopping off at Sekopololo for packets of chlorine for their cisterns. There
was a moment that took me by surprise as we were leaving to resume
whatever it was we were doing. I hesitantly asked Nelson if he wouldn't
wear his kepi when he was out in the sun. He owned one, I knew. He
was normally out in the noonday sun bareheaded, except in the depths
of summer. He looked at me. The back of your neck worries me, I said.
It looked cured. You probably don't wear the thing so you can avoid
looking like the French Foreign Legion, subconsciously, I said. But
please wear it. He still hesitated. I want you to last forever, I said, and
then my eyes filled up. Chronologically he was closer to death than I
was, and the thought was unbearable for a minute. It was not the last
time this would happen. He was immediately good about the kepi.

I was trying to be casual and as provisional and patient as I could, but
as we continued promenading and visiting a lot with people that day a
quirk of his seized me that I felt would destroy me. It was this. When he
was given something liquid, soup or a beverage of any kind, he would
swill the first sip around in his mouth for a noticeable period before
swallowing. It was an unconscious thing of some kind, a tic. I couldn't
stand him to do it. I knew it would be insane to say anything on such
short acquaintance, but there was no way not to. I had never previously
been with him continuously enough in convivial situations to have this
tic impressed on me. Table manners are fraught for me. I resisted my
reaction. My mother had made me a demonically fastidious and correct

eater, clearly abreactively to her own inner chaos and loss of control when she was faced with something to eat. There were periods when she would eat out of sight of me and then serve me my food and sit opposite me to monitor and correct my table manners. Up and down Tsau we went, taking tea or juice in various settings, myself embroiled in what to do about this gross thing he was repeatedly doing. I wanted to know where it came from. Even when she was supposedly sated and finished I could feel rays of greed steaming from my mother as I ate. Something rose in her every time she saw food, whether she was full or not, which meant to me later that this was a trait in someone who was definitely not meant to reproduce, because such a trait indefinitely replicated would mean the world gnawed down to its core, but in fact she had managed to reproduce and the result was me. For the time being I conquered myself.

Toward evening there was a general meeting where Denoon announced the readings on the main storage cisterns. The readings were wonderful. Even the men felt free to show they were happy, a mood helped by the fact that a heifer and two tolleys had been killed by lightning and would be donated for a town braai. I stood next to Denoon like a what? a consort? Why was I walking around with Denoon and being gracious instead of attending to things I could enumerate that needed doing? I comforted myself by reminding myself how rare such rain prodigies were.

There was a small hitch, it developed, regarding the dead cattle. Dineo and Nelson met over it, and no one said I couldn't bystand. The heifer that had been killed belonged to the Baherero. In a slightly anomalous arrangement the Herero cattle, though kept with the municipal herd, were vested in the Herero group separately. There was an arrangement obtaining to defray feeding and veterinary costs, through Sekopololo. In any case the Baherero had decided not to donate the dead heifer to the braai but to sell it to Sekopololo for the purpose. This was rather late in the day. All the animals had been field-dressed by then. Denoon was unhappy and wanted someone to argue with Martha, the Herero spokeswoman, to try to get her to keep to the precedent of making donations in cases like this. I was interested in the way Dineo diverted Denoon from doing anything, which was mainly by patently, to me, humoring him about how unfortunate this was but at the same time stressing that it could be seen as another vindication of her longtime belief that the Baherero would pull up stakes and go back, however they could, to Namibia whenever the government yielded to their insistence that they be allowed to go back taking all their cattle with them rather than leaving them behind. Someday we are going to wake up to see nine empty houses, she said. This was by way of being a subtle reminder to Denoon that his wager—that the Baherero in Tsau would stay even if the rest of their nation decamped for Namibia—would be strengthened if this small matter was not turned into a cause célèbre. He yielded.

It was dinnertime and I still could not get this man to stop touring the by now completely terminal cleaning-up efforts. When I whined a little he murmured something about seeing Tsau as an organism showing it could repair itself. Self-repair was important. It was the opposite of social decadence. And did I know the moment that Ignazio Silone had decided he was no longer a statist type of socialist? There was an essay on the exact moment, a classic, in fact. A flood had occurred in the mezzogiorno, and the local village people, who had always in the past undertaken to do their own disaster relief and reconstruction, instead this time—owing to the growth of the welfare state—sat down in folding chairs and watched in droves while the carabinieri did all the cleanup.

Do you know who I'm talking about? he asked me point-blank. I was straining to get the neuron to fire that would tell me who this guy was. I almost knew, I thought. It didn't come.

Then he looked intently at me and said Don't be in pain if you don't know.

Then he explained who this man was, what pleasure I had facing me when I read a novel of his, *Fontamara*, which he even thought he had around somewhere. By now we were at last back in the octagon.

Supper was ready by the time he'd established he was unable to find *Fontamara* anywhere. I didn't mind cooking while he searched. I love someone who takes a serious tutelary attitude toward me, so long as he's not doing it just to turn out another member of his cult. It has to be ecumenical. The idea of having someone want to improve me and fill me up with new ideas rather than punish me for my lacunae is tonic. I see myself as quite perfectible. It always surprised me how few pygmalious, polymathic men had ever been interested in sprucing me up, given that I'm so interested and available, and that, as everyone notices first about me, I remember everything.

As we were eating, my face got hot when I realized that I had come within an ace of saying Yes, Silone, the fascist or profascist. I had been thinking of Céline. I thanked god my mind had failed to provide. Silone was an icon of humanist socialism.

Just to illustrate the depths women live at emotiono-intellectually: it occurred to me briefly that I ought to confess my near miss over Céline. Can This Marriage Be Saved? I thought, to josh myself out of my cravenness. I had been saying that to myself all day, as a matter of fact, when I realized I had things to do other than roam around with Denoon sampling civic joy but that he seemed to be in his element. Can This Marriage Be Saved? was a column in a women's magazine my mother occasionally shoplifted from our local supermarket, which she would study fixedly, every page, as though this was the manual that was going to teach her how to become a normal person.

There was more about socialism, free associatively, as we ate and washed up. It was mostly against socialism as an orientation or aesthetic or feeling instead of socialism as being about concrete institutional propositions that could be shown to work or not work. A form of stimmung, I said, which he liked. There was a socialist magazine whose charter issue had the epigraph Socialism is the name of my desire, from Tolstoy, over its manifesto. They had no idea what they were revealing about themselves, Denoon said. Socialism was becoming a bibelot. Student socialism was essentially an art school phenomenon. He shuddered to think of how few socialists there were who could define marginal utility. And so on.

That this man loved to talk was obvious. Also, I was appropriate for him, as a listener if not exactly as a discussant, although that evolved pretty quickly. He had been an isolated limb of the West for long stretches. I was a denizen of the same academic subculture he was from. When I got up in the middle of that night to go out to the latrine I inadvertently woke him. As I got back in with him he asked if I felt like talking, being quick to say that it was all right if I didn't and wanted to get back to sleep. I think this was prefaced with his saying I was stimulating. Of course it was fine, how not?

It was just that he wanted me to not misunderstand him when it came to socialism: he could be considered a socialist in the noumenal sense of being for a society where human self-realization and liberation were a general outcome and not an outcome only for the most talented or driven or unscrupulous in any given generation, and their heirs. He wasn't going to bore me with all his specifications for the devices you had to put together to give you such a consummation devoutly to be wished. But also I mustn't be confused about him and unadulterated capitalism or think he thought anything but that the limited liability corporation was a virus that was devouring the world. Underneath everything in America he sometimes imagined there was a subliminal sound like an orange crate cracking when you stand on it, except that this sound never stopped. When Nelson really got rolling and interested in what he was saying at night he liked there to be a light on, just a touch, one candle, I now discovered. We need socialism, correctly specified, he said, or rather we need the soul of it or its noumen. But then nervously he said When I say we I don't mean to be incorporating you into my construct in some subtle way, by the way. It's all right, I said: I'm not *not* a socialist, if that's any way to describe yourself politically. You could call me a nihilo-liberal. He laughed. I meant it, though.

It turns out that being in a symposium lying down in the small hours when all you want is to be asleep is a little akin to being asked to bleed to death. I ultimately developed a slight capacity to intersperse dozing with a murmur here and there before I dropped off that was satisfactory, and a murmur when I came back to consciousness again briefly. I was fading. The problem was that calling yourself a socialist put you in the same pew as people who had a purely reflexive concept of what socialism would be: it would be whatever came after capitalism was undone, and it would be beautiful. The mind the new left had been the most at the feet of took the position that all you needed to know about the oncoming free society was that it would be like the feeling you get from great art, beautiful music. This was decadence. Undergraduates had supposedly been going to be the midwives of the new society. Marx was the original offender with his attacks on the people who had the temerity to physically try out a particular concrete stab at the common life. He started naming them. Here I drifted off, only to come back to a more musing stream, particularly about me. I had gone to sleep with his arm around my shoulders, and he was patting me now to make a point. He was so happy we were both nonreligious and empiriocritical, because it was no good for a person to go along with a partner's strong convictions against something like socialism or religion as an act of will when in fact there were private residues to the contrary, residues of credulism. I assumed this was a meander fed by his parents' terrible mismatch or possibly Grace retaining Episcopalian feelings underneath it all. She looked Episcopalian to me, despite the fact that undoubtedly she had presented herself to him as his own tabula rasa. And the last of it was about purification, somehow, and was there a general human need for something called that, and wasn't that the element religion stuck its taproot down into, once it got started otherwise? Here was when I learned in passing that he had been an altar boy. I remember asking if by purification he really meant atonement, something I could understand better, a need to expel guilt over the thousands of transgressions you discover you've committed as you get older and more ethically acute. That wasn't what he meant. People could have done nothing and still have this other need. I was out of stamina. I fell deep asleep. There was something interesting afoot in the underbrush here but I missed it. In the morning I woke up being kissed on the leg.

I Should Tell Everything

My story is turning into the map in Borges exactly the size of the country it represents, but I feel I should probably say everything.

There was the ambience in our place after dark, which I think of as blond. The base was the yellow candlelight everything transpired in. I had inveigled Nelson to let me put up café curtains over the peculiar windows, custard yellow being the only color available. Why, he wanted to know, on a precipice, totally without neighbors? I said So that if anyone drifts by at the wrong moment they can't see my breasts and genitals and your penis and anus. He laughed and said But how about *your* anus? I overlooked it, I said. We looked very golden naked, and I think pretty good, although not perfect by any means.

People act more deliberately by candlelight. Your gestures are slower. I felt like an illustration, at times. Other things contributed to the honied atmosphere. Possibly the absence of an overabundance of reflecting surfaces was one. In America even the most spartanly furnished apartment is full of reflecting surfaces, from windows, through the glass in framed pictures, through the sides of your toaster, through actual mirrors. In fact the frequency of mirrors goes up, as a trompe l'oeil maneuver to make you feel you have more space for your money, as the actual square footage of what you can afford to rent goes down. I have done it myself in certain of the broom closets I've been reduced to renting. On the street it's shop windows and bus windows playing their part in the conspiracy to keep making you monitor how you look. Before Tsau, I knew something was wrong with it: I kept losing my compacts in high school until I stopped carrying them, thusly copying my mother in at least one trait. Of course I was still bound to mirrors as recently as crossing the

Kalahari, when I went into shock when mine was lost. Mirrors are bad. Africa is nothing if not matte, and that returns you to yourself, unexpectedly.

But I should tell everything. The underside of the thatch over us was golden-brownish, the unweathered side, and the karosses we'd spread liberally everywhere were medium brown to pale tan. One panel in the big kaross we had on our bed was auburn, exactly matching my hair. It was from a horse. Nelson was very deliberate, sexually, for a man, for whatever reason. I told him he should write a book called How to Undress a Person Other Than Yourself, which was an homage to the delicate and nonfoisting way he would undress me all the way down before touching his own clothing. At first while he was undressing me he would say Sh when I tried to undress him back, make things a little more mutual. Sh meant not to do that. After four or five times I was afraid of two things. One was that this was going to be some frozen onset ritual that meant hysteria somewhere in his past. The other was that this was revealing him as one of those congenital bores who think silence during sex is holy and who usually turn out to be men who have either barely or nominally escaped the effects of intense religious processing during their formative years. And of course I had just learned Denoon had been, however briefly, an altar boy. I was afraid I had an ex–burnt offering on my hands. But luckily neither was at all true. I guess I was overreacting to the politics of feeling that I had to always let myself be passively undressed, complicated by the fact of life of not minding it that much erotically. He liked my book title. He also liked a much later conceit for a title for a book by him, What to Do with Your Hands While You're Making Love. He knew how to touch.

What else? What hurt me? There was very little. Only that when he was apologizing about the ambience, viz. that we couldn't have anything to drink and he would have liked to provide a little something if he could, the fact was that he could have. This is in retrospect and still irks. At the time, what did I know? Of course I also withheld something on this subject. There was plenty to drink in the village if bojalwa was up your alley. I knew, but he didn't, that there were two functioning shebeens in Tsau. They were rather covert, but they were functional, and not only for the men. All this is symbolic only, because a drink before dinner is decor to me, and decor is a subject I have in perspective. I knew Nelson was very identified with the temperance tendency in Tsau, so I put out of my consciousness the feeling that he might have had the forethought to make an exception in my case by having a jug of Carafino brought in for him on the Barclays plane. He apologized for the limited range of the repertory of tapes he had to offer as background music for our evenings, mentioning in particular that he wished he had a cassette of the Academic Festival Overture, Brahms. The tacking on of the identifier Brahms silently killed me.

Undressed he became very laissez-faire. He was fundamentally sexually secure. The Herero beast had ended up on the market, not being donated for the braai. I was taking advantage of this little spike in the availability of beef and making a lot of soups and ragouts for us, as well as putting up quite a lot for biltong. Something about all this amused him. I got it out of him. You think I'm middleaged, he said, and red meat is good for my libido. I virtually had to cross my heart to convince him this was a piece of sex folklore I'd never heard of. There was nothing wrong with his libido. By the way, he said, I am old: I remember when science fiction was called scientifiction, which is old. He said You could call my autobiography I Remember Kolynos. What Kolynos was I had no idea, although it sounded vaguely classical or like a Greek place name. It was a major toothpaste from the 1940s. I said You are old, Father William, whenceforth Father William became part of our idioverse. He always laughed when I resorted to it, and, nicely, never felt any need to remind me that I was not, myself, younger than springtime. Ah, of course, he said in the middle of talking about being old, No wonder science fiction replaced scientifiction: it has one less syllable, so that's one more for George K. Zipf and the Principle of Least Effort. George K. Zipf was one of his intellectual gods. Re autobiographies, I said, A friend of mine who was teaching creative writing had a student who was writing hers and wanted to call it When Hair Styles Were Different, which I've always regarded as some kind of high-water mark for innocent banality. He liked it. I had no complaint about Nelson sexually in any way age-related. By laissez-faire I mean that anything went, once he was undressed. He would kid, he would say anything. Take me in your legs, was something he might say in a moment that you would think was supposed to be serious.

There was great sweetness to everything. I called it mellifluence, to myself. He let fall that he had been celibate for two years. I positively did not solicit or dig to get this. The thought was a source of excitement to me. Before he said anything, it was evident he was enthusiastic about us sexually. But this added. His drought was ending through me. Honeymoon is the word that inevitably comes to mind, but it certainly doesn't apply: we were both working all day every day, normally, and also without saying it we both knew we were superior to the term. He had in fact had an actual honeymoon with someone, and where had that led? I think we both unspokenly wanted to transcend certain social homilies about coming together. There was never a lot of individual fixing up before we made love.

I was the first with compliments on the sex side, saying I felt like someone who was just coming out of a maze. To which he said It may feel like that, but you're entering another one right away instead. I see that this is only in a meta way about sex. But then he praised my hair and breasts, two good choices. In fact, about my breasts he said something to the effect that if individual parts of our bodies went to specific heavens my breasts would be hand heaven.

If he erred it was on the side of being more consultative than he needed to. He was solicitous. I could be on top to my heart's content. Up close he had more hair on his shoulders and back than I had realized. He must have been fatter at one time, because there were striae on his buttocks and the sides of his upper legs. I loved our early sex. If it could be done I would drop down into reliving it over and over like those rats that press a pedal connected to their pleasure centers and press it until they die. This is only to say I wish I could relive it, god help me. This is too extreme. I become extreme, at times, still.

In the spirit of saying everything, he was uncircumcised. He had a significant penis. At first I had to deal with feelings that a smaller penis would have been more relaxing for me. There was a history to this. At some level an average or slightly less than average penis is always going to be a relief to me, thanks to my mother's berserk attempts to infect me with a specific sex fear. She must have had an unusually small introitus, assuming the whole thing wasn't a fantasy. She claimed she'd been harmed in a relationship with a man whose penis was simply too big for her, too wide across, as she put it. A woman should always find out if this was the case with a man lest she fall in love and be in for physical suffering. My present theory is that this was probably a fantasy concoction obliquely related to her becoming obese, justifying it, where fat becomes a form of armor against the possibility of all sexual approaches. But maybe she did have an abnormal introitus and this is unjust. She compared the hurtful penis to a Lebanon bologna and a rolling pin. Denoon suggested this scene might be transposed from a real molestation incident in her childhood, which had never occurred to me.

I think she also tried to warn me about uncircumcised men, but not insistently enough to leave a mark, evidently. I did examine his member fairly closely when we first made love, to his amusement. I was holding a candle up next to it, and he asked me to be careful re the molten wax. He asked if I knew that prostitutes in Gaborone, the more hip ones, carried lemons in their handbags which they would squeeze over the penis of a prospective if they were worried about small lesions or sores being present, an adaptation to the detestation by both sexes of the use of condoms. You know many things, I said, but not that I don't need that. He was holding a little jar of Vaseline. His wife had always used it, or something like it. He was embarrassed. I asked If the prospect flinches, what happens? Is the deal off or is the lemon juice considered a disinfectant? He said he didn't know. Clever of you not to know, I said.

In the act he was very orthodox, which was what I wanted. I wanted him to be solid in what I think of as the foundational part of sex. His endurance was good to the degree that I sometimes held myself back for a long time, although not often. The man had been celibate for two years, was a consideration. I asked him if he used particular images to retard himself. He said yes but didn't want to tell me what they were. I tried to encourage him by telling him a thing I do to move myself on, if I need to. There is a certain type of swing for young children that used to be common in parks in Minnesota, consisting of a square of piping with a canvas sling affixed to the front and back of the upper rim. There was quite a bit of direct pressure on your je ne sais quoi. My mother specialized in taking me to parks at dinnertime or even later because she was likelier not to encounter anyone there for her to have to talk to or act normal toward. She would talk to herself while she pushed me hard and interminably. I was tiny, but there were certain moments that were rapturous and erotic. It seemed to have to do with how long the swinging lasted. In retrospect I'm astonished that no one was ever prompted to inquire about this strange woman. We weren't always the only ones in the park, and my mother talked a lot. I was surprised when I discovered there were people who didn't talk to themselves pretty much nonstop in the privacy of their own homes. I thought it was part of adulthood. Nelson was interested in my story but still wouldn't tell me his images, saying it might be bad luck. He was very noisy, for a man. This is not a complaint. These bosun's chair swings were suspended by chains, not ropes, and the sound of the chains squeaking together at the peak of the highest rises, just before the strain came off them as you rose above the crossbar, is a sound that helps if I can reimagine it. His groans of release were a cross for me between music and food. I was convinced I could hear sadness going away when they came. I felt I knew he was sad about something he was unlikely ever to admit, but that these were moments when I could hear it going, being overwhelmed.

Afterward he would sleep like the dead, almost instantly afterward, it seemed to me. It was a tribute. He might try to converse for a while, but I was kind and let him plunge. I experimented some, as in seeing how loud I could talk or sing when he was asleep before he would stir. I perused him. He had the usual vaccination scar and one from a mastoidectomy. I had more scars than he did. Depending on how he was lying, I could take his sac in my palm and watch it slowly heave around, one of my favorite phenomena for its power to ground you utterly in the biological substrate of being. He was graying, but concentratedly, in his nape hair and behind his ears, more behind his right ear than his left. My utopia is equal love, equal love between people of equal value, although value is an approximation for the word I want. Why is it so difficult? Assortative mating shows there has to be some drive in nature to bring equals together in the toils of love, so why even in the most enlightened and beautifully launched unions are we afraid we hear the master-slave relationship moving its slow thighs somewhere in the vicinity? It has to be cultural. In fact the closest thing to a religion I have is that this has to be cultural. I could do practically anything while he was asleep and not bother him. I wrote in my journal, washed dishes in slow motion if we hadn't gotten around to them. I was emotional a lot, privately. I wanted to incorporate everything, understand everything, because time is cruel and nothing stays the same.

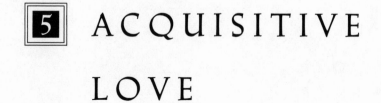

5 ACQUISITIVE LOVE

The Bathing Engine

The bathing engine was good for us. We were using it in fairly cold weather. Denoon would make the fire under the boiler and I would run out in my kimono when the tub was full of hot water. We would get in together and I would slide one of the litani mats aside so that we could look out into the desert. Denoon took the back position and I would recline against him. The bath hut was dim in a particular way that obscurely bothered me at first. Then through free associating, with Nelson, around why I felt that way, I was able to transcend. That made the bathing engine sessions auspicious. Confessional or difficult times between us came up there.

I would smolder over stupid things. In cleaning up I had found a copy of a radio message he had sent out in February after hearing that Bernadette Devlin McAliskey had been shot. It annoyed me that he knew her, that that was the level he moved at. I even imagined that maybe he had had something to do with her, since she was so superbly political, his kind of woman, and so on. We cleared that up. I was able to help him with his depression about Poland. He was expecting the Russians to invade and produce a bloodbath. Solidarity had been pretty much repressed, but he was still expecting the Russians. I gave him a useful rule of thumb. I said In the case of Poland, which would be more dramatic and historically interesting—for the Russians to invade the way they did in Czechoslovakia or for the government to manage things on its own with imprisonments and halfway measures and so on? He agreed it would be the first. So my rule of thumb was that of any two possible historical outcomes that you could possibly be aware enough of to obsess on, by some huge odds and for some unknown reason it would be the less dramatic and interesting that was likeliest to occur. This is one of those conceits that happen to be apposite, for the most part. He liked it well enough to urge it on me later once or twice when I was having similar megrims.

Being deliberate with each other was mutual. I had not done the usual swan dive women do when they start a promising relationship, which is to just deliver all there is about ourselves, the entire midden of past relationships, your first sex, your hopes, your dreams, the entire midden in a backhoe. We were wary and going through a more male process, which resembles two people sitting opposite each other and taking turns putting soupçons in the scales blind justice carries around and trying to keep the pans level. He was parsimonious because he was a man. I was parsimonious because I knew I was dealing with a feminist to whom a heart-laid-bare swan dive would seem stereotypical and also because I had had a shorter and, to say the least, more restricted life. So I felt it might be intelligent to ration my res gestae a little. I wasn't the one who had someone like Bernadette Devlin McAliskey to send a get-well telegram to or who got six-page letters from Hungarian socialists named Kornai, another name I had just added to my syllabus. The most famous person in my ambit was Denoon himself. But in the bathing engine the ratchet would turn a click or two toward greater openness. He was, for example, apparently worried about rifles.

Has anyone talked to you about rifles? he asked me.

About rifles? No. The main topic is still the rainstorm. Tsau is as full as a plum, and so on.

No one is saying Sekopololo should be stocking a few rifles?

No, and what is this about?

Probably nothing, but tell me if it happens.

I think it was to get off this subject that he, luckily as it turned out, brought up the question of what it was about the particular atmospherics of the bath hut that made me a little anxious.

What light is this like? he asked.

Well, it turned out that it was like the light in a treehouse some neighborhood boys had built, which I had been allowed up into in order to play doctor. There was a tarpaulin across the top and most but not all of the way down the sides, although you could get virtual privacy by sliding sections of cardboard carton over the open spots. There was a nice view. We were quite a way up. Access was via slats nailed to the trunk of one of the trees. My mother crept up on us. She wanted to know what was going on up there. I forget what we said, but it couldn't have been the right thing, because she decided she would climb up and see for herself, with the inevitable result that the rungs popped out of the tree under her weight right away, inspiring her to start howling like an animal. Come down! she screamed, all the while in her rage and berserk strength plucking the remaining rungs out of the tree, destroying, naturally, our only means of downgress. We could get a little way down, then had to hang and drop to our fate.

You were terrified, Denoon said.

Oh indeed, I said. But at least she never hit me. I was inviolate that way. Property was another matter.

We lay there silently for a while. Light breaks where no sun shines, he said, quoting something.

Already the feeling in the bath hut was different for me.

Vervets

Shortly after this I did begin hearing about rifles, in connection with a vervet monkey population explosion in the eastern wards.

I mentioned it to Nelson while we were eating dinner and I was getting him to admit he looked incredibly improved since he'd let me cut his hair. It was short, almost en brosse, parted over the left eye. I had teased him gradually into it by showing him how he looked with his long hair fanned around into pageboy bobs and so forth and calling him Prince Valiant.

He knew about the vervet problem. Male vervets are particularly distracting because their favorite pastime is to sit on your door or windowsill and display their electronic blue or lime green testicles, an act they intersperse with helping themselves to food items. I said that what I understood was being proposed was buying a couple of rifles to have available for hire at Sekopololo for situations just like this. I had been lobbied gently and had expressed myself as thinking it wasn't unreasonable.

Guns are not a good idea, he said, very curt. Then it was Who, exactly, talked to you?

Reason with me and I might tell you, I said.

He didn't want to. He wanted me to accept the general proposition. I was firm. I took a lighter tack, telling him about my pacifist friends in Palo Alto who had forbidden their little boy to play with toy guns. By the age of five he was so obsessed with guns he turned everything into a gun.

He would bite his toast into a gun shape. He aimed his banana at you at breakfast. This could be similar.

But it seems I was being infantile. There were serious reasons not to, among them the paranoia about Tsau in certain quarters in Gaborone. Certain people in certain ministries were in the pay of the Boers, who were convinced that somehow Tsau was giving aid and comfort to SWAPO, if not the ANC, or both. Everything that came out on the Barclays plane was monitored. He wouldn't tell me how he knew any of this. In addition, hunting was illegal where we were, in the Central Kalahari Reserve. Only the Basarwa were allowed to hunt, and then only with bows and arrows and blowguns. He would appear to be getting set to violate one of the founding conditions he had agreed to.

I thought that was all, but in a minute he went on more vehemently. Couldn't I see how it would go? Suppose we got a waiver and got a couple of rifles in. Then we would need a few more. Then the main thing the men would be doing would be clandestine hunting instead of attending to the heavier work they were doing now. The guns would be checked out by the women for legitimate nuisances like the vervets and they would be passed on the sly to the men. I was an anthropologist, so I must know that the oldest male racket ever invented was hunting, I of all people. Didn't I know how laughable the nutritional contribution male hunters made to the common diet was, everywhere? Which didn't stop them from acquiring status with the women in honor of their long hours drinking and lolling around out in the bush. So he was going to oppose it as long as he could. He was very unhappy.

So what were the women supposed to do about the vervet plague?

They should stop taking the line of least resistance and instead think of something. What did they do in the villages before there were guns? There were plenty of predators in the equation, which ought to take care of it over time, if people could be patient.

The vervets will spread, I said. They're already showing up around the kitchen.

Then poison! There was someone he could write to.

You're too rigid, I said. You try to preempt everything.

No, what I'm trying to do is preserve for as long as I can what's exceptional about this place so that something will survive once the hacking and trimming start.

Then I said, which I should not have, People say you have a rifle yourself.

Who told you that? he said, apparently outraged. I hated his murderous expression with its inner taint of shame. There was something worse in it. It contained the message that I was operating ultra vires. This stung me where I was already chafing.

Well, was it true he had a gun, or not? In fact it was. He hardly even knew why. The construction crew had left it with him, all right sold it to him, rather. It was for some emergency purpose. It was just an ultimate precaution. It was like having a fire extinguisher. And he wanted to know, seriously, whom I had heard it from.

I evaded that and asked him why in the name of god he didn't just take the thing and appease people by shooting a few vervets. I said Your deus ex machina is sitting on a shelf somewhere and you won't use it.

He was against shooting things. He tried to make a joke of that instanter, though, saying he kept the rifle around in case somebody tried to rape his mother or sister. In fact he was against shooting anything, against hunting, against killing live things with guns, he personally, and he was not going to loan out his gun, either. He was sorry he had the thing.

This is pure ideology, I said. This is the middle of the Kalahari Desert, where nature presents you with threats that require guns—in this case the vervets—but there are going to be others, believe it.

He was upset, but I admired the efforts he was making to calm himself down, involving structured breathing.

I got up and stood behind him. I said Would it be conceivable to continue this discussion while I was touching you? I put my hands on his trapezii. They were granitic.

This made him practically explode. He shook me off. Who was I to talk about ideology if I was bringing this encounter group crap into everything? This was pure Californian. Probably next I would want us to hold hands.

It was a calumny, of course. It made me mad. He was conflating the normal and friendly practice of calming someone down by massaging their trapezius muscles with an entirely different thing I had mentioned bemusedly and in passing on another occasion—a hostility-reducing technique I had heard of wherein you and your antagonist hold hands while you ventilate something painful between you, some grievance. I'm certain I mentioned it critically, although I may have said I thought it was vaguely interesting.

It's nonviolent aggression, he said, to which I replied Funny, it seems to me to be exactly in the stream of various little inventions you seem to have managed to get inscribed in the texture of things here, such as signaling for English, to mention only one. And what you're really saying is that it's inconceivable that you, a male, could take the hand of a woman and hold it during a serious argument, not even just to see what would happen. One thing I can tell you, and you can go into your stupid Californiad again if you want to, is that most women would be willing to try it. His riposte was Don't you want to know which kitchen utensil I feel like right now? By the way I am not from California, I said. I have nothing to do with California, other than attending Stanford.

Then it came to me that I could save him, if he would let me. Stanford had the full panoply of slightly ridiculous upperclass sports including skeet shooting. I had tried it. I knew how to shoot. If there was nothing unusual about his rifle, I could solve the vervet problem for him, he wouldn't need to apply for a waiver, there would be only one so it would be easy to manage, I would be responsible, etc.

Is that voilà, or not, I said. I could tell he was going to go along with it. He didn't like it a bit, but he saw it was a way out.

I imposed one condition, though: he would stop asking me for names, because it made me feel like an informer.

The rifle was a magnum seven millimeter, mainstream.

All right, he said, then, compulsively, I don't kill things.

I do, I said, sometimes.

Specimen Days

▶ *The vervets are going. Today shot 3 more and Prettyrose and another woman tried the rifle. Faint praise from N, ostensibly because there are only soft nose bullets for the gun, which mangle the target, so there is no point in skinning the dead animal, and the fur, which is probably good for something, is lost. My right ear is roaring and hors de combat despite the wadding. My deltoid hurts. Again a gallery developed, primarily male, animated by a Mongwaketse, Hector Raboupi, ca 35, glittering eyes, signature fur hat with jennet tails dangling in back, cheeks that bunch into knobs when he smiles and wheedles, teeth separated, like pegs. Drops into English without giving the request sign and also spoke* to me in Afrikaans for a little joke. He wanted to shoot and I said no. He said You are teasing on me. Idly unbuttoned his shirt while he was observing, ostensibly to get at something that was biting him but in fact to let show his sculptured torso. Something told me to shoot only the males, which was simple because of their iridescent testes. I disliked the actual killing but liked being part of the solution. Raboupi hates me.

▶ Raboupi again. I answered his English with Setswana. He is the postmistress's longlost brother. He says he is from Bokspits, which is not where I recall Dorcas being from. HR a migrant in RSA gold mines until, Dineo says, he was thrown out for fighting. He works for cash in the tannery. He thinks the mine compounds are the bright lights. He must hate it here. N is interested in him and concentrates when I repeat anything I can remember Hector saying. Why in the act someone seems to prefer one breast to the other is probably interesting. His foible for the right is not really pronounced. I am oversensitive because my right nipple is slightly higher than the left, making me stand compensatorily when I'm naked and I remember it. This will pass.

▶ I thought it was time to show interest in birdlife again and roamed quite far SW down the sand river, alone, too far. Looking back, there was only the blank side of the koppie, no sign of habitation. Panic came: all the fears I manage to keep separate fused on me: sand will cover Nineveh, Tsau is so strange it can't last, the land is so fierce, I am not being helpful to N, I should shut up more, something was going to happen to N if I didn't act perfectly, I am putting myself between him and Tsau, which he will never forgive, and so on. Seizure of hysterical appreciation for my parasol, so beautifully carved, the thong and strut mechanism, the batik chevron motif on the shade. I got parched hurrying back. Something would have happened to Nelson, it had happened, I was psychic, et al. But he was all right, he was preoccupied. I went to the pathetic library and calmed down.

▶ Last night, N: My lower self hasn't felt so good in years Your lower self, meaning what I think? Below the waist. Why couldn't you have said ever? I meant ever. Then a silence, and then N: I love having you go around naked in here. I never had that. Grace is uncomfortable naked. Then more silence. N: I probably get this from my father who subscribed to Sunshine and Health for years. It was to torment my mother, who *would never say anthing. He said he subscribed for the poetry. One of his favorites was O how I love to sleep out in the nude, wake up in the morning feeling gude. It was aggression. He got away with it because he subscribed to everything. The only reason he married a Catholic was to have a permanent martyr in striking distance. Nelson, you don't get it: I walk around like this because I think it's dirty. We laughed. N: Here is a man with advanced ideas, left, left wing pals, a humanist, and all he could think of to do with his life was see how much some limited woman from a tradition he was part of and hated and had gotten over could be made to suffer. He felt strongly about literature, by the way, and even ended a friendship with a crypto-Trotskyist on the police force over whether James T. Farrell wasn't a greater writer than James M. Cain. The drinking was also aggression. I like him to praise my body but also hate it because it makes me want to scream that I am going to be old flesh someday and then what?*

▶ *Doing dishes when N came up behind me and began feeling me up, friendlily. I said You may not be aware of the first commandment of feminism, so may I tell you? By all means. It's Don't grab or fondle the beloved's private parts when her hands are occupied, especially when they're menially occupied. This is not a rebuke, just a word to the wise. He stopped immediately and apologized. I said Usually it happens that men do it when the beloved is cooking or at the sink, suggesting that the sight of a woman engaging in domesticity is aphrodisiac. He said he thought the first commandment of feminism had to do with never using the imperative form to a woman unless she was in the path of a runaway bus. I was pushing the edges of our paradigm by using the term beloved. It went by unnoticed.*

▶ *I told N about the shebeens. He half knew, he said, but he looked surprised to me. We are both sick with kissing. My lips feel bruised. We have been kissing like adolescents for the last two evenings, intensely, to the point where you begin to feel anthropological about it à la an extraterrestrial voice saying Why are those two people mashing their oral cavities together and why is one squeezing the other's milk glands even when nothing comes out? Not knowing about the shebeens bothered him, or half knowing, to give him the benefit of the doubt. There is no village this size in Africa that doesn't have one or two, I keep telling him. But there had been an understanding with the charter women. Someone should have said something. So it went.*

▶ He disdains celebrating birthdays. Why? Because they celebrate pure duration. Revolts are all right, though. The Casas Viejas Revolt? and Bastille Day. Don't you celebrate anything in your life, Nelson? I haven't done anything to celebrate yet. You floor me. And I named his whole series of projects, names that are famous, listed in textbooks, discussed. He considers them failures. I said What about Tsau? Not yet. We want candor in the men we want, but not bleakness an outsider could easily mistake for perfectionistic posturing. I said You consider them failures? Have you informed your fellow stars in the development firmament or the groundlings who are still studying them in graduate school lo these many years? He could have said more about why he thought these were failures, which I wanted him to do and was inviting. But he fell grim, and I thought Reculer pour mieux sauter if you know what's good for you. All I added was Do you know how many people would die happy if they could fail at your level?

▶ 2 days tutoring English with the kids, which makes me maternal, which I do not need, so made myself do two afternoons in the laundry. N's concerned about people settling into doing only one or two categories of work, or only one, like the cronies who rule the kitchen. Raising and lowering credits works only up to a point. N says the phenomenon is mainly among older women and is not some general effect of the principle of least effort—that is, earning credits for the thing you know how to do the best and thus need to expend least effort on—but that if he's wrong then maybe they should think of some rule or custom that would limit the number of days straight in a row you could do one thing. I said that would be against freedom, unfortunately. Not if a group imposes a rule on itself and understands why it's necessary. What planet are you from? This is like Russia, where you have to wait fifteen years for a car because it's to the common good to dig the world's longest canal before anything else gets done. Also you may have heard of the instinct of workmanship, which is, I think, what I was alluding to priorly. But he was obstinate that Tsau was different. The example of the kibbutz, where the women ended up doing washing, cooking, and childcare, irked him, but the explanation socalled was that males ran the kibbutzim whereas here the base was female. I think I planted a seed, no more than that. A thing that corrupts N's worldview is his own demonic energy, which is what socalled greatness may in fact reduce to. He's unnatural. He can work six hours flagstoning or paving, scabs of cement stuck all over his body, a bite to eat, into the bathing engine, and he's all set to work late into the night

reading and writing and using his abacus. But clarity has to go with
energy. I think what I want is the feeling I got when I first read David
Hume, when I felt something like cold light bathing me. How much of it
would I feel reading Denoon as of today? Denoon has no copies of his
books here, I discover. He deprecates them. The past is a bucket of ashes
undsoweiter. In the morning I feel like a slug at times, N never. I have
never been the first one up, to date, which has to change.

▶   Somehow impress on N he is too fertile with ideas for the assets at his
disposal here. Projects within projects yielding other projects. I am cast as
the apostle of stasis. How would I like to live in a place like Gumare, and
so on. He is only trying to establish a propensity to keep trying things. He
is continuing with his ostrich ranching mania. I said You're going to go
out and trap ostriches, but how are you going to get a breeding pair? You
can't tell the sexes at the distances you'll be working from. You have to
get underneath them, practically. They're immensely strong. There are
people here who know how to catch them. Such as the great underem-
ployed hunter Hector Raboupi? Possibly. They said the same thing when
I said we could raise guinea fowl. Now that's thriving. Then he said Would
it be a good idea for us to set aside a fixed period every evening for arguing?
I let that go. The ostrich idea is with the mother committee.

▶   Gleanings re Grace. Her great beauty started it. Are you especially
susceptible to great beauty? was my question. I must be, he said. She tried
repeatedly to live overseas with him and to give up or suspend her career
in architectural history and preservation, but he would always urge her to
go and curate when the opportunity arose, or to develop as a consultant,
the original idea. Her desire to please was excessive: he had to convince
her she didn't have to say she enjoyed sex per anum. She said the only
question was if he enjoyed it. It made no difference that women have no
prostate and so have greatly less anatomical basis for enjoying it than
men. She plainly hated Africa but never said a word against it. She tried
to be interested in vernacular architecture, unsuccessfully: her heart and
mind were in the Baroque. He thinks two miscarriages in Tanzania, one
concealed from him. She was shy about nudity and he loves my whoresque
ways, but when pressed, yes, there can be something a little erotic about
conventual and hypermodest ways. She was attracted to Vedanta the last
he knew. He thinks she may end up religious because of her phobias re
cleanliness and contamination. Once they get going, all religions manip-
ulate and pump up human hysteria about contamination, a subject he

would appreciate more discussion of with me. I think I know a lot about lustration, if I can recapture it. She had an eyecup and rinsed her eyes with a solution, but not because she had conjunctivitis—to prevent it. She would pore over him for whiteheads. Her first reform for N was to never keep his comb in any pocket he carried money in, for hygienic reasons, and once he'd said no, he caught her subsequently clandestinely scalding his comb. She was obsessed with depilation. Severe menses. An example of how distressed she got around menses: he found her weeping and finally got her to explain: it was because if she lost something he would come to her aid and they would find it, but when he lost things she was never able to add anything to the search that helped. She had no interest in reforming him, the comb mania aside, and she only made the one attempt. My antennae vibrated: what was he meaning to say? Did they argue? Very little, although they once argued over whether dance was a major art form or not, he negative, to a point of hurt feelings. Symphonic music should be on during sex, she felt, especially Sibelius. She was a member of a recorder consort. In sex she had two modes: number one, she is a normal not particularly sexy person being soldierly, trying hard to get into state two where she becomes almost a nut or dissociated person, wild breathing, sometimes fainting, throat sounds: getting from one to two is the eye of a needle, the aperture growing smaller, probably due to their increasing separations, he says. Had he noticed my nipples are slightly off axis? He hadn't. He denied everything. He said I shouldn't complain. Why? Grace has a supernumerary nipple. He wanted me to know he was not criticizing Grace, only describing. You can always find something nice to say about a girl, his mother instilled in him. If you can't find anything else nice, you can usually say she has nice skin. Grace's very good skin has come up inter alia more than he may be aware of. The skin of the rich is different, I say. Her family is wealthy, so ipso facto she must be too, but he is vague about the magnitudes, which I marxistly interpret as meaning they are substantial and also as one reason parting was apparently mostly such sweet sorrow, his claims to the contrary notwithstanding. He sees his mother's advice as machiavellian in that the motive behind it was that it would get around the junior high school girls that here was someone who always had something nice to say about a girl and this would mean he had a greater chance to find his right mate, not make the wrong choice, important because divorce would kill her, his mother, for one thing. If you failed to find your true mate it was life in death. Each woman is a copy of the Virgin Mary that the world is smearing and trying to ruin. Grace collects lacquerware and majolica, or *did. She is subject to rose fever. When she begins a novel she feels she has to read it straight to the end: he could sleep through her doing it, but in the morning she would be drained. She depended on his literary taste. He bemoaned the paucity of first-rate short novels and novellas in English, which is what her fixated attitude to novel reading led him to search out for her. They tried every variation of interim living together: visits, six months together six months apart, reconciliations, everything. Any cruelty I saw toward her in Gaborone was an act to get her to let go and face the need to find someone appropriate for her while she is still beautiful and possibly still fertile, with luck.*

What Country, Friends, Is This?

Since the job of getting up night soil from the privies takes a strong back, I was volunteering for it once or twice a week. This endeared me to some of the older aunts, which was nice. I also liked doing it because it could be seen as a concrete riposte to the question Mais qui videra le pot de chambre? which was the question, as I understood from Denoon, that had bedeviled the French anarchists in the nineteenth century whenever the reorganization of society on a voluntarist basis was proposed. The answer to the question of whether I was identifying not only with Denoon but with his weltanschauung is yes. Complex propositions being supposedly confuted by the simplest of questions never ceased to annoy him, as when pacifists were asked by the British draft boards during both wars what they would do if someone tried to rape their sisters. Presumably the scales were supposed to fall from their eyes at the brilliant simplicity of this thing they had overlooked. I loved the answer Sir I would endeavor to place myself between them, which some notable person had given.

I was at a house on Queen Nzinga Way, just starting to work, when two children ran past in great excitement, stopped, and came back. They were looking for Rra Puleng, but in his place I should come with them to see about two makhoa coming amongst us with a weapon.

This was baffling. I knew that a dentist was due to fly in in two weeks, but no other visitors were authorized or expected. I knew what was in

Nelson's daybook better than he did. Tsau was a genuine forbidden city, by and large. I sent one child to look for Denoon at the gum tree lot, then went with the other to see who these intruders were. The great underlying civic fear was that one day Tsau would be attacked by Boers. The South African Defence Force came over the border to destroy houses and people with sufficient frequency that South African refugees were having difficulty finding landlords willing to rent to them in Gaborone and Ramotswa. And there were Boers raiding and killing nearby in Namibia. Mangope's Bophutatswana agents were everywhere. The intruders had been sighted on the road from the airstrip. We took shortcuts. Along our way the consensus was that Boers were invading Tsau. The warning bell began to peal.

There's some misunderstanding, I thought. I was sure I was correct when we got to the road and it was blank as far as the airstrip.

But immediately there were cries coming from our right, from a knoll outlying the koppie, where the cemetery was. A spur from the track to the airstrip led there. Whatever was going on involved shouting and flailing. We sped toward the cemetery.

Backing down the spur toward us were a man and a woman, whites. I thought I saw the man in fact sheathing a sword, if such a thing was conceivable. They were heavily burdened with shoulder bags and valises. Some women and children were following them, not being threatening in any way obvious to me, although they were agitated and were shouting questions at them. The couple saw us. We are UK! the woman shouted. Tell them!

Our visitors were Harold Mace and Julia Rodden. They almost clung to me. I felt I knew his name in some connection. They were actors and they were married. They wanted me to understand that they were nothing irregular: they were being sent about by the British Council to read Shakespeare at schools and whatnot. They showed me something from the British Council. The British Council had booked them. They went where they were booked. Someone here must be aware of them. Was there a district officer? The pilot had deposited them summarily because his schedule called for him to reach an airfield where it had been reported that the night lighting was down, so he'd had to hurry to arrive there before dark. He'd fairly thrust them out, they said.

The cemetery had obviously unnerved them. They were sorry if they'd trespassed, but they had thought they were meant to go that way. Here Harold gestured at the oddly decorated baobab tree that dominated the cemetery. I could see how they might think it had some beckoning or official significance. And I could see why, coming unprepared into the cemetery, they'd been unnerved. Five women were buried there. Each plot was paved with cement in about the dimensions of an oversize ironing board. There was a flat metal box set where the headstone would normally be, and in the box was a ceramic death mask of the deceased. There was a clear glaze baked onto the masks. On the lid of each box was a two- or three-hundred-word life of the departed, on vellum and pressed between panels of glass sealed all around with some hardened waterproof tarry substance. It was strange the first time you lifted the lid and looked into the box, and saw a mask, not only because of the glistening face confronting you, but also because an anchoring staple was fixed over the mask at the brow, its shanks going deep into the cement, giving the brief impression that this was a person somehow bound down or constrained. There were no religious symbols evident on any of the boxes or the pavings, which must have resonated oddly with Harold, given that he was wearing, I noticed, a fairly major gold crucifix around his neck. Then when your gaze strayed to the baobab, you saw, on the main limb overhanging the graves, five ruby red cast-glass objects, elongate, like tears or gourds, the size of gourds, more like giant drop earrings than anything else. There were holes in the necks of these glinting red pendants through which the chains attaching them to the tree limbs were threaded. There was something ineffable in the extreme about this baobab display. You thought of teardrops, blood, Christmas tree ornaments, pawnshop signs, traffic lights. Beyond this there was the sheer arrestingness of the baobab itself, with its surface more like living gray hide than bark, and the frenzied, clutching look of the limbs concentrated at the top of the trunk. Baobabs have always looked more like monuments to me than like vegetables of any kind.

I felt the fine Italian hand of le dieu caché in the design of the cemetery. Nelson denied it was his idea. The mother committee had evolved it, according to Nelson, and he'd merely gone along.

It was true about the sword. Harold had drawn his rapier, which was one of the props in their act. He was very apologetic about it. He kept explaining. He seemed unable to refer to the cemetery as anything other than The Necropolis. They had been in the necropolis and had seen figures, seemingly armed, rushing toward them. In fact one woman had been carrying a hoe, was all. I'm afraid I am not longsighted, Harold said.

Julia wanted me to know that they had no fear of remote places. They had just performed at Moeng College, did I know where that was? It was in wild mountains. The High Commission had never given them to understand there was anything particularly different about this place, Tsau. I was by then informing them bit by bit that Tsau was in fact different, that it was a closed project—which I tried to elucidate for them —but I kept reiterating that everything would be all right and that their visit would be enjoyable all around. I wanted to preshape things as much as I could before Denoon broke the surface. I knew he was going to see a plot. He was certain for some reason that the British High Commission particularly wished Tsau ill. He was always ready to cite chapter and verse on the British High Commission, more than any other embassy, working hand in glove with the South Africans. He claimed to know for a fact that among British intelligence types the paranym for Africa was the Zoo.

I made introductions. I think they were frightened of Dirang Motsidisi, who had been in the original intercepting party. A dung cart arrived to take luggage. There was a water jug and a damp towel in it, which Harold and Julia made use of, taking off their pith helmets and tamping their necks and faces.

Physically, these were interesting people. They were middleaged but very impressive and fit-looking. They were middleaged in the way actors are middleaged, which seems different. Harold was a fine figure of a man. He was made for tights. I loved his big, martial jaw and full head of gray hair worn leonine. It was crimped across the back where the helmet band had pressed. His eyebrows were the color of brass. He had carriage. They both did. They seemed like dancers. Julia was wiry and small, with a headstrong-looking face. She was fatigued. The flesh beneath her eyes was soft and looked crosshatched. They were both in safari kit. I knew she had no breasts to speak of, despite the brave cups in her shirtfront. Her upper chest was bony. Her hair was gray-blond, cleverly streaked, cut shortish. Harold was not perfect, on closer scrutiny. His magnificent nose had a slightly dropped septum, which would have made no difference except that the interior of his nose was rather vermilion, so you noticed. Also there were a couple of liver spots on his forehead which hadn't been visible before he had performed his mini-toilette just now. They must have been touched up. His eye whites were congested, but that could have been due to fatigue and nothing worse.

As I led the way into town my personal fixation on the relationship between looks and fate revived. How old was Julia? My mother's age, roughly? What was I going to look like in twenty or so years? What was the kind of roughing it I seemed to be committing myself to going to do to me? What was the consequence going to be of living where you kept running out of moisturizer? What was Harold's story? Clearly his physical envelope qualified him for something loftier than being a strolling player in places like this.

They seemed to like me. Julia's voice was her creature. It had an adorable rasp to it. Harold had a rich, capacious voice I could tell would be capable of great projection. Then there was Nelson's fine voice. I was assigned to be the only lakhoa in Tsau with a nondescript voice. It was true that they seemed to like me, but they were showing not the least surprise at finding someone like me in a place like Tsau. I don't know exactly what I thought they should think, what more wonderful situation I was clearly more appropriate for, someone so youngish and smashing as myself, but I was a little undermined.

They were especially British, which worried me. They weren't incidentally British, like British aid workers you might encounter in Africa. They were paid exemplars. Nelson's hostility to Britain started with the British refusal to do sanctions against South Africa and stretched backward through items like their letting Mussolini through the Suez Canal so he could invade Ethiopia, which according to Nelson wouldn't have happened otherwise. He was encyclopedic. By 1898 Japan was the only Pacific country the British had failed to force the opium trade on. And if you mentioned anything favorable you'd be reminded that if you put it in the box with everything else and shook it all up, what you would come out with would still be the British Empire. Also he referred to himself as a birthright Fenian. This had osmosed to him through his father from an even more diehard nationalist uncle, so diehard that he had briefly been a blueshirt and gone to fight alongside the Germans, the great enemy of his enemy. Of course, for his father, that had been going too far, and when the uncle visited after the war there had been cataclysmic scenes, drink-based and violent, ultimately.

I had a slight coup. Harold had calmed down. He said Place—the Seacoast of Illyria, and then What country, friends, is this? I said Twelfth Night. I'm not sure how I knew, since Shakespeare is a blur to me, Hamlet and Macbeth excepted. Harold noticed that I knew, nicely. I took them straight to the guest quarters at Mma Isang's. My excuse for not taking them up to the plaza first, for formalities, was that they needed desperately to rest and get hold of themselves.

Foreign Bodies

An hour later I was trying to impress on Denoon that he was not dealing with evil people here, so far as I could tell. As I'd approached the octagon I'd heard the thudding of the generator and guessed correctly that Nelson was radioing Gaborone for explanations. Somebody who'd witnessed Harold and Julia's arrival had run to him with the essentials. Nelson already knew more about the visitors than I did, viz. that Harold had played Richard the Lion-Hearted's best friend in a BBC-TV series in the sixties. The explanation for their presence was that there was someone new running the British Council and also that the person at Local Government and Lands who should have known enough to block the visit was on holiday. The government was being apologetic. We would have Harold and Julia for four days, no more.

He seemed to be reconciling himself to the intrusion, albeit with little side trips into grumbling about Shakespeare. The chronicle plays were royalist propaganda of the purest sort and did I know that in them only kings were allowed to speak from a seated position? Proroyalism was the secret core of the impotence of British socialism. It all came down to something as intractable as not liking it that America emerged from so unsatisfactory a culture as Britain. I feel about England the way Blake did, he said.

He wouldn't come to meet them right away. Dineo could meet them, and I should be in charge of them for the time being, which was what Dineo had already suggested to me. In the meantime he had an idea—something he wanted to work on, which he would tell me about later. He looked pleased with himself in a way that I'd come to perceive with a certain amount of apprehension.

Toward three I picked up Harold and Julia and took them on a tour of Tsau. They had napped. I had them each bring a change of clothes along—my plan was to end our tour at the bathhouse, where they could clean up for the reception and dinner the mother committee had decided to put on.

Tsau impressed them, although it was clear being impressed with

Tsau made Harold unhappy. It's so clean, Julia said, so almost Swiss.
She asked good questions, and it was clear she grasped the fact that Tsau
was a brilliant machine intended to reroute social power to women in a
variety of ways. She was very probing on female-only inheritance. I was
eloquent. I explained that the next stage of the equity system would be
the setting up of satellites of Sekopololo in major villages like Maun,
enclave branches, starting with the same kinds of poor and destitute
women who had made Tsau, and that ultimately Tsau should ideally
evolve into a training center and vatican for the broader movement, if
all went well. Here I was adumbrating on my own hook a bit. But surely
something like this was going to happen. Harold was deliberately super-
ficial in his reactions, saying, whenever some feature of the place struck
him as particularly eccentric, What country, friends, is this? His remarks
kept verging on the implication that Tsau was a sort of theater, artificial.
I love the costume, he said. He was a little offensive—as in referring to
the cart boys and girls as porters—but this came from disequilibrium.
He kept wondering aloud whether the Overseas Ministry had put funds
into any of this. Wherever I introduced him someone was sure to ask if
this was the swordsman everyone had heard about, which he didn't like
much. Where are your churches, may I know? he asked me at one point.
I told him there were no churches, although certain groups met informally. Even when he was being dismissive, there was something playful
about the man that I liked.

I took them into the bathhouse and showed them how it worked. It
was reserved for them for a half hour for their exclusive use. Harold was
being mysteriously funny and started to say something, but Julia took
control and thanked me and led him in. When she let go of his elbow
there was a white pinchmark where she'd been gripping.

So where are the foreign bodies? Nelson asked me, later.

Washing up, I said. He had been writing something that he put away
quickly when I came in.

In passing he accused me of already starting to sound more British. I
denied it, but I know I'm susceptible, and it may have been true. I
accused him of already sounding more American, or more prolish, in
fact, which meant talking more like the proletariat than usual. This had
turned up earlier, when he was telling me with obvious pride how many
of his chums had been blue-collar-family boys. He'd denied it. But what
I was accusing him of was not a canard. It was real. He was preadapting.

Shaxpur

At first at the reception dinner Harold was like a statue. We were gathered in the central kitchen annex, a low-ceilinged but spacious enough room that felt claustral because the ring of tables we were seated around came close to the walls of the room on three sides. These tables were brainchildren of Denoon's, with leaves that folded out cut in such a way as to make each table wedge-shaped, so that the table ring could be smoothly and solidly effected. I once saw something like it in a King Arthur movie he claimed never to have heard of. Harold's coldness was very unfair to the mother committee. They had outdone themselves. We had goat curry, coleslaw, red rice—not my favorite, but popular in Tsau, the red deriving from beetroot juice—and a sort of soda bread that was baked on special occasions only. Denoon was being quiet, too. So naturally Julia and I were, to compensate, being overgracious. It was about as I'd expected between Nelson and Harold. Sotto voce earlier Nelson had informed me that Harold was dying for a drink to the degree that he had asked a couple of mother committee members if there was to be wine or not. Also Harold was a vector of empire, he was not to be trusted, and so on.

Julia was digging Harold to get him to participate, which led finally to his blaring out in his rich voice to the table of thirteen women and Denoon Does anyone have a question about Shakespeare the man, of humble origins dot dot dot. He had been told that most of the women understood English but that he should speak slowly, which he was doing, initially.

The women were shy. It was leaden in the room.

Denoon said By Shakespeare you mean Shaxpur, which he said with a flat a, then added insult to injury by spelling out.

You could see Harold bridling.

Denoon persisted. But tell us anything about this man, he said.

I couldn't believe that this was going to be about the authorship of the plays. There were ways to talk about Shakespeare that would have gradually included the women and conveyed something. It was evident that Harold was pleased at the turn things were taking. He began to eat the Jell-O he'd been ignoring.

Do I detect a scent of Bacon in the air? Harold said, going into a sniffing routine that was ludicrous and baffling to everyone except the four whites.

The case for Francis Bacon being the author of the plays is better than the case for Shaxpur, as you may or may not know, Denoon said.

Ah, Bacon to skewer! Harold said. What a rarity! What a find! And where else could one find such a rarity? Where else could it survive?

Harold and Nelson were clearly cheered up at the prospect of wrangling over this. They began. Julia made a couple of attempts to torque the exchanges around to a more general intelligibility, but the titans seemed determined not to be more inclusive, no matter what.

I hated to listen to them. In fact I was interested, but by seeming to follow too closely I was afraid I'd be abandoning Julia in her attempts to keep some semblance of connection going via side conversations with various members of the mother committee.

These men were not ignorant. The exchange was civil, at first, but very intense and substantive. Harold conceded it was odd that there were no books or papers of any description included among the chattels in Shakespeare's will, but not that there was anything arresting about references to the circulation of the blood in three of the plays despite Shakespeare having died twelve years before Harvey published his theory whereas Francis Bacon was an established intimate of Harvey's and would have known all about this theory. It signified nothing to Harold that Bacon had written as if it were one continuous name Sir Fraunces Bacon William Shakespeare in one of his notebooks. What about the fact that Bacon's crest contained the figure of Athena shaking a spear? This connected with something I missed re Bacon's watermark turning up in the paper of some of the first folios and also with Shaxpur never having had a family crest, although the evidence was that he put an enormous amount of time into trying to get one. Nelson presented and Harold refuted each of the reasons a pantheonic member of the nobility would feel the need to disguise being something as lowly as a playwright. I found Harold convincing on this. And so it went. Only once did Harold challenge the factuality of something Denoon was contending. This was that Macbethus Tyrannus! was written in the margin of a history of Scotland in Bacon's library, in Bacon's own hand. But then he seemed to believe Denoon and took the position that it was sheer coincidence. Nelson denied it meant anything that when the First Folio came out the preface referred to the author as dead, whereas Bacon was still alive. A preface can say anything, he said.

We have these lovely plays and poems, Julia said to the table at large, so why does it matter whom they came from since we have them, and wasn't there someone who proved that Homer was probably a woman?

I think there was more to her point, but Julia never got to finish because the duelists joined together to explode this notion. I for one do not contend that the idea of Homer being a woman was anything but a practical joke of Samuel Butler's, god knows.

Next Harold was attacking from the rear, after leading Denoon into admitting that there might be something to be said for the candidacy of Edward de Vere, maybe as much as for Bacon. To which the catch was that then Nelson's choice as the author of the plays was either someone who had defended torture, Bacon, or de Vere, who had murdered a cook in a fit of pique. The idea was that any reasonable person would want the author to be other than a villain or monster.

Mais non, according to Denoon. This was all about abstract justice or truth, I forget which. He wanted Harold to know that he, Nelson, was far from an unqualified fan of the plays, particularly not of the chronicles, which were reducible to royalist propaganda, although they were gorgeous in places. And he would feel the same concerning the authorship of Ralph Roister Doister, or of The Duchess of Malfi if there was evidence pointing away from John Webster.

Nelson flung himself back into what he considered his area of strength—uncomfortable or dissonant facts. He was not reading the tenor of the rest of us. How is it that when Hamlet is accused of being insane he says: Set me the matter to restate, which madness would run from? Wouldn't this be an unusual conceit or test for a wool merchant and landlord like Shaxpur to know anything about? Of course in Bacon's notebooks there were pages of entries about mental illness, including a proposed test for madness identical with the one in Hamlet.

Just then Dineo activated a social mechanism I knew vaguely about but had never seen used. At a signal from her, all the women but Julia and me rose. And then we followed suit, bemusedly. The idea was to shift seats, and specifically to shift seats so that Nelson and Harold, who were at nine and twelve on the circle, would be moved next to each other. Denoon realized what was happening, probably not surprisingly, since this exercise had him written all over it. The woman sitting between them withdrew. Denoon shifted over, like a good fellow, and he and Harold were side by side.

The assumption behind the exercise was that disputants made to sit in close proximity to one another would cool down, usually. The principle was identical to the one in the handholding stratagem he'd been so dismissive of, but no matter. And they did calm down that night, although later I found out it was because of something Harold broached during musical chairs. There was supposedly a manuscript of a fragment of a play about Sir Thomas More, author unknown. The fragment itself was in four fragments, each in a different hand, and the last or D fragment was in the hand that wrote Shakespeare's will. This was something totally new to Nelson. It stopped him. It wasn't that he disbelieved Harold on this, but he needed more details, time to try to imagine how this datum might be made to fit his anti-Stratfordianism.

The peacock fight apparently having concluded, Julia and I concerted to give a précis of Taming of the Shrew. I translated here and there, to be sure the picture was clear. Scenelets from the play were going to be performed around the village the next day and we hoped the members of the mother committee would do a modicum of audience preparation for us. Harold and Nelson began listening to us, Harold even chipping in, finally.

Getting ready for bed that night, Nelson was generally apologetic about the way the evening had gone, but strewn among the apologies were questions for me as to what I had ever heard in re the More Hand D evidence. Not my field, I told him. I knew nothing about it. The light was only off for a couple of minutes before it was back on so he could dash off an airletter to an academic friend at Cambridge on the subject. His friend must be world famous, because I'd heard of him. Then I fell asleep.

I woke up an hour or so later with the light still on and Nelson still writing. But this was something else, a surprise for Harold and Julia he would prefer I not ask him about because it was going to be a surprise for me too.

Perfidious Albion

Things were developing amiably enough over the next couple of days, I thought. Harold in particular got steadily more accommodating, agreeing to use his rapier in shadowfencing routines when the children begged sufficiently. I was the interlocutor and translator for the spot performances—or suites, as they called them—that we put on before various groups. The costuming and props made a great attraction: Harold wore a jerkin and a doublet, and Julia had a change of gowns and a toy lute she plucked to counterpoint some of the poetry. She also sang Dowland and Purcell. Harold and Julia worked entirely from memory, which was commented on. And I think they were pleased at how closely people seemed to be following, to the extent that there was hissing and ululating from most audiences once they had my translation of Petruchio's conquest-of-Kate speech. In fact, once he saw the reaction he was getting, Harold darkened his reading of the lines I will be master of what is mine own / She is my goods, my chattels, she is my house / My household stuff, my field, my barn, my horse, my ox, my ass, my any thing. I did begin to notice that certain people whose presence I would have expected at the performances were turning up absent. Circuitously I found out that they were with Denoon, in rehearsals for something, a play to be put on by Rra Puleng and the mother committee especially for the visitors, as thanks. I decided not to know more about this. My plate was full. Nelson would have told me everything that was planned, if I'd asked, I did later establish.

Suddenly the news was that there was going to be an extra day of Harold and Julia. Nelson had arranged it by radio. It had to do with what he was cooking up, obviously. He asked me to inform them that there would be an extra day and not say why, which I refused to do and which Dineo ultimately did.

On the penultimate day of their visit we had their final and biggest performance, for the whole village at once, whoever wanted to come, in the plaza. Essentially it was dinner theater, people sitting on mats and eating mealie while against the backdrop of the darkening Kalahari Harold and Julia strutted their hour. I translated. I was hoarse when it was over. We were a team by now. They knew instinctually when to pause for me. It was very smooth. Denoon was in and out. I wanted him to dislike Harold less, despite Harold's provocative tendencies, such as being sure to appear between performances wearing either a crucifix or an ascot with a cross of St. George stickpin. These tendencies predate you and aren't aimed at you, I tried to tell Nelson. I liked Harold. Earlier that day I had come across him sitting under a tree reading Andrew Marvell.

The thanks and farewells were nicely handled by Dineo.

I became aware of a contained hubbub to the rear left. The audience, which had started to rise to disperse, was asked to sit down again, and people complied. Something had been going on offstage earlier, I realized, which I'd thought at the time was rude, because it had been distracting during the Hamlet and Ophelia amalgam, which you had to follow fairly closely. Anyway, I had returned to the audience and was joined there by Harold and Julia, still in costume. It was a little cool. Not everyone had come prepared with shawls and afghans for this addendum, but there had been forethought: people were passing out shawls and even extra mats. We took some and tried to make ourselves comfortable. An announcement was made. We were going to see a brief program that would show our thanks to Harold and Julia. Harold wasn't comfortable sitting on the ground. I asked him if I should get him a chair, even though it might make him feel a little conspicuous to be the only one sitting kinglike above the rest. So be it, he said, and also urged Julia to accept a chair, which she declined. They argued a little, and somewhere in the exchange I heard her use the phrase Childe Harold, for my benefit, I think. I got Harold's chair and he sat in it. The proscenium was suddenly dramatic: we had blazing torches, four of them, on staves set into metal stands, grouped two on each side of the center spot.

I was torn. I knew Harold and Julia must be hungry and that it was up to me to go off and do something about it, but the feeling that I needed to stick close to them was stronger. Baskets of ground nuts were being passed around, which I took as a sign that what was coming would probably be brief, so I stayed put. Julia ate ground nuts, but Harold passed. Nelson gave the signal for the games to begin. I don't know what I expected. I think I expected something gentle that might be called The Apotheosis of Tsau, something poetical and historical.

In retrospect I have sympathy for Nelson, knowing what his intentions were. There is such a thing as being so driven to act that you blot out the gulf evolving between the incident you find yourself creating and the ideal incident the depth of your feelings entitles you to have. Also, the image of William Blake was somehow ghostlily conceptually entwined in Nelson's idea of what he was doing—Blake the defender of the essence of England against the traducers who were turning it into mere empire. Nelson adored Blake. And in defending himself, when we went over this later, it was his identification with Blake he used against my accusation of Anglophobia run amok. The idea of the performance had been to present to Harold and Julia, emissaries of England the mother of empires, the feelings of some former subjects of the crown who were now undeceived and no longer humble—as those feelings might well have been articulated by people acculturated to express themselves in terms of formal drama. This may seem elaborate, but I want to be fair to Nelson. The script for the occasion came out of several sessions where members of the mother committee were encouraged to free associate on the subject of the British Empire—with Nelson stirring the pot, interpolating considerably more than he should have, I'm sure, transcribing, and then editing the whole. I never fathomed how he had proceeded so far without cognizing how embarrassing a product was resulting. Because it was embarrassing.

I was truly embarrassed, which I think may be why my memory of the overall event is what it is. I looked away. I willed it to be over. And so on.

Two boys came out, my friend King James and his best friend, Edison. They were in traditional dress—goatskin capes, breechclouts, seedpod rattles on their ankles. They posted themselves truculently, one in front of each of the torch sets, leaning on staves clearly meant to represent spears. We had actual spears in our stores house, of course, but no actual weapon was ever going to be released into real life if Nelson had anything to say about it. And of course real spears would have been vastly more effective. A girl came out, Adelah, a darling who would be leaving us soon for the government secondary at Kang. She was shadowed by a bulky presence, a woman completely swathed in black and carrying a flashlight with which to aid performers in reading their lines. It was getting fairly dark. The presence was Dirang Motsidisi, and the black swathing was meant to make her inconspicuous, unbelievably enough. Even her head was somehow veiled. Prettyrose Chilume joined the central group, her violin fixed at her throat, ready to be played. There

was something transfixing about the tableau against the fading glow of
the desert, the torch flames wagging. The audience settled down unusually quickly.

Then began a declamation, I think it would be correct to call it, by
Adelah, a declamation against England. Prettyrose wasn't there to do
Lady of Spain but to produce harsh saccades to underline the different
indictments of perfidious Albion being shouted out. The boys also provided emphasis by stamping their staves and feet. To me what was interesting was that what I was hearing was a complete inversion of the
traditional Tswana praise ceremony for the chief and his subchiefs usual
on festive occasions, wherein the royals are exhaustively likened to cattle, a great compliment.

I hope I can give a decent approximation of what went on. There was
a concentration, understandably, on the war in Zimbabwe, which was
just over, as, in *England* you had a killer slave, but you let him to be free
to kill amongst us at Lesoma, where seventeen Tswana soldiers he shot
down, and this slave was Ian Smith. This was about an actual famous
massacre of Batswana soldiers during a raid into Botswana.

It went on with *Now* today Ian Smith is the forward-leading man
running away with excrement on his heels from fear.

England you gave away Ghanzi Ridge to Boers and as well Tati Farms
to Boers, and rich farms in Tuli Block as well to Boers who mischarge
Batswana as to oranges from those trees to this day. All this was in
English.

England how could you leave us with no roads, whilst you have many
roads crossing all about England? There was more along these lines.

Then *England* you wished to hand over all Botswana to the Boers but
were stopped from betrayal by your queen when Tshekedi made her to
prevent you from this.

England you held President Sir Seretse Khama away from us above
seven years.

England when you brought your churches upon us even your pastors
could take some slaves from the Bakhurutshe and Barolong and sell them
for money in Natal, because in that time you were hard as teeth to us,
the same as Boers or Mzilikazi.

There was more, but less than there might have been. I was relieved
that it had been so succinct. Harold was looking around in a way suggesting an interest in offering a rebuttal if some appropriate modus presented itself.

The spectacle had been received with a fairly uniform puzzlement, I thought, amounting to annoyed dumbfoundment in a couple of cases at its discourtesy. As I was organizing Harold and Julia to come away with me for some refreshment the word was passed that we should sit down again. Clearly we weren't through being entertained.

The Lamentations of Women Brought to a Finish, Full Stop

Five women lined up between the torches. Four were holding flashlights in the air above their heads, and the fifth was carrying an implement impossible to make out at first, which proved to be an oversized flail, almost a caricature of the real implement because it was so large. When someone came out and deposited an object like an ottoman in front of this chorus I knew what was coming. The object was in fact a foot-high segment of tree trunk crudely sewn into a cowhide casing. The woman with the flail would shortly be abusing it. The flashlights were switched on and trained on Dirang Motsidisi, still dressed as she had been but with the veiling around her head pushed down. She was now a principal. The flail was handed to her. I was right about what was coming. We were in for an installment of The Lamentations of Women Brought to a Finish, Full Stop. I hoped and prayed it was only an installment. From time to time I had seen installments done, rehearsed. It was an ongoing production which in its entirety would probably never be performable because it was so epic.

I felt like shriveling and concurrently felt disloyal over my embarrassment, seeing myself as callowly identifying with the white West and turning my back on the person I lived with because his attempt to tease out and concretize the voice of the formerly oppressed was too hubristic for me, at least when I had to witness the attempt not en famille but in the company of educated members of the West cultured in ways I happened to be impressed by. We all love hubris in a mate but we prefer it to be in moderation. I know what was happening with me. Something about Harold and Julia was reviving all my sensitivity about my education. I look more educated than I am. I know how many thin spots there are and how much of what looks good is sheer memory. Harold and Julia were regressing me. They were beautifully educated and I wasn't, ergo they represented the ideal observer, jointly. It was excruciating that Nelson was insisting on this second extravaganza, the innocence and good intentions of which would be inaccessible to Harold and Julia because on the surface it could be so rowdy and peculiar.

I appreciated what Denoon's strategy was, and that it was innocent, so that why ultimately I somewhat freaked is hard to explain, even given everything I've said. Obviously Part the First of what we'd been treated to you could imagine being entitled A Fiery Raspberry to Decrepit but Still Perfidious Albion, and Part Two, now in the overture stage, The Lamentations, would be a demonstration of the new live post-Albionic culture of liberated Tsau. So what, if through The Lamentations Denoon was skirting making a spectacle of our bodies and ourselves, us women? Why was this so suddenly intolerable for me?

The Lamentations ritual, which is what it was, was a hybrid thing. It was both artificial and spontaneous, both foreign and domestic. It was ritualistic in that its format was fixed—although the flail was a new touch, an improvement, and I suppose an escalation over the switches or lengths of rope I had seen used in previous outings when the ottoman was being lashed for emphasis at certain junctures in the performance—but the content was only partly fixed. The germ of The Lamentations was notes taken by people attending a set of lectures I am tempted to call seminal, given by Denoon, on the history of the oppression of women. These notes had been expanded by the women to a master list of iniquities, and every household had a copy of the list in a special wallet hung next to the rondavel door.

The popular attitude to The Lamentations was pro, on the whole. I do know that in the one case of a woman whose wallet of tribulations had been eaten by a goat, I should say allowed to be eaten by a goat by her husband, who was responsible for keeping the goats out of the house, there was a rather severe penalty assessed against him that everyone agreed with except me. People were supposed to bring their lists to sessions of the evolving Lamentations spectacle. Many did. Denoon's cadre was faithful about it and knew just how to inject historical injustices appositely into the proceedings when vox populi got off the track, got fanciful or notional or brought up injustices not strictly traceable to men or nongermane in other ways. The agon was always the same. A lead woman would start reading out particular injustices, a chorus and the audience would yell out Shame!, the audience would be encouraged to volunteer additional personal injustices—there were some favorites that people wanted to hear over and over—and there would be ululating, the ottoman would be lashed, periodically there would be declarations that such things as were being mentioned would never be allowed to happen in Tsau. Men who came to the sessions were polite but tended, I noticed, to drift home early. The pattern was for The Lamentations to start out in English and then for Setswana to predominate, as emotions rose. As I say, I had nothing against The Lamentations. I embraced them for what they were, for their being didactic and sociocathartic, for the bawdiness that crept in, all of it. But still I wanted to run away. Denoon's attitude to The Lamentations was too pious. This was going to be evident to Harold and Julia. The Lamentations was deeply amateur, almost burlesque, but Nelson's demeanor during it was as though he were listening to a tone poem, some sententious piece of music by a composer like Messiaen, like my mother sitting piously frozen while she listened to something by Messiaen once she had decided that of all the phonograph records I had taken out of the public library for her this was the one that was meant for her soul. It was holy. It contained the holy. Once I knew she liked it I saved my allowance and brought her her own copy, one of my worst mistakes because whenever it was on, the whole downstairs was supposed to be frozen in silence, so she could listen correctly. Everything I did made too much noise, including, once, gargling. She listened to the thing endlessly, it felt like, during certain periods, like a drug. I had been trying to impose music appreciation on her, working from some list I had, and then she stopped dead at Messiaen. And it wasn't anything to do with Messiaen in the sense that she wanted ever to hear anything else by this master of her soul's heart. In fact she recoiled from the idea. It was just this one religiose perfect endless composition and only this. The look in Denoon's eye was milder than hers during Messiaen, but it was still cognate. I hated him to be rapt, ever. When he was, I would remind myself that no one is perfect. Christ himself, for instance, never saw his doctrines extending as far as the condemnation of human slavery. My reaction may have been due to feeling totally overbooked on the woman question, especially as it applied to reconciling my supposed nobility and independence with the requirements of my campaign to get Denoon, who was seeming more and more like the store of all value to me, whatever my cavils. I wanted Denoon in an increasingly absolute way I was losing control over. No doubt the last thing I needed emotionally was to be convinced—or reconvinced—that every society you look deeply enough into turns out to be yet another male conspiracy against women conducted with assistance from the victim class itself. I was doing something and I was going to do it and I suppose I felt there was no point in philosophically paralyzing myself. Anyway, the sight of Harold sitting down again like Canute on his throne and looking around for me to explain to him what on earth was now going to happen was too much for me, and I fled.

I realize now that a thing that happened that morning had put me in a volatile state, quite obviously. I thought I'd conquered it by defining it as pseudo. It's only recently that I connect it to my bolting act. This was a pseudo epiphany regarding Nelson. I saw the tree of life on his front for a second and got hot in the eyes and weak all over. He had come in naked from sponge-bathing in the courtyard. As he turned in the doorway he was ventrally lit by a shaft of sunlight that made the way his body hairs were matted, chest and belly and so on hairs were matted, look like a perfect tree of life, with the exfoliation on his chest the canopy, the pressed-together belly growth the trunk, his escutcheon and genital area hair—he had quite a bit of hair on his actual scrotum—the root, and the whole genital package the treasure or casket or rare gem the roots of the tree were twined around. I got a grip on myself and warned myself that if I was seeing Nelson's flesh as a billboard for Yggdrasil, I was having the pseudo epiphany of all time. But we are fools, and the moment was unquestionably a contributant to my hair-trigger state of being as The Lamentations began.

I retreated as far as a privy in back of the kitchen building. I hid out there. The excuse for my absence was going to be gastric distress not further specified. Why I bothered to sequester myself during The Lamentations is, in retrospect, a good question, since as the event tediously ran its course I began proposing my own tribulations, as a distraction, to fit into the gaps in the cycles of cheering and groaning. This is my way. A lot of The Lamentations I knew by heart. In my own private pageant I had masses of women vilifying the State of Maryland for having Fatti Maschii, parole femine, deeds are like men, and words—weak things— are like women, for its official motto. I was fairly miscellaneous. I ranged from the case of the first woman gynecologist being forced to attend courses disguised as a man, and then having to practice as one, on through the woman who invented the astrolabe being stripped and tortured to death by a male mob led by the patriarch of Alexandria, and when I sensed I was cleaving to a rather elite level I went for the generic class of women east to west in Africa who had routinely been forced to let male relations fuck them in exchange for trifling little loans, not to mention a study I read some years back about the percentage of American women owning small businesses who, credit being unobtainable by them, earned their original stakes by selling their only material asset, their bodies. It was easy to monitor The Lamentations and know where you were, because somewhere toward the end there would be cries in English and Setswana of a favorite line of Nelson's from Blake: Every female is a golden loom. That moment came.

It was all dissolving as I approached. Two late contributions that struck me as not quite in keeping with the spirit of the event rang out, one being No more to drink only always bush tea! and the other being No more only to be using block soap! The first referred to Sekopololo's resistance to stocking socalled white tea, brands like Joko available from South Africa, out of fidelity to the idea that we should continue drinking the locally gathered rooibos tea, which was free and perfectly good, albeit without caffeine. The second related to Sekopololo's similar chariness when it came to ordering commercially produced soaps, again because we were supposed to be happy with the local homemade soap, its feeble lathering capacity notwithstanding. Somebody was out to provoke a little. That was interesting.

Denoon was off with the performers. It was truly over. Once again Harold and Julia seemed to be my lot: I was the logical one to do something since no one else was, and here they were, wafting toward me, Harold looking especially superior to everything and Julia looking rather numbly appeasing. Harold had wanted to say something, but, he claimed, only by way of thanks, and that hadn't been arranged, which increased my guilt feelings, because if I hadn't sequestered myself I could have seen to it.

So I said to come to dinner in a half hour, that it would be just entre nous, at which they half melted with relief. In truth I may have invited them because I thought it would be easier than facing Nelson alone with the fund of questions I had built up burgeoning. There was also defiance in it in that I was fairly sure the last thing in the world he would choose to have happen that evening was a prandial confrontation with the people he had been aiming his shafts at, at least in the Perfidious Albion segment. It was defiance saying to me that if I wanted to have people in I should be able to. He would be welcome but not as a boor. He was going to have to be nice as a courtesy to me. He was going to have to be nice out of his best instincts, not via negotiation with me. With men it takes too long for me, as a usual thing, to come face to face with the nature of what I've actually gotten into. Is this the man? was the question that was always with me. Nelson would be lovely to people of my choosing as a courtesy to me if for no other reason, or I could draw my own conclusions. Of course in this case I was choosing guests specifically not to his liking. But tant pis. He hated what the British had done in Africa. I appreciated all this and also all his buried anxiety about his origins at every level, from the mother of empires through his mother and father. But nevertheless. Why should I give in to his hysteria over being a created being instead of some self-created neat original? I would love to be original. I would love to. There are things you can do something about and things you can't. I was determined that Nelson was not going to be someone with a neurotic stance toward his origins. That way lies madness.

Anyway, Harold and Julia would turn up in no time to partake of I knew not what at that point. But I sped home and began deciding what canned delicacies to sacrifice for the occasion. Our last can of consommé was going to go for onion soup. I was feeling reckless. I pulled down items, like some smoked oysters, I knew Nelson would bridle at laying out. Oddly and to my great relief he was all mildness about their coming for dinner. I sensed he was nervous that I was going to take up the question of the point of the Albion exercise, at least, and that he was glad not to have to look forward to being alone with me, even if it meant more Harold. Combined with any rays of indignation proceeding from me was the symbolism of my having a knife in my hand while I sliced onions perfectly thinly, like a machine of some kind. I slice very thin and I slice very fast. It's a gift I have. Nelson helped minutely with dinner.

I heard our guests outside. I said to Nelson The only substantive thing I want to beg you to let alone is religion. The man is an observing Catholic and not an adolescent you might consider it reasonable to proselytize. If you want to argue about England you're on your own, but do it on the merits and be scholarly, the way you can. He said something like it was never too late for reason, which I took to be apropos my request about arguing religion, but in such a murmur that I took it as compliance.

This is more a collation than a normal kind of dinner, I said when they came in. In looking at what I had wrought, I realized I had just been putting one thing next to another and come up with something signifying nothing. Also I had concentrated on what was quick. There were chapatis, toasted sprouts, tabouleh, the oysters, the French onion soup, goat's milk clabber to go with the tabouleh. There was no entrée, strictly speaking. I decided to boil some eggs.

Evidently Harold had more than one crucifix. This one was silver, also very large, a Maltese cross. Denoon admired it and asked Harold if he knew who had the world's largest personal collection of crucifixes. Harold had no idea, but when he was told it was Boy George he seemed genuinely delighted to know that, not offended in any way I could tell, and then I saw why: he was just into the foyer of drunkenness. That was also why Julia seemed so scattered and tense, sans doute. In a trice Harold was producing from a knapsack the source of his joy, which was a bottle of rare Scotch, Oban, a little more than three quarters full, a gift. Ah, Denoon said, trying not to look my way.

Harold seemed very happy. He stalked around our place, peering condescendingly at different things and saying whatever he was saying in a voice audible only to himself. I don't know what he'd expected, but he was clearly and stupidly pleased to see that technically speaking we were among the poor and that however he lived, it was at a level above this. Julia wanted to be gracious. She followed Harold around and said countering things. But he wanted more to drink. Do you see what this is? he said, holding the bottle up close to Nelson's face, Oban. I hope you will join me, and you also—he said to me—as Julia will not do, her only fault. But there was a surprise. Her hands were full of mugs. Ah well, this one time, she said. He had begun pouring. He looked blue murder at her and poured a trifling drink. More, sir, please, she said. He complied only barely. He looked at her, astounded underneath. My drink was also derisory. Denoon he lavishly supplied, and himself.

Denoon hesitated over his huge drink. Here I have some responsibility. I think he was about to give some shred of a piety vis-à-vis not wanting to indulge in something, an evil that he was forever urging the avoidance of in Tsau, but I preempted and said They're leaving tomorrow, trying to show that a drink tonight hardly mattered. I thought we could all be normal together, just possibly. I think I also wanted to show Julia at least that there was no question of Nelson needing my permission re a drink before dinner. Because I think Nelson had been on the point of looking, in some way he thought would be covert, for my permission, which was not tolerable.

Julia was looking agony in my direction. The sky at dusk is so luminous, she said, and wandered off and out into the courtyard as though to look at it, despite the fact that night had fallen and I had batteries of candles going. I never drink, Denoon said to Harold, then drank hungrily. He was transformed with his first couple of swallows. I could tell. His sensitivity to alcohol had to be genetic. Julia called me out into the yard.

Give them some starters, she said. The oysters could be starters, I proposed, but that was no good because Harold disliked seafood unless it was plaice fried stiff. Then she wanted to know when we could get soup out, at the soonest. I estimated it would be twenty minutes and this seemed to send her into distraction. She stood in the doorway, looking in at Harold and Nelson, then came back and went so far as to get down on her hands and knees in order to blow into the firebox of the yard stove, to forward the soup, as she put it.

Are they getting on? I asked.

More than well, she said. Then: I think he would eat cashews, if you have some about.

I didn't have any.

Several times she said Well, I must tell you. But she stopped each time before saying anything more. I had to stop her from, in her agitation, pushing more sticks into the fire than made sense.

I don't know about your husband, she said, but Harold is very susceptible to drink. This is so wretched for me, but I am very worried. Harold likes your husband very much, and he might say something I am very worried could, er, flow back. To the British Council.

Nelson is not my husband, I said. I didn't want to go further into it than that. She gave me a long look, a surprised look.

How do you conclude he likes Nelson? I asked her. They seem so opposite. Before she could explain, I remembered I had a Gouda cheese, not too old, sitting in its carapace on a shelf somewhere. Gouda is durable. I ran to get it. This could be the answer to the appetizer question. But something had penetrated its red shell. The cheese was hard, a kernel of its former self, wizened. That was my news for her.

She said You see, when we finish a booking we have an agreement that, all right, he can—er—be himself, um. But because we like you so very much, well, and this is more drink than he, you see, I worry, we must eat, truly, how are they? She was as disjunct as that.

I said I was there long enough to hear Nelson explaining the origin of his bête noire World War I, where history went wrong.

Harold loves history, she said.

I said Well, he is getting an explanation of why the war that ruined everything began. I had heard this one before. The proposition was that the Czar had caused the war by calling for a general mobilization intended to stop a general strike going on in St. Petersburg. The Germans and everybody else had misread the mobilization, and voilà. Nelson collected historical inadvertencies, the accidents underlying the supposedly inevitable or foreordained. I can't remember them all. One had to do with the supposed historical enigma of the persistence of Judaism as an entity in a world so hostile to it. There were two parts to this. One was that the existence of Judaism as a distinct religion was attributable to the accident of the Seleucids overthrowing the Ptolemies, because if the Ptolemies had kept control of Palestine the hellenizing process which had already captured the town elites would have worked its way out to the rustics and run its course. But the Seleucids with their fanatical confrontationalism had radicalized the Jews, and the rest is history. The second part of this is lost.

It's a very poor idea, trying to instruct Harold in anything, especially the historical, Julia said.

She was right. I said At this very moment your husband is taking the position that if Nelson is correct about the First World War then it's the socialists after all who're really to blame for it by going on strike when they did, which is hardly Nelson's interpretation.

Denoon came out with a flashlight, and I thought for a moment he was about to help us with the fine detail of cooking in the dark, but no, he wavered off into the bush, walking not quite as I was used to.

She saw something in my expression, because she clutched my hand with both hands and said And nor is he my husband, Harold. England is hard. I don't think you know. There is no regional theater, nothing like. So we do this. My husband is dead. Harold is a homosexualist, you see, and we agreed we would say we were married. There was a ceremony of sorts. Because you see the British Council prefer very much to make use of the married for overseas work like this. Nelson slid past and into the house, carrying something.

She wanted to tell me everything. I tried to listen. There was a tortuous story about favoritism at the BBC. I had things on my mind. The main one was the question of whether Nelson would hold to his promise to stay off the subject of the Catholic Church. The Church fascinated him, and his thesis about it was that through stumbling into the celibacy requirement for priests it had created an accidental sanctuary for homosexuals whose concentrated talents would result in a capital-accumulation mechanism second to none, since the assets of the Church could never be in danger of being dispersed to the heirs of its dramatis personae. Thus, through celibacy to temporal power and invincibility. He loved to talk about the Church, and I was afraid drinking would erode whatever barrier his promise to me constituted. It was institutional permanency that fascinated him, the unmoved movers historically. And Harold was so floridly Catholic. The irony involved in the Church both stigmatizing homosexuals and covertly and brilliantly exploiting their energies was going to recur to Nelson and be difficult to resist. And it occurred to me that another angle of attack might be suggested by Harold's also florid antisocialism. Nelson had a teasing analysis of the Church as a model socialist institution that I'd heard him trot out before. This would be more manageable on my part, if in fact he succumbed to temptation.

Julia was dishing up soup before my very eyes. It wasn't as hot or as married as I like French onion soup to be, but I deferred to her anxiety.

We went in with the soup. It seemed to me that both Harold and Nelson were responding benignly to the alcohol. In fact brotherhood was in full flower. Our men had found common ground on an astounding issue, Shakespeare, agreeing that whoever wrote the plays was amazing because for any of the credible candidates, including Shaxpur, writing was a part-time activity, subsidiary in his case to acting and wool gathering, as Denoon put it. He meant, of course, wool factoring. They were even beginning to agree to disagree, I gathered, about men in relation to women, sequent to an exchange of pleasantries about the Lamentations spectacle. Harold wanted a hearing for his denial that men were harder on women than they were on other men, only a hearing. In other words, denying the reality of gynophobia, I thought to myself. Go ahead, Denoon said, fairness incarnate. Also coming up was a hearing for the proposition that women were as bad as men, given the opportunity, as indicated by the fact that the most murderous and depraved period in Turkish history was the wellknown socalled Rule of Women, when concubines ruled various sultans from behind the curtain of the seraglio. We adore women, Harold was maintaining.

I got us all seated and ready to address the soup. Harold and Nelson had ravished the Oban. It wasn't clear to me that later on I would still be able to get myself heard. I had been through scenes not unlike this in my other life. Before it was too late I wanted to register myself on the subject of gynophobia, so I told a story I told Harold he might find illuminating on the subject, something to think about, at least. I said I'd once lived in a co-op house at Stanford with nineteen other people, male and female. One of the members of the house had been a woman named Betty. Then a man joined the house who owned a dog named Betty. So naturally the practice grew up of making clear, when it was apposite, which Betty we might be referring to by saying, if we meant the dog, Betty the dog. I was subconsciously waiting for what happened to happen, and it did: in an exchange in which someone mentioned Betty the dog a guy said Which Betty the dog? Was this anything but seizing an opportunity to express freefloating hostility arising from some primal substrate? It so happens that Betty the woman was probably the best-liked and best-looking woman in our house, and in fact the guy who was insulting her had gone out with her a couple of times.

I didn't elicit much with my anecdote. There was some pro forma nodding. I don't know how closely anyone was listening. But I didn't have to feel like a fool for very long. Denoon was being peculiarly agreeable and passive. Shortly I saw why. He was ashamed of something, and here it was: two bottles of Cape Riesling with bits of earth still clinging to the labels. They dated back to the Italian construction workers and had been cached against a special occasion rising. It was hard for me not to think of special occasions in the past involving just the two of us when a taste of wine would have made a nice addition, but no, instead the wine was unearthed in honor of a visiting male no one would be likely to mistake for a comrade of his. There was no justification for it other than Denoon's feeling that he had to reciprocate for the Oban. I was not happy.

Denoon began pouring generously all around. Almost as though it were a chore he swallowed down whatever Oban remained in his mug, so that he could get properly going with the wine. Julia nudged me under the table. She declined wine until I signaled her that it might be a good idea for her to assist me in diminishing the supply, as feebly attempted before with the Oban. I was making the assumption that these two bottles were all there was. Nelson was indicating that that was the case. But how could I be sure? Wasn't it just as possible that he was trying to reassure me that however tonight developed I wasn't going to have to endure something like it ever again? I felt traces of pity, his shame was so patent.

Harold was developing the standard canard about the ingratitude of women regarding the unappreciated efforts of men to provide for them, even knowing that women in the long run are going to outlive them by a long chalk. Where was the hatred in that, on the part of men? Everything men accomplished in society was for women, for acquiring the attributes of all kinds needed to attract them and maintain them in as much comfort as could be managed. And was it not illuminating that, as much as women might complain, when they had got the suffrage, what was the result? Giving the vote to women had been the one thing needful to bring about a new and perfect world, so the previous generation had been told, but what have we here? Women voting to affirm the world as men have made it in every respect, albeit with something a little more for crèches. You endorse us, really, he said, do you not?

I had my artillery ready, but I was waiting for Nelson. I thought, he knows reams more than I do on this. Where was he, while Harold ruled the waves with half-baked vignettes of women in power behaving exactly like men? A man should be rebutting Harold. Of course Nelson didn't know it, but Harold was acting, playing sort of paterfamilias. Speak, I was thinking toward Nelson, or forever hold your peace.

Then Nelson came up with Do you happen to know which country in Western Europe has the fewest women in parliament and cabinet, both? He sipped wine vigorously while he waited for Harold to guess. Harold wouldn't. Greece, Nelson said, and a close number two, the United Kingdom, very close. Nelson's expression told me that this feeble thrust was supposed to calm me. But this statistic was nowhere near the point Harold was making. If this was Denoon inter pocula I needed to know it.

This in no way refutes me, Harold said. Julia asked me on the side if it was true, and I told her that Denoon was always right on his facts and figures.

Ultimately it was my continuing silence that got Denoon to realize he had to perorate. Nelson roused himself. He really let fly, and all for me. I knew he was encyclopedic on the woman question and that night he proved it. He said to Harold You mention Turkey groaning under the rule of women, which is an old chestnut, but I wonder if you know that all during this supposed reign of terror the kadeins, that is, the favored concubines, even the most favored and sovereign ones, had to join the nominal sultans in bed by crawling from the bedroom doorway on hands and knees, over to the bed, then kiss the coverlet, and then crawl up underneath it from the foot until they got level with the sultan? This was nota bene for me because Nelson had come to bed that way a couple of times and I had not known there was a referent, I had been under the impression he was just being funny. I think I prided myself that his playful side was developing under my benevolent influence. But his being able to strike back so specifically against one of Harold's major canards was the main thing. I loved that. I lose detail here because I had to organize more food for us. The men had eaten about as much of the soup as they were going to. It was unlikely Julia would be much help. Thanks to her pitching in with the wine reduction strategy, she was becoming visibly more relaxed.

Nelson was masterly. He drove home two theses. One was that despite apparent differences every society can be analyzed to show that women are in essence being shaped to function as vehicles for male imperatives and the physical reproduction of male power. He didn't carry this thesis into its most perfected form, in which he shows that in strictly biological terms man is a parasite on woman. This would have been too much for Harold. The second thesis was that because of the history of crushing and molding of women, men have no idea what women are or what they might be if they were left alone. One proof of this was the spectacle of male marxism searching high and low for the liberatory class that would lift human arrangements into a redeemed state—the proletariat, the students, the lumpen, third world nationalists—in short, every group around except for the most promising one, a majority group at that, a necessary and sufficient class an sich, the mass of women, women suitably enlightened and thus für sich. Then he brought out a pet contention, which was that among the thousands of credit and producer co-ops in Africa, the ones that tended not to be looted by their officers or to have fallen deeply into debt were the ones controlled by women. Then he rested.

Nelson was not succinct. And he was repetitive. But the power was there and Julia, for one, was seemingly getting it. Nelson knew his audience. He was gingerly with religion, barely treating it as causative in the case of female circumcision. She made him repeat the estimate of seventy-five million victims alive and suffering as of then, not seventy-five million since the origins of the outrage. I think the only other reference to religion in that whole segment had been in his windup, in which the Trinity of Plunder—Church, State, Capital—got alluded to. Julia seemed mildly spellbound. I saw her repeat rather wonderingly to herself certain phrases, of which Trinity of Plunder was one.

It was a ringing finish. Even I was moved, as much of all this as I'd already heard. As always there was something new, which served to remind me how lucky I was to have someone so encyclopedic for my own. This time it was the image of Chinese brides under the old regime lying in bed and waiting for the groom to descend on them while hundreds of banners fluttered over the marriage bed saying May you produce a hundred sons and a thousand grandsons.

Come out with me, Julia said impulsively, undone, I thought, by the preemptive drinking I'd urged on her. I didn't want to. I needed to understand more of what was going on. Denoon semidrunk was terra incognita. I looked at him and found him doing something he had olympianly observed his father doing inter pocula—that is, picking up the nearly empty wine bottle and bringing it close to his face and grimacing as he studied the label, as if to mime the sentiment What in the name of God liquid is this I have been drinking? He had presented this to me as a sure sign of sotdom in a person. Now he was doing it himself. Please come, Julia said. The implication, I thought, was that her need was personal, as in being escorted to and made comfortable with our out-house. So I went with her.

Julia pulled me almost to the precipice. Obviously this was not about what I'd assumed it was. We stood in the starlight. She commenced with a long, heartfelt look. Clearly, small women get stewed faster than ampler ones. You must, she seemed to say. I asked her to explain. It was that I must seize him, marry him, this man. She was dazzled with Nelson. She couldn't think why I hadn't married him, since it was plain that he loved me, the way he deferred to me, his manner. I mustn't miss out over anything silly. She had been married. Then a second theme emerged: especially I must be calm about drinking. She could see I was unhappy with it. But she had been married to a man who had drunk to the point of unsteadiness at times. He was dead now. But he had been a fine man. And he and she had been great friends with William Empson and Hetta his wife, Empson another great man and someone who would overdrink, but William and Hetta had been very happy together. Did I know the books of William Empson, or his poetry? Nelson reminded her of Empson in the subjects he could inform upon, and William had lived in China and here Nelson was living in Africa. I didn't know who William Empson was. I thought he had something to do with Basic English.

I thanked her and assured her I appreciated what she was saying. This kind of thing was in fact the last thing I needed to hear, but her sincerity was touching, and the fact that someone so British would be so open and intimate was too. Now she needed the loo. I took her to it and waited for her and we went back to the fray.

Harold and Nelson were closer than ever. Unbelievably, they were rejoicing in both being Irish. Harold had confessed that his true given name was O'Mealia. Julia was not amused by this, I could see. And there was another slight bombshell for me: Denoon was mixing up his personal gods. Suddenly I was hearing what a Fenian his father had really been, underneath. Until that moment I had been under the impression that Nelson's attitude toward Irishness was the same as his god James Joyce's —viz. that Ireland was a sump and a cracked looking glass and so on. Suddenly his father's Fenianism was positive. I realized I was even hearing positive references to Nelson's worse-than-black-sheep uncle, who had gone to Spain to fight alongside some fascist blueshirts led by a madman called O'Duffy against—against!—Nelson's other gods, the Spanish anarchists, the wonderful Confederación Nacional of whatever it was, CeNeTé is all I remember, the wonderful Cenetistas. I could hardly believe I was learning in extenso what a true Fenian his father had been, because I remembered clearly the fact or story that he, Nelson, had been so appalled at the one or two forays his father had made into Irish cultural gatherings with folkdancing and so on, instancing them to me as examples of how far his father had been willing to go to get cover for drinking himself blind, before deciding that eisteddfods, which is Welsh and the wrong term, but the Irish equivalent, were too bogus and embarrassing to be borne even in that holy pursuit. And then where was the terrible fistfight between his good old fascist uncle and his good old father that had taken place when his uncle had turned up threadbare in Palo Alto after the war, his hitherto beloathed Uncle Niall, hitherto until just then? But there were parallel wonders, I gathered, involving Harold, who was both a British Empire loyalist who believed the IRA, especially the provos, should be suppressed root and branch, and a son of Eire, however crypto, who also admired their spunk or grit or whatever Briticism he used, their tenacity. What was this all about with Nelson? I was shocked. Was this about loving Uncle Niall for the intensity of his beliefs, however imperfect? But I thought if I had learned anything from my life to date with Nelson, it was that credulism, believing in believing, was beneath retrograde. But why else would he be referring so nonjudgmentally to his suddenly so colorful and nothing more Uncle Niall?

Now there was also new news, from my standpoint, to the effect that the last Nelson had heard, his Uncle Niall had been working as a courier for the IRA. So he had been functioning as a shuffling old murderous factotum well into the sixties or even later. Was there a faint note of pride in Nelson's voice? I couldn't believe it, since Nelson's day-to-day presentation of self had him maintaining that the struggle in Northern Ireland was the best candidate since late colonial India for a purely nonviolent campaign, two years of disciplined satyagraha and the six counties could join all the others in one big madhouse. What was this celebration of joint Irishness by these two men about? Was what I was facing the revelation of yet another, inner, more standard, less interesting Denoon, almost an anti-Denoon, manifest only thanks to the solvent effects of alcohol, his proclaimed enemy? How could this be? Could the inner man be more generic and mundane than the man I embraced and who embraced me? Is that what all this meant, or could it all be understood in some more benign way, an excursion, load-shedding, something like that? Or was it just weakness of some kind being amplified, raised into a second self, through the power of the perfect male actor, Harold? Or was Nelson just expelling toxins accumulated in the course of living too solitarily for too long in the bush? Also was this inner man an old man like Niall, a residue of something that had been overcome, or was he fetal, a homunculus, something yet to be? It all made me feel like getting critically drunk myself, immediately, so that our revealed selves could meet and get to know each other and waltz. I felt desperate and like screaming out What is wrong with this picture? Except that what I felt was that what was wrong was my presence in it.

People weren't eating sufficiently. In an inspired state I got up and began a commedia, wherein I rifled our larder for every canned and jarred delicacy I had been hoarding, these constituting the analog to Nelson's Riesling, undoubtedly. I'm not absolutely certain I knew what I was doing. But it was symbolic language saying All right, if you won't eat what there is then what about this? and this? and also this? You prefer to just drink, but will you when you see this and this and this? The joke ultimately was on me. I thought I was putting out a shaming overabundance of food, but drinking makes you hungry and virtually everything seemed to go—the mandarin orange segments, the anchovies, the hearts of palm, the white plums, the fig paste. These were treasures. Only toward the end did people seem to notice what lengths I had gone to. No one commented on how utterly miscellaneous the spread was.

The talking died and eating in earnest took over. The evening ended when we were stupidly full.

We were meditative, finally. I think that what was dawning on Nelson was the realization that the next day it would be just us again and that certain questions yawned before us.

These Things Are Nothing

I purposely left Denoon asleep behind me the next morning, getting myself up and out swiftly and silently to escort Harold and Julia to the plane, which was due very early. I hoped Nelson would still be asleep or just surfacing when I got back. We needed to talk, and we would get to the heart of the matter sooner if nobody had been busy building elaborate rationales and defenses.

All the way to the airstrip Harold kept looking over his shoulder for Nelson, whose fan he had clearly become. I told him Nelson had gone to take care of something urgent but might make it to the airstrip before they left. Harold wanted Nelson to know that this place of his, meaning Tsau, was extraordinary. Julia was touching. I wished her well. In fact she was on the threshold of becoming wellknown at the level of Nyree Dawn Porter, after starring in an endless television series based on a Maria Edgeworth novel, as I later found out. I was happy and relieved for her.

It was all gracious. They were nice with the women and children who had come along to say goodbye. My mind was on Denoon throughout.

But in hurrying back to the octagon to get things straight, I went through a strange evolution, a mutation almost. I was using what amounts to a mantra to calm myself down, something like We are still acquiring each other—meaning to avoid being premature. I was over being clenched about the Lamentations and Perfidious Albion exercises, which I had managed to reframe as cases of simple overweening in trying too hard to make a point, the kind of thing I might do myself if I had the same degree of passion as Denoon and were in the same position with respect to resources. But now there was last night at dinner. Had all Nelson's overpowering bonhomie vis-à-vis Harold been in vino veritas? What bonhomie was this so powerful that it had led to the unearthing of an almost sacred cache of wine it wouldn't have been amiss to produce at least one bottle of so we could toast a couple of significant personal events I could think of. Also what was this huge susceptibility to alcohol? And what was this nostalgia for an uncle who was a certifiable fascist?

And how did this nostalgia fit with Nelson's heretofore immutable position that pursuing anschluss—his term for it—by armed action in Northern Ireland was a perfect example of choosing the strategy that was exactly the reverse of the one strategy practically ordained by history to be successful in the circumstances, id est mass nonviolence à la Gandhi in India? And where was the subtending irony he was so prone to mention in his right mind: that the result of all the suffering in Northern Ireland if and when the anschluss happened would be all power to the priests and the cretinate, their dupes? Now he was all roseate toward Ireland. I was even more right than I thought. At the time I was unaware that in his closet role as a poet manqué he had written a poem beginning Night falls and the Irish cease beating their children, which was apropos Ireland at the time of writing being the world's largest importer of a certain type of cane used by the nuns and brothers for beating children in school. But what happened is that as I jogged I felt all my questions leave me, for no reason. It was like entering a warm cloud and coming out the other side changed. I think it was profound. One minute I was tremendously vexed and the next I was dead certain the correct thing to do was leave Denoon alone. I had passed through a cloud of unknowing of some kind. It was crystal clear to me that I had delved enough, full stop. The everyday man he was was fine, full stop. I should stop evaginating him, to use a term I had gotten from him and demanded he stop using the second time I heard him do it, because it was stupidly provocative and not funny, even though all it means technically is to turn something inside out.

And there was actually very little to pursue when I got back home. Nelson was all abjection and apology. He should never drink. I was supposed to help him forever after if he was tempted. Reciprocation had been behind his producing the wine. And this was wine he had been saving for something genuinely momentous, whatever it might be, in our future. He had made me some toast and Ricoffee. He would sit down with me, but there was no way he could eat anything himself, the way he felt. He was his father's son. Never before or since have I felt myself become tranquil so abruptly and causelessly. I can look back and say that it was some physicochemical way station on the road from the state I called acquisitive love to the state of love itself, I suppose. It felt ordained. Something was saying These things are nothing, Ecce homo.

The first thing I felt I had to do was convince him he was absolved insofar as the Albion and Lamentations spectacles were concerned. Your problem is that you want to do everything, be everything, an impresario, I said. Try to remember that nobody can do everything. He looked wry and said Except Leonardo da Vinci: did you know that on top of everything else he could do he was one of the great singers of his time, with a beautiful singing voice, and that he won first place in a competition at Milan over singers from all over Italy and won it accompanying himself on a new type of lyre invented by himself, made out of silver, in the shape of a horse's skull, which gave out powerful and ravishing sounds of a kind never heard before?

Then more about alcohol. He rejected it. He hated it. It gives you pseudo insights such as how absolutely astonishing it is that creatures who have to go so frequently to the toilet to void their wastes have managed to create such complex civilizations as we have, he said. Hear hear! was my attitude, but softly.

Slowly he was getting ready for a normal day. He began shaving. Hector Raboupi had been by while I was at the airstrip. Nelson got agitated telling me about it. Raboupi was claiming lions had been seen. He was raising the cry for guns again. Raboupi had gotten almost apoplectic when Nelson proposed that if there were truly lions around we should call in the game scouts from Maun, because that, according to Raboupi, would make the men of Tsau look like small boys. Finally he had sent Raboupi off after telling him that he had to bring proof there were lions around, such as droppings. Nelson nicked himself. I took over, and he let me finish shaving him, a first. I had to make him not talk while I finished up. It was nice. He wanted to kiss my breasts, but through my blouse, he wasn't asking for more. There were more apologies.

Admit one thing, I said. Admit you like to fight in the generic male way, you liked fighting or contending with Harold because you like fighting with other men, specifically, which is more fun than contending with women or fills some other need. No, he said, no and no.

You do know, I said, that Harold is gay, by the way?

All he said, after a pause, was How do you know that? He looked offended or hurt.

I told him how I knew. He wanted to know when I'd known for certain, and seemed a little relieved that it wasn't until I was told. But all this had an odd effect.

He sat down fairly abruptly. He still had soap on his face. The state he seemed to be in wasn't meditative, a state I'd seen him in enough times to identify for what it was. This was something else—sheer cessation, stasis. I prayed that being hung over had something to do with it. It was alarming.

Nelson did have a trait of occasionally branching off into an intense static condition of empathy for some victimized group he hadn't thought about in a while. It was a trait that was en route to the borderline of neurosis, in my humble opinion, and was part of his ongoing great question, the question of which contemporary evil was the actual worst and therefore the one you should really be directing your life effort against. This business of dwelling on abused groups was like driving through the mountains with someone likely to stop and brood at every overlook, even though night was falling and the inn lay far ahead. The first few times he fell into these broodings it made me feel I was dealing with someone very pure, someone who in fact needed protection, shielding. I connected these bursts of brooding to his mastery of the statistics of every injustice known to man, such as the number killed in concentration camps under Tito or this year's figures for dowry bride murders in India.

He came out of his stasis saying something about what an abyss it must be to be homosexual in a society whose every gesture of law and culture makes you feel unclean. It was a form of crucifixion. He himself couldn't imagine anything more perverted than being forced to act against your sexual orientation.

I was just beginning to appreciate how deeply hung over he was. He took my hands and said An alcoholic promising not to drink again is roughly like anyone promising never to fart again, I'm aware, but never again, so help me, I swear.

I appreciated the impulse behind what he was saying, but I wanted one thing clear. I'm not an involvee, I said, and I'm not your mother. You'll see me react to the way you are when you drink, if you drink, but never in my life will you see me wagging my finger. I have no interest in controlling another human being's vices. I said My reaction was about never finding a reason to offer to dig up some wine just for us, or for me, even, but you say reciprocation, plus already having begun drinking, did something to your judgment, which is fine. I said that I also thought he associated me with the cardinal virtue of sobriety. I said Let's just regard the whole episode as overdetermined and forget it.

This worked out to be a genius thing to say, evidently. He was relieved. We held hands across the table. Sail away, I thought, this being my personal phrase for moments of feeling perfect and at ease. I more sing it than say it, mentally. I only use it in extremis, so to speak, when

I have to face the fact that nothing is wrong. I don't know if the phrase comes from some cheap pop source. It may. I don't know when I had used it last.

I was having an overwhelming experience of joyfully being with someone and not wondering what he or I should do next to maintain this. Nobody was entertaining anybody. Remorse is powerful with me. I said While everybody around here is apologizing I want to apologize for something myself: I want to apologize for calling my mother the Colossus of Duluth. He smiled, but he wanted us not to talk. This was extraordinary for him too, then. For me the feeling was like being in a bath and being fed at the same time, or thereabouts. But this also traces back to Nelson, who'd mentioned the theory of someone he admired that every abstract painting you instinctively admire is in fact a picture of a biomorph in a perfect environment for it, a homolog of the womb. As I recall, this was something he'd mentioned as an example of paradox, because the author of it was a literary fascist terrible in almost every other respect, although admittedly very smart. We must have been talking about bad people dot dot dot good ideas, how to deal with that, how to deal with taintedness, a theme of his.

I don't want to hear the answer to this, really, I said, but if you were in a room full of women, thirty or so women, or ten, and you saw one of them and felt a deep attraction and you had a magic ring you could touch that would make people fall in love with you but not one by one, only in a broad zone, and this was the only way you could be sure your target woman would fall in love with you, sweeping all the others of various degrees of attractiveness along with her and presenting you with the problem of turning them off, probably hurtfully, would you still do it? I don't know where this came from, to this day.

He said of course, no. Still he wanted us not to talk. I had the clear sense that he wanted the feelings this silence together gave us. My fear was that I was going to show I was less tolerant of perfect silence than he was, or than he assumed I was. Sail away, I thought.

Things intergrade. I had another touch of the feeling the next day when I got a fullfledged endearment from Nelson. When I got it I felt faint, which shows the level I was coming to this from. I had a klang association with being in a house where the mother is an accomplished cook and four dishes are in the oven at the same time, including baking, rolls baking, and the united fragrance is perfect. Which reminds me that as a child when I was invited to anyone else's house for a good meal I had a secret fetish of putting something from each item on my plate on

my fork each time I took a bite, which must mean something. Nelson
was being sexually attentive post Harold and Julia. The endearment was
more a conclusion on my part than an endearment direct and nonpareil,
but still I clung to it when it happened. Nelson was up first that morning
and when he heard me stirring he said Ah the voice of the turtle is heard
in the land. So then am I your turtle? I asked. You are, he said, my dear
turtle. He seemed to like thinking of me as that. He used the term
affectionately later that day, and then on and off later on. I think he was
grateful to me that morning over a discussion the night before during
which I had been frank with him about cunnilingus. I'd told him I
appreciated it but that he should relax about it. He'd gotten into a pattern
of regularly descending every fourth or fifth outing. I explained to him I
enjoyed it but only really enjoyed it when I felt it was undertaken out of
being genuinely overwhelmed in that direction. Otherwise he should
know I preferred our usual face to face but with the nice, graduated
approach he had. He was relieved. They always are. There's something
infantile somehow about cunnilingus except at the right moment and
the right interval. The subject is left communicating with the vacant air
during it, for one thing.

Where Were We Going?

I think I was tentatively starting to pride myself on having a generally
good effect on Nelson. He agreed, at least insofar as his attitude to
keeping up with the news was concerned, something he was perpetually
striving to keep from turning into a mania. He had conquered it as far as
print went, because although he still saved all his Economists, he had
disciplined himself to read them in batches, working backward from the
most recent issue so that tributary pieces in earlier issues could be
skipped. This was an old intention of his that had been honored more in
the breach before my arrival. He was spending far less time trying to
catch Deutsche Welle or the World Service than initially. In fact we had
missed the attempt on Reagan's life as a contemporaneous thing, about
which he was grateful. I can't tell you, he said, the amount of time I
would have wasted, while it looked like he might die, trying to figure out

which clique or faction was going to turn out to be behind this thing. It was all moot when he first heard about it, and he had saved hours of his mental life, indirectly thanks to me.

I also thought he was tending to be more truthful, or rather more truthful more quickly. There was one contraindication to this, when I asked him, lightly and en passant, how old he was, and he palpably hesitated before answering. We were working in the gum tree plantation. I was stunned for a second at his apparently revealing himself to be someone who thinks age is important. No truly adult male does. Then he said the only thing that could have saved him, which was that he didn't know how old he was. He thought he was forty-seven, but he might be a year older. He had been born at home. His mother had already gotten pregnant, he gathered, by the time she began living with his father. His father had been trying to make a living as an apprentice to a man who sold redwood mulch and made coffee tables out of redwood tree boles and on the side did serious woodcarvings. This was in a collapsing utopian colony founded by Finnish socialists in the nineteenth century, mostly abandoned by them, and feebly recolonized by Depression unemployed people. It was in Washington State, in the woods. Nelson's father had delivered him. The birth certificate was gotten after the fact, in fact long after, and his mother's sensitivity, as a good Catholic, may have had something to do with the date entered.

Then he amazed me by saying I know you think I was about to lie to you on the subject of my age. The opposite is true. The lie would have been just to save mental time, I suppose. But I think we can both stand it if we, if I, stick to the absolute truth from now on. This was said with an undernote of How do you like that? almost, I thought, that was faintly threatening.

It was threatening because it dared me to advance prematurely into questions I knew would be difficult for him. They were inchoate or global, many of them, but they were all pressing to me. Where were we going? was one. What was I supposed to make of his recent allusions to the truism that people who worked in development created situations that were supposed to be good enough for the locals forever but not for their Western animators, who would be leaving shortly for the fleshpots of home, everyone should understand. But did that mean he intended to be the exception? And if so, I had questions about that, because the exceptions to going home were the religious. They were the only ones who fought being torn from their projects in the mean streets of the world, and lurking in their motivation had to be—and Denoon saw it this way too—something self-punitive. He did seem to be loving Tsau more. In part it was the freak rain, the sense of an unusual surplus making daily life enormously easier. I kept looking at the going-versus-staying conundrum from different angles. Of course I am and was in revolt against the cultural diktat—which is what it amounts to—that women are by nature sessile and men are footloose and that when they find the right man women are supposed to go against their sessile instincts if they can't anchor their male alongside them and go wafting along after him, to wherever. But here Denoon was being too sessile for my taste. You could say I felt slightly torn.

A paradoxical result of Nelson's declaration was that I was more reluctant to pursue things with him than before the edict. I wondered what was going on, since I hadn't asked for anything so drastic from him. But there it was, and also it was supposedly obtaining without my having said Ah, me too, because I'm not a hypocrite.

I was sleeping unusually well in Tsau, as a result, I assume, of the substantial component of physical work I was doing daily, but my underlying insomniac nature still got galvanized from time to time, especially when in the middle of the night I'd discover Nelson gone somewhere, usually briefly, but not invariably briefly. He did go off, as I knew, on personal retreats of a day or two, without much preambling. That was a given with him. But there were more than a handful of times when I would wake up and find him not present.

I made the usual assumptions about where he might have gone, at least for the shorter absences. There was also the delicate matter of our both being pretty much on the sendero leguminoso, dietarily, as he put it, so that there was some flatulence to deal with, simple flatulence. It seemed to be cyclical, but it was definitely there. In our first days together we had individually found reasons to go outside for a minute, especially after we'd gone to bed, to avoid the antiromance of it all. But that got to be too much. We developed a fairly decent modus, I thought. He might say, when I was the author, Also sprach Zarathustra, or Ah, a report from the interior, as though he were an ambassador or proconsul. These and some other coinages evolved as we became more comfortable with each other. This condition does have to be worked through between lovers. I know of a marriage where the first hairline crack that led to full collapse appeared when the husband claimed that flatulence was only a problem when he did the cooking.

A few times I said nothing on his return. Then once I said Where do you go, mostly?

Well, mostly it was to the latrine, but not always. Sometimes it was to muse on the landscape, to moongaze.

I was persistent. I asked But do people come and meet with you late at night ever?

Sometimes yes, he said, but only occasionally. There was some of that—meeting outside of channels—before things settled down at Tsau and we got the committees really working. The Tswana are secretive, in case you hadn't noticed.

Forget I said anything, I said. But then I said, like a deranged person, Tell me what you did about sex all the years here when you were seeing Grace infrequently, shall we say, what you did aside from sublimating. This question had been en route to my lips from ancient times, and the moment of asking it was like the moment when you know for a certainty that nothing you do, no posture you get in, is going to keep you from retching. I was ashamed, naturally.

I give him credit. He was direct. I masturbated, he said, not as a regular thing, or I went to two or three women in Gaborone who aren't exactly prostitutes and are my friends, and the real question you want to ask me, and to which the answer is no, is if I slept with any woman in Tsau. So. And the beautiful Dineo is included in that.

Too much is enough, I said. Let's change the subject. I was over-wrought, and it continued, partly because he was showing so much noblesse toward me, and how little if any quid pro quo was expected from my side. This I took as nobly and subtly acknowledging that the storage tank of lies and adventures on the male side is so much larger, generally, than the one on the female side that there was no onus what-ever on me to reciprocate. I was thinking Well, masturbation, how not? but how often, on average dot dot dot. But that would have been genu-inely too much, so we went on to business as usual, both of us about equally upset.

He was still upset when it was time for my abacus lesson. He was skilled at tutoring, but that day he was impatient and not clear. In Tsau everybody ultimately learned the abacus. Business meetings at Sekopo-lolo were alive with the click of the beads. It was required, like learning to butcher. I loved the abacus and still use it. Why isn't this amazing instrument taught in schools in the United States? I asked him. Because it doesn't create dependency, was his answer. No batteries, no electricity, and one abacus is all you need for your whole life. He had plans for an Abacus Society for all of Botswana and beyond into Swaziland and Le-sotho. I absorbed nothing during that session.

A Diagram

About here I began to be more fragmentary. I was doing my journal less assiduously, I think because doing it felt slightly counterromantic, although that wasn't what I told myself. This wasn't in response to pressure of any sort from Nelson. He had at worst a quizzical attitude toward my diarizing: he was also flattered, at least that was the way I took all his Boswell references. Somewhere shortly before this I'd done something Nelson took exception to, strongly. And that incident may have had some impact on my eagerness to write things down.

I must have been showing what struck Nelson as more than a passing interest in different people's backgrounds, their affiliations, who were the devout Zed CC's and who were pro Boso, and so on. I really was doing this more in the spirit of asking myself about women who interested me, trying to get him to confirm the correctness of the croquis résumés which I was amusing myself by coming up with to pass the time when I was working at something dull.

I remember we were talking about the Botswana Social Front. I was curious as to how they must feel about Tsau. The ones I had talked to in Gabs had been for nationalizing everything except cattle and giving a social wage to everybody, working or not. They had a huge youth wing, I knew, and a women's organization. They had two people in parliament and were, although I didn't know it at the time, on the verge of electing mayors in two of the large towns. Martin Wade had approved strenuously of them, I hadn't failed to notice. The Bosos I'd met fell into two categories, those who were nice but fervent in a way it was hard to take seriously and those who were cold, rigid, and eager to be in some position where nobody would talk back to them, ever.

Ah, Boso, ah yes, Nelson said. He went on, copiously, even after I reminded him that I knew somewhat of his attitude to Boso, since he had been debating one of them, Mbaake, the first time we met. I was hearing what I already knew, to wit, Boso was Jacobin, corrupt at the top, the rank and file ingenuous, the top dogs taking money under the table from the tribal chiefs—or giving it to them, rather—and from the Russians and from De Beers and from the South Africans. Did you ever meet Pamane, the Boso supreme secretary? Nelson asked me. All I knew was that he was a dentist. He said Then probably you don't know why he's so revered by the student left, which is because he has apparently memorized the last volume in the Marx Engels Gesamtausgabe, the *Chronik Seines Lebens*, which is a day by day listing of where Marx and Engels were on any given day of their lives and what they were doing. This is what they worship. He'll even give you the book and you pick out a month, I think it is, and he tells you what Marx was up to, like a mentalist. This is what they worship! Here in the dry heart of dying Africa, in a country famishing for welders, plumbers, borehole mechanics! You talk about savant idiot—he's it. The students want to be like him. So does the whole industrial-class level of the civil service. And he isn't a dentist, by the way, he's a chiropodist, a further irony in that you have so few foot problems in Africa because people still go barefoot a lot and commercial footwear is the main cause of foot problems, so that his medical specialty is probably the least needed one he could have picked out.

He said Anyway I got this up for you. He produced a folio-size sheet of thick paper folded in half or thirds. He unfolded it at me, saying that he had put work into it.

It was a political diagram of the population of Tsau, as I understood it, or more properly an affinal diagram, because families and tribes and other affiliations were among the attributes keyed. It was in several colors.

Something impelled me to make him not show this to me. I violently didn't want to see it. I hadn't asked for it.

I pushed it away.

He was stung and annoyed and repeated that he'd put work into it.

Don't get upset, I said, but I don't want to see it, that's all.

I don't know what my impulse was. It would be facile to say it was pure solidarity with the women, for instance. But I would have left the premises rather than look at this thing. I wonder now if in some oblique way it made me mad that Pamane's memoriousness had been trashed, since if I have any distinct mental virtue that would be it. What was so despicable about Pamane being able to remember a remarkable amount about someone he admired, rightly or wrongly?

In any case, my saying no provoked a peculiar enraged act that took me totally by surprise. The act was like a strongman performance in the circus, it was so deft and definite, so practiced-seeming. What he did was, in a lightning way, crushingly fold the chart down into a square packet the size of a deck of cards. Then he dashed out into the yard and thrust the packet into the throat of the mudstove.

I followed and squatted down near him in order to catch what he was muttering to me while he solicited the paper or cardboard or foolscap or whatever it was to burn. He seemed to be saying everything was all right.

I made him out to be saying You identify, which I love. You identify.

I said I don't know if I identify or not, but in fact I don't think it's that. I think your document smacks of something.

He stood up and dusted his hands off, his face very flushed, still. You identify, he said. You're a woman. You think my chart is manipulative.

I thought this was pretty reflexive of him and told him so. I reached into myself, which being oversimplified by someone else helps with. It's principle, I said. Your diagram is part of something I don't like. These people have a right to be anything they want and for that not to be noticed or recorded by you except in passing. Are you an anthropologist? What is this?

He seemed astonished with me.

I said My mother thought Negroes were funny. I've escaped from her. She knew nothing. How many black people were there in Minnesota? She got her idea of black people from the radio, Amos and Andy, Is you is or is you ain't my baby? She'd say that to me when I was being naughty, with a big ho ho.

I was worked up.

I said This reminds me of her and reminds me of dossiers. You think you're neutral, you think what you do is neutral because you're not British or a Boer, because you're American and we never did much in this particular neck of the woods. But it's the strong and the weak, or that's what this feels like to me. I'm sorry if I'm being incoherent.

You're so strict, was his last word on this, turning away deeply unsatisfactorily to me with my need for a cincture at the bottom of every event.

He started to go in but stopped and came back to embrace me. I'm yours, he said, I am.

The only thing I didn't like about that was the suddenness of the transition from evident rage to this. I hate bouleversements in general.

Diving

His I'm yours stayed with me and became more gravid in my mind over the days. I took it as a sign we were close to the point where it would be as painful for him to lose me as for me to lose him. Whenever I felt that that might really be true I tried saying Pride goeth before a fall to myself, sonorously, not with great effectiveness.

Wherever it was we really were, I did notice that I was more interested than ever in the exact terms of his divorce, not that I felt it would be smart to reveal that. And I felt our sex was going differently. Sex can be various things, but in my experience the usual thing it is is considerate work on the part of both parties, with Alphonse and Gaston–style routines—after you, no, after you, mais non—this being the standard among educated people. But then there's another kind of sex, that's more like despair on both sides. My own name for it is blank sex. It's sex without an order of battle. No program goes with blank sex. My closest nonsexual analog for it is from repeated diving. When I was a girl I would go to the municipal pool in the summers and get into uninterrupted diving, off the board and into the pool and back up onto the board again as fast as I could: chain-diving. This was from the low board only, so that the circuit would be the shortest possible. The idea, I think, was trying to link the experience of being in midair as closely to the next moment of it as you could humanly achieve. Or it may have been the moments of plunging I was trying to link up. What you wanted was a certain inner teeming feeling produced under cover of ostensibly testing yourself on the number and quality of dives you could make. I was always surprised that there was no one to notice what I was so manically doing and try to moderate me. But then I used feints so that I could continue. I would sometimes nod or shake my head as though I were responding to someone in the area where the mothers sat, mine not included, to throw anyone who might think I was being excessive off the track. In blank sex everything tangible about your partner is transformed into something that excites and weakens you, seems irreplaceable, his breath, even physical defects, and all these things are somehow necessary for your physical survival or salvation, and yet you know you can never possess them even as you caress them and try to convince yourself that contact with them in the heat of sex is the same as claiming them, having them forever, which in your heart you know is untrue, and thus the tonus of despair.

Blank sex is only possible between adults—that is, it's not a reflorescence of onset sex à la adolescence, which is intense but so expeditionary and educational that sadness and intimations of finitude hardly come into it. But then you do get experience and you get older and sex is going to continue and it does continue and then sex is what it is, average, until the time comes when everything about it changes.

There was more blank sex lately, which was wonderful but also not wonderful in that it was enervating. Postcoitum you might be left in a crystalline mental state but with no physical executive power to speak of. We would resume our duties in Tsau, but I was always afraid people would be able to tell, that they'd be able to see through to my essential languor, no matter how hard I tried to bury it in brisk movements and responses. It was a drawback that midday was usually the time this broke on us, because we had to go out and interact so proximately to our occasion. But sometimes I even felt the effects lasted overnight and would be visible to the ideal observer should she be passing through, perchance.

Masepa

Your hair grows like a fiend, I told Nelson. I liked cutting his hair now that he had stopped being resistant to fairly frequent trimming. He was even goodnatured about letting me take my time about it for the purposes of a touch of art. I was going very languorously that afternoon, a Saturday, for the aforementioned reason. I had gotten him over to accepting a longish crewcut as his style for the present, despite the fact that it did nothing for his incipient male pattern baldness, which the pulled-back ponytail had been made for. But he was unvain, essentially unvain, I was gradually having to admit.

Dineo glided onto the patio, out of nowhere and out of breath, beautiful as always, her image reminding me that I would never be one of the truly lithe. She was wearing a long white tunic and black wraparound underskirt, very severe for her, and a tight powder blue turban. There were no greetings. She spoke past me directly to Denoon in machine-gun Setswana, which I strained to understand, coming up with the unlikely interpretation that someone was coming to us bearing masepa, meaning shit.

Nelson had gotten up so fast at her approach that I had stuck him minorly with the point of the scissors halfway up his neck. Nelson began thrashing at the cut hair on his naked shoulders and telling me urgently he wanted his shirt. I am not going to run like a child for your shirt, I said, or like a valet, unless this is an emergency, which it isn't. All this was out of the side of my mouth. But I changed my mind when I sensed he was clearly unhappy and feeling distinctly unhorsed over something. I got his shirt, but casually.

Toiling up toward us was a procession led by Hector Raboupi. Dineo said to me in English Raboupi is bringing lion spoor to show.

Suddenly Denoon wanted a different mise en scène than he had just seemed to want. Now he was back to wanting to be sitting down and in the midst of getting his hair cut: he wanted to be interrupted. He slashed my hand away from pressing on the little blood bud on his neck, hurting me with the sharpness of the blow. He threw the shirt I'd just brought him onto the ground. He caught my hand with the scissors still in it and brought it back up into cutting range. He held his hands up and pushed out, hard, toward Dineo, obviously miming her to fade back beside or behind the house, which she ignored, I was pleased to see. Deal with yourself, I almost said to Nelson.

Raboupi and his sister and four other women and six or so men hove into view. He was triumphally dragging a burlap sack.

They arrived.

I thought it was interesting that it was Dorcas, a woman, he directed to bring the sack forward and peel the mouth back, to reveal a few dark spiny clods of supposed lion dung. Dineo went to look.

This was Raboupi triumphant. He was wearing his fur cap, with the tail brought forward over his right shoulder, a signifier of pride or teasement, I'd been told. It was a cool day, but he was wearing a cowhide vest in lieu of a shirt, and the vest was not fastened up. This was winter. He was the only one in the group so lightly dressed. The other men were wearing jerseys and watch caps. I noted that somehow he had acquired a pair of new-looking gleaming black riding boots.

So, my sister, what shall you say? Raboupi said in English to Dineo.

I wondered what tack she would take. There was no question this was lion spoor, because of the quills. Lions are the only animals that eat porcupines.

This is very old spoor, Dineo said in English and then again in Setswana.

If a group can snarl, this one did. Dineo shrugged. Raboupi went passionately into just where and when the spoor had been found.

Denoon twitched to remind me that I was supposed to be cutting his hair, which was difficult for me since it was a done job. But I fiddled on, as instructed.

Denoon lazily asked why they had come to this place when the matter was something for the mother committee.

Raboupi was quick. We are going to every place with this to show, not just this place. After now you will see us roundabout so all can see.

Dineo murmured that then the mother committee would be expecting him to come at the soonest.

Denoon was impatient. He was conveying the feeling that he expected Dineo to say more.

Enfields! Enfields! Raboupi's group was chanting. They knew the particular rifle they wanted. Raboupi was doing a recitative on the well-known incompetence and tardiness in arriving of the government game scouts.

Dineo seemed frozen.

There can be Enfields for hire, Denoon said alternately in English and Setswana, all business.

Still Dineo was passive.

Nelson said, projecting patently theatrically, I thought, all in Setswana, You must meet with the mother committee to see if they say some Enfields can be stored, a small number, and put out for hire when there is some need.

I was electrified at this, because I knew Nelson knew that what Raboupi wanted was for Enfields, or whatever rifle could be gotten, to be regular items in stock at Sekopololo, which would mean they would filter out into general ownership through women to the men who lived with them. So rental was a brilliant idea. Of course it cut against his role as guardian of the social surplus, guns being as expensive as they are. But I knew Nelson, and this was flexibility on the part of the man who liked to say that the best definition of the state was Lenin's The state is bodies of armed men. The rental scheme would keep the numbers of guns in play finite. He was improving. It was also since me that this guardian of the social surplus had given up his objection to importing bras, when he had previously taken the position that a strip of cloth artfully passed around the upper body like an X was essentially all that was required. I had said to him that his notion of the postlactative breast was so defective it was laughable. His finishing flourish to Raboupi was to say that he was turning his own rifle over to Sekopololo in perpetuity to begin the scheme.

Dineo came more center stage to cheerlead belatedly for Nelson's proposal, which it was clear Raboupi was surprised by and not enchanted with.

He and his party withdrew pestered by King James, who had turned up complaining that Raboupi had refused his cart services.

I think I felt delighted with the rental resolution. I could tell Nelson had been annoyed at Dineo's not taking a more forward role in laying things out, but there was nothing reproachful showing as they summed up once Raboupi was gone. Why did I have the feeling that he had partly gotten this proposal going so quickly as a kind of demonstration to me? All seemed well. There might be trouble over how many rifles should be bought, Nelson thinking we might get away with two or three, Dineo thinking we might need to go for five or six, but it would be worked out. We all looked ruefully at one another and that was that, I thought.

Psychisms

In a couple of days Nelson was morosely rethinking the rifle scheme, strictly entre nous, compulsively I thought, adumbrating ways it could be strengthened, rules on how many guns could be out for hire at any one time, and so on. Then it was on toward the dark scenarios that having the guns for hire might escalate to. First the guns would be checked out during lion scares, on anybody's report that lions had been sighted. Then there would be some incidental hunting of permitted species, like warthogs and rock rabbits. Then there would come a time when a deal would be struck with the Basarwa who were better and better established in their little settlement behind Tsau on the sand river, and the deal would be that Raboupi's men would shoot impala and wildebeest and the carcasses would be traded to the Basarwa on some basis, with the bullet wounds altered so that the carcasses looked like arrow or trap kills. Everything would appear legal. And then the Basarwa would barter the meat with Sekopololo, but there would be kickbacks to Raboupi. And then we would be well en route to establishing a permanent leisure hunting class among the men, than which nothing could be more traditional, more parasitic. Something like this was bound to happen because only the Basarwa could legally hunt large game inside the reserve. Of course I was thinking that nothing is totally bad. We could use more animal protein. He knew my position on that. The nurse was saying that there was too much anemia. The only exceptions to the severe restrictions on hunting by non-Basarwa had to do with lions and leopards, which could be shot if they directly threatened persons or livestock. The nice thing was that Nelson came to me with his compulsive scenarizing, which in effect was asking me to help him rid himself of it.

First I came up with all the cavils I could think of, the flaws in his assumptions about what would happen postrental. But in fact, underneath, I saw his point. I did come up with one idea he liked: the rule should be that women were always included in any hunting parties and women were to be trained in the use of rifles and incorporated into every facet of what was ostensibly going on. This provision obviously couldn't stop the particular devolutionary process Nelson was afraid of, but it seemed to me that it might slow it down. I made my case. Do you get it? I asked, when he was taking too long to brighten up.

Gotcha, Buthelezi, he said, a pun on the name Gatsha Buthelezi, and another good omen. He was showing more willingness to be jocular about serious things. Gotcha was another entry in a jeu I had initiated between us when for no reason I had described some position he had taken as Highly Selassie or Fairly Dickinson or that some notion of his was Utter Pradesh. He had been longsuffering at first about this game, but lately he'd been more willing to join in the fun and had introduced inversions, such as Ansermet, Ernest.

But alas, even with good-faith efforts on his part, he resuccumbed to gloom over the rifle question. Again he as much as said Help me with this. Again we sat down together. Before I even had time to try for some new approach, he was saying he thought he knew what it was that he couldn't overcome.

His problem was, in his words, metaphysical. He was being very confessional. He had a conviction about Tsau that could only be called metaphysical, which was that somehow Tsau would prosper only if it, as a created or guest organism superimposed on a large organism, the desert, an organism that could be hostile, would or could prosper only if it took what it needed from the desert in order to be there, and nothing more. He was the one who described this as tantamount to an idée fixe. I was sympathetic throughout, although a little confused. After all, this was the same man who referred to organized religion as organized superstition. This is superstitious, he said. If rifles came in, the fear was that there would be competitive and unnecessary hunting and killing on behalf of the population that already had enough, the people of Tsau. There was a brief divagation on the Basarwa, pointing out that the only people who had made it in the burning desert for thousands of years were people who always asked forgiveness of the deity of the species they had taken the life of a representative of, and who only and always took as much as and not more than they needed to survive. Very hangdog, he said I have the feeling that I'm right about all this in a baseless way, which I need to expel if I can, and if I should.

He then went on a tack I had difficulty relating to what he'd just presented. There were things about his mother, who was so intuitive. I gathered I was supposed to be the voice of reason on this. There was a story involved that he wanted me to hear.

About his mother: the fact is that he would say she would have to be considered psychic, genuinely, but at a trivial level. As in knowing twenty minutes before guests were going to arrive, when she would begin bustling to prepare, and so on.

I said Totally unexpected guests or expected guests who happened to be late?

Both, he said, both. If they were late, she had started preparing late. She would know. Also she could find lost objects, a useful gift since for his father losing things had been almost a hobby. Nelson said There was a period when the domelight kept coming on in our car when it was locked and parked in our driveway and we knew it had been off the night before. This trivial poltergeist phenomenon drove his father the archempiriocritical materialist crazy, and not because he was worried about the battery being run down. You should have seen it, Nelson said. My father went through a period of damn near paranoia directed at me and my brother. He made sure he had the only keys to the car safely in his possession and went out of his way to see that the car was locked tight every night and that the domelight switch was set at off. The mystery went on sporadically over a period of a few weeks, then stopped. My father eventually associated my mother with this oddness, and it did seem to be true that sometimes the light went on when my mother was in the vicinity of the car, taking out the garbage or putting mail in the mailbox. Then he had the wiring taken apart, without the garage finding anything.

He said She was clairvoyant, but not flamboyantly clairvoyant, so to speak. She seemed to know where you were when you weren't home, whose house to call, for example, to locate my brother, who was someone who could be anywhere. She was a sort of physical medium, I think, and ironically enough her attitude to her powers was that they were nothing, they were coincidences. She had the traditional Catholic attitude toward the paranormal—it was illicit and probably demonic. And of course to my father the paranormal was all bunk, all charlatanism. His suspicion fell on me because I was learning to do a few card tricks at the time.

He said The coup de grace in all this came near the end of my father's life, when he had gone abstinent and become very meek toward my mother. His liver was gone, and he was dying. I think he may have been on the point of becoming actually pious, but he managed to die before that could happen. In any case there was nothing he could do for my mother that was too much, including taking her to Europe so that she could inter alia visit shrines and cathedrals she had read and dreamed about her whole life, including Notre Dame, the jewel in the forehead of her idea of Catholic Europe.

They go into Notre Dame and for the hell of it he decides he'll buy some of those centime votive candles they sell in racks in the back and take them up and light them and add them to the array already burning that you see up at the end of the aisle. My mother buys a handful of candles, and he does too, and they go up. He stands waiting while she places and lights her candles. And then he takes his out and not one of them will light. Not one of the wicks will take the match. He goes back and gets more, a selection from the different zones of the rack, but the result is the same. He takes some back to the hotel and three candles light right up. She was all wonderment and astonishment, I gather. And when my father asked me how I could explain it and I said maybe it's a reverse poltergeist effect, that is, instead of repressed feeling showing up in spontaneous fires in the curtains and woodwork, which is the standard explanation of the poltergeist phenomenon, maybe you produced a fire suppression effect. He was very unhappy and he wondered what good a college education had done me, because of the bunk I was coming up with.

This account is something I now associate with another remark of Denoon's, to which at the time I paid no attention, to the effect that when you're really happy and doing the right thing with your life, including morally—for example not living in evasion—in that situation you should expect to have repeated trivial instances of the odd happening to you. You'll have correct intuitions. For no reason an obscure or archaic word will come into your mind and in a week you might discover it's exactly the word you need for a difficult passage in a piece of writing you're doing. I remember wondering at the time if he meant to be saying that the more rightly you're living, the more odd things will be peripherally happening to you, so that as you get to actual secular sainthood you'd find matchbooks levitating toward you when you need a light and your weight going down no matter how much Black Forest cake you eat.

I know now that I should have plunged to the root of all that in the man, because I was the right person to do it, believing in nothing as I do unless it is proved to me to my entire satisfaction, and the first thing to be proved is that nobody is lying, nobody lying, nobody wanting to lie, nobody lying—my utopia and good luck to me.

I thought that by listening to his story of the candles, I'd done all that was expected. But Nelson wanted to know what I thought, seriously.

So I told him I thought probably someone was lying, telling a story. I asked Is it possible this was a folie à deux somehow proceeding from your mother? I have never made a more unpopular suggestion. My idea was to reconstruct exactly and from whom and in what he had gotten the original story, but he was more than resistant.

But who was lying? he said. There has to be a reason for lying!

No there doesn't, I said, and that's the problem.

The rifle question then did seem to go away, but whether I had done more than reinforce a certain fatalism he was feeling on the subject, I don't know. I am exactly the wrong person to discuss the psychic realm socalled with. I have no sympathy. I'd thought, on the basis of everything he'd said up to then, his manifest attitudes to the notional and the church up to then, that we were birds of a feather, but clearly there was an inclusion or residue or cavity of the sublunary in him. I hate the mysterious, because it's the perfect medium for liars, the place they go to multiply and preen and lie to each other. Liars are the enemy. They transcend class, sex, and nation. They make everything impossible.

The Better Happiness

The question of when you're living rightly and not in evasion with a capital E, which had emerged proximately to our talk about his mother's psychiana, began to preoccupy me subliminally because I was feeling very happy, day to day, and I felt Nelson was saying that there was some definable difference between brute happiness, which can occur to anyone anywhere, and this other and better happiness whose reality he had insidiously half convinced me of. The better happiness arises out of a sense of alignment between your powers and the world's woe, so far as I could tell. Or at least this is a necessary condition for it. I tried to get at this a little by asking if it wasn't slightly Hegelian. What a mistake. He hated Hegel and told me in detail why. It went deep with Nelson. It even ended with a sort of quiz, he was so anxious that I not in any way mix up his notions with anything related to terrible Hegel.

I was happy. How was Nelson?

One datum I had was that he was having, recently, a recurrent dream he associated with feeling high or very good. I always had to be careful handling his dreams, because I found them so transparent, this good luck dream not excluded. It was a landscape dream. He is at a height above the landscape, either on an overlook or in the air over the main item in it. He's looking down onto a wooded countryside, a wilderness with a circular lake at the heart of it, the lake featuring a round island at its center, and in the center of the island a circular pond. The unfailing association for this dream was with the good junctures in his life. Could this be anything but a breast analog? I'm sure that's what it was, because his association for what was going on down on the island and around the pond was, he thought, he surmised, perhaps naked young women lounging or going for a dip. If this scene is anything, it's a breast inside a moat. The island was described as mounded, not flat. I hinted at my interpretation, but he seemed not to want to go where it was pointing. This is another example of the complexity of his dream constructs: he's in the Grand Vefour, he's been seated, but they've run out of silverware.

I think what I was experiencing was a period of freedom from basic

striving, made even sweeter by small things like feeling freer increasingly
to come and go in Nelson's various realms, such as the glassworks—
which since the maiming of his apprentice had been essentially his sanc-
tum sanctorum—and such as certain tenderer areas of his past. There
were fewer checkpoints between incidents in the present and interesting
nexi back in his personal history. For example, lately he was pleased with
himself sexually, especially when it happened that I might have to request him to desist, let me rest. Somehow this led to the evocation of his
father as a sort of 1920s armchair sex radical with a locking glass-fronted
bookcase containing *The Man Who Died*, by D. H. Lawrence, about a
sex-mad Christ, and Edward Carpenter's *Love's Coming of Age*, a sort of
bible of that milieu, and *The Body's Rapture*, by Jules Romains, wherein
someone's penis is referred to as The Lord God of the Flesh, which
Nelson found hilarious of course. Naturally he found a way to penetrate
this collection. How the sacred reading cache fit with his father's having
chosen for a mate someone so hermetically sealed off from cultural tastes
like his was a serious question. It created a bond, was Nelson's thought,
something his father could lacerate himself with equivalent to his mother's separate and different suffering. Nelson was certain his mother
thought sex was strictly for procreation and that any other application
was sinful, something to be endlessly atoned for. He was equally sure his
father had been unbrokenly faithful throughout their marriage, although
I wouldn't trust an alcoholic to be faithful for a minute. What have they
got to lose that they haven't already lost? We talked about how wonderful
it must have been, say circa 1923, to be under the impression that once
sex freedom dawned in the world human institutions would relax into
utopia.

Another sign of being in equilibrium must be repeated feelings of
equanimity about things that would normally bother you. I was enjoying
work that was by definition boring, like passing bricks up the hillside as
part of a chain of women so that the catchment system could be repaired.
Then I even enjoyed some rather grueling forays out into the desert to
harvest grapple plant. This was actually one of the sub rosa products of
Tsau, and it was another case of being honored by being asked to join
the teams, which were made up exclusively of senior—and so presumably more trustworthy—women, and women for the most part without
male collaterals of any sort on the scene. Tsau received a huge price for
the plant, whose leaves went into a potion supposed to cure impotence.
The buyer was a consortium of West German health food stores. The
truncate, exoteric name for the teams was Kokotsetsa, the Upholders,

but the true, esoteric full name was Upholders of the Far Fallen Down Penises of the Europeans. I only went two or three times on day-trip gathering expeditions; in fact other teams scoured deep into the country-side, overnight and longer. The take for Sekopololo was fairly astound-ing, which I was delighted to find out because it demystified things and assuaged my drive toward a marxist interpretation of every institution that manages to persist over time, id est where does the money come from? I think marxism should be called cui bonism, from cui bono, which is what it comes down to. That year the harvest was immense. The runs I made were really gleaning exercises, decided on because of the unusual rain, which meant that this late second harvest was a good idea.

I put the climax of this period at my return from one of the grapple plant expeditions, probably the last. It was toward two or three in the afternoon. Nelson was nowhere, no one had seen him, so I sought him in a place I knew he liked, a ledge on the south side of the koppie, high up, overhung with mopane trees, and there he was.

There he was, on a goatskin, prone, furiously reading his Nonesuch Blake, doing something he was always haranguing the world, through harangues to me, to do—that is, stop and read during the prime part of the day, not when you're at the end of your strength and when reading competes with television and paying your bills. In the good society you would see people reading during the heart of the day: there would be provision for it. Nelson was lying on the goatskin with two pillows under his chest, wearing canvas shorts, no socks or sandals, and a bulky black cowl sweater I didn't know he owned.

I crept up. His legs were in three tones, pale below where his knee-socks came to, and then darker, then darker yet where a strip of shadow fell across his upper thighs. I had read a certain amount of Blake in a dutiful way in the course of things, and it had seemed clotted and recur-sive to me, so I had never thought much about the poetry except for the three or four short lyrics everybody likes, and certainly I had never attempted to memorize any Blake at all. What remained with me was what remains with everybody, Tyger tyger and What is it that in women men desire?/The lineaments of gratified desire. What I almost idly wished for as I crept up on Nelson was for some apposite line out of the whole blur and ruck of William Blake to come to me. That would be perfect. And lo, out of nowhere, and thanks to cryptomnesia being a real capac-ity, I retrieved the line He rested on the Desart wild. I felt mediumistic. Nelson rolled over in shock. It turned out that he had just been going from browsing the Four Zoas to reading the Additional Fragments and Notes section, where in fact my line came from.

This must be the right life, I thought.

The Batlodi

At the ostrich pen: two stanchions were bent far outward and the diamond mesh fencing between them had been pressed down into a chute over which our breeding pair of ostriches had decamped. Nelson suspected human agency, I knew, so I spent some time hurling my weight against one of the still-standing stanchions to prove to him that nothing I did made traces anything like what we were seeing. It was life and it was what everyone had told him: ostriches are insanely powerful beasts.

His mood wasn't helped by Raboupi appearing out of the boskage, taking an interest. Worse was that our two newest residents, the batlodi, the bad girls, were with Raboupi. These were sisters, late adolescent, related to the minister of Local Government and Lands, and they had been inside-parties in a longterm robbery of stock from a bottle store in Mmadinare owned by a Chinese. Against his better judgment and as an unavoidable favor to the minister, Nelson had agreed to accept them as parolees. This was to be a once-only exception. The minister's idea had been that all the batlodi needed was a spell of healthy country living away from the discos and bright lights of periurban Gabs. Patently this was a joke. The girls were very hard. And they exploited a certain ambiguity in the feelings of some of our people toward crimes committed against Chinese or Indians, I should say larcenies to be more accurate. The Batswana hate crime, especially intragroup. They will drop everything to chase down a pickpocket and surround him, yelling and imprecating until the police arrive. And they are more than swift with cattle rustlers out in the sandveld. But a lot of the Chinese in particular are disliked as bosses and shopkeepers. The batlodi had a faint feel of celebrity about them. They had been caught through their own reckless boasting. They would be with us for only six months. They had immediately attached themselves to the Raboupis and our malcontent nurse and a few others distinguished by a critical attitude toward Tsau. The batlodi were highly sporadic about regular work. Hector and the batlodi melted away toward the tannery.

I think Nelson liked being convinced that with the ostrich escape, he was at worst a victim of avian force and cunning. I could be married to you, he said, then quickly went on to praise my good sense, ask what thoughts I was having about my thesis, if any, and generally imply I was impressive and could do more things in the world than I probably thought I could.

The Basarwa

Another reason for not worrying unduly about the escape of the ostriches was that more fresh and dried meat was coming into Tsau. This had nothing to do with the Enfields, yet, which were still on order. Sekopololo was bartering for meat and for honeycomb with the Basarwa, whose encampment on the sand river had gotten very permanent-looking and populous. In the past they had camped there intermittently, the usual pattern, leaving when the lice and fleas got too bad. No one had paid much attention to them, they were so evanescent. There were eight families in the camp. Our children were also dealing independently with the Basarwa: the Basarwa were superb at locating anthills, fresh ones, which our children were bringing back chopped up in their dung carts to feed our chickens, who were suddenly doing very well, better than ever.

Denoon began to wonder about the terms of the barter deals, their fairness or lack of it. Sekopololo was importing more salt than it ever had, and for the first time quantities of pipe tobacco. These were, of course, the key trade goods the Basarwa wanted. Unequal exchange, as a general thing, disgruntled Nelson. I asked him if he knew that there were Peace Corps volunteers who saved up their worn-out shirts and jeans and then took them on the train to Francistown and when it stopped at Shashe traded their rags, actual rags, for terrific woodcarvings produced by the Basarwa destitutes living in a little colony run by the Mennonites near the rail line. We may be convinced that this is objectively wrong, I told him, but unfortunately the evidence is that the Basarwa are delighted with the deals. His ideal of exchange was for it to take place only when all parties were in surplus, hopelessly enough. His inquiries into how barter was going were a little resented. He is pressurizing us, a couple of women in Sekopololo had said to me. I passed the word to him.

I wonder what the Basarwa thought of Nelson, because he began dropping in on their camp, but in rather a moonstruck or disembodied and shy way. Sometimes he would sit in the brush on the slope above the camp and seemingly study them. He couldn't speak their language, and the fact is he made no attempt to learn any of it, beyond the basic greetings. The camp was doing decently. Because of the rains everyone credited me with inspiring, the sand river was a good source of water, yielding more than they were used to when they dug their seep wells. The Basarwa were another universe. They were somehow too much. They fascinated him. He contrasted the strain and devising and committee meetings that went into making Tsau run with the workable planlessness he saw in the Basarwa setup. What was his responsibility to the Basarwa, however that might be construed? He was confused. He knew Tsau had some responsibility, even though the fact that the camp was becoming more dependent on Tsau was nobody's devising. I think a problem was that he had had eight years of Tsau with only the most glancing visitations by the Basarwa. If they'd attached themselves to Tsau during the beginnings, when he was fresh, it might have been easier for him. I think inwardly he was supplicating them to be gone. When we talked about them the discussion invariably led sideways into the most absolute questions, such as how you tell that one society is genuinely superior to another, granted both are equally uncruel. We were dealing with the Basarwa on terms Nelson thought were unfair, on our side, but putting that aside, what did we owe them, medically for example, and how helpful longterm was it going to be for them to make use of what we could offer? He was just at the wrong ebb for all this, I think.

Now when he went missing I had a new place to look for him, one that was closer to home than some of the others—the pyramidon, which is what he called the summit of the koppie, or his ledge, or the glassworks. It got surreal, in that I would go to look for him and find him brooding from the brush overlooking the camp, and I might sit for a while and watch him watching.

I suppose I should fault myself for keeping my distance on this issue for as long as I did. I liked to watch the Basarwa too. It was like observing fairies, they seemed so nice with each other, so tentative and patient. And of course why would I want to disturb any connection he felt with a specimen of a society so close to his ideal in the matter of not injuring the earth? When finally I felt he was too much in the grip of a romance about the Basarwa, I tried to tell him that in fact there were more offstage killings male on male and more wife beating than he might be aware of. But good luck: he knew this wasn't my field, which I had to admit. He didn't really want to hear it, and he had on his side the evidence of his senses, which was that life in the encampment was so pacific it was practically treacly.

A few times I was able to watch Nelson during one of his silent visitations to the camp. They accepted him with the same attitude they might have shown toward a heron or stork wandering through their site. Free time was what kept coming up with Nelson after these visits, how much free time does a society guarantee to all its members and not just the preferred classes within it? I reminded him that as far as free time goes, the Basarwa men had rather more of it than the women did. I brought up my information about the degree of concealed violence there was. Then the phrase "organized innocence," out of William Blake, slipped moonily into the conversation.

There was never a true resolution of his feelings about them, or of mine, to tell the truth. In my mind I can still see the camp with utter clarity. I see the eight dome-shaped huts, the lattice showing in places but mostly covered with a mélange of reed, bark, sacking, scraps of polyvinyl sheeting that looked suspiciously like the ground shielding we used in the nethouses. I see the central campfire, kept smoldering all day by what looked like a completely random system of attentions to it, and fed into a blaze each night. There go the men filing off in the mornings sometimes, and sometimes not, according to rules you would love to be able to figure out and which you felt you might someday divine just by watching long enough. There go the women, off to dig up tubers or gather other varia, the chores getting done by groups that seemed to agglutinate differently each time you watched. They were always chatting. I've slightly gentrified the camp I carry in my mind: it was slovenly, but I don't see that.

Denoon was cogitating, cogitating. We had to do more. There were certain health conditions we had to be more aggressive about. I associated a couple of nights of loud bruxism with his having gone over earlier in the day to the Basarwa camp. The Basarwa can disorient you. I know two colleagues who did fieldwork with the Basarwa and who afterward struck me as different, more meek or dreamy than they had been, in a sense, and they were always eager to justify more fieldwork, more going back.

Pine Nut Soda

An amazing episode, I thought: Nelson sat down with me and said Instead of going to the mother committee or back to Sekopololo I'm going to complain to you about something, the composition of our requisitions lately, the trend, and that'll be the end of it.

I said So am I not supposed to do something with your complaint?

Nothing. This is by way of an experiment. Before I kept on complaining about the brassieres I talked it over with you and you convinced me. Also you convinced me I was wrong opposing white tea, camphor oil, and what else? Hair thread. But now something else is getting me. First of all, we're letting ourselves run low on bonemeal and cordage, but that's not it, it's going to register with somebody before we're in trouble. Then I noticed a new import item, Pine Nut Soda, which struck me as the last straw. But that was only the first last straw. The next last straw was Milk Stout.

I stopped him in order to defend Pine Nut Soda, if not Milk Stout. It was true the soda cans took up inordinate space on the plane, but for what it was, it was doing good things. Sekopololo was making it available at an astronomically high credit rate because people wanted it for special occasions, where it was treated almost as champagne. It was for special occasions. When it was traded it went into the solar refrigerator at the infirmary to chill, and people were delighted. I assumed it was about the same with the Milk Stout, although the premium for it would be even higher and admittedly the market for it might be more predominantly the men. And it was alcoholic, granted, whereas Pine Nut was not. But I reiterated, and truthfully, how Sekopololo was thriving on these commodities, in terms of the work people were willing to exchange for them. He grimaced.

He said I don't want a defense of these things from you; what I want is to stop thinking about them by telling you about them. I mean it. This is what I'm saying. I don't need to feel that mistakes aren't being made. But I want to feel that I don't have to dot every T, you know what I mean. He was embarrassed. I want to stop with things at this level, I think. I think I should. And this might help me. I essentially want my mind elsewhere.

This may be wise, I said. I was flattered, deeply.

The Summarist

We were strolling near the kraals at dusk and watching the bats come out everywhere. Denoon could be eloquent about bats, their wonderful dung, which got collected from the numerous cylindrical bat hotels he'd had affixed to trees everywhere, bats and their insect-destroying qualities, and so on. Anyway, we were rich with bats curving and diving and piping everywhere at dusk, coming out from the koppie and over the flats, even as far as the kraals.

Near one of the dip tanks we ran into three women carrying spades for no purpose I could discern. Dirang Motsidisi had her arm around the shoulders of an obviously distressed woman, Mma Sithebe, our summarist. Acting as a sort of lookout, I decided, was Idol, the kitchenmaster. I liked her although the dynamic she created in the kitchen was not for the faint of heart, because she was a volcano of abuse and mockery which paradoxically kept her co-workers in a state of permanent hilarity. It was a little like the House of Commons when heckling is in order. And people did riposte. More than once I'd heard Idol's voice compared to the screams of mating leopards. I'd made good-faith tries at working in the kitchen and been unable to take the incessancy of the raillery. But there was a core of regulars who seemed to love it. Outside the kitchen, Idol was very quiet, and very tender with her little granddaughter.

What the summarist did for a job was turn up by appointment before different work groups and read to them, either at breaks or, if the work process was quiet enough, while they were at it, but never for very long, never intrusively. It could be something in English or in Setswana, whatever people wanted. She had a range of things to offer. Tsau was supplied by a virtual cottage industry Denoon had stimulated at the university in

Gaborone. He paid students to translate various classics into Setswana in their down time. There was Austen, Kafka, some Dickens, some Thoreau, lots of a poet he liked better than Yeats called Edwin Muir whom I had never heard of until Tsau, who is in fact magnificent, some Blake, needless to say. He stuck to short texts, mostly, excerpts. The only African writers I'm sure were included were Chinua Achebe, Wole Soyinka, and Ayi Kwei Armah. One of his translators had abandoned a major project, *Wuthering Heights*, halfway through, just when people had gotten interested.

The idea of a summarist had come to Nelson through contact with one of the down-on-their-luck radicals his father had put up from time to time, this one an anarchist cigarmaker from Cuba whose union had hired unemployed actors to read Calderón and Kropotkin to them while they rolled cigars. The chronology of all this is inexact in my mind. But Nelson's father during a good patch had been sent as a perquisite to have fun in Cuba under Batista by some advertising company or other, or possibly he had won a prize. In a burst of drinking bonhomie and heavy tipping he had gotten to be friends with some of the waiters he'd met there, who had given him a complimentary subscription to their union newsletter, Solidaridad Gastronómica. He remembers his father looking crushed when what was clearly the last issue came in the mail, the union having been extinguished by Fidel Castro. Naturally Castro hated them because they were anarchosyndicalists. So despite their having fought valiantly against Batista, Castro destroyed them, expropriated their credit unions, shut their cooperative restaurants, and created a diaspora—particles of which turned up now and then on the Denoon household doorstep to be waited on hand and foot by Mrs. Denoon. Nelson liked to call Fidel Fidel Catastro. Nelson described his father as being promiscuously left, a fan of the left generically, in the sense that to get his approval you could be any variety of leftist so long as you were rank and file. It didn't matter to him that your leftism was at loggerheads with the variant or tendency of leftism of the person he had invited you to take potluck with. That is, you could be an old Wobbly and be invited to dinner with a stalinist stevedore, your deadly historical enemy. All you had to be was real, not a piecard, meaning bureaucrat, and not an academic, either. I gather that one reason his father had very little use for the Socialist Party was that they were all schoolteachers or pharmacists, supposedly.

Mma Sithebe had a clear, steady voice, she could translate from English to Setswana or the reverse quite decently, and she was uniformly nice to everyone. Her nine-year-old son, Sithebe, was studious and was also pleasant. There was nothing invasive about Mma Sithebe. Even when she summarized current events at cream teas or other common meals, which she sometimes did, she was almost apologetic before commencing, and she was always brief. She was our town crier. There had never been the slightest sign that anyone was anything but happy with her, even when it was her task to roam around calling out reminders about meetings or classes, or when she named people who were defaulting on inoculation schedules at the clinic, or when she announced deadlines for the multifarious contests always being promoted. Now, we learned, three enterprises had voted against her coming to them in the future, on the grounds that they would rather have conversation among themselves than have makhoa literature forced upon them. The three women had set out to intercept us with this. Mma Sithebe was distressed. They say they have no need of me, she said. Dirang said Dorcas Raboupi was behind it, at least as it touched the laundry and the fabric print house. Idol had defeated a similar maneuver in the central kitchen.

Denoon gave a puzzling performance. He tried to convince Mma Sithebe that this would blow over, that he had heard only fine things about her. He seemed to want to say that these actions were not really directed at her, they were directed at him, through her, but he put it all so vaguely that even I had difficulty getting his drift. Why did I feel the three women were much more militant about this than he was? There would be an answer, he kept telling her, and people might change their minds. He would think of something to do. It was a weak performance by Nelson, his weakest, and so felt we all, I was sure.

6 LOVE ITSELF

This Is How Depraved You Can Become

 Nelson began looking peaked, then got lethargic. I knew something was definitely wrong when I invited him to not come to the table once or twice and he let me bring him his dinner to eat propped up in bed. I thought this was the consequence of overexertion resulting from a day of work grooming the airstrip, which was something supposed to be done periodically by a levée en masse, like a quilting bee. There had been a decent turnout, I thought. But he wanted to have it all done within one day, as apparently it had been in the past, and he had driven himself too much in order to attain that, raking and grading late into the evening with only a few hangers-on for company, finally.

I was taking his soupbowl away and handing him a damp cloth when he said, astounding me, I would never leave you. There was no context immediately evident. As a stone neurotic I naturally fastened on why I was hearing would instead of could: didn't this mean there was a trailing clause lacking, like a phantom limb, which would reduce to his saying he would never leave me once some as yet unattained level of intimacy was reached? Wouldn't could have been preferable, more definite, more present-based? I was agitated.

I was agitated because what we were both trying to do, I think, was arrive at love manifest—that is, love being established between us to both our satisfactions without anyone having to go through the horrible bourgeois ritual of declaring love, he for his reasons, I for mine. He was sensitive and knew that the last thing I wanted was a horrible sotto voce I love you and then on into a flurry of hungry kisses to bury the robotic nature of what he'd felt he had to say. I assumed that of course he had declared his love to Grace at one point. Inescapably declarations precede not only the few marriages that make it but also all the farces and divorces there are. Judging by British television, the practice has been given up on over there by now except in situation comedies and among the rural.

He closed his eyes and began to writhe and mumble and sweat almost immediately. It was a plunge into another state. His brow was hot. He

was having an attack. Already he seemed to be in the outskirts of delir-
ium. And this is how depraved you can become: I bent over him for a
minute listening to see if something about love might not escape—or
anything that might shed light on how to interpret his I would never
leave you, anything to show me if that statement itself had integrity or
had only been a first spattering from the storm that was now on my
hands. Might he repeat the phrase, but with could instead of would,
showing me I'd misheard?

I got badly frightened and tried to wake him up. I shook him, which
instantly seemed wrong. I think I pulled on his ears, I was so distraught.
He would rally, but only for a minute, then flop back comatose. It was
unplanned, but in my fear I told him I loved him, fairly loudly, a few
times. Nothing was helping. I ran out to get the nurse.

Dineo was already occultly in our house and taking care of things by
the time I got back with the nurse in tow. I must have attracted more
attention than I thought during my search, stopping people and so on
when there was no one at the infirmary. Word had reached her and here
she was. Nelson seemed better too.

The nurse was very good. I tried to be helpful and brisk, but I was
fighting surges of feeling faint. I felt incompetent. I know first aid and I
know a fair amount about the body, but all of that had left me, apparently
because the patient was Nelson. I felt like a peasant next to these two
women. Dineo was in a beautiful caftan decorated with ankh symbols.
The nurse was thin and strong without being overbig, unlike me, with
my big shoulders and all. I had to hide that I was in terror that Denoon
was slipping away. He was clearly very sick and might be sicker than they
were saying. He was sick, someone I had never seen sick, and what had
I been doing with my life lately except parsing everything going on with
us like a maniac?

I wrote down what they said I had to do—there was in fact some
medication in the house—and lo, my handwriting was the handwriting
of someone else: my mother. This was more proof to me that I was
doomed, metabolically doomed. Living with Denoon had already made
me fatter than I'd been for a good while. And now abruptly it was intolerable to have these two women, these in particular, in our house, in
our privacy, witnessing but not understanding that there was an unresolved war going on between two different aesthetics of what comfort
was, for one thing. I wanted them to leave and said No in a virtual scream
when Dineo said she was going to send someone to stay with us.

I've been overwrought in my life, but this was a revelation. The culmination was my rushing out to catch them before they left our patio to tell them both, sobbingly, that I loved Nelson, which I wanted them to know, and that I would do everything, everything.

Then it was all right. I was with Denoon for forty-eight hours straight, reading to him and doing as I'd been told and jumping under the covers to hold him when he began to vibrate. His malaria dated from Tanzania, and these bouts were infrequent, never more than one per year, he said. He was back to his lucid self permanently by midnight the first night, although a few times he came out with aperçus not clearly related to anything going on around him.

Everything was all right. I'm convinced I was drawing power from some new source. I fought off three serious attempts by women to come in in numbers to stay with us while Nelson recovered, which is the Tswana way: the more people there are in the sickroom with you while you convalesce, the less likely it is the badimo will snatch away your soul. But I managed to get rid of everybody without offending anyone and began to feel that if I could manage that situation I could manage the world. Someone as a treat brought cold Pine Nut Soda, innocently. Nelson drank it and said it tasted beautiful. I had news for him I had to withhold: Dineo wanted me to be the one who let him know a rule had been adopted saying that he was welcome to come to committee meetings only when he was specifically invited, except for the committee as to names, to which he could come anytime he pleased. He was being rendered emeritus whether he liked it or not, I gathered. It was interesting that I was chosen to be the messenger for this news, and I even wondered if the change would have happened at all if I hadn't been there to convey it, the ideal conduit, although I may be inflating myself here. It was nothing when I did break it to him, seemingly. He was gazing at me with love following some ministration or other, and the gaze continued while I gave him the news, and afterward, such that I was able to believe him when he said it was nothing. I was everything, or we together were everything, was the implication. Every day was soft.

A Reduced Footing

Once he was restored I was free to have an attack of urticaria. I felt
hideous not only because my face is always the first thing affected when
I get these attacks but because my mother also gets hives, so it seemed
like another gratuitous foreshadowing. But the outcome was something
only possible between people in a state of love in that Denoon really
seemed not to notice. And it certainly had no effect on his physical
interest in me. When I finally noted offhand that he seemed not to have
any particular reaction to my eyes having virtually disappeared thanks to
adjacent tissue swelling—I was overstating—or to blotching on some of
his favorite parts of mine, he admitted that in fact he had noticed but it
had led him into thanking god I was a skin reactor. Humans react to
stress in three ways—through their organs, their muscles, or their skin
—he informed me, only gradually picking up from my hyperpatient attitude that I was fully up to date on this piece of pop psychosomatology.
But he went on with it. The luckiest are the skin reactors, because the
range of topical medications they qualify for is so huge. So he was relieved that I was in that category. Inter alia he was letting me know he
appreciated that my stress was probably his fault, or his malaria's fault,
and he was grateful for what I had done for him more than very much.
Concluding, he said My category is organ reactor. I'll say, I said, attempting a lewd reference. It went past him. He was all concern. He took my
hand. The treatment for urticaria is the same as for malaria, he said—
that is, the passage of time.

I think he was almost disappointed when my hives faded as precipitately as they did. He wanted to reciprocate my taking care of him. The
irony was that the hives cleared up after his suggesting that I might speed
up their exit by willing them to go, in a conscious way. He suggested I
visualize my body as a paper doll with blotches and then as a paper doll
without them, blank. He even made some joke mesmeric passes over me
while I carried out his mental exercise to humor him. In the morning I
had to laugh, the improvement was so distinct. We were both surmount-
ing everything, it seemed, without strain, with a feeling of automatism,

almost. Even his being put on a reduced footing with the committees wasn't affecting him to the naked eye, although all the news of the day for the period when he'd been out of it had to be gone over and nailed down, to be sure there was nothing included that was something from his deliria. I think he thought his removal was something he'd imagined. He appeared unworried about it, though. There were going to be elections soon, and then a general meeting, a plenary, where everything always got settled. For myself, I wasn't unhappy feeling that the forces of circumstances were moving him toward thinking of a future in someplace less remote, although I kept this strictly to myself.

I can't say I was perceiving any serious ambivalence in him about someday leaving Tsau. Or possibly if I was seeing any, I was dismissing it as my mistake. When I praised Tsau once, over something I forget that impressed me, he went into a sort of aria asking how Tsau could fail to be terrific, since it was the pyramidon at the top of all his prior failures, socalled. He gave the entire sequence of truths learned, project to project, such as controlling the scale, working in the vernacular, cutting expatriate staff to near zero, locating yourself remotely enough to avoid premature disruption, balancing collective and individual incentives, basing your political economy on women instead of men—his theme song, Every female is a golden loom. I had heard it all before, but this time it was put together in a lighthearted way. He did tack on, of course, that if Tsau were really perfect the proof of the pudding would be its originator being unable to give up living in it, but then he went on to say nothing is perfect, so that if this was significant in a precursory way, I missed it. I read it as valedictory.

Accouchements

Among my mistakes was going twice to accouchements.

I went out of curiosity initially, and to sharpen up my midwifery, in which I have an actual certificate. I no sooner set foot in the birth house than I was deluged with complaints about Nelson, making me wonder if this wasn't the real reason for my being invited to attend. He must remain away, was the main demand. Apparently he haunted the environs of the birth house during accouchements, in a proprietary way understandable to most of them but still a thing they could do without. In fact it was an improvement on his earlier conduct, which encompassed attempts to be present during births and to urge fathers to be present during births. His will may have been good, but I was amazed he would run headfirst against so fixed a tenet of Tswana culture as the belief that if the male eye landed on a newborn's head the baby's fontanel wouldn't close. No one but me knew how apprehensive he got when a delivery was due. He was overflowing with horror stories about mothers typically getting to the hospital too late, after the child had turned in the womb, the child having to be decapitated to save the mother, about caesareans resulting in death owing to wretched aftercare, stories relayed by a woman who had been a maternity nurse at Jubilee Hospital in Francistown and told to him primarily, I think, to induce him not to want to insert himself into such gruesome scenes.

In Tsau you gave birth sitting up in a massive peculiar wooden chair with raisable stirrups to hold you in a knees-up position. The chair was a beautiful piece of carving and joinery, and there was something about the fact that all the babies in Tsau descended into the world via this chair that was extremely moving to me. I kept thinking that this was how things became sacred. Also I had a fugitive feeling of wanting to sit in the chair sometime just to see how it felt, particularly how it felt when the trap in the seat was unlatched beneath you. I supposed I was lacerating myself. I felt both that I wanted to sit in the chair and that I had no right to do it. The chair was set up on a U-shaped platform so that the attendants could get on their knees and slip under the mother to help the baby out, with or without employing a wooden chute that locked into place to guarantee against the child being fumbled and dropped. Tubs of flowers were always moved inside the birth room on the principle—as I understood it—that the first things the eyes of a newborn saw should be beautiful. I was told that sometimes the mother would supply a particular piece of printed cloth or weaving or picture she loved and that it would be held up for the baby before the child was held near the flowers. The room was immaculate, red tiles with a hatched surface on the floor and slick red tiles halfway up the rondavel walls. There was another of Denoon's notional crank-system fans high in the vault, but I never saw it used. Everyone was barefoot, always, for deliveries.

I don't know what I found so wrenching about the experience. It wasn't the pain and mess of childbirth, which I was already familiar with and which at Tsau seemed so much less anyway. Childbirth in the vertical position went so straightforwardly and apparently so much more easily for the mothers that I felt essentially like a bystander. An hour or two was the longest any recent delivery had taken, and there was some amused conjecture that the mother had prolonged the action in order to get some dagga to smoke, which was allowed. Even the nurse who supposedly hated Tsau was heard to say once that she wished she could come back when it was time to deliver her own child. There was a little ceremony after the umbilicus was cut, in which each woman placed two hands on the child and told it that it had landed in freedom and that everyone there was the child's mother. This was not an overpowering ceremony in any way. It also contained the wish that the child's mother should never falter. When it was over, the team went in a body to the bathhouse to clean up. That was all. But both times I left feeling depressed and hostile and labile.

After the first delivery I went home and yelled at Denoon when he did nothing worse than ask for reassurance that the baby was normal and healthy: he was obsessive, he should stop haunting the birth house, he should stop being impossible and prepare himself for a different report someday because that was in the cards, undsoweiter. After the second I was as bad. I forget what set me off.

There was no point in being emotionally riven every few weeks, so I said I was going to stop attending, which seemed to relieve him, which set off another surge of feeling against him.

At no time was Denoon less than understanding and consoling. He was loving, whatever I did, even when I wanted to rant about my life being difficult, my feeling disadvantaged even though I came from le-fatshe la madi, the country money comes from, my hating being self-evidently pitied by women who had so much less.

Chez Raboupi

Nelson was convinced Raboupi was using the Basarwa to screen what he called private-property hunting. It was true the Basarwa were coming up with considerable game lately, wildebeest in particular. And the rifle had been checked out ostensibly for use in lion watches. Nelson was certain that wildebeest killed at the nearest pan were reaching us after Raboupi and his men carved out the bullets and gave the liver and tongue and the fat around the heart to the Basarwa. He was convinced it was true because Raboupi had definitely been missing from his usual workplaces, the tannery and the blockyard. Nelson hated to admit it, but Raboupi was a demon worker and his absences made a difference in the amount of work done.

I was with Nelson when on impulse he stopped one evening at the Raboupi place to have a word with Hector. There were people in the house, among them the batlodi, whose hard loud voices were distinctive. It was dusk, early dusk, not late enough for us to be considered uncivil for knocking at a household where the welcome light was unlit. He wanted to thank Raboupi for something, was the unlikely story he gave me.

We knocked and at first there was no response. Then we heard suppressed talking and an evil laugh, and then Dorcas came to the door barebreasted, a towel around her neck but the ends pushed between her breasts so that everything showed. There was no excuse for it. The nights were cold. Tswana women go barebreasted in the countryside when the weather is hot, or they may do it en famille more than I'm aware of. But this was a mixed lot of people crowding up behind her to see how Denoon would react. Also Dorcas was very westernized. It was done to affront. She was cheaply asserting her crude version of Tswana earthiness and disdain.

I was enraged, but Nelson was cool. He asked for Hector.

Go and find him in the blockyard, she said.

I am just from that side, Nelson said. Hector has been away from the blockyard since Tuesday.

Is it? she said, pretending to be surprised.

Tell him I came by to thank him for a service, Nelson said, and then we all said gosiame, meaning everything was fine, and the encounter was over.

Actually Raboupi had done Denoon a favor recently.

What's this? Denoon had said when he saw for the first time one of the Basarwa grandmothers in town, standing like a sentinel near the Sekopololo porch. She was in the usual assemblage of rags and skins, looking ancient and smiling the Basarwa smile of absolute innocence.

I told him that lately they had been coming around and into the plaza one at a time and doing the same thing there that they do at the Kings Arms in Ghanzi—that is, standing around until somebody gives them some food, and if nobody gives them food in a reasonable time, starting to dance in place with their eyes closed and humming to themselves. That usually mobilizes a donation. They can dance for hours.

He tried not to look at her. Trading is one thing, he said. This is begging. This can't be.

I asked him why it was a municipal problem here but not in Ghanzi, where they officially just ignore it. No, something had to be done.

So when he asked me who the best Sesarwa speaker in Tsau was I told him the truth: it was Hector Raboupi, far and away.

And now as we were leaving the unpleasantness with Dorcas, I learned that Raboupi had indeed gone down with him to ask the Basarwa not to come into Tsau to beg. Nelson assumed he had made himself understood. He was genuinely grateful to Raboupi.

I heard again that things would get sorted out at the plenary.

A Proposition

One morning at shapeup two women approached me and asked in a hushed way if I would go to see Dineo to say if I would stand in the election for the mother committee. I was incredulous. I told them no one had asked me, to which they said that just now they were asking me. We say you are very pleasant and you are strong for women, they said. I told them how amazed and pleased I was, but that I couldn't decide such a thing quickly, especially since it would be saying I would be in Tsau for at least one year more. And I would have to speak with Nelson.

I brought the proposition up at the wrong time, I suppose. Nelson had pitched himself into a phase of dawn-to-dusk heavy manual labor. He was working extending the trail grid on the high south side of the koppie. He would come in at night, wash, eat, and sleep like the dead. He felt this was therapeutic for him. He thought it might work akin to Russian sleep therapy, where when you're artificially kept asleep for a week—through brainwave manipulation, with an IV hookup, natur- ally—you wake up with your melancholia in abeyance. One of his tests of a sound society was the existence of arrangements letting you switch off into periods of intense physicality when you felt the need. The aerobic exercise craze in America was something he saw as a sad substitute for this option of heavy work, and wasteful in that you produce nothing socially useful while you do it. I knew he was tired, but I felt under pressure from the mother committee to say yea or nay, so I brought it up while he was nodding over his demitasse.

He was surprised at the offer but, I discovered, absolutely determined to say nothing one way or the other as to whether I should accept. He would discuss neither it nor anything to do with it, not even something so germane as the question of whether or not this was intended to compensate for his having been made occasional at mother committee meetings. No, it was a tribute to me, was all he would say, and it was my affair and something I should decide strictly on my own. I strained to imagine what principle or scruple could possibly be at play in his attitude, but came up with nothing. I really pleaded. We have to discuss it, I said, because everything is connected.

I was left groping. Was the idea for me to make a decision that would tend to settle things re his future without his participation when he felt divided on the merits of competing courses of action, and was this a situation it made sense for me to slide along with? I hate a vagarious temperament in men, which this was not: it was something else, but not necessarily something I liked a lot better. I hated the idea of being ananke for him, or being the shape the yarrowstalks took when they fell and which he had in secret committed himself to obey. Despite my saying it revealed a taste for stasis, he continued at points to quote Zeno's arrow in my heart, I float in the plunging year—never very relevantly that I could see. What did it mean? Fate is our destiny, was a bétise by some major politician that he had happened to notice. In fact beware being great or important and ever saying anything stupid with Denoon around, because he would remember. The most he would say was Do it or don't do it. I reminded myself of things he'd said about the ideal relationship between a man and a woman consisting of alternation between who gets to be yin and who gets to be yang, where one partner acts with force when he or she feels it and the reverse when not, whereupon the other picks up the cudgels for a while. American women hate this idea, he'd said. Not me, I like it, had been my position. But why was this sudden attack of laissez-faire of his being stimulated by my little situation with the mother committee? It was beyond me.

I dropped it with him, then, and decided that if he could be inert so could I. It was pique. I said something noncommittal to my contacts on the mother committee, who left me alone afterward on the subject, and gradually the whole proposition seemed to fade away. When Nelson evinced some mild interest in what was happening I put him off, saying no one had followed up, which was the truth.

This Is Intimacy, I Said

A new thing was my sense that the impulse for wordless lounging together was coming as much from him as from me. We had had foreshadowings of this during times together in the bathing engine, but with nudity as an ingredient and the natural terminus put to events by the water cooling, it had been different. Now we would just lie down in the late afternoon or evening, fully clothed, not necessarily—in fact often not—with a precoital feeling going, and not even read or remind each other of things that needed to be done. He gave up always having a notepad and pencil at hand. Our lying down together was noninstrumental. I sensed and he confirmed that he preferred me not to be reading anything too absorbing while we were lying down, because it took me away. Poetry was fine because there were gaps between poems when I was present again. I couldn't credit this. It was too flattering.

About this time the question of true intimacy—how to define it, did we have it or not—blessedly went away. Sometimes as we were resting Nelson would roll over and confront me with a manic smile that made him look like the logo on a funhouse. This was to give me the opportunity to reassure him about his teeth and smile. This is intimacy, I said. He knew that one reason he smiled less than other people was his feeling that his teeth, which were a little jumbled at the sides, were unattractive, and when he smiled his face felt swollen to him, unnatural. This is intimacy, I said, and dredging up vintage fantasies about having sex with identical twins is fake intimacy, although that constitutes ninety percent of the male concept of it.

Most of the activity around the mother committee elections clearly went on during the afternoons we were engaged in our new extended siestas, because it was almost a surprise when the elections were over. Denoon surprised me by insisting on getting down to the plaza to read the results in the freezing dawn rather than waiting to go by at midmorning. And he surprised me by having no particular reaction to the results. There were a few new women on the committee, but aside from Dorcas Raboupi advancing to the second chair I couldn't detect any startling change. Dineo was still chair.

The signs that there was less equanimity in Nelson than met the eye must have been around, but in my flattered state I was mostly missing them. They were wavelets.

We were in deep winter, but thanks to the incredibly long growing season in the Kalahari were still getting greens out of the nethouse, albeit only escarole, and only escarole as tough as sacking. Nelson wanted it exclusively in salads nevertheless. He could be insistent. I don't know how many times I said This belongs in soup, minced, with onions. But no, we had to endure it in salads, and why exactly? Because people should eat something live or raw at every meal. I ascertained that this was something other than an avatar of my saying that the consumption of leafy greens in Tsau needed to be encouraged. He meant something else. It came to me then how unfailing he always was about picking off a cherry tomato or a sprig of parsley from our doorside tubs after a meal, or in seeking out a pinch of whatever we were sprouting that week in the event it hadn't been an ingredient in our last collation.

Was it that he wanted to eat perfectly as some kind of moral body English for everybody else in Tsau? Was it magic thinking?

It wasn't that. No, he said, what I think is you should eat something fresh—not much, necessarily—just something at every meal.

Was it a sort of magic thinking connected with the rather uneven appreciation of sprouting manifest in Tsau? No. Nor was it anything I had said about enzymes, our needing more fresh food as we grow older because we produce fewer enzymes physiologically as we age. No, it predated that, he said.

He supposed this had to be called an intuition. Somehow it had come to him. A noetic experience, not to put too fine a point on it.

So this tic about always something fresh could be called revealed science, I said.

I've rarely seen anyone so delighted with a phrase. So much so that apparently he was willing to forgo having escarole only in salad thenceforward. Some could go for soup. This was the way it was in those days. We seemed to coast over everything, up and over, a good thickness of rushing water between us and the boulders underneath.

For me love is like this: you're in one room or apartment which you think is fine, then you walk through a door and close it behind you and find yourself in the next apartment, which is even better, larger, more floorspace, a better view. You're happy there and then you go into the next apartment and close the door and this one is even better. And the sequence continues, but with the odd feature that although this has happened to you a number of times, you forget: each time your new quarters are manifestly better and each time it's breathtaking, a surprise, something you've done nothing to deserve or make happen. You never intend to go from one room onward to the next—it just happens. You notice a door, you go through, and you're delighted again.

This feeling of progress to better and larger was present in our conversation too. I suppose that in a sense the size of the items of his personalia I could now unreluctantly bring up obscured my view of smaller but still critical subjects that stayed difficult for us. And of course every topic I ventured was in reality a Trojan horse containing the questions What are you thinking of doing next? and when? and where do I fit in? Probably that was why it felt so congenial to get him on to the very large question of what a person should best do with his or her life. He was willing to return to this again and again.

As a boy and pre-Gandhian he had had no doubt that the best thing you could do with your life was assassinate Franco. Certainly he had had no doubt it was the best thing his father could have done with the end part of his own life. But then in retrospect it was better that Franco had died naturally, with the falangists sated and out of gas, so that Spain could move to normalcy without spasms of reflexive killing on anyone's part. His intensity about Evasion, about justifying your life, was so unusual in someone at his stage of the game that I was always struck. Of course how it could be that Tsau wasn't enough of a crown and pinnacle for anyone's life was beyond me. He was prickly about it and not willing to talk very deeply about Tsau, because, I gathered, it was too soon to sum it up as a success or failure. We talked about peonage in India, which is growing. He listened, but said tackling peonage would mean another physical project probably, and Tsau was his last project, full stop. He bridled a little when I pointed out that in these discussions he always seemed to present himself as someone radically closer to the end of his working life than someone at forty-eight had a right to feel. What about writing? He could tell me about writing. Writing without personal advocacy, if I meant political writing, was pointless. He had written something he would be glad to show me, something he had put into the right hands, something that in retrospect was absolutely correct. It had been an attack on the ANC embracing dual power as a strategy. Dual power amounts to seizing a cellblock while the rest of the prison remains in the hands of the bourgeoisie or the whites or the fascists, whichever. The great apotheosis of revolutionary dual power had been in Italy in 1920 when the workers had seized the factories in the north and held them just long enough to terrify the bourgeoisie into lining up behind Mussolini. There was no second act for the factory occupiers and none for the ANC once they got hold of the townships. Dual power in the South African context was a recipe for repeated decapitation. I could judge for myself how successful his argumentation had been, since the ANC was more yoked to dual power strategies than ever. I didn't know what was or was not important in discussions like this, so I went off and wrote down what I could in my journal while what he'd said was still fresh. He was still brooding when I returned, but was willing to talk more.

He said that there was actually one writing project that if carried out successfully would be enough to justify anyone's life. That would be a convincing essay against violence, against participating in official violence, ever. He had the noumenal form of the essay. It would be brief, it would be secular. The text would be printed on India paper in thirty languages. It would make a book about the size of a deck of cards. There could be a foundation to distribute it to everyone, on the order of the Gideon Bibles, internationally though. Of course the problem was that the essay itself would have to be a thing of genius, of compression, of inspiration. It would be like asking oneself to sit down and write not only a poem but a great poem. It would have to be like Thoreau on civil disobedience or Hume on causality. The fact was, he said, that this essay already existed in him, in his mind and feelings, but that was the problem: it was a conviction about violence, against violence, that overwhelmed any text he had ever tried to confine it in. The text was always pallid and weak compared to what he knew and felt, which was the proof that he lacked the genius to externalize himself on this issue. With this text you could cut the roots of war, of armies, and so on. Telling me this he got slightly flushed.

I was having trouble being sure how completely serious he was, especially when he seemed to remember that there was one other project that would justify his life however everything else he had done to date got ultimately judged. This would be to do something about flight capital, secret accounts, to do something conclusive to make the banksters stop helping the Wabenzi, the kleptocracy, by making bank secrecy illegal everywhere. I didn't know who the Wabenzi were: it was what the Kenyans called the African civil servants who drive Mercedes-Benzes. If you wanted to accelerate African development by some unimaginable multiple, bank secrecy reform was what a serious person would put his best effort toward. Of course that would involve lobbying, going through the UN, setting up an organization, and he had sworn an oath to himself that he was never going to sit in an office again in his life. So that apparently was that. How seriously in all this I was being taken was not my question at that time.

It ended nowhere. In retrospect I regret being so passive. But I wanted to hear everything. I think I tried to be more probing about the bank secrecy idea—it had some feeling of reality and possibility about it—but I was deflected by his asking from nowhere if I didn't think it was interesting that there was no term equivalent to cuckold to apply to women when they were being betrayed. Was it because the condition was so far from exceptional that no particular term was needed? He knew of no language in which that was not the case.

I love your mind, I said.

A Shift in the Scenery

It seemed we could ride up and over everything, not excluding the to me rather bold maiden decisions of the new mother committee to postpone the plenary and admit men to full membership in Sekopololo. Men could work for credits now instead of only for pula, which was an economic advantage to them, but they were still ineligible to run for any office or serve on committees. And there was no question of any change in the system of female-only inheritance of chattels and homesteads. I tried to tease Nelson by comparing men in Tsau to Jews in the Middle Ages or Indians in Fiji, with respect to land ownership. I was being polemical, and I was quick to add that I appreciated that the difference was that men in Botswana, on past performance, deserved it, unlike the Jews or Indians, obviously. He wouldn't be drawn. The mother committee was shifting the scenery around quite a bit, I thought, but he was remaining serene.

Except that he did want to talk, however calmly, about the postponement of the plenary. His point was that there had to be a plenary. It was the custom to have at least one a year. He said more than once We have to assume they're going to change their minds. Everybody had liked plenaries in the past. It was important to collect the whole social body together periodically. Batswana loved kgotla meetings, so they should love the plenary, which it was just like. He felt strongly enough about this that he had gone to the length of socially letting fall expressions of disappointment that the plenary was being postponed, obviously with the expectation that they would be passed along.

Letting his opinion be known around the plaza a few more times seemed to be enough for him. He stopped bringing up the plenary altogether, which was what I wanted.

So naturally I brought it up again myself. I had something to say that I thought might put the whole question to rest in a profounder way.

I think I put it confusedly.

I said: One thing about yourself that I think you don't appreciate is the complexity of why people tend to accept things you lay out for them as good ideas. Don't get mad, but in a way your lifework could be described as getting people to do things you regard as improvements, better for them. You have great powers of getting people to do things the way you want. Only partly is that because the things you come up with are sensible in themselves. The rest of it has to do with something benign about you, unusually so. You seem good. You seem unselfish. Even people who are really at loggerheads with you see it, although it may drive them even crazier against you when they do. Also you look counter to what you are, since you look more like an unemployed wrestler than anything else, which incidentally adds to your power. What you are operates cross-culturally, for some unknown reason. I may be trying to say that possibly the plenary is less important in a structural way than you think, and that it should sink or swim but you should hold back from using your powers to try to get it reinstated. What I want to feel is that you've divorced yourself from it.

This is as I reconstruct it. By the end of it I was confused about what, really, I was trying to say, other than quite obviously declaring appreciation tantamount to the most abject love.

His reaction to this was to say Light from the caves! This was a standby he used to greet solecisms or cant.

I was overwhelmed with the desire to apologize, which I suppressed.

An Impassioned Lecturette on the Enclosure Movement

When Nelson said in so many words that he loved me, I should have felt it more as the major benchmark it was, the thing long sought, than I did. We were living as though he had already said it, for one thing. And for another it seemed to me that something about his almost always appending a phrase like heart and soul or root and branch to his declaration made it more literary and less real. Something fell off a shelf in the middle of the night and when I said What was that? he said The scales falling from my eyes. I love you.

He started talking about movies with me, gamely but lamely, because he was worried he'd insulted the cinéphile in me by earlier saying things like Only a fool could think an art form is significant where your emotional response to it is signaled to you by mood music. He made good-faith efforts to think of movies he'd seen but forgotten he'd liked, like *Dead of Night* and *Fame Is the Spur,* neither of which I'd seen at the time, unfortunately. He was going to get better movies for Tsau, not just the kung fu films that were so popular: I should think about what classics I might like him to try to get. I remember saying to him Explain to me how I can love someone who has never seen a movie he liked enough to see twice? This had even been a point of pride with him, and it derived from his huge antipathy to repetition of experience in general, to which he attributed his recoil from the prospect of university teaching. I had tried lately to get a little deeper into that famous aversion of his.

I was also getting sensate confirmations thick and fast. It was cold and we were cutting back on using the bathing engine because of that and also to set the usual noumenal good example re water use, which resulted in cooperative rather sloppy indoor showering and sponge bathing. I actually had to admonish him to slow up on the worshipful and hyper-intimate aspects of our lustrae unless he was willing to be a little less sparing with the briquettes we used for our heating fires, which were kept minimal, also as an invisible Kantian good example. !Gum, we would say, shivering and lumbering around in our anoraks and layers of sweaters. He was sexually very available. The number of erections coming to

my attention was, for someone his age, outstanding, I told him, willing
as ever to stoop to any depth for a smile. !Gum is winter in Sesarwa.

This especially I prized: once when he was refusing to let me help
wash up after dinner I decided to read something while he finished, but
there was nothing to read immediately visible so I mock-complained, to
which he said You can read my fichier if you want to. This was a surprise.
His fichier was an oversized oilskin wallet he kept next to his bedlamp
and in which he stored excerpts and quotations that spoke to his essence,
in essence, all transcribed on two by five cards in his neat handwriting.
Nothing he'd ever said had specifically laid out that these were private
materials—in the way my diaries were, for example—but the tender way
he handled this wallet when he wanted to find something in it told me it
was at least personal. My hood is up, is what he was reinforcing with this
offer, clearly. I was flustered because I felt reading hungrily would seem
unseemly, so I was brief and consequently remember only a few things
in any detail. There were his warhorses à la Zeno's arrow in my heart,
and Society—an inferno of saviors, but there was also a quotation from
Rousseau that struck me as central and which he later let me copy for
my own information, and which I still have: The problem is to find a
form of association which will defend with the whole common force the
person and goods of each associate, and in which each, while uniting
himself with all, may still obey himself alone. And there were several
long passages from a book on the enclosure movement in England, about
the one village that had the good sense never to enclose its common, a
town called Laxton, which survives into the present: I remember it was
described as a proud village, a happy one, and a prosperous one. This
led to a discussion or more accurately an impassioned lecturette by Nelson on the enclosure movement. He was against the enclosure movement! What manner of man is this! was all I could think. The enclosure
movement is hardly something you can still be against in any personal,
burning sense, you would think. But he was!

There was even more being done for me. Nelson was cooking more
dinners than he had been recently, soups or other one-dish propositions
by and large, but I love soup. Keep talking to me, he said a few times
when I thought we had covered something and I was moving off to
attend to something not in his vicinity. For someone always afraid she's
overtalking, what could be more reassuring? Also he was responding, it
seemed to me, to my encouragements to get beyond his stimmung when
it came to women in general, which I found ideological. Women are not
semisacrosanct. I informed him our nurse was still fighting against iso-

lated outcrops of the traditional method of weaning children when they got to be two or so, viz. putting snuff on the nipple or telling the children worms were coming out of it. How nice was that? I saw progress when he made jokes of the following sort: at breakfast by mistake he took my pile of various pills rather than his, mine including Enovid, and then that evening when I pointed out what he'd done he said That explains why all day I've been unusually sensitive to the needs of others. There were a handful of retroconfessions unprompted by me. One was that he felt he'd been a prig in one of his responses to me. I'd said something like Don't you ever get the feeling you'd like to get out of here just for a few days and act like a pig, eat steak and profiteroles and dress up and go dancing with the kind of funheads who like to go dancing, drink whiskey sours, in your case one just before dinner and one glass of wine with dinner, out of consideration for me? He'd said no and now he took it back and of course he could go for a steak chasseur. He also said he was sure he'd implied that he'd read *Middlemarch*, but the truth was he'd only read two thirds of it, or a half.

As if to complement the impression of a barrage of lovely things occurring we had on two successive nights displays of unusually brilliant shooting stars. Everywhere people agreed this meant great changes coming.

A Pedestal for Something

The woman who ran the meat tree was one of ours, very pro-Nelson and Dineo. She served up all kinds of news and gossip from her customers, so it paid to stop and chat even if the meat offerings were not exactly what you had in mind. I was reminded how circuitous everything in Tsau was when I gathered from what she was saying that Rra Puleng had fixed it for the summarist to continue reading and announcing everywhere, just as before. So he's still machinating outside proper channels, I thought to myself. How interesting. I bought two hares because she had so many and it was late in the day. There seemed to be a steady flow of hares from the Basarwa camp lately. This was good because the situation in our rabbit domes was unpromising again.

Then I was converged on by several women, good friends like Mma
Isang and Dirang Motsidisi among them. What followed was odd and left
me thinking This is a pedestal for something. We were going to walk
homeward together, so I had to wait while protracted transactions went
on over hares. A conversation began, in the echt traditional way, with
inquiries about key relatives. Was my mother keeping well? She was a
poor person, wasn't it? I had no father, wasn't it? This really set me back
because I'd discussed my pater absconditus situation with only two people in Tsau, Denoon and Mma Isang. Wasn't it so, that no moneys were
being sent to me from my home? Other questions established that if I
returned to lefatshe la madi there would probably be no one to pay me
for my studying about birds and that I would have to go for lowly work
as in serving up drinks to men. I was a little irritated. They began commiserating almost before each individual drawback was acknowledged. It
seemed to me I was getting oeillades from Mma Isang and Dirang to play
up any sadness or forebodings I had. The scene was a contrivance. We
were back and forth between English and Setswana. I was uncomfortable
and wanted to leave not only because of the oddness of what was going
on but because I had what I thought was a consummate entry in a stupid
comedic competition Nelson and I were engaged in. He'd started it. Just
to annoy me, and based on my age and milieu, he asserted that I had to
be a fan of Bob Dylan. This had come up in the umbra of allusions to
the difference in our ages. I was such a young person that naturally I
was a fan of the great bard of my age cohort, with his wonderful elegant
grasp of the lyric, as in Lay Lady Lay, or as in his whining queries as to
when we all might expect cannonballs to be forever banned. Denoon
liked this conceit so much that my protests were wasted. I think at one
point I defended as pretty good the line The pump don't work 'cause a
vandal stole the handle. Somehow this led to a Ping-Pong competition
re completions of the phrase The band can't play 'cause dot dot dot. We
had gone through the simple completions like 'cause a strumpet stole the
trumpet, or a bum stole the drum, and were at about the level of Jean
Arp stole the harp, or a wily crone stole the xylophone. I wanted to
spring on Nelson that the band couldn't play because Vera Hruba Ralston stole the tuba for Halston. Since he knew nothing about movies he
was sure to assert Vera Hruba Ralston was a name I made up.

It was hard getting Nelson's attention, he was such a hive of industry
of late. When I commented on it he quoted a line of Blake from a catalog
to an exhibition of his pictures I remember as Now after such long

slumbers I once again display my giant forms. The exhibition was a failure, as I recall, and Blake went back to engraving ads.

In any case Nelson was back at work in his spare time on a contrivance about the size of a beer keg that I made the mistake of referring to as a light fixture. No, it was more than that, much more, it was something in notional Latin like luminon, lucinant, noctiluminant. The polyhedral carapace was panels of amber and lettuce-colored glass set in a metal framework. Within was a revolving honeycomb entity involving mirrors and certain cells which were crude lenses that would swell the beams of light. A ring of vanes around the top would let the slightest breeze turn the inner entity, at whose heart burned a lamp that would run for twenty-four hours on two quarts of sunflower oil. The idea was to be able to raise and lower it from a mast in the plaza or, better yet, one on the summit of the koppie. But probably it would be for the plaza since decorating the top of the koppie would have to wait until the committee as to names ended the deadlock on what the koppie should be called. Denoon had originally wanted the koppie named the Fulcrum, until he had been convinced that there was no equivalent word in Setswana. His proposal to use a word in Sekalanga that might be stretched to mean fulcrum had been met with furious objections. Even in Tsau the Bakalanga were considered foreign, more foreign than the Baherero. Then he'd proposed Tshiamo, Justice. But there was suddenly an iron consensus for the koppie's being named for a person, a woman, possibly some woman from the charter days of Tsau. Factions had formed, and there the matter stuck.

I loved to go down to the glassworks and write letters or read while he tinkered with this ornament, sanding glass or buffing or drilling and setting it. Concentration was important when he was at this, so I wasn't supposed to talk while he was busy unless something in his train of thought led him to laugh out loud or say something on his own. Then I could partake. He started laughing once because he had just had an epiphany in which it suddenly became clear to him how comical a word foolproof was, with its associated imagery of objects or machines so basic no flailing oaf could damage or misuse them. This was !gum, moreover, and the glassery was usually warm because of the furnaces Nelson used. There was immense tablespace there, whereas at the octagon I had to elbow his impedimenta aside whenever I tried to do personal clerical work. The glassery was domestic. The thatch on the building was recent, I gathered, since a faint smell like cinnamon or sherry came from it.

There were generous windows looking east to the kraals and the mealie
fields. I could duck out and visit my boy Baph.

I realized the luminon must be the object he'd referred to earlier as
something he'd given up working on because he'd concluded it would
take forever. I couldn't resist saying At the risk of being what you hate
most, that is, psychologistic, at least tell me we both see this object you're
making as a form of undoing or of some process related to putting the
bottle castle your father smashed back together. I thought at first he
hadn't heard me, but then he said I'm not a complete fool, am I? So
what? he said. He seemed calm. I thought but didn't say that what this
bauble would most resemble once it was up was a lit-up macropineapple
or one of those mirror-chip globes that tell you this is a prom and not
just a regular dance. That sent old feelings cascading through me, about
dance avoidance. We had established that we were both nondancers,
historically. With me it was a feeling of bad faith about dancing, especially close dancing, with someone you had no intention of letting sleep
with you. Dancing is erotic for me. Dancing was unpleasant for him
because it got him hot, or I should say had when he was adolescing and
still in the shadow of the withdrawing batwing of the church. It was a
minor bond between us.

His back was to me when he said We could stay here. He may even
have been fully out of sight: all I have is the voice. We were in the
glassery. I may have been facing the landscape, trying to catch a glimpse
of my animal, which I could sometimes do if he drifted to the far end of
the kraal he was in. I know I stayed fixedly wherever I was and tried to
replay what Nelson had said, to be certain he wasn't saying something as
innocent and local as that we could stay an extra couple of hours at the
glassery if I sent to the kitchen for some soup and scones, rather than
going back for supper to the octagon. But the inflection was wrong for
that. This was what it seemed to be and it was pivotal. I felt cold. I had
to deal with the way I felt, somehow, without saying something that
would turn out to be fatal, something assaultive re his lifework, Tsau.
Also, why did I feel so cold?

By stay, I said, you mean stay indefinitely in Tsau, us both.

That was what he meant.

But what about Jews? was my absolutely peculiar first thought. I felt
panic. Staying in Tsau with Nelson could hardly be considered durance
vile, but there were no Jews there. All of my best friends were Jews. The
only male colleague friends Nelson ever alluded to with signs of feeling

were Jewish, I had happened to note. Then there was a surge of feeling about my mother. I would never see her.

Nelson came over then and we embraced.

How smart are you, fundamentally, I was thinking, if you love some-one who produces these tests for you? Because I felt it as a test. This was not the drift things had been taking.

I went on a diversion. But how could you qualify, how could you stay in Tsau, I asked, since we're not citizens?

There was no problem. There was a provision in his contract with the government specifying that he and any dependent of his could elect citizenship—but not dual citizenship, he was quick to point out. In fact the government had been pleased, he thought, when he'd proposed it. This also was news to me, and another rung in the ladder of tests I felt I was climbing. I'm trying to be fair to myself and what I felt when this news came. I was in tumult. I wanted to know why everything comes out as an ordeal, a test. Tests have been my bête noire all my life.

I said But what about your status otherwise? The rules are that men only get to stay in Tsau as dependents, relatives. Same for Sekopololo. You can't just say koko, I want to be a member, and get in. There are rules.

I could through you, he said. It would be like this. As my dependent you could be a citizen and as your dependent I could live here and belong to Sekopololo. It would work. You could be chartered in terms of the rules, technically: you have no money, you're unemployed, in fact with your student loans you're a pauper. Your mother is not a resource.

I maintained my neutral to slightly positive attitude façade fairly well until he mentioned in passing that he had recently assigned all his roy-alties in perpetuity to Sekopololo. We hadn't discussed that. He de-scribed it as only a gesture, but to me it was preemptive. I felt betrayed by it, but equally I felt I was betraying Nelson with my reactions, my apparent grasping at the negatives of staying on in his creation.

I fought myself back to a casual level. I remember Denoon as now back at his workbench and holding a piece of glass up to the light. He looked absolutely beautiful to me at that moment, more beautiful than he ever had. This is a serious man, kept saying itself to me. Other men aren't. What I was suddenly afraid of was that this moment was our perihelion, the closest we would ever approach or be, and that everything after this would transpire between bodies farther apart. I was thinking that if you looked back over the trajectory of every mating once it was over, there would be an identifiable perihelion. I couldn't stand the idea

that this was ours. I didn't know why I thought it was, even. My eyes
were hot. I had to leave. This is all hypothetical, I said, keeping it declar-
ative and trying to keep any note of entreaty out. But I knew better.

I wandered out to the kraal. The odd thing about the fait accompli
Nelson was covertly presenting me with was that I hadn't noticed it
assembling itself chunk by chunk before my eyes. A case in point was his
recent recurrence to the theme of development projects always seemingly being good enough only for the locals to live in and never for the
founders and donors, for long. Then there had been the conjunction of
his murmurings about how rapidly the surplus was accumulating in Tsau
—notwithstanding that it could be accumulating even faster if people
would only be a little more ascetic—and the bleak general evolution of
Africa over all. Then there had been Nelson's reversal on the subject of
my thesis. Before, he had been saying I should go for something new.
But now he was thinking it was salvageable. What did this mean? One
thing it meant was that if I stuck with my carcass thesis I wouldn't have
to go back to Palo Alto to negotiate a new one, do new fieldwork, be
away from him for a long time and dot dot dot who knows? possibly get
interested in someone else. All I had seen, up until now, in those discussions was his flattering interest in my academic tsuris.

Then, irrationally, it was the graveyard, everything about it plus the
prospect of ending up there, that chilled me. I knew what I would hear
from Nelson if I alluded to it: If you don't like a particular custom or
usage here, you can change it, or try to, you can propose your own.
That was the central virtue of Tsau, supposedly. The same applied to
culture. Tsau was Paris compared to ninety-eight percent of the villages
of the world. I would hear again how deeply he believed in the village
qua village. Any book or periodical in the world could be brought into
Tsau. There were villages in Austria today less culturally open and advanced than Tsau. I would hear again that in Tsau we had everything
we have a right to demand in a continent as abused and threatened as
Africa: decent food and clean water, leisure, decent and variable work,
self-governance, discussion groups on anything, medical care. These
were not lies.

I did something infantile: I let the wind blow into my mouth. I did
that and then in the same vein, and feeling like a Chekhov character, I
said to Baph My question to you is Who is composing this life for me? I
hated being emotionally disheveled so suddenly. I hated my volatility.
Was this a form of premature retirement I was being summoned to join
Nelson in? How could it be? He was still in his forties, however barely.

But of course everyone reaches that point, some sooner than others. Was he that tired? And what was the name for the madmen who crouched on top of pillars in the Libyan desert in the name of purity, some going blind in the process, and whose name I knew I knew. The name Monachists came to me. Then I put my face against Baph's neck and stopped talking.

What upset you? Nelson asked when I came back in. Nothing, maybe my mother, I said, evading, when what I really wanted was to shout at him about the gigantic quid pro quo he was presenting, as in We can be together forever but only on the head of a pin, in Tsau. I was tired of the good news and the bad news always linking up. You win a honeymoon but in Beirut, you win a retirement chalet but on top of Kanchenjunga. I wanted to stride around and kick his sacks of rare sand. And I felt I absolutely must avoid getting into discussing the merits of Tsau as a venue according to its position on the depressing spectrum of where the poor have to live worldwide. Or into discussing futures suggesting that his place was anywhere but with the poor forever: that was definitional of him and in any case I respected it, although I reserved the right to adumbrate ways you could be with the poor without necessarily being at their elbow year in and year out. I had a retrograde gust of feeling or yearning toward being religious, so that I would be able to believe that my suffering in itself, separate from anything else I might do, metaphysically lightened the sufferings of the poor. But religion was beyond me anyway and I had been dragged farther away from any berserk clutching at it I might be reduced to, by Denoon's on and off stream of aperçus and imprecations on the subject. He was fuel to the flame. And his most recent recensions on religion, to the effect that the taproot of religion is perennial irrational individual self-hatred, had been especially trenchant to me. Religion might originate through thunder and lightning and wondering what the stars are, Nelson had been saying, but once it gets rolling it's about self-hatred, which is why religions crossculturally always exalt and beatify people who continually hurt themselves or allow others to hurt them. I think this had been touched off by a pope recently blessing a devout bathing beauty who had crossed the Alps on hands and knees to see him. Another tack never to take was that Tsau was effectively, by African standards, middleclass, so was his continued presence being justified as necessary to its remaining so? his white presence? mine included.

I thought I was being superbly contained, considering what I was feeling, until Nelson said So this is what one hand clapping sounds like, which was an evident reference to the lukewarmness over staying forever in Tsau I thought I'd been masking so well. The proposition was serious for both of us, which I could tell in various ways, from the primary to the trivial. Among the trivial was an onset of rather sharp itching in my escutcheon, an established accompaniment to moments of major foreboding. At the same level was Denoon using the amalgam GodJesus in connection with swearing one thing or another. He would never coerce me or anyone, if that was how I was feeling. He was sorry if I thought that. He loved me. I shouldn't be upset. Then he confessed for the second time he regretted giving me the impression when we were discussing *Middlemarch* that he'd finished it. Before I could remind him that he'd already confessed this he was going further, saying he'd never even begun it, that he knew what was in it only from what he'd picked up from women discussing it. But now he was going to read it, he swore. Here a blur ensues. We went on to other things.

 **STRIFE**

In Retrospect, Where Was I?

 In retrospect, where was I when strife came to Tsau, and what was I doing? I keep asking this. How inert was I? Could I have done more to deflect the future? I think so. I have no excuse other than my inner absorption with the prospect of staying on in Tsau, wrestling with it, trying to look clearly and deeply at it, find the right and true referents for it, and not keep recurrently seeing it as sheer exile.

I had battles of my own to fight. Statistics such as that in the United States a colgrad needs to be in a city of at least a million in order to be able to count on having five close friends would assail me and have to be countered with reminders that in Tsau I would have one perfect friend, for a start. What city in America could guarantee me that? And repeatedly I had to push back value reversals: things about Tsau that had been giving me pleasure, like the oceanic skies or the quintessence of solitude you attained on the summit of the koppie, were suddenly malign and frightening. Or I had to fight back moments of conviction that this was all coldhearted and a test. And always there was the struggle not to be sordid, not to will myself to be engulfed by blinder love, slave love so strong nothing spatial would matter.

At moments everything seemed like a conspiracy against me, to force a choice, like Denoon's theory of the characterological collapse of the male in the Western world, America in particular. As women get stronger and more defined, men get more silly, violent, and erratic overall. I more than agreed. I was a walking contribution to the statistics the idea reposed on. But why go on about this more than once, if the inner point was not to get me to feel panic about who else I could get if I abandoned Nelson, the clearsighted man, obviously one in a million, exempt from this piece of sociology? Then, was it only happenstance that he was dropping aperçus about the superiority of small and powerless countries like Botswana or Ireland morally as places to live? However oppositional you are in a superpower, you partake in the routine misery being inflicted through its CIA or equivalents, secret wars, arms sales driving the third world mad and sowing dragons' teeth unto the last generation. I felt like

saying Ireland, yay! But in the nick of time I remembered the priest-
ocracy.

I knew what I needed was exactly what I couldn't have here: a woman
friend I could discuss Nelson with, confide in. There was the political
barrier of my identification with him. That would always exist. Also
standing in the way was the Tswana institutionalized madness about
secrets. Secrets are for the family only. Outside the family, secrets confer
dangerous power to the hearer over the divulger. When I say the Batswana are opaque I mean things like the young woman at the national
bank, high level, whose husband had been in England for four years
straight getting a doctorate in biology: she was perfectly cheerful, was
famous for it and for not having boyfriends. Of course in time every
culture will yield to someone saintly enough, supposedly. Of course I
had recently been driven to talking to my donkey, and what did that
mean? There were two women in the United States and one, possibly, in
Sweden I could conceive of making an emergency life and death confessional help-me phonecall to. But there were no phones in Tsau and
never would be until I was in cronehood, if then. Would life in Tsau be
me forever wandering up and down the interface between the main two
races I would never understand, Bantus and the male? This was when I
was at my lowest.

I tried America has taught me to overestimate my importance in the
scheme of things. I tried this often. I fought off image seizures of new-
lywed wives in movies confronting more than humble apartments and
putting their fists on their hips and saying This place has possibilities,
which would lead into surreal fantasies of how I would revise and redec-
orate Tsau to my own individual taste, long and involved fantasies.
Mostly I tried to find some equilibrium around the feeling that Nelson
had in fact been talking more exploratorily than conclusively. But then
he would unhorse me by reminding himself of dead undertakings he was
going to revive—promoting sauerkraut and croquet were two of them.
And during all this he was being especially perfect and solicitous.

I think I must have known there was a hump in the arras. Dineo
seemed stricken over something private once or twice. Possibly I could
have picked something up if I'd lingered in the robing room after a hunt
for a rock python, which I joined. But I didn't stay to socialize. I was in
too great a hurry to resume observing Denoon and brooding on the
results. And writing my broodings down. And reading what I'd written,
back and forth, back and forth.

The Night Men

An epitome of both how conflicted I became and how perfect Nelson was being toward me: I woke up one night at three a.m. and woke him up to tell him he had to stop reading poetry to me as a nightcap for the time being because it was unfair. It was unfair because having poetry read to me is the equivalent of manna and he knew it. We had done it a lot during our first weeks together, then there had been a caesura when it became sporadic, and now he was reading Whitman to me every night, beautifully. He agreed instantly. Anything I could in any way, shape, or form consider coercive on his part was out. In the midst of this I was seized with guilt and wonder over having a man I could safely wake up in the middle of the night with a particular concern and get an agreement or get calmed down and never hear a murmur of objection out of. Every other man I had regularly spent nights with was like a wild animal over his sacred sleep, because—had I conceivably forgotten?—he had to work the next day, in caps, as if I didn't. I lay there. In Nelson I had someone who would not merely tell me my nightmare was only a dream, which I tended to know, but would to the best of his ability trudge through my attempts at analysis with me. Where was I ever going to find that quality in someone again in my life if I gave him up? He was already asleep again and so crazed was I that I woke him again to apologize and take it back, and even that was all right with him. I told him I felt like pure shit. It was no help reminding myself that men sleep better than women in every culture known. In the morning I apologized again and let him make love to me standing up, my least favorite position, as a treat for him and a penance for me.

I went to a menarche party for Golepe Setlhabi, a girl of twelve. I had been to one before. These were more musicales than anything else, for women only. There was kadi to drink, which was new. I sang By the Rivers of Babylon when my turn came. We gave Golepe a collective gift, a sheepskin. She was overwhelmed, genuinely. So I was overwhelmed. The sheepskin had been my idea. Real gratitude in others for something you do for them or give them is tonic. I was exhilarated. Of course I'd had some kadi. Here was an unmixed good, it seemed to me. Adolescents in America are so jaded a reaction like Golepe's would be impossible. Why would I leave a place like Tsau? What was wrong with me? Why wasn't I more sensitive to the simple pleasures? Was I more jaded than I wanted to admit, and could Tsau be a cure?

I was glad when my inner maundering was interrupted by the summarist's putting in an appearance. She reminded everyone to be sure to attend the coming great discussion as to god, to see who would gain the prize. This was the first I had heard of this event. Tsau struck me then as very precious and various. I went home to ask Nelson what this event was, very positive for a change, almost hyper.

Now I realize that the first bruitings about the night men occurred at that party. It seemed like nothing to me. Certain men, part of Raboupi's entourage but not Hector himself, were in effect being prostitutes, spending the night with some of the younger women for gifts. I think I asked if they used contraception, which was the only serious social point of concern that I could see, and was told Yes. Someone claimed the batlodi had conceived the enterprise, although I doubted that. Given the demographics of Tsau, it was not a surprising development. It had started with token gifts from competing girlfriends and escalated. I believe the discussion was truncated when it became clear I was following it despite its being in rapid sotto voce Setswana.

If I thought anything about this it must have been that it made Tsau seem like a slightly more interesting place. I don't remember thinking anything in particular, nor would the idea that this was a development I or anyone could conceivably intervene in have occurred to me. I remember the brilliance of the stars, my optimism.

Parlamente

I asked Denoon what this function I'd heard about was. It sounded like a debate.

No, it was different. It was syncretic. These were periodic mass freeform meetings, which he would interlocute. Each one was on a single large subject. Colliding presentations were given, there would be heavy questioning and intervention from the floor, then a prizewinner would be chosen in a novel way: people would shift physically to the side they favored. Another feature was that the entire proceeding had to unfurl with everyone remaining seated on the ground, no matter how heated things got, until the very end, when it was time to shift permanently for the headcount. Staying seated had been taken from the Zulu indaba format. If you got to your feet in anger your side was dishonored, disgraced. Nelson called these things moots. I told him moot was wrong unless an adjudication was going on, which happened to be the one item sticking in my memory from Ancient Law. He was impressed. The Tswana term for these meetings was either parlamente, the loan word for assembly of talkers, or phutego, meaning public meeting. They were apparently leisurely and drawn-out affairs, with people bringing mats and even napping a little at times. Food was provided by Sekopololo seriatim, to encourage people to stay till the end, Nelson finally admitted. He said These things are looked forward to immensely. As to past topics, he mentioned Master and Slave and What Is Work? or How Should We Work? You should have one on Whither the Local Bushmen? I said, thinking of the growing ambiguity of their relationship to Tsau. There were more of them. More and more they were coming to the infirmary. His reply was to groan at me. I'd missed the point about the scale of the questions the parlamente was for.

I was a little puzzled over the choice of the existence of god as a topic for the parlamente. Tsau was average for Botswana with respect to religious attitudes. So far as I could see, there was no problem with excessive religion, with sect competition getting out of hand, no manias breaking out. In fact there was more mild agnosticism in Tsau than anywhere except the largest towns in the country. There were three or four informal Bible-reading congregations. The Botswana Social Front sympathizers could be scathing toward the few devoutly Christian women, especially the Zed CC women, but the logic of their own position was odd: for image reasons they were what they called protraditionalist, by which they meant they were for the herbalist part of the traditional witchcraft belief system but somehow not for its essential element, to wit, the belief that the source of the maladies everyone suffers is hurt feelings or ill will among dead ancestors. There were no religious classes in the schools other than a hair-raising history of religions course put together by Denoon and emphasizing massacres and anathematizations. Tsau seemed to be secularizing in a trendless way, very gently. Popular science was popular.

All was well. There was no mediumship being practiced. There were no processions. And overarching everything was this diffuse cultus around the wonderfulness of women. Everyone deferred to this. Even the batlodi and Dorcas Raboupi and the other sour cultural reversionaries or dialectical materialists, depending on which camp they were in, partook. The one thing I would have assumed was potentially problematical was something nobody in fact complained about—that is, the prohibition of religious edifices. It had been gotten into the charter, somehow. Any congregation could operate informally but could never have fulltime paid pastors or leaders, nor could it ever have a permanent building devoted exclusively to it. The argument for this had something to do with the notion that churches remained benign when they were informal and in the hearts of their adherents but became aggressive and divisive once they possessed property and officers. This was put in the context of a general prohibition against all clubs and political groups having buildings, for the same reasons. I understood the hubristic but nobly hubristic impulse behind the prohibition. My feeling was that in the heat of the miraculous escape from destitution Tsau represented, women arriving would naturally agree to something like this, barely noticing, but that over time resentment ought to be simmering madly. Yet there was absolutely no trace of it. So to me this particular parlamente sounded either supernumerary or like a deliberate quest for sleeping dogs to annoy.

He said something apropos my obviously overlong meditation on all this.

I explained why I was puzzled.

He was vague. He had had very little to do with the choice. It had come out of the mother committee. It was a useful thing to do because it gave everyone a chance to see what things were breeding in the hinges of shadows, the place where shadows bend, meaning what doctrinal involutions were establishing themselves in the hothouselike recesses of the different Bible groups. Also a tranche of the older boys and girls would be leaving to go to secondary school at Kang, where they would be targets for the Scripture Union. This is like a rinsing, a rinsing off that needs to be done periodically. He said Try to look forward to it.

Thick Calm

Different things made me not want to go to this particular parlamente. One was Nelson's insouciance and generalness about what the
event would structurally be: I couldn't get answers to the questions of
whether teams were involved, who would speak when, whether he would
be lecturing first or at all. There was too much spontaneous order being
assumed. I always want to know the rules, because there always are rules.
People who tell you there aren't tend to be hiding their knowledge of the
rules for their own advantage. Then also he was clearly trying to flog up
major attendance at this parlamente, or so I concluded from the hyperactivity of the summarist with her incessant announcements. You were
almost afraid she would jump out from behind a tree to remind you one
more time to be sure to come. But Denoon was telling me that the size
of the crowd was a matter of indifference to him. Denoon was in a state
I was beginning to think of privately as thick calm. He was seeing everything sub specie aeternitatis, all of a sudden.
    I was careful to point out to him that at the same moment he was
arranging what would amount to a shot across the bows of undue reli-
giosity, he was, behind the arras, pushing a sort of milky cult of the
foremothers, centered on the cemetery. I was sympathetic with what he
was trying to get at. I admired him for trying. He was trying to do
something about the bottom layer of the Tswana mind, which consisted
of the conviction that our ancestors hate us, watch us, and are touchy.
Via little picnics and observances in the cemetery, he was clearly trying
to propagate the cartoon that the five charter mothers buried there were
mothers of us all and were powerful and were loving toward us, the
living. Thus he would be crowding out very slowly the main source of an
underlying kind of paranoia in Tswana culture, presumably. If you believe that the dead hate you and that all your afflictions come from
offending them, this is what *we'd* call paranoia, a structural paranoia: he
was right. I said to him Your foremothers cult is mariolatry of a sort, like
the way the Catholics use Mary to soften a cosmos run by a punitive god

and his pal Satan. It's religion, I said. He said No, it's ideology. He was made extremely uncomfortable. I wanted to say that blaming your ancestors for all the bad luck and illness bound to befall you in a dire terrain like Botswana was probably pro survival, group survival, in that it directed rage and suspicion backward and mostly away from contemporaries, except, naturally, for the occasional unlucky witch.

I understood what he was trying to do, but also Of all things in existence some things are in our power and some not is a truth. You can be only so promethean before the consensus is you're a nut. What was to be done?

When Whitemen Come Amongst the People
It Is Always for Lying

The morning of the day of the parlamente I got a disabling headache. It was a classic. I get headaches, but out of wanting to resist being a stereotype I rarely mention them, so that when I do complain I'm credible. Nelson was attentive and clearly unhappy at leaving me in my duress. But he went. I insisted. I lay there feeling totally razed until, at around three in the afternoon, when the meeting would have been in progress for two or so hours, I was seized with the conviction that if I didn't go I was going to miss something critical to resolving my feelings about the prospect of staying in Tsau. I took four Compral and went, trying, futilely, to time my steps not to coincide with the thudding in my head.

The parlamente was al fresco. There were about a hundred people packed in a crescent around the porch of Sekopololo. Burlap canopies had been stretched above this area. Everyone was sitting on mats. Denoon was on a strip of mat back against the porch, sharing it with Dineo and a sharp-tongued aunt, Mma Keridile, who was in charge of the municipal herd. Bolsters had come from somewhere. There was food being handed around, bean salads and scones, and hot tea, which was welcome. It was a little chilly. People were bundled up. I found a place to sit where I could lean against the trunk of a thorn tree, at the edge of the crowd, out toward the view of the desert. There was no particular pattern to the distribution of the crowd, except for the cluster of men around Hector Raboupi directly in front of Denoon. I liked the mixed lolling and disputation idea, and the vaguely Near Eastern feeling coming from being on rugs and under tenting. The tan light was soothing. So was holding my mug of tea against my forehead.

The way it worked, as I gathered, was that beforehand people had submitted statements or assertions on the general subject of god and religion. These were on cards which got shuffled by Denoon or Dineo or Mma Keridile before one was selected to be read out. The writer would acknowledge. Then people would respond, sometimes substantively and sometimes with deprecative shouts. The point in having three interlocutors was to rotate the function of selecting people from the floor to reply. And you were supposed to signal your desire to comment by holding up a twig. Maybe half the audience adhered to this protocol, half the time. Also the chairs were authorized to summarize or supplement contributions and to determine how long a particular point was to be pursued. Clearly also the panel was balanced in terms of viewpoint in that Mma Keridile was a believer of some kind, probably a Zed CC, Dineo was neutral, Denoon was the village atheist. You could tell which chair was in charge of the current phase of the proceedings by his or her tenure of a glass bar like Mma Isang's and a little metal hammer to strike it with in order to punctuate the flow. Most of the older children were there, looking excited. There was coming and going in the crowd, but not much.

I arrived as Denoon was reminding us that parlamente was not intended to raise one idea or belief up to oppress others but for all views to show in the light. Now for a time we would proceed in English. I was relieved at this. The idea of exerting the concentration necessary to follow closely in Setswana, with my head hurting the way it was, was painful.

There was a statement before us, to wit, that it was wrong that in only one village in all Botswana was it true that believers of god could not raise up a building, this village of Tsau. There it was. The very issue I had been told endlessly was under control, not an issue, was plainly on the table.

No, someone said, this rule was correct because in the religion of the people before the coming of the makhoa there were no churches required. But also the rule was correct because not even BNP or Boso could raise buildings, which was best because such buildings would be signs and proofs of division amongst the people. Mma Isang's contribu-

tion was that if Tsau was a village for women, then why should a church
be raised if no church could be seen in any corner of Botswana where a
woman could be seen to be the priest or pastor. She repeated this in the
form of a rhetorical question to the crowd, asking for the name of any
church of which this was not true. It was a fusillade, highly organized,
and there was more. The stalwart Dirang Motsidisi pointed out that we
know from scripture that the Lord Jesus was very much rude to his own
mother, Mary. This could be proven time and again, so why must we
rush to raise churches in such cases? She followed this with We must
always remember that whole tribes were at one time given by chiefs to
be under one church, such as the Bakgatla given by Chief Lentswe to be
under Ned Geref Church, whose name we know today from crushing
down African people and in South Africa saying all the while apartheid
is from the Bible. Where were the seconds for the pro edifice view? This
seemed to be a true rout. I was certain Nelson and Dirang had orchestrated it. There was no question it had been artful.

My pal King James piped up with Until it comes when god speaks the
same rules to every church there should be no churches of differing
kinds raised up. Because churches disagreed very much, yet all said they
were the churches closest the lips of god. Nelson glowed at this, and at
Even there are churches found who say you must talk as poultry or dogs,
just senselessly, to show you are of god. I gathered that this was a thrust
at some pentecostal tendency in Tsau not known to me.

That wasn't quite all on the subject, though. One group, which was,
I noted, referring to itself as the Friends of God, contended variously
that god deliberately made false creeds abound in order to force people
to find which was the true one, the implication being that Zionist Christianity was the true creed. A few of the Friends of God were carrying
mini New Testaments and using them rather than twigs to signal when
they wanted to be heard.

A majority laughed politely at this contention of the Friends of God,
and out of this laughter the voice of the Ox, Dirang, rose at its most
clarion. We must not waste gum poles and mud blocks to raise any
church at all, because really there is too much disagreement, she said. If
you stay to Kenya the Israel Church Nineveh will tell you you must
speak in any words of nonsense god sends to you, as even small boys in
Tsau can see. If you stay to Zimbabwe you can be told by followers of
Maranke that to pray you must kneel but with your eyes held open and
your hands raised up and not closed together and you must turn to the
east whence Christ will return from and you must make a loud sound in

your nose like Zulus finding out witches. This produced a ripple of grumbling. There were some Zulus among us. Then she said In Malagasy there is a church of vomiters who teach out that we best worship god by vomiting, so you must practice to vomit, because in your vomit will be found sins and devils your eyes cannot see, so thus you must ask your moruti, who can see everything. Then she repeated that she was not disrespecting any view but surely everyone could see that if one church tells you a man can have only one wife and another says he can have many, and each have buildings to gather and plot in, there would soon be trouble. Her final point was a hit: she reminded us that there were many villages in Botswana with more churches than fleas and yet in those villages also would be found thieving and too many prostitutes to look at.

I realized I was thinking of the pro-Denoon people as loyalists and everyone else as the opposition, whether their differences sprang from ultratraditionalism or genre marxism à la Boso or reflexive centrism. This is interesting of you, I thought. I realized how natural it felt to be dividing the women—sisters—into winners and losers when I heard myself inwardly ranking the loyalists, with myself included, the winners so far.

There was a fairy ding from the chair and everyone got up to stretch. The signal to rise had come somewhat after the fact, I thought, since Raboupi's men had been getting up even as Dineo was concluding a homily to the effect that if god was our author he would expect us to make use of our brains without restriction, even as touching views as to god himself. She was her usual oddly splendid self, in a purple sheath split fairly high along each side seam—which permitted her to maneuver on the ground comfortably—and a coarsely knit white cardigan and a black turban whose broadened tails could be arranged around her neck scarfwise. It was intriguing. Denoon was dressed in a way I believe he felt made him look more non-Western. He was back to his headband, which was actually functionless now that I was keeping his hair short. He had on his pasha pants, and he was wearing a boxy plain light blue dashiki over a black turtleneck sweater. I looked closer. On the right breast of his dashiki was a large food or drink spot. My reaction was weirdly strong: I was ashamed! I was guilty of letting him come to appear at a function wearing dirty clothes. Of course I had been lying with a cloth over my eyes when he left, but still. Then I was doubly ashamed, the second wave being over the extent of my identifying with Nelson. I had long ago seen the archetype of pathetic identification and sworn to learn something from it at the time. It had been in a crowded coffee shop in a Greyhound terminal in Yreka in the redwoods in northern California. I was sharing a table with a young local working-class couple. They had ordered omelets or scrambled eggs cooked so incompetently they looked like omelets. The husband must have been ravenous, because he managed somehow to furl an egg mass the size of a potholder onto his fork and swing the entire thing into his mouth. Obviously my horror showed. His wife turned red at my shock. Then she furled her own egg up defiantly and neatly in exactly the same way as her husband, intending, I'm certain, to suggest to me that this was merely a regional way to eat eggs and not something boorish and particular to him. She had done it instinctually. What this is is servility. I told myself Never forget it. And there I was, flushed, wanting to go up and somehow block people from seeing the spot on Nelson's shirt.

I stayed sitting, afraid that if I got up and started walking around I might jar my headache back to its heights. A new hors d'oeuvre had come out, which somebody brought me. It was smoked bream cut into chunks, with thorns stuck into the pieces to facilitate neatness. It was decent. I'd heard that Herero herdsmen were detouring to Tsau and bringing sacks of smoked bream down from Lake Ngami. If we could get this with any regularity it was good news. Animal protein was a fixation for me in those days. I noted that people seemed less gingerly about the bream than I would have expected, the prejudice against fish-eating being what it is among the Tswana.

When things resumed, the new chair was Mma Keridile. After a vote we went into Setswana. Even chewing too hard seemed to set my head off, so I had to concentrate on masticating my bream ultratenderly. I drifted during a rather diffuse rally by the believers, consisting of set answers to the one question of why churches were in fact needed, answers like To prevent us from evildoing and To say where we shall be once we are dead. The constituency for this was sparse and, I thought, about out of gas, when Denoon felt called upon to add something that was being left out. His point, which he pursued prometheanly in Setswana, was that a better way to look at a religion than through the particular beliefs that compose it was to see how much repetition it expected of its most faithful adherents. By this he meant the sheer numbers of times per day or week a particular text would have to be repeated or service attended. Every church was there to see if you were doing enough repeating to be satisfactory. Built-up churches were engines to enforce repetition. Repetition is what we use to put a child to sleep. This was all too spun out, but on it went. Whenever there is a church edifice it is in fact there to give you a place to come and repeat something, and you will repeat as you are told because every church says it is your father's house and we are used to obeying our fathers. The reason for repetition was to make our minds sleep. And it would be good to remember that the big competition between churches was not only over doctrines but also over seeing which one could be foremost in the number and kinds of repetition it could impose on its faithful. I felt for Denoon. All this was heartfelt but indigestible. I knew this theme. It went deep with him. I had heard priests described as superintendents of repetition before. Repetition was a problem everywhere. American television, or irrelevision, as he slightly annoyingly wouldn't stop calling it, was based on it. Genre was a covert form of it and genre was overrunning literature. And so on.

I was clearly not alone in having missed the signaling that was supposed to precede Denoon's being allowed to declaim for so long. There was a shouted protest from Leta, the worst batlodi.

She continued with This is lies! She herself was violating the rules by plunging straight into English without getting assent, which drew comment.

Why are you speaking so long with saying we must not have beliefs whilst you are thrusting beliefs upon these people from long before when we first came here? she asked.

People said Shame! but she went on. Always you are giving forth beliefs, yet you are a lakhoa and we say why is he not giving forth beliefs to makhoa rather than Batswana?

I was amazed. She was very junior to be putting herself forward so aggressively, and her status in Tsau was interim and dubious to say the least. And there was ingratitude. By accepting the batlodi Nelson had saved them from jail time.

All this came out in the partial chorus that rose against her: She is impudent, She is a new person who is soon gone, Where is her mother to see this?

She said You see because when whitemen come amongst the people it is always for lying, as we know from when they came with New Testament put down in Xhosa and Pedi that was saying it must be one man one wife as you can see written. And then in time they could no longer keep hidden Old Testament with proof of many kings with many wives at that time. And you must make that woman stop with writing, as I am not on for examinations, I am speaking my heart.

She was pointing at me. It was like a blow. I had taken my notebook out and was getting a few things down. I had done this publicly often enough, without anyone objecting, although I suppose that usually people assumed I was under the rubric of recording something about birds. Before anybody had to defend me I stopped, ostentatiously.

Leta stopped then. Denoon was silent, feeling chastened, no doubt. He looked worried.

I sensed a larger attack gathering. Dorcas Raboupi seemed to be creeping between several groups. When I perceived the attack forming, my headache vanished completely, occultly.

The rest is sketchier than it should be, because I was stopped from noting things down in situ and it was a fair while before I could get back to reconstructing the event. And then the event itself took such a swerve toward furor.

First there was an ineffectual flurry of dinging. In a way I experienced that as a tolling for something lost. I had never seen anything in Tsau as uncivil as what Leta had done. I was full of clear energy. I wanted to fight, not that I had any special right to and not that doing it would have been anything but counterproductive, granted my status, meaning my link with Nelson and my race too, I suppose. But still I wanted to fight. I was tremendously galvanized. And my head was perfect.

What had been in preparation was a potpourri of falsely spontaneous grievances ostensibly brought into being by Leta's salvo. Nothing had anything to do with the subject of the parlamente. The attempt was to inflate the churchbuilding issue into an umbrella unrelated issues could shelter under. Say how he has interfered amongst our underclothing, was a facetious reference to Denoon and the brassiere imbroglio I overheard. I think this was humorous and probably not meant to be part of the developing potpourri, but one of the batlodi also overheard it and brazenly shouted it out, even though that issue long predated her arrival in Tsau and everyone knew it. There were four or five foci of objections spread throughout the crowd, the most active one being among the people around Hector and Dorcas. Everything critiqued Nelson in one way or another, but the protest was always directed to Dineo, with Nelson referred to in the third person, which was an insulting strategy in itself.

He has made us to eat from a wheel, someone said. This had been mentioned to me. At an early point Nelson had tried to introduce the lazy susan into household mealtime protocol as a delicate way of promoting a more equalized access to food, protein in particular. Nelson was well aware of the statistics on household males, senior males, getting the first pick and the lion's share, then the women, then the male children, then the female children. He was perfectly right, because the statistics about men hogging the food in the third world, and I don't mean only in Africa, are horrifying. I could understand Nelson's feeling that here they were, engaged in wringing food and drink from bare rock, in a sense, and he was seeing it reticulated directly into a stratified consumption pattern which anyone seeing it from the outside would want to do something about. I don't know how sensitively he'd promoted these lazy susans, but they had fallen out of general use, although we did encounter them on occasion when we went out for corso, where they might be in use for serving sweets. It was an elderly gentleman who had raised this complaint, so presumably he had personally undergone the wheel and it had clearly left a mark on his soul. I was pleased that there was at least a little negative trilling by the loyalist women after he spoke.

There was another complaint, a feeble one, and sidelong, that Nelson was frightening the children with pictures of monsters in the water we must drink. This referred to a feature in some of his popular-science lectures, where slides of water were magnified and projected on a wall so that all the animalcules there are in unboiled water could be appreciated. I suppose it was an oblique way of protesting all the emphasis on hand-washing and the rather comic civil surveillance he tried to keep inflated to monitor it. Denoon even privately jokingly referred to the monitoring as his campaign of terror against unwashed hands.

Someone then said He at one time forced us to run amongst ourselves like phuti, meaning deer. Nelson later explained to me what this was about. He had tried to promote a few village-green-style sports, mainly kickball and some limited footracing. Kickball was still played in a desultory way down by the kraals and was a game particularly popular with a group of the aunts. What I said when he told me about the games was that surely organized exercise in Tsau was slightly nugatory, Tsau where people are on their feet morning to night doing work that's primarily physical, not to mention the perpetual up-and-down-the-koppie process. I said Life here is thoroughly aerobic. He agreed but said that everything was an experiment and that he had never understood why field sports had to be limited to the young. They could take place in a slower way, but he saw no reason why the impulses behind people wanting to do games should go away. If I was wrong I was wrong, he said. And in fact the very mild form of kickball, where the ball is rolled to you and you run to base and back to home, if you can, after the kick, had survived on its own.

Denoon seemed satisfied not to answer each thing: these were patently such mock objections, I suppose he felt, that he could let the derision most of the complaints provoked answer for him. In fact he seemed almost beatific, probably because everything seemed so civic to him. But I knew better. I decided to creep near my enemies, the Raboupis. Why not? Dorcas could slide around anywhere she pleased.

I got close enough to hear an exchange between them, Hector hissing that someone must say about the streets made too small for cars to ever go, and with steps up to interrupt, to which Dorcas made a motion that said No. I got closer still. Hector said Say about the mokete. Mokete means big party. Again Dorcas silenced him. He was working to keep himself in hand. Mokete rang a bell with me. People had been talking about wanting to have a big celebration for Tsau. After all, eight years had passed since the founding. Denoon was in favor in principle but he was always arguing postponement until the right time, when Tsau would be ineffably more complete, better. People had deferred to his feelings, but less readily, lately, it seemed to me.

I wanted there to be more support for my beamish man. What was going on was caviling. Women were doing it, by and large. Why weren't the loyalists louder in defense? What was this place, I was thinking, if people were unable to see Nelson for what he was, someone pure?

Thank god, I thought, when two children spoke up to defend Nelson —King James and a younger boy, whose name I've lost. I was remiss about recording the names of the children thinking that because proportionately there were so few of them and because they were all so vivid to me at the time, I would always remember them. I remember King James said that because of Rra Puleng, Tsau was the village in Botswana with the most less of snakes. This was in English. We were speaking mostly Setswana but jumping back and forth between it and English hors protocol now. King James's heart was in the right place, but this tribute was received mixedly, since it may have been Denoon's idea to organize the snake women, but it was the women who caught the snakes. Then again it may not have been Denoon's idea at all. I realized I had just been making that assumption.

Hector tried to start a wavelet of sneering at this, but again Dorcas stopped him, to his evident unhappiness. Children are so popular in Tsau that treating them with whatever is the equivalent for children of uxoriousness for wives was the rule. Hector's desire to stimulate a contagion of complaints was being thwarted. I had the distinct feeling that the crest of whatever he might have expected had passed.

We were almost in the clear. The dais was proceeding with the next act of the program. This was a good choice, I thought, because it was boring: we were having something very much like a book report on the monastery period in the Middle Ages, mostly in England. The point was being made, not subtly, that the monasteries were good examples of church edifices being permitted for one purpose and then accruing power and becoming quite something else. Mma Sithebe was reading this report from sheets of paper, and she was a perfect choice for the job, with her strong, clear delivery. Dineo ran this presentation well, with some interpolations and questions of her own. We were in Setswana. One reason this exercise was calming was because it was history and not something anyone could argue with. Also lists are calming, and we were presented with long lists of taxes and penalties imposed by the monasteries on their serf populations. A few injustices were particular hits: the heriot was one, in which the monastery gets the second-best animal owned by a dead serf, after the lord of the manor takes the best beast. An intervention established that, yes, even if a serf left only two beasts, the church would still take the second, plunging families back into destitution. This was perfect information, considering how the Tswana feel about their cattle. They hissed the merchet, which was the tax you had to pay if you married someone not chosen for you by the priest. I knew it was the Catholic Church in particular that Denoon wanted never to stain the premises of Tsau, if he had anything to say about it. The Church was his favorite infernal device, and he hated everything about it, with particular emphasis on Catholic population policy in the context of African poverty. He claimed to know for a fact that the archdiocese was already looking for ways to sidle in.

Also calming was the malty odor of bogobe arriving in a tub from the kitchen. Its place in the program had been moved up by an aside from Dineo. For the Tswana, bogobe is the real right food. I even wondered if the bream snack had been a feint, giving people a food item they knew they were supposed to like but weren't actually enamored of and which, if it did anything, would only whet the social appetite for something as counterexotic as bogobe.

Mma Sithebe kept on with it. Probably owing to the overlap in my painkillers, to which I'm abnormally sensitive, I began to feel rather exquisite. My ears were ringing. Usury came up, and how the priests preached against it and practiced it at the same time. There was something about only priests and lords being allowed to keep rabbits, the rabbits having the run of the fields and gardens of the serfs, snaring being forbidden. Somewhere in this bricolage was a reminder that because women were barred from choir service in those days, the idea of procuring sopranos in perpetuity by castrating boys and then training and keeping them had been adopted by the Church and had spread from there throughout the Holy Roman Empire, even as far as the people putting on operas. The event was seeming brilliant to me, Dineo brilliant, Nelson brilliant, with his wonderful patience. This was not a thing to be ashamed to be auxiliary to. Have faith in the mind that thought of this, was the dazed sort of injunction I was giving myself in my elevated state.

We broke for porridge. Since it was getting dark, hurricane lamps were lit and placed here and there throughout the crowd, giving a sort of family campfire ambience to the event as we reassembled for what ought to have been an amiable conclusion to things. I was mellow. Appreciate the absence of pain, I was telling myself. I reminded myself how struck I'd been when Martin Wade said that once you'd been in prison you never forgot it and that the feeling of day-to-day life, however hard, once you were not under restraint, was always sweet. That was the kind of thing that should be kept in mind. Another hint that I was overmedicated was that I had no appetite whatever, even though I'd eaten very little all day.

Denoon was the chair as we resumed. There had been a reshuffling among the opposition. Dorcas and the batlodi and their other cadre women were settled in a ring around Hector and his male cadres, four or five of them. They had moved up en bloc and were only eight or so feet from the dais mat. I was certain this meant something disagreeable, some new thrust in embryo.

The last subject was apparently to be the afterlife. Three or four questions had been sent up from the crowd. I remember thinking the questions were good, even the ones defending the afterlife, and that Denoon had his work cut out for him.

He began with a virtuoso overview of the paradoxes involved in fitting the main hells and paradises and limbos of the leading religions into any single continuum. This was good for closure because it allowed him to be both encyclopedic and funny. En passant he displayed facts such as that in the Muslim paradise the beautiful houris who wait on the heroic dead pogromists are specially created beings who have no genitalia. There was always something fresh. I knew that there was a Jewish hell but not that it's actually physically next door to paradise and that the saved can look forward to peering over the wall to watch the damned in their sufferings, if they like. Tackling the afterlife was clever also because by not attacking a particular religion but instead juxtaposing the incompatibilities in all the different lives to come, all religions were made to appear childish and wishful.

Suddenly it came to me where he was going with this. He'd been polishing an argument he was quite proud of but which was too complex for a group discussion, in my opinion. He'd tried it out on me. The argument was that even if you could demonstrate, somehow, the existence of god, there was no way you could rule out—and in fact you had inadvertently strengthened the case for—the existence of many gods. In other words, any arguments confirming the existence of a god simultaneously undid the contention that there could be only one of them. This is as I remember it. And since all the great surviving imperial religions, except Hinduism, were monotheistic in an exclusivist, and contradictory, way, this argument was supposed to let him illuminate a critical disjuncture facing people when they undertook credulism or, as he sometimes more gently put it, credism. I'd told him that this was all too Thomistic to be useful. But my saying that seemed to make him feel I was falling below a certain standard he had for me, meaning I was rather dimmer than I should be or, worse, than he'd thought I was. This was the true elenchus, the coup de grace, he said, and I was failing to appreciate it. So this was what I saw about to be bracketed to the afterlife piece, his pièce de résistance. Well, it was what he wanted.

The overview was finished. The bridge—if I was right—that was to lead to his set piece on multitheism was a dialog, now just beginning, between Nelson and Mma Isang, who had joined him on the dais mat. We were continuing in total Setswana. With the dialog, the trouble began. At first I thought I was hearing an animal sound coming from some source not apparent to me.

But then it became clear. I couldn't credit it. Each time Nelson's turn came in the dialog, Hector's group, just the men at first, made an obstructive sound. They started in a low groaning mode, but got louder and more organized-sounding each time. Mma Isang could say anything, and nothing would happen.

Nelson dinged his glass object and tried again. They kept it up. Dineo took the dinger from him and got immediate silence. I don't think she grasped yet that the chant was solely by men and solely directed at Nelson. She said something general about courtesy and how late it was getting.

Nelson began again, and again the growl came. I badly wished I could be next to Nelson to be sure he understood this was something specifically orchestrated by the Raboupis. It was dark and he was in fact more nearsighted than he liked to admit. Also I wanted him to be certain to let a woman handle this, please.

Again Mma Isang was permitted her turn. When Nelson spoke he tried to ignore the chant and raise his voice to get above it. But they matched him. There was a point to what they were doing that went beyond showing contempt for Nelson. They were demonstrating that any woman could speak but that no woman could prevent them from obstructing Nelson. I think Dorcas didn't care for this, although this may be overinterpretation on my part. The obstruction was cold. There was no armwaving. Even while the chant was going on the chanters projected stillness, normal attention.

There was more of it. I was bursting to intervene.

I saw it clearly. The women had to act to contain or stop this before it unraveled to the point where it would be up to Nelson to stop it. Something atavistic was developing. Nelson's being steely in the face of all this was beside the point. He was in a vise. If he let the chanting silence him, Hector had won. The growl had evolved into nonsense syllables, which on closer inspection were not nonsense: they were chanting bo-so, bo-so, bo-so.

I took another Compral, dry, chewed it up, and swallowed it assisted by saliva and nothing else. This itself was irrational. Also irrational was putting into Setswana in my head Denoon's theory of male gangs, their inevitability, how deeply he saw into them and how essentially unhostile his view of them was. He had belonged to gangs, or cliques that were ganglike. I couldn't remember all of it. But young men needed gangs as an experience to pass through because, as I reconstruct it, power in the family unit is given, you have to obey regardless of the qualities or lack of them you perceive in your parents, your masters. In gangs there would be a sorting out based on some sort of competition, at least. I don't know today if this is a parody of what he'd said or not. But then you would pass through the gang stage. The reason I took the last Compral was because I felt a tickle inside my head that suggested my headache returning, which I couldn't permit, because someone was going to have to act, probably me. I had a piercing ringing in one ear. There was nothing relating to women in Nelson's theory of the normalcy of gangs, of course, because we are on our own, in the real world, as I put it to myself.

Denoon tried a couple of times more. Some of the small fry evidently thought the blocking chant was funny and shyly joined in. Their mothers reacted instantly to make them stop: in fact for the first time ever in Tsau

I saw hands being raised threateningly in the direction of the cherubim. An apprehension of the extremity of what was going on was spreading, resulting in the female contribution to the proceedings largely dying away as people listened more intently to see if they could possibly be right about the turn things were taking. Direct unadulterated intermale conflict had become for us a novelty, with something transfixing about it. I felt that myself. We were not used to it. It even brought out a fleeting regression in me, like wondering if this feeling I had would be what I would feel at a prizefight where two brutes were consummating their entelechies by bashing each other into unconsciousness while I ate peanuts. When I was fairly tiny I went through a brief mania about prizefighting, wishing I could see one in person. Nelson was trying again. I shook myself away from the toy chest of my psyche and tried to think. The mutterance this time was the loudest yet.

Dineo said something feeble to the effect that it was bad if people could not be heard. The response was sarcasm from someone in Hector's claque: But we hear all you are saying so very well, mma. I could feel the scene tipping over. The darkness was speeding things up, or rather the anonymity that went with it, and so were shadows around the lantern lights. We had to conclude somehow. It was cold, and that was another reason people needed all this to come to an end, as well as being an explanation for their upsetting passivity: they were letting the disturbers of the peace produce a condition someone would have to use fiat on so we could all go home, I told myself. But the dais seemed paralyzed. Nobody was moving toward closure. You are playing as animals, Dineo said directly to Hector, who said back If you can say we are animals then you must tell us who is forcing Batswana to live as elephants. This was said ringingly, in English for Nelson's particular benefit and then in Setswana so that no one would miss the point.

The reference to elephants baffled me, as did the wavelet of approval the comment got from elements not limited to the group around Hector. Dineo explained it to me later. Elephant herds are matriarchies from which all adolescent males are expelled and only a handful over time allowed to return and function as adult companions. The females are careful to keep the males they let back in outnumbered and cowed, and they rather cavalierly exploit the satellite expellee males who mope along after the herd, using them as guards and sentries. Later I wondered whether the murmur I'd heard had been not pro Hector but pro-elephant society as a model for Tsau, which it was assumed we'd find scathing. I could tell Denoon had been stung in some way. I understood how aggressive Hector was being but not how recklessly and in what tender directions. The paucity of men in Tsau was a real issue for many of the queens but was seen differently by most of the aunts. Nelson's power base was in the aunts, I think it's fair to say, with a salient of support among a minority of what I would call the most advanced younger women. It was Denoon's position that gender imbalance was structural and it would self-correct down the line, but only at a point when female primacy had been established as normal. There was everything to be gained by keeping this issue from becoming anybody's action item, which of course Raboupi geniusly sensed.

Nelson was vibrating with rage. He was now up on his knees. If Hector succeeded in provoking him to get to his feet, I saw a debacle. The bo-so bo-so chant began again. In perfect Setswana, Nelson tried to say against the chant A strange beast is sending its breath across Tsau, and now we are hearing the name of the beast, and it is Boso. This beast is known to be chewing the shadows of certain chiefs who are drunkards and wifebeaters. This beast declares it loves the women of Botswana so much, yet can find not one woman to take her place among the men who tell it what dance to do. This is not a living beast at all. No, though it makes sounds such as goats make, as we hear at this moment, it is no more than a skin thrown over scoundrels whose design is men at ease again, with women serving. This beast is known to take money from the Boers in Mafikeng.

I saw that Hector was in a crouching position. Whatever was going to happen would be worse than what would happen if I acted. I was born to intervene, obviously. What I should do came to me.

I got up and performed a fainting fall. It was good, but I still cringe at the little outcry I felt I had to embellish it with in order to make sure I was noticed. Still, clearly my act was the pretext the forces of good had been waiting for. The event was over. I was the center of an exaggerated rassemblement. People had been in such a hurry to get to me that another diversion had been created: a hurricane lamp had gotten knocked over and set fire to a blanket briefly. There was no going on. Denoon's being baited to his feet had been converted into a dash to see what was wrong with me.

I reassured everyone with lies about not having eaten, knowing full well that the true cause would be assumed to be pregnancy. People were already acting knowing as I showed them I was okay again, completely steady on my feet. I agreed to stop in at the clinic. Nelson was acting stressed and paternal. He badly wanted to get me aside, but he was the one who put the most pressure on for me to see the nurse.

We went. In the distance I could hear Hector laughing. His laugh was distinctive.

Oh, but There Was No Debacle

The next day, once he was convinced that my faint had been a feint and that I was truly all right, suddenly Nelson was not interested in talking about the symposium. I sensed this was because his interpretation of events up to the point of my intervention was going to be radically different from mine, meaning ipso facto that we differed on whether I should have intervened at all or not, id est whether I had made a fool of myself at least insofar as he was concerned. I was frustrated. He was being unjust. There were things to be learned from yesterday, such as how he'd felt for the interim during which he had to entertain the idea I might be pregnant. And was the sanguine way he was acting today about yesterday the way he'd felt then? And if so, how could that be?

But he immersed himself in his map of Tsau project, erasing perfectly good—I thought—sections and penciling in legends in handwriting even more microscopic than mine in my journal. He was semisacrosanct when he was at work on the map. What could I say, since making the map was my idea? First he put an hour into looking everywhere for the art gum eraser. I had begun to hate the map on other grounds. It functioned as a meditative device for him lately, negatively from my standpoint, because when his sessions of sweet silent thought were over he would usually come forth with some grandiose thing that needed to be done right away or that should have been done earlier, when Tsau was started.

As day turned to night I got more incredulous that I was plainly not going to get the slightest credit for staving off the physical imbroglio I'd seen coming.

I brought him tea and set it down nonobtrusively, then when he said something I mistook for an opening, something like Ah shit!, I thought Ah, this must be the return of the repressed, that is, yesterday in all its glory. So when I asked if he wanted a scone with his tea, and he said, being scrupulous, How many are there?, I replied Oh, many, many tekel upharsin. I thought he would get this as my lead-in to presenting my interpretation of the implosion of yesterday's event as handwriting on the wall, meaning that it was perhaps time to think concretely about moving on. But it produced only puzzlement.

And all Ah shit! meant was that he was annoyed with himself for forgetting to include somewhere in yesterday's presentation the only contribution to science ever made by religion, namely the invention of logarithms by a Scottish lord nuttily obsessed with figuring out the dimensions of the New Jerusalem from inane clues in the Book of Revelation.

Oh spare me, I think I said. Yesterday was a catastrophe trying to tell us something like that Tsau is an organism trying to deal with us as foreign bodies. Yesterday was only the latest trope.

Please, he said, showing incidentally how pleased he was to have gotten perfect points on two pencils, meaning that now he could resume with the map and I could recede.

This is denying me, I said. You don't listen. Where were your protectors yesterday except for yours truly? If you had gotten up and pushed and shoved Hector or done whatever, dealt with him physically, then what? And don't tell me you weren't ready for it, ready for demolishing this whole sitting down and reasoning-together tradition you revere so much, or used to. Did I save that or not, that tradition if not you personally? Say something.

But he began writing or tracing, whichever it was, again. You're in another world, I almost shouted. Why can't we talk about what was a debacle?

Oh, but there was no debacle. It was incomprehensible that I thought so. But we couldn't talk about it right then.

Whatever false consciousness is, you're developing it in spades, I said.

This was my unkindest cut, and I knew it. He tried working for a few more minutes, then got up and left the octagon for a midnight ramble lasting a couple of hours. I went to bed.

I was asleep when he came back, but not for long. I got a harangue. He was wound up. The symposium had been positive. Why couldn't I see this? Tsau was evolving. Tsau today was only a foreshadowing of what it was going to be ultimately. He would be whatever Tsau wanted him to be, needed him to be. This was a new formulation. I was astonished. What did it mean? This was new. I pressed him in my usual gingerly way. Does this mean that if Tsau wants you to end up as the village atheist while she goes her merry way, while she or it turns into something entirely different, you're up for that because it would be such a privilege just to be there to witness for the old idea of Tsau? I was being rough, because I was involved. I must have been very rough, because he changed his mind about staying in bed and went out for another midnight ramble. As he was leaving the second time I called after him I hope you remember you were the one who said the answer to the question What is the meaning of life? is The meaning of life is abnormal psychology. I doubt that he heard the whole thing, in his hurry.

He was back beside me when I got up the next morning. I made oatmeal and thought my kitchenizing would rouse him, but it didn't. I ate alone, looking at him, wishing I had power, some kind of power.

I Measured Dimensions Not Standardly Taken, Why Not?

His not responding in any way to my breakfast activities led me into a brief and I think genuine mania. I think that was the effective cause although something else might have done it later on.

I sat fixatedly staring at him. I moved my footstool around and stared from different distances, getting into it, getting into not washing, sitting there in my yakuta, not getting dressed, feeling aggrieved. How could I believe he was truly asleep? I knew his habits, his sleeping modes especially, since my insomnia gave me such amplitude to study them. I deserved to be talked to about yesterday. If my intervention was stupid I deserved to be comforted. I needed to be kept from succumbing to a certain metaphor for marriage I was recurring to too often, that is, of marriage as a form of slowed-down wrestling where the two parties keep trying different holds on each other until one of them gets tired and goes limp, at which point you have the canonical happy marriage, voilà.

There is a condition you can precipitate in yourself by staring intensely enough at another face, or even your own. The face reorganizes itself subtly. The condition resembles the feeling you get when you look at a face upside down until it seems correct, a real face with eyes where the mouth should be, a possible kind of face. The face you're staring at reorganizes itself into another face. The Rosicrucians encourage you to stare at yourself in a mirror by candlelight in a dark room until your face changes and you get a glimpse of yourself in a previous incarnation. Actually I knew about this from Nelson, whose father at the very end of a lifetime of florid atheism became a Rosicrucian and performed this very exercise so excellently that Nelson heard him yell with fright. The story was that he had seen himself as a bearded man imprisoned for his beliefs in a dungeon. The whole subject of his father's fall into Rosicrucianism was painful for Nelson. Somehow his father had gotten into it as a crutch for his final abstinence from liquor, but then he had begun believing its tenets, going so far as to take up chanting mystic vowel sounds supposed to vibrationally lift the mind to a higher state. This was a morning and evening thing. He would begin with low steady sounds like Aum and Ra, which were all right, but he would end with a piercing nasal cry of Ain! which could be heard on the lawn.

I was staring at Nelson, and there was a flicker, and then something made Nelson's image seen smaller, as though he were receding. It was instantaneous, but there was no question about the reality of it as I was seeing it. What I saw was a distinct event, not on the scale of a cartoon character shrinking or anything remotely like that, but a shift, a recession away from me. I reacted with chills. I knew the answer had to be brain chemistry in essence, but I still felt shaken and weak.

Try not to interpret everything, I warned myself as I concluded instantly that I knew what the experience meant. As things were going, I was going to lose Denoon, one way or another. This was my unconscious taking the bit between its teeth in a friendly way, for a change. I was going to lose Denoon because I wasn't acting intelligently. And I was acting unintelligently because there was too much of him I didn't understand. And I was failing to understand because the situation of trying to learn while I was in the act of living with him recapitulated my difficulties in absorbing material in lecture settings as opposed to absorbing material from a text, from something I could reread and underline. And this illumination yielded a subillumination to the effect that I had to reduce everything about Denoon to writing, classify it, so I could learn Denoon the same way I ever learned any subject decently. This did not seem bizarre to me in any way.

My project came to me with insane clarity. My previous piecemeal treatment of Nelson had to go. It had been wrong simply to strew bits and fragments on him through my Tsau notes-cum-ongoing-analysis of my unique self. I needed to cull and put together under the right headings everything I had on Nelson so far, and I had to get more. What I had on Nelson had to be inadequate and misleading. He was the one who talked about protean behavior, namely the tactic in almost all mammal species of jumping erratically and randomly around in response to being chased. This could apply to him. I had pursued him. There was no argument about that. So a lot of what I'd captured was undoubtedly not what it seemed.

As a task, this project was perfect. Of course, this is as I see it now. It was perfect because of its penultimacy. It was concrete and it was urgent, but it was the act preceding the final act or decision, which would have to be postponed, necessarily.

I wanted to begin right away—in fact it felt urgent to begin right away. Whatever the mental equivalent of flailing around is was what I was doing. I knew it but couldn't help it. Somehow I had to get the true dimensions of this man. The word "dimensions" galvanized me. The minutiae of this are important. My attention was caught by Denoon's beloved retractable steel measuring tape. It was Swedish. It had been everywhere with him. The reel case was the size of a compact, but the steel tape seemed to come out of it forever. The quality of the tape was amazing: it was like silk but indestructible. He loved his measuring tape. It was on the floor near his head, where he could reach it. It and his slide rule and his hunting knife were equivalent pet things. The hunting knife I was ambivalent about because he wore it around too much and also because by using it in mundane little chores he rendered them overdramatic, in my humble opinion.

I know there are lines in the Greek lyrics that describe the frantic state of mind, derived from love, I was entering. You burn me, someone says to Eros, and in one epigram someone complains that Eros is inside him and he feels his limbs being shaken by Eros's wingbeats, approximately. I crept over to Denoon and lifted the blanket. He was deep asleep, naked as usual. He was sleeping the sleep of true exhaustion. He was on his left side, his right arm stretched out as though reaching for something and his right knee raised. He looked like a hurdler. I was going to measure him.

I wanted him to wake up and not to wake up, both. I was pulling his blanket off but I was keeping the place dark, not opening the curtains. I was going to measure him, but gently, not letting the metal tape measure touch him, lest the cold of it startle him.

I measured dimensions not standardly taken, thinking Why not? I measured across his buttocks. I measured his right calf. I wrote the numbers in ballpoint pen on the palm of my hand, like a Motswana clerk in a small general dealer shop. I was being outré in other ways too. I never sit around in the morning in my yakuta. The yakuta was for sex. Sitting around in a kimono was too much like my mother clinging to being not dressed for work as long as she could. But there I was. My hair was a wreck. Either he was genuinely sleeping the sleep of the dead or he was faking: whichever it was, I had to know, because my personal motto should probably be You lie to me at your peril. I measured his fingers, still keeping the tape from touching them. I decided I would measure his penis.

Obviously I wasn't delicate enough because voilà he was awake, explosively. He pushed me away. It was understandable. I was a shadow to him and was no doubt conforming to some invasive hag archetype we all carry around within us. Also he'd caught the glint of the metal tape and hadn't had time to process exactly what metallic thing he was seeing. Then also I give him credit for sensing I wasn't in normalcy, the proof being that it was no problem for me to wait until he spoke first, even though I was the invasive one and the convention of the female speaking first when an unresolved conflict has gone on long enough was alive and well in our house. Ah good, I thought, another thesis topic although unfortunately not in my field, id est proving that women are almost invariably the appeasers when fights occur that lead to stalemates. Nelson was alarmed. Finally he said something like What was that?

I believe in the existence of situational genius and that I occasionally possess it. An explanation of what I was doing leapt into being. It was that I was planning to make something for him, clothing, pants in fact, a surprise, so I'd been measuring his inseam on the q.t., I was sorry, his pants wardrobe was useless for getting an idea of how long a normal pair of pants should be because it consisted of pantaloons and shorts, and I was sorry.

He apologized for startling me with his reaction. I could see he was simply going to accept my explanation and not probe to see if there was any element of provocation in what I was doing. Something in his attitude convinced me, in the state I was in, that reducing him to paper was the right idea. I needed to proceed with it. I wanted him to leave the house so I could do that. I hope never again to undergo the state I was in. I even remember one peculiarity of it: I was aware more than usually of the edges of my field of vision, my lashes, the ghostly nose we forget is always there.

Religion, the Most Effective of the Placebos

Surprisingly, the conviction that getting Nelson on paper was urgent was just as strong in the days following. Denoon Evaginated was the secret working title for my compilation.

There was a significant amount about Denoon in my journal for me to extract and collate, for which I needed index cards or paper that could be cut up to serve as index cards. There were no index cards available. In fact we were in one of our chronic general paper famines. We had orders in for all kinds of paper, but inevitably they were the items left out of the consignments of sundries the supply plane brought in. In my journal I had no more than forty blank pages left, and these were not expendable because my diarizing was going to go on simultaneously with my anatomy of Nelson. An example of my focus was my strolling in the vicinity of the school one gloaming and being tempted to slip in and pinch one or two exercise books from the handful we had left. But I remembered how proud we all were of the absence of stealing in Tsau and controlled myself.

It occurred to me I could use aerogram blanks, which the post office had plenty of. In a way, that was perfect. I could appear to be writing to friends when in fact I was doing otherwise. Nelson for some reason liked the idea of my writing to friends, or possibly what he liked was the appearance of my having as many friends as my quote unquote letter-writing implied. Seeing me writing even inspired him to do more than he usually did vis-à-vis dinner and housekeeping, which was already substantial, though, it now came to me, not as substantial as he'd origi-nally led me to expect. He thought I was referring to my journal for current incidents to include in my letters. It was admittedly a little reck-less of me. The only drawback to the airletters was their price, but some-thing about that felt right to me. I put fictitious names and addresses on my airletters and even sealed them up, only to have to later open them and cut up the sections for classification.

It was surprising to see how many sections I had that bore one way or another on Denoon and fatherhood, or more specifically on Nelson and his father. Was this because I was interested in any clue that would tell me whether or not he was germane as a father-of-my-child prospect? There was too much on fatherhood. I had to compress it. For example, I had a surplus on the contention that good father-son relationships are predicated on the father having some expertise or maestria to pass on to the son—nothing about daughters here—preferably something wherewith the son can make money, although sports or philately or hunting and fishing will do. Because his father was in advertising there was nothing vocational to convey, advertising being a fraud and something his father was ashamed of in any case. Pathetically, along these lines, he realized his father had tried to tell him about something he did know, drinking, or rather how to get away with it, as in avoiding hangovers by taking two aspirin and drinking all the water you can hold before going to sleep when you've overindulged. This was along with other advice at the time Nelson was leaving for college.

Religion was another hypertrophied facet. It was everywhere. He was adamant about the Catholic Church. Even if he acknowledged for a second that there might be some progressive Catholics in Brazil, say, his next question was sure to be Why is it it never occurs to the Pope to excommunicate a serial murderer like Pinochet? or something similar. According to the Koran, when Mohammed went up to heaven to meet Allah he asked Allah to reduce the number of obligatory daily prayers to whatever it is today, fifteen or sixteen, which Allah agreed to as a mark of approval. But did this belong under Religion or under Repetition, another very oversupplied category? Or where did religion, the most effective of the placebos, go?: under Religion or Humor? At this point I decided to let the category alone for the foreseeable future, which was, in retrospect, dumb of me.

Humor was tough for several reasons. Sometimes something I'd collected would seem to me to be humor and other times it would seem merely median sardonica. Did his singing go under Humor? He liked to sing a parody of The Impossible Dream, in which he ate the inedible meal and drank the unpotable beverage, and so on. The question was whether it should go under Humor or a character trait like obstinacy, because while I'd smiled the first two or three times I'd heard him sing this, I finally had to signal that I wasn't finding it very funny, and finally that I wasn't finding it funny at all. But he was still singing it off and on, trying to get my approval for ongoing refinements in the lyrics. Other areas of his humor were slightly invasive as well. For some reason he continued to think it was funny to pretend I liked the music of Bob Dylan, when in fact all I had admitted at an earlier point was that I liked It Ain't Me Babe. He would murmur-sing How many times must the cannon balls fly Before they're forever banned, and then shout Wuxtry! Wuxtry! Historic Agreement! UN Bans Cannonballs Forever! Flintlocks Next! And of course out of my supposed adoration of Dylan came our longrunning match on why the band can't play. There were many more reasons than I'd remembered. Mine were consistently more hubristic than his, I noticed. He was not really ever going to evolve much beyond a strumpet stealing the trumpet or Jean Arp stealing the harp. Gender may be involved more than I recognized. He told me something he'd said jokingly, to which his wife had taken exception. Two people they knew had been living together for eight years and had decided to marry. So Denoon said to them Marriage is wonderful, this is great news, I know you'll find the addition of the sexual dimension to your relationship a great improvement to your life and a real eye-opener. He seemed surprised that I agreed with Grace that this was low-level. I'd put down very few of my own sallies, except when he'd seemed to react inordinately, as for some reason he did to my I'm attracted to you as to a magnate, or you attract me like a magnate. I persevered with this category. And not to venture too far into the underside of our household humor, he also laughed inordinately when I was getting into bed and slightly farted and he said Is that the way you greet me? I replied quick as a flash That's the only language you understand. Neither of us could figure out why we thought this was funny, but we both did.

The physical description I assembled is a masterpiece of some kind. I doubt that there is a more minute physical description of one human being by another anywhere. I wish I had never done it.

I Love a Demystified Thing Inordinately

I was improving on my texts as I went along, adding asides and priorly left-out associations.

That the fact that I was creating material almost as fast as I was classifying the material already in hand didn't bother me meant some-

thing—either I was at heart a congenital academic or the prospect of
indefinitely delaying coming to a conclusion about living with Denoon
was not unwelcome to me. Neither interpretation was flattering. One or
both were probably right, but this realization was completely weightless,
somehow. I kept on, drivenly, with that mobbed feeling your brain gets
when you're cramming for finals in nonelectives. Meanwhile the issue of
the night men was turning crescive without my noticing.

One morning three women I particularly liked came to get me for an
arch raising. They were Mma Isang, Mina Hlotse, who was our best
midwife, and Prettyrose Chilume, who was physically so slight that her
contribution to the actual labor of arch raising was basically spiritual,
even though she pulled and shoved along with the rest of us. I was always
asked. That day we were supposed to raise an arch over Our Mother
Street, the mother being not the Virgin Mary, as I think I'd been bemusedly assuming, but Mme Mpopo Kalighatle. This was an average
arch, about twenty feet high and seven wide, made of gum tree logs
enameled red and black in alternating bands, with the street names
carved into the crosspiece and painted with tar into which multicolored
glass fragments had been pressed while the tar was still sticky. Raising
the arch involved pushing the crosspiece up using claw-tipped poles
while the uprights were slid into the pits dug to receive them. The main
problem was the weight of the poles. You needed a few fairly sturdy
women in the crew. These events were largely celebratory. A few words
would be said about the virtues of the honoree, which, in Mme Mpopo's
case—I was about to learn—included an unfailing willingness to work
wherever she was needed most and an aptitude for intercepting children
about to wander out into the desert. She'd died two years earlier. Her
name came up often. She had a genuine reputation for great benevolence, and I wished I had known her. A new thing was that men were
offering their services at the raisings, claiming that they could do it faster
and more safely. In fact there had been a time or two when the arch had
not gotten to apogee at first try and had flopped back, narrowly missing
someone's foot. But women are nimble. Whatever we lack in hoisting
power we more than make up in agility at getting out of the way of
toppling structures. We were perfectly able to manage the raisings on
our own.

I was scribbling away when mes amis said koko. It was a relief to feel
obliged to knock off, since I seemed to be in quicksand anyway. One
problem I was encountering in making my compilations was deciding
when some striking remark of Nelson's was more than it seemed to be at

first blush, determining if perchance it was meant to convey something in an aesopian way to me. I might be looking for something even deeper than that, some warning or cue, some little nothing from the bowels of his mind, something to pay attention to because his unconscious was my friend, because Nelson loved me. Just then I was trying to see the relationship between Nelson's cynical observation that the meaning of life in every formulation seemed to reduce to finding or inventing a perfect will to be subject to, the relationship of that to scanting remarks about la femme moyenne sensuelle—which we agreed I was not, of course—finding her raison d'être in the love of a male as close to alpha as she can get. Then, to add to that, I had a handful of asides alluding to certain self-evident similarities between happy marriages and socialism, or just between marriage as an idea and socialism. Did he mean the two are similarly impossible, something as blunt and cheap as that? But that led to the bolus of whether he was or wasn't, himself, a socialist. One, he hated his father for being, merely, a prosocialist, a fan of the concept: that was utterly clear. Two, Nelson referred to himself from time to time as a socialist, but meaning something particular by it: his socialism was closer to the noumen than anybody's. And in the same jeremiad he could be referring to himself as a socialist in one breath and execrating genre marxists and social cubists in the next. His socialism was socialism, their socialism was militant nostalgia, and so on. Anyway, I didn't mind leaving all this for the nonce.

Mma Isang was hurrying us. I asked why and was told it was because a decision had been made to set up the arch without notice, which would prevent certain people, the baruledi, from coming to try and help. It would all be finished before the baruledi were even awake. Since baruledi means roofers or roof repairers, I was at sea. My friends were surprised that they had to explain it to me. The baruledi ba bojang, thatch roofers, were the night men. Thatch repairing was a bawdy if rather oblique euphemism for the service they provided. Clearly, resentment against the night men, on the part of some of the women, was getting substantial.

They are uprising against us, Mina said. It is all because of Raboupi. They just uprise against us without fear. You can see so many queens just defending about them.

There are now as many as nine night men. Mina named them. Raboupi wasn't one of them, but it was suspected he took a cut of the take. I asked more questions. There were some reasonable controls on the practice, at least. Mina said that the baruledi would always, now, bring protection from the clinic. And it was established that they were not to idle forever in order to be invited to meals: they had to leave when they were asked to go. I thought that the objections to the night men might arise from service being withheld from the aunts, generally. But that wasn't happening, as I should have known. One of the attractive things about African society across the board is how old a woman can be and still be some younger man's sex pal.

Apparently what was disliked was a growing blatancy about the enterprise. When I asked them how it was I hadn't noticed all this if it was so major, they shrugged, saying I overlooked it because it was hidden under a shadow, an ironic Tswanism meaning it wasn't hidden at all, ergo I was just not paying attention. They grumbled on as we proceeded, but I was relieved, oddly, about the whole thing. The notion that sex was nonpresent as an issue in Tsau, or was being transmuted wholesomely and wonderfully into something neutral and socially positive had always felt dubious to me, not to put too fine a point on it. I love demystified things inordinately. Also I loved it that the whores in Tsau were men.

The actual raising was very rushed, in fact, and throughout there was a subtle feeling of getting away with something. Several women spoke in praise of Our Mother Mpopo, each one in a very telescoped way— considering what the norm for occasions like this is. And lo just as we finished a little detachment of Raboupists turned up. They were welcome as spectators. Their group demeanor suffered slightly when the group was joined by a copain emerging blinking from a nearby rondavel not his own. We reacted kindly. We were already leaving.

I ran into Nelson as he was trotting down toward the site of the concluded event, his grapevine having belatedly functioned. I had to tell him it was over. He was genuinely unhappy. He'd prepared remarks a week ago or more. He had been deeply fond of Mpopo. There were things to say about her that only he could have said. He asked me who'd spoken. He'd known Mpopo better and longer than any of them. And so on. He was very distressed.

He had a right to know why the arch raising had been unannounced, so I told him. I wanted him to know that his not being included was an artifact, not something deliberate. In retrospect this was reckless, I suppose, but in mitigation I think I was under the impression I'd already mentioned the night men to him, however glancingly. It's possible I had but that he'd been in his occasional, rare actually, though less rare recently, Stepford husband mode, only appearing to hear me. Maybe I hadn't mentioned it.

His reaction was beyond disliking being the last one on the block to hear. He was trying to conceal how shaken he was. My thrusts in the direction of levity were a waste. I said he should look on Tsau as finally normalizing, first via the development of begging, thanks to the Basarwa, and now with prostitution.

We had to sit down somewhere. At first he didn't want to talk. Then he wanted to know everything I knew. A sure sign he was in extremis was his pressing down on the top of his head with his fingernails, as though a column of force was trying to emerge from his fontanel. He did this twice.

I Hear the Biography of Edward Lear

He stayed rattled all day and into that night. I thought sex might help and I showed I was approachable. I don't remember exactly how that foundered, but it had something to do with my hands, which were pale blue from an afternoon in the fabric printery. We got off the track, although this was far from the kind of thing that would normally derail him. Their heads were green and their hands were blue and they went to sea in a sieve, he started quoting. He loved Edward Lear. So did I. But did I know what an unhappy life Lear had lived, how his homosexuality had forced him to live out his life in places like Corsica? No, and he told me, in extenso. Slowly this developed the flavor of an incident from my past when someone I knew to be personally desperate seized on a book he had been recently reading and I hadn't read and proceeded to tediously summarize the whole thing as a means of evading the central misery we both knew was there. I never need to read the *Autobiography of Lincoln Steffens*.

Why Do You Look This Way?

I don't know how long it was, exactly, one day or two or three, three being the most it could have been, until the end of things began in earnest.

Whichever night it was, at dinner Nelson was silent, which constituted a total prodigy between us. He had been spending time closeted with Dineo, enough time to make me uncomfortable. The word was that he had been making inquiries about the night men.

I said Why do you look this way?

How do I look? It took him an effort to say even that much.

You look dissociated, almost.

Not that I said it, but my model for the way he was looking was my mother in certain of her troughs.

Then came a ghastly effort to appear animated and normal, ruined by his voice being sepulchral.

I finally got out of him what he had been discussing with Dineo. It had nothing to do with the night men. Hector Raboupi had gotten someone pregnant, a minor.

He had been planning not to tell me who, astonishingly. I got it out of him by reminding him I had friends who would tell me anyway.

It was Adelah Makhise. She was thirteen, a child. I loved her. She was darling and very smart. She was preparing to transfer to the government secondary at Kang. I was sick with rage. I wanted something done. There was a complete reversal going on. Now I was marginal with rage over this and he was supposed to soothe me and contextualize, whereas before it had been my role to calm him down over the night men. This had nothing to do with the night men or prostitution. It had been a simple seduction, apparently.

But Nelson was very wrung out. He had no surplus, nothing to give me. Everything he said was pro forma. And the worst part was that I developed the conviction he was more interested in observing me than in helping me. I felt I was being studied.

I know how random I must have seemed. I wanted to know everything, but in no particular order. Was Raboupi planning to marry this child? Nelson laughed. This set me off even more. The one place in the world something like this should never happen to Adelah, to this wonderful child, was Tsau. What was Raboupi's punishment going to be?

You know the culture, Nelson said. That meant the most that Raboupi would have to do by way of recompense was pay Adelah about forty pula per month, assuming she even requested it. But what are the women going to do about it? I wanted to know. There had to be better answers than the piddling forty pula. Raboupi should be punished, humiliated. There should be something like the practice in ancient Rome of creditors hiring mobs of people to follow deadbeats everywhere and identify them for what they were. I even remembered what that was called—the convicium—thanks to my cryptomnesia. I guess he was used to hits like this issuing from me from time to time, but I took his lack of reaction as meaning something more. My point was that a social invention addressing cases like Adelah's was lacking here. Who was to blame, if not the person in Tsau whose second name was social inventions?

Then, so amazingly, right in the midst of this he said Sometime we should talk about whether Boswell hated Johnson, which I can prove.

I don't know if this was deliberate protean behavior à la cornered jackrabbits or if it was simply adventitious. I had to strain to see what it had to do with anything. For a while he'd been teasing me about my Boswellian relationship with him. And lately he'd asked me for my Oxford paperback of The Life, which he had never read. In those days I carried my Oxford Boswell everywhere as a fallback in case I broke a leg somewhere where reading matter was a problem. I'd started The Life several times, never getting much beyond Johnson tutoring his schoolmates in Latin in exchange for their carrying him on their backs to school. It took three of them to manage it. Then Nelson seemed to be going on about Johnson's pulling strings at the British Admiralty to get his freed-slave manservant involuntarily returned to him after he'd run away to sea, as an illustration of the nasty side of Johnson Boswell was consistently revealing. I refused to talk about it. It was news to me, if true. This was not what we needed to talk about.

You're giving me cognitive dissonance, I said, so stop it. What's going to be done about Adelah?

Organize something, he said, continuing in the distant tone I hated and that felt so hostile.

I'm white, I said. What can I do? What about her mother?

Nelson said the news was that she was not so upset. It wasn't that there was great disgrace involved. He said Dineo thought Adelah's mother might have already gotten a gift of money from Hector which would have reassured her that he was prepared to do his duty. Hector had a surprising amount of disposable income, some of it from the game meat scheme he'd worked out with the Basarwa. Nelson was watching that, he reminded me.

Abortion, I thought. I knew the nurse could do it. There were other women I was sure could do it. But how far along was Adelah?

Around four months, Denoon said, and if you're thinking about abortion, it can't be done.

Because she's too far along, you mean?

It may be less than four months, he said, but it still can't be done.

You mean because someone has asked her and the answer is that she wants to have the baby? Because if that's it, let me talk to her before anyone says no on this, please.

No, he said, standing up, very white. No because an abortion is all we need. It's illegal. We have enemies in Gaborone doing nothing but waiting for us to break the law. An abortion would give them just what they want.

I said Oh, then the little arrangement over meat between Raboupi and the Basarwa, which is an illegality tout court but involving men, is all right. But an illegality by one or two women on behalf of a young girl is not all right—am I following you? How attractive is that?

All we need is the Christians against us, he said. If our game deal gets out it's not good, but the people who run this country own cattle and they know that the boys out at the cattle posts do certain similar dubious things once in a while.

I said something hotly about realpolitik. Humiliatingly, he corrected my pronunciation, but without responding to whatever my gravamen was. I realized I had never heard the word spoken. I had only seen it printed.

Do whatever you want, he said, being extraordinary and childish, I thought. But remember there are two things Gaborone right left and center never forgives—cattle rustling and abortions.

It was too much for me when he said Of course we could always expose the newborn. I knew it was sheer provocation and was well aware that he was the one who lobbied to get a street named after a woman whose main activity had been rescuing abandoned infants all over West Africa, but still it was insufferable.

I couldn't stand being in the same room with him at that instant.

Clearly the feeling was mutual. I felt I was doing him a favor by being the first to leave the house, and when I came back almost immediately in order to rummage up a torch, he was clearly getting ready to go someplace himself, lest I come back before he was ready for détente, no doubt.

I didn't care. Nothing was good. I left again and forged my way deliberately carelessly through rough brush, all the way over the shoulder of the koppie and down to a spot where I could contemplate the night fires of the Basarwa. I got a few scratches, going. It was cold and I was underdressed for it. It felt right to sit hunched up in bitterness, looking down at the Basarwa, who had nothing except lice but were happier than we were. The fires fade steadily and then brighten when they're replenished, when it's coldest, toward dawn. I stayed for that. I was getting a sore throat, and that felt right too.

Foul Play

I went directly from my crow's nest to the plaza. All I wanted was to pick a job someplace that would be warm, like the kitchen or the laundry, and simple, so I could vegetate while I worked. Something was funny, though. There were more people in the plaza than there should have been at so early an hour. And there was uneasiness. I was struck again with how true it was that a village like Tsau is an organism of sorts, and that I was becoming more and more a part of it. Something was communicating dread, something was up. I needed an interlude. I still had thorns and twigs in my hair. Just then I saw something I had never seen: Dineo running, the skirts of her gown pulled high up, her enviable thighs flashing and depressing me. She ran out of the edge of my vision and into Sekopololo.

There was a troop coming up Gladys and Ruth. I had never seen anything like this in Tsau. It was military. They were ululating and jogging in a cadenced way, a Zulu war jog. They were going to be exhausted when they got up as far as the plaza. Where am I? I thought. Other women left the plaza, rather quickly, I thought. The war jog conveyed something. Mma Isang materialized and came up to me. She

said They are in a rage of fury. This was the last English I heard for a
while that morning. Dorcas was leading the war party. I thanked god
when Dineo came out, composed, all in black, black turban, hieratic-
looking. She would do something. There were men with Dorcas, just
behind the batlodi and her other regulars, but no Hector that I could
see. Dineo was looking around for Dirang, asking urgently, Where is the
Ox? I wanted tea. There was a mechanism supposed to get tea out about
now that was not working. Tea was late and Dorcas was coming, disheveled, unlike herself.

I was thinking how theatrical we would appear to someone suspended
in the middle distance and facing the plaza, with women on different
levels of the upper flights of stairs, arranged like players in a student
production of Antigone.

Dorcas arrived with her troop. There were thirty, at least. If this was
her core group, it was growing. Immediately Dorcas began shrieking at
me in particular. Where was Rra Puleng? And why was I standing there
shivering—what was wrong with me?

Mma Isang said She is here for work. What are you making this
turmoil about?

Dorcas then produced something I had seen Batswana women do
only at funerals: she went into a violently undirected flailing and hand-
fluttering fit and had to be held up for a moment before she could
carry on.

My attention was divided. Some of Dorcas's people ran over to the
plaza bell. There was a scuffle. The Ox was guarding the bell for our
side. Dorcas herself seemed incoherent. She was shrieking questions at
me and now and then at Dineo. Where is my brother? was the main one.
She seemed to think I knew where her brother was, but she also seemed
to know that something terrible had happened to her brother. She was
saying a vision had come to her of Hector, dead, murdered. That was
her first version, as I heard. There would be others. She made a raking
motion at me and said You are dirty. I assumed this was about my
unkemptness of the moment, but she meant more. Her group was
crowding in on me.

Under stress my Setswana isn't what it should be. I tried to say that
she shouldn't be so excited, or that she was too excited, but I mixed up
gakatsega with gakatea, which meant I was telling her she was too angry.
This was inflammatory, and she began appealing to the sky and the earth
to say whether or not she had cause to be angry, she of all people.

I really hate being surrounded. I pushed my way out of the circle around me, and fairly roughly, but I felt two imperatives. Ululating is one thing from a distance and something else altogether when it's being directed at you, hatefully, up close. I had to get away from that. And also I was fixated on getting some food to eat, an egg, a scone, anything: my blood sugar was too low for what was happening to me. I ran over to get next to Dineo on the Sekopololo porch.

This was nobody's finest hour. Dineo was going in circles, ducking into the Sekopololo office and coming out again, starting to scrawl notes on scraps of paper, waving them around and finding no one to take them, finally crushing them up.

Do you know what any of this is? I asked her. She didn't seem to. Miraculously she had a platter of hardboiled eggs on her desk. I snatched myself one and scratched off the shell.

From the porch I could hear Dorcas giving another version of what had happened. This story was that she had heard Hector leave his rondavel, the smaller one on her plot, after someone very quietly called him to come out. She'd thought nothing of it, because he would sometimes go walking at night, to the tannery to see about chemicals and shifting hides from one bath to another. So she had gone back to sleep and slept hard because of overworking of late, and when she had heard a cry outside she made this cry a part of a dream. But now she knew it was her brother's cry. And even if she had awakened at the cry she would have been fearful of going out because of so many enemies always hovering against Hector. But in fact she had slept on and only in the morning had she realized that the cry she had dreamed her brother made was in fact his voice, saying he was killed. And then when her brother's men came for him as always, and he was gone, she knew now he must be found dead.

I began to be afraid in a shameful way. I wanted to say I have nothing to do with this place, I'm on my way home, my bags are packed, virtually. Dorcas was finishing in a genuine crescendo of hysteria. I was choking on my egg for a minute. It shames me, but I thought with terror that Nelson and I were the only whites within a radius of two hundred miles.

Dorcas's group lurched and then swept confusedly offstage right, Dorcas shouting that Hector's body had been put among the rocks and that Dineo should call out the snake women to search. They were leaving, at least. I was relieved until I realized they were making for our place. I said urgently to Dineo that we had to follow them. She was making a list. We must have a committee. But she stopped writing and said she would come. I was already running after them. Nelson slept naked and he might not be up yet.

I got to the octagon to find smoke rising from the donkey boiler and Dorcas and her followers converged around the bathing tent. I thought it was odd of Nelson to be going to the trouble of firing up the bathing engine, especially since I obviously wasn't being included, but also because it was a lot of work in cold weather and the tub cooled off almost before you got soaped up. It was a shock to me that evidently the women had gone into our house to look for him.

The mob, which is what this was becoming, was shouting into the tent for Nelson to come out, stalking around it, some women ululating right into the canvas.

I tried to manifest calm. I must have succeeded. They let me through and into the tent, not happily. I probably projected absolute determination to get in there and got a response to that. There was a thing about Denoon, undoubtedly rooted in his living in the periphery and alone for such long periods of time. He went around naked more than average. I was used to it. I'm averagely casual about going around naked in front of established boyfriends, but around Denoon I eventually took to being more modest. He was unusually responsive to female nudity. He claimed it was generational. Men his age had spent their first twenty or so years waiting to see a naked female in the flesh, undsoweiter. Anyway, I had generated a wardrobe of kimono-like garments which I had distributed around, one in the privy, one in the bathing tent, my prize yakuta in the house itself. I got into the tent and there was my Nelson, naked, moist to the waist, having hauled himself out of the tub when the commotion began. He was forcing himself into my garment, in his dislocation. He wanted to talk, urgently, naturally. He had looked for me during the night, and so on, and he wanted to know what all this was about, what was happening. He was between bemused and alarmed. I told him to stay put until I could bring him his bush shorts and a shirt and sandals, not to move an inch, I would manage it. I tore my garment off him, somewhat wrecking it. He was not going to be seen in this floral thing if my life depended on it. Later he denied that when I'd burst in he thought at first I was one of the furies besieging him, but in fact there had been such a moment, just a flicker, but real, which hurt me to see.

I put my head out to announce that everything should wait until I came back with proper clothes for Nelson. As I did, someone pushed in,

Dorcas, out of control again. I had routinely pulled the plug on the bath, assuming that there was clearly not going to be one now. Dorcas screamed, pointing at the water running out, saying He must not wash and we must examine him for blood. People began copying, shouting Blood, blood. Nelson stood there in the corner, his back to her.

I was trilled at when I came out of the tent. I went into the house and grabbed up clothes and came back with them. There were more women in the tent. I stood in front of him while he got properly dressed. No one left. I was enraged.

I said in English to Nelson Do you understand that they claim you did something to Raboupi, as in killing him? He nodded. He was aghast. But he did understand.

Dorcas said to me You are not allowed to speak, as from this moment.

These were bullies. I said to Nelson Don't let them touch you.

Let us see your hands, they said to him, as to marks.

Nelson looked directly at Dorcas and asked if he had ever harmed her in any way, then ruined it by saying he was speaking as a brother. This was insane of him, or course, and just what she wanted.

Rra, my brother is just lying murdered, which she shrieked, pronouncing it the South African way, murder as murdeh. That was very odd, but so was everything, my whole world. A lot of progressive Batswana in Gabs like to sound South African, prefer to be taken as South African because they think it makes them seem more sophisticated, but here in Tsau it made no sense.

Nelson was completely appeasing. I said to him—against people telling Dorcas that I was talking, in disobedience to her dictum—you have to clean up more, your hair is insane, you look like a fou, you have to insist. But no, all he wanted in life was that whatever this was going to be it would be nonviolent. This was right, undoubtedly, except that sometimes bullies vanish at the first sight of counterforce, but we were white, so he wasn't wrong in the circumstances. As I was backing out of the tent, not through the door vent, because that was blocked, but through the side, some bitch stepped on the hem of the side wall to try to make me get down on all fours. I heaved the thing up like Atlas. This was new, unthinkable.

There were more men around, I noticed, but it was interesting to me how tightly they were being kept to being spear carriers. Women were actively waving them back from any involvement with the tent. Here I was wanting to fight just a little. I embrace the physical. I think in my hysteria I wanted to be the one-woman whiff of grapeshot. When I was an adolescent I was always the one who wanted to organize my girlfriends to go into the heart of the crowd in St. Paul on New Year's Eve, granted the men collecting there would be reliable North Europeans more into puking than into grabbing and kissing, à la San Francisco. But still. I told them I would guarantee no one would touch us. I don't know what I meant, but I believed it. We would be safe, somehow. Three and then four of my friends came with me, finally, and no one touched us, in the heart of the worst St. Paul had to offer. Four came with me in my senior year. No one touched us. I think all this came to me, and then: You can control men, but what can you do now? Think! You are lost.

There was one further interesting mêlée before the cavalry, the loyalists, arrived in force and we could consurge back down to the plaza. Dineo had dismissed school. Many children arrived with the loyalists, potential witnesses, I realized, a moderating presence, brilliant.

Timing is all. The actual tannery manager was Moffat Dabutha, who was also a top pawn of Hector's: he made as if to restrain Nelson, tie his hands with some thongs. He was exceeding his authority. Dorcas ignited. She ripped the thongs out of Moffat's grasp and wound them around her wrist, repeating that only women may touch their hands to Rra Puleng. Some were, in fact, prodding him toward the sandpath down to the plaza. There were new currents here. Dorcas was operating nakedly, commanding men and women alike. I think this had something to do with the amazed inertness of our side when they were faced with the dynamism Dorcas was orchestrating and sustaining. Nelson's utter passivity was also undermining for us. He was starting to go with his tormentors, numbly, and with only one sandal on. I fixed that. I brought him his other sandal and made everything wait until he had it securely on.

I was feeling less regressed by then. I wanted to communicate to Nelson that he was wrong to take what was going on as any kind of legitimate frenzy. There was foisting and theater in it. All of this would dissolve when Raboupi turned up. He had to be somewhere around. At that point I was incapable of taking seriously that foul play had anything to do with his absence, if he really was absent at all.

The pushing stopped and we all went down to the plaza at a stroll.

Groups and committees were already mobilizing. The main snake women were meeting. I was not being included, not surprisingly. The justice committee was being called together, which was going to be pointless since they were used to dealing with matters like cattle gates being left unlatched, at the most earthshaking. Also the justice committee consisted of three very old women, our oldest, and their deliberations were extremely slow.

The alarm bell was banging.

Nelson went voluntarily to sit and wait in a room in Sekopololo. He must stay in one spot, he must be under guard, Dorcas was shouting. He must not roam about at this time. And pointing at me, she announced that I must not be allowed to stay with him or speak to him. Some of the loyalists said Gosiame, meaning they were going along with this, while others said no, I should be with him. I paid no attention. I went inside and sat myself in a chair outside the door of the room Nelson was in. Dorcas was now certain that the voice she'd heard summoning Hector was Nelson's. Word kept coming in that Hector was not in this venue, nor in this, nor in this. I was going to suggest a sabbatical once this was over. Dineo went in to talk to Nelson. I couldn't make it out. Nelson was speaking in Setswana. Other people went in and out. Nobody would look at me.

I had a moment of panic about our house, our things. I knew people had been inside our place, and I was diffusely afraid they'd found something that would be dangerous to us, although what that might be I had no idea. I had to go and check. But everything looked undisturbed, except for the transmitter, where some wires and leads at the back of the set seemed to have been pulled out. But the radio was not my province and I wasn't certain I was seeing things correctly. I tried to get a clear mental picture of what the damage might be so I could pass it on to Nelson when we were able to talk, which I was determined was going to be soon.

I went back to my post outside his door. Spring had come. It was a superlative morning. There is no more beautiful season in the Kalahari.

A Cell

Don't pay any attention to this, he said.

But this was a cell! There was no other word for it. They had brought in a pallet, a covered bucket, and a water jug and cup. He said This is voluntary. They need to do this. They know I don't know anything about Raboupi: I was asleep.

We embraced. He asked me to stop acting tragic, if I didn't mind. This was nothing and would be over soon. We said we loved each other.

Do you at least have privacy when you use that? I asked, pointing at the bucket. People had been going in and out fairly freely, not knocking.

I don't know yet, he said, but in all probability.

I described the state of the transmitter as best I could. He seemed to think that possibly a section of lead was missing, possibly not, but it didn't matter since he had spares for everything.

Nothing is going to happen to anyone, he said. But I could feel effort behind his saying it.

You have to fight more, I said. He barely let me finish. His smile had never seemed so transcendent to me. I hated it. This was a performance of his reposing his trust in the entity or organism he had created, and I was just supposed to sing along. I knew his tropes. This one reduced to a sickly fatalism. He was saying If this my child or creature fails me, then I have failed and I have done it to myself, so that must be what I deserve.

I went outside and came directly back to say There is the most beautiful weather, can't you come out for a second and just stand there and inhale? No, was the answer: there were meetings going on. He pretended it was his choice.

I had theories about Raboupi, the premier one being that if he was genuinely missing, it was something faked up between him and Dorcas. Then: what about friends of Adelah's? I hated Raboupi myself. What about Basarwa, who were undoubtedly being cruelly cheated by him? It was no use. He wouldn't speculate. Time would take care of it. There were a few things I could bring him, if I didn't mind.

Nelson Is Very Calm

Tsau was distracted with meetings, with the snake women filing in and out of the plaza on one search after another, with rumors.

Nelson stayed under office arrest—the only term for it I can think of —for two bad days. Attitudes toward me were unstable, but I didn't care.

All I did was loiter, essentially. Everything was arbitrary: sometimes I could walk straight in and see Nelson, and sometimes I was refused. When I did get in, I found him very calm, meditative. I had to suppress impulses to tell people things they should know about Nelson, such as that he needed to wash his upper torso thoroughly every day to keep him from developing a rash under his chest hair, which was quite thick. He claimed he was allergic to his own sweat, but I knew it was bacterial because witch hazel, which we were out of in Tsau, always cleared it up in a couple of applications. His message to me was unchanging—this would all be over, the mills of the gods were grinding, the thing was to be patient.

Routines slipped. The Barclays plane came and went, and no one met it. I was the one who, after wandering down to the airstrip, brought to the attention of the powers that were the fact that there were crates and items sitting on the ground waiting to be picked up. Somebody unknown, once, began ringing the alarm bell. Never had this happened before. There was a generalized feeling of transgression affecting us. Mma Sithebe and Mma Isang were subtly trying to keep track of me and keep me reassured. I had no appetite. I was unable to plan.

In the end Nelson was discharged from office arrest for reasons of convenience. He was needed to get the transmitter back in working order so that Dorcas Raboupi could file a charge against him with the police in Gaborone. The damage to the transmitter was real, but it was trivial: he remarked that it must have occurred because people moved things around without being careful. He made nothing of it. And the police made nothing of Dorcas's confused appeal to them. A male relative making himself scarce without notice was nothing. They were sure he would turn up. Dorcas went into too much detail. Her assertions that Nelson should be put under investigation because he was the one who knew more than anyone at Tsau what caves and fissures there were and how by shifting a rock a dead body could be concealed forever were simply uninterpretable to the police. So that was a misfire. I think Nelson would have volunteered for a third night of office arrest unless I'd made a move. He was very mild about captivity. He was very much enjoying reading the *Tao Te Ching*, which he had asked me to bring him. You have to stay here with me, I said, because I'm becoming paranoid: I get the feeling the house is being watched, and I'm afraid to be here alone. I need you to stay with me.

There would be more meetings. There would be a hearing.

Our first night back together was odd. He wasn't interested in sex. I was. Odder was that he couldn't seem to make himself help me with my panic, my need to have us acknowledge we were on a precipice together. I wanted that, and I wanted for us to pool everything we could think of about Hector and his possible fate, to try to solve it, to comprehend it. And as if that weren't enough, I also wanted it made clear to me, in any form he could do it in, that I was living with the man I thought I was, someone of absolute delicacy in regard to human life, innocent of any connection with any injury to Hector Raboupi. Women supposedly want to marry men taller than they are on the subliminal assumption that the taller they are, the more adequately they can be expected to function as protectors, for which read killers, if need be. This was never me. Not that it proves anything, but Nelson and I are the same height. I wanted a pacific male: I suppose I always had, but he had made the need definite and intense. Wonderful, I told myself, the way you're multiplying your desiderata as you get older, Brava! Stupidly coexisting with this value was an emotional trope that said that in matters of violence women could have latitude, because of history, which turned violence by them against men into reprisal actions.

But I was getting no help from Nelson. All he wanted was normalcy.

There was nothing I could do. On Hector, he wouldn't go beyond saying he was certain that the disappearance was something Hector had staged, with help, and that the truth would out. We would have to wait for the next act. He was very tired. I had to relent. It wasn't enough for me to feel convinced of his innocence: I wanted him to show he felt as strongly as I did that if there had been a crime, it was critical, to say the least, to find out who was responsible. But of course he was staying with the position that this was all an illusion. He wouldn't speculate. I could, if I wanted, was the best I could get.

My ignoblest hope I managed to keep to myself, which was that after this was over, the prospect of disengaging himself, ourselves, from Tsau might be brighter.

Duplicrats and Replicans

Tsau oscillated for another week. The mother committee offered a five hundred pula reward for the body of Hector Raboupi. Everything was disrupted. Children and teachers left school to go on searches. Even the Basarwa were brought into it. When all this led to nothing, it was time for hearings before the justice committee.

Written statements had been taken from a dozen of us, describing everything about our movements and observations the night of Hector's disappearance. I was essentially no help to Nelson in terms of an alibi. He had been out that night. At the time when he was presumably back, I was out. We had had difficult words. Great interest was shown in all this, naturally. The justice committee was extremely thorough. The permutations in Dorcas's account were noted. There had been a careful physical examination of Denoon at Sekopololo just after his removal from the bathing tent: although he had various minor scratches and bruises on his arms and trunk, all were consistent with the accidents the kind of physical work he was doing might have resulted in. The conclusion was that no one could say what had happened to Hector. Two possibilities were that he had gone off for some reason to Tikwe, a flyspeck of a settlement forty-five miles north of us, or to the Herero trek route thirty miles east of us, which was in use at this time of the year. In any case his disappearance had been reported to the district commissioner at Maun for him to proceed with. It seemed to be over. Dorcas and her friends were admonished to stop repeating accusations. This was received darkly by them. They were especially unhappy when it was pointed out that Raboupi had been away from Tsau without notice to anyone for up to three days at a time in the past. Dorcas vehemently denied this, but it did seem to be the case.

Adelah miscarried. I have my own opinion as to how genuine this was. Dineo loved her too. So did Dirang. We all did. Now she could go to school. I gave her a locket. She said she would write to me. The weather was beyond perfect. It must really be over, I said to him when I heard he'd been requested to come to Sekopololo to help with accounts.

His drive for it to be over was so strong and pathetic that I fell into line. Now we can go, I said. Your work is done and Tsau is a normal place: it has beggars, prostitution, and crime. The Basarwa were the beggars, the night men were the prostitutes, and I was for the moment taking the stance that Raboupi's evanition might in fact be a crime. He bridled hugely. I apologized for being flippant.

I knew what was happening. He was trying to take asylum in professionalism. Tsau, after all, was his profession. The message was that I should stick to my lares and penates while he got on with his work. A brain surgeon doesn't consult with his wife on how to attack a tumor just because he loves her and she's a lovely person. Also the message was that it was time for me to see myself not so unqualifiedly as a colleague.

That was it for then. Never mind that I could see him filling up with sadness like a shirtcuff inadvertently dipping into an inkwell. One way he had of reminding me of how much older than I he was was by recalling that when he was in grammar school they had had inkwells set into each desk, and ink monitors to fill them. You had to be careful not to dip your sleeve into them. I was post-inkwell. So much of my imagery comes from stories and asides of Nelson's it shocks me. I don't want it. It isn't as though my own life hasn't been fairly vivid in its own way.

Cues not to entertain the idea of getting Nelson back to America rained on me. I forget what the issue was, unless it was neither the Democrats nor the Republicans having anything to say against South Africa going back into Angola and murdering hundreds at Xangongo that August, but I was getting bitter references to the hopelessness of American political life, the two parties should be called the Duplicrats and the Replicans, and so on. I was tempted to say Then why don't you go back to the U.S., the flagship of the thing you see destroying the world, be a man, jump into the fiery furnace, run for Congress or start a movement or something. And I felt like adding that that's what I'd do if I were a man with all his attributes and felt as strongly as he seemed to.

Clay-Shuttered Doors

Denoon's response to even my feeblest attempts at asking burning questions reminded me of one of my favorite adolescent reading experiences. He was like the mother in *Clay-Shuttered Doors*. A mother gets terminally ill and is on her deathbed. But her family gathers around her and somehow their love and need for her are so kinetic that although she actually dies this love force somehow reanimates her. She's not fully alive and there are oddities about her that prove it, such as her breath being ice cold. She manages to drag around the house for a week or so, responding to simple questions and the like, making scrambled eggs but nothing more complicated. Then it's all too much and she dies all the way. This was Nelson in that period. We had two or three very nice passages of rain. In normal times this would have elevated him enormously. But he was pro forma toward it.

He answered my questions in good faith, I thought, but in a labored and not fully engaged way. It seemed like such an effort for him that I thought I might precipitate something untoward if I kept it up, so I fell back on my all-purpose recourse of scriptomania and made a list of all the questions that I might someday ask, when he was himself again and we could solve things according to the dictates of reason, the right questions to ask to elucidate the matter of leaving Tsau versus staying forever. These were questions like Would you be planning to stay if you had children to raise? That would have been a disastrous question, I realize in retrospect, because it suggested that he had created something second rate but good enough for other people's children, or it suggested I might think so, if he and I had children together, or a child. It would also have struck him that I might, through this question, be subtly asking him to get me pregnant, asking please to be allowed to define myself in the world by offspring of his and their no doubt similarly worldshaking accomplishments to come. I have no idea if I'm maternal or not, but this wasn't the way to find out. Another question might have been Would this be happening between us if we were legally married?

Since the questions I was entertaining were for my eyes only and could always be triaged, I felt free to get ultra vires if I felt like it. Some were what he hated most, pop psychological, as in Is there anything that might be helpful to you in deciding about this if you looked at your parental constellation, id est the idea that you might be carrying out a paternal mission, converting his philoradicalism into the real thing, and at the same time creating a society your saintly mother would be proud of, in which women are supposedly never harmed by men and where temperance is queen, which also retroactively rules the cause of your father's downfall out of existence? I'm not quite the deadly enemy of pop psychology I'm afraid I let Nelson assume I was. I'm a true eclectic. In fact I once even vaguely thought about becoming a Transactional Analyst, because they had wonderfully simple certification procedures and I don't think you can argue with the idea that internalized family dynamics are to some degree or other critical in what we are. This was during my continual search for economic fallbacks. Nelson never fully appreciated how determined I was not to fall into poverty in America, into debt in particular. I knew what that was. Even when I went ultra vires there were limits. In none of my questions do the words midlife crisis appear, for instance.

Another question I had was Supposing I were more vocationally clear and driven and less skeptical and ambivalent, how would that affect this? It wasn't that I was no longer interested in nutritional anthropology. I am and was. And I knew that with a modicum of luck and encouragement I could blow on the embers and get the son et lumière back, probably. But pursuing Nelson had filled the skies of my mind with another edifice. I would try to revivify my feeling for anthropology from time to time, even carrying my efforts into little fantasies of pulling out, going alone and whole hog back to Stanford and into a new thesis and a new thesis adviser and lo and behold having Nelson without warning turn up, having followed me across the world to be with me. But if he didn't come, what then? And what about having to deal with the dynamo women who were taking over in anthropology, the ones who had been smarter and who had done it better, who would be really en route, some of them with husbands they loved, who loved them, children already? And what would I do when it turned out that the most interesting thing I could tell anyone was anything I was willing to divulge about the great social genius Nelson Denoon, who was rumored to have been very attached to me at one time?

This moment in my life wasn't good and had to end. To live in Tsau decently you have to attend to small things. Distraction can hurt you. I got slipshod about checking the bedclothes for scorpions, for example, and felt something on my ankle one night and that was what it was. I knocked it away before it could sting, but it was a warning to me.

My dreams were not helping me in any way. In one of them I had a suitcase and was entering a house that was like a child's drawing and in one of whose windows I had caught a glimpse of a name anthropologist, male, who had once expressed an interest in me but who was, I had found out, bisexual. When I got inside the house it was a place where I had lived briefly with my mother, a rickety cottage on the outskirts of a quarry. There was blasting at any time of the day, two or three times a week. In this house there were no level surfaces. You would get used to it but then the next time they blasted, things would slide in a direction you weren't adapted to. My mother in a deluded attempt to spruce the place up had pried down the lath covering the joins in the beaverboard panels that made up the ceiling and had tried to spackle and repaint the whole thing to create a more seamless effect, because, as I recall, she hated the feeling of being under a grid. But unfortunately the outcome was that as the grout between the panels dried out and the blasting continued, little bits of stuff and dust would drop down on you, especially, it seemed, when you had your little friends over for a tea party. Anyway, that was the house I was back in, in my dream, although nothing seemed to be going on and there was no sign of my mother.

One night I looked at my right hand and noticed a callus like a little knob just above the first joint on my middle finger, and a padlike thickening on the tip of my index finger that I'd been unconsciously picking at lately, all due to incessant writing. This has to end, I said to myself.

A Branch of Tsau Is Needed

One morning he was up before light. He was gathering things together and putting them in a pack. I'm leaving, I thought I heard him say.

Naturally I was electrified. He looked altered. He was purposive. If he was packing, I should be packing too, n'est-ce pas? I was afraid to say or do anything that would threaten the construction I was placing on things.

But he undeceived me in a flash. He knew what he was going to do vis-à-vis Tsau. He was going to go, now, at once, to the minuscule hamlet of Tikwe. Tikwe was forty-five miles to the north of us. In the stretch of desert between us and Tikwe, there were no settlements whatever. He, singular, was going. He was looking for my water-points map.

He would be going to Tikwe for a specific purpose. It was time for Tsau to have a sister colony, an affine of some concrete sort. The lack of a sister or daughter colony was at the root of what was wrong in Tsau. People had to be confronted with the need to spread the idea of Tsau rather than merely reposing comfortably in it. There needed to be exchange. Exchange would concentrate the public consciousness in Tsau on what Tsau truly was. People in Tsau had gotten too casual and spent too much time writing letters to poor relations elsewhere, essentially lording it over them. In Tikwe he would see about setting up a branch of Tsau, or at a minimum explore bringing back a couple of women as interns. Tsau had the wealth to begin to expand modestly, and this was modest. Also he would be able to see if there was any news of Hector in Tikwe.

Sit down while we eat something, I said. I could smell danger all over this project, commencing with his mode of conveyance. He was going to borrow—this was his word—a horse. Tsau owned two horses. I knew this was something that had to go through a committee, and he was not planning to go through a committee. He was departing immediately. He was speaking in short sentences and sentence fragments, I pointed out to him. I said Being this terse is proof this whole thing is precipitate, isn't it?

I was frank with him. This is action for the sake of action, I told him. There was no risk, he claimed, and if there was, it was a fraction of what I had faced in coming to Tsau. He knew this patch of the Kalahari inside out, whether I believed that or not. In any case he wasn't going to argue the central proposition, because that would be time-consuming and he was definitely determined to go. If he was wrong, so be it, it would cost him a week and then he would be back to rejoin the waltz and I would have been proven right about something yet again.

I could stop you, I said. I could notify people. I love you, which you're exploiting: you know I won't stop this. But I should. I should, just to stop you from talking to me in this particular way ever again. I am not your audience. Remember that. I'm dead against this and I love you, but nothing I say can have the slightest effect on you, can it? We both know it. This is patter you're giving me, and you're the supposed proclaimed enemy of the idea that women are just pontoons for the various male enterprises coming down the pike, but look at this. What would be wrong with going tomorrow or the next day? The problem is that the women would make difficulties for you. They are not going to love your absconding with one of our horses. This is going to be left for me to handle. In fact you need me to be here, which is why I can't go along if you have to leave without notice like this. Isn't this right? If we took both horses without a by your leave, there would be hysteria to the skies. But with me left behind I can rationalize, I can explain, I can invent the reasons why this had to be done without notice, and so on, right?

I made him let me check on his food choices, which were adequate. But he had forgotten both the first aid and the snakebite kits. He found them.

I am trying to save this place, he said.

But you don't deny anything I'm saying, do you? I asked.

No, he said.

This is wrong, I said.

Why Was He Doing This?

I talked to myself after he left. He wasn't a fool, so why was he doing this, or why did he feel so absolutely that he had to do it? I was full of staircase wisdom. Maybe the conviction was establishing itself that people wanted him to go, actively in some cases, clearly, and more passively in others. So that by this action he would reverse everything and create a new role for himself it would take them awhile to fathom and object to. So that he could stay. I could have raised this possibility with him. I could have raised the possibility that all the approval for and orchestration of our getting together as a ménage had been directed at the same thing, something permitted to happen premised on the prescient idea that I was younger and would be likely to have an agenda that would pull us both away sooner rather than later. I could have found some way to get under the closed surface of his patter. I could have made him argue, somehow.

I even ran a little way out with the idea of catching him and telling him to take Baphomey instead of one of the horses, because people would be less upset about it, even though Baph was technically Sekopololo property, like the horses. I had given Baph to Sekopololo. But I realized there was no way he was going to be willing to arrive back in Tsau riding on an ass, with or without Tikwe in the palm of his hand. He would want to look equestrian. I went back to bed. I think now that I still might have been able to catch up with him and make him reconsider, but there was also the fact that the idea of Tsau's becoming more a model and propagator of the equity system sooner rather than later was itself respectable. It was something that had been talked about. So I went back to bed.

A Heresy

The uproar began at noon, when the absence of one of the horses was noticed. I made mistakes immediately. I got down to the plaza after the fact. I was on my way to see Dineo to tell her what had happened, but timing now suggested this was a bad idea and that I should dissemble.

Dorcas was there, infuriated, sensationalizing the missing horse and saying Denoon was out in the desert taking Hector's body with him to hide there.

I was afraid. Fear made me say I had been asleep and knew as little as anyone else.

These people are always asleep when crime is going forthwards, Dorcas said, screamed, rather.

Dineo pulled me in, and I told her the truth immediately. I emphasized how I had argued with Nelson but that he had been immovable. I had to write a statement. I felt for her. She was upset.

The weather was peculiar, a white low sky with wispy black underclouds like ink dispersing in water. That night it rained. I thought of Nelson in the desert, thinking it would probably take at least two days for the journey. I slept badly, waking up when the perfect phrase came to me for what Nelson had done, the phrase I could have used to stop him, maybe: On s'engage et puis on voit. That might have stopped him. Being classified was one of the few things that ever did. Or maybe it would only have encouraged him. I found his main sunglasses on the desk. He had others, but why would these be here?

In the morning I walked down to the kraals to see Baph. There was an ostentatious guard, men and women, posted. I suppose the idea was to keep me from helping myself to either Baph or the remaining horse. I probably shouldn't have made that visit.

The justice committee was convened again.

I thought to myself I am in danger of going crazy if this goes on for very long. I had been dropped out of two discourses, one with Denoon because in a crisis we were not really collegial and also because of not being a man, I am convinced. And I was being dropped out of discourse with the women of Tsau because of not being an African and also because of my connection with the increasingly suspect Nelson.

I tried to be internally militant and to disdain the present circumstances of my life because they were boring and I was not born to be bored. Of course in Setswana there is no word for boring or bored, which Nelson had pointed out to me as an example of Tswana soundness. But then where was Nelson, my friend, whatever his weaknesses, now that I needed him?

You are boring to me, was the heresy I wanted to shout into the faces of the squinting rabble who were following Dorcas around. You bore me to tears. You are consigning me to a boring position. You are interesting only from the standpoint of someone interested in boring people. You are less than uninteresting. You are boring in the way you interact. I am not asking you to be characters in Proust, but I am mentally asking you not to surveil me, which is the most boring thing you can either do or be subject to. All over the world in the privacy of their huts anthropologists are turning up their hands and saying This is boring. Life should not be boring. There is a person here who is not boring, Nelson Denoon, and you together have driven him into a state where he is out in the desert, and the desert is always dangerous if you go out into it alone. I also am not boring. You may think you aren't boring because you're courteous a lot, when you feel like it. In my humble opinion courtesy is the ancien régime everywhere if it goes off and on like a traffic light. I made my own discourse.

Where Was He?

He was supposed to be gone a week at most. A week can mean five days or seven days. And when seven days had passed I was frantically telling myself that he had probably said About a week.

After the fifth day I was frozen with anxiety. I was convinced something terrible had happened to him. My writing project seemed pointless, worse than pointless if something had happened. I should be doing something physical or practical. The effort it took to keep my handwriting from looking atypical was frightening me. I signed up at Sekopololo to distribute seeds around town for the spring planting in the kitchen gardens. At certain houses they closed the door to me when they saw who was calling. I persisted anyway.

The weather had been irregular, some days bright and some ominous, with a little rain. I went up the koppie every morning and evening to see where it had rained, where the dark patches were that would turn green first. Also I was looking for Nelson. I tried to remember what he had told me about a Frenchman in the seventeenth century who had had one and only one occult power, which was to be able to predict accurately when ships would be arriving at Toulon. He couldn't predict or prophesy in any other way. Nelson's favorite mystics were individuals who had one freakish talent that was fairly pointless. In the fifties there was a character who seemed to be able to get little fragments of scenes onto photographic plates by sheer concentration. Usually Nelson's heroes ended in poverty and ignominy. The Frenchman who could see ships around the curvature of the earth, which was what he claimed he could do, never attempted to make money from his gift. One of Nelson's major qualities, all of which I was appreciating strongly in my present state, was that if he knew something you didn't know, he would tell you all there was, and there was no part of it he would shade or leave out because it fit badly into his own belief system. Why did he know these things? He believed in aleatory reading. Through his academic friends he had stack privileges in all the great libraries—this must be a slight exaggeration—and often when he was back in what I would never dare to his face to call civilization he would go straight to the nearest university library and stand up for eight hours, wandering and reading until he had it out of his system. Now where was he?

I had been twice to Dineo to try to get her to authorize a party to search for him. She said that they knew him better than I did and that they were aware of many times when he had gone off like this to one of the pans or along the sand river. She was sure he would be back in good time, and in any case there was the complicating matter of his taking the horse. There really was no excuse for it. I spent an entire day on the koppie, with my binoculars. There was nothing to do. Maun and Kang had been radioed. I was the only one who was distraught.

Nine Days

I appealed to Dineo to let me have my donkey back. They could take all my credits. They could set any value on him they wanted. If my credits were short I would owe the rest and work it off nonstop. I reminded her that I had donated Baph to Sekopololo in the first place, which should have counted for something. She wanted to do it, genuinely, but now, especially, she couldn't approve it on her own. They would have to meet on it.

What enraged me was that everything had to be so consensual, even in what I felt was a crisis. I kept saying Show me the rules that say this or that can't be done; where is it written down? But there was very little on paper. Everything was inscribed in what people recalled.

In the midst of imploring Dineo I said something so grotesquely stupid it pains me to think of it. I said: You have no idea what you are doing —you are condemning a *delightful person* to death with this. I trailed off because she gave me a look of scorn I will never recover from. I was reaching the point of seeing everything in Tsau as an obstacle to my need to find and save him.

Finally it was nine days. I could find nothing better to do with my funktionslust than go up to the top of the koppie and sit there near hysteria, wondering why there was no way of bringing the Botswana Air Force into this. Why was there no person in a high place who could get me out of this, no special friend? What lack in me had produced that situation, that my only true friend was out in the thornveld with nobody helping? King James and his sister sought me out and brought me snacks, dried papaya.

The Eleventh Day

I talked to several women who had been part of the grapple plant harvest, and to some of the snake women, to see if they would consider going with me at least part of the way toward Tikwe. None was eager, except softhearted Prettyrose Chilume, a sensitive plant, fine in a group but not appropriate to go in a duo just with me. I needed a hardier companion. All my attempts at finding someone to go with were reminding me of how frightened I'd been during my crossing from Kang and how potent the residue of that fear was.

The radio was impossible. I did get a promise from Wildlife that they would attempt to contact game scouts who had passed through Tikwe sometime in the past week. This was followed by silence.

I read through my compilation on Nelson like a madwoman. It was insidious. All it did was serve to convince me that Nelson was the man, Nelson was the one I should cleave to, wherever he wanted to be. Brilliant, I told myself, how brilliant to come to this conclusion under these conditions. One thing that was absolutely certain was that this was not a man who would let someone he loved go off on an exercise supposed to last five or six days but lasting ten and then not summon up a force to go out and secure her.

However afraid I was, there was no question I had to go out, at long last, to find him. I began kitting up.

People tried to dissuade me. Dineo said an official search party would be going out soon. But she couldn't say exactly when the party would be ready to go.

I made an abortive effort to enlist two Basarwa men. I couldn't make myself understood. I cursed myself for not learning Sesarwa. Hector had been the local master of the language.

I got myself as ready as I could. There were no water-point maps of the area, that I knew of, except for the one I had brought with me and which Nelson had taken with him. I was ready by high noon of the eleventh day.

I was furious with Tsau, furious with the people stopping work to somberly watch me go, furious that they were letting me go off into what was undoubtedly going to be a liebestod if not a farce. Is this right? I wanted to shout at them, along with We're only here because of you! and This is love!

It was love, but it was also, to some degree, pride. I knew this because I was thinking of my friend Anna as Tsau dropped astern. Anna went to Provincetown in the dead of winter one year in order to rusticate herself in somebody's unused summer house so that she could finish her thesis before the deadline got her. She was working like a demon but inevitably got a little bored and went out seeking some sort of distraction, something free or cheap, because she was broke. She decided it would be a nice idea to go up the Provincetown Memorial, a thing like the Washington Monument or a minaret, on top of a hill overlooking the Atlantic. It was closed for the winter, naturally. But there was a guard or caretaker there she undertook to presume on to break the rules and let her go up. Go ahead, then, the guard said with an odd undertone in his voice, and he opened the door to the spiral staircase leading hundreds of feet up to a gallery where you could peer through slits at the sameness of the sea in all directions. The desert sea, I thought. So he opened the door for her and said This is at your own risk. She soon saw why. After the first ten or twenty steps the spiral staircase was coated with flows of solid ice, like something by Gaudí. Driven by pride, she climbed this frozen waterfall. She inched her way up in her slippery shoes, clinging to the railings every step of the way, stayed for a second at the top to let sleet blow into her nose and eyes, then inched back down to the bottom, taking forever, hours. Thanks, she said cheerily to the amazed, and by this time anxious, guard. With one misstep she could have ended up an envelope of broken bones. The muscles in her arms and legs hurt for days. This was pride at its most monumental. She had done it, she guessed, because the guard had clearly tricked her and had expected the satisfaction of seeing her do an about-face when she discovered the condition of the steps. Now there are more women working for the National Park Service. Anna didn't make it academically. I plan to contact her.

Spikes of Alarm

I strode due north, desperate under every heading and incredulous that everything in my life, every maneuver, had combined to make it absolutely necessary that I march out directly into the jaws of death, alone, no one beside me, replicating the one experience I had learned was the one above all I should never again undergo—that is, being in a place where you were on the same footing with vicious wild animals, or rather where they are the superior power. I wanted to be out of the reach of the eyes of Tsau, not to be visible to anyone there.

At the last minute a young girl had brought me a rifle and shells, issued just as I was leaving by Dineo. The gun depressed me because it was confirmation that what I was doing was hazardous and because it was heavy. I weighed the idea of sending it back. Slung over either shoulder it was unwieldy and would slow me down. Finally I put it transversely through the top of my backpack, and that was better.

In only two or three miles it was already grueling going. The ground was softer, thanks to the rain, than during my previous expedition, at least in certain tracts it was. I was wearing the wrong kind of socks: they were Nelson's, not mine, and they had a tendency to inch down into my boots. At least I was away from Tsau, and the world could relax into boring vistas, an occasional baobab constituting an extreme of interest.

I used my binoculars. There were too many inscrutable objects scattered around the landscape. In one case I went a long distance off my route of march to examine something that turned out to be a crumpled sheet of rotting tarpaulin. I was looking for too many different things. The remains of a fire, a body, his, or the carcass of a horse, a tent—he had taken my pop-up tent at my insistence—or some other piece of improvised shelter: these were all the kinds of things I was scanning for. I kept having spikes of alarm each time I thought I saw something. So far everything seemed to be innocent, on inspection, although inspection consisted in too many cases of simply staring harder and longer at the particular thing.

Gradually I became demoralized when I realized I had done my own version of On s'engage et puis on voit. I had no forward plan. This was about as far as I could get from Tsau before I would have to stop and go back, in order to be in Tsau before nightfall. I had no tent. On foot, I could never make it to Tikwe in less than three days, especially with all the scanning I was doing. I wasn't a Bushman who could sleep in a tree. I had been planning, self-evidently, on finding something in my first thrust. I was a fool. The best that could be said of my mission was that it had been a way of ascertaining if Nelson was lying hurt or dead close enough to Tsau to be recovered from our end.

I was sure he was dead and then alternately that he was alive, lying somewhere with my name on his lips. The impasse I was in led to the bizarre urge to write things down about him that were coming to me now and that I realized were not in my compilation. Of course, this was no time to be writing. It was irrelevant. But I hadn't gotten down Nelson saying Unhand my behind, followed by Do I have a way with words, or not? Or that when he was in an enamored state over a junior high school classmate, a young woman referred to as the Blond Dago, he had gotten into the shower with his pajamas on. There were other, more intimate things I knew, that I'd left out out of sheer decorum. This had been wrong. Also I had very little in my compilation about marriage. I remembered something that was probably key. He had said I never get married unless someone asks me. I needed to be in a library, the only one at my table, my polished blond parquet table, wonderful light, foliage swaying outside the window with normal birds in it.

Horsemen

I was so self-involved that when an actual anomaly appeared I failed to notice it until it was on top of me. Horsemen came threading through the brush toward me. They had been approaching for some time. There were six of them, coming very slowly. They were Baherero, looking rakish as usual, miscellaneously dressed, some with leather slouch hats, others with fur hats or rag turbans. The lead rider was lapped in cartridge belts about the torso. In fact all of the horsemen were armed. Something was exciting them: my gun was. I had taken it out of my pack and was leaning on it.

They can tell me something! was my first thought. But that would only be if they knew Setswana. There were enough Herero women in Tsau who would have been willing to tutor me in Saherero, but I'd never taken the opportunity to learn, largely because I thought that when the Herero dispute with the Botswana government over their cattle was solved they would pull up stakes overnight, including our Hereros. The only Saherero I knew was the greeting, Wapenduka. They nodded when I said it, but they wanted something more. They indicated they wanted me to lay my rifle down and step away from it, which I did, not gladly. A seventh rider was bringing up the rear, traveling even more slowly: something bulky was being dragged behind the horse on travois poles. I had to see what it was, even though I was telling myself it would have to be supplies, not to assume more. I was shaking. Two men dismounted. They wouldn't let me move until one of them had his foot on my rifle.

The dismounted men spoke a peculiar and meager Setswana. I realized why it was peculiar. They had had their mesial incisors knocked out, per the cultural requirement of their tribe. Even before they said the word mmobodi, meaning sick man, I knew what was on the travois. I ran to the travois. I pushed back the flap at the top of the long canvas bundle slung between the poles and it was Nelson, looking inhuman but breathing, his face terribly swollen, sunburned, white crusts around his lips. I had to look away. I looked back at the double track the points of the travois poles had cut in the sand. He must have been immobilized for some time in the sun, but clearly he had found a way to keep his eyes and forehead shaded, because above the root of his nose the burn was less severe. I wanted to unwrap him, feel his limbs, give him water, but just as I was reaching to unlace his shrouding the rider moved, pulled him away. I yelled something. I made them halt long enough for me to see how hot his forehead was. It was not extreme, if my touch could be trusted. But then, amid a lot of shouting, the rider started up again, pulling away from me. They were making for Tsau. With the burden that horse was slow, I gathered they were saying. Gomela go shwa, He is sick but will recover, someone said, pushing me back from the travois. I think this is what they said. I was insane. I wanted to push the travois.

I was saved. He was alive. These people knew what they were doing, and my mission was not to become a handful and prevent them from doing what they were doing, which was making for Tsau with Nelson as

fast as they could manage. I began apologizing. They began leaving, as
a body. I think one was asking me how far was Tsau, but I had no idea.
I think one offered to have me ride behind him, but I said no, thinking
that I would slow things up, and the best thing was for them to get to
Tsau as fast as they could, to our enemy the nurse. I would jog along
behind the travois, since it was going the slowest, and with luck I should
be able to keep it in sight. I had to jog pretty quickly, from the start, and
even then I fell behind, which maddened me, because I wanted to urge
the lead rider to go ahead alone, at a gallop, to let Tsau know and get
help coming from the opposite direction. I jogged harder.

I was saved, but I was steadily falling behind, courtesy my Enfield, so
I decided to relieve myself of it intelligently. The riders were too far
ahead of me to signal anything to. They could have taken the rifle for
me. But good luck to that, since they were far ahead and I was falling
farther back, since the travois was going faster than had seemed likely.
So an intelligent thing to do would be to discard the rifle by depositing it
in the branches of a tree, a tree in some way distinctive, one of the larger
white thorn trees, possibly. The Baherero would stop and look back for
me occasionally, which I was desperate that they stop doing. In no time
there was the right tree, one I would always remember, smack on the
due north heading to Tikwe, nonproblematic, so I stuck the rifle into its
branches as high as I could reach and good riddance. I could find it
again, no question I could.

I was saved, but had Nelson been conscious or only semiconscious?
He had said something when I said his name and my name, I was sure.
But had he? He might be saying things no one was paying the slightest
attention to as they pulled him along like luggage. I could catch up. In
fact I was closer than before I'd ditched the rifle. So now off went my
backpack and this and that, everything except for my canteens. I had
two. I realized shortly I needed only one. My binoculars were nugatory
too now. I dropped them. I drew closer to Nelson. There should be a
universal language. English was taking too long. I would tell Nelson this.
I had always thought Esperanto and Volapük and all of them, Basic
English, were jokes or rackets meant to create sinecures, but that was
wrong. I could have been adequate if the horsemen had been able to
communicate with me in more than nine words, and I with them. Maybe
Esperanto was not the answer, maybe something simpler was. I would
never mock the proposition again. It could be made compulsory, universal. I could work on it with Nelson from someplace like Bern or Carmel.
I ran toward Tsau.

Now He Was Perfect

When my lagging got more extreme, one of the riders was detailed to wait for me and insist I get up and ride with him. The main party, with Nelson, went on ahead. It took awhile for my man to work out the drill. He had to improvise some cushioning for me, using a putrid blanket, since his position was that we couldn't both fit in the same saddle, which was in fact nonsense. He decided to jettison and cache one set of heavily loaded saddlebags from among the several he was carrying, but then changed his mind and put everything back the way it had been. He was very agitated regarding the whereabouts of my rifle. It bothered him that I didn't have it, and it was evident he felt it was up to him to do something about it, like going back and trying to retrieve it. It was worth a fortune, of course. All our transactions were conducted ninety percent in sign language, which slowed us seriously. Finally he gave up on the rifle. I think he was convinced I was crazy, not someone he wanted on his docket for longer than was absolutely necessary. We set off and arrived not much more than half an hour after the others.

Nelson was already in bed in a compartment in the infirmary. There was unguent all over his face. He seemed to be asleep. I lifted his sheet and he was naked, which irrationally bothered me. Fortunately his penis was nothing to be ashamed of. His left arm was splinted and bandaged, and there was a shorter splint on his right leg, near the ankle. I'm ashamed to say that his loss of weight was one of the first things that registered with me, not because it was alarming but because now he was perfect, his ribs defined but not overdefined, his belly slightly concave: he was the weight I'd been willing or wheedling him toward since we got together. I went over him again. There were bad abrasions on his right leg and his back and neck. Kakelo, for all her reservations about Tsau, was being impeccable and even slightly tender, I thought, in her ministrations, although her tenderness may have been a cover for the collective guilt they were all going to have to bear for not listening to me about sending help sooner. Everything had been done for him except for cleaning up his feet, which she let me do. I wanted to be reassured that he could talk, but she preferred me not to press that, saying it was urgent that he be let to sleep. He had taken juice, and he had recognized everyone, was the story. I was very faint and cold and was intermittently under the impression that I couldn't make out colors. Kakelo read off everything she'd found wrong with him so far. The main injuries were a broken left arm, which he'd set himself very cleanly, and a broken ankle. There was some infection in the scrapes above the ankle, but not very much. There was sunpoisoning. His temperature was just above one hundred degrees. His collarbone might be broken, but perhaps not, we would see.

A chair was brought in for me, and then a pallet, and then beef tea. There was a crowd outside, I knew.

I thought I might lie down for a minute, and did, but wrenched myself up when I realized that before I did anything else I should go to the octagon and bring back a pair of clean undershorts and cover his shame with them. I knew it was ridiculous and I knew all there was to know about Tswana casualness toward nudity of every kind, but I felt impelled, partly because he was too beautiful. His beard was beautiful and when he was well I was going to make him let it grow high into his cheeks like this. He was the Idea of himself.

After I'd reclad his loins my breathing normalized.

I slept fitfully, getting up a few times for the purpose of putting my face against his chest, listening to his heart.

There were birds nesting in the infirmary thatch, something I'd never noticed.

Fantasies Vis-à-Vis His Seed

The next day I was an obstruction to everyone. I don't know if his imago was igniting martyr and saintly prisoner associations in me or what it was, but I was full of fiery feeling for Nelson. I was militant when someone came in with a libation she refused to characterize for me but which turned out to be beef blood, or largely that. It was worse when Kakelo was noncommittal and refused to bar this person or this remedy forever from Nelson's sickroom.

Also I had an agenda for them: I wanted them to make him awake and alert and talking. I was tired of hearing how well he had talked to everyone last night, before I got there. He had slept enough. While they carried out my agenda I would be there monitoring and managing to be physically in contact with Nelson, by touching him or taking his hand, at intervals of between ten minutes and a half hour. I was overflowing with helpful either/ors, on the order of either he says something intelligent by noon and not just someone's name or we arrange for a medical evacuation. We had medevaced a woman with bleeding fibroids, I pointed out, but here we had the founder of this place in an unknown condition and were not getting on the transmitter because Kakelo was saying he only had some breaks and exhaustion. She got out a medical book to prove to me that he wasn't concussed. I wouldn't read it, not a paragraph, not a sentence. I wanted a rule made that no one could come into the room other than Kakelo or me unless I said all right. This was connected with desperate fantasies I was having vis-à-vis his seed, assuming the worst had happened. It humiliates me to admit that I was wondering if I could get him erect and then get over him and capture his seed. I could only contemplate doing this if first I established I could get him erect. And I could do that only if we had privacy. I would think of a ruse to get Kakelo off the scene.

Now comes the ultimate with me. When you're on the borders of shock you have waves of intense sense perception, it seems. I had one, and it involved the way I smelled and ipso facto must look. A spear entered my mind. I was too fat, not good enough for him physically, not equal, the way he looked. My triceps were going to hang down like hammocks, about which nothing could be done, it was already happening. Excuse me, I said. I went running to the octagon. People wanted to speak with me, but I shook them off. He was an icon of beauty, and what was I? I got home and found whatever I had in the way of makeup and made myself up, meaning just lipstick and mascara, I hope. I don't know exactly today what I did to make myself beautiful. My dread was that he would wake up and see me and hate me and either die or turn to someone else. This was the state I was in. At that time I was probably at most ten pounds over my high school weight, to give an indication of how askew my perceptions fundamentally were. Obviously how I looked had taken precedence over how I smelled, because I did nothing about that. Also, walking, or, as I was given to then, running, was extremely painful, because I'd neglected to remove my boots after my excursion, and my feet were swollen because of Denoon's socks not fitting. The problem had been that his socks had been clean and mine hadn't, because once I moved in it became prime for me to see he always had clean things, and I had slipped when it came to myself.

In my makeup I caused a hush.

Nelson had, yet again, been awake, coughing this time, in my absence. But lo, he was asleep again. And in fact they wanted me to sleep or rest or wait in another compartment, if I wouldn't mind. But first they wanted me to eat and to take something that would calm me. I ate porridge, refusing pills of any sort, but they had outsmarted me and put powders in the malted drink I drank, sleeping powders. I went straight to my new room and had vertigo and was gone.

His Hands in His Lap, Palms Up

There he was, sitting up in a chair in the shade outside Sekopololo. He face was still glistening with unguent, but the swelling was much better. He was wearing pajama bottoms, there was a white cotton throw over his shoulders, his chest was naked, his hands were in his lap, palms up, one hand nested in the other in an odd style. You can use the word delighted all your life and never know what it means truly, or inly, as he occasionally liked to say. But then I knew. I ran to him and crouched down and put my arms around him. I was weeping. He looked at me, but nothing more demonstrative than touching my hair was done, I gathered because there was a crowd of fifteen or twenty people around, paying their respects, saying hello, just watching, keeping us company for a while, and he wanted to be decorous. Several women told me to be soft because his collarbone was bruised hard.

Are you all right? I asked, the inevitable question.

I am, he said. His voice was fine, steady and low.

I pressed my cheek against his mouth and he made a kiss, but not right away.

I was stringing disparate questions and sentiments together: Can I get you anything? Thank god, thank god. You look good, you look well. When can we go home? I elicited smiles and murmurs from him.

Instantly it was time for Nelson to go back in. Kakelo was there with Dineo.

Dineo said He has answered every question as to how he comes to us as he is. And when he closes his eyes it means to cease talking while he can rest.

Nelson had closed his eyes.

I let them take him again. I was ready to rally myself, clean up, renormalize. It bothered me that Nelson seemed limited to a purely responsive mode with people. He had initiated nothing. But this must be proof of the depth of what he'd been through, I told myself. In any case I had an audience with Dineo coming, in which she would tell me all she knew and incidentally take up the matter of what was going to be done about the rifle I had lost and the horse that had been taken and was now dead: Dorcas was making an uproar about both, apparently.

The Smile

Below are three dialogs from Nelson's convalescence, the first two from different stages of his stay in the infirmary, the last from the first night we were back chez nous. They go in ascending order of normalcy —that is, from the least normal to the most. The first two are reconstructed from notes made immediately after each exchange. The last is actual transcript from a tape. I resorted to taping when I finally sensed the extent of the bouleversement in Nelson I was witnessing, one proof of which was that he had no objection to my taping every word that fell from his lips—quite the contrary, in fact. All his irony about my Boswellizing was gone. Where I say the Smile I mean that his response is a particular smile, very tolerant or forgiving and structurally condescending, but not meant that way. The protocol for an audience with the Dalai Lama involves the audient's agreeing to a fifteen-minute period for the exchange of benevolent glances before any substantive talking begins. Even the Pope had to agree to this. The Smile is what I imagine people in that situation coming up with. A feature that shows in the dialogs is that I become more upset as he becomes more equilibrized. And throughout I seem to be concealing my decision to stay with him in

Tsau, if that was a bona fide decision, which is explained, I think, by my understandable interest in getting some hint from him that that question was working its way from the depths of his mind to somewhere near uppermost, where it had been before his, to my way of thinking, misadventure. My withholding my inner decision is of course something I look back on with hindsight telling me that my blaring out at some point my yes to staying might have changed the course of events. In fact I couldn't do it.

The first dialog began after I'd been telling him yet again how I'd gone from hell to heaven, losing him, being in Tsau with Dorcas raising the winds over his absence and what it had to mean vis-à-vis Hector, the main implication being that Nelson was a fugitive from justice, the general seethings over the taken horse, no one listening to me, and then getting him back alive. He was healing absurdly rapidly, his face losing its swelling and joining his body in a perfection I could do without. Even the little lozenge of fat that seems to appear after you're forty on the side of your nose was gone. His weight loss was anchored by his current diet, which was largely soup, broths. I think I would have made a perfect gay man, my appreciation for the male form being what it is. Nelson was becoming the pygmalion object I would have carved for myself as a physical mate. We were twinned, me with my response to his corporeal self and he with his self-proclaimed receptivity to the female shell, the beautiful ones, that is, naturellement.

He was still in his original windowless room at the infirmary during the first two dialogs, still under observation. I wasn't supposed to close the door when I was in camera with Nelson, although no reason was ever given to me for the proscription. I have no doubt the idea was to deter me from bothering Nelson sexually, in his delicate condition. He was being treated like a godlet. If I did close the door, it would be unobtrusively popped ajar by an unknown hand.

Three Dialogs

1. Are we all right?
   He nods.

I need you to say it, not just nod it.

Yes, we are, he says.

Is it still so tiring for you to speak up?

No, he says, more strongly but still marginally for normal discourse.

Then do we love each other? because I dot dot dot love you. I said the words dot dot dot in an attempt at lightheartedness and also to remind him of the days when he had seen fit to tease me about the caesuras in my conversation—as when I was too slow to make my point—by saying dot dot dot, just as I had. The point in those days had been for me to realize that I had to hurry to keep up with his fine intellect, the brain of a person so keenly attuned to things that movies were a bore for him because of that flicker of black between the frames that he, unlike the groundlings who saw movies as seamless things, was aware of. I don't know why this particular claim to fame remains such a burr under my saddle, but it does. But in any case it was his turn to be the provider of caesuras. He was slower and more hesitant than I had ever been at my worst. But I had the feeling he wasn't really trying, which had never been true of me. I know I was being unfair, in the circumstances.

That day he had let me brush his teeth instead of his doing it himself. He could do it himself. I had offered to do it just to see if he'd let me. This was an epitome of the way he was.

Please tell me everything that happened.

The Smile.

Nelson, do you want to walk around outside?

He said No. But without giving a reason.

Nelson, tell me yourself what happened, or give me a sketch, at least. They're making things up about you, like that at some point when you were lying helpless you were protected by *bees*.

The Smile.

I was tired of not hearing the whole story from his mouth. Kakelo and Dineo were together in the position that he should be protected from having to tell the story over and over to every comer. Reportedly he found telling the story very difficult, although anything longer than three sentences, on any subject, seemed to be a trial for him. I had talked to Dineo and others and I knew the vulgate on his misadventures: he'd lain injured on the ground for eight days before being found by the Baherero. He had been halfway to Tikwe when a boomslang had dropped out of an acacia onto his horse's neck, or alternatively it had struck the horse in the neck from the side as they passed too close to a tree limb. The horse had panicked, thrown Nelson, broken its leg in its thrashings to escape or shake off the snake. When it happened they were in a patch of slippery black sand locally called black cotton soil, which I think is a kind of marl, or sand with marl mixed in. Snakes are supposed to be more common in black cotton soil areas, which was a piece of lore I was surprised he was unfamiliar with. All his supplies were on the horse with the exception of his canteen. Nelson was on the ground going in and out of consciousness. The horse was a shuddering hulk maybe twenty or thirty yards from him when he came fully to. It had been maybe an hour and a half. He was badly sunburned, and an arm and a leg were broken. He dragged himself fifty feet to a termite tump built at the base of a tree and set his arm and fainted again. That night he dragged himself back to the horse and got all his provisions and impedimenta off it and then cut the animal's throat with his hunting knife. There was no rifle with him, which was his way of making a certain point, I suppose. Then in a paradise of pain he had dragged himself back to his tump, not once but twice since he had to make a return trip to the horsewreck in order to get everything there was that he might utilize for purposes of surviving. Then it becomes fabulous. He had been delirious and had had visions of presences or a presence, a female presence, who had been involved somehow in his immunity from the attentions of the black-backed jackals who had come to devour his horse before his very eyes the next day. Also, bees had been involved in discouraging the jackals. There were different versions. Bees had discouraged either the jackals or the boom-slang, which was still dangerously in the vicinity. He had had various insights of a certain grandeur, which he had only been willing to hint at so far to others. There was more and worse. He had put his ear against the tump and heard what the termites say, or heard their songs, which were magnificent. This, for me, was like finding myself wandering around in the Midrash. Dineo had left it out of her account, along with most of the other signs and wonders—she knew me—but I was hearing them elsewhere.

I mentioned a few items that were on my mind, water management being one of them, the question of how he'd survived on so little water. On water, he was gnomic. He had reduced his need, somehow, by becoming like something else, something that needed little or no water, possibly something dead.

I asked Will we discuss these things later in more detail?

The answer was, incredibly, I believe so.

There was an impasse in the making, so I stopped. Regression under stress is hardly unknown, I reminded myself. Then I warned myself to

remember that Nelson's mother's alltime favorite piece of music, which
she'd played endlessly on the piano in his presence, was The Lost Chord.

2. It had been too unnerving to stay all day with Nelson in the infirmary
waiting for signs of normalization, so in the spirit of the scientific discovery that smiling when you feel terrible actually makes you feel better, I
went back to the shapeup at Sekopololo and took almost any assignments
that needed doing. This was my most endless week, in a way. I felt like a
machine throughout. I had to supply two statements about the loss of
the Enfield, the first being considered not complete enough.

I didn't like the social mood in Tsau. There was anxiety, and people
were short-tempered. I didn't like the morning levées around Nelson,
with people leaving little items for him.

Kakelo was sick of me, because I wanted to know why, if Nelson still
needed to be in the infirmary despite his going from strength to strength
physically, she wouldn't consider evacuating him to Lobatse, to the psychiatric wing of the hospital there. She just looked at me. There was an
expat Italian at the head of psychiatric services, and he spoke almost no
English. She lectured me, not unkindly despite her annoyance. Nelson
was doing well. The only reason he was still in the infirmary was because
he wished to be there. Whenever he said he wanted to go back to his
house he could go. This was true.

Nelson wasn't reading, which was a sign of something significant, to
me if not to Kakelo. I had brought him a sheaf of Economists. Worse
than his not reading was that once when he saw me coming he snatched
up an Economist to feign reading with. This was like an arrow in my
heart. I still see it.

This dialog began with me telling him something that normally would
have interested him. The Baherero who had saved him had been en
route from a new enterprise based on the growing spring game kills along
the cordon fence north of us. The migrating wildebeests were making
for their usual watering place at Mopipi at the far end of the Kuki fence,
where they were getting the shock of their lives because the lake at
Mopipi had been drained off for diamond-washing operations at Orapa.
So the animals were turning the corner at the end of the fence and
heading for their only other source of water in the region, Lake Ngami,
far in the opposite direction, so far in fact that when they arrived there
they were so dehydrated and weakened that they could be beaten to
death by children with cudgels. It was a massacre. They were dying by
the hundreds. The Herero in Gomare had come down to capitalize.

They were air-drying and brining the meat in volume, and taking the position—since they were under the same ban on hunting as everyone else—that this was salvage meat derived from animals already dead of exhaustion. This was essentially true. And the game scouts were permitting it. So the Herero were selling and bartering their biltong wherever they could, coming as far south as Tikwe, us, and the rest camps along the trek route. Even though wildebeest requires the most doctoring of any game meat to make it palatable, I thought we should take it. The Herero were not the ones who had drained the lake to wash diamonds with. There was a pittance of zebra and impala biltong available along with the wildebeest, offered as a kind of premium, I gathered.

Having gone over all this for him, I concluded with So that's how your life got saved—through the commercial impulse. They took their biltong to Tikwe, but there was almost nobody there and whoever was had no money. Too bad there wasn't a branch of Sekopololo there so they could have struck a deal. So they headed for Tsau and found you. Does this interest you, Nelson? Because it doesn't seem to.

Certainly.

Certainly was a word totally external to our idioverse. It was from another dimension.

Well, should they be encouraged to come this far next time?

He didn't know. He thought there seemed to be sufficient meat coming into Tsau already, one way or another.

A gleam came at me out of this. There was something far more deeply interfused, and I thought I knew what it was. I seemed to recall that in the soups he was eating lately he was finishing everything except the bits of meat.

Are you not eating meat, suddenly? I asked him.

He sighed.

I said You like meat. You did like it. Are you now not eating meat?

At length what I got out of him was that he had no general position about eating meat, but he was in a phase where, at each meal, he was in a sort of absolute way following his inclination as of that meal. And so far his inclination had been not to eat meat. He supposed his inclination could change. I felt like saying that as someone likely to be preparing some substantial percentage of his meals in the near future I was curious to know how long this phase might go on. I felt like shouting at him Youth wants to know! which was the name of some educational radio program he'd professed to be a child devotee of.

I asked Do you think you might be depressed?

His answer was no, and I was almost relieved, because if he'd been willing to say yes I would have had to think immediately about where to seek professional help in a universe where there were no decent choices. I knew that the Italian at Lobatse was impossible. And I knew Nelson couldn't go to South Africa, where there was presumably some ilk of mental health establishment, for ethical-political reasons.

Are you the opposite of depressed?

Closer to that.

None of my timid sorties into irony or the jocular were working. I couldn't shift him back into his normal historical voice. His convalescence was always in front of me, muting me. Also everyone else was showing so much patience and tenderness toward him that I was afraid of setting myself apart. There was even shrinkage visible in the Raboupi faction: people just outside the core were being more pleasant, showing up in the levées, and so on.

Since he seemed to be saying he was in a protracted high, I pursued the idea of his considering that brain chemistry, the euphoric toxins you get when brain fat breaks down if you fast for long periods, might be something to talk about in an exploratory way.

Here another way of blocking me made its appearance. We were in his cool dim room and he put on his sunglasses. I took this as primarily a defense against any more searching looks from me and as a signboard behind which he could resume what seemed to be his central interest as of then, namely staring into himself. The irony was that he had never been partial to sunglasses and that I'd made a small nuisance of myself theretofore with reminders and urgings to him to take them with him or put them on.

I did get the answer to one burning question. Why are you still in the infirmary? I asked. He was healing like a movie cartoon character, it was so fast. He could get around. There was only a little supportive bandaging on his formerly cracked or broken leg. Was he staying there because he felt he could recover faster there than at home with me?

Well, it was yes and no, which exfoliated into the position that this was probably the best place for him to be thinking about the things that had happened to him. Allegedly, I said to myself, allegedly happened.

You have to come home, I said, you have to be back with me.

I hadn't had any intention of saying that, but I did.

I said You don't know how much I have to hold myself in, with you here and me just visiting. You have no idea. When I washed, took care of, your feet the first night I thought of saying Your feet are killing me, which I repressed. That little joke. I was afraid. Don't you think that's slightly funny? Your feet are killing me? I was afraid even to say it under my breath. I thought if anyone did anything wrong you might die.

One disconcerting discovery was that apparently he had gotten to like the pajama pants the infirmary supplied him, so much in fact that he had requested that some copies be made for him out of stronger cloth, some heavier white cotton we had. And to wear with these he'd also had made a sort of sleeveless top on the order of a roomy vest, also white. What was going on? I'd brought him a pile of clean laundry, and I realized that the only things he'd chosen to wear were his white tee shirts. This too shall pass, must pass, I told myself.

3. Coming back to the octagon was as arbitrary a decision as lingering at the infirmary had been, so far as I could tell. He hobbled in and sat down.

We went through the preliminaries, or I did, about how it felt to have him back. I had overprepared the event. Our place was pristine. We had fresh bed linen, clean curtains, and the rugs and karosses had been aired and beaten. I had overprepared the event, and myself, in the sense that all this refurbishment had been driven by the anticipation that with his return to the octagon everything would revert to the way it had been before he left for Tikwe. I was emotional. I was compulsively scanning for signs that everything was going to be all right. It was essential that we be back to normal. Anytime I willed myself into thinking of not being with Nelson, all the physical strength went out of me. He seemed to appreciate all my cleaning up, although I thought I saw a quizzical shadow pass slowly over his features when he fingered one of the karosses. Our karosses had shed quite a bit. I hadn't known you had to beat them a lot more gently than rugs.

I was trying to preempt everything. On his pillow I'd laid out a sleep mask, against the possibility that it might take him a little while to get used to sleeping next to an insomniac again. He looked quizzically at the sleep mask. My policy was to keep everything light, amusing. I said Do you remember the first time you saw me with my sleep mask?

He was making a good faith effort to remember, but it was taking too long. Throughout this whole time I was fighting against images of someone I had known who, post acid, could take ten minutes to roll up a shirtcuff because the aesthetics of the procedure were, in his illuminated state, so exquisite.

I said The first time you saw me with my sleep mask you took it off me and put it on and went around crashing into the furniture and said Tonto, give me the scissors, the outlaws are escaping!

The outlaws are escaping, he said meditatively. This was a new tic also. He seemed to consider a repetition of the last clause or phrase I'd just said to be an adequate contribution to an ongoing conversation.

I said I remember it because I think it was maybe the first time you went out of your way to make me laugh by acting stupid and going beyond your urbane sort of humor. Remember we've discussed this?

Then he remembered. I am grasping at such straws, I thought. Which led to the epiphany that there should be some comical game going, like our The band can't play because dot dot dot. This would turn the clock back. There was an idea for one lurking in my mind, if I could entice it out.

Do you mind if I tape us? I asked. This was mainly to gain time. I half thought he might very well say Are you insane? Why? To which my answer would be that it was celebratory, just my way of capturing something important, forget it.

Tape us? Certainly.

Certainly what?

Certainly yes, tape us.

I was slow and obtrusive about setting up to tape. I put the recorder very near him. He was sitting at our dinner table with his hands again in the nested palm-up configuration that I hated so much. Everything was more than okay with him.

One inchoate idea for a game had involved a child's questions to mom, and mom's clever deflective responses, such as the child saying Mom, why does Dad always sandpaper his fingertips before he goes to work at night? To which Mom has an ingenious response having to do with the better to do such and such and provide for us. But all I had was the question to mom, not mom's brilliant collaborative-with-evil lie, and without mom's response there was no game. But then there was another possible game, which my feeling of grasping at straws reminded me of. This game was The Intellectuals Have a Picnic. They have a picnic and play games that are their equivalents of Pin the Tail on the Donkey. Grasping at Straws was one, Knocking Down Straw Men was another, or Setting Up and Knocking Down Straw Men, and Putting the Cart in Front of the Horse, and Kick the Cant. Then there was just a stray shard from The Band Can't Play series, having the band not being able to sleep because Teutons had stolen the futons. But there was nothing good enough to insert. And I was taping mostly silence, which just in itself was unbearable, the cost.

The outlaws are escaping, he said for the second time. This I couldn't bear, and I began to weep behind his back. He must not have heard me, although I can make it out on the tape.

I had no idea where to take hold of things. Certain traits I wanted desperately to stop in their tracks, like this repeating business. I wanted to say Are you repeating after me because you want to savor certain lines or words? But I was afraid noticing it openly would concretize it some-how, make it harder, not easier, for it to go away. Even my acid friend eventually lost interest in his shirtcuff.

We will, someday, sit down and just go through everything, won't we?

He seemed to nod.

Doing it soon would be good, because people are making things up that are ludicrous.

They'll stop, he said.

No they won't, I said. Not until someone can say with some sort of authority that this is what happened and that this is a fable, such as you. Or me.

It was a mistake, he said.

What was?

Going into it. People are going to forget about it.

Do you think you're different since Tikwe?

Do I think I'm different. Yes. I don't know. I was different before.

This was going to lead to a paradox of some kind. I had no appetite for it.

Just tell me this, I said. Just tell me if this is right, that something momentous happened to you on the way to Tikwe, you think.

Something momentous. I think so.

It was up to him to elaborate. I could have made him do it, led him to do it. But the sense that I represented the forces of interruption was too much for me, the sense that I was keeping him from certain sessions of sweet silent thought, sweeter and more important to him than any-thing else on earth.

We sat in silence.

I hated life.

Conspiracies

In my attitude toward Tsau I was stuck at a paranoid level. All I did all day was revolve the permutations of the explanations for the lurid impasse I was in. There were explanations in which everything that had happened was connected, like parts in a complicated machine. There were explanations in which everything critical that had happened to me was accidental. Certain things could have been charades. Dineo's dilatoriness about letting me organize help for Nelson could have been a result of the fact that she somehow knew he was all right someplace. Possibly all this was an ordeal designed for me, something to test how much I wanted this man. Or possibly Nelson wanted me out and gone. Or possibly I had just been a catspaw of forces that had favored my getting together with Nelson in order to move him along the path to departure, stimulating him to speed it up by my ordinariness and consumerism and need to get back to the country money comes from. Or possibly Dineo had disposed of Hector in order to break up Boso and stimulate Dorcas into going somewhere else. On it went with me. Possibly the original idea had been to use me to get Nelson's case of founder's disease out of the vicinity and into a project on some other continent, leaving the women of Tsau to evolve in their own way. But maybe the new revised passive Denoon was another story: maybe he was now someone who could be useful in his present form, a Prince Albert in a can for Dineo. Or was it conceivable Nelson had disposed of Hector and out of remorse dumped himself to either die or improve and come back shorn and tractable, speaking only when spoken to, being good, already up and hobblingly doing little chores, a man as good as a woman. That was conceivable. I laved myself in conspiracy and in the process felt myself closer to the central or historical Nelson, with his very patent—to me— view of the world as a place in which conspiracy is routine. I don't mean that he was an obsessed assassinationologist of the standard kind you run into in the States. With him it was more an assumption of the mundanity of conspiracy. He was offhand about it: of course there was a conspiracy behind the John F. Kennedy assassination, he might remark, unless it makes sense that Lee Harvey Oswald would advertise himself as a marxist by having his picture taken holding up copies of the Militant and the Daily Worker at the same time, two papers whose party lines in regard to Cuba were violently opposed at a time when he was supposed to be a member of the Fair Play for Cuba Committee and so, strictly pro-Castro. Then there was the Shakespeare conspiracy, although on that he was more of a zealot than in some other cases.

Africans have a particular way of interacting with the insane, and I thought I could feel myself drifting into that kind of regard. My best friends among the women kept treating me like a child: Rra Puleng would be fine, he was fine.

I was volatile. One day I was shaping up to work in the kraals dawn to dusk, and the next I was refusing to do something minor, something I had agreed to do in prehistoric times: I think there was a prize for the person who had taken the most books out of the library and I had agreed to do the tally, but somehow in my present state I felt it was an affront being asked to do this. I couldn't explain why.

Dineo, I decided, was going to be the key to the exit.

Whatever hesitation there was in my mind about getting Nelson out of there and in reach of someone who could identify his condition for me was diminishing day by day. If he was improving, it was unbearably slowly.

I would go to see Dineo. First I would invoke what I felt had been an implicit friendship between us. Then I would remind her that I was formidable too and that I was ready to bring the American embassy into getting Nelson out if I had to. This would be against everybody's will and interest, Nelson's included, but I knew how to operate the radio and I could make it happen whether anyone liked it or not. I could lie to the embassy if I had to. Of course by going the route of force majeure I would tear up any chance I would have of ever coming back to Tsau. I wouldn't be forgiven. I tried to have a proposal ready for each of the likeliest objections. I wanted him x-rayed. I had to get out of a matrix that was becoming untrustworthy and impenetrable, so that I could trust my own thoughts again.

From the outset Dineo resisted so strongly that I was taken aback.

There were changes in her office. The interior had been freshly cal-cimined. We met in a white glow. It was midmorning. In the old office all the chairs had been uniform. Now hers had a taller back and had

arms. She looked imperious. She was wearing her headscarf in a new
style, with the tails brought together over one shoulder and secured with
a medallion clip. Tea was served to us, which surprised me.

The first surprise was that she wanted us to speak only in Setswana.
People would be coming in and out, and Setswana would be best. I don't
know why that put me off my stride so badly, but it did. It was a statement. Also I had been set for her to be warmer, or at least more silken
toward me. Instead she was being rueful and direct and looking me
straight in the eye. I know by having us speak Setswana she wanted to
avoid any suggestion of collusion between us, but still I hated her for it.
She had never been my enemy.

We talked in general about how well Nelson was coming along. This
was her view. I made the distinction between physical and psychological,
and she appeared to be listening to me. Then she said that although she
could see Nelson was quieter than before, she wanted me to know that
the nurse had told her that anything of that sort should be put down to
convalescence, the aftereffects of the trauma, something that would lift.
She also slipped into the stream of our talk a few hints that there could
be questions of favoritism if someone with a medical condition perceived
to be as minor as Nelson's were evacuated to Gaborone. Also she made
clear that she understood from Rra Puleng that he was not at all interested in being moved.

She was being clever. At no point was she refusing me. But she was
resisting.

I decided to be frank. I said I had often wanted to remind her about
her showing me in the bathhouse the scars that meant she could never
bear children, and how I had taken that as a gesture of friendship toward
me, to show that she was not a possible mate for Nelson, if that was in
fact something that was crossing my mind.

She nodded. She was not embarrassed by this.

I said that then I had wondered if the reason she and others had been
encouraging me to be with Rra Puleng was because perhaps an attach-
ment to me would lead him to think more quickly about going away with
me and leaving Tsau in the hands of its citizens a little sooner.

She was very precise as she denied this. She spoke so formally that I
almost felt it as an invitation to read through what she was saying, not to
be literal. She did deny any thought of the kind I was mentioning. She
was speaking for everyone in Tsau. She was sure that no one except for
some unfortunate people who in any case might not be for long in Tsau
could have wanted anything other than that Rra Puleng must stay in

Tsau as long as he was pleased to. All of this was in the same strangely precise delivery.

I'd already started in this direction, so I continued. I probably put this badly, but what I said was that she must see—given the idea or suspicion I'd just admitted—that it was only natural for me to wonder if, now that Nelson seemed so much changed, and so passive, there might be perfectly understandable reasons for him to be wanted in Tsau, with or without me. I had to repeat this with some changes to be sure that I was getting everything into it in Setswana that I wanted to be there. I was brave.

She was very cool here. She wanted me to understand that she could see how I would have such fears but that there was nothing true about them, any of them, about any fear like the one I had expressed. But she felt it would be the worst thing for Nelson to go off before he himself felt it was the correct time for it.

She alluded to the problems of the dead horse and the lost Enfield. This whole time, she was thinking I would have to sign a document of liability for the rifle, and if I went away with Rra Puleng we would both have to sign for the horse. Or possibly only Nelson would have to sign. She would consult with the mother committee. I thought I saw daylight coming. She said she assumed Rra Puleng and I would be leaving our things if we went off. I said eagerly Yes, yes. I had nothing to leave, essentially, that I cared about. All I wanted was my notebooks. Anything else they could have forever.

Early on in the discussion I felt I'd been successful in conveying that there were lengths I was prepared to go to that would be painful for me. I was loaded with propositions I never had to use, thank god. I was ready to tell her that I was going to marry Nelson and I was a Catholic, a lapsed Catholic who had just recently unbackslid and that of course as a Catholic we would need to be married in a real Catholic church, of which there were none in Tsau. I was gambling that Nelson was so limp that if I told him we needed to go to Gabs to get married he would do it, like that.

I felt a stab, thinking this. That was really the problem. Nelson was in some unreal state of acceptance. He was agreeing to everything, it seemed, with the one exception of requests that he go through chapter and verse of his ordeal. But anything else, at all, he would do for you. It was dangerous.

I wanted this interview to be over with before I lost my hold on myself. Why was she so beautiful and exactly how old was she anyway?

What was I going to be in eight years or eleven or thirteen? I wouldn't age the way she had. This was my physical high noon, in all probability. I knew it.

Then she dropped into English, just for a moment. It was rushed, and what she said was that she would be most concerned if certain of the donors were to visit with Nelson in Gaborone before he was fully recovered. She mentioned two names in particular. I knew who one of them was. The other she identified for me as the present representative of the Swedish International Development Agency.

I don't know what I said, but it was what was needed. I made a circumlocutious pledge to guard Nelson, rusticate him in Gabs the way she had in the infirmary, manage his contacts until he was himself again, which, with the help of the doctors I could definitely find or summon to Gabs, wouldn't be long. I half implied, to assuage her fears about donors prematurely stumbling on him, that Nelson might well be in Gabs for only a few days, if it was decided that he ought to see someone in Harare, say.

She would have to talk to the mother committee, of course. But I knew it was set. He was going away from Tsau with Scientiae Athena, otherwise known as me. I would restore him. And that would restore me.

The next day, strangely enough, facilitating rumors were percolating around. There was something about complications and the need for x-rays. And people had heard something suggesting that I was in trouble with Immigration and had to go to explain my long stay in Tsau and correct everything.

A Sabbatical

There was a hint of valedictory sentiment in the air during our departure, which was a little odd since this was only supposed to be a sabbatical. I was full of emotion the circumstances forbade me to express. There was a crowd at the airstrip to see us off, which included Dorcas and the batlodi, who were very contained about whatever they were feeling. They had been the objects of a special mollification process: word had been passed that a primary reason for our trip to Gabs was to deliver a packet of depositions on Hector's disappearance to the Criminal Investigation Division, at long last.

Getting Nelson to agree to the excursion had been no problem at all. I'd deemphasized the medical side of it, although I did mention that the nurse was recommending it, which was true. I had a rather grudging referral note from her. In fact it would make sense for me to show my face at Immigration. I suggested that he had some business pending with different ministries. He agreed. I brought certain folders to him that he specified and he began stirring through them, but not in his usual way. He was so desultory that it was painful to see it.

On the plane it was bliss, a thunderstorm we had to pass straight through notwithstanding. I copied my indifference to the buffeting storm from Nelson. Apparently I was being a fool, because when the pilot left the control cabin and came back past us to leave, his face was chlorotic. Being with Nelson then was like being with a distracted older brother. There had been no real sex since Tikwe, and this felt almost like a kinship prohibition to me now. I began to be generally hopeful. In the plane I confessed I'd left most of his emperor of ice cream wardrobe, his vanilla vests, tops, and pants, behind, except of course for what he was wearing. Everything else was his regular gear. He smiled about it, but in fact it wouldn't take me long to find there was some slyness afoot, because he'd packed his own supply of white raiment without telling me about it.

With us on the plane was another medical evacuee, an Indian shopowner who'd been on holiday at Island Safari Lodge in Maun. He'd been bitten by a hippo, or rather the aluminum skiff he'd been cruising in had, and he'd been injured. He was met by a throng of family and friends, the matrons wearing the most unflattering garment ever to befall the female midriff. There was no one to meet us, which should have been a relief. I'd worked hard for it to be that way. But at the same time I felt a tremor of disgust with the world that somehow the fate of this man, my beloved man, hadn't come to somebody's attention in Gabs, because something was seriously wrong with him and he was important.

Time Is an Ape

I thought I should give silence and sequestration and nonconfrontation at least a week. That is, I created a vacation from everything for us.

There was only nominal pressure from Nelson for me to try to line up something for us in his old haunts in the Old Naledi squatter settlement. We spent one night in the President Hotel and by checkout time the next day I had a leave house for us for a month or maybe more. It was a big, lavish, newish walled layout assigned to the American embassy's admin officer, who was away on a short course in Mauritius with his family. There was a cook and a yardman. The swimming pool was empty in deference to the drought, which had been ferocious in Gaborone. Tsau seemed succulent, almost, compared to Gabs. I mentioned to someone from Meteorology how well Tsau had done with rainfall, and he seemed dubious. He quoted me the figures from Maun, which were much lower. The implication was that I was telling him fairytales. Everyone around the embassy was extremely glad to see me. I had apparently done a superb job of ingratiating myself earlier on. Helpfulness toward me reigned. Of course a part of it was that the embassy wanted to get au courant with the mysterious Denoon's activities. But they were proper. They knew all about the privacy agreements he'd extracted from the Ministry of Local Government and Lands. But the embassy was indirectly providing our housing, after all, so it was not untoward for people like the pol-econ officer or the USAID director to drift by. The yardman turned them away, according to our instructions. Nelson wasn't ready to see anyone yet.

I did errands that week—shopping, going to Immigration to cement relations—at a run. I ran because I was so unsure about Nelson. I was perpetually afraid I'd come back and find him gone, recovered in my absence and gone. He was essentially doing nothing that I could see. People who wanted to see him he referred to as the curious. He got up late. He walked around the garden. He ate small meals. He bathed or showered a couple of times a day. He napped. He would listen to music if I suggested it and set up the stereo and chose something. The only basic change was that he was reading again, which was the good news. The bad news was that he would only read one book, the *Tao Te Ching*, which he had brought with him, that book and only that book. I had begun to hate Lao Tzu. It was impossible to get a discussion going, however tangential, relating to the Tao. I gathered that the whole thing was too sacred, too central to what was distracting him. We slept in a vast bed. He went to sleep every night at eight o'clock. Sex was not rearing its lovely head.

I wanted to supply just a little in the way of delicacies available only in the capital, but Nelson was showing a marked preference for the food of the people: bogobe, other porridges, maas, all the staples of our existence at Tsau. He never told me to stop getting the Wensleydale cheese or the occasional cup of crème fraîche, but he took only token tastes, mostly, then asked for his porridge and maybe a piece of fruit. I wasn't made to feel guilty about my European eating propensities. I could do what I liked. I was eating a little too much at first because I felt I ought to finish up what he was declining to more than taste.

That week yielded exactly one unsolicited comment or statement from him, although he continued answering everything that was put to him. That one unsolicited comment was, I think, Time is an ape. I think this is what he said. I asked him to repeat it and he just said Never mind. I would have pursued it except that I'd sworn off all pressure for the week, just to see if he might slide back toward normalcy.

After the embassy nurse came over I was depressed, as depressed as I'd been. She took him into the bedroom and I could hear the repartee. It sounded completely normal. It would, naturally, since it was just Q and A. I had told her point-blank that I wanted something from her that would let me refer him to a psychiatrist somewhere. At least I wanted her to see if she could get Nelson designated a stop on the circuit the embassy medical officer in Pretoria made from time to time. She came out effusing about him, apparently not only because he was healing so wonderfully but because he was himself such a wonderful person. He had been using a knobkerrie as a crutch, and he could stop that anytime he wanted. She would schedule him for x-rays but only because I seemed so determined on it. She wished she could find more Americans his age with his blood pressure. Psychologically this was just a man who was relaxing in order to heal. He was fine. His reflexes were like an adolescent's. All this was conveyed to me with an unsuppressible, wistful, jealous but still Christian look that said what a lucky dog I was to have this man. She went on to show me that she fully empathized with how it must have been for me when he was missing. She was about forty. She was unmarried. By the time she was leaving she was more concerned about me than about Nelson, with my incomprehensible fixations and misinterpretations, as she obviously saw them. I wondered that she didn't find it odd that Nelson never joined us but stayed sitting on the bed where he'd been left, thinking about something or other, deeply. She gave me an over-the-counter sleeping pill that was risible. I did confirm that the only psychiatrist in Botswana was still the Italian in Lobatse, with this addendum: he was a Yugoslav, who mainly spoke Italian. Her look confirmed everything I had already concluded re hopelessness in that direction. After she left I felt like killing myself for not mentioning that the only thing Nelson had volunteered all week was the sentence Time is an ape, and how would she like that in a boyfriend? Why could I not bring myself to say the words nervous breakdown?

There was one false dawn that week, when someone turned up at the gate whom he seemed to want to see. Nelson was sitting embowered in the blazing jacaranda. He recognized the face at the gate and got up with alacrity, actually, to stop the yardman from sending this guest away.

I watched from the kitchen. The visitor was a pathetic fixture in downtown Gabs, a refugee from Lesotho, a high school teacher who had been tortured after the Chief Jonathan coup in the seventies. He was in his forties and he was a gargoyle. One eye was half closed with scar tissue and there were terrible scars on his neck and down his chest, which you could see because he never buttoned his shirt. He walked with one leg dragging. Torture had made him a gargoyle. Apparently Nelson had known him. Hiram was his name. He got a little stipend from the UN High Commission on Refugees and lived in a shed behind a Canadian's house. He was always being stolen from. Expatriates would take pity on him and give him food and clothes, especially when their tours were up, which the local thieves had figured out. He forgot to lock his place up half the time, so he was always being robbed. Mentally he was not quite right. He was always smiling. He wrote things, strange manifestos and so on, in Sesotho. You would see him circulating around Gaborone, and occasionally he would beg. He would go into an office or a shop and beg for writing paper, never money. Children were afraid of him. He was usually wearing rags.

In came Hiram. They sat down facing, knees almost touching, on lawn chairs, myself thinking that now I was going to see my love galvanized back into himself by this icon of man's inhumanity to man. I was willing to bet on it. This would remind him. This was his walking and talking raison d'être.

One thing about Hiram was that he was voluble. He had a strange, hissing voice, and he was voluble in a way you could hardly make out, but once he had your eyes he kept talking, soliciting you, nexing with you.

But lo, not at all, this was real! Hiram was silent. This was like the exchange of benevolent glances between the Pope and the Dalai Lama. Neither party said a word. Nelson rested his hand on Hiram's shoulder for a long time, then took it away. At the beginning of things, Nelson had made me write down the name of a book, *The Power of the Charlatan*, from which had come a phrase he'd used a couple of times and that I'd inquired about: e nosatu et sta ben così: I've smelled him and now I feel so good. At some point in Italy there were charlatans who sold sniffs of themselves. I crept out to hear if they were talking at all. It was still silent benevolence. After fifteen minutes Hiram got up to go. The event was over. I sped back into the kitchen to throw food items into a sakkie for him and grab one of Nelson's better unwhite shirts, and I managed to catch him just as he was turning the corner at the end of our street. Nelson was back in his bower.

This also was the week I found my first four or five indisputably gray hairs. I was shocked. I thought they were supposed to come in by ones for a while, then twos, and then much later in threes and genuine arrays like this. I blamed my surprise on a certain inattention to my appearance that had taken root in Tsau, and on the bleary inadequate mirror and lighting I had available for my toilettes there. One of the hairs was oddly coarse and semicorkscrewed, and I pulled it out, but then stopped. There is the joke about finding a little golden screw in your navel and unscrewing it and then having your anus drop out onto the floor. My equivalent of that, after I tugged my premier gray hairs out, was the descent of a pseudo insight that gripped me for a day or two until it disappeared. The insight was that Nelson's whole mien was an act intended in a kind way to get me to relinquish him, go away on my own initiative, because he was too old for me and in fifteen years there would be trouble, pain, however we parsed it, wherever we went, whatever we did: there would be inevitable tragedy, it was a terrible idea, like marrying a Negro was supposed to be in the forties. So it seemed brilliant just then to let the gray remain, to not look any younger than I had to.

I was being driven to the edge by Nelson's seeming normal, for one reason or another, to everyone but me. The nurse, Rita, had given a religious interpretation to his experience, I was sure of it. I knew she was Catholic. I knew they'd murmured back and forth about the meaning of life during his socalled examination. This was not someone who could tell the difference between enlightenment and a nervous breakdown and elucidate it to me while she was at it. Then as to his stasis and dolce far niente: Europeans will go into villages in Africa and not infrequently see people not at work at anything discernible, not doing a task or hurrying en route from one task to another. There is what to us looks like lavish standing around, alone or in silent groups, people sometimes but not always leaning against a tree or a wall in a sort of self-communing state. And then you have the ultrarural population, people on cattle posts tens and hundreds of miles from anywhere, without amusements of any kind that you can imagine other than listening to Springbok Radio or Radio Botswana if they're lucky enough to have a radio. When you see them these are not depressed or unhappy people, or bored people, insofar as anything like that can be determined from the outside. So to the Batswana all Nelson would seem to be doing would be partaking subtly in that particular lifeway. Nothing odd about that. Of course the premise of Tsau was to break poverty in the village by replacing stasis with its opposite, contests and meetings and inventions and dynamism. But nobody around here was thinking about that.

No, he was just all right, meaning just fine, to the locals. The resident help had almost nothing to do, we were so undemanding and so few, so they leapt into the breach and devoted themselves to his wardrobe, starching and ironing and bleaching his vanilla costume, for example, into a blinding state of perfection. He didn't object. This was slightly a judgment on me by all concerned, I felt. Why had I let him go around in so much lesser a state of splendor? He looked so splendid, groomed up this way. It helped that his weight was perfect. He was growing a beard, but shaving meticulously every day, so as not to let beard shadow creep up into his cheeks. I waited out the first week. I gathered that what he anticipated was going back to Tsau, soon, apparently, and presumably with me.

The first week was up and I was inwardly girding my loins for strife, uprooting his mode or making him say what it was, making me understand it.

We were having mint tea at the dining room table when he said, almost as an afterthought to my questions about things that needed to be done in Gabs, We can be married.

Then he said it again: We can be married here. And then he added
And we can have children.

I burst away from the table and went off to our room. I wept but I
was enraged. I left the door open to give him the chance to come normally after me and see what was wrong, what he could do.

From where I was I could see him still sitting at the table, looking
vaguely after me but not rising. What was this? Was it a byproduct of
collapse and regression into a kind of simpleminded protohusband role,
or was it enlightenment and his inner self telling him it was time to
multiply with me, or was it the last worst slash of the knife at me, a trick
to disorient me and make me let go? Was he incapable of seeing this as
an act of force against me, this reversal of every position he had ever had
on the subject and an exploitation of what he certainly knew was a highly
particular vulnerability of mine, in my situation? He had torn me away
from midwifing in Tsau in order to help me keep my natalist impulses
from starting to churn, which incidentally would have run athwart his
bias against having children, there being so many unwanted ones in the
world. And now this.

Anyway, with that he had unnerved me and I was in no condition to
start on the interrogation I had been preparing myself for. Could he have
done this deliberately to derail me?

Psychology

I think it was weakness that made me want to reknit for a couple of
days before I made the assault on whatever his new belief structure was,
that and the news that there was an actual trained psychiatrist briefly in
town, a Sri Lankan on consult at the Ministry of Health. Nelson had
been willing to see the nurse. But there was no question of his going to
Pretoria or Johannesburg, because that was South Africa. So mightn't
he see Dr. Pereira if I could arrange it? Pereira would come over. Nelson
wouldn't have to leave the house.

At breakfast I went at it obliquely.

I mentioned that there was a Sri Lankan psychiatrist in town.

He said Sri Lanka, that could have been a paradise after the English left except for two mistakes. One was canceling English as the official language, which drove the Tamils wild because they were having enough trouble in the civil service without having to learn to write their memos in Sinhalese. The other mistake slips my mind.

I was alert, waiting for more, but he fell into silence again.

Having gotten Dr. Pereira's name into the atmosphere, I swung into some overkill on psychology, remembering Nelson's hostility to the discipline and his hatred of clinical psychology in particular, a specialty he thought of as about as respectable as colonic irrigation. I may have played a role in exacerbating his feelings here—not that much help was needed—with the horrible true story of something that had happened when my mother and I lived in the gatehouse of an estate a clinical psychologist couple had rented the rest of. One of their patients, a woman being treated for shyness, had frozen to death in their parking area one winter. She had had car trouble and hadn't wanted to bother anyone. She'd been in treatment with one of them for five years. Also the psychologists were cryptosurvivalists, and we would see vanloads of canned goods and staples being delivered in the dead of night and stuffed into various outbuildings. Nelson and I had been peas in a pod on the subject. I'd torn out an item in the Economist to show him, reporting that the two hundred top psychologists, department heads and deep thinkers and top-dog practitioners, had been asked to list the most important theories or discoveries in the field in the last twenty-five years. And there was total disagreement among the lists, no consensus anywhere, absolutely the only uniformity being that if they'd discovered or proposed something themselves it would likely appear on their list of the top five advances. So now I was about to beg him to let himself be psychologized for my sake.

I did a roundabout rehabilitation of psychology. Had I ever told him, I asked him, about my discovery in my mid-twenties of why doing mental work would suddenly become much easier for me at about three in the afternoon? I had been talking about grammar school with someone, and how much I'd hated it. Then through that the click had come. Everything in grammar school had been coercion and boredom, which ended at three when school let out. After that my concentration was the same morning, noon, or night: all I had to do was remind myself that I was no longer at Horace Mann.

And then there was the story of my aversion to supermarkets. I would always become faint when I got up to the checker, slightly faint. My aversion cost me money, because it was so distinct a thing I'd go long distances and be willing to spend more in order to shop in little mom and pop places. Then one night when I had no choice I went to a Safeway. As I got to the checkout a woman going out the main door changed her mind and came back in my direction. She was an older woman, dressed in a particular way, and I was already in the penumbra of feeling faint, which seeing her deepened. She came back and got whatever she'd left behind on the counter and left. Her face was obscurely terrifying to me, like a death's-head. But then I relived a moment when I'd been on line in a supermarket with my mother and a neighbor woman came up and made a furtive urgent gesture for my mother to come aside so she could tell her something. And as I watched them go I knew what it was. I must have been ten. This woman's son had obviously ratted on me about some sexplay I'd initiated. I was known as the Fig Tree Girl among the little boys I preyed on and delighted in the shelter of a particular fig tree. Testicles fascinated me. Then there was my mother coming back looking like the most revengeful and, worst of all, most disappointed monster in the world. It was her disappointment that slew me, because she was seeing me as not normal, me her darling. Once I recaptured that moment of shame I could shop anywhere.

Light from the caves, Nelson said.

I got back to Pereira. Would he see him?

Certainly, Nelson said.

Dr. Pereira Attends

In came Pereira—a Tamil, from his coloring. He could give Nelson twenty minutes. Going in he was very brisk.

He had been totally unwilling to have me tell him what I thought Nelson's situation was. I had barely gotten the words hyperpassivity and decompensation out of my mouth when he reminded me that he was very well used to diagnosing any kind of personality inversion.

The twenty minutes stretched into more like ninety minutes.

I could not believe the outcome. I felt like shaking him. He was small.

Nothing was wrong with Nelson, who was in transcendent mental health. And he, Pereira, was going to find some brochures to lend us, because Mr. Denoon was very very interested in a very fine school of Hinduism in fact created by a woman, the Marathi saint Muktabai. In all the country of Botswana there were many Hindus, but all were ignorant, to his knowledge, of the very fine bhakti school. All the great persons of bhakti were women, or many of them.

Pereira looked sternly at me. I am lacking a wife, he said. And I tell you if this man came to say This woman right here you should marry, I would go straight to her.

He was hoping to find time to see Nelson again.

War

I gave peace a chance for one more day. War was coming.

There were just a few foreglints of the dies irae. One was I lost patience over his attitude to meals. He had some inchoate idea that meals should be aleatory: there should be an array larger than would be usual of different things to choose from, with an emphasis on cold cooked grains, and one should eat homeostatically each time—a little of this, none of that, a little of this, and so on. Congratulations, I said, you have just invented the cafeteria.

I made myself get ten hours sleep the night before the war.

When I got up, I reassessed. It had to be. He was minimally more talkative, but it was still basically only responsively. He hadn't made one phonecall. He'd talked vaguely about needing to go to a couple of the ministries but hadn't taken any steps in preparation.

I fixed myself up more than usual. Breakfast was in silence. I needed protein for what I had to do, and ate eggs and cold sirloin tips.

He was hyperclean and splendid in his white raiment.

I was having my period, a heavy one. I'd stopped taking my pills for a while, why not?

I said You know we have to discuss things. I led him to a round metal table under a big acacia. We sat facing each other across it, in flareback wicker chairs.

First I got his agreement not to leave the table for at least one hour no matter what I said, how offended he might get. And that if he left for the toilet or a nosebleed he would come back. He was agreeable.

Is this roughly the picture of what happened to you?: you were en route to Tikwe and not paying attention and you rode under a tree and either one or two boomslangs dropped down on your mount.

Two, he said.

You were in black cotton soil, and so when the horse reared up and slipped you went half under him, which is when you broke your arm and ankle. And then the horse struggled up, with a snake still biting into its neck, but it had a broken leg and fell again.

Fortunately you were wearing your canteen—unfortunately in that you cracked some ribs landing on it.

You passed out. But later you came to.

You were unconscious long enough to get a bad burn on one side of your face and neck.

I got upset as I spelled all this out. I had notes on a pad on a clipboard.

You dragged yourself fifty feet to a termite mound that was under and half around a small tree. You saw your horse lashing around and making terrible sounds. You managed to kill it after this. You were in pain. The termite mound was like a recliner, a sloping shape.

At this point he volunteered to narrate, if I would turn the recorder off. This was new and, it seemed to me, positive. He wanted the tape recorder off because it would make him feel he had to go too fast.

I said Go day by day as much as you can.

He would try, but I had to remember it was all a continuum to him.

He put his palms flat on the table as he began, and he told the whole story with his eyes closed. I felt he was rising from some inner depth to do this, that it was painful. At points I could tell he was pressing his hands down hard. I myself was pressing my fists in against dysmenorrhea now and then. It was extremely peculiar. I felt linked to him, as though together we constituted some sort of mechanism.

He went slowly. I am condensing. He said the first scene he has clearly is in twilight, when he first smelled and then saw black-backed jackals converging on his horse. What he got to watch was this beast being torn to pieces. It was like hell. He has fragmentary recollections of having dragged himself back and forth from the horse earlier to get his food pack, in terror of the boomslangs, which had vanished by then, apparently. He was certain the jackals would come after him once they were through with the horse unless he did something.

At first the jackals ignored him, but then two of them came straying over. He had the conviction that terror, his terror, would doom him and that the first thing he would have to do was make himself into a nonreacting entity: that is, stop thinking and make himself as much like the ground or the trees as he could. He had to stop sending out waves of fear and supplication. It was a process of deidentification, he called it. It soothed him to have this task.

He found it hard to talk about how he got into this deidentified condition. It was a formula, a certain order of images he made himself experience. It was an inner contortion. It had to do with making himself not feel the passage of time. In any case the jackals left him alone.

I pointed out that another explanation was that the jackals—there were only four of them—had gorged themselves and that also he wasn't quite yet their favorite food, carrion.

I could be right, he granted. But he did feel he had gotten into some genuine state. And after the jackals left he continued experimenting with it, thinking that lions might be next, probably would be next.

I was in his mind. He was determined not to die, because of me.

He had set his arm and had tried to set his ankle break. In neither case had the skin been broken.

He had the full canteen. He would limit himself to three mouthfuls of water a day. He had retrieved one of the two food parcels he had brought before the jackals came and ate the other along with the horse. He had mistakenly used up one trip to the horse for the purpose of gathering anything he could use for shielding against the sun. He'd gotten more than he could use. My tent was unworkable and he had torn the canvas off it to use for protection. He couldn't explain to me why it was unworkable, and I concluded finally that in his pain and panic he'd given up too soon on it.

His supply of food consisted of scones, dried pears, biltong, some mongongo nuts, and one orange. The idea, of course, was to husband this, something made easier by his discovery that when he went into what he was calling his interval state, when he was willing himself to be deidentified, he would lose both hunger and pain.

Then he went for a highly summary and bland account of the next eight days. He rested, he slept, he practiced his interval state, he was lucky, the Herero found him. He had had dreams he could tell me about.

I knew I was being maneuvered. There was more to be gotten at. But I let him think I was accepting the diversion of talking about dreams.

It was transparently a diversion away from the experience or visions or messages other people had alluded to his having talked sketchily about, that is, away from the very things that had made his misadventure so momentous.

He remembered two vivid dreams, both about the earth in the future. In one of them mankind has spread throughout the galaxy, and the earth has been converted into a mortuary planet. Various features of the old, inhabited earth have been sold to members of the galactic elite as personal family monuments. The Eiffel Tower is one, Niagara Falls is another. The remnant population of the earth is totally employed in monument-tending. In the other dream the earth seems to be given over totally to art. He dreamed he was having lunch next to a gigantic fountain while metal sculptures slid across the sky overhead on cables, their arms or wings spread. But he did see these as purely literary dreams with nothing noetic about them, didn't he? Certainly, he said.

Finally we went back to the chronology. Along about the fourth day there was a new dimension to his interval state.

It may have been a hallucination, he said. You'll think so.

It was a sinking inward and experiencing the body as a polity, was the way he put it after a lot of groping for words. He experienced the body as a confederation of systems that were in their own ways conscious or sentient, sentient being the better word for it. Anyway, it was a set of systems the mind could enter into a relationship with, an indescribable relationship, but friendly.

My position was that this was not, strictly speaking, a hallucination at all. It was more an inner dramatization of something that he already intellectually understood to be the case in a primal way—e.g., cells signal back and forth, certain organs could be looked at as city-states. In short, the idea that the body is a hierarchy of systems is something that got dramatized dot dot dot.

Ah, but not a hierarchy, he said. Not a hierarchy. Don't make me say things I didn't say.

I had to watch my limits. When I asked So did you enter into shall we say a new or friendlier relationship with these elements? all I got was a shrug and a longish look of disapproval.

In a moment he was benign again. I was free to have any interpretation I liked on anything he said. He wasn't placing a great deal of stress on anything.

What other revelations were there? I asked.

He was silent. I thought this might be as much as he was going to say.

He wanted to tell me something before we went on. He would make it brief. If he were a writer this would be a short story he might write. You have a husband and wife. They are like night and day in terms of health.

I was hearing a fable.

The husband never gets sick and the wife is permanently ailing. You read the story and you observe that the husband never complains and the wife is always complaining.

He has nothing to complain about, with his good health, I said. Or are you trying to get at a chicken and egg proposition?

Listen to the story. The husband praises things, appreciates things, says so all the time. He might go so far as to praise his tools, his saw, say, his log-lifter. They live in the country. His wife is mired in not liking much of anything, aside from her ailments. He's like the Basarwa are, apologizing to the animals they kill and praising the totem of the genus, thanking it.

I let him take his time. I had wanted him to talk, and now he was.

The husband goes out of his way to try to demonstrate to his wife that she lacks a certain thing, which you could call gratitude. He has a philosophy of gratitude of a certain explicit or even crude sort, which he rightly or wrongly thinks may be at the heart of the difference between them, his better luck. But a thing about his philosophy of gratitude is that it has to be spontaneous, or come spontaneously, to work. It can't be a rote thing like saying grace. He feels all he can do is exemplify what he feels, because, and this may be irrational, he feels that if he instructs her or catechizes her into it, not only will it not work for her but he himself might then lose the benefits of his attitude to the world. By the way, both of them are atheists, so this is not about religion. But how this story ends is a problem. One way it could end would be his telling her, and her laughing. And then they both begin to decline.

I said Well, didn't you say they were both elderly to begin with?

Maybe I implied it. But in my mind, in my story, they are.

A fable, I thought. No, a parable, god help me.

But I am very good with dreams and parables.

I said So the husband says goodbye to a hardy old age. I don't know what to say, really, except that I think this is your way of telling me not to ask you about things you feel prohibited from telling me for cosmic reasons of some kind, to which I say what you once said to me and made my hair stand on end with: Thought looks into the face of hell and is not afraid. That was you, wasn't it, from Bertrand Russell? I loved it. Thought looks into the face of hell and is not afraid. Loyalty to this is why you stipulated that they're atheists, and why you wince when I use the word revelations, I guess. I think this story is silliness. If only the wife is smart enough to read his body language and copy him they can live another what? nineteen months beyond their allotted span, or something? I am sorry, but this is just plain Don't bother me, in spades, and I hate it, hate it, hate it, reject it. I don't care.

I said I can't help reading between every line, can I?

So there are certain private magnificent things you could tell me, but if I were perfect I wouldn't make you tell me. Because of the consequences, and so on. But I'm not perfect. Tell me this: will you be punished by some vaguely female force or image or power if you tell me everything? I'm just guessing here, but tell me. And don't think I don't love you for telling me this story, which is an act of friendship as well as being whatever else it is.

Go back a step, I said. Try and see this just as documentation for someone you love.

He really groaned.

I said Tell me the worst thing you're not supposed to tell me, as I construct it, because something might happen we both would hate.

With his eyes closed, he said Consciousness is bliss.

I said This is something you know and feel? As opposed to something you were told or got as a message?

Again he groaned and said Yes, yes.

Was this literary or was it real? It seemed real. All my questions à la Then how are you ever going to get anything done? seemed callow, or worse.

Here was my beloved envelope looking into his palms. Why was parsing all this up to me? which it was.

I knew suddenly what he was really like: he was like a fortune-telling machine you put money into for each message or prophecy you got, the head being behind glass, encased.

This is something you feel even as we speak, I assume. Say those words again.

I will.

But he was pale and looked almost disgusted. This was the most excruciating part of the morning. He looked exsanguinated. I was being driven into seborrheic hyperactivity. I touched my nose and it felt anointed. A desperate protojoke tried to emerge premised on how difficult it would be for me to be led around by the nose, it was so shiny. Meanwhile the revenge of the womb was ongoing.

It was violative, but I had to make him say more. The gist of what I got out was that over the days, he had been allowed to have this experience of consciousness as bliss and finally to keep it, protract it, take it away with him as part of him in his reconstituted state. This element of allowance or permission was what bothered me the most, since it implied personal agency on the part of some undisclosed party. And I was right. He had had a vague sense of a presence always near, mostly behind him, and he would say female, if he had to assign that kind of quality to it. The word ethereal evidently caused him so much pain that I felt I had to apologize.

I wanted to know if this consciousness change was part of any other, larger conclusions about the secret of the universe or of nature or if it had anything to do with his conceit—I let myself use that word—about the confederal nature of the body.

No, there was no doctrine coming out of this. Every part of what had happened to him was separate.

I asked Might there be a connection, though, that you just haven't forged or come upon yet?

The Smile.

I tried to slip in an insinuation or two about Taoism. The Smile again. Taoism was a nondoctrine, not to put too fine a point on it. He had always been a sort of Taoist, he said. I was making a mistake in trying to reduce any of this to some established schema. He could see where I was going, and it was a waste of time. I of course was thinking that his mother's Mary fixation, osmosed to him as a child, was seeping up in all this in the guise of the hovering eternal feminine I had made him, by bitchlike persistence, disclose and talk about however minimally.

I was going to have to let us stop. But first I took him back over this bliss-consciousness development. He was halting and recursive. It was impossible to formulate it further for me. It was an overwhelming feeling when it was at its strongest. It was on the order of sexual pleasure and had to be controlled, actually—kept down. He claimed he was holding it down, keeping it at a subdued level even at that moment. One of his tasks was to learn how best to do this—in fact, it was one of his main tasks.

An image came to me from a philosophical discussion about torture we'd had a year or so before, something practiced by the Manchus in which an incision is made in the victim's stomach and a piece of the intestine is nailed to a tree and the victim is lashed and made to circle the tree, unwinding his entrails as he goes. I was being the Manchu.

I produced a kind of last straw for both of us for that session by asking if I could watch him while he relaxed his control and let himself feel this new state of being he had discovered. I knew it was invasive when I said it, but I was desperate to get to some kind of conclusion I could penetrate. I felt slightly sordid and took it back right away, seeing the expression on his face.

When I asked him—looking for a little forgiveness—if he didn't think he would feel better once all this was out, external, he said no.

It was time to stop. I got up. He had just lately given up the knobkerrie he'd been using as a crutch. He asked me to get it for him.

He suggested we not eat lunch together, if I didn't mind. He would prefer to eat separately. I was hurt, but I was also convinced by his manner that his motivation, whatever it was, was not punitive, not in the least.

Satanic Miracle

After lunch he was willing to resume, but sitting side by side in our wicker chairs rather than facing. I'd moved the table away. We were in the same spot, al fresco. It was hot and bright. He apparently felt strongly about our continuing our conversation there, where it had begun, instead of indoors. I was for indoors for reasons of privacy. Because of the drought there was a ban on using hosepipes for garden watering, so the yardman was ubiquitous with his watering cans throughout the grounds. His English was rudimentary, though. An odd thing was that he professed to not be able to understand my quite good Setswana except with difficulty, whereas anything Nelson said, however murmurous, he got right away.

Nelson took the helm more that afternoon. I let him. There were long gaps, when he was doing the narrating, that I could use to reprise the questions I was asking and reasking myself, the main one being what was I going to do with him? Where had his comic side gone? was another.

And why was everything between us so asymmetrical—my having urinary frequency versus his never having to pee, his appetite being tiny and precise, mine being pretty much out of control. And what exactly would he be to Tsau if he went back in his present mode? This was a very interesting question. What exactly was I supposed to do now? Should I stay with him and pray for a remission? Should I give him an ultimatum and somehow get him back to the States the same way I got him out of Tsau, even though it seemed everybody was certifying him as more lucid than thou? Should I marry him as he was, sweet, and take some kind of pleasure in his wifely qualities and satisfaction in my association with his past glorious works and the future glory of what Tsau would be seen as when it was thrown open to the world? Should I kill myself, seek professional help for *myself*, give him another six months of my nets and snares and shock therapy, stay with him on the assumption this was a maneuver of some kind on his part and that he'd turn to me some night with a smile and lucidly explain why all this had been necessary? Which? What? I grasped an unfortunate truth: his willingness to be a father was operating on me, confusing me, weakening me. He was appealing to my maternalism on two levels. He needed to be taken care of, self-evidently. And there was also the real thing: I could be the mother of the children of this brilliant, unique man. And then I would always have them, whatever else happened.

I must have said This is too much, because he said What is too much?

Nothing, I said. I realized I was doing something women did only in nineteenth-century novels. I was wringing my hands.

I should tell you about the lion, he said. I think you heard a parody of what it was like.

A lion found me, a male, a rogue, solitary, as the sun was going down that night.

It came toward me after nosing around what was left of my horse. By the way, streams of ants as big as my thumb were covering the carcass, and more were coming all the time.

The male was advancing on me, then I felt the presence I told you about behind me. This upsets you.

Well. At the same time from a tree off to my right a horde of bees came out and formed an arc in the air between me and the lion. They made a sound louder than I've ever heard bees make in my life.

I know this is amazing. I have no proof the whole thing wasn't a hallucination. And I know you never see bees around at sunset.

The thing is that the lion surprised me and terrified me so much I had no chance to go into the interval. I was pumping out fear.

The lion came close to me twice. Within six feet. The second time he was stung around the eyes. I passed out. I woke up in blackness later and I think I still heard the bees. That was the night before the day the Baherero found me. I woke up, and the scene was quiet. And there was another odd thing. The stench of the carcass had been torture. That morning it was gone. In fact I thought I smelled something almost like cosmetics, if I smelled anything at all, coming from that direction.

You agree everything could have been a hallucination, in theory, the lion, everything, don't you? I asked him.

Certainly, he said.

I could tell from his expression that this admission was pro forma, which took the heart out of me. This amounted to saying whenever it was convenient, Of course, anything could be hallucination. If that was the plan, then where were we? Nothing was going to be scrutinized. I had the sensation of my chest cavity filling up with gravel.

I said But the feeling you have about consciousness, this is not a hallucination.

No.

So it must mean something about the other events that went with it.

It may.

I said Do you think the world should be taught how to achieve or at least know about this kind of consciousness you have?

He said Not necessarily.

I was flailing around. I was coming from different directions. I asked him if he thought he was normal, considering how little he was doing in the course of a day.

He thought so.

I knew he wasn't normal in at least one respect because of an unconscionable thing I'd done the night before. I'd gotten into bed naked and we'd begun embracing, all in silence—which was atypical. And I'd discovered what I wanted to discover, that the same things made him sincere as always. But then I'd stopped and moved away to my side of the bed. I moved away gradually enough for him to protest. But he let me slip away without any semblance of pursuit whatsoever. This was accommodation gone mad, at least in terms of our protocols. This was the man I'd learned the phrase A standing prick has no conscience from. Why had I done it, when I was fifty percent certain the outcome might be what it had been? It was plucking at an old generic fear of mine about marriage in general, maybe my most fundamental fear. What happens in a marriage if your husband is no longer sexually compelled by you? What happens in your heart when you sense he's pretending to want to do it? How old are you when this happens? The whole thing is unbearable.

I said And you think your going back to Tsau is what everyone there wants. You have no suspicion they might not mind so much having two fewer faces, white faces, hanging around?

He was never more puzzled. Why, what did I mean? Almost everyone at Tsau came to him before he left to say he should come back as soon as he could once he was rested.

More than came to me, then, I said.

You were included, he said.

I don't know why this delusion or fiction in particular so undid me, but I went into a mad scene so embarrassing in retrospect that I've repressed half of it.

I was manic and global. Everything was a last straw. I went up the hill on passivity and down again. How did he define love, in his present state? Did he deny he was insanely passive? Also did he think the capacity to get pleasure out of sheerly being awake was something: (A) everybody had at one time had but they'd lost? (B) animals had but we didn't and he like a shaman had gotten from his experience and a little help from the eternal feminine? (C) something that people like me could be taught and would he teach me? or (D) if he tried to teach me and I failed to get the hang of it would he or would he not say that might create a hairline crack in our relationship? granted that he loved me more than life itself. Did he think I enjoyed being driven out of control like this? Or suppose all this was quote unquote real, did he imagine I wanted to spend the rest of my life with someone marching in the direction of total perfection as in the case of someone so homeostatic he had the eating habits of an angelic being of some kind? I think at this point I compared him to an exotic flower, a bromeliad, because during his time in the wilderness he had lived on light and air, virtually, the way they do. I had added up the food he'd had available and it was negligible, so he was a bromeliad and not a human being.

I was circular. In my display the pattern that developed was that I would say something irrational and then walk away, then come back, be irrational and circular again, then drift away, slightly farther each time, finally finding myself going into the house at one point. The help was transfixed, but I hardly cared. I kept going farther afield and coming back to see if he was all right and if there was any change, had he thought of anything to say to me to stop all this from uncoiling this way. There was nothing I could do. I said to myself I could have fallen in love with a Catholic, whose beliefs were more outré and more numerous than anything my poor Nelson seemed to be believing lately. But of course I couldn't have unless he was presented to me in the costume of someone else, a rational person, unless I had fallen strictly through the commands of the flesh, which can happen but more with men than with women, no matter what the conventional wisdom says. But always he was just still sitting there, his hands tented. Think what you're doing, I said to myself. Was I showing him madness, my madness, my worst self opposed to his?

He pointed out, on one of my return swings, that my period was showing on the seat of my skirt. That I attended to, and when I returned he was rising, not abruptly or in any way dismissively to me, to go in to take a nap. It made me feel more epiphenomenal than ever.

I followed him into the bedroom.

Can you see in any way that this is hell from my standpoint? I asked him.

Yes.

But is it making you personally suffer, to any degree, through your bliss?

Certainly. This answer followed a long pause.

I left him to his nap.

I went to the hideous mall and to the main shrine of the expatriate depressed, the Botswana Book Centre. Mordant whites went there more to touch books than to buy them, the exchange rate being what it was. I'm thinking particularly of Peace Corps volunteers, I suppose, with their limited living allowances. There was a huge staff at BBC. The Batswana at the cash registers were the swiftest in the world. The rest of the staff, in blue dustcoats and carrying feather dusters, was the reverse, more like a functionless chorus grouped along the back wall, chatting and sitting on books. It was hectic when the Rand Daily Mail and the Johannesburg Star came in but otherwise the place was quiet and dreamy, just what I wanted.

Someone that everyone was talking about was in the next aisle from mine, her head down as she studied a book I saw was the paperback *Development as the Death of Villages*. This had to be beautiful Bronwen Something, a State Department intern who was over in Gaborone short-term to work on the trade fair held every summer. It was a customary

position, and since the American participation in the exercise was fairly
nominal, these pcps, as they were for some reason called, had rather
little to do. She wasn't the first pcp I'd seen reading at three in the
afternoon in the Botswana Book Centre.

I recognized what Bronwen was immediately. She was my satanic
miracle. I knew it. Her image seemed to leave a print on my sight when
I looked away from her. She was reading Nelson's book with ferocious
concentration. I could tell she was believing it.

Ripeness is all, was Bronwen. People had said you would know her
when you saw her because she looked like the ingenues in the Coke ads
of the nineteen forties, the perfect blond ones. She must have been
genuinely beautiful, because fluorescent light, which makes the rest of
us look cadaverous, only made her look luminous. She had hair the color
of custard. I doubt that she was twenty-six. She wore absolutely no
makeup. Conceivably her underlip was a little overfull. She was shorter
than I am.

I got interlocking satanic inspirations. This woman would be awed to
meet Nelson. He would love her for her honey-colored hair alone. She
could have Nelson. I had had the Nelson she was reading the words of.
What there had been of him I had in my mind, in my memory, in my
notes. Maybe she would love the present Nelson even more than she
would have loved the original. We could see. We could find out. I could
bring them together. This led to my second inspiration. I could bring
them together at a celebration for Nelson he would never forget. I would
open the floodgates. Something had to change in my life. If I was unable
to get him back to himself singlehanded, then maybe the curious descending all at once on him could do it, along with Bronwen Something.
He wanted to be Adamic, then okay, leave it to me to round up an Eve.
He hated surprise parties, and he hated birthday parties. His birthday
was in the wrong part of the year, but this could just be my mistake. I
could orchestrate this. It could be done. I had been kept from taking any
kind of real action for too long. Now I could act. It was intoxicating to
think of all this. She was the right one: unknown to her as she plowed on
through Nelson's book, she was the center of a web of male glances,
black and white male glances. Some of them even saw that I saw, and it
meant nothing to them. They kept staring, so what was I? People were
arranging what they had to do so they could rest their eyes on her. I was
nothing. I was nothing despite my superior bosom, and she was some
pure flamelike thing with her part perfectly straight and perfectly white,
her custard-colored hair up in valences behind her absolutely perfect

ears. I felt almost simian. I have definite down on my arms, no more than average but it is a little darkish, and her arms were like polished dowels of some kind. I would drop her in his lap. He would have the option to ignore her. He would have the option to be enraged, to accuse me of anything, pimpery. That would be something. We would see. There was a suppressed furor going on over Nelson's sequestration. Everyone would want to come. Let them, I thought. She never looked up. She was not a rapid reader.

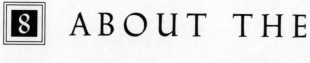 ABOUT THE
FOREGOING

The Call

 I don't like it here in Palo Alto. For a while I was able to sustain myself by self-congratulation. Severing myself from the spectacle Nelson had become to me had been a success, as I read it, a stupendous thing. It gave me strength. Everything worked for me. A way I could contrive a thesis out of my Tswapong Hills data and some haphazard data from Tsau came to me. I have an extension. The department was delighted to see me. I went to see my mother and controlled everything. I was never insulted once. The most partial of answers satisfied her for a change. She is in the bosom of a Lutheran cult and likes it: they operate a nursing home on a freezing peninsula, where she works in the mailroom for room and board, essentially. She can stay there forever if she wants to, she says. She considers she has her first white-collar employment ever. Everything was yielding to my hand. I kept saying Freedom. I was riding a wave of fire at first. I went to a parasitologist, who said I was cleaner internally than the average middleclass American.

Of course this demonic phase had to end sometime, and it has. The wonder of my escape from Africa, as I so often couched it for myself in the beginning, is less sustaining to me. Now, apparently, I would rather think circuitously back and imagine ways that the necessity to sever us could have been avoided. Or I have time fantasies. Supposing we had met in the eighteen nineties, say, when there was nothing ambiguous about socialism being the answer to everything. It would have been obvious that the collective ownership of the means of production was all that was needed to make us happy. That would have been a medium for us to embrace in. We would have been perfect militants. I come out of fantasies like this furious with actually existing socialism, vacuously enough.

The demonic phase was on an adrenaline continuum with my lutte finale surprise party for Nelson. It almost arranged itself. Everyone wanted to come, the extraordinary Bronwen most of all. She was on the qui vive re Nelson after picking up on all the speculation at the embassy concerning him. That was why she'd looked up *Development as the Death of Villages.*

As an infernal device the party was perfect. Once I'd started issuing invitations the die was cast. I had to go through with it, however fainthearted I got. I'm not sure now what it was I really wanted, other than to see him either alter before my eyes or be confirmed as what I was afraid he had become. Just to have him infuriated with me, in a personal way, would have been a treasure. In the beginning I tried to honor my promise to Dineo to protect him from certain unfriendly characters in the donor community. But ultimately there was no way I could. They all heard about it—Brits, Boso people, a closet Trotskyite in the Friedrich Ebert Foundation. The Libyans call their embassy the Jamahiriya, meaning nonembassy or people's bureau or whirlwind, I forget which: two of them were coming. Apparently Qaddafi had pervertedly incorporated some anarchist tenets into his political bible, The Green Book, an act which Nelson had found extremely offensive, so perhaps those embers would have a chance to reignite. I realized the guest list was very light on anyone who might be called Denoonisant, except for lustrous Bronwen. So much the better, I thought. With Bronwen I played a complex game of self-presentation intended to lead her to think of me as someone not necessarily happily associated with this great man, someone possibly coarse, possibly uncaring toward him, someone not legally married to him, in any event. I thought so often of Grace, Grace pushing me toward Nelson. There was even a full moon the night of the party.

One thing I made sure of was the alcohol supply. There would be ample hard liquor, good brands. The cook-maid who came with the house would emerge, in her green uniform, with salvers of samoosas and drumsticks from time to time, in the style usual in top-dog socializing.

At the lutte finale I was invisible, or, more accurately, visible only at the margins, never at the center. That was for Bronwen. Nelson came out from his late nap. The forty guests erupted from behind things, shouting what they were supposed to.

Of course all of the above is really about the phonecall and the What is to be done? question. Somewhere in everything I remember lies the answer to how I should decide. At this point, oddly enough, I have the money to do whatever I decide is required. Of course a month has passed since the call, and I haven't decided. Instead I've done what I do best, made an academic study of myself centering on the last two years, made myself a field of academic study with only one specialist in it. The lutte finale was about resolving doubt, I thought, but it would be exactly doubt that could wrench me out of here one more time. The reason Achilles can never lay hands on the tortoise is the same reason a month has passed while I've studied the question of why I have yet to act. There is always new material to be integrated into the study of me. Each moment of thought demands multiples of moments of classification, analysis, parsing. I tried to suppress the gravamen of the phonecall, which was so interesting of me, wasn't it?

Nelson's conceit about god being in control of the content of life and the devil being in control of the timing is so useful, especially as applied to the question of what to do about my phonecall. Normally my slender means would have decided for me. For most of my life that would have been the case. But right now everything is working for me, and paying too. I got a TA-ship right away. The Association of American University Women chapter in San Mateo heard about me and asked me to give a little talk. But I have no slides, I said, and I'm so busy that if I do it I'll have to have an honorarium. Gosiame! They loved it that I had no slides, that I could paint word pictures and induce people to experience Africa the way I had, viz. not as a picture-taking robot only there to reduce everything to visual documentation while the gists and piths of authentic local life evanesced unnoticed. Other clubs are burning to get me. I attacked tourism, à la Nelson Denoon: Your warriors shall be bootblacks, your potmakers shall be chambermaids, and so on. Gosiame! I was quoting Nelson up and down. He sounded fascinating. He was still known. When I left the U.S. for Africa he was probably about even with Ivan Illich on the clerisy's fame meter. The clerisy is a word I got from Nelson which turns out to be indispensable, like others of his. Now Denoon's probably a point or two lower than he was, but his name still resonates nicely.

You move from circle to circle. I had mystery going for me. At the faculty level I would say only a little about Nelson, on the grounds that Tsau was a sealed project, I was under an unofficial obligation not to say so much until Tsau was declared open, and so on. My exact relationship with Nelson I left vague. I dressed pretty much for the part, wearing ostrich-egg shell-chip chokers, for example. Circles interpenetrate. When word got around that Tsau was a female polity, then, voilà, feminist organizations lined up to book me. By the time they found me it was already established that I got respectable fees.

Before I could even begin to worry seriously about livelihood I was offered a halfway decent job, which I took and still have, at this moment. I am in the academic demimonde. I am an editor and manager for a marginal publisher of doctoral dissertations languishing because they're too specialized or because they fall outside the desiderata of the regular university presses. I am in charge of Third World and Female Area acquisitions.

Maurice, who owns this business, has money he inherited, although he has less than he started with because Gretchen, the woman he formerly lived with and who persuaded him to start this enterprise so that she could fleece it discreetly, got a good deal out of him, that way and otherwise. He's a very dreamy man interested in the Middle Ages, so interested that one of his first injunctions to me was to keep him from unbalancing the list in that direction: I am supposed to build up the more trendward side of things and to at all costs resist his antiquarianisms. I remind him of someone, and he spends a good deal of time in his office trying to think of who it is. He has an unpublished thesis which he won't let me see. There's a wonderful sound system in our suite, and one of the first things I was presented with when I took the job was a memo asking me to list any favorite classical recordings I might like to have played for us. Our offices, in Belmont, are in good taste. I did produce a list of old favorite records in self-defense, after I realized how unvarying the playlist was going to be, how much plainsong and continuo I was going to have to enjoy. I need a strong woman, he likes to say. He has once or twice complimented me on my shoulders. I may have a new fall-back vocation as a dominatrix, at least if the current middleclass and higher decadence continues to unfurl at the present rate. I'm in control of my hours here. This is not precisely Guilty Repose, but it resembles it.

Being in America is like being stabbed to death with a butter knife by a weakling. Brazen Head is the most popular president ever. People think I have very interesting political slants. So much is siphoned from Nelson, so how should this make me feel? I seem to be all things to all women. Feminists like me because of Tsau, socialist feminists like me because of the cooperative side of Tsau, professional women, nonsocialist feminists, like me because of the private property and incentive side of Tsau, and lesbians like me because I never go around with men. There are no men, so far. People see me as women-identified, something new, and seem to be proud of me for it. The left is prolapsed, insofar as I can judge. I can't find an enemy in my milieu anywhere. If you have ideas that rise above Power to the people! you qualify as someone who should write a book for the Monthly Review Press.

The below is all Denoon. These are my commodities. This is what I say, with attribution, in one form or another. There are three major, dire, world-historical processes going on that your ideologies—a word I always use in the pejorative, like my man—are not letting you pay attention to. I keep rediscovering how inadequate for analyzing the nature and depth of the impending general planetary crisis both class analysis and vulgar feminism are as exclusive filters, by the way. The main process going on could be called corporatism unbound, with the term corporatism understood to include the state corporations of the Eastern bloc, although these are turning out not to be competent variants of the main type. What is becoming sovereign in the world is not the people but the limited liability corporation, that particular invention: that's what's concentrating sovereign power to rape the world and overenrich the top minions who run these entities. The perfect medium for the corporation is an electoral democracy where nobody—in the mature systems—bothers to vote, parties disaggregate, labor unions decompose, corporations control who gets into parliament, accountability disappears. A second major world-historical process is the invisible war of states against nations, recognized states against nonstate tribal nations, a bitter war, bloody, one without rules, breaking out even in regions where everyone assumes the game is over: East Timor, Chittagong Hills, Roraima—there are so many sickening examples to give. Third is the destruction of nature accompanying the ascent to absolute power of the corporate system. Then I give my own emendation, a less pessimistic one, which is, slightly embarrassingly to me, seemingly the most popular. Mine is the jagged and belated but definite rise of women into positions of political authority. I take this seriously. I am embroidering a bit if I imply that Nelson ever took it as hopefully as I do, but he wanted to and was just afraid, I think, to really believe in it because of the implications of events like Margaret Thatcher monstrously sinking the Belgrano. He was afraid that the lateness of the rise of women was its own doom—not that he wasn't trying to promote it nevertheless in his own molecular way at Tsau. So the above makes me interesting. I leave every group I speak to with at least this thought—that a true holocaust in the world is the thing we call development, which I tell them means the superimposition of market economies on traditional and unprepared third world cultures by force and fraud circa 1880 to the present, and that this has been the seedbed of the televised spectacle of famine, misery, and disease confronting us in the comfort of our homes.

They love me for it.

But back to my phonecall, because inhering in it is the cultural ghost of the whole perplex of women waiting in agony to be phoned by some man or other. I didn't leave Africa to come back here with the covert purpose of waiting for a phonecall that would set me dancing and playing maracas. I left to leave. In junior high we were forced to read a short story about a girl who meets a boy when she goes ice skating and who then goes home and waits in agony for days for him to call. This is a famous story by a woman named Maureen Daly, who got elevated into the very top level of women's magazines by it. The story is called Seventeen, and I think she was sixteen when she wrote it. The story won prizes. I had a very strong reaction to it. It sank into my soul and I vowed never to be her or anything like her. I vowed this. Also—and this is something I just now realized, thanks to the phonecall that's driving me to the edge—it has to do with why, when I could have, I didn't go after Nelson and stop him while he was still on his horse and heading for Tikwe. I had time. And I started to, but somehow I couldn't do it. I realize that I was very moved, but in the wrong direction, by Jean Peters running out to stop Emiliano Zapata from going someplace he was determined to go. I may be confusing two different scenes, in one of which she presses a freshly ironed shirt on him, pleadingly, or tries to. I hated her. This would never be me. I wasn't going to be Jean Peters in *Viva Zapata* when in fact the sensibility on the horse was who I really was. That was me.

Of course when I say my phonecall I should be saying message instead, which is all I have, because I was out when my mysterious friend called. Text is literally all I have. The call came to the office, and why the call came to the office is unmysterious, because I've written to enough people on business stationery for this number to get into circulation. There was the money order I sent for the Enfield. There were my notes to Adelah and to Mma Isang. The receptionist thought the call was from a woman but wasn't absolutely positive. It wasn't a clear line. The caller's accent wasn't American. There was no identification given. There was no request for a return call. And there's nothing more to be gotten out of the receptionist. She's sick of being quizzed. What is to be done? as Lenin so aptly put it. I think I need a maxim of some kind. Nelson's—insofar as they're apposite to this situation—are all so uniformly nothing but wry, as in Nothing ventured nothing lost, that they don't help me.

Why do I still regard it as surprising that he turned to her, even though I had deserted and I had thrust them together and we all know how absolute his need is for the eternal feminine when he gets into trouble, such as being stalked by lions, or a lion, to be fair. Why, just because I had left him naked to his enemies? They were being civil enough, actually. Was it just that I'd let in so many of them? He could have called out for me, of course, something that might have made all the difference. I could have swung in like Wonder Woman and cleared the place and said everything was my mistake, the party was off. But no, he was going to be the unmoved mover. I was actually observing the proceedings, on and off, from within the draperies and other demeaning vantages. Hell is closed and all the demons are here, he liked to quote from Marlowe. I was febrile. I was thinking So this is what he wants! Not only is she beautiful and not only are there bookmarks hanging out all over from her copy of *Development as the Death of,* but she's punctual. It was, as usual, difficult to read him, expert though I am. He was sweating lightly, more than the warmth of the room called for. He could have sent someone to find me, detach me from my duties masterminding the finger food relays. Of course at times I was outside looking at the moon. Even when it ended no one came to look for me. I could have been found. She went into our bedroom with him, conducted him. I sat in a rocking chair the rest of the night. I began cleaning up toward dawn, picking up each beer can and ashtray individually, delicately, trying not to make a sound. I thought of Grace and finding her and suggesting we move in together.

One factor I should take into account is that America is driving me more insane than I already am. I know this because sometime last week I felt anguish because I don't own a zester. I needed one urgently so that I could get little spirals and coils of carrot and jicama on top of the larmen soups I was eating for lunch that week. Then they would be attractive and I would like eating them better and my weight would go down. Another factor is that we seem to be in prefascism of some kind. The right is at the center everywhere. There could someday be a TV series set in the specious present called I Was a Liberal for the FBI. Of course if I'm a serious person the question should be What is to be done? by me about prefascism. Talking to people would be one answer. But that leads to nothing other than making them think I'm fabulous. The import of everything I say is that we're locusts, all of us here in the white West, but that never comes through. I recur to Nelson so much it makes me sick. What am I doing? There are only two kinds of work in the world, he once said. One kind on balance adds to the work other people have to do, the other kind on balance lessens the labor of others. What am I doing, or which am I doing? Youth wants to know! and suppose you say Okay, then, I'll write, I'll talk. Everyone tells me to write a book. So you

say Okay. But too bad about the language. On television a commentator
the other day described someone as morally devoid and a politician called
someone a spineless puppet, in the same sentence praising his own stead-
forthness. His constituents demanded their freedom of rights. They said
We want our voices spoken. And of course where is the man who could
laugh alongside me at this and help me to not keep dipping into despair?
I need the man who said Lyndon LaRouche should be called Lyndon
FaRouche instead.

All of which brings me back to my message. I read it, and what does
it tell me to do? It says either nothing or a great deal. It says Hector
proven alive Manhope police agent. It says Bronwen sent from Tsau
after one week.

I was on all fours cleaning up around their bedroom door when she
came out in the morning looking as though she'd been inducted into
something so very exalted. She almost tripped over me. She had the
decency to look ashamed. I kept on polishing. She went back in. I had
the place clean as a jewel for them. My knees were burning by the time
I got through. This will fade. I made sure fresh orangeade was waiting in
the breakfast nook before I left.

So: What is to be done, Lenin?

One possibility is that I should find a way to have sex before I decide
anything. I am living asexually. I can get sex. My celibacy is known and
is highly exciting to certain oaves on my periphery. What could be more
pointless than what I'm doing, id est developing a sacral attitude toward
historical sex with Nelson? Nothing.

The message was allegedly from a friend, and the call was placed in
Gabs. I have no friend in Gabs, really, but that hardly means anything,
because the call could have been made on or in behalf of someone
someplace else, or by someone visiting Gabs.

One thing I have definitely ceased with is slavishly reading through
the corpus of great books I unfortunately missed that he enlightened me
as to the importance of, at least until I decide What is to be done? All it
does is make me hopeless. His greatest of neglected books was too much
trouble, *Human Behavior and the Principle of Least Effort*, by George K.
Zipf. It's full of equations. Also, apropos being furious with actually
existing socialism, I am giving up on reading socialist apologetic of any
kind or stripe. I thought maybe I could convince him, if we ever met
again, that socialism was curable and we could be socialists together and
life could be like Berlioz on the stereo. This is an extreme of my extremis.

This is another item calculated to drive me mad. An epitome of how

Nelson haunts me is his presence in the question of my weight. I may have left out that when I was hounding him on the details of his illumination in the desert and especially the fine detail of his discovery that the human body is a sort of confederation, I asked him if he thought I might be able to control my weight better if I ordered my body or my fat cells or whatever entity I settled on to cease absorbing lipids for a while. He balked at answering because he thought I was out to trivialize. But finally he did answer Yes, possibly. And then I pressed on and asked Well, would it be preferable to give my body an order to be slenderer or to ask it nicely to be slenderer, which? And I wouldn't let him get away with saying that he didn't know which would be better, commanding or requesting. But then he said Either one, with requesting probably better. So I've been doing this, and since I started I'm down six pounds.

The first part of the message is straightforward enough. Where it takes me is not. G's being pronounced as H's, Manhope has to mean Mangope, the dictator of the bantustan across the border that would someday like to engulf Botswana because they're all Tswana after all, and there are five million of them under Mangope and only one million in Botswana. The Boers love Mangope's irredentism and keep it pumped up. So this news, that Hector is a police agent working out of Mafikeng, leads in many strange surprising directions. It makes his amazing vanishment out of Tsau something that could have been arranged quite easily by the South Africans. A helicopter could have come down from the Caprivi Strip, for instance, and picked him up out at one of the pans. So it could have been meant to get Nelson ejected so that the South Africans through Mangope through Boso—and no doubt ultimately through a born-again Hector—could carry out some geopolitical maneuver for which they wanted Tsau as a base.

An interesting synergy is that the arrival of the message coincided with my decision not to go on with my Denoonian lifetime reading plan, which followed my strange surprising discoveries in the *Tao Te Ching*. I had never touched the *Tao Te Ching* until lately. This is an instance of the patchiness of my education. If I ever had touched it, that might have made a difference. I wonder. But then I haven't read the Rig-Veda yet, either. My attitude to the East is out of *The Lotus and the Robot*, from my youth. What I thought when I got into the Tao was that I had the explanation of Nelson's fall. He had made an intellectual mistake! In a moment of vertigo he had embraced something that in his right mind he would have recognized as propaganda, imperial propaganda, a noxious thing albeit very poetical. Halt! cria-t-elle, I thought, when XXXIV hit me: *The way is broad, reaching left as well as right / The myriad creatures depend on it for life yet it claims no authority. / It accomplishes its task yet lays claim to no merit. / It clothes and feeds the myriad creatures yet lays no claim to being their master. / Forever free of desire, it can be called small; yet, as it lays no claim to being master when the myriad creatures turn to it, it can be called great. / It is because it never attempts itself to be great that it succeeds in becoming great.* That sent me back through the whole text. Halt! I kept thinking. Another gem was *This is called subtle discernment: The submissive and weak will overcome the hard and strong.* Then there was *I shall press it down with the weight of the nameless uncarved block. / The nameless uncarved block is but freedom from desire, / And if I cease to desire and remain still, / The empire will be at peace of its own accord.* Which I put together with something earlier: *When the uncarved block shatters it becomes vessels: / The sage makes use of these and becomes the lord / Over the officials.* Halt! There was more of the same. Take XLIII: *The most submissive thing in the world can ride roughshod over the hardest in the world—that which is without substance entering that which has no crevices.* For a day or so it was clear to me that all Nelson needed was Scientiae Athena to come back and illuminate what he had become on a dark night. He had become an impostor. The *Tao Te Ching* was a textbook on how to be one, and what kind to be. Or had Denoon always been an impostor without my noticing it, starting with so eloquently leading the world to expect Tsau was going to be some liberating municipal bromeliad running on sun and sweet breezes when in fact although the place was bristling and glittering with solar hardware how much did it do? A little water heating, some cooling, some grain drying? There was his marvelous personal solar crucible, but that was a toy. People had solar cookers but barely used them. And what was Tsau to him, really? Who was Tsau for?

Something had happened in the desert. Had he decided to prolong that thing for his own reasons, such as putting me to some impossible test, which I had failed, making me obsolete, and then had he prolonged his state in order to get rid of me or so he could relax into Tsau in some whole new mode involving dressing in white? So now was he sorry about it? Was this message from him: had he made the call or had it made? This was where my mind was. I've been over and over the list of candidates for secret caller so often it makes me sick. Could Dineo have organized the call? Would the idea be to tell me that all's well at Tsau and I could come back, or more likely that I should descend and take away the increasingly irrelevant Nelson? Or on the other hand was it a

genuine nervous breakdown thanks to his own whole particular foregoing, his mother, his father, the Tao, the events that precipitated the trip
to Tikwe, the horror of his experience in the desert? But then I thought:
you left to leave. Staying in his ambience like this is stupid and it is
lacerative. I told myself I am hardly going to save him via a marxist
interpretation of the Tao, although stranger things have probably happened. Who else could have sent the message? Could Z have? And what
had lustrous Bronwen been about? Irritation this intense is intolerable.

The Bronwen part of the message reads Bronwen sent from Tsau
after one week. That means Bronwen is no more.

And of course what finally enrages me is that it feels highly possible
to me that I have been maneuvered by a liar somewhere in all this. And
the thing is that Nelson knows that you lie to me at your peril. I will not
have it. He had ample warning. What is to be done?

Je viens.

Why not?

Glossary

S: Setswana   A: Afrikaans

ANC	African National Congress
Baherero	members of the Herero tribal group
bana	children (S)
basadi	women (S)
Basarwa	members of the San, or Bushman tribal group
batlodi	bad people, spies (S)
Batswana	inhabitants of Botswana. A single inhabitant: Motswana (S)
biltong	air-dried game meats (A)
BNP	Botswana National Party, the (fictional) governing party in 1980–81
Boso	familiar abbreviation for Botswana Social Front
braai	barbecue (A)
chibuku	commercial maize beer (S)
colgrad	college graduate, abbreviated in speedwriting ads
cooperants	development volunteers
CTO	Central Transport Organisation
CUSO	Canadian University Services Overseas
Diamond Police	special police branch devoted to diamond-smuggling suppression
expat	expatriate worker
gosiame	all-purpose term meaning variously: I agree; Okay; Everything's fine (S)
graywater	rinsewater
karosse	mat or rug of pieced furs or hide
kgosigadi	a queen or chieftainess (S)
kgotla	traditional village council of (male) elders and representatives of the chief (S)
klang	as in "klang association": the first thing that comes to mind when the analyst directs the patient to unmediatedly associate with a particular word or image
koko	knock, knock. Said to announce oneself on arrival (S)
koppie	island-mountain. Isolated stony hill
kraal	corral (A)

lakhoa	European (any foreigner). Plural: makhoa (S)
lefatshe la madi	country of money, country money comes from (S)
lolwapa	courtyard of traditional homestead (S)
Mainstay	South.African cane liquor
mealie	cornmeal (A)
memcon	memorandum of conversation (U.S. diplomatic usage)
mma	mother, senior woman (S)
mmamogolo	old woman (S)
mme	my mother (S)
nethouse	open structure of shade-netting over beds of plants
pan	craterlike depression (in the Kalahari desert)
paraffin	kerosene
permsec	Permanent Secretary
pula	the national unit of currency, rain (S)
rondavel	traditional round, thatched hut (squaredavel, ovaldavel—contemporary variants) (A)
rra	sir, father (S)
SADF	South African Defence Force
sakkie	plastic sack
Selous Scouts	elite counterinsurgency group in Rhodesian Army during the war of independence
Setswana	the national language
SWAPO	Southwest Africa Peoples' Organization
UDI	Unilateral Declaration of Independence (regime under which Rhodesia prosecuted its civil war)
UNDP	United Nations Development Program
Waygard	commercial security guards
Wits	University of the Witwatersrand
yakuta	Japanese bathrobe
Zed CC	Zionist Christian Church

Note: The author has taken the liberty of borrowing the place name Tsau, which belongs to a village in Ngamiland, for the women's settlement in the Central Kalahari.

Acknowledgments

I'm grateful for material support during the writing of this book from the Guggenheim Foundation, the American Academy of Arts and Letters, the National Endowment for the Arts, the New York State Council on the Arts, and the Rockefeller Foundation, for a Bellagio Residency.

For love and encouragement from earliest days I thank my dear friends Dorothy Gallagher and Sylvia Roth, and Ruth Gonze—my loyal sister-in-law, critic, and advocate. For steadfastness on my behalf or for varieties of help at crucial times I'm grateful to my friend and father-in-law Edward Scheidt and the late Ruth Scheidt, to Tom Disch, Dan Menaker, Ben Sonnenberg, Henry H. Roth, my editor Ann Close, my agent Andrew Wylie, Sam Brown, Alison Teal, Elizabeth Udall, Lynn Luria Sukenick, Bob Nichols, Phalatse Tshoagong, Dick Mullaney, Mzichoe Mogobe, Elizabeth and Dick Voigt, Bob Hitchcock, Bill Picon, my brothers Chris, Nick, and Robert, and my late sister, Cathy. For his bravery in persevering in the making of literature under conditions of unimaginable hardship Jacob Khalala is my talisman.

A Note on the Type

The text of this book was set in Electra, a typeface
designed by W. A. Dwiggins (1880–1956). This face
cannot be classified as either modern or old style.
It is not based on any historical model; nor does it
echo any particular period or style. It avoids the
extreme contrasts between thick and thin elements
that mark most modern faces and attempts to give
a feeling of fluidity, power, and speed.

Composed by Dix Type Inc.,
Syracuse, New York
Printed and bound by
R. R. Donnelley & Sons,
Harrisonburg, Virginia
Endpaper map by Mia Vander Els
Designed by Anthea Lingeman

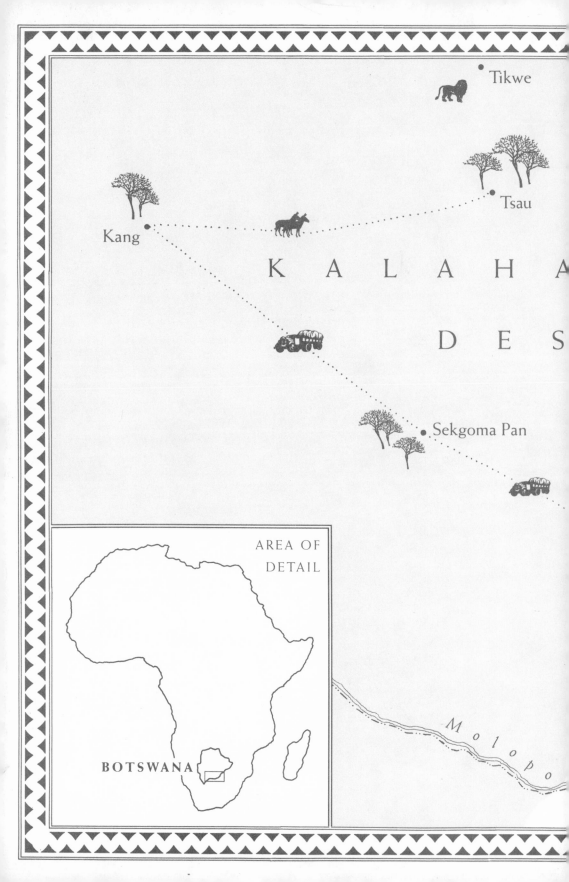

Tikwe

Tsau

Kang

K A L A H A

D E S

Sekgoma Pan

AREA OF
DETAIL

BOTSWANA

Molopo